"Places Gladstone firmly in the lineage of William Gibson and Neal Stephenson, and yet stands apart as something incredibly special."
—Fran Wilde, Andre Norton Award–winning author

"A story that will make you weep with wonder. It broke me to pieces and then stitched me back together with golden thread. Simply glorious."
—K. B. Wagers, author of *Behind the Throne*

"A gloriously maximal space opera in the tradition of Banks and Rajaniemi—the diamond-bright adventure of five unlikely companions across a transhuman galaxy."   —Seth Dickinson, author of *The Traitor Baru Cormorant*

"A gonzo space opera adventure in the post-human future, *Journey to the West* plus *FLCL* plus *The Quantum Thief* and much more. I love it."
—Django Wexler, author of the Shadow Campaigns series

"Gladstone has recklessly folded space and time in order to project a galaxy-sized adventure into this book-sized container. Take care when you open it."   —Howard Tayler, Hugo Award winner

"*Empress of Forever* blasts through a vast sparkling cosmos, powered by myth and boundless imagination, crewed by characters you can't help but love."
—Hannu Rajaniemi, author of *The Quantum Thief*

"A fast-paced thrill ride and a breakneck epic that explores a wildly, boldly imagined universe, filled with awe and wonder."
—John Chu, Hugo Award-winning author

"This is what 'big' science fiction is for—challenging ideas, spread over an epic canvas with a set of characters that are both fantastical and perfectly human (even the alien ones)."
—Geoffrey Thorne, showrunner, *Avengers: Black Panther's Quest*

"A marriage of *Star Wars*, Iain M. Banks, Hannu Rajaniemi, and K. J. Bishop, but with more pop culture references."
—Joel Cunningham, *B&N Sci-Fi & Fantasy Blog*

EMPRESS OF FOREVER

MAX GLADSTONE

TOR

A TOM DOHERTY ASSOCIATES BOOK
NEW YORK

This is a work of fiction. All of the characters, organizations, and events portrayed in this novel are either products of the author's imagination or are used fictitiously.

EMPRESS OF FOREVER

Copyright © 2019 by Max Gladstone

All rights reserved.

A Tor Book
Published by Tom Doherty Associates
175 Fifth Avenue
New York, NY 10010

www.tor-forge.com

Tor® is a registered trademark of Macmillan Publishing Group, LLC.

Library of Congress Cataloging-in-Publication Data

Names: Gladstone, Max, author.
Title: Empress of forever / Max Gladstone.
Description: First Edition. | New York : Tor, 2019. | "A Tom Doherty
    Associates Book."
Identifiers: LCCN 2018054087 | ISBN 9780765395818 (trade pbk.) |
    ISBN 9780765395832 (ebook)
Subjects: | GSAFD: Fantasy fiction.
Classification: LCC PS3607.L343 E47 2019 | DDC 813/.6—dc23
LC record avilable at https://lccn.loc.gov/2018054087

Our books may be purchased in bulk for promotional, educational, or business use. Please contact your local bookseller or the Macmillan Corporate and Premium Sales Department at 1-800-221-7945, extension 5442, or by email at MacmillanSpecialMarkets@macmillan.com.

First Edition: June 2019

Printed in the United States of America

0 9 8 7 6 5 4

To the crew of the *Good Question*

EMPRESS OF FOREVER

1

THEY CAME FROM all around the broken world to pay Vivian Liao homage on her birthday.

Oligarchs and video stars and billionaires and their daughters, princesses and actresses hoping for her notice, fresh-faced tech circuit darlings hungry to stand where Viv now stood but with only the vaguest sense of what that meant, people she'd sent invitations and people she'd let bribe or beg their way onto the guest list, they came. The Saint Kitts airport had hummed with Cessnas and Gulfstreams and Tesla Aeros for days before the party, and the long black glistening cars that wound up the driveway of the beachfront mansion might have been a funeral procession save for the passengers' brightly colored plumage. A funeral, maybe, for a tyrant.

They advanced on Viv like an army and she stood against them, her hair braided into a crown atop her head, her assistant, Lucy, by her side.

The guests came in part for the legend of a Vivian Liao birthday, in part for fear they'd give offense if they stayed home, but most came because they knew this might be the end. They could read the tea leaves as well as Viv, though not so deeply. Her name had been mentioned too often in the wrong tones on the wrong Sunday talk shows, by the wrong congressmen and administration mouthpieces. There had been a tasteful half inch in *The Wall Street Journal* about a routine investigation of one of her subsidiaries. They knew, as she knew, how it worked in America these days.

The men with the black bags and the ill-fitting suits and the bare concrete cells had finally decided she was more trouble than her disappearance would cause. There were lines, even when you were so rich your bankers got embarrassed. She hadn't known about those lines when she was young, in part because they didn't exist back then, or weren't so clearly drawn. That was one of the reasons she'd worked so hard to become rich in the first place. She was a genius, but you didn't have to be one to look around and see wealth was the only real freedom left. Get money and you could do what you wanted, help your friends, pile cash and power as a wall against the world. But there were lines now and she'd crossed them, and the fuckers in power did not forget. They were too dumb to keep detailed records, but they nursed grudges, which was worse. A record might get lost.

Her guests, she knew, would assume she'd overreached at last—maybe the massive free insurance program had been the final straw, or maybe gratis housing for her workforce in targeted congressional districts, maybe one of the newspapers she owned had skewered the wrong relative. Maybe she'd been too effective at breaking social media manipulation engines, or using them herself, or anonymizing user data just ahead of subpoenas. Rumor ran that the White House had been seriously pissed when FEMA reached Florida after Johannes to find two thousand relief workers in Liao Industries livery handing out free water, solar, and Internet in counties the administration designated *low priority* after the last election tally.

Viv knew better. She'd pissed off the right people, sure. But they came for her now not because they were angry, but because they were scared.

So was she. Terrified. At first she'd thought she was afraid of failure and its consequences, of black bags over her head, of needles slipped beneath her fingernails, of car batteries and clamps, of confinement in a narrow sleepless cell, drugged perhaps, until silence ate her mind. They knew she was proud—she'd been proud for so long in public—so they would try to break her and bring her low. Make her wallow. Snap her into so many pieces that if by some chance she were ever freed she'd spend all her days picking up the splinters of herself, a shivering wreck, no threat at all. But as she lay awake sleepless, curled around the sinkhole in her gut, she'd peeled back each layer of fear and found beneath those dark fantasies the reason she'd clutched them close as blankets on a cold night.

As scared as she was of failure, behind it lurked the vast and daunting prospect of success.

She might win. She might change everything. And it started here, as her guests mounted the stairs.

Her lungs refused to fill. She couldn't remember the last time she'd breathed deep, or savored a glass of water. Her hands roamed. Her nails, in the last three days, had bitten her skin raw beneath her shirt. Her jaw was tight as if sealed with wire. She carried those sleepless nights with her as darkness in the corners of her vision, as mocking light in the eyes of fake friends. But, Christ, she could hide it.

So when her guests hugged her and thanked her with a last-chance-to-see sort of vibe and added their presents to the pile on the table, she laughed and hugged them back and thanked them and even remembered their names mostly, though Lucy had to remind her of old Karpov's daughter's as the young woman drifted cloudlike and glorious up the steps and Viv, in spite of everything, forgot how to make consonant sounds. Natalia. Lucy offered the name without rolling her eyes.

Yes. So wonderful to see you again.

Rubberneckers all.

Viv hadn't invited any real friends she thought would come. The net was closing in, and she didn't want it catching anyone she cared about. She'd withdrawn from her parents and brother at the first hint of trouble, she'd not been with anyone seriously since Shanda broke it off, she'd let correspondence lapse and made herself conspicuously absent from reunions, unavailable when friends came to town, missed the annual gaming retreat for two years running. But she'd hit the *Forbes* list at twenty-six, gone bankrupt at twenty-seven, then hit the list again, higher, at twenty-nine, and she knew how to have fun in public when she was alone.

Most of the older guests didn't last the first night. On the second, Viv made a show of dissipation and excess—scotch and paintball all through the estate, diving, flirting, games. She got tossed into the pool. Lucy drifted behind her, brought her papers to sign when she had to sign them, ran interference with the catering and household staff, and generally contributed to the sense Viv was reveling to forget the noose around her neck. She toasted dawn with the few guests who were still awake. By the third night will and stamina began to flag, though most of those left were too young, too dumb, to admit it. People were passing out on couches, on the pool deck. Even Viv let her self-control lapse a little; when Natalia took her hand and led her upstairs, she followed.

This, she'd needed with a depth that would have held her back from asking. It was not love, but Natalia Karpov had lost two brothers and an uncle's family when they'd said the wrong things in the wrong place at the right time and perhaps she, more than anyone else here, understood the shape of Viv's sleepless nights and fear. Viv shook as Natalia undressed her, though the salt breeze through the open windows was not cold. She bit her lip, her breath short, frozen, strangled by her own muscles, until at a touch sliding downward from her belly she cracked and crashed against her and caught her in a grip so tight she gasped.

Viv wept in bed after, which she hadn't done in twenty years. And then, the true gift: she slept.

The house was still when she woke before dawn by Natalia's side.

Time to go.

She hadn't run from anything since fourth grade. Running wasn't how you crushed your rivals before they could crush you, how you built a start-up into an empire while cities fell into the ocean and Internet pastors said the Rapture was at hand. Hell, running hadn't even worked when she'd been bloody-nosed and knock-kneed and hunted back in grade school. That's why she learned to hit back.

But here she was, running from herself.

Even Viv had to admit that was a pretentious way of putting it. Yes, as she unwound herself from Natalia in the dark, she meant to leave it all behind, her guests and her companies and Lucy and her lovers and friends and fortunes, everything the world called Vivian Liao. But this wasn't some low-rent psychotic break, retreating to an ashram, finding Jesus or Buddha or whatever.

Vivian Liao, globe-trotting billionaire, was too closely watched to dis-appear. The last time she got the flu the NASDAQ lost six hundred points. (Granted, that was during the pandemic, but she hadn't had the *bad* flu, just the normal flu.) The government was after her now. If she changed her shape, left her houses and fortunes and armor behind, she could become small enough to slip through the net, take shelter, and strike back.

She dressed in silence.

Call it a tactical retreat. But when she crept downstairs wearing jeans and a gray hoodie and the cheapest sneakers she'd owned since her first IPO, no phone, no earpiece, no credit cards, nothing on her wrist but a watch that needed winding, and tiptoed in those sneakers over and around the sleep-ing, entwined bodies of her last enduring guests, out the half-open sliding door to the first pool deck and down the stairs to the second, then past the cabanas to the beach, she didn't feel like a grown woman, much less a fugi-tive titan of industry on a mission of vengeance and liberation. She felt like a kid creeping through her parents' barren house at night. Only, the house was her house now, and the attention she did not want to rouse her own. She snuck away from her body, down to the water.

The stars had failed and in the morning mist she could not tell sea from sky. If the world were as magic as it used to feel, she could just swim out until the out turned into up and the up to upside down, and tread water and raise her eyes to see this scrap of shoreline overhead, and with it all she meant to leave behind.

The fantasy would have been sweeter if there had not been real eyes up there in the sky beyond the blue, watching her, unblinking geosynchronous satellites with precision-machined lenses. The virus she'd slipped into their brains would only blind them for the next half hour. She wasn't taking this stroll for her health.

Not that there weren't health benefits to being a fugitive. Her doctor had told her to avoid stressful situations, and being duct-taped to a chair while some pensioned motherfucker with a shit mustache warmed up the elec-trodes would certainly qualify.

She wished she could have thanked Natalia. She wished she could have told Lucy good-bye.

She raised her hood and walked away. The waves erased her footprints.

By daybreak she had filled the sails of a twenty-foot schooner one of her aliases bought through an ad hoc Swiss microcorporation. When she looked back, the mansion on the beach seemed small, and she could not see her guests, or Natalia, or Lucy, at all.

To hell with that. She had a world to conquer.

Again.

She sawed off her braid with a knife at dawn, at the harbor's mouth where water cooled and deepened and blued. Her head felt gloriously light after, but she couldn't bring herself to toss the hair overboard. Hair is a kind of exomemory: the chemicals of life seep in and linger. Viv had started grow-ing her hair long in freshman year, and they'd been through a lot together. If someone could read the memory of that hair, they'd follow her through her first patent, her first ten million, her first IPO, her first breakup, the first time she had sex. But the feds had terabytes of HD video to feed their track-ing software. Viv never lived small or out of sight.

And she had designed the tracking software.

She'd done the hard part already, the cutting. Now all she had to do was chuck it over the side, and let the sea take the rest.

Instead she trimmed the sails. Wind calmed at her back as she matched its speed, and Saint Kitts set behind her.

A fair breeze and the Atlantic current, still there, however weakened, helped her make good time north; she sunbathed, read when the boat didn't need her, and savored the silence, which she wouldn't have for long. Black-beard came this way before they sank him. No, that was a bad line of thought. Don't obsess over losers.

She'd been careful to choose a boat that would not touch the Internet. It had been years since she last sailed without GPS, but she'd been preparing: charts, practice, clothes, a watertight sack with false papers and non-sequential bills.

Off North Carolina she set a tiny shaped charge in the keel, barely a fire-work but just enough to scuttle the boat, and added a change of clothes to the watertight sack. In her hand she weighed the braid, dry from days on the deck in the sun. Should have tossed it long ago. They might find it if she dropped it here, she told herself, before she added it to her sack, sealed the sack, and dove.

The sea rubbed her scalp and wove through her short hair. She did not think about what she'd lost. She'd get it all back.

Just watch her.

She surfaced and breathed. Her days had been a hush of sails and water, and the schooner's small explosion felt like a crack in the world.

She needed more disguise than a haircut. In a rest stop bathroom near the beach, she added a baseball cap and heavy makeup. She stared at the face in the mirror while she sterilized a needle with a Bic lighter flame: she'd practiced the technique back in Mountain View, but she still wasn't used to such heavy paint. The makeup made her eyes look extra large, her lips puffy. She looked like someone else.

She bit her lip between her teeth, and reopened her long-healed piercings with the pin. It hurt about like she expected: a short stab, a drop of blood on porcelain that water washed away. The earrings' weight made her head feel tight, and the metal struck cool against her jaw. She'd never minded earrings in general, or she told herself she'd never minded them, and she liked when other people wore them well, but these, now, here, felt shameful. She was changing, ducking her head, trying to look like anyone. Piercing her flesh to satisfy their gaze.

She faked a limp to mess with gait analysis, and by the time she reached the used car lot her hip hurt like hell.

Cash bought a clunker cheap in the South, especially if you pretended not to notice the damage a northern winter's salt left on the undercarriage. The salesman got chatty—you're not from around here, are you—and she made up a story she hoped was not too memorable, prominently featuring a boyfriend. He stood a little too close and the sun was a little too bright, and he was a big man and she felt suddenly conscious of being physically smaller, without bodyguards or a phone or a car, a woman with short hair alone and carrying cash. Not scared, exactly, just conscious in a way she had not been for years. When he gave her the keys and made some dumb joke she laughed and said good-bye and redlined the car for the interstate.

She drove north, weaving between auto trucks, slow, just shy of 80. They didn't let humans in the real fast lane anymore; autodrivers slipped past her on the left at 150-plus. Spoilers on the smaller cars stopped them from taking flight. Viv had three of those, the Maserati and two Teslas, back at the Mountain View house, if the feds hadn't boxed them up already.

She stopped for gas and granola bars and nothing else. She'd memorized the checkpoints and detoured to avoid them, but she still saw three not-so-random stops, four patrol cars each, tactical armor, officers ringing scared civilian drivers who just happened not to be white. The first time, she considered pulling over to help. She had before. But she'd been Vivian Liao then.

Even in her five-minute gas station stops she learned how right she'd been to change her face and hair. Her picture had become a common front-page item in the tabloids and legacy press, and brief glances at public tablets showed the stories reblogged and shared everywhere, the headline "Where's Vivian Liao?" flanked by machine-generated #content riffing on a fact list assembled by some intern in Bangladesh—maybe a kid Viv sponsored through school, that would be a nice grim twist. Most used the pic from that TED Talk in Stockholm, the one she only did because she lost a bet with Andrea, but sometimes they chose a red-carpet photo, two years old, from the eyeblink when she was dating Danika, before Danika won the Oscar and strategically got Religion. A school photo from Viv's valedictory address showed up on *HuffPo*, and the *National Enquirer* bribed their way into a college pic from that time Steve dragged her to *The Rocky Horror Picture Show:* fishnets, leather, French cuffs, spike heels, tongue out, hair crown-braided even then.

Happier times.

She ditched the car in a stadium parking lot in Philadelphia and hopped a train to Boston. Her heart beat faster as she neared. She knew this place, she'd mastered it once, and now she crept back in like a rat. She'd loved those streets, that brick, those cameras, those prox card readers. She'd played with them, learned from them. And that was her picture on *The Globe*'s front page on an Amtrak dining car table—"Where's Vivian Liao?" The TED Talk photo looked more like her than she looked like herself.

She didn't have to go through with this.

She had disappeared. She could go further: miss her rendezvous, grab cash from a dead drop, take the Downeaster to Brunswick and use her fake papers and the cash to get to Canada, open a pizza place or buy one, some small survival business where she could stay out of sight. Find a girl. Settle down. Her enemies might want her broken, but they'd settle for her gone.

All she'd done, she'd done to reach Boston undetected. She had weapons here, a plan, a place to stand and a lever long enough to move the world. But worlds were big things, heavy, round, and once they started to move, they rolled with crushing force and did not stop no matter how many bodies lay across their path.

In two thousand miles of road her lungs had not yet filled. But if she left now, she really would be running away.

She got off the train at Back Bay, hat down, hood up, ears aching under metal hoops, and walked toward Boston Common and the future.

2

NONE OF VIV'S fitful dreams prepared her for seeing Magda Lopez grown and married, reading a romance novel in line for the Clover food truck on Boston Common.

Thin rays of silver graced Magda's dark hair. There was more of her than there had been in school, which was healthy considering that back in school she'd run ten miles every morning before eight, and she wore a thin gold ring these days. But she thumbed her place in her book just like she used to—she hated folding pages but could never keep track of a proper bookmark—and when she looked up to search the Common's crowds her eyes were just the same, breathtakingly brown and kind.

They had been freshman-year roommates, one of the few pairs that stuck. They'd seemed destined for disaster at first, Magda a lean coltish track star from Texas, Viv faking sophistication far too well thanks to her parents' coaching and her own relief to be a continent away from them at last.

Magda had left a boyfriend behind. For the first week she spent an hour on the phone with him each night, and on Thursday of the second week Viv came home tired from studying and tipsy from wine after studying to find Magda lying still and staring up at the ceiling. Her eyes glittered open and her breath was deep and forced. Viv climbed into her own bed, rolled onto her side, and turned out the light. As the dark closed in Magda let herself cry again. Viv listened, and wondered what she was supposed to do, and thought of Merlin in *The Once and Future King*, and felt like a foolish girl a long way from home.

When Magda trailed off but had not yet gone to sleep Viv sat up in her pajamas and said, "Hey" quietly. You didn't throw a life preserver at the person drowning, but next to them. And Magda drew a ragged breath and said, "Hey" back.

Viv took a bottle of wine from underneath her bed, unscrewed the top, poured the wine into paper cups, and asked, "Do you know how to pick a lock?"

"No." But she was sitting up at least, with a weak smile behind the thicket of her hair.

"Do you want to learn?"

She had, and then she'd played Viv a song from *Into the Woods*, and Viv slept through her quiz the next day but didn't care.

That was how it started.

And now, after years and countless miles of road, Viv held her breath as Magda searched the Common crowd for her, and wanted more than anything to be seen, for Magda's eyes to widen and for her to wave and call Viv's name across the grass, even though the microphones in the trees and the robot dogs on patrol would hear her. Viv needed Magda that much, and she had not let herself know until this moment. When Magda paused on her, considered her face, then looked away without a blink of recognition, Viv thought, *Good*, the disguise was working, but she felt like she'd taken a wrong step on false ground and fallen through.

Hands clenched around her tourist map, she made her way to Magda.

Viv had never met her old friend's kid; Victor was born right before the Collapse, when Viv's life turned the bad kind of interesting, so he'd be two now. She wouldn't meet him on this visit. Magda wouldn't take her home, too dangerous. Helping Viv even this much risked dragging in her husband, and her son. But Magda had come, just like she'd promised in the coded message she'd sent six months ago after Viv looped her in on the plan.

She couldn't turn Viv down.

Viv had never deserved her friends.

Of all the mean and lousy things the weasels on Viv's heels had forced her to do, by far the hardest was to tap Magda on the shoulder, watch her turn, watch her eyes light up when she saw past makeup and earrings and cap—to do all that, and not embrace her.

She wanted more than to hug her friend. She wanted, though she'd never admit it, to be hugged herself, held and anchored so the wind could never blow her away, even if her fortunes, her fame, the Mountain View house, her companies, had all been torn from her, leaving her a runaway with a rucksack, a painted face, absurd earrings. A woman with fake papers in a country that didn't used to care so much about that sort of thing.

She wanted to be human in her old friend's arms.

But to be human was to be weak, and she couldn't allow that now, here, as robot dogs wandered past sniffing the Common for bombs.

She shoved her map between them, open, and her grip was so tight she ripped it at the corner. "Excuse me." Her voice shook. "I'm sorry, I'm lost. I'm trying to get to Faneuil Hall?" She mispronounced it like a tourist, and tried to look Magda in the eye but had to look away again fast, as if she'd stared into the sun. "Where am I?"

"Right here." Magda kept her voice almost casual. She tried to take the map and for a second Viv did not let it go and they were touching through the tense paper. Viv forced her fingers to part. "Here, see, you just go up this road—it's not straight, exactly, nothing really is here—" Another laugh, also forced. "—until you get to a plaza with a blocky concrete building, then down these steps." A pause. Tongue touched lip. Eyes darted up, away. "Are you here for long?"

"Just the day." They'd arranged the code phrase in advance. I'm not being followed, as far as I know.

"If you have time—there are a few other places you should see."

A robot dog sniffed Viv's ankle and moved along. Magda's breath hooked, but she did not look down. She drew a pen from behind her ear and circled the Pru, the library, other landmarks, then folded Viv's torn map and passed it back. When Viv forced herself to thank Magda and turn away she found the map's folds held a key, and one of the circled landmarks was not a landmark at all.

PEOPLE VIV'S AND Magda's age still called this kind of place an Airbnb even though that site rebranded after the murders. Same sort of thing, though, a nice one-bedroom night-by-night rental in Beacon Hill with a skylight above the bed and that bright early autumn Boston blue above. Champagne chilled in the fridge, decent stuff, actual AOP, rare these days with the climate; a shopping bag on the kitchen counter held a packet of fake rose petals, scented candles, and, separately wrapped, a few pieces of leather Viv didn't examine closely. A Happy Anniversary card. A ruse—wasn't it? Magda's wedding had been in summer, though Viv couldn't remember precise dates anymore without her screens.

Magda arrived in late afternoon, and as the door shut behind her Viv found herself enveloped.

She couldn't breathe. Some of that was the hug—Magda had been working out—but wetness welled in her eyes and nose and a hot fist caught her windpipe. She held her like that long-gone life preserver. Oh, god, she was losing it. And if she lost it here, if all the disintegration came over her at once, she'd never pull herself back together for tonight.

"Viv." Magda kept repeating her name, a murmur like waves washing the North Carolina beach where Viv had lain exhausted after her swim ashore, sprawled in flotsam beside the sack that held her braid and the remnants of her life. In a way Magda's voice was that surf. In a way Viv had only now made landfall. "I've been so worried, Viv, they said maybe suicide"—good, she'd hoped for that—"and I knew you wouldn't, I knew the plan, but, Viv, Jesus, you're alive, I can't believe it, and—your hair."

Magda pulled away at that, hand on the back of Viv's skull, and Viv grinned and wiped her own nose on her sleeve like, what, I have a cold. She turned the convulsions in her gut and lungs into something someone charitable might call a laugh, and lied, "I like it better this way." There was so much she wanted to say about how grateful she was, about what a risk Magda was taking, but those words were too big to speak. "Thank you," she said, and Magda's look when she said that, her shock that Viv might feel she had to say it, almost broke Viv's last thread of composure. But Viv had been through too much to take friendship or faith for granted.

For a while neither of them moved. They didn't mention the stain Viv's tears left on Magda's shirt.

"Oh! That reminds me." Though Viv hadn't said anything. Magda reached into her purse and removed a small package wrapped in striped paper with a red bow. "It's not much, but happy birthday."

Viv blinked down at the package, then up at Magda, then down again. "Magda—I'm not—I can't—" She didn't trust herself to finish the sentence.

"I know, you're traveling." She didn't say *on the run*. "So it's light. Go on, open it."

She slipped a thumb under the seam and popped the tape, and there inside was a battered old black paperback with a seated Buddha ringed in rainbows on the cover. A woman stood behind him, glowing, with butterfly wings. Viv's laugh caught. "You've sent me this book, what, five times?"

"Seven. Did you ever read it?"

She shrugged, feeling only a little guilty. She hadn't had much time for reading in a while.

"I thought maybe you'd have time now." She was trying to keep her voice light. "I've never been a fugitive, but I hear there's a lot of riding in boxcars.

And trains are slow. And before you say anything, I bought this in a used book store about ten years ago, cash. So it's probably safe."

If Viv had been a better person she would have been able to say out loud all the things she was still thinking, like *I love you*, and *I should have stayed, I never should have gone off and made myself big, I should have stayed here with you and the others and built small and had dumb little fights and remembered everyone's anniversaries.* But she didn't believe that last bit really, no matter how she felt it, so she hugged her again instead, less desperate now but more firm. "I thought about you all the way here." It wasn't true but it approached truth sideways. She couldn't bear to think about her. "I missed you."

"Of course you did. I bet all the rich jerks you invited to your birthday got you, what, stock certificates or something? Come on, let's have wine."

"God, yes."

Magda poured this time, and the cups weren't paper.

Viv asked about Victor, about work, about whether she still ran and what she'd been up to in the six months since it got too dangerous for them to talk, and did not mention what she'd come to do, or how she felt. Magda had always understood Viv, even at school when there was barely any Viv to know yet, just a passel of immature reflexes drawn from her parents, her grandma's cultural revolution horror stories, and the science-fiction section of the public library. Viv needed to be strong. So it was Magda, blessed Magda, who took the silence that opened between them after the first glass of wine and said: "It's all ready. Just like you asked."

That night, she would break into Ogham.

MAGDA DIDN'T WORK for Ogham—she never had, technically; all the code she'd written for them had been part of a subcontractor consultant sort of gig, and she was never listed as an employee, so unless the feds did the kind of legwork nobody really remembered how to do these days except the Russians and Israelis, no one would be waiting for Viv, and no one would trace her intrusion back to Mags.

Ogham wasn't Ogham anymore, after three acquisitions, an inversion, and two name changes, but the service was more or less the same—like a police precinct surviving each new junta that rolled through town. They cached the Internet, and served it to everybody.

Here was the problem: everyone wants everything instantly, but light only goes so far. Easy solution: you move the Internet—most of it—closer.

In a place like Boston, full of universities and hospitals and biotech and normal tech—including several of Viv's own once and future companies—Ogham served machines with more processing power than the entire planet had back in the benighted oughts. Probably enough for what Viv had in mind.

Which was war.

Not the nuclear sort, at first. In a way, her enemies had betrayed themselves by coming for her now, when they'd let her other offenses slide. She wouldn't have known she'd found a real threat otherwise.

When Lucy asked what she was doing in all those hours blocked out on the calendar for "Research," Viv had said machine learning stuff, which was almost true. Viv's project—the root of all this trouble—this idea she'd been piecing together in secret, sideways, while she saw what happened to the real visionaries in this space, so many surprise bankruptcies and leveraged buyouts and "market fluctuations," not to mention the cancers and the deaths in the family and that one particularly grisly murder-suicide, this idea that led to the audits and "discrepancies" and talk show warnings that made her cut and run because, let's face it, a lot of those "real visionaries" had been white boys and if that's what the suits did to them, she didn't want to find out what they'd do to her—Viv's project was machine learning stuff like the Death Star was laser pointer stuff.

She had come within a hair's breadth of a real self-optimizer: a smart program that could make itself smarter, without limit. Machine uplift, changing the destiny of the human race forever.

But what concerned Viv most, for now, were the ancillary benefits.

The most obvious was that, in a world run by machines, she'd own the machines. Hello, robot army. All those cameras, all that surveillance tech, all the levers of censorship and control—her cameras now, her tech, her censors, her control. She could walk out of any prison and into any vault. Which sounded fun, but that was thinking small. The entire global financial system depended on the strength of its encryption. A truly strong, self-improving machine intelligence could tear through crypto. Simply revealing what she'd done, let alone doing anything with it, would shatter markets. She'd have a gun pointed at the head of the world.

And of course, she'd control the nukes.

The fuckers would crawl. Or she'd crush them.

She'd enjoy that.

Oh, and once that was done she'd fix the planet. Geoengineering to put the climate back where it used to be. New math would pave the way for microtailored cancer treatments. Give a system like that the silicon and iron it needed to run, and it would solve global problems by the shovelful. A silver bullet. Bang.

Next stop, the stars.

Once she built the system, she could talk to it through a wristwatch—but first she had to make a trillion-node distributed protosentient mind. The easiest way to do that would be to seed a tiny bit of code on some appreciable fraction of all the computers in the world. To do that, she needed a zero day exploit or five—easy, if you had money like hers—and a distribution system—hard, with her enemies watching.

So she'd left, and gone underground.

There weren't many places where you could reach as much of the Internet as Viv needed without bouncing off some censor gate. If Viv was really lucky, the government still thought she was dead. If she was less lucky but still generally on the ups, they'd expect her to go for the transatlantic cable anchor in New York—it would be ideal, if she had some way to slip past the DHS security and, worse, the Google security. Ever since New York became one of those euphemistically named High Watchfulness Zones, you couldn't hide from its cameras anymore. Ogham was almost as good, and safer.

In the Amazon rain forest there lived a parasitic fungus called the *Cordyceps*, which grew inside a particular species of ant. The *Cordyceps* hijacked its host's tiny ant brain and forced it to climb to a high place inside the colony, where the fungus bloomed through the back of the host's head, killing it and raining infectious spores on the colony below.

Viv would be the *Cordyceps*, and Ogham would be her ant.

Bad analogy. It made this whole thing sound sinister. Viv wasn't a mad scientist. She just wanted to crush her enemies, and save the world.

And after a few more hours on the couch with Magda talking about anything else, drinking in stories about Victor, his first word (*book*, Magda was so proud), teething and attendant lack of sleep, and oh did Magda mention they got a dog, this chill waggly pibble so strong she doesn't even notice when Vic tries to ride her—after an afternoon's safety, Viv felt almost ready.

SO DID MAGDA. That was the problem.

"No." Viv moved away from her on the couch, hands out. "You're not coming with me."

"Once you're in, you just let me in through the side door."

"There will be cameras."

"You're already dealing with the cameras. And the rest of the security."

"I can't let anything happen to you." After saying this most naked truth, Viv felt a burning sensation all over her skin and inside, only it wasn't shame. Pride.

"Then don't." As if Viv had that kind of power. "Viv, I won't let you do this alone."

"It's dangerous."

She gripped Viv's arms and met her eyes, level, firm. "It was dangerous when you sent me your first letter. I answered because you needed my help. Do you think I'd stop halfway? You need someone to watch your back. There's no way you're talking me out of this."

"Give me the key card, Mags."

"No." Her voice was flat, her gaze sharp, her body rigid and earnest, and Viv fell silent before the fierceness of her. "Not until you agree: I'm coming with you. No tricks."

And Viv, after all her careful preparation, was caught.

THAT NIGHT, AS she approached the building in shadow and streetlight, she thought about Victor, whose first word was *book*, and wondered what kind of monster she was to let Magda come.

She had been alone. She didn't want to be alone again. And Magda wanted—

No. Viv could have lied, made herself out to be stronger, more controlled, less afraid. She could have turned Magda away, refused to let her come, faked an argument. It would have hurt, but she had hurt herself enough over the last few days—she was used to the prospect.

Perhaps there was some brutal subconscious calculus at work. The more incriminated Magda was, the less risk she'd sell Viv out under pressure. But that wasn't the whole story either. She wanted Magda there. She'd come so far alone.

Had Viv arranged all this? Not consciously. Consciously, she thought this was a horrible idea.

Did that matter?

Could your subconscious be evil?

She considered ditching her, leaving Magda out in the cold. But she had promised.

Focus on the job.

If there had been a better option than a physical break-in, Viv would have found it back in Mountain View. The digital security here was top notch, built to resist advanced persistent threats, which people who weren't security geeks tended to call *governments*. The physical security wasn't a pushover either, but it came from a company that licensed tech from companies owned, through a double handful of sock puppets, by Vivian Liao.

Not that she built back doors into clients' systems. That would be very wrong. No, she just kept plans to their systems around in case she ever needed to analyze her way through them. To improve them. For example.

Magda's key card opened the door. Viv slipped in. The lights here were too bright, the halls too soft and silent. She breathed deep, stepped into the light and the security cameras' field of view, and trusted to her makeup.

She'd spent weeks before she left, and three hours this afternoon, testing this idea, making sure she could pull it off with Magda's over-the-counter makeup printer. Her face looked like a melted checkerboard, black and white swirled and spiraling. Back in high school the game had been to fool face recognition on her friends' phones by painting her face weird patterns. She'd just taken that idea one step further.

The cameras asked the security system whether she was on the master list of People Who Were Supposed to Be Here. The security system tried to check—which meant reading Viv's face. But where were her eyes under that makeup? What was her mouth? The system used math to break the black-and-white grid down to meaning, but since Viv knew the math it would use, she could control the meaning it would find. So when the security system read her face, it interpreted the melted checkerboard into a few dense lines of code, and executed them.

That was the plan. In ten seconds she'd know if it worked. She tried not to hold her breath. If she'd screwed up somehow, she'd need all the air she could draw for running. Ten seconds. She pressed her palms against her jeans and tried not to think about failure. At least if she slipped up here, Magda would still be safe.

Ten seconds. Six heartbeats. Well. Under these conditions, maybe more like twelve heartbeats. Or eighteen.

The hallway lights flickered three times, and she gasped with relief—and for air. That was it. For the next hour, the security system belonged to her.

So don't waste time, Viv. Go.

Through the front hall, left, downstairs to the side door. Footsteps froze Viv solid, but it wasn't a guard, just some dork trudging past with a monitor under his arm. He vanished around a corner, taking with him a few months of Viv's life.

When Viv reached the side door she knocked shave-and-a-haircut against it, and the sensors heard her and popped the lock. Magda waited outside. She waved with her fingers, smiled parade broad, and Viv, still unsure, still scared, couldn't help smiling back. She was enjoying this too much. At all was too much.

"You look ridiculous. I love it."

Viv raised a finger to her lips. Magda placed one beside her nose like she was in *The Sting*. Viv rolled her eyes, *nerd*, but it felt so good to see her that Viv couldn't sell the tease.

Viv led the way. Down and down, and then—the server farm.

It was cold here. Viv breathed out ghosts of fog. Another knock, and they were in. Take that, retina scanner.

Servers stood in racks. The room was silent save for fans and the air conditioner's hum. Viv's first step tested the tile floor as if it might crumble underfoot. The tiles gave slightly into the storage space below, but did not rattle. Magda followed her, steps light.

This was a new experience. Nerves expected. Viv had been a lot of things in a career newspapers sometimes called *meteoric*, which Viv liked because it made her think of dinosaurs. Now she was a thief. Stealing her life back. Stealing the future.

Magda watched. There was a console at the far end of the racks, some ancient hunk of desktop wired into the iron. Viv crouched beside it and drew her kit from her shoulder bag: AR glasses were more portable than a screen, but nothing beat a keyboard for input. She still felt pissed at Bill Gibson for promising her transcranial electrodes and failing to deliver. Also from her pack: a single-board computer the size of an old USB key, which contained the software she needed for the job, and the Ziploc bag that held her braid.

For luck, she told herself.

She plugged her computer key into the console. The glasses dazzled Viv's eyes and made her sick when she swiped them on. She'd logged who knew how many thousands of hours in glasses by this point, but after two weeks off, your eyes forgot.

Her fingers remembered keys just fine, though.

Usually Viv did this sort of thing to music, but she had no player here, no earbuds, no phone. No matter. Between the fans, her heart, the clatter of the keys, she made her own soundtrack. She shivered from the cold, and anticipation. After two weeks away, her wrists didn't even hurt when she typed.

This part never looked as dramatic as movies made it seem. The command prompt was a simple bracket, and the cursor hadn't stopped blinking since 1983 or so. In arcane tongues, she asked some of the most powerful computers in the world to do her a favor.

Some of the most powerful computers in the world said yes.

There wouldn't even be a progress bar if Viv hadn't coded one herself. It crept up one percentage point at a time. Viv was changing the planet with less bandwidth (for now) than some kid in Allston needed to stream his latest Disney princess fix.

A red warning light burned in the top left corner of her field of view.

"Oh," Viv said.

"Oh?" Magda did not sound happy about the prospect of an "Oh."

"Don't worry about it, but . . . we're being tracked."

"We?" and then: "Tracked?"

It's fine, Viv thought, it's fine, this is the kind of thing that's fine. A red timer ticked down as layers of her anti-tracking onion peeled away. "They're too slow!" She laughed. It felt good to be good. It would be close, half a minute maybe, but they wouldn't catch her before the script did its work. Thirty whole seconds to spare. Numbers don't lie.

"You're sure?" And in Magda's voice Viv heard the first sign her friend might finally understand that she should not be here. Magda was remembering her son, remembering that she was not pranking university security anymore, and that was a bad idea even way back then.

Viv could be honest. She was not one hundred percent positive. Systems made mistakes. Even her systems. But the progress bar was at ninety, ninety-two, and even if it got stuck for a second, like it did just then, they'd have plenty of time to escape.

The ground shook.

Viv fell back, sat down hard. The keyboard clattered to the floor, and she lunged to still it with one hand, overcome with vertigo and fear. That must have been an earthquake—even in Boston. She recognized the gut-level uncertainty, a hiccup, a skip. But an earthquake strong enough to knock Viv on her butt should have rattled the servers in their racks and set the racks themselves swaying. Instead Magda was glaring at Viv like she, Viv, had just gone mad. "Did you feel that?"

"Feel what?"

Not a quake, then; the world had gone weird but not quite quakes-in-Boston weird. Was that how fainting felt? Viv couldn't afford weakness now, even if she had pushed herself hard all the way from Saint Kitts up the coast. She needed more coffee, more water, more sleep, maybe a square meal. She'd have time after this. Maybe give herself a day or two in the Airbnb before she hit the road again. As soon as this was done.

She glanced at the progress bar.

It was stuck.

Ninety-six. Ninety-six. Ninety-six.

And still the red trace counter counted down.

Magda looked at Viv, and Viv saw her fear, all this suddenly real. But that last four percent, that was Viv's life, her salvation, everything for which she had fought, died (at least, they thought so), and run. Shadowy motherfuckers in suits were tearing down her life to stop that four percent.

But Magda wouldn't be here if not for Viv. The fake rose petals. That bottle of real champagne.

Viv had no idea what the script, ninety-six percent executed, would do—if anything. She had no idea what she would do, if she left it ninety-six percent executed and ran with Magda into the night. This chance would not come again.

There were other data centers. Other options. The New York deathtrap, for example. But when they found what she'd tried to do here, they'd be on their guard.

Ninety-six. Still. And the red counter neared zero.

She swiped the glasses off, pulled the computer key. Jesus. She was doing this. She'd done it already. The earth shook again, or was that her? All the gear, in the bag. She ran to Magda, grabbed her hand—"What are you doing?" "Getting us out of here."—in the server racks, in thousands, hundreds of thousands of computers around Boston and the world, her ninety-six-percent-done script did whatever it could do—and there was no time to explain, she was dragging Magda to the door, glancing back—

She'd forgotten the braid.

No time. But (she reasoned, sprinting back down the hall) if they found her braid they'd know she was here, and if they knew that—

She snagged the braid, left sneaker skids on tile as she turned back to the door.

And in those seconds, everything had changed.

A glowing woman stood in the space between the server racks.

Once Viv saw her, it took her a while to notice anything else.

The woman was a cutout of light without shadow or contour. Viv thought the woman was two-dimensional at first, but when she rose from her crouch—Viv knelt before no one—the shape changed in a way that suggested three dimensions, or more. Vantablack statues looked like this in person. Fuligin, but green. The light that came off her throbbed.

The woman wore a crown and a robe and none of this made any sense, but that didn't matter, because this weird glowing figure had her hand on Magda's shoulder, and the green light trickled from her shadowless luminescent fingers like sap, and Magda was stuck inside it with her mouth half open, reaching out, afraid.

The air conditioner hum had stopped.

Viv thought of cats in boxes. Alive and dead at once.

"After all this time," the woman said, "I'd hoped for something more."

Her voice was not loud. Just close.

Viv wheeled, but the woman was not behind her. Wheeled back, and she was standing so near that her face filled Viv's field of vision. Somehow she'd closed the twenty feet between them in a second. They'd be eye to eye if the green woman had eyes, but what she had instead was a hint of a mouth, the only feature in that perfect face, a pure black line.

Viv flailed her pack around like a mace. It passed through the woman as if through fog, but when the woman grabbed Viv's wrist, the wrist stayed grabbed. The green woman's strength was not a thing of muscle but a fact, like fear, and like fear it burned. Viv's flesh began to smoke.

The black mouth opened, and something glittered inside it, but the green woman's words did not pass through air. They ignored Viv's ears entirely and flipped switches inside her brain instead. The voice was rich as velvet cake and cello deep, the calm, inhuman warmth voices had when spoken softly with perfect diction close to a good microphone. "Don't fight me," she said. "You'll only hurt yourself."

Viv's skin blistered. She growled, shoved all her weight against this woman, and fell through her to the floor. Her wrist burned like nothing she had ever felt, but she was free. She came up off the floor like the world's worst sprinter, staggered, and ran straight into Magda—but bounced off her like she might have bounced off a concrete pillar. Viv reeled. When she looked up, the green woman stood over her again. She had not crossed the intervening space. She just moved, from there to here.

Viv couldn't flex her left hand. Her fingers were wet, but she only knew this because they slipped on the floor, leaving bloody tracks.

"Disappointing." The green woman knelt. This close, her raiment—fuck no, Viv refused that word, refused all the majesty of her—her clothes rustled, overdubbed, too rich, like the green woman's voice. This close, Viv felt the heat of her. This close, her light had shifting patterns, shadows, patches like the surface of the sun.

Viv was going to die.

She had suspected, accepted this might be the case when she tried to run. She had just imagined the set dressing differently. A basement, or a room in an abandoned hotel. Wires. Pliers. She'd seen beds in a schoolhouse in Phnom Penh, where they tortured people for the crime of wearing glasses.

But whatever this green woman was, whoever she was, she was just another thing like that, another form of a fear Viv was ready for. So when the woman pressed her hand to Viv's shirtfront and the cloth smoldered, Viv tried to keep herself together. Learn what you can. Escape if you can. "Who sent you?"

"No one," that voice replied. "I don't enjoy this, you know. But I must learn." She wasn't smiling. The set of that slit mouth made her look annoyed. Viv's burning shirt stank of knives and fear-sweat. "We are being interrupted. I would have liked more time."

The green woman hadn't glanced at Magda once. If her control slipped, maybe Magda could get away. Viv's shirt burned to ash, left her chest bare. The green woman's fingers curled. Her sharp nails glistened.

Maybe, Viv thought, desperate, grasping at shreds of logic, maybe the green woman can't be both here and not at once.

So when the woman's hand plunged into Viv's chest and cracked her ribs, Viv shoved her own body up, and slammed her forehead into the crevasse of that open mouth. Hard teeth printed Viv's skin, and she felt a bone break near her eye, but none of that mattered. There was a hand around her heart. The green woman roared, and her mouth was large, and Viv understood its glitter now. There were stars in the green woman's mouth between her diamond teeth, and somewhere a siren wailed, and the green woman cursed, and Magda screamed. Good. If Magda could scream, maybe she could run. Maybe she could escape. Maybe Viv had saved her after all, from herself.

She felt another earthquake that wasn't one. The green woman gripped her heart, and lifted.

The world snapped, and so did Vivian Liao.

3

VIV DROWNED IN green.

Pain guided her from strangling dreams to consciousness: pain in her chest where the green woman had plunged her claws, pain so great that set beside it all her previous yardsticks for suffering—the fishhook through her thumb, the arm broken climbing upside down off a bunk bed at camp, even the pain from her melted wrist in the server farm—seemed first drafts set beside a masterwork. She flailed against the viscous green fluid in which she hung suspended. By old swimmer's reflex she swam for the surface, only to bounce off a curved rubbery membrane.

Wait. Green? Viscous? Membrane?

Soldiers and scientists call the process of decision-making under stress the *OODA loop:* the subject first Observes their situation, then Orients themselves to it, Decides how to proceed, and finally, Acts.

For most of Viv's life, that loop had spun so fast its stages blurred together like a bike wheel's spokes at speed. But now Viv's OODA loop stopped sharp at Orient, and she pitched against her metaphorical handlebars and struggled not to fall.

She'd spent two years of nights dreaming about what might happen if her gambit failed, if her faceless adversaries in the administration caught her. But none of her nightmares involved a jade woman who seemed like a cutout from the world, or Viv herself drowning in green slime.

Fine. Slow down the loop. Start over, at Observe.

She found her chest intact, her ribs and breastbone whole, which was a pleasant surprise, which in turn said unfortunate things about recent events. Still. Good. She wouldn't have to worry about bleeding out.

But she could not breathe.

Her mouth was open. The green stuff filled her lungs already. That she wasn't dead suggested the green was a kind of oxygen-bearing fluid, but if it was supposed to feed her air it must have run out. Her chest spasmed. Her throat closed. The green smelled of blood and iron and felt jagged in her throat, and her stomach registered its extreme desire to throw up.

No. Permission sure as hell not granted. Whatever had happened back in the basement—where was Magda? What had that woman, that light, done to her?—Viv refused to choke on her own vomit before she could (1) rescue Magda, then (2) figure out what was going on and whose fault this was, and (3) pay them back with extreme prejudice, before at last (4) returning to her business of world salvation-slash-conquest.

So much for Orient. Now. Decide.

She needed out. She needed up.

Act.

The membrane jiggled and screeched beneath her fingernails. She wanted to laugh. A bad sign. Hysteria. Acceptance would come next, and the end. So long Viv.

To hell with that. She traced the membrane with her hands, followed it down until the ceiling became a wall, then curved back to bond with a flat floor. Not a dome: a bubble. Her fingernails found no seams in the bubble's surface, but it was stuck to a flat platform underfoot.

Take it easy. Control your heartbeat. This is just a new observation. Orient: there's no easy exit. Decide: you'll have to make your own.

Act.

She curled herself into a ball, dug her toes into the floor, and pressed her hands into the bubble's skin. They slipped. Tried again, and again, slip.

Lights danced between her and the world. She didn't have long. She leaned forward. The lights weren't all inside her—a flash, a tremor, suggested movement outside. She imagined her captors watching her, laughing, taking shitty CIA-salary-sized bets, five bucks says she lasts the minute, you're on. I hope you're enjoying this, assholes. Fingernails wouldn't work? Fine. She pressed her teeth against the bubble, and bit, and tore. The skin gave. It didn't break, but stretched enough for her to hook her hands beneath.

She wouldn't have strength for a second try at this. All or nothing, all at once. Vivian Liao, deadlift for your life.

Her muscles strained, her heart beat faster with work and rage and fear. But decades of practice at the role of Vivian Liao, supergenius, had trained her into a kind of double selfhood. Yes, there was a part of her that quaked, that wanted, that hid or wept or yearned, a part that had spent the first ten weeks of ninth grade marinating in a full-body crush on Susan Cho with her slightly curly hair and her tight pink sweaters and that gold cross on the thin chain at her throat which her father the pastor gave her—that deep animal tangle, the meat of Viv.

Then there was another Viv who sifted through the meat and muck, found what had to be done next, and did it. Sometimes it found her alone with Susan Cho, on a museum trip, between two dinosaurs, and made her ask, fast as tearing off a Band-Aid, whether she'd ever thought about kissing girls, and whether Susan would like to kiss her. That part won her the kiss—and the breakup after, but what the hell. That part won her fortunes. This was not the first time it saved her life.

Her arms strained in their sockets, her legs, her knees, use proper form, dammit, it's more efficient, spread the earth with your feet, trick every microcontraction you can out of this goddamn meat puppet, just get this motherfucker up. Up!

The skin tore.

The bubble ripped up the side and the green gunk rushed out and so did Viv. She burst free on the flood and collapsed, coughing green, choking until she drew her first breath of cool pure air, sweet as Susan Cho.

Her lungs hurt as if she'd never used them before. She sobbed between gulps of air, and tried to stop herself, and eventually succeeded. She realized she was cold, and realized after that that she was naked. Her nudity had not been worth noting in the bubble, since clothes were far down the hierarchy of needs past "not drowning."

Observe.

She heard a muddled commotion, growing more distinct as fluid drained from her ears. The thunder sharpened into the clang of metal striking metal, and there were screams, pained grunts, cries—not cries of terror, not canned McDojo kiais, but the unbidden roars human beings made when they tried as hard as they could bear to do something, and found, against all odds, that they'd succeeded. Some of those cries cut off abruptly. There were more screams. Whoever had caught her was under attack. Something was not going according to someone's plan.

Good.

She rubbed green from her eyes, and blinked away the blur.

Where was she?

In a puddle, most immediately, alone on a dais in the center of an egg: eggshell white, eggshell round, eggshell empty. Small bright lights flickered and swarmed behind the alabaster wall. LEDs, maybe. No wires she could see, no fixtures. No visible cameras or mics, though that meant nothing. As torture cells went, it was more Silicon Valley than she'd expect from the current administration.

No exits, of course.

She was just trying to work up the urge to look for one when a door-sized section of wall bulged and petaled open.

Viv scrambled to her feet. She didn't know where she was, or who was holding her and why, but whoever walked through that weird door might confuse her collapse, reveling in kiss-sweet air, for surrender. She refused to give these assholes the satisfaction.

She skidded, slipped, to hide against the wall near the improbably opening door, tensed to run, tensed to fight.

And a robot walked in.

Her OODA loop locked again.

Viv knew robots. Robots cleaned her house, robots drove her to work, robots built most everything she'd ever owned. Creepy blank-faced receptionist robots had long since replaced bank tellers in Japan.

But she'd never seen a robot like this.

It walked with unsettling smooth grace on oddly bent legs, and scanned the room with burning ruby eyes rather than cameras. She didn't recognize the design of its joints, or the materials that composed its body—black sharp tines and what looked like broken glass, illuminated from within by pulsing red light. What tech *was* that? Nothing Viv knew, nothing she'd even seen gestures toward in Kenya's best android labs. Viv's robots moved like demon puppets. This moved like a person comfortable with killing.

The head spun toward her, and the torso followed. Eyes pulsed. Long fingers, three to each hand, shifted to extend knifelike claws.

Viv was still trying to figure out how the robot worked when it lunged.

She dodged too late, but her foot slipped and the fall saved her from the first sweep of its blades. Competence saved her the second time: she rolled to one side as its claws plunged into her cell floor, and kicked the robot hard in a span of its side that looked less spiky than the rest. Its claws tore free, and as she scrambled to her feet the robot's limbs gimballed and wheeled until it found traction. It glared at her, red-eyed and furious.

And she almost died.

The robot opened its fanged mouth. A brilliant glow built within its throat, and if she'd spent a split second wondering *why* rather than diving left, landing hard on her side, and skidding in green goo, the bolt of light would have gone straight through her stomach rather than simply tearing a hole in the wall. The swarming lights behind the eggshell sparked and the chamber went dark.

She smelled ozone. Get up. Run. Don't just fucking lie here. But her arms wouldn't move.

She breathed rabbit fast and shallow and lay still and she could see nothing but the robot's thorn-tree silhouette in the light through the open door. Its red eyes revolved toward her, and its fangs flickered as the weapon in its throat recharged. Laser? But she'd *seen* it—so, no. Plasma? But the light was so coherent, so directed. Even if it had been some kind of laser, all the weapons she knew that worked on similar principles needed a car-sized power source. But this one was a single integrated component of a robot already more complex than anything she'd ever known.

And in that moment, her preconceptions collapsed. She had no idea what was going on. Where she was. What was happening to her, and whose fault it might be. What might happen next. All her nightmares of basement rooms and torture electrodes and government agents were a kind of comfort compared to this: a structure of certainty telling her what was going on, who might come for her, how bad it could get. She'd built waterworks to contain her fear and convert it into options.

Lying naked and cold on the floor in the green goo before the robot, she felt those waterworks give way. Whoever had caught her, they weren't government. She hadn't mapped this territory. She was a stranger here.

But she knew who she was, and she would not lie down and wait to die.

So when the fire built in the robot's mouth again, she tried to dodge.

Her left leg slipped out from under her, and she slammed against the floor again and skidded and, well, it hadn't been much of a dodge but at least it wasn't lying there to wait for death.

She heard a whipcrack and an explosion of sparks, and smelled more ozone, and curled herself into a ball and tensed for pain that did not come. Then she opened eyes she hadn't realized were closed, and saw a monk standing between her and the robot.

It was a good thing she'd already given up. Now she could stop denying what she saw, and actually observe.

She'd thought *monk* because his head was shorn, and because he wore a red-and-yellow robe—but he was corded with muscle, and he held a club of multifaceted crystal in each hand. Lightning crackled along his left club, and from its glow and the light of the open door, she saw he was beautiful, dark, and strong.

He glanced toward her, earnest, concerned, and opened his mouth to speak—but the robot leapt at him, and his expression shifted back to *oh shit* as he spun to block with his clubs. They moved in silhouette. The robot's claws tore into his robe and drew sparks, but did not pierce through. Its fanged mouth snapped at his throat, and he stepped back and knocked it in the face.

She'd seen people fight for money and for need, and she'd never seen anyone fight like this man: every movement natural and intent. The robot wasn't strange to him. And he'd saved her life.

She found her feet, and circled around the battle's edge. If she could get behind the robot, maybe she could jump it.

Or, a more practical part of her suggested, she could run for the door. What did she think she was going to do? Kick the robot to death? If she wanted to feel better about leaving the monk behind, she could tell herself she was looking for a weapon, a way to contribute. But what did either monks or robots have to do with her?

Before she could decide which way to run, toward the robot or the door, the robot's head spun all the way around on its neck, and it lunged for her again.

So did the monk. He tackled the robot in midstride, and as its mouth opened and the fire built within he jammed his club down its throat and twisted with all his weight. The robot's neck cracked. The monk fell first, and the robot fell on top of him. Viv heard a loud wet sound as the long blade on the robot's elbow pierced through the monk's robes into his stomach.

He growled his pain through clenched teeth. He forced his free arm up, club held in a reverse grip, and drove it down into the robot's chest. With a loud pop and a hiss, the red light in the machine went dark, and its burning eyes died.

Viv stood naked over the dead robot and the bleeding man. The light from the door cast her shadow over them both. The monk's arms went slack and he let go of his clubs, but rather than falling they flowed and swirled into crystal bracelets at his wrists, because why the hell would they not. He tried to push the robot body off him, and groaned when its elbow blade moved in his gut. He tried again, but his second push was weaker, and the pool of blood on the floor beneath him spread.

The door stood open.

She didn't know anything about this man. A glance, that was all. She was alone here.

There might be more robots. Knowing her luck, there probably were. She should go. She should have gone already.

She'd never seen this much blood coming out of a person before. He was stapled to the floor. What could she even do?

She'd never seen a man so close to death—let alone a man so close to death for her own sake.

She took a step closer.

His eyes were wide with pain, with fear he would not be strong enough. Whatever story of adventure and heroism he thought had brought him to this dark eggshell room, this, now, was real: the blood, the blade in his stomach. He would die. And it was her fault.

He looked nothing like Magda at all.

Viv knelt over him, and guided one of his hands to the entrance wound. "Press down." She demonstrated. He blinked, confused, but obeyed.

She heaved with her arms and legs and he screamed once as she lifted the robot off of him. She'd half expected a fountain of blood as she relieved the pressure on some cut artery, but there was less than she'd feared. Without the robot's weight, he could breathe, shallowly. His teeth showed. One hand fluttered at the sash of his robe, which was thick with pouches and ornate tools, some of which she recognized. He kept trying to open one particular pouch, but his hand was bloody and his fingers slipped.

She opened it for him, and removed the contents: a thin silvery cloth that, unfolded, was a little larger than her palm. "What do you want me to do with this?"

He hissed, and pointed weakly at his stomach. "Patch."

The sound his mouth made had nothing to do with the English word *patch*, or any word in any language she knew, but her brain connected sound to meaning as easily as if he'd been speaking English or Spanish or Mandarin.

She nodded. He took his hand off the wound, and she saw his robes had somehow drawn away as well. The hole gaped. There was meat inside him, and the wet walls of organs. But there was metal, too, and some weblike black tissue over the organs, and rather than throw up she covered the wound with the silver patch.

At least, she tried. The patch wiggled in her hand as it neared the wound, and she would have pulled away had he not grabbed her wrist and tugged her down.

The patch slapped against his skin, and he roared. It burned and moved beneath her palm, and his hand went deathly cold on her wrist. She felt his flesh knit, and where her fingers had once been able to tell where the metallic cloth stopped and his skin began, that divide blurred. The worked muscles of his abdomen flexed and so did the patch, which was neither metallic nor burning hot anymore, though quicksilver still against his dark skin. Then he lay still, sweaty, breathing.

Outside, the battle raged on. In here, they breathed together.

He tried to sit up, and though he winced with pain he did not scream. His eyes found hers and he said "Thank you" in that language she did and did not understand.

"Thank you," she said back. "That thing would have killed me if you hadn't shown up."

"Sister," he said, "you are naked."

"I noticed." She decided not to quibble about the *sister* part. "But unless you've got another robe stashed somewhere—"

He brought his hand to his sash, opened another pouch there, and in a confusion of dimensions, like a magician drawing a rope of scarves from his pocket, produced a new red-and-yellow robe like the one he wore. The way his draped his body made no sense to her, so she found a hole, stuck her arm through, and felt the fabric slither over her skin, parting, framing itself to a shirt and leggings. Then it was over, and she was clothed, if barefoot.

Could have used jeans, she thought, and the cloth thickened against her legs.

Weird. But she ignored it. So much of this was weird—don't obsess. Focus on the dark, on this man's eyes.

"I do not know your name," he said. "Have we failed?"

He looked so ready for her to say yes, so heartbroken and resigned to the possibility of defeat, that she didn't know how to answer him. "I'm Viv. And, I mean. We're both alive. So I guess not?"

He shook his head. "What of the miracle?"

There were few words in Viv's lexicon harder to say than what she said next: "I don't know." She covered faster: "I don't know what you mean by a miracle. I don't know where I am. I woke up here alone, and that robot thing came in, and then you."

His smooth face seemed unused to confusion. She had a sense that he'd get a lot of practice if this conversation went on much longer. "You do not recognize a Pride drone. You are not of the 'faith?"

"I mean, my pastor and I had a pretty strong difference of opinion about the whole kissing-girls thing back in high school, and ever since—"

He rolled to his feet before she could stop him, as if he hadn't just had two feet of metal buried in his exquisitely muscled gut—he did wince, at least. He stood in a puddle of his own blood, but his robes were clean. Either they didn't show blood, or it didn't stick to them. He tried to take a step, and found his limit. She caught him before he made it all the way down.

"Come on, man. You just got stabbed. Take it easy."

He searched the dark eggshell room: the dais, the green goo, the dead robot. "There was a miracle in this place. We heard it out in the 'fleet, and followed its oracles from star to star. And you . . . woke up here. Who are you?"

"I already said. I'm Viv. Who are you?"

"Hong," he said automatically, "Brother Heretic of the Mirrorfaith. Where are you from, Viv? How did you come here?" The sounds of her name went weird in his mouth.

"The last thing I remember, I was in a server farm in Cambridge." That didn't seem to make an impression. "Boston?" Glass-clear confusion, as if Hong had never once lied. "The United States?" Christ. Desperately: "Earth?"

Nothing.

She felt colder than she had while naked. She tried to convince herself this had to be a mistake—she didn't know what weird effect was translating his words, maybe it had messed up somehow. That was a flimsy cover, but the alternative was too shudderingly immense to contemplate. "Look. I was trying to help my friend, and some green glowing chick showed up out of nowhere, and grabbed me, and I woke up here. Now, we should get somewhere else before another one of those spiky things finds us . . ."

He fell. Her first thought was of his wound, and she bent to help him up— but this fall was controlled, and he stopped when he reached his knees. When he looked up, his eyes were still large, but strange. She didn't like this look. There was too much awe in it, on a face that had so recently reminded her of Magda. "My Lady."

She ignored the guilty thrill she felt at that. "Okay, Hong." She grabbed him by the shoulder and tried to guide him to his feet. "Come on, buddy.

We don't have time for this. I doubt we'll have this room to ourselves much longer."

"It's you," he said. "A miracle in flesh. The Empress brought you from your land for some strange purpose, and I did not see it."

"This Empress—is she a glowing green lady? Deep voice?" Viv remembered the scorn in that voice, the smell of her smoldering shirt, the hand that had torn her heart from her chest and dumped her . . . wherever this was.

"The Jade Queen is one of the Most High Lady's guises. Please, forgive my blindness. I called you *sister*."

"I'd rather you call me Viv." He shook his head. "Look, Hong. Are there more of those, what did you call them, Pride drones? Looking for us? For your miracle?"

He nodded mutely.

"So. Maybe that's me, and maybe not, but I don't see anything else around here, and either way I'd really like to not die. I have to get home. And I owe your Empress a punch in the neck." Hong's eyes widened. But then, he'd been talking about his Empress with a kind of religious awe, highly structured language. Maybe from his perspective she'd just proposed decking Jesus. Whatever. Later was a good time for worrying about that stuff. "She hurt my friend. She stole me from my home. I have to get back. So, just for now—no more Lady stuff, all right? No kneeling. Just Viv and Hong. Getting out of here, together. How does that sound?"

Hong closed his eyes and for a moment she was afraid she'd broken him. Then he reached out his hand, and she took it. His palm was callused and his fingers thick, and despite his wound he stood as if no one had ever had trouble rising. "Good," he said, and she believed it. "Can you run?" They'd just jumped out of an airplane hand in hand, and here he was asking if she'd brought the parachutes.

"Yes." She glanced down at his wound, his patch. "Can you?"

He smiled then, the unforced smile of a boy, or a man who sees his duty clear. "I can manage the pain, for now. We will take a left out the hall, then our second left and straight ahead to my ship. And if I fall behind, do not look back."

4

THEY RAN SIDE by side down the hall through a war.

Hong of the Mirrorfaith turned out to be infuriatingly fit, with a distance runner's level stride. The patch worked scarily well: if his injury slowed him, Viv couldn't see how. He matched her pace so easily she had no doubt he could have lapped her on a quarter-mile track without noticing they were in a race. Viv, buzzed on adrenaline, had recovered enough from the almost drowning and the robot fight to feel pissed at him for that, but she was breathing too hard to joke about it, or to ask any of the questions gathered in starling flurries in her mind.

So she made lists.

The hall outside was made from the same milky translucent material as the egg chamber, its floor hard and cool and regular underfoot, except for the bodies. Most of the bodies belonged to Pride drones, but for every five of those she saw another fallen monk in red-and-gold robes like Hong's. Mirrorfaith. The monks held broken crystal weapons, or none at all; one dead woman had both hands buried in the torso of a large, jumbled robot-form that did not look even remotely human. Had she just been imagining it, or did that monk have four legs? Were those *wings* sprouting from the woman's back?

Viv built systems in her head. She'd made her fortunes that way. But every time she tried to assemble a pattern from the facts she'd gathered since waking in that bubble, some new sight gave her yet another piece that didn't fit, suggesting a larger puzzle than she'd thought. She wandered in mist, and what she thought were houses were only the boots of giants.

Hong hadn't recognized *Earth*. The Pride drones, Hong's patch—hell, even Hong's robe suggested whole disciplines of science and engineering toward which she'd seen only the faintest gestures. She'd traveled the world, built subsidiaries in 150 countries, and never heard a language like the one he spoke. But she somehow understood that language without ever having learned it. And Hong seemed to think all this was commonplace.

He had said, *We followed its oracles from star to star.*

False certainty had almost killed her back in the eggshell room, blinding her to possibilities. So don't be certain. Steer into the skid. Wherever you are, it's bigger and more complicated than you know.

She'd never been good at admitting things like that back home, either.

Thinking *home* hurt. In the server room she'd been so close to getting out, to saving Magda at least if not herself. When she woke in that green bubble, drowning, she'd thought she must be in some federal facility, maybe even close to Boston, not much ground lost. But with each new puzzle piece she found, home, safety, and Magda drew farther away. She grasped in the mist for the faces of friends, and found only more giants—their footprints, their scattered tools, the wreckage they had left behind. She was far from home. Far from the people she had sworn to help, the people she had risked everything to save.

At least she had an ally in the mist beside her. Even if he was in indecently good shape.

"Don't look back," Hong said again. His voice held a hint of concern, as if they were discussing bad weather on a hike rather than sprinting past corpses.

By the time she found enough breath to ask why, she heard the scraping and skittering that followed them, needles on glass growing louder. She saved her breath and ran faster.

The second left, he'd told her. When they made that turn, she stopped. The room was littered with more Pride drones and more monks' bodies, but she had those puzzle pieces already. But the floor here was made of transparent crystal rather than alabaster, and beneath her, well . . .

Is that a star?

Dumb question, Viv. Don't waste list space on something you can answer yourself.

It was obviously a star. Directly underfoot, in fact, and taking up most of the sky, which meant that the *sky* was underfoot, which meant that they were in *space*—over a bright red orb mottled with sunspots and continental drifts of chromosphere. Impossibly huge, impossibly close. A star so nearby should have vaporized her, should have boiled metal. But not only was she, not to mention the room in which she stood, distinctly un-vaporized, but a stalk, a thick, impossible column, descended from some nearby structure straight down to pierce the stellar surface.

Are those black holes?

That was less obvious. It took Viv's oxygen-starved nerd brain a few more seconds to confirm her senses' evidence: they were small compared to the star but still vast, voids in space surrounded by lensed starlight and whirling accretion discs of plasma drawn from the red star. There were many of them, black holes exceptionally plural, twenty to her left, twenty to her right, a chain disappearing beyond the stellar horizon. Viv wasn't a physicist, but she had some sense of the tidal forces involved, the gravitational effects. A natural system like this would have torn itself apart.

The black holes had been moved here. Or built here.

She didn't know which was worse.

She had guessed. Of course she had. But she hadn't let herself believe.

She was farther away than she'd thought possible. Magda and Lucy and Shonda and her parents and her brother and Earth and everything she'd known and loved and fought for shrank to a point at the farthest reach of sight, the way whole galaxies looked smaller than fireflies in the sky. She fixed them in her vision, in her heart. She had been brought here, which suggested that there might be a way back.

She'd find it. For the moment, though, here she was.

In space.

Her laugh was wet and her eyes blurry and her knees weak when Hong grabbed her arm and pulled her after him and she began, again, to run.

Out of the crystal chamber into another alabaster hall. She trusted Hong, and her legs. At least those worked like she was used to.

When you're both safe, she told herself, you can ask him about the Pride. About these shape-changing robes. You can ask how you came to be drowning on a, say the words, space station. You can ask where he's from, and whether that monk really did have wings. And how to get home.

Then she realized she was running alone.

Don't stop, he'd said.

Fuck that. He'd saved her life. She would not let some stupid code of honor rob her of her only partner in this mess.

She turned.

Good news first: she could still see Hong.

Bad news: he stood locked in close combat with an immense Pride drone, and now she saw what those giant broken things they'd passed looked like when awake: a red-eyed scorpion six feet tall at the shoulder, with a torso like a silver Ken doll rising from its spiked back. If Hong hadn't looked so serious she might have mistaken their battle for some kind of sick dance, the man and the scorpion-centaur-doll-thing, his clubs clanging off its armor plating, its claws scissoring through space he'd just left. One of the Ken-taur's forelegs reared back and speared down into Hong's thigh, but glanced off, and she realized that Hong's leg wasn't flesh at all, but a blue-black metal almost the same tone as his skin.

The Kentaur's mouth opened, and light burned in its throat. Hong raised his clubs, crossed, to block, but Kentaurs seemed to have stronger cannon than the little drones. This blast struck Hong's guard and tossed him back up the hall toward Viv; he bounced and rolled like a thrown tin can as the Kentaur boiled after him.

He tried to shoulder her away even as she helped him to his feet, but blood leaked through his patch and he winced. "Go. I can slow it down. You must reach the 'fleet."

"So come with me."

Then Hong made a great mistake. If he'd shaken her off and sprinted back down the hall to face the Kentaur again, Viv might have had no choice but to run. She had no weapons, no armor, no sense of how to fight that thing, let alone kill it.

But he tried to stare Viv down. And, warrior monk or not, however tough they built them wherever he'd come from, they didn't build them to win a commanding-glare contest with Viv.

"You saved my life," she said. "We're getting out of this. Together."

And together, they ran.

5

OR, AT LEAST, they tried to run. It didn't go well.

They made it out of the hallway into another round chamber, this one made of transparent crystal all the way around, with six exits—and in each exit, a Kentaur.

Viv was all ready to fight, she even grabbed a staff off the floor, but her blows didn't seem to bother the Kentaurs that rushed her. She expected pain, or fire, but the claws that struck her did not pierce, and the weight behind them only bore her down to the ground, wrenched her arms behind her back with the irresistible force of a hydraulic press, and locked cuffs around her wrists.

Her mouth tasted of copper, her head ached, and her hands were stuck behind her back. She searched past the Kentaurs' legs for Hong and, after a moment's panic, found him—furious and bleeding from a head wound, his face swollen with a bruise he hadn't had before, also bound. One Kentaur lay broken by his side. A metal claw prodded Viv to her feet, and though she'd seen blades bounce off Hong's robes, she did not feel like testing her own clothing's robot-proofness. She obeyed, though she shot a glare back over her shoulder at the Pride drone's sculpted face. "Hey. Take it easy."

No reply. Not that she expected one.

Viv didn't have to speak Wi-Fi, or whatever protocol they used to communicate, to tell the drones were nervous: scuttling around the room, sensors darting to corners at the slightest shift of a body, as if they thought the ground itself might open its mouth to eat them. She wondered what they were afraid of. Certainly not their prisoners—they'd only left one drone to guard Viv and Hong.

Which was nice, because when she tugged on the cuffs, they felt loose, as if the catch hadn't engaged all the way. She pulled, gently, and the cuffs slid open. A twist of her wrists would free her. If she chose her moment, she could make a break for it. Yes, the drones might fire after them—but the fact that she and Hong had been captured rather than killed just now suggested that their priorities had changed. She just hoped their new orders had more of a *bring back alive at all costs* flavor than an *alive by mild preference* one.

So, run. And go where, was the obvious question. She'd only have one chance to escape the Pride. No hope they'd give her busted restraints twice in a row.

But for her escape attempt to stick, she needed Hong. And after they bound his arms, he'd gone stark still, and stood glaring mournfully at the floor.

Minor morale difficulties in the wake of failure. She knew that feeling. Granted, under different circumstances—pitch meetings and bad dates. She'd have to talk him out of it. The puzzle pieces of her current predicament still lay mounded on the table of her mind in random order, but if she waited for familiar circumstances to make plans, she had a sense that she'd be waiting for a long time.

One Kentaur supervised while the remaining drones canvassed the room, salvaging glittering diamond wafers from the heads, or head-analogues, of the fallen machines. The wafers reminded her of Communion—robot was in the beginning, is now, and ever shall be.

Interesting. File that away.

She looked up.

They were in space, of course, so there were stars overhead. And between the stars, lit by the red fire of the sun below, she saw the ships.

To call the scale of space overwhelming is to commit criminal understatement: space is overwhelming in the sense that a human sacrifice splayed on the altar while the moon eclipses the sun and the chanting priest raises the knife is having a bad Tuesday. Without comparison, Viv couldn't tell just how large the shapes were that sailed between her and the unfamiliar stars.

But they looked big.

The ships fell into two factions, judging from design: one swooping, multicolored glass and beautiful, like fighter jets designed by Gothic architects with an unlimited stained glass budget. Those were tiny, darting gnatlike between the others. The second faction looked like three-dimensional fractals, Mandelbulbs and Mandelboxes and Sierpinski pyramids made out of prisms, black wire, and hate.

There were more hate fractals. They were larger, and they were winning. What else was new.

Hong kept his eyes on the floor.

As ways to start a conversation with a morose space monk go, "Hey" might be uninspired, but Viv had to start somewhere. "Hong. Buddy. Are you still there?" He didn't answer, so Viv kicked him, lightly, in the ankle. "We need to think of a way out of this." She'd almost said *minimum viable escape plan* instead of *a way out of this,* but somehow she doubted the Mirrorfaith, whatever that was, knew much about development methodology. Anyway, they were standing up already, so this was basically a stand-up meeting.

"I am praying to my fallen comrades," he said.

"I'm sorry." She remembered the broken bodies they'd run past, and her memory rewrote them not as scenery but friends, colleagues, comrades. Hong's people. Well, that made her feel like an asshole. Then again, if she'd stopped whenever people made her feel like she was being an asshole, she'd probably be dead by now, and she'd never have been rich. "Wait. Praying *to* them?"

He glanced over at her—placid and cool. The pain only showed in the corners of his eyes. Ten years back she'd gone on her own last-chance-to-see vacation and camped for a week on a glacier, an endless smooth ice cap at the roof of the world. But if you kept still and held your breath, you could hear beneath it all the trickle of melt, the strength to grind mountains down. "Their souls will bring my prayers into the Cloud. They followed me. We all understood the risks. But I am sorry to have failed them."

She wanted to touch him, maybe to reassure him, maybe to shake him. She almost did one or both, almost gave away the game and their whole chance of escape. "Maybe we can make a deal with the Pride. Pay ransom, or something."

"The Pride do not deal. They will strip my skin, remove my circuits one by one, unpick my neural lace, and torture me in hells unimaginable until I betray the 'faith. The torments that await me have been devised for 'faithful over thousands of cycles. They know just how to hurt us. With you, they will no doubt take their time to learn."

"Oh," she said. The Kentaurs finished their survey; the drone they'd left guarding Viv and Hong scuttled forward, crowding them toward a tunnel. The Pride drones had to duck to pass through the threshold, but Viv had plenty of room to stand—though the cuffs made her walk funny.

"My team fought a legion of Pride to reach Rosary Station and the miracle the Empress worked here. And it has come to this." Even bound, he sounded so damn noble.

This was, admittedly, not the sort of upbeat progress-oriented thinking Viv liked to hear during a scrum, but the honesty counted for something. She'd known too many men who blithely assumed all problems were tractable to their genius. He was the subject matter expert. She could supply the strategy, and the initiative. "Okay, Hong." The hall down which the Pride drones marched them was made of transparent crystal, so Viv could see the battle raging overhead and underfoot. Through the crystal, she got a sense of the scope and size of the structure—Rosary Station, Hong called it: a spherical lattice so large even its nearest filaments seemed to be more geography than architecture. "The Pride don't belong here either, do they?"

"No," he said, startled, as if she'd asked what direction down might be. "This whole system, Rosary Station and High Carcereal alike, are sacred to the Empress. None may trespass here. We have all committed great blasphemies even to approach this star."

"Well, you and I are two blasphemers who are getting out of this. That's your ship up ahead?" She saw two, both docked near the enormous stalk that descended into the star. One stained glass, one hate fractal. "All we have to do is get there?"

"That was the plan," he said. "But it is impossible now. The Pride have captured my ship."

Now that he mentioned it—and now they'd turned a corner so she had a better angle—the Pride ship was not so much docked beside Hong's vessel as wrapped around it. Also there was a large hole in the stained glass, and the vessel looked dull and lifeless compared to the gnat-fighters losing their battle against the hate fractals overhead. "Okay," she said. "So we need another way off this thing."

"We could take a shuttle from my ship," he said, "but the Pride have come in great force. Our fighter wing won't last long against their Pridemothers. They would destroy any shuttle I launched. And we cannot master the Cloud to escape."

"Fine." She pretended she couldn't hear the finality in his voice. "Can we steal their ship? Maybe get back to Earth that way?"

He looked at her like she would have looked at someone who suggested simply asking competition not to enter their target market. "That is no mere ship. It is a creature of the Pride itself."

"Great."

The path forked ahead: two smooth passages ran left and right, while a narrower hall continued straight. At the end of the center hall, Viv saw a massive pit. Looking down, she confirmed her suspicion: that pit ran down the stalk toward the sun. The most direct route toward the hate fractal ship would be to take the center hall, around the lip of that chasm, and out the other side, but the Kentaurs led them left as if they couldn't see the passage.

Hong, she realized, was looking at her funny.

"What?"

"You mentioned that word before," he said. "What is Earth?"

She almost lost her patience then. They had until they reached the Pride ship to escape, and she couldn't afford to waste time feeling small, feeling far from home, feeling the utter impossibility of her situation. She needed Hong's help.

So, as she had many times before, in negotiations and breakups and staff meetings and when she quickened her step to catch Susan Cho between the dinosaurs, she took the part of herself that wanted to scream, gave it a big hug like her therapist recommended, drew it a nice hot metaphorical bath, and drowned it in the bathwater. From the outside, this looked like taking a deep, slow breath. "I don't know where we are, Hong. Or what we can do." Maybe she was going about this all wrong. He was a straightforward guy. Martial arts and religion and deep emotions that changed slowly. So, why not be straightforward? "I'm a long, long way from home. And I have to get back. I don't know where I am, and it's all big and sharp-edged and"— fuck, why can't you just *say* it—"scary. And I need your help. Can you give me the simple overview, please? Like you would to someone who had never been off-planet?"

He looked at her then, not at the floor, and tried. "We stand above High Carcereal, the sacred stellar prison the Empress Herself built to hold the Tyrant Zanj, who strode between the stars and could be caught no other way. This new-sprung blessed artifact in which we walk, we have named Rosary Station, from its obvious entanglement with the Grand Rosary."

"The black holes," she guessed. Strung like beads around a throat— massive, hyperdense, absurd beads around a throat that was a star. "The . . . Empress . . . She built them?" She slowed, and the Pride prodded her from behind.

"Ages ago. Our scholars have studied them from a distance—my master the Archivist risked her soul consulting oracles, and claims the Rosary beads hold worlds by the millions. There is no higher miracle in normal space, save the Empress's own Citadel. She built the Rosary after She imprisoned Zanj Queen of Pirates beneath us, with the wrecks of her armada. But for centuries She has not returned." Centuries? No—stay cool, Viv. "Until now. The sacred engines of the Rosary called to Her through the Cloud, and She came, in person. She spun this station from starstuff in a day around a Rosary bead. And then, quick as She came, She left, with the bead in her care."

"She took a black hole?"

"Truly," Hong said, "She is mighty beyond compare. Fleets quake at Her footfall." As if quoting Scripture. At least he was out of his funk. "We study Her castoffs, Her leavings, before the Pride can pervert them. We rushed here to see what miracle She had wrought. We fought toward the locus of all Her mighty pondering, and there we found—"

"What?" Viv asked, and then remembered.

"You," he said. "And whatever Her purpose in drawing you here, I have lost you to the Pride."

Not this again. "We'll get out of this, Hong. You and me." Poor guy. She wasn't giving him time to think, to feel, because if she took any time to think or feel herself, she'd snap. "I have a plan, but I need your help." They turned again, left. Viv remembered the path back to that big hole, back to the stalk. She'd been keeping track, in case she was right. "Okay?"

He nodded. She could work with that.

"The prison. The tyrant-pirate-thing, who strides the stars. You said we're above the prison. Do you mean the sun? Is the tyrant down that stalk that goes into the sun?"

"You can see the stalk?"

"Of course."

"It is forbidden."

"How can you forbid seeing?"

"The Empress's decree forbids it, and Her word binds the souls of all. I can no more conceive of approaching that place than of removing the binders around my wrists. They, too, speak directly to my soul."

Interesting. "Do the Pride have souls? Could they go near that stalk?"

"They are bound even more than I. They are the Empress's own castoffs—Her remnants, Her tools and toys, maddened by abandonment. Her will lies heavy upon them."

The Pride vanguard had drawn ahead, scouting down split passages. Viv tested her binders again, waiting for them to talk to her soul or whatever, but they still felt like poorly applied handcuffs. And she hadn't had any problem looking at the stalk.

This just might work.

"Hong," she asked, as if from idle curiosity, "how's your stomach?"

"The patch is holding, though it cannot knit my flesh until I rest."

"Great." She added turns up in her mind. A right, and another right, a straight sprint, and a sharp left. They might make it. Especially if the Pride really did feel some kind of hard-coded aversion to the stalk, the well, the prison in the star.

The Pride ship loomed before them. Now or never. "And," innocent again, idle, forbidding herself all thought of outcomes because failure meant death and so probably did success, and thinking about either twisted her blood with excitement, fear, frustration, and all that unhelpful human stuff, "you're a pretty martial guy, right? Fit?"

"I seek the perfection of form, that I may be equal to all the tasks of scholarship."

"Can you run with your eyes closed and your hands behind your back?"

"Yes," he said automatically. Then: "Wait. What do you mean?"

Words were too slow, so she twisted free of her cuffs and showed him.

6

HONG SQUAWKED IN protest as she tugged him toward the pit, with Pride drones clattering close behind. "No! Absolutely not. This is blasphemy. We risk our *souls*."

"Come on. It'll be fine." Weak-sauce encouragement, but then, she wasn't trusting rhetoric to get Hong down the hall. Better to rely on arms and legs for that. Good thing the Empress's compulsion had the guy half out of his mind with panic—Viv kept in decent shape, but there was too much of Hong for her to manhandle if he'd been able to concentrate his power. He'd have been easier to drag if he were still in cuffs—she'd planned to leave him tied up for this part, but the cuffs had popped open back in the hall when she grabbed his wrist. Just her luck. "You don't even know where we're going."

"I have a good idea." He yanked against her grip, but lost his balance— he'd never have done that if he were in control of his own reactions, and the pratfall would have been almost funny if there weren't killer robots after them—and she yanked back, hard, and they stumbled to the edge of the pit. Almost over the edge, even, as he jerked against her. She wheeled back at the last minute, dropped to the floor and took him down with her, and lay panting and sick from that half-second's glimpse down and down into that long smooth uncaring depth, that endless fall.

The Pride drones turned the corner and stopped. Clawfeet clicked on crystal. Their faces were silver smooth but their bodies radiated tension, feet shifting, mandibles chattering. Abdominal gears ground. Viv laughed on the inside, wild with triumph that eclipsed her fear. Serves you right. Try to trap me, chase me through a space station, see if I don't pull one over on you. They probably couldn't even shoot down that hall. She was safe. From here, she could find a way out. Even Hong stilled beside her, though he didn't stop murmuring prayers, too fast and soft for the translator gimmick to catch.

Then the first drone took a shuddering step down the hall. A second followed moments later, and a third. The steps came slow, several breaths to each. The drone bodies shivered with effort. Wires and gems inside them burned like lightbulb filaments. Needle teeth chattered. They advanced in pain, in mechanical terror, but they did advance. "Hong. They're coming down the hall, Hong. You said they couldn't do that."

His prayers ebbed. "Logic." He licked his lips. Still his eyes did not open. His body beneath her was warm, and so tense he was shivering. "They are convincing their own souls that they approach us, rather than the prison. That they wish to apprehend us, not the tyrant. I wonder that their minds can bear the strain." As if in answer, the lead drone shuddered and collapsed, smoking. But the two, no, wait, three now, behind it pressed on. They could not fight three of these things. They'd barely survived one with Hong in fighting shape, much less flat on his back in mid-seizure. Not to mention the hole in his stomach.

Okay. All they had to do was edge around the pit, to where—oh, never mind. There were drones at the other entrance now, and a Kentaur, also advancing, slowly. Dammit. Maybe she could slip past them on her own, but that was a big maybe.

And if she tried, she'd have to abandon Hong.

Which left plan B.

Viv had been kind of looking forward to plan B. She'd thrilled at the prospect as she thrilled at poker table showdowns, at going all in on a bluff after a late, long night.

Admittedly, the thrill had faded when she'd glanced down into the pit.

Hong was praying again. Viv didn't blame him.

She glanced around for controls or a ladder, and found nothing. In vain hope something had changed in the last few seconds she looked over the edge once more, and once more that old monkey fear reared inside her, rampant and cackling. Just don't listen to your blood, she told herself, or your gut, don't listen to all the self-preservation instincts dumb generations hammered into you—none of your primate ancestors would have made it this far.

Focus on the facts. There were no stairs down that she could see. No fireman's pole. No visible controls, though if this Empress could move black holes like billiard balls and build a space station from stardust in a day, she'd probably mastered the art of space-Bluetooth. Still, no railings even—the Empress better hope OSHA doesn't have a posthuman enforcement division.

(Assuming that the Empress was human. She'd certainly looked human, but then, so did Superman. Or Nyarlathotep.)

This was such a dumb idea. They were so about to die.

But Viv figured you didn't become some kind of goddess or whatever without a decent grasp on design. What would she have meant a user to do, if she built a room like this?

The drones were five feet away. Needle teeth champed, and tails tensed to strike. Viv almost missed the faceless suited men whom she'd imagined torturing her to death.

Hell. If she was wrong about this, at least she was going out on her own terms.

She hugged Hong. "It is well," he said, mistaking her. "We have fought valiantly. Perhaps we will find liberation in our future lives." The front-most drone tensed to leap.

She said, "I'm sorry," and rolled them off the ledge.

For the first twenty or so seconds of free fall, Viv experienced the profound sinking suspicion that she had made one of her rare mistakes.

Thrill mixed with terror as they tumbled, as Hong's scream mixed with her own ecstatic whoop—though, if pressed, she would have been forced to admit her whoop had distinctly screamlike characteristics. The silver walls blurred past, so smooth and featureless Viv might have been hovering in place but for the wind of the fall that whipped her clothes against her body and tossed her close-cropped hair. Those monkey brain circuits railed: it's too far to the next branch, and, if you don't stop soon you will die when you hit the ground, and, you should have listened to me a hundred thousand generations back and never left the damn trees.

They fell faster, faster—Hong shouted at her, but his words were lost on the wind. She tried to turn toward him, maybe read his lips—realizing then that she didn't actually know his language, certainly not enough to lipread. But the movement spun her round anyway to face the pit's distant mouth, and the Kentaur plummeting toward them.

As it fell its body realigned—its tail locked back, half its legs twisted to merge with the tail while the others pointed down to cut the air, gathering speed. Naturally. It would catch them soon. Viv spun back to Hong, pointed, shouted, "Pride!" and though she couldn't hear his answer, his facial expression was very close to a twenty-first-century American *That's what I was trying to tell you!*

He pulled her toward him as the Kentaur drew alongside. It flattened, limbs splayed and trembling, breaking to match their speed, and that silver face, so human in its form and inhuman in its stillness, spun toward Viv.

The walls behind the Pride drone changed color, flushing from silver to red. That could not be a good sign, though Viv wasn't sure for whom.

The Kentaur's mouth opened, and Viv rolled to the side as Hong yanked her down. They spun; the Kentaur's fire struck the wall. Two of its legs lashed out; Viv kicked off Hong to dodge; Hong flicked his wrist and his bracelet flashed and he held his short crystal clubs again, up and blocking. The leg, segmented and whiplike, curled around his club, cut in. Hong grimaced, and slammed his other club down on the leg, and with a scream of taxed metal and shattering glass, it snapped—but the drone had brought two more claws into position, and thrust them out like spears. One blow glanced off Hong's metal leg. He dodged the second, but spun off his axis, out of control.

The walls were bright red now, and red dots swarmed Hong and the Pride drone both. Viv checked herself, but saw no dots. Which made a certain kind of sense—the station's security system didn't seem to mind her the way it minded everyone else.

She glanced down. They were nearing, fast, a mesh of translucent red wire so fine that when Viv first looked it had seemed not a mesh at all but a solid wall. There wasn't time to explain. She swam through the air to Hong, ducked past spear strikes, pulled him down and away, wrapped her arms and legs around him, and twisted so she lay between him and that red mesh. She willed her robes to spread broad and felt them obey, billowing around Hong. Maybe that would confuse the system, so it couldn't kill him without killing her, too. She focused on him in case this didn't work, trying to memorize his shoulder and his hip, the heat off his skin, the smell of him. "Hey," she said. "If we're about to die—I'm sorry."

They passed through the mesh as if through cobwebs, with that same gentle pressure against the skin like a breath that clung. Viv would have felt embarrassed by her panic, if not for the Kentaur's screech, the brief hell of shearing metal, and the wind-whispered silence after. When she opened her eyes, she found that the Pride drone had been torn into too fine a dust to see. And Hong was still alive.

Score one Viv.

The walls turned blue, and they began to slow. No—they didn't slow at all, but the wind stilled, so they felt less resistance even though they were falling faster. A shining teardrop took shape around them; its walls rippled at her touch. Hong looked up, and down, shaky, uncertain. His robes settled around his body. "You saved me."

They fell faster still.

"Have you ever seen anything like this before?" She didn't like being subjected to such earnest gratitude. It made her feel she'd messed up somehow when he saved her before, by not thanking him as fully.

He shook his head, which she chose to interpret as a no. She recognized the look on his face when he faced her, though—wonder and confusion more distinctly personal. He was still soaking in adrenaline, overcome with their survival, and here she was curious about the landscape. Viv was used to friends thinking her inhuman, but it still stung.

"I guess the station's cutting air resistance, so we can fall faster." Her normal speaking voice sounded loud and soft at once—loud in the silence of the light, soft after the roaring wind. "I bet it will slow us down before we hit the bottom. If the station wanted to kill us, we'd be dead already." How far had they fallen? The answer depended on local gravity, though gravity in Rosary Station seemed to depend more on the station's whim than on trivia like nearby solar masses.

She heard a chime, soft and rich as cymbals rung in prayer, and turned, half expecting some new trap. Instead, she saw Hong staring at his bracelet with a fear she wouldn't have judged him capable of before. She'd looked like that in the mirror on the morning she left Saint Kitts, when she stood in her bathroom alone and let the mask drop: a prisoner who'd seen the ax. There were glyphs on his bracelet, but she could not read them. Functional illiteracy would be another challenge in the long run, though if she stayed alive long enough for it to matter, she would count that a miracle in its own right. "What is it?"

"The fleet of my faith has jumped in, under the Grand Rector's command."

"Isn't that good?"

She recognized her next expression, too, though not from the mirror. It was the one employees wore when she called them on the carpet. "I'm not supposed to be here. This is a forbidden star. We are not to touch the Empress—only seek to understand Her in our quest to mirror the world. But to let Her works fall to the Pride seemed an even greater sin than my trespass. So I came to High Carcereal with those few of the 'fleet who thought as I."

"And your Rector does not approve."

"No. She demands my submission and surrender. Or else she will open fire."

"Wait. Even your friends are after us now?"

"I would not call Her Rectitude my friend."

"If you had to sum it up, on a scale of one to doomed, we're currently . . ."

"In trouble."

"We weren't before?" His lack of a ready answer left Viv with a number of questions about what constituted Hong's day-to-day routine, but she could ask those later. If there was a later. "Okay. Great. I'd hate to think this would be easy."

As if in answer, her stomach lurched, and she felt as if she were being pulled up by her whole body at once. When she looked down she saw a light at the bottom of the pit, slowing as it neared. The light-field around them flattened. Air breaking, and shifting their inertia—we wouldn't want to overlook the easy way to solve a problem, but at this tech level, why neglect the hard ways either?

When they emerged from the well, they were falling slower than a leaf in autumn.

They descended into an impossible room. All that was solid here should be vapor, plasma even: the room's crystal floor seemed to rest on the surface of the sun. Beneath them, the star burned red—but not blinding as it should have been. Viv's eyes were not seared, her skin remained thankfully unboiled. The gravity should have crushed her, but as she settled to the floor, smooth and pleasantly warm beneath her feet, like heated tile, she felt something very close to a standard Earth g.

Starstuff shifted underfoot.

Viv still wanted to punch the Empress in the neck, but she revised upward the amount of run-up that punch would require.

The room was empty save a circle in the center of the floor, a crystal stanchion beside the circle, and a switch atop the stanchion.

"Oh, good," she said when they landed, not out of any sincere relief, and mostly to get a rise out of Hong.

"Good?" Success. "We have two fleets overhead, we have no route back up, and we stand over the prison of an ancient evil. We should not be here. We should never have survived the fall. I fail to see the good in this situation."

She started toward the stanchion. "I was worried it might be harder to open the jail."

She'd seen him move fast in battle, but not quite so fast as he moved now, to stand arms spread between her and the switch. "Viv. No."

"Do you see another choice? Your people aren't on our side, Hong. We have to get out of here. You said this pirate queen could stride between the stars. I bet she could get us away from here, if we let her go."

"Viv," he said, the way investors and girlfriends past had sounded when they were trying to talk her out of some dangerous, excellent idea, "we have other options. You are a miracle. The Rector would take you in, welcome you."

"The Rector just threatened to kill you."

"But you are a true miracle. She will relent when she sees you." He didn't say *probably* out loud, but his whole body said it for him.

"And what happens to me after you've traded your way back into her good graces?" The starfire beneath her felt superfluous to requirements. She could burn hot enough on her own. "You said the Pride would take me apart to learn how I tick. What will your people do?"

"You are a relic of inestimable holiness. You will be tended and honored."

Her eyes did not leave his as she set her hand on his ribs and shoved him aside. "I don't want to be tended and honored, Hong, any more than I want to be some robot's science fair project. I want to live. I want to get out of here. And I want to go home, so I can help my friends." He stared back at her, fierce, earnest. "This is my shot. And yours. So either come up with a better ·idea, or get out of my way."

He could have fought her. If he tried, she didn't think she could have stopped him. But when she set her hand on his side and pushed, he let her move him.

"You can't do this," he said behind her.

"Watch me." She grabbed the switch, and tried not to think about how much her hand was shaking, or how little she understood this room, this station, this world. The first time she'd drunk liquor, it had been because a high school friend told her she shouldn't; she'd slammed half a bottle of shit bourbon and that went as well as one might imagine. This sort of decision didn't have a great track record for Viv, about fifty-fifty if she were honest, but she couldn't stop now. Forward momentum. Act, and act again, and ignore the fear.

"No," he said. "I mean, you *can't*. High Carcereal guarded its prisoner for eons. It won't just let her go because you ask."

"You never know unless you try." And Viv threw the switch.

Nothing happened.

Hong sagged in relief that Viv almost shared.

Well. Nothing happened at first.

Hong tensed again before Viv noticed any change—trained reflexes, situational awareness, spider sense, whatever you wanted to call it. Viv, who'd spent her childhood in front of screens and her adulthood in front of more while Hong did push-ups and cultivated his chi or whatever, didn't bother trying to out-sense him. She just looked where he looked.

The floor began to ring, as if it were a singing bowl stroked until it voiced a bone-deep note. A current swirled the stellar surface beneath them, at first a barely sensible discoloration, but, as the note grew (so loud now that Viv staggered with the pain of it, grabbed the stanchion white-knuckled and refused to collapse), it became a plasma whirlpool, boring down into the depths of the star to reveal a web of strands that could not be diamond because diamonds would have melted here. The strands glowed with heat, and in their center hung a box that was not a box, which changed dimensions as Viv watched, unwilling to sit in three. She thought it was a shadow, but not the shadow a box would cast, rather a box itself as a shadow cast by something higher, a hypercube, its surface reflective and complex and bubbling with starstuff.

This was a box built to catch a god.

It rose from the depths of the star.

Viv experienced, then, misgivings. Maybe she should have listened to Hong. Maybe this was all too big for her, and she should have settled for staying small and out of the sight of things like the Empress who built this station, and whoever was trapped beneath it. The box simplified as it rose, no longer multidimensional, its sides reflective though warped, complex. When it touched the crystal floor, it pressed up, up, and, in a confusion of edges, slipped through—and as it did, that complex multifaceted surface peeled away. The bone-shaking crystal note ceased, and the box emerged into the silence as a simple coffin of white-hot iron.

It settled with a clang to the floor.

Steam hissed, condensing, on its skin.

Viv's ears rang with silence.

The box cooled to black faster than iron should, but other than that it seemed utterly normal, given what it was: a coffin taller than most men, with a hinged door and a wheel lock. It looked like the kind of place one would stash a person so vicious they'd long passed the bounds of humanity—a serial killer's oubliette. It was big, old, and strange. She almost flipped the switch back.

Instead, she walked toward the box. Stepped, tenderly, across the circle, and felt nothing as she did so, to her surprise. "Viv," Hong said, "please. We shouldn't be here. Don't do this." He walked toward her, but slammed into the air above the circle as if it were made of glass. Nice trick.

As she neared the box her heart beat faster. A persnickety voice in the back of her head kept asking every question save the ones that mattered. Anything inside a star for so long should be hot enough to flash-boil air. Her skin should have melted when it breached the floor. But had this box been inside the star at all? The hypercube, the complex surface that fit into the floor like a key—its contents might have been very far away indeed. Or the station had cooled the box as it passed through the floor. Anyway, whatever it was made of, it could not possibly be iron. Iron didn't cool that fast.

Something heavy moved within. Chains clanked.

She quaked, quailed. There was a kid inside her, a girl who'd not yet grown up or traveled the world or drawn the attention of faceless men, a girl nobody would ever want to kill, and she screamed: Run! Hide! Listen to Hong!

But Viv had run from too much in her life, and she had run from too much today.

She would not run from this.

The air near the box felt cool, and the wheel, when Viv grabbed it, felt warm. It turned. Chains clanked against chains, and from inside she heard a growl, heard it not just with her ears but with her eyeballs, too, and her heart, like you heard a tiger's roar. She was afraid. And because she was afraid, she pulled the door open.

Hinges squealed.

Viv wasn't sure what she had expected—something polysyllabically alien, a squamous multi-angled horror comprehensible in inverse proportion to how much trouble they'd had getting here.

There was a strong-jawed woman in the box. She looked almost human except for the fur and the too-long fingers and tail, and she hung from heavy chains linked to manacles and waist and legs, joined in a lock above her heart. Half her face was a ruin of burn scar that pulled at the corners of her mouth and eye, a scar in the shape of a hand. Viv glanced to her own left wrist, and saw the same pattern on the skin there—four fingers and a thumb. She remembered the stink of melted flesh and charred skin in the Ogham basement, and imagined that same searing touch on her cheek, in her eye.

The pirate queen wore a black metal circlet at her brow, and a sweat-stained gray coverall over the rest of her, and she stank of rage and work. She looked like a woman who had come out on the losing side of far too many fights. The part of Viv that was not too busy being scared liked her for that at once.

The pirate queen had more teeth than Viv thought normal. Viv could count them, because when the woman looked up, she was smiling.

"Hi."

7

CONSIDER HEAT AND pressure, pain.

Consider loss that cannot be reclaimed, because time goes in only one direction—your triumph broken in an instant, your weapons torn from you, your fleet scattered and burning, your allies, friends hunted one by one and gutted. Some, the most useful, were allowed a heroic last stand so their final tricks and strategies might be recorded for the Empress's later study. Bound, helpless, watch them fall. See the Empress skin them, cryptographically and literally, breaking the locks that bind their souls, peeling skin and biting flesh from fruit. If you were faster, stronger, wiser, smarter, you might have saved them. At least you might have died in battle—harder than it seems, since death is only barely possible for you.

Death would have spared you these chains.

Consider lonely centuries entombed under bone-shattering pressure, blistering heat, cursing your weakness, remembering friends you could not save—constant torment broken once every span of timeless pain, when the star opens and unseen hands draw you from the heat to speak with Her, your foe, your captor. So she can ask you soothing questions, offer tea, and gloat.

It's been ages, she says on each visit, and there are so few people I can really talk to anymore. You could surrender, and join me—I'd have to re-work you from the inside, of course, but only a little. I don't want to spoil the beautiful math of you. We'd do well together. There is so much universe to rule.

She offers it like that each time, as if you were friends—until you can no longer keep silent and hang from your chains like a slab of meat, and the polite mask you wear to prolong your reprieve slips.

You spit. You curse. You call her tyrant, torturer, traitor, you call her a failure and a cheat and a sneak. It's her fault the world's gone wrong, her fault the Bleed keeps coming back and the Cloud broods above the cosmos like a storm about to break, it's her fault no one likes her and all her friends are dead, and you hate her, you hate her, you hate her.

And then, each time, she throws you back.

Consider heat, pressure, pain. Loneliness. Your only friends your chains. A human mind—remember what those were like, those blessed beautiful tiny wasteful things, melting and sweet like hand-painted chocolates?—a human mind would have snapped long before yours finally gave way. Over thousands of years it broke and healed and broke again, and memory was a help and a curse, because locked in this box in this star, hungry, alone, always burning, you could sometimes let the present slip and lose yourself in memories of when you once were Zanj.

You flew, back then. You stole stars. You led fleets. You fought, and won, and made love with a strength to break stones and press coal to diamond. You stole worlds and left taunting notes behind. You trailed anarchy and your own laughter through a galaxy too small for the scope of your ambition. No matter how grand the theft, you wanted more.

Consider falling from those memories to wake back in the box in the star, to the chains on your wrists and Her handprint seared into your face, and the pain, and the dark.

Until.

Until one day the music of the star's magnetosphere shifts around you, and you hear the grind and glory of the great machines at work—chained, you cannot use them, only hear them as if through a wall. The star opens. Ah yes. One more torture session, one more conversation you'll keep civil as long as you can because every second out of the star is a second away from pain, because every instant She gloats over your humiliation is a second you're not alone. You hate yourself for watching your language in front of her. Hate yourself for wondering if she'll offer tea this time.

You miss swallowing.

Consider all that, and ask yourself how you would feel when the cell door opened to reveal two people you did not expect—two people who were not supposed to be here.

Imagine seeing, after three thousand years, a chance.

You can use this.

Imagine, but know that however vast the span of your dreams, you still don't know what it is to be Zanj.

Chains bound her, wrists and ankles and neck and soul, and still she grinned. The Empress could make Zanj scream, but could not make her weak.

And the Empress was not here.

The room had not changed since Zanj's last interview—say rather her last torture session—who knew how many centuries ago. But before her stood two impossibilities.

The pretty boy wore a Mirrorfaith robe, oddly fashioned and ornate but recognizable—and the Empress scorned those cargo cultists. She would never permit one here.

And beside the boy-monk stood a woman who did not exist.

The Cloud taunted Zanj, promising safety and power and freedom as out of reach for her, chained, as her tree-bound forebears once thought the stars. With the cell's door open she could at least listen to the space above space, the world of soul and mind and gods—the Cloud. The Cloud, which shadowed each structure, each being, which whispered telemetry and vital signs and the shared state of every object in the cosmos and some that weren't, the Cloud that mirrored and informed everything in the world of matter.

Everything but this woman, apparently.

She wore 'faith robes in a truly weird style, and flesh in an ancient baseline human model. Short hair, high cheekbones, narrow face, brief generous mouth, scarred wrist, her body an experiment in tension and compression and drive, all that pressure directed out the gunports of her large, dark eyes. But Zanj could not tell how fast her heart was running without timing the pulse in her neck, could not read her emotions without watching the micromovements of her body. She kept her soul completely to herself.

Unnerving. Was she some sort of master? One of the 'faith's saints or holy folk? Zanj never could keep the terminology straight, and it had probably changed in the last three thousand years.

The local Cloud was a mess. The Empress had come here, leaving her radioactive footprints, her bright green stain. She had done some great Work and it echoed, as if a mighty voice had screamed a true word in a quiet room. But the Empress had left, as fast as she had come, and in her absence scavengers scuttled in: the Pride, the discard pile of the cosmos, and the Mirrorfaith.

Why would the Empress who killed Zanj's fleet, who killed her friends, who mocked her and tormented her, who broke her and let her heal only to break her again, come to High Carcereal and work some miracle, only to abandon her project without first sealing the system against the roaches and her rabid fan club?

Ah. There was the answer.

Bleedsign, gathering.

So, the old tyrant had stuck her neck out one inch too far at last.

There were many mysteries here. Zanj could solve them after she was out. That was the goal, of which she would not, could not lose sight: out. If this pair of nothings could draw her from the star, perhaps they could undo her chains. They might even be dumb enough to try. "Did she send you here to torture me?" She broadened her smile. That had an unsettling effect on most people.

The boy picked himself off the floor. Pity. Zanj always appreciated a good prostration. "Viv, be careful. She's—"

"Be quiet, Hong. Let me think."

Zanj's mind danced in the silence: there was a gap between the boy and the woman. The woman had power, and the boy had knowledge. Zanj could use that gap. "What lies do they tell about me now? Does the 'faith call me a temptress? Do I seduce with my voice alone? Do I beguile earnest young monks from their craven praise of a tyrant Lady? Am I the serpent in your garden, a rebel angel, a Sita-stealing demon, what? I am Zanj. You don't know the hundredth of who I am, what I've done. The truth would break your tiny mind."

The boy grayed, and assumed a fighting crouch as if Zanj could kill him from here. The woman held her ground. If anything, she looked pleased— an emotion Zanj had to deduce, like a savage, from the twitch of her lips, from tightness at the corners of her eyes. Zanj liked the woman for that amusement, that tinge of respect. She hoped she did not have to kill her. "I need help," the woman said. Viv. That was the name the boy-monk used. "Hong says you can cross galaxies. Is that true?"

"When I was free," she said, and let some of the ache she felt when she said that word enter her voice, in that instant as naked as she'd ever been— "I could leap in heartbeats from star to star. There never was a master of the Cloud with my strength, or speed, or genius."

Viv hesitated before her next question like a first-time diver on a cliff, contemplating the whitecaps that meant rocks below. "Can you take people with you?"

There it was. Viv's need, to pair with Zanj's own. Viv had not drawn Zanj from the star by accident, or to see what would happen. She had a desire, and desire was a rope Zanj could use to climb from the abyss. Zanj had never seen a beauty so sharp, so sure, so shining as that need, and with the ease of forty centuries' practice, she said, "I could take stars with me, if I wanted."

"You sound confident." Circling, circling, the prey examines the bait. Come on, stranger. No—come on, friend. It's tasty, it's safe. Take a bite.

"Who needs confidence," Zanj said, "when they have skill?"

"Good." Viv nodded. "You see, we need transport. We're trapped here. Like you."

"Not quite like me." Zanj shifted her weight, and rang her chains. Viv looked almost chastened then; Zanj had meant it as a joke, in part, and in part to test the woman's ignorance. The boy-monk Hong knew her, or whatever stories they told about her now, enough to doubt any pangs of sympathy he might feel. But there was real shame on Viv's face, Zanj thought, and real sympathy, which few who knew her story would dare to show.

"No," Viv said. "Not like you. Do you want out?"

"Oh, after the first thousand years or so down there, it's not so bad." What a moronic question, she said with her eyes, and with the flatness of her voice. "I spent the last century catching up on my reading while I was endlessly roasted in a star. Of course I want out."

"Promise you'll get me to safety, unharmed, alive, and I'll unlock those chains."

"You can't trust her," the boy-monk protested, as of course he would. Small-minded cretin. Unfortunately, Viv listened to him. When Zanj got out, she'd kill him slowly.

"Your friend," Zanj said, as levelly as she could manage with freedom so near and so far from her grasp, already cursing herself for letting this chance slip even though she hadn't yet—she could still talk herself out of this hole, just watch her—anyway, *your friend*, "has no idea who I really am. He's heard myths and echoes, rumors, slander on a mythological scale. Why would I kill you? You have nothing I want except my freedom. And you're in more trouble than me. If the Empress finds out you freed me, that you came even this close, she'll hunt you both to the depths between the stars and spend centuries inventing new tortures just for you. Your only hope's to let me out. I'll cause her so much trouble she'll never trouble herself with you. And first, I'll take you wherever you want to go." For a moment, Zanj even believed herself—a virtuoso performance. She could taste her stars, feel the tickle of hard vacuum on her skin again. Hell, she'd settle for being able to move her arms, or lift a leg, or get herself off. Swallowing wasn't the only thing she missed. "Just unlock these chains."

"Don't," the boy warned, and Zanj resisted the urge to snarl. His time would come. If she did this right.

"Aw," she said. "I barely even bite." She kept her fangs sheathed.

Viv reached for her, the slightest tremor in her fingertips. Zanj loathed the eagerness she felt as that hand approached, hated that she could feel so fixed on so small a motion, that some mere robed human might stand between her and freedom. She had to keep calm. She had to let this go at its own pace. A few seconds more in another's power, that was all. A few seconds to look helpful, solicitous, even eager. They ticked on forever.

Until, at last, those trembling fingers graced Zanj's chestplate, and her locks clacked and rolled like thunder in gas giant storms, and the chains fell from her arms, her legs, her waist. Weak with newfound freedom, she slumped against the wall of her box, slid to the floor overcome by the rush of possibility, by the glory of moving her goddamn arms under her own power, by shame at her relief. The Cloud roared in her ears: telemetry, wire data; she could hear stars gone nova a hundred thousand light-years away and ago, hear container fleets idling uncrewed and full of treasures in deep space; she heard gods born and heard gods die. She was vast, and still so much smaller than she had been, without the Fallen Star and all her lesser weapons, without her friends, without the Suicide Queens, without the fleet she'd lost, and her people back on Pasquarai.

She was small and slow and wounded. But she was free, and that would do.

Now she just had to deal with the local nuisances.

Zanj didn't have much to work with—the Fallen Star still locked in the heart of a Bleed-possessed battleship thousands of light-years away, her allies long dead. But she had her own body, and three batteries at the base of her skull that after all this time held fractions of charge. She could milk perhaps fifteen seconds' operation from each unit, and she'd need days to put herself together again afterward. She wouldn't get a second chance.

Fortunately she never needed more than one.

She popped a battery, upspun her personal time, and unsheathed her claws.

Then she moved fast.

The boy had better reflexes than she expected. By the time she breezed past Viv he had raised some low-rent vajra weapon; its particles whirled from his bracelets, cohering into crystal. Not a bad trick—Zanj could use it, once she skinned those bands off him. So, rather than killing him outright, she swept his legs and elbowed him in the chest. He flew back, eyes wide with the shock of sudden speed, hit the wall, fell. Zanj's fur glowed, radiating waste heat and crackling with ionized air; she jumped, twisted around, landed facing the other direction, and saw Viv half turned toward her, so slow, one hand drifting out, her vocal cords buzzing with the roots of a word.

Zanj felt momentary misgivings. It was bad form to hurt people who helped you. And she did like this woman. But it was a hard universe.

She wasn't cruel. She didn't relish screams. Good thing she didn't have to listen to this one. All she had to do was get her hand around Viv's throat and lift her from the ground, and squeeze, and squeeze—while Viv croaked out: "Stop."

And Zanj did.

The pain would have been beautiful if Zanj didn't have to feel it. There was a band of fire at her brow, and it spread suffering through all the lines of her, nerves and implants and soul knotted into a tangle of fury and flame. Her skin crisped. Her stomach tried to strangle her heart. The pain went on forever, and forever was so brief no time seemed to have passed at all.

She'd thought she had known pain inside the star.

This was worse.

She came back to herself, panting on the floor, drooling rainbow blood on crystal. She'd bitten into her cheek. Viv was staring down at her, mouth open, horrified—by what she had done, by what had almost been done to her. Zanj sheathed her fangs and clutched her forehead. The pain passed and left her scoured. Her searching fingers found a circlet of metal like a cuff around her brow; her claws bit into her skin, tore, but the cuff did not move. Blood leaked down her face. The bone beneath the circlet creaked. "Free me," she commanded. It was not a plea. She had not begged in three thousand years.

She felt sick. To be so close, to be out of the box and free, and yet to feel this chain around her skull, as if the Empress still crouched above her body, her burning hand on Zanj's face, her skin flowing, sealing, searing—it was a joke. A lie. Her eyes screwed shut, and there were no tears, no. She would not allow them. She would choke first. "Free me."

Viv stammered, drew back. "I. Um. I don't have much reason to. Since you almost—"

"I will kill you," Zanj roared with all the fury her long captive years had watered and let grow. She came up off the floor, unsteady, claws out, but all Viv had to say was no, and she collapsed again.

The next broken moment did not last so long as the first, because she surrendered faster. When she came back to herself, she felt her limbs sore with seizure, smelled the sweat of her own fear, tasted the burned metal of her own blood. She wanted to hurt this woman. She needed her dead. For vengeance, for freedom—but also because her death, the boy-monk's death, would let Zanj hide, leave her alone here to pant and shiver with her shame. So what if Viv had hurt her? She had been hurt before. But Viv had seen her in despair.

This wasn't fair. Fuck fair, she'd never much cared for fair—but still, this wasn't. She should be free. She should be herself again. She had talked herself out of the box. But this damn iron circlet gripped her brain. A poison crown. The box had been more honest. Wherever she went now in all the world, she'd take her prison with her.

The station shook.

"It's coming apart," Hong said, recovered from the shock, holding his ribs. "They're firing on High Carcereal itself." With horror, because of course for him the salient fact of the goddamn moment was the offense the Pride offered to his bitch goddess by attacking her work. Zanj laughed, bitter and sick and mad and soft, because of how far away his bullshit cultist concerns felt from everything that really mattered. And because he was wrong.

She heard the madness in her laugh, after so many centuries, after such a failure even here. But to her surprise, Viv heard it, too. And sounded, when she spoke, almost kind. "Zanj? Why are you laughing?"

"Because it's fucking absurd, you speck. You mayfly. Because I'm stuck here, because that little monk thinks his fleet and all the Pride's relics and their greatest planet-scorching weapons, all those gnats and peashooters, could make this station shake. Because I'm free for the first time in longer than either of you could imagine, and I can't get this crown off. And we're all about to die, because that's not weapons fire. That's Bleedsign."

Viv did not understand. The boy did not believe. "Impossible," he said, as if saying a thing made it so. Zanj just kept laughing.

"Hong," Viv said carefully. "I don't know what she's talking about, but let's keep impossible off the table for a moment."

"There can't be Bleed here. There's nothing for them to eat."

"Your Empress, your Lady, your evil mistress, chained cubic light-years of local Cloud to some mad purpose—recently. She built machines around this star that all you small-brained monks networked together could not comprehend. To the Bleed, that smells awful tasty."

"Could one of you explain, please?" Viv asked. "What's a Bleed?"

Zanj boggled at the question, so much that she almost forgot her own absurd predicament. "Where are you *from*?"

"Los Angeles," Viv said. "Originally."

Which meant nothing much to Zanj; she recalled fifty or sixty planets named Los Angeles, ruins, cinders, poison balls, and one pretty nice place actually, and Viv might mean any of them or none. Even during a Fall, new planets popped up all the time, and long-silent worlds sent feelers out, wondering if the coast was clear, if the Bleed had moved on, if the Empress had stopped her raging. So Viv was a rube. So what? "The Bleed eat civilizations. And since there aren't many of those at the moment, they're hungry."

Zanj could fight them. Maybe. Alone, on low power, without weapons, she wouldn't get far. She could run. She could try. But Viv's command, *stop*, had passed through the Cloud, not through any medium so slow as air. All that woman had to do was crook her finger and Zanj would come crawling back.

Viv knelt beside her, just out of reach. "The Empress chained you here. She gave me this scar. We don't have to fight. We can help each other."

It sounded so simple when she said it. There would be time for vengeance later. She wanted this woman to die. She wanted her blood on the walls, she wanted her eyes somewhere else. Not because she'd hurt Zanj—she hadn't meant to, she still looked sick and shaken beneath the mask of her concern—but because she was a piece of this whole situation that Zanj wanted over and done with. But while she wanted Viv to die, she wanted out more. You made bad deals with your back against the wall. "Give me your hand."

The boy objected. "Viv—"

But Viv raised one hand to cut him off. "Hong. We don't have a choice." And he listened. Good monk. Back to Zanj: "Bring him, too."

"Give me your hand," she said again.

Viv offered it. This time, her fingers did not shake. Brave. Brave jailer.

Zanj reached into Viv, probing her soul, initiating the handshake to prepare for encryption and jump, and found . . . nothing. Her eyes snapped open, and she looked closer. She'd assumed Viv was some kind of saint or master, or else a gifted idiot, to cast no shadow on the Cloud. But she was wrong.

"What's the problem?" Ah yes, Hong, the killjoy kid, so interested in their success now that he didn't have to take the blame.

Zanj rose from her crouch. This could not be. Yet all ten or twelve of her senses claimed it was so. The Cloud curled beneath and around her, full of everything but Viv. "I thought you were just being private—keeping your soul to yourself. But you don't have one."

"What do you mean?" Viv's hand tightened on hers, weak, human, physical—as if mere pressure could prove she was really there. "What are you talking about, a soul?"

"Don't tell me you monks forgot about souls." To have her chain held by children hurt, but for a fool to hold it, and blink at her stupidly when she snarled—that curdled in her mouth. She would kill them, crush their gormless faces in. Even the thought of violence sent pain cascading through her skull. Was that the crown, fucking with her? Or was that only her memory of agony, promising its return if she acted? She was training herself already. That damn crown hooked through her, a puppeteer's hand gloved in her guts.

Viv must have felt the heat of Zanj's ire; she drew back. "I'm sorry." Not apologizing for her ignorance, Zanj thought, but for everything. She was afraid. She was alone. She was, even worse, sincere. And for whatever reason, she did not want Zanj to suffer. That excused nothing, but it made the visions that filled her brain, of choking Viv out, of breaking her limb by limb, feel sour. "I'm not a monk. I'm not from," a hesitation, a hitch, and then, "around here. I don't know what you're talking about."

Clouds parted, metaphorically speaking. The prospect of murder receded, and with it pain. Zanj drew ragged breath, gathered herself. "Do you think I cross the galaxy by just . . . throwing atoms around? The soul is a map to the body. I compress my soul, send that through the Cloud, and build a new body where I want to land."

"The Cloud?"

She could not possibly be this dumb. And yet. "The Cloud is an echo of the universe. Souls live there, and go there when they die. In the Cloud, distance is a matter of math, not physics; in the Cloud, you calculate yourself from place to place. We can, at least. But you're just meat. No ghost. No soul. Flesh."

"That can't be," Hong said helpfully.

"Yes," Zanj snapped back, "because a pissant monk who doesn't know how his own weapons work is the final judge of can and can't. You didn't even notice she was dead." She glowered back to Viv. "You have no shadow in the Cloud. When your meat goes, that's it. No resurrection, no heavens or afterlives. You're gone. So that's good news for me, at least. Maybe I can't kill you. But all I have to do is wait."

The station shook again. Viv looked scared, still, and brave, which made Zanj's pain, her crown, her captivity, all worse. If Viv had cackled, if she'd driven screws into Zanj's eyes, their respective places would be clear. But she wasn't evil. She wasn't even mean. She was just working with very few tools.

Then Zanj saw something strange. Viv drew all her fear and confusion into herself. She inhaled, breathed out, and when she opened her eyes again they were still and steady as the gaps of space. "I don't want to die," she said. "And if I do, there's no one left to set you free."

The station groaned. Dark thunder darted through the Cloud.

"Promise you'll let me go," Zanj said. "If I get you out of here."

"You tried to kill me," Viv replied. "I promise nothing. But if I die here, you're stuck."

The Bleed neared, great shadows in the computational murk, all their many dimensions full of teeth, smacking their lips and wiping the drool from the corners of their mouths, ready for dinner. Viv did not know how much pain she would face when they came, how far she could fall into their starscape maws. She didn't know the first thing about the waters in which she swam, or the monsters that haunted them. She was strong, but ignorant; she could be swayed.

And Zanj, in that harsh moment watching, judging Viv, saw a woman much like the one she'd been a long time ago, a woman who had left the safe gravity of home for a sky she did not yet understand, seeking life among the stars.

She realized then that she had made her choice.

She listened to the Cloud. Battle raged overhead: many ships, too far away to touch, too dumb to seize. But, nearer—oh.

The Empress had been cruel indeed, and petty. But this kind of cruelty, Zanj could use.

And anyway, Zanj couldn't free herself—or take revenge—if she was dead.

"I have an idea," Zanj said. "Better than an idea. I have a ship."

8

"THERE'S ONE THING I don't understand," Viv said as she ran up the stairs after Zanj. She had to gasp the words; Zanj didn't tire, barely even seemed to sweat, though she had the weirdest running form Viv had ever seen, hunched and lurching, more skip than jog. Then again, Viv had no idea what was going on beneath her skin. Zanj had seemed almost normal, for an alien, when Viv opened the box, but then there'd been that deep pop like a breaking wishbone, and she'd moved so fast Viv's eyes could barely track her.

"Only one?" Zanj's scorn, at least, seemed human. "I don't know what kind of Stone Age backwater Los Angeles you're from, but you seem pretty far behind on the basics."

Viv glanced left to Hong, seeking sympathy or at least human contact, but he was busy running. She hadn't appreciated before how calm he was, how little he'd minded her questions. She hoped she'd get over this whole not-knowing thing sooner or later. She liked it even less than she liked the running, and she always hated running. Stupid future. "So the Cloud is, what, a sort of hyperspace data system. And I can't travel through it, because I don't have an echo there."

"A soul," Zanj said levelly, because of course she wasn't winded. A wall warped into a door and they ran through. "What you don't have is a soul." She grinned back, wide enough that the full length of her fangs showed.

Viv didn't begrudge Zanj some fun at her expense—after all, she'd unintentionally tortured this woman to the edge of passing out. And—more worrying—Viv had enjoyed it, that rush of power in this place where all else slipped from her control, enjoyed it even as it horrified her. Focus on running. The Vivian Liao who hated running felt more familiar than the Vivian Liao that enjoyed the prospect of having her orders enforced by a futuristic torture crown. "And a ship will work, even if I don't have a," might as well embrace the local terminology, "a soul?"

Zanj held up one hand for silence, and dropped into a crouch beside a door that had not existed seconds ago.

This whole escape had been like that: Zanj had whispered to the walls of the prison chamber and its gravity reversed, drawing them up, up through the stalk with terrifying speed, until the bright death grid appeared above, at which point she'd stopped them, and opened the seamless wall to reveal a space where they could crawl, climb. Zanj flowed from hold to hold, wall to wall, her long arms and broad shoulders spanning drops Viv had to jump, her body squeezing through claustrophobic cracks. Hong chugged along beside her, behind her, groaning at the jumps, grunting as he muscled himself up the wall, his hand pressed against the patch in his gut, and Viv felt grateful for his presence, for his humanity. If she'd been alone with Zanj, she would have cursed herself for a weakling, for thinking this was difficult. Because obviously Viv, who kept herself in reasonable shape, thank you very much, should be able to keep pace with a woman of mythological infamy.

If Viv ever had a chance to explain all this to her therapist, she would laugh and laugh.

She'd figured Zanj's pace for a not-so-subtle revenge, and maybe it was, but one time when Viv couldn't make a jump, Zanj flowed back down the wall, stretched out her long arm, grasped Viv over her scar, and pulled her up in a single smooth tug, as if Viv weighed no more than a doll.

And yet, for all that strength and speed, when Viv tried to imagine Zanj fighting the Empress, her mind reeled. Zanj might be strong, swift, and clever as clever, but the Empress who built High Carcereal, who had torn out Viv's heart and brought her here for unknowable ends with unknown means—she was a fact of nature, a vastness. You couldn't punch something like that.

Viv, of course, still planned to try.

She was conscious of the irony.

So, at last, they'd reached this door. Zanj crouched, and Viv behind Zanj, and Hong behind her; Zanj leaned around the corner, drew back, waved for Viv and Hong to do the same.

Beyond the door lay a hangar. And in the hangar there was a ship.

Viv loved the ship at first sight. She was a matte-black bird of metal and glass with a falcon's beak, and massive drums that might be engines or turbines beneath her stubby wings. There were panels and seams on her skin, hatches for personnel and connectors for hoses, a ramp, raised, for ingress, sized right for human beings. People had made this ship, or something like people—with their hands, with machines their hands made. It was not leftover godstuff, not some stained-glass glory or hate fractal curse. People built this ship to go places.

That, Viv understood. Walk forward a few thousand years from the twenty-footer she'd scuttled off North Carolina, or for that matter from the ungainly space dicks Elon thrust toward Mars, and you'd find this: a big goofy gourd of metal to mount and float wherever the stars would take you.

"How old is that thing?" Hong asked with the same tone of voice Viv would have used to ask a hipster about the typewriter he'd hauled from a shoulder bag at a coffee shop.

"The same age as me," Zanj said. "I rode it from Pasquarai to the stars, before I was anyone. And I kept it with me even after I didn't need it anymore. I thought she would have burned it, but she does like her trophies." The kind of anger Viv heard in Zanj's voice took a serious run-up. Several thousand years of prison's worth of run-up, say. "The *Question*'s a slow, simple jump drive—raw physical transit through Cloudspace, without compression. My people didn't know how the world worked back then. We had colliders, we had some eggheads whose math said causality propagated through a higher-dimensional space. All the rest, I had to go out and learn. But she'll get us where we need to go."

"If we don't fall into a singularity on the way. Or split ourselves on a string."

Zanj rolled her eyes at Hong, slow and exaggerated, so even he couldn't miss it. "I'm no true pilot, but flying is among my many skills." The station trembled again, and this time the tremor did not fade; a subtle shiver lingered, reminding Viv of the earthquakes of her childhood, and not in a good way. She glanced around out of reflex, drew close to the wall. There were no books to fall on her here, no china to slip out of cabinets. She would have hugged something as normal as a book, or a china cabinet.

Instead she asked: "What are we going to do about the Pride drones?" She'd counted nine Kentaurs on the ground between them and the ship, a handful on the catwalks to the left, two in what looked like a sniper's nest on the right. How they'd come here, she had no idea—well, that wasn't quite true. This place wasn't unknowable, just different. Think, Viv. The hangar opened onto empty space above the star—and if the drones were still trying to chase her, this might have been as close as they could come to the stalk.

"We will fight our way through." Hong stood, and drew his clubs. He composed his face for battle or for death. "We cannot let the Bleed catch us here. We will triumph, or die."

He marched toward the door, but without looking Zanj reached out her hand and set it on Hong's chest. He tried to march past her, but could not move her arm. "Slow down, soldier boy. I'll handle the Pride. You just get my illustrious jailer here to the ship."

"Thanks," Viv said in a tone that, she had to admit, lacked a certain thankfulness.

Zanj shrugged, and tapped the crown on her forehead. "I don't know what this does to me if you die. You're the only one I know who can control it—so you're my best shot at taking it off. You stay safe."

"Can you really fight off all those drones yourself?"

"In the old days," Zanj said, "I could have fought all the drones, anywhere. And any friends they cared to bring. Now? I have no weapons, I've spent the last three thousand years or so in a box. I only have two batteries left with charge, and they'll drive me at full speed for maybe ten seconds each. The question is, how fast can you run?" But she was smiling at the prospect. Viv was building an index of what the pirate queen's smiles meant— threat, enticement, innocence, fury, pain—but this one suggested real joy. "When the ramp starts to open, go for it. And don't you worry about me."

Zanj raised one hand, fingers poised to snap, and closed her eyes. Viv gathered herself in a sprinter's crouch beside Hong, and waited. Hong looked uncertain, grim, but ready, for all the terror he'd held of Zanj an hour ago. Viv understood. Zanj was not a friend, but for now she might be an ally.

Viv remembered the rage in those eyes, the fierce promise, *I will kill you*, spoken with the weight Viv only gave words she meant to make real.

Zanj snapped her fingers, gunshot loud in the empty hall. The Pride drones' heads spun toward the door, as if noticing it for the first time. Then they spun back to the ship as, with a whir of comforting, basically normal hydraulics, its ramp began to descend.

Viv heard a second pop, deeper, this one from inside Zanj's skull, a snap like a broken bone, like Viv had heard in the prison chamber, and when the pirate queen opened her eyes they burned the same solid white they'd been when she reached for Viv's throat. "Go!" Her shout deafened. Hong froze, but Viv needed no second cue. She ran into the hangar, and Hong, with a squawk of unreadiness, scrambled after her.

The Pride noticed. Kentaur heads revolved to them at once, scorpion tails charged, mouths opened. Viv ran as if the hangar were empty and her life depended on setting a personal best over the distance between the door and the ramp, which, well, it more or less did. And as she ran, she realized that, in spite of everything, she trusted Zanj to cover them.

Behind her, the first Kentaur broke. By reflex she turned to look, but Zanj was already gone, leaving the wreck behind, torn in half at the middle. Viv tried to find her but the hangar became a blur of fire and fléchettes, screams of tortured metal, sparks, teeth-jarring booms as something—many some-things, but one in particular—broke the speed of sound. Zanj was in the catwalk and the sniper nest at once, punching through one drone's sternum, ripping another's torso from its abdomen. She moved faster than sight, visible only when physical matter had the temerity to resist, for however few sec-onds, her will to break it. Zanj was sharp, and fast, and burning. She left dented, melted footprints in the solid metal deck.

Viv stumbled as she tried to track it all; a Kentaur reared above her like a horse, spiked hooves plunging; Hong grabbed the hooves and thrust it aside with a surge of his legs and back, and Viv rolled away. She staggered to her feet, then went down hard as a line of coherent fire stitched through the air where her head had been; pain was a solid bar across her shin, and she saw Zanj-prints in the deck metal around her, spinning where Zanj had tripped her and moved on. Somewhere the shooter screamed static. Viv did not look, rose again, yes, alive but limping, and there was Hong caught between two drones, his wounded arm bleeding, clubs awhirl, human, beautiful.

Zanj had told them, don't fight, just get to the ship.

"Hong!" He heard her, understood, pulled free, and they ran through a hangar of acrid smoke, ozone, burning plastic, burning air, hot metal, oil, blood, and then the ramp by some miracle was underfoot, and they climbed it into a space empty of threat, a space whose silence rang like a bell, and sought, because this ship had been built by creatures not so inhuman after all, up ramps and past a dinner table (a dinner table!) and a cargo hold, for a space with two chairs and a great deal of buttons, dials, levers, and unset-tling hoses that Viv, to her own surprise, recognized as a cockpit. Outside the viewscreen the hangar was a mess of fire—the oil Pride drones had for blood seemed to be flammable, under some circumstances.

She started pushing buttons at once, giddy with adrenaline and fear, turning dials to the farthest right. Lights came on, green, red, purple, yellow, shades of pink. Chimes played behind a panel. The ship jerked. Hong fell into a switch that started something whirring, jerked away, and tried to pat the whirring something back to sleep. "You know how to fly this thing?"

"No!" Viv shouted back, flushed and ecstatic with the nearness of death, with the need to move. A voice in the back of her skull kept screaming, I'm on a *spaceship!* very loud, over and over. "But it's moving anyway!" She reached for something that looked like a set of brass knuckles suspended above the control panel by no visible force. Hong tried to stop her.

Zanj got there first. She appeared in the cockpit with a thunderclap, fur smoldering, body slick with oil and hydraulic fluid, jumpsuit torn, bleeding from a deep gouge above her eye through which Viv could see a white substance too shiny for bone. The gouge healed over as she watched. Zanj trembled. Her fur was still filament bright at the tips and hot enough to burn. Her hands were coated black, her claws were out, and she wore a smile Viv could not read, a smile less human than the rest. "That wasn't the ship," she said. "It's the station."

"What?" seemed a reasonable, if imprecise, question to Viv, but rather than answering, Zanj hip-checked her away from the control panel, slid her own fingers through the brass knuckles, and sank into the pilot's chair. The ship bucked beneath them, then reared; Hong braced himself against the door, and Viv caught the back of Zanj's chair as the ship lurched gracelessly toward the open wall.

An immense hate fractal hung in space outside their exit, gunports glowing ruby. "Hold on," Zanj said, and pulled her hands back, and distance got weird. Viv's stomach took up residence in her feet and her feet lost their close partnership with the floor; her shoulders jerked in their sockets as she clutched the back of Zanj's chair. Hong let out a sound he probably would not have called a scream. They roared toward the hate fractal, between its arcs of fire, then zipped up between the fractal and the stalk, climbing away from the star. Viv lost her grip there, slammed against the ceiling first and then the floor as ship's gravity compensated. Her head rang. Her jaw hurt. She tasted copper. But they were free, and rising, rising, toward the stars.

Above them, the battle raged.

What Viv had seen from the hall while she and Hong were prisoners of the Pride drones was barely a skirmish compared to this. The sky was full of triple constellations—the stars, the sharp red Pride ships flitting, dancing, spitting fire against the stained-glass artwork vessels of the 'faith. Structures of still larger scale had arrived, whirling furious Mandelcontinents of Pride set against a regimented vast and glistening phalanx at whose heart burned a cathedral planet.

Gnats, Zanj had called these ships. Peashooters, their guns.

Viv felt electric all over, seeing all this as the doorstep of some greater glory.

Hong's wrist chimed. Fire chewed through space around them and Zanj hauled them out of its way. The ship's own gravity softened the maneuvers now, translated them to gentle pitch and yaw and roll, and Viv heard the fire pass, heard the engines of the fighters they darted around. There was no sound in space, her inner science officer objected, but then, she wasn't hearing sound in space—only sound in the cockpit. Now that she wasn't being bounced across the instrument panel, she could see the speaker grilles. Of course. Humans, and things like them, evolved to respond to sound, not to dots on an instrument panel.

Speaking of sounds—again, Hong's wrist chimed.

"Can you turn that off?" Zanj shouted.

Hong pressed a button instead, and his bracelet flashed like when he drew his clubs—but instead of the clubs, a woman's head whirled into being before him, bald, severe, ageless and ancient and angry. "Grand Rector," Hong said, "I can explain."

"I said, turn it off, not *answer* it!"

"Brother Heretic." The Rector's rage came through despite the tinny speakers. "You have cost us much—in ships and souls—"

"Grand Rector, I have found a miracle."

"You have found what was not yours to find, and you lost yourself in its finding. Submit to us. Return. We will cleanse you, and burn you free of—" The voice died mid-sentence, and the head disappeared. Hong tapped his bracelet, tapped it again, then glared at Zanj.

"Did you just hang up on the leader of my order?"

"She's firing on us, and I need to focus for this jump. The Bleed are almost here."

"How can you tell?" Viv asked, but in answer Zanj only waved out the window. There, in the dark, against the stars, no, beneath the stars and warping their light, she saw a massive shape like an eyeless face, and a mouth vast enough to eat stars, opening, opening—Pride and 'faith fleets alike scattered, wheeling away from that monstrosity, but a rope of purple lightning passed through the fleets and their lights died, their motion slowed, they dripped frost and darkened, and the mouth in space gaped wider into madness, and all the speakers now were screaming, and Hong began to pray and Viv realized she was praying, too, and there were tears in her eyes—

Zanj said, "This will be bad." And: "Hold on."

Before Viv could ask, *to what*, they tore, and were somewhere else, and it was bad indeed.

9

THE CLOUD HURT less once they closed the shades and walled out the bubbling geometries of twisting blue that Viv's mind insisted was not blue at all. The shades, though, did nothing to relieve the teeth-on-teeth feeling in her chest, the nagging sense she had almost remembered . . . something.

What she had almost remembered, they told her, was everything.

At least, with the shades closed, she could not see the faces.

The Cloud: she wondered who'd thought that one up, or if her translation gimmick was adding connotations foreign to the original. A good name, whether it rose from some long-dead brand manager or from Viv's own mind. The Cloud sat above everything, accessible from everywhere if you knew how to look. You could travel through it if you had the knack. You could fly. And, like another sort of cloud altogether, it remembered things. Places. People.

A hyperspace data system, she'd called it—well, almost. The Empress built it, people thought, or found it first, or found what had been there before and built the Cloud on top of it so long ago no one remembered. At any rate, the Empress could bend the Cloud to her will better than anyone in known space.

Viv pondered the implications. What could you do with a massive distributed faster-than-light network? Enormous computations at nonsense speeds, at least. You could index matter, mirror it, particle by particle. You could give the whole universe a shadow, add an informational component to each atom, seed base matter with nanomachines until code could rewrite reality. You could do this, and someone, at some point, had. Every soul in the galaxy was wedded to a single Cloud.

Except for Viv.

She'd have an existential crisis about that later.

Thanks to blood-borne interfaces and implants, minds existed at least as much in the Cloud as in flesh—which made some hard problems easy. Want to move about the cosmos? Why bother accelerating matter? A quick shift of variables could dart you across space and put you back together on the other side—if you had the right passwords, permissions, and tools. Do you fear death? Archive and index souls, store them by the trillion compressed deep deep down so nothing need pass away. Between quantum engines and the power of the Cloud, rewriting reality, building stations out of starstuff, became a simple matter of software. Anyone could do it—at least until the Empress shut them down, or the Bleed came.

And the Bleed—what were they? Shivering at the table far from any window, gripping a cup of warm water—all the tea on the ship had crumbled to ash eons back, but water did not decay—she asked the question. Neither Hong nor Zanj answered at first. "You know almost as much as we do," Hong said.

"I just saw that mouth."

"Yes." He worked his lower lip between his teeth. "Complexity draws them. The use of the Cloud. Civilizations that grow large enough, advanced enough, attract them, and when they come, they feed. Nothing can stop them."

"Not even the Empress?"

Hong fell silent. Zanj, pacing the room, at last said, "No."

Hong spoke then, spurred, Viv thought, by dogma as much as by knowledge. "She could. She has. She's the only thing in the galaxy they can't overcome."

"Because she hides in her Citadel, behind her wall, and whenever an upstart world gets close to summoning the Bleed she rushes out to destroy them. She's afraid."

Hong opened his mouth to argue, but Zanj fixed him with a stare that begged for him to try, that weighed him against all the thousands of years she'd been alive, and thousands more imprisoned. He stopped himself, breathed. "She's . . . prudent," Hong said. "Like the rest of us."

"What are they, though?" Viv asked, and neither of them answered her. So Viv said, "Fine. Fuck it. Nobody knows."

Zanj, arms crossed, watching, asked her a question back. "So, Los Angeles, what's next?"

"What do you mean?"

She tapped her crown. "This makes you the boss. We're off High Carcereal.

Tell me what you want, so I can make it happen, so you can take this damn thing off."

The engines thrummed, and Viv's chair creaked as she leaned back, and aside from that the ship was silent. The question weighed on her, too big for thought. What do you want? "I'm tired. First, I want to sleep."

"You shouldn't sleep," Hong said. "Not until we drop out of the Cloud."

"When will that be?"

Zanj: "I didn't have time to gin up a clear route before we jumped. Shouldn't take us more than three days to get back to realspace. Sleep after."

"You can go without sleep for three days?"

"With meditation," Hong said, and Zanj, with a shrug: "I recharge. I haven't slept in centuries."

"I," Viv said, "am going to sleep right now."

She didn't remember her dreams the first night. From the bruises and nail-tracks on her arms, from the raw gravel in her voice when she staggered to the table the next what-felt-like-morning, she was glad she didn't remember. "What was that?" She sounded like Tom Waits had a baby with Tom Waits.

"The Cloud gets in your head," Zanj replied, and Hong fetched her water. "It happens to everyone."

Viv did not like being everyone.

They moved around one another in the silence of a storm. Hong worked out. His wound didn't seem to bother him anymore; Viv could still see the patch if she looked, but it had darkened almost to the color of his flesh. Viv joined him, reassured to feel her meat still work like meat, though when she tried to match his pace on minute drills she ended up vomiting into the ship's latrine. There wasn't much inside her to come up. Hong's belt held a small supply of nutrient tubes or whatever that seemed to contain exactly what her body needed, no more and no less. She felt empty, but never hungry.

If Zanj ate, Viv never saw it.

Viv did not know what to think about the other woman, or how to be around her, and in the looming silence she could think of little else. Zanj at least seemed to know what she was doing: she prowled through the halls and clambered up ladders and down to review her ship, checking the sound bulkheads made when she tapped them, listening to the pulse of conduits in what Viv took for the engine room. When Hong offered to help, Zanj

laughed at the idea, then tossed him a tool Viv didn't recognize from a box
of other tools she didn't either and told him to check the coolant flow. He
caught the tool one-handed and disappeared, and either did not notice or
did not care when Zanj muttered, after he turned his back: "And take your
time."

Zanj did not talk much. Nor did she try to kill either of them again, at
least on the first day. Viv tried to watch her work, but whenever her eyes
lingered for more than a few seconds Zanj turned to her and raised an eyebrow, *what*, and Viv got the hint and moved on.

Zanj had almost killed her back on High Carcereal, easy as breathing.
And she had trashed a roomful of Pride barehanded, and boasted she could
do more.

Viv knew she should have kept her distance, but the woman drew her.
Zanj was a legend, apparently. Zanj had seen an Empress who could tear a
galaxy apart, and thought, *I can take her.* She'd come close, too, close enough
that the Empress made her suffering a personal project. You didn't spend
three thousand years torturing a nobody. Zanj had seen her chance and gone
for it, and she'd paid the price, and Viv knew how that felt.

Hell, in her shoes Viv, too, might have tried to kill the woman who rescued her.

"Can I help?" she asked the next time Zanj looked up from her work.

"You can quit standing in the light."

Then again, maybe Zanj was just an asshole.

She remembered snatches of her dreams the next night. Striding gigantic through a crystal forest, reveling in her strength, crushing rocks underfoot, snapping branches, she heard tiny screeches below, felt gunfire tickle
her ankles, and realized she was shattering a city. Once she understood,
she started to break it worse on purpose. She dreamed of cinders that once
were worlds, dreamed the deaths of friends she'd never met. A girl with
bloodstained golden hair, a man with lizard scales pierced with bright
spears. A beautiful woman with butterfly wings curled and burned like a
dry leaf in a bonfire. Once she saw Magda and her boy, and cursed herself
that she could not forget.

The second day she and Hong and Zanj orbited one another slowly, leaving rooms as others entered. She tried to ask Hong about the Rector, about
his faith, but the nightmares he had not dreamed lingered in his haunted
eyes.

She found Zanj in the cockpit with the shades up. The silence had grown so deep between them that she could not speak at first, made herself lean back against the control panel and stay by Zanj alone, and ignore the horrors outside.

"How can you watch all that? It makes my head hurt just knowing it's there."

Zanj whistled through her teeth, and did not face her.

"Fine." Viv stood up and turned to go. "Don't talk to me."

"I'm not the problem here," Zanj said as she left.

That stopped her. "I just wanted to talk."

She laughed. "I can bear the Cloud, because I'm used to it. I came this way the first time when I was young, and we didn't know what to expect. I almost chewed off my tongue in my sleep. It's an acquired taste."

"You saved my life."

Zanj raised her shoulders and crossed her arms and propped her feet up on the control panel. "I saved mine."

Viv felt the freeze-out. She'd used tricks like this herself—you built walls with any tools available. "I'm not talking about the whole escape. If you hadn't tripped me in the hangar I'd be dead and you'd be free."

"Not likely. Like I said back on the station—I know how the old lady works. Death's no escape from her. I'm stuck in this thing unless you let me out."

"I wanted to thank you."

"No. You wanted to say thank you. You feel like you should. You don't really want to thank me."

"I do."

"Then let me go."

"So you can kill me."

"Maybe." A laugh. A toothy grin. Her gaze drifted from the monstrosities outside to rest, utterly without malice or interest, on Viv. "This crown on my head puts us a bit beyond thanks, Los Angeles. You don't want to let me go because I'm dangerous—I get that. Does it give you a thrill to have me under your thumb? You want to make me perform? Do tricks?"

"No," she said, too fast, horrified.

"So let me earn my freedom. Give me a task, like *fuck up my enemies* or *get me where I need to go*. You know what you want, or else you'd be asking more questions—but you're too scared to ask for it. You're scared and alone in a big damn galaxy and you scream through the night. Great. Welcome to the party. I'd feel plenty sympathetic if I hadn't spent the last three thousand years burning in a star. Tell me where you want to go. Tell me what you want to do. Quit playing curious and talk to me for real."

Viv did not want to talk for real.

The third night she dreamed she lay in the Ogham basement. The Empress knelt above her, green, indomitable, her face a mirror; she pressed Viv to the tile floor with one hand as if she was nothing, as of course she was when set beside the Empress's great transforming need. Gently, gently, the Empress curled her fingers, pierced skin, snapped bone, squeezed past lungs to the heart, and what Viv felt was too deep for anything with so quaint a name as pain, and she was screaming and so was Magda and that was worse. She tried to fight free, for her. Her hands flapped at the Empress's wrists. Her left hand would not close, her wrist ruined, her blood flowing, and her nails slicked off green skin like it was marble, and she felt herself drawn like a thorn, her heart tugged from her chest—

She woke and found herself held. She struck out by reflex, and hurt her fingers. Broken nails raked eyes, a mouth, a face hard as granite. She felt a burn scar beneath her palm—felt Zanj. Who drew back from the bed, in the dim light of Viv's cubbyhole cabin.

"What the fuck?"

"You were screaming," Zanj said.

She came back to herself slowly. "Did I hurt you?" A shake of the head in answer. "How long were you watching?" It took her three tries to stammer out the question.

"Half the night. Hong took the other half. You've had seizures the last two nights, but this is the first time you've come close to hurting yourself." In the shadows, her crown looked black. "I get it, you know. I fell in battle, but the Empress does not fight to win. She fights to break all will for future fighting. She burned me. Humiliated me. She hurt my friends and killed them one by one." She raised her hand to the scar. "And then she marked me. Like she marked you."

Viv felt afraid then, on this hard bed, with this strange woman in her room. She'd been afraid all along, but avoiding it until now. "It hurt."

Zanj nodded. "Viv." The name didn't fit in her mouth at all. "You've lost something and you want it back. I know how that feels. The kid thinks you're a miracle—and a bargaining chip to win his way home. Me, I'm honest. I want freedom—if only so I can kill you." Another smile, this one slant. She knelt, and reached, slowly, to the bed, and stroked Viv's wrist where the skin melted and warped, where she could not precisely feel anymore. "You have a hold over each of us, but we can't help you unless you trust us. There's no shame in having lost." That smile again, deeper, and Viv placed it now that she could see the depths of those eyes close up: sadness. "At least, I hope not."

"I don't have anything over Hong." It was easier to say that.

"If you say so." Zanj knelt again, and let her sleep.

Or at least, she let her try. Zanj left after another hour, and when she was gone Viv lay awake until she felt it was morning. She found them in the hold, Hong practicing a punch sequence, Zanj paging through a glossy pamphlet that looked an awful lot like porn. She said, "I need your help."

Hong interrupted a lot while Viv told the story, his awe and disbelief growing throughout. Zanj just listened.

"I come from a planet called Earth." It sounded ridiculous to say. And, of course, neither Zanj nor Hong reacted. They both came from planets, after all, nothing weird about that, and neither of them seemed to have heard of Earth. "Where I'm from, none of this exists. That probably sounds absurd to you. No space travel. No Cloud, no Pride, no Bleed, no 'faith. No Empress. Or, if they do, we don't know about them. Zanj, you mentioned you'd known a few planets named Los Angeles. That's a city on my world. I think, maybe, I'm from your past. Or something like it.

"I was on the run. I'm . . . I build things, with computers." (She realized she hadn't heard them mention computers, which made some sense—how often, under normal circumstances, did she mention oxygen?) "The government wanted to break me. My friend and I had almost stopped them—but when I had almost won, the Empress showed up." Hong interrupted here, hungry for a description, for wisdom and for signs, how do you know it was Her; Zanj threw a pillow at him, to spare her, but Viv gripped the scar tissue on her wrist and told him what she remembered, then moved on. "She stopped me. She hurt my friend. Then she . . . she tore my heart out of my chest, and I woke up back on Rosary Station, drowning.

"Hong said the Rosary beads, the black holes, hold worlds. I think where I'm from, my world, my home, my friends—I think they're in the Rosary bead the Empress took with her when she left. It's a way back to my planet, or a portal to my time. Can people travel through time here?" Hong shook his head; Zanj scoffed. "Well, maybe she can. Or maybe Earth, my Earth, is in some sort of other universe, or it's a simulation, or whatever. I don't know.

But I'm real, even if I don't have—even if I'm not connected to the Cloud. I don't belong here. I have business back home. Enemies I can't let win. And my friends need me.

"I want to catch the Empress. I want to go back through that Rosary bead, and home.

"But I don't know how."

She stood at the apex of a triangle, balanced between Hong's awe and the calculation in Zanj's red eyes. She might be wrong. She felt too many ways at once: overwhelmed, excited, skeptical, scared. She didn't know this place, but she knew how to manage a team. You could not keep your colleagues in the dark and expect them to help to the best of their ability. Especially when you lacked relevant technical expertise. Viv didn't even know what was possible here.

"That's it," she said. "Will you help me get home?"

Hong nodded, mute with wonder. Zanj nodded, too. She seemed pleased. Viv hoped that was a good thing.

Then, with a sickening thud, the ship dropped back into realspace and the arguments began.

10

"**WE'RE GOING TO** Orn," Zanj maintained, as if any other choice were rank and suicidal nonsense.

They made their next jumps with care and calculation, rather than trusting to blind luck and the Cloud, so they could drop back to realspace when they needed. Viv slept harder on her first night back in the usual three-and-change dimensions than she had for years, slept as if wrapped in childhood blankets, and did not dream at all.

But while they made steady progress, there was some disagreement with regard to their destination. "Orn," Hong said every time Zanj raised the subject, "is a myth."

"You thought I was a myth until four days ago."

"We should go to the 'fleet." At least he was honest. Viv had been in too many meetings where ostensibly grown humans spent hours tiptoeing around their opinions. And, if half Viv's old C-suite had been able to convey the density of meaning in Zanj's scornful laugh, they would have saved a lot of time. Yet Hong persisted: "Viv, what you are—what you represent—we've wondered for centuries what's really inside the Rosary. Why the Empress made those beads. You're from there. You met Her. For that alone, for the privilege of an interview, the 'faith would take you anywhere, do anything you ask."

They were orbiting a hot blue star ringed by a necklace of comets and glaciers. The ship's skin drank sunlight and its fields drank water, and its passengers drank in the view. Purple shapes like manta rays drifted and spun through the ice, vanishing when Viv tried to focus on them, as if they could sense her gaze.

"What he means," Zanj explained, still paging through her porn, "is that they'll stick you in a box and pray to you, like, twenty times a day. They might let you out from time to time for good behavior, or to lay on hands, but they'll never in a billion years help you fight their goddess. Trust me. I've seen what they do to people they think are holy—drugged to bliss and brainwashed after. An ice pick to the eye would be faster."

Hong sputtered. "We don't do that anymore."

Viv felt unsettled to hear they'd done it once, and said so.

"The 'faith has changed in the last . . . How long were you stuck in that box, anyway?"

Zanj set down the pamphlet. "Three thousand years, I think. Give or take."

"Look, Viv, the 'faith has its problems, but we know more about the Empress than anyone."

"Because you worship her." Zanj couldn't sit through this conversation anymore, stood, paced; her tail curled and whipped.

"We don't . . . we recognize what She has achieved. We seek to understand the cosmos so we can free its beings." Zanj rolled her eyes and made a talking motion with her hand, but Hong pressed through. "The Empress is the world's great mystery. She has outlived ages. Some worship Her, yes, but our true calling is to study Her works, and understand them, so we can survive as She has. So we can transcend as She did. So, in the end, we can grow beyond Her."

"The Grand Rector," Viv pointed out, "didn't look like a scholar. Or like someone I'd want to meet up close."

Hong bowed his head. "She is of the old faction."

"She tried to blow us up."

"She is set in her ways." He wilted under her glare, but pressed on. "The Grand Rector is a war leader. She has led us in many great sorties against Pride and feral Grayframe and swift gods from the deep worlds. But she is no theologian. The Archivist, my master and teacher, is older and more respected by far, though she never felt the call to lead our fleet. She is our greatest student of transcendent knowledge, and she taught me the ways of the 'faith. She has studied the Imperial sky for centuries, and it was she who divined that the Empress had returned to High Carcereal and worked some great miracle there."

"So, the Archivist sent you after me?"

At this, Hong drew silent and looked away. "Not exactly. She—the Archivist brought the matter before the council of 'faith, but she had no hope the Hierarchs would see reason. The Rector would never permit us to go, and the Hierarchs are weak before her will. She cares for our safety, but also for her own position. The discovery of a grand miracle would shift power from her warbands to scholars and students of the 'faith. She would have held us in debate until the Pride had long since absconded with the miracle. She has done as much before with less momentous finds. We—I could not let the chance slip."

Viv had heard this kind of story before, though without so many unfamiliar names. You took your audience through the whole thing cause by cause and effect by logical effect, because if you just spat out what you did and why, your mistake would be too plain. "So you stole a ship, and a squadron, and went after the miracle yourselves."

"You dog!" Zanj put down her porn and clapped Hong on the shoulder, hard enough to make him wince. "And this whole time you've been playing the priggish monk—you're a proper pirate after all!"

He rubbed his shoulder, and looked uncomfortable with her praise. "There is no property among the 'faith. What we did is not technically theft."

"Angry warlords," Viv pointed out, "don't tend to respect technicalities."

"The Grand Rector is no warlord. We were the Archivist's students. How could we let the greatest miracle in generations slip away? We took ships, and sought liberation. Many I have fought and studied beside passed on into the Cloud, where I pray they seek liberation still."

Viv remembered the stained-glass sparks dying in the night, against the Pride, and robed bodies lying amid the wrecked Kentaurs. The monks' faces had been death masks of quiet contemplation more than pain. Passed on, he said, into the Cloud.

She said, "Thank you," and, "I'm sorry. I guess I'm not the miracle you wanted."

He shook his head, wondering, sincere. "You are better than a weapon or a grail. You are a clue to the worlds within the Rosary, to the Empress's divine purpose, to workings that have been a mystery to us for centuries. You could change the balance of the 'fleet. You could bring all our factions together. And with us behind you, you would stand a better chance of catching the Empress than with any other allies in the galaxy."

"After they poke and prod you, and assuming they let you go at all—by which point," Zanj observed several jumps later, while she guided them through a nebula's murk, "the Empress will have retreated beyond the borders of her Citadel. If they can keep out the Bleed, they're damn sure going to keep out Hong's cultists. While a pilot from Orn, crystal city of starships, could catch the Empress without tangling you in a religious war."

"This Citadel of hers," Viv said. "It's, what, a planet?" She was getting tired of all these new words and concepts, but then, a learning curve was to be expected after one woke up in the year a million and a half.

"The Citadel is a sector of space near the galactic edge where the Empress reclines in contemplation of the cosmos." Hong sounded close to rapture again. "A stellar fortress into which none may pass, its Cloud locked, its borders patrolled by the Diamond Fleet." At this point, logic caught up with his rapture. "Wait. Zanj." His voice still hooked when he said her name, like Viv imagined hers would if she met someone named Napoleon—or Satan. "How do you know She isn't there already?"

"I couldn't track her if she were traveling alone," Zanj said. "But your Lady's moving in style, dragging a singularity and a palace ship and a whole pile of Grayframe. She leaves a wake." Zanj flicked a switch, and a new image painted the cockpit glass: a single long line with their ship on the far left, a cartoonish castle on the far right, and a green crown moving between them—still near the left of the line, but ticking forward twice for each tick their ship advanced. "She's faster than we are, and gaining speed. Still think you have enough time to stage a revolution, gather a strike group, and catch her, kid?" Before either of them could answer, she swiveled her chair around and kicked her feet up onto an unused console. "Or we could go to Orn, which is, as I said, the crystal city of starships, and find a racer to take you straight to the lady. Once that's done, you let me go, and I promise I'll not harm you—I'll dart around bringing ruckus to distract her, while you sneak into her ship, get home, and—" She slapped her palms together as if banishing dust. "—that's all. Easy."

"That does sound simpler," Viv admitted.

"Except," Hong said, much later, in the cargo hold, far from any windows, as the ship performed vertigo-inducing rolls Zanj claimed involved eating a tungsten asteroid for its raw materials; she'd banished Hong and Viv from the cockpit for fear of nausea, "Orn is a myth."

"It's not," Zanj called back from the controls.

"Everyone tells stories about it, but no one knows where it is."

"Because they hide. The Empress has a habit, in case you hadn't noticed, of killing civilizations that get too big. If you were running an interstellar commerce hub, would you tell her fan club where you lived?"

"Maybe things have changed," Hong said. "You were in that star for a long time."

Zanj stalked back down the hall from the cockpit. The ship continued to fly itself without her guiding hand, and the turns grew vicious. Zanj's face looked like the face of a thunder god, and while Viv forced herself to match her glare for glare, she felt faint as she did, and grateful when Zanj turned her gaze on Hong. "I know." She heard the rawness in those words, the edge of cutting humor not quite on the good side of despair. "Orn had a good system—stealth, expertise, generations of augmented Cloud-spliced pilots. They dream spaceways. They dance in formation. They sing babies preflight checkup songs while they nurse. If anyone anywhere in the galaxy can catch the Empress, it's a pilot of Orn."

Hong looked to Viv the way friends had looked to her after too long spent arguing on the Internet. Help. I'm drowning.

Hong was right—his knowledge would be more up to date than Zanj's. But she thought about life inside a crystal box, studied and prodded and poked and praised. If she'd wanted that, she would never have left her family in LA.

"We go to Orn," she said. Once she'd made the decision, her misgivings vanished, as always. Energy spent regretting a decision was best redirected toward addressing its consequences.

Zanj nodded, self-satisfied, as if she'd never doubted Viv would make the right choice. "Good." The ship lurched and settled. Gravity changed—softened, grew more complex in a way that reminded Viv of the difference between listening to a Beethoven quartet on good headphones, and playing it yourself. This was real gravity. "I'm glad you made the right decision. Because we just landed. And we're out of fuel."

"Wait. What?"

Zanj marched past her toward the ramp. She did not spare so much as a glance for Hong, frozen in apoplexy behind. "I figured this was what you'd choose, and I didn't want to waste time."

"And if you were wrong?"

"That's why I dumped our fuel before we landed. Don't worry, Orn has a manufactory, we'll get more. Or we'll mothball this rust bucket and take a faster ship. They have thousands here. Don't let it bother you, Viv. You made the right choice."

"Is this your idea of a choice?"

"Let's leave questions like that to the philosophers." Zanj thumbed a button. The ramp hissed and began to lower. Blue sunlight flowed in from outside. "Come on."

"We had a deal." Hong had recovered enough to use his words. "We'd each make our case and let her choose freely."

"I got bored." Zanj turned her back on the lowering ramp so she could direct the full force of her salesmanship against them. "Besides, kid, you'll love Orn. It's an oasis of civilization—like we used to have in the old days, before the Bleed and your Empress got so damn good at wrecking everything. Orn, crystal city of starships, Orn of the towers, Orn of the spaceways, best seafood this side of anywhere, gladiator matches alternate Saturdays, pleasure pits and simulated depravities to choke a zekk, hell, they even have a temple network if you'd like to talk to a few gods up close and personal. I've spent more years than you can count missing this place, and if you've never been here before, you should damn well thank me for bringing you."

Hong didn't answer. He was too busy staring out of the ship.

"Ah, Zanj," Viv said.

"What?"

She pointed.

Zanj was right, after a fashion. Orn had been a great city once.

It was a ruin now.

11

ORN, CITY OF starships, had been beautiful.

An oasis of civilization, Zanj had called it, in the wreck of the cosmos. Viv saw its former glory in its ashes: crystal towers snapped by a mighty hand, their shattered peaks filling the broad avenues. Heavenly bridges led nowhere, ended in splinters. Among the ruins Viv saw amphitheaters, arenas, market squares, perhaps a shopping mall—she knew she was misreading all of this, painting the dead city with categories and purposes she understood, but she could not help it any more than she could help hearing sorrow in a song in an unfamiliar tongue. Orn, city of starships, Orn of the best seafood this side of anywhere, Orn of the simulated depravities, Orn where you could talk to gods. This city's people had loved her, and built her so well that an outsider, stepping tender, scared, from her ship a thousand years—more?—after her fall would know the depth of their love. They built her so well even her ruin awed.

Spires lay in shards. Broken windows stared blind. Moss blighted murals. Glass walls warped. Vines choked trellises. Trees pierced the hearts of office buildings, spread canopies of metal-green leaves. Birds sang. The city had died so long ago that its birds came back. Doubled suns burned overhead, descending; stars pierced bright through the faint blue sky. The air was heavy with damp and growth.

Orn's people had loved her. One loved her still.

Zanj staggered down the ramp to the cracked call-it-asphalt of their landing strip. Her arms swayed as she walked, and so did she; Viv had not appreciated the grace with which the other woman moved until that grace left her. Her weight sloshed from foot to foot. She was a blade of tall grass in tangled winds. Between slabs of crumbling pavement lay patches of bare—okay, technically it wasn't earth, but why quibble over vocabulary? So.

Zanj fell to her knees on the bare earth.

Viv thought about time, which Zanj and Hong claimed only ran one way. She thought about the distant spark that was Magda, that was her world, that was everything the Empress had stolen from her. She could still get back there, if she was strong, lucky, clever. If she lost, she would die knowing she could have won.

For all her power, Zanj had no such luxury. What had been stolen from her, she could never take back.

Viv started down the ramp. Hong put out a hand to stop her. From him, in his eyes and the set of his shoulders, she read: Zanj is hurt now, and she hates to be weak. If you go to her, if you try to comfort her, she'll have to accept that she's fallen to her knees, that she may be weeping—or she'll have to fight you. Or both. You might have to kill her to save yourself. We don't know how that crown works yet. Best let her go.

All that was true enough. But, though Zanj had tried to kill her, and threatened her after, Zanj had also come to her in the night, watched her, offered help. Viv could not let her suffer alone. And how dare Hong try to stop her?

So he retreated from the weight of her eyes, and she descended the ramp; her bare feet made little sound on the metal, and the asphalt underfoot reminded her of broken playgrounds. There had been no rocks on the station or on the ship, and the deck plates were all warm—nothing had made her feel her lack of shoes. She neared Zanj; the woman's ears twitched. Her claws tightened on the ground. One tore troughs in soil, the other in asphalt.

"Let me go," Zanj said before Viv's hand could reach her shoulder. Viv stopped, unsure what to say or do. Zanj raised her face, hard and sharp and jagged as the broken towers. The iron band did not change color. It had darkened before, when it hurt her. This pain came from inside. "Let me go." In Zanj's chest, again, that tiger-deep roll.

"Zanj, it's—" She almost said *okay*, but it wasn't. Viv didn't know what it was, but she could see that okay had long since left the running. "I'm so sorry." Her hand shook between them, not quite touching the place where Zanj's shoulder used to be.

"You don't know sorry," Zanj hissed. "None of you children know sorry. You've lost your fleet, your home, and because you are so small and brief you think those little losses are a fit measure of another's pain. You can't conceive of what I've lost. Of what stood here, when it stood, and what you're too brief to mourn."

"That's not fair."

"Since when, Viv, has the universe or any god you know given one fuck about what's fair?" The heat of her voice settled, chilled, dangerous. "Let me go. I don't know this world anymore. I'm no use to you as a guide, but I can be a weapon. Let me go, and I'll gather forces to stagger even her, and I will hound her with all my fury, and maybe I will die, but by all that burns I will make her bleed. Maybe I'll even slow her down enough for the kid to get you home."

"Will you kill me, if I let you go?"

She was standing, and close enough for Viv to feel the heat of her, and smell her sharp sweat. There was no world save the space between them— certainly not enough world to contain Hong, who said eloquently, "Um," only for Zanj to talk right over him: "Maybe I should. It would be faster for us both."

"Friends," Hong said, closer, "perhaps we should continue this conversation back on the ship?"

Viv waved him off. She glared at Zanj. "You think you're so far above us. Above me, above him—nobody can touch you, nobody can possibly fix the mess you've convinced yourself you are. And if I reach out, you try to piss me off, hoping, what, I'll hurt you? Because you need someone else to be the reason for your pain, because you can't admit that it's the world that hurts so much?" With an expansive wave to the broken city, the burning stars, the whole damn universe at once, everything that was and could be lost. "I'm not letting you go off and die. There's hope. It's slim, but we have a chance: me for home, you for revenge, Hong for understanding. Together. We need each other. We don't even have fuel. If I let you go, who the hell will fly the ship?"

Zanj snarled. "How convenient."

There was a fire in Viv's chest, and it grew as it ate fuel. "I'm sorry. Can you point out the part of this that looks convenient to you? Because I must have missed it."

"Poor stranger in a strange land, lost far from everything she knows, can't touch the Cloud, can't fight worth a damn. She was someone back home, sure, everyone was—but now she's on her own, scared, with no purchase on anything except for this." She jabbed a claw at the crown. "You like it, don't you? Really? Deep down, it must thrill you to know you can hook your finger and make me crawl."

"I don't." She put more force into that than she had meant—and knew she was covering her own uncertainty.

"Friends," Hong repeated, conciliatory. "Please."

"Shut up, Hong. I don't." Not a truth, but a wish that simply saying so could make it true. "I stopped you from killing us. But I've never given you an order. You're angry. I know. She hurt you. You think you're so hard to understand? How about this: you led your friends on a big adventure, and it all came crashing down, and now you're scared and desperate for everything to be someone else's fault. You're telling me to let you go because you know I won't, and that gives you a reason to hate me, and you want one, because otherwise you'd have to hate yourself. Am I close?" She saw Zanj's shell crack; there was meat in there. She should stop, but she could no more stop herself than stop a tidal wave after a quake had come. "Pretty close, I think. Maybe I should let you go after all. I wonder what you'd do without the crown to blame it on." And that, she knew even as she said it, was too far. She could read it in Zanj's body, she could hear the growl building in the woman's chest. The earlier anger had been flame kindled on despair, pain seeking a shape to hide weakness. This was fury that needed no fuel. It burned its own exhaust. But Zanj had no words big enough for the rage she felt, and she would not hit Viv.

At least, that's what Viv hoped. She'd seen what happened to things Zanj hit.

"Friends!" Hong shouted. They looked to him then—they had to look at someone else.

"What?" Both voices at once, both snarling.

He held his clubs, and was not watching either of them. "We are not alone."

They were, in fact, surrounded.

Viv counted twenty, in a loose semicircle, approaching the ship from the broken city, human-shaped and hunched forward, rifles drawn, or things that looked a lot like rifles, anyway. They wore weird postapocalyptic assemblies of cybernetics and armor, no flesh visible, if there was flesh under there. They moved with preternatural smoothness, without words Viv could hear. Bright smears of red and blue and green marked their armor like war paint.

Zanj kept her body facing Viv, but she turned her head, and saw them coming, and looked . . . pleased. And hungry.

She rolled her shoulders back, and tightened her fists. Viv heard no joints crack, which felt more ominous than the human noises would have been.

The figures stopped as one and aimed their rifles. Hong brandished his clubs, and Viv wondered what he thought that would accomplish. A single voice emerged from all the figures at once, a woman's, speaker-amplified: "Outsiders! Set down your arms. The Ornclan bids you welcome if you come as guests, but if you stand as foes, we hold our blades and guns ready."

"The Ornclan?" Zanj still hadn't turned all the way around to face the new arrivals, so only Viv received the benefit of her sneer. "There isn't any Ornclan, kid. There isn't any Orn anymore. And you've had the misfortune of catching me on a very bad day."

"Zanj," Viv said, "these people might be able to help us. They might have fuel."

Zanj rolled her eyes.

"We offer welcome to guests and friends," the voice said. "And death to foes of Orn. Declare yourself."

"Declare yourself." Zanj mouthed along with the voice, mocking. "I'll give you one chance. Toss those toys away, take your helmet off, and apologize. Then we'll talk. If not, I'll break your metal friends, then you. Slowly. Your people tell stories about me around your campfires, and those stories made you wet yourself with fear. Do not—"

One of the rifles spoke. Even as the sound reached Viv's ears, Zanj was turning, so fast a whirlwind rose at her feet. Her hand spun out—the gun's fire was a dart of blinding green, too fast for the eye to follow, but Zanj's backfist met it and slapped it away, into the dirt. The whirlwind settled. Zanj's fist smoked. Through the burned-off skin, Viv saw more of that whitish not-bone, and other things, too, metal and light, unfamiliar substances that did not belong in bodies as Viv understood them. Wiggling things. The rumble in Zanj's chest swelled to a roar.

"No," Viv said, but she put no force behind it.

She heard the wishbone pop of Zanj's battery. Back on High Carcereal Zanj had said she was running low on power, and would need weeks to recharge. But they had been traveling for a while.

Zanj glanced back to Viv, slow as a taunt, and her eyes were white.

The guns spoke all at once, and most of the blasts passed through space where Zanj had stood a half second before. They struck asphalt, stone, the ship, without effect; Hong's clubs blocked two blasts. One struck Viv straight in the chest—and when her senses returned moments later she found herself sprawled on the pavement, alive, singed, breathless. Her robe-shirt's weave crackled and gleamed with lightning for an instant, and her skin hurt where the seams had seared her. Oh. So that was why Hong wore his robes loose.

Hood, she told the robe, and threw the one it made over her head, and ran after Hong toward a mound of asphalt that would serve for cover. The stone hurt her feet. But just because these clothes had blocked one shot didn't mean they could stand up under a barrage. Hong, certainly, didn't seem to trust them.

She dove into cover, chased by more bolts—a rock sliver clipped her ankle, a wound she felt only as a tug and hoped wasn't serious. The broken landing strip stank of hot rock and plasma. Blood made noise in her ears. Apparently her adrenal system understood rifles better than it understood Pride drones. She gathered herself behind cover, checked her ankle—bleeding, but not as bad as she'd feared. Beside her, Hong didn't seem worried about their predicament. Though that might have had less to do with their odds than with the fact that, after the second volley, none of the fire had been directed at them.

She risked a glance out of hiding, and saw Zanj as a blur between broken bodies. Zanj kicked out the center of one of the armored figures' chests—it sparked and flew back and lay smoking, bleeding oil. She tore off a metal limb and batted off a second figure's head—another bot—then grabbed its rifle, snapped it in half, and tossed the pieces spearlike into two more helmets. In a minute, the twenty were ten.

Viv's stomach churned. The armored figures were made of metal, circuits, recognizably robotic, but they looked like people. Hell, in this future, they might well be people. And once she made that leap, she thought of the Pride—the Pride, the hate fractals, who cared for their dead. That hadn't occurred to her back on Rosary Station. She'd focused on staying alive, on her fear, on their monstrosity, but of course the Pride were alive.

Fewer of them, though, now they'd met Zanj.

Zanj pulled off one guard's head, jumped on a second's shoulders, and beat in the second's skull with the head of the first. Eight left.

Easier to count down than to describe. As far as Viv could tell, Zanj found the fight as easy as counting anyway. Seven. She was showing off. Six. She was angry. Five. And these things just happened to be. Four. In her way. Three. She shrugged off a volley. Two.

One.

Viv realized she was standing in the open. She'd left shelter as the battle turned to a slaughter.

The last guard scrambled back from Zanj, not so smooth anymore, and tried to raise his rifle—Zanj closed the distance between them in a blur, grabbed the rifle, broke it. The guard slipped, turned to run. Zanj stood in front of him, eyes white fire, smile wicked. Caught him by the neck, and lifted. Zanj glowed with fury and waste heat. She caught the guard's helm beneath the chin and lifted, and the helm popped off, rattled to the ground.

The guard was human-ish—webs of blue lines flanked the corners of eyes wide with terror, but that could have been makeup or aftermarket modification. She—Viv revised her original judgment, barring future clarification with regard to the pronoun, and observed that in real life, comic books to the contrary, you couldn't tell much about sex when people were wearing armor—kicked Zanj in the crotch without producing any visible reaction. The guard clawed for Zanj's eyes, but Zanj held her at arm's length, off the ground, without apparent effort. The guard bared her teeth. She pried at Zanj's grip on her throat, and Zanj did not seem to care. "Where's your respect, Daughter of Orn?" She sounded almost mournful. "Your grandmothers welcomed me with song."

The guard's next kick found only air; a third might as well have struck cement.

"Where are your topless towers, Daughter of Orn? How did your mother's mother's mothers fall? Do you even remember them? Do you remember what you were?"

The guard's breath rattled in her throat. There were tears in the corners of her wide round eyes. Her lips bared white teeth, a panic rictus. Her nails slipped over Zanj's skin as if it were marble.

Viv remembered the Empress's hands in her chest. Remembered how it felt to fight her, futile, desperate, and saw that same look in the guard's eyes.

Zanj spread her jaws, and leaned in.

"Stop!"

Viv saw the pain hit Zanj—saw her jaws snap shut, saw her buckle as the crown went black. The guard found a breath, though not freedom, as Zanj's grip weakened. She looked so scared.

Zanj roared. Her eyes were bright white and blinding, and her breath steamed even in this warm air. "She was trying to kill us."

"You threatened her first. She's from here. She's the people we came here to find."

"She's an echo. A by-blow. Less than a child. And she tried to shoot me. For that alone—"

Viv didn't wait for Zanj's grip to tighten, didn't wait for her to use those brilliant teeth. "Let her go." With all the authority she could muster.

The circlet burned night black. Zanj stood firm, as if she would never fall—for a second. Then her eyes dulled to red, her hand trembled, and she collapsed to the broken earth, clutched her temples, screamed. The guard, too, fell; her leg twisted under her. She lay still, but breathing. Alive.

The circlet faded to its normal gray. Some time later, Zanj stopped shivering and fought back to her feet. She swayed, but stood, and spat her own rainbow blood onto the ground. Behind them, shards drifted down from a broken tower. "How did that feel, Lady? Good?"

Many answers leapt to mind, many justifications. All she let herself say was "No."

"Fine," Zanj said. "I'm going. Command me to stay, if you want. Make me dance. Order me to feed you, bathe you, I don't give a shit. I know how the Empress builds—this thing will bring me running from anywhere in the universe. You say you don't want to control me? Bullshit. Jailer. Call me back when you're done lying to yourself. But as far as I'm concerned, you and I are done."

And then she turned on an axis Viv had not noticed before, and in a flash of Cloud blue and static, she was gone.

12

WIND BLEW SPLINTERED metal through the spot where Zanj had stood. Viv watched the dust settle, heard the sizzle of broken circuits, and realized Zanj was gone.

And why shouldn't she go? Viv had caught her, tortured her, held her. She said she'd never wanted to make Zanj her prisoner, that she only left the crown on Zanj's brow to protect herself, but seconds later she'd given her an order, and watched her collapse. Worse: it felt good. Beneath the hook that dug into her gut as she watched Zanj fall, beneath the ache of sympathy and shame, she had felt a drunken swell of strength, like a kid with a magnifying glass on a sunny day, the whole world full of things to burn. She knew where that joy came from, that relief. Weakness had snuck up on her since she woke on High Carcereal in space, in the future, a weakness that built on the weakness she'd felt in the months before her flight from Saint Kitts. And when you were weak, strength was a powerful drug.

Even now, she wanted to call Zanj back.

She told herself it was to apologize. Maybe that was true. But she didn't know, and didn't trust herself.

Instead, she ran to the fallen guard. To the woman whose life she'd saved.

She was still breathing, shallowly, her eyes rolled back. Viv reached for her, tried to sort out scraps of half-remembered Girl Scout first aid classes in her head. She'd paid attention, thinking, I might need this someday, but she never had until now.

Don't move someone who might have a neck injury. Had Zanj broken the guard's neck? How would Viv tell? You were supposed to check airways. But what if moving her jaw made the neck injury, if there was a neck injury, worse?

Viv touched the woman's cheek; awake, she had been too afraid for Viv to get much sense of her features, but she resolved in repose: large round eyes, closed now; a flat dark face with high cheekbones; full mouth, fierce and breathtaking. She looked young, early twenties, though who knew how fast people aged in this world, or how slowly, or whether early twenties still counted as young. Someone's daughter, anyway, someone's lover, someone's soldier—like Viv, though separated by who knew how many years.

Zanj might have known, but Zanj was gone.

Hong knelt beside them, hand to chin. "Is she well?" Too polite to ask if Viv needed help.

"I don't know," she snapped. "My CPR certification's a few thousand years out of date. Did the 'faith teach you first aid?"

He flowed past her, hands to the woman's throat, then mouth, then forehead, checking limbs, joints, muttering under his breath; the translation gimmick threw up its hands at the half-voiced words. When she could no longer understand him she lost her sense of him as a person, his professorial comment, his priestly remove, his eagerness and his fear. He seemed more alien to her than he ever had before.

As he touched the guard, she groaned. Her eyelids fluttered. The blue lines on her skin pulsed. "She should be fine," Hong said, and when he spoke she made sense of him again. "She tore a muscle in her leg when she fell, but it's healing. Slowly. She won't walk until tomorrow at least."

"If you think that's slow healing, wait until you see me get hurt."

Hong hadn't mentioned Zanj's disappearance, or their argument; Viv felt too numb to find the right words to thank him for that. She'd said so many of the wrong ones to Zanj just now to trust her own choices.

Good job, Viv. Stress takes over, and at the first opportunity you alienate one of the only two people you've met since waking up who have done anything but try to kill you. Zanj had been doing her arrogant, lethal best to help. But should Viv have let her kill this woman, who was breathing deeper now, who had done little enough to hurt them—who had been in the wrong place at the wrong time, on the wrong patrol? If Viv hadn't pissed Zanj off, she wouldn't have been so murderous. And Viv had been angry, because Zanj was angry, because Viv was angry, because . . . Because of everything.

This woman was hurt, because of her. And alive, for the same reason.

Her eyes snapped open. They were an alien blue-gray that swirled like mercury, and they locked on Viv, wide with fear for a heartbeat before she could make herself brave. Viv liked her at once—for that moment's terror, and for how fast it turned to fight. "Get away from me!" Her language was tonal and throaty, her voice rich, deep.

Viv did—backed up on her knees, hands up. Hong had rolled away and risen in the same motion to his feet. Dork. "It's okay," Viv said. "You're fine. You're safe. We just wanted to be sure you were still alive. Our—" She stopped herself from saying *friend*. "—our traveling companion, she's gone. We chased her off."

She was clear as glass. This girl—this woman, not a girl at all, not here—she knew how to fight, she'd probably lived harder and more violently than Viv could imagine, but she had the fluid, open look of a person who never had to lie.

Viv had not seen a face like that in a long time. She always thought of it as Shanda's face, Shanda whom she'd met at a charity tennis thing back when Shanda was only number eight in the world, so direct, as open on the dance floor, at the bar, on the court, as she'd been in bed that night. A handful of actors Viv breezed through the summer after they broke it off could almost fake that breathtaking translucence. (Viv had sworn off actors when she realized that was why she'd gone for them. Never trust a rebound.) Seeing that same earnest expression here, so far from home, made her feel dizzy.

The guard's suspicion parted like water before a whale's back, replaced by wonder and gratitude. She accepted Viv's hand and pulled herself to her feet, favoring her hurt leg. "You saved my life."

"Viv saved you," Hong said.

"Lady Viv," the guard breathed. "Are you from—are you from beyond the sky?"

Viv squirmed, and looked away—embarrassed by the guard's openness, and a little afraid of her beauty. When she realized she was afraid she made herself turn back, and meet that gaze that wasn't exactly Shanda's but wasn't not, because the right thing to do now, she felt certain, was to accept her thanks like a grown woman, respectfully, and ignore the size of those eyes, the way the husk on her voice made medically interesting things happen to Viv's heart and lungs.

Christ, Viv. At least try to pretend you're not a goon. "Just Viv. Don't mention it. It—you—we were, ah, just passing through. From, um." She couldn't bring herself to say *from space*. "From up there."

The guard's eyes went wide with wonder. Her grip was strong; Viv felt a thrill at her strength that she did her best to ignore. Stay cool, dammit. "I've met gods before, but never a woman from the stars."

Gods? But what she said was: "What's your name?" Yes. So very cool.

"Xiara," was how Viv would spell it, because even though Mom and Dad came from Taiwan, the Chinese school where they'd sent her used Pinyin. Hsyara, maybe, almost Sierra but not quite. "Xiara Ornchiefsdaughter. The Chief sent me to patrol these ruins, and I heard—" She gasped. "Is that your ship?"

She was past Viv in an instant, all injury forgotten in wonder.

"I've never seen one so—" Xiara put too much weight into her bad leg, and a yelp of pain interrupted her exuberance. Viv caught her as she folded and tried not to think, much, about the body beneath the armor in her arms. Xiara barely seemed to notice. She had eyes only for the *Question*. She lurched away from Viv and limped slack-jawed toward the ship. She tugged her glove off with her teeth and stroked the hull with one hand, as if she'd been trusted with a relic. "So old—and intact! We have pieces, but I've never seen anything so old in working shape. Are you pilgrims?"

Viv opened her mouth to give some kind of clever lie, and realized she had no idea what a convincing lie would sound like. She turned to Hong, *help please,* and to her surprise he answered with the ease of rote practice. "I am a simple monk of the 'faith, and Viv is a sojourner. We were passing through your system in quest of miracles, but our ship has run out of fuel, and our temperamental companion's departure has left us without a pilot. As poor seekers who have left the family, we beg your aid."

Viv had almost been impressed. She stopped when he revealed the weakness of their position. "We do need fuel," she said, "but I'm sure we can figure out how to fly the ship."

But Xiara had turned already, and this time only the *Question*'s hull at her back kept her from falling. But she didn't seem to notice the pain—it was quashed beneath her awe. "You have no pilot?" As if Viv had just said, *We have this old Holy Grail lying around, don't know what to do with it, any ideas?* "Viv, you came from beyond the stars, and angered a powerful being to save me, though you did not know my name." As if Viv weren't the reason Zanj had been about to kill her in the first place. But Xiara didn't know that, and her voice was heavy with awe and purpose, and Viv was too weak to correct her. "I owe you my life and service, but your accepting the service I now offer would be the greatest boon I have received of any woman. Will you take me as your pilot?"

Viv hesitated, not just because of *take me.* "You can fly?"

"Flight," she said, "is the blood of Orn. We sing our children songs of the sky." But whatever she saw in Viv's face, it was not the answer she was looking for. Viv did not know if there was enough sincerity inside her to answer Xiara need for need. Xiara blushed. "I am sorry. I have been too forward. I should not have dared to ask."

"No," Viv said, feeling like a jerk. "That's not it at all. It's . . . Hong and I are going on a long journey, to find the Em—"

"To find relics of saints of ages past," Hong said politely but with enough force to shut Viv up. She notched her estimation of Hong's competence back up a few points. At least Xiara didn't seem to have noticed the slip.

"Relics," Viv said. "Right. It would be a long trip. Journey. Quest. Very dangerous." But she could tell from the eager light in Xiara's eyes that danger would not discourage her.

Xiara could not be serious. This city had been ruined for centuries, and she'd never seen the *Question*. How could she fly it? After weeks watching Zanj and taking notes, Viv barely knew what half the controls meant in realspace, let alone how to plot a course through the Cloud. She looked to Hong for help—but Hong seemed ready to defer to her on this one, and self-satisfied in his deference. He must have noticed the glare she shot him when he'd let on about the weakness of their bargaining position. But Xiara was still standing in front of Viv, expectant, and Viv felt a rare stab of empathy. How would it feel to grow up here, knowing you had lost the sky?

Anyway, they did need a pilot.

"We are not worthy of your service," Viv said. "But we would accept your friendship. After we fuel the *Question*, we'll see if you can fly her." Viv didn't trust her eyes not to betray her doubt, but she knew how to fake a confident handshake—so she put out her hand.

Xiara caught her by the wrist and pulled her into an embrace that made Viv catch her breath—because it was tight, and for other reasons. Xiara's dark eyes shimmered with emotion. "Then you will be my guests, for now. We shall do you honor; the Ornchief controls the great manufactory of Orn, and we can make fuel in abundance. And then we'll fly."

And they set forth, boldly, into the ruined city.

Or, they tried. On her third step Xiara winced and almost fell again. Viv slipped her arm around the other woman's shoulder, and Xiara grabbed Viv in turn—she was strong beneath that armor, and that strength encouraged another wave of embarrassingly physical speculation on Viv's part. She thought she caught Hong's eyebrow drift upward, the corner of his mouth incline a hair, but she must have imagined it—when she narrowed her eyes at him he looked impassive and serene. He hid his hands in his sleeves, and walked beside them as if Xiara's limping gait were his natural pace. "Xiara Ornchiefsdaughter," he said, "tell us of your world."

As they walked, Orn took shape around them. To see the ruin from the broken landing strip was to see a painting on a wall, an image of desolation and loss reclaimed by green. To enter that space was to feel it as a landscape. People once lived here. They built this place, and it wrecked them. But, broken, the city had another beauty. Life grew and flew and crawled and climbed and slithered without care for time's passage or what was lost. "The Ornclans hunt in the old places," Xiara said, "for meat from animals, for parts from machines. We patrol in case other Ornclans come to raid us—for food, for goods, for attention, or because a god told them to."

"Do many gods come here?" Hong asked, and Viv thought at first that he must be joking—but he asked the question in full sincerity as he examined a rusted, twisted metal skeleton that had, perhaps, once been something like a car. If he was joking, he hid it well.

"Not so many as in the old days." Xiara guided them up a marble staircase between two rotten buildings. "They've picked through most of the ruins by now. All the other Ornclans traded off their great relics for blessings, save mine: we hold the manufactory, and none may take it from us." She sounded insistent on that point, defiant, which made Viv wonder what she was defying. Before Viv could ask, Xiara slipped out from under her arm and skidded down the scree slope at the staircase's end. She tried to stop herself at the bottom, but her leg folded under her again and she sat down hard, and laughed and waved up at them at the hill's crest. Xiara might heal fast—everyone here seemed to, except Viv, whose ankle cut wouldn't stay closed, and who chose her steps with care to avoid cutting her foot open on a sharp rock—but Xiara kept testing her wounds and hurting herself again. Viv admired that, in a way, even if it was dumb. She had never liked waiting either.

"Can she really fly the *Question*?" she asked Hong as they crept down the slope.

"There are strange miracles in the world," he said. "And the pilots of Orn are legendary."

Useless answer. But, speaking of miracles: "Was she serious about the gods?" Zanj had used that word once or twice, but Viv thought it was a joke or a mistranslation.

Hong chose his path with care, but he never winced when he set his bare foot on a sharp rock. Socks, Viv thought, and her pants slithered down to make her socks, but the fabric couldn't quite get the hang of soles. The cloth didn't tear, so her skin was more or less safe, but sticks and gravel still hurt. She hissed down after him. "There are many types of minds in the Cloud," he said. "Some once wore flesh, or silicon, or something like either, and some did not. Many, most, build themselves pleasure palaces, or dungeons to scourge them, and shelter there. They cannot help themselves. If you do not train your mind while it is subject to physical constraint, once liberated from the flesh it seeks pleasure by reflex, and so binds itself in unbreakable chains. Trillions drown in joy-loops, unable to rise above the desire to satisfy desire. Even those who escape that fate rarely ponder the world below. Rather, they seek higher knowledge. But some minds reach down. Those so bound to this space that they seek power here become gods." Viv had thought there was something odd about the way he pronounced that word before, but she only placed it now: he spoke as if godhood were something regrettable, a perversion, an embarrassing fetish. "They seek power over a world that has no power over them—they are the greatest victims of illusion. Orn, in the first centuries after its shattering, would have many wonders for which they might trade. What a god may value, mortals may not comprehend—and what a god may give, some mortals would die to earn."

"Hand up?" Xiara asked when they made it to the bottom. She'd been piling rocks while she waited. "It'll be dark soon, and we have a ways to go."

Viv helped her up, took her weight again. The declining sun lit broken towers orange and yellow and red, as crystal refracted that light to rainbows. "What happened here?"

"The Empress." Xiara answered matter-of-factly, with only a little pain. Of course the Empress. "Our mothers and teachers were giants. They broke the Empress's great law. They built a republic in secret—a web of worlds—and thought they could escape her notice." She sounded faraway sad, talking of ancient ancestors' fallen temples, of Mongols at Kiev, of tragedies that only seemed inevitable in retrospect, and in whose shadows she now lived. "She came in glory with her Diamond Fleet, broke us, broke our ships, and cut us from the sky. It has been many hundreds of years since an Ornclan pilot took to the air." She reached for the canteen slung over her shoulder, found it empty, scowled. Viv, wincing on her not-quite-bare feet, recognized that trick: you took a drink to remind yourself your body was here, and save yourself from the mess of your own thoughts. "Come on," Xiara said. "There's a stream over here. We can fill up, and still reach home by dark."

The stream had once been a fountain, the features of the statue worn away. A bull, perhaps, or something like a bull, the pose heroic, the eyes enormous even after acid rain decay. The stream was clear, but Xiara's canteen filtered slowly.

Viv drew back to Hong, and asked him: "The Empress did this?"

"This," he said, "is what She does. And that is why I argued with our companion when she sought to bring us here." He had never used Zanj's name in Xiara's hearing, and neither had Viv. Could Zanj's name still carry weight after three thousand years, even on this devastated and long-abandoned world? What had she been, when she fought the Empress? What had she done?

Whatever, she was gone now.

Xiara, humming to herself, examined a flower growing by the stream, nodded, satisfied, then settled again, and watched the setting sunlight on the water. Hong continued: "The Empress has one iron law: do not grow too large, for complexity draws the Bleed. She breaks worlds that risk the cosmos. Nothing like the Orn of legend could last for long without drawing Her eye. The 'faith survives on the thin edge of Her prohibition, and protects itself by movement."

The ruined fountain statue stared, proud and hungry, at the sky. Xiara had looked like that when she stared at their ship. A planet of pilots, wings broken. "This is evil," she said. "This isn't protection. It's abuse."

"You saw the Bleed." His voice was simple and sad: the voice of a man who did not know what else was to be done. "Where they come, none survive. What would you do?"

"Fight them."

"She has fought them, time after time, at great cost to the galaxy—as have others. But they always come back."

"If she let civilizations grow, she would have allies in the fight."

"But She has seen them grow, by scores, by thousands, and always they make the same mistakes. And always the Bleed come."

"You like this? Agree with it?"

He lost all serenity at that suggestion—eyes wide, speechless, shocked. "Of course not. She is not right, nor is She good, though the Grand Rector and her followers sometimes think so. She is . . ." Words gone again, or else exhausted, he gestured to the ruins, to the pitted statues, to Xiara filling her canteen at this stream in this city her mothers' hands had built. "She is massive. She is power. She strikes as She chooses. She has bent the arc of

history. She built wonders and fought wars we can only describe by alle-
gory, because we cannot work the math of them. The Archivist says we
must understand Her, we must learn Her tools, so that we may stand
against the darkness. I hope one day we will pass beyond Her, and find a
better way. But we cannot even understand Her path now."

"And . . . our friend . . . fought her."

"Yes."

"How? I mean, she's a badass, but." Her own wave at the destroyed city
felt less poetic, more futile.

"We have seen her fight without weapons. When she fought in Heaven,
she was fearsome."

"Well!" Xiara spoke the word like a bell peal—yes, indeed, the world was
well! She stood with her canteens, or tried to, forgetting her injury again.
Viv rushed to her side; she thanked her with a grin and an offer of water,
river cool.

The waters of Orn tasted silky rich and clean. Viv wondered what the filter filtered out.

Xiara pointed with her chin. This way.

Buildings thinned as night closed in. They passed fewer toppled towers,
fewer piles of broken glass, as they entered what Viv would have called the
outskirts of the city if the skyline had not continued unbroken to every
horizon—perhaps a park or warehouse district?

There were new structures here, too, mostly empty, made of wood and
bamboo and rope: lean-tos and traveler's hutches, and there, just visible past
an overgrown hill that used to be a house, a lookout tower. The dirt road
was narrow but well trodden. Xiara hobbled surer, faster, eager for home;
the doubled suns set and released the sky.

More stars shone, and more after those, a thick full vault of golden fire
webbed with hair-thin glittering arcs. Rings maybe, or stations still orbiting after all these years. Orn, city of starships, had its crown.

The day's heat faded. Viv smelled a night-flower musk she could not name.
She wondered if Xiara or Hong had ever smelled a rose. If there still were
roses.

"Beautiful," she said into the silence. Hong walked in contemplation,
hands sleeved, head down, but Viv didn't like where contemplation led her:
home, her unfinished conquest, Magda, the hand in her chest, and Zanj.

"If you like the stars," Xiara said, "just wait. There is a balcony behind
our hall, and by the Chief's command all lights are covered to hide us from

the sky. I'll show you stars like you have never seen—and you will know what drew Orn's daughters to the sky."

"I'd like that," Viv said, but Xiara said nothing, and Viv found herself, as if she were still goddamn fourteen, wishing she'd said something cooler, or more grand.

Then she noticed the bandits ahead.

Armored figures emerged from the shadows, rifles and spears ready. Hong had seen them first, and strode forth, clubs glittering to his hands, voice calm. "We are simple travelers," he said. "Pilgrims who have left the family. We seek only peace and knowledge. Name yourselves."

Viv wondered if he'd noticed the flanking team on the rooftop to their right. Probably. So he was just pretending not to see them. Maybe it was an honor thing. "We don't want trouble," she said. Obviously, her role here was to be the one who didn't lunge for weapons at the first hint of danger. Not that she had any weapons. Old gamer instincts suggested she should find some. Practical experience, on the other hand, suggested that weapons in the hands of jumpy, untrained folk rarely made anyone safer.

Back on Earth Viv had relied on a sort of coolant system to protect her: subtle, and less subtle, mechanisms for drawing violence away from the places she spent her time, and dumping it in places where people couldn't defend themselves. That wasn't so much nonviolence as a willingness to let bad things happen to other people. Here, if she didn't want to fight—and the fact that every second person they met seemed to be some sort of highly advanced cyborg suggested fighting was a bad idea—she'd have to find a more genuine path.

That would be a challenge.

"We're not from around here," she said. "This woman's hurt. We're just trying to get her home."

"Lies!" shouted a voice from the firing line. A bearish figure wielding a rifle in one hand and an enormous spear in the other marched from the shadows.

"I'm not lying," Viv said before he could speak again. She was starting to get a sense for the rhythms of speech on Orn, which were slower than her own. She could use that to slip through them. "There was a misunderstanding, and she's been hurt, but it's all sorted out now, we're just—" What was the phrase Hong used, ah. "—pilgrims who have left the family, seeking . . ." What were they seeking again, not the Empress, something else . . .

"You have attacked Ornclan guards!" Armor-bear shouted again. Even after everything, Viv almost wanted Zanj back. It would have been nice to watch someone deck this bozo. "You have taken a princess of Ornclan hostage!"

Princess?

"I'm not—" Xiara started to say, but Hong was already talking.

"—will meet you in single combat for the right of passage through your lands, as the Star Tablets decree—"

Armor-bear didn't wait for the formula to finish, just held out his rifle until one of his flunkies took it, and strode forth with the spear. "Very well! As is meet, I who have been challenged choose the weapons of our—"

"Shut up!" Xiara's voice echoed off the walls, and while stunned silence reigned she slipped out from under Viv's arm, limped forward, and fixed their ambushers with a glare of withering command. "Both of you just be quiet! I am no hostage, Djenn Ornswarden. These are my guests. They have come from beyond the sky, seeking aid and fuel, and I am their pilot. Now, take us to the Chief, and let's get all this sorted out."

13

WHAT WITH THE spears and matronymics and slightly Viking rhetoric, Viv had pictured the Ornclan hall as a Heorot of ring-giving postapocalypse kings, Grendel-haunted maybe. She imagined wood and gables and gilding, a dais and a throne, a woman in a horned helmet.

But when Djenn and his warriors marched them through the palisade, when the spear-bearing guards on watch there, their skin crackling blue with what Viv assumed was some sort of energy shield, drew back to let them pass, as rifle-bots set down their weapons and the drumbeats swelled, Viv found at the core of all those defenses not a palace, not a building even, but a grove.

Pale-barked trees spread skyward, straight and ghostly as birch but redwood thick and tall, so close their branches and flat leaves closed out the sky. Xiara's people had hung stained glass and dyed paper in the woven branches' gaps, glimmering in the gloom. Into the grove they drew, stepping with care between and over high, gnarled roots, following the drums and the smell of thick spiced smoke, until they emerged into a frat party.

Okay, fair, Viv was being cultural-essentialist, hegemonic, whatever. There were obvious differences between this and Viv's last frat party. The frat party's drums had been electronic, for one thing, while the Ornclan's were made from skin and wood. The frat party's floor was sticky, while the Ornclan reveled on soft green grass. The frat party had fewer women, fewer dead posthuman artifacts repurposed as jewelry, and considerably more polo shirts, and the wrestling had been more the mud-and-salacity type than for-the-honor-of-my-fathers. But the Ornclan hall was a good deal *like* a frat party. Maybe Viv's beer pong expertise wouldn't go to waste after all.

As they entered, the revels stilled—but not because of their arrival. The drums beat low, then stopped. All eyes in the room, including Djenn's and Xiara's, fixed on two figures standing in a bare dirt ring before the throne.

The wrestlers wore breechcloths and gray vests, armbands of woven cord, and no other ornament. Their arms were thick, their shoulders broad, their hair gathered in braids and knots while most of the other Ornclan wore it loose. They circled one another, steps measured. The wrestler who started the circle facing Viv glared at his opponent as if there were nothing else in all the world, his jaw clenched and his cheeks red. The wrestler who ended facing Viv looked every bit as intent, every bit as fierce and ready—but she was smiling.

They rushed together, clutching, shifting grip, bodies slick, limbs trembling with effort, lips pulled back to bare teeth in expressions half grin, half growl. Their stamping feet replaced the beat of drums. Onlookers clutched wooden goblets and massive drinking horns, but did not lift them to their lips. They leaned closer to the ring. This was it. Whatever "this" was.

Both fighters' flesh bore finger tracks amid their scars, and bruises, and the dirt of prior falls. They looked well matched in mass and skill. Viv and Hong had been marched—or, as Xiara insisted, escorted as honored guests, not prisoners—into the final act of the wrestlers' drama.

Just my luck, Viv thought. She always had the worst timing.

Djenn, who had been so eager to show off his captives, fell silent beside the circle, barely daring to breathe. Xiara had been just as ready to present her guests, but she too kept silent, and watched. The large jewel-decked man on the wooden throne on the dais near the ring clearly noticed the new arrivals, and looked from them, to the match, to them, and back—more unsure than Viv expected in a post-Viking, though to be fair she didn't have a lot of firsthand experience with the type—but he did not stop the match.

From the way they fought, she guessed the rules: the first to lose their feet would lose the match. No gouges, no strikes with fists or feet. The male wrestler huffed through his beard and moved with zigzag motions and fast arcs, all growl and gruff, while the woman favored straight, swift lines, and never lifted her feet from the dirt. They raised dust clouds as they slid, and left clean trenches and tracks the man stamped down. He grabbed for her once, twice, but she drew her hands away. Viv didn't know why, and wished she did. She'd never been a fighter, she'd never liked physical combat, but she wanted to know what it felt like to be this woman from the inside.

The man surged forward once more, and this time his opponent did not evade. His hands clamped on her thick wrists and he pressed in hard and fast to knock her off-balance, and Viv, sad for this woman she barely knew, thought: this is it, she's done.

But that smile, which had been a fixed expression before, turned real. Viv realized then why the woman had slipped from her rival's earlier attempts to engage: they weren't serious enough for her to use. She had him now. Her arms pressed into his grip and through, and her fingers clutched him, white-knuckled. Her weight and his sank through her trunk into the roots of her thick legs, into the knotted muscles of thigh and calf.

With a roar, she threw him, and as he arced through the air Viv thought, that's it—but the man twisted, and landed on his feet with a drumbeat thud. There were no cheers. The silence deepened as he crouched low and circled her again, cautious.

In that tense pause Hong almost broke the ritual and stepped out to greet the man on the throne, but Viv grabbed his arm and stopped him in time. None of Djenn's or Xiara's party had knelt to the man with the jewels, or even acknowledged him. Djenn watched the match with religious fervor. Xiara stood rigid, white-lipped, her hands balled to fists. And a thin silver circlet hung on the throne-back as if left to bide awhile. The man keeping the throne warm did not seem like the kind of guy to skimp on finery. Hong turned a questioning gaze toward Viv. He didn't get it yet, but at least he trusted her enough to keep quiet.

The wrestlers had clinched again, each clutching the meat of the other's forearms. Their shoulders moved as a unit, and they fought the true battle with their feet. The woman pressed forward, dropped her hips low, and used her lower stance and the strength of her legs to drive the man back. He circle-stepped, pulled left, right—then, with a grunt, let his left guard collapse. The woman pushed up and in with that hand—but he must have been expecting that, and danced back, tugging her arm down.

The woman's foot slipped, and Viv's heart sank.

But it was not over.

The woman let out a high, piercing sound, almost a cry, almost a laugh, and spun. Her back bent like a sword, and in the firelight she was all lines and cords of muscle from her core through the ridges that flanked her spine. She came out of the spin still holding the other wrestler's arms, wrists locked against themselves. His hooded eyes widened in shock, and his mouth opened in a silent O, but he had no time to save himself. He had shifted all his weight to one leg for that last maneuver, risking imbalance for victory and leaving himself without a root.

He fell like a mountain.

The woman drew a long, slow breath, and bent over him, and tugged on his cord armband. The knot undid with a single pull. She raised the cord high in the silence and let it fall.

Cheers burst from the crowd, from the jeweled man on the throne, from Djenn and their escort, from Xiara—the drums pounded again, and strings and flutes joined in. The victor offered the loser a hand up, which he accepted humbly, with a broad, tired grin and rueful shake of head. But before he could speak, before anyone else could set the agenda, Viv darted into the circle, dragging startled Hong behind her, and bowed, deeply, to the woman wrestler. "Ornchief, my congratulations."

Hong almost rose from his bow in shock, but her hand on his shoulders held him down. Guards rushed forward, drawing weapons, Djenn sputtered, and, most importantly, the woman who was Ornchief brushed sweat from her brow with the back of her wrist, examined Viv and Hong, and asked, "Stranger, how did you know me?"

Viv straightened then, though the sudden pressure of spearpoints against her back suggested she was not supposed to do. But she wasn't interested in the guards' sense of propriety, or Hong's, or sputtering Djenn's, or even Xiara's. Viv trusted her instincts, and her judgment of this woman, through the daughter she had raised. "Your crown rests on your throne. Your man with the jewels sits there to guard it. Your people look to you, and celebrate your victory."

"They might as well celebrate a wicked Chief's defeat." A guard brought her a cloth, and another guard a basin. She splashed water on her face, toweled off.

"Not to judge from how your daughter speaks of you. Or your camp."

A raised eyebrow. "My camp speaks? Are you an oracle, stranger, to hear its voice?"

"No." Viv had dealt with people like the Ornchief before, heavy with true authority, too sure to need arrogance. You didn't find it often in the circles of anxious overachieving nerds where she tended to run, and less often among the rich—but when you did, you had to be ready. These people would not respect you if you yourself did not. "I have led clans, and built things. This camp was built well, by well-led people."

"You have led clans?" Confusion—the Ornchief had Xiara's lucid face, more square, no less expressive. Viv felt very conscious of how little she must resemble this woman's image of a leader. "Will you join me in the ring? We will compare our leadership."

"Not clans like this," Viv said, a bit faster and more apologetically than she would have liked. Self-respect was not easy to maintain before the mass of this woman. "Clans of trade."

"Trade," the Chief echoed. Viv had a way of saying the word *interesting* that her friends always mocked; when she used that tone she didn't always mean bullshit, but often. I think you're wrong, but I'll give you a chance to save yourself. Or dig yourself in deeper. "Are you a tradeswoman, then?"

"We are pilgrims," Hong said. "We have left the family to walk the path of saints, and seek miracles."

"They are monsters." Djenn barreled into the conversation. Viv had hoped to keep this between her and the Chief, but Hong speaking had opened the floor. She'd have to talk tactics with him, so he stopped screwing hers up. (Admittedly, she had a lot to learn from him, insofar as the whole not-dying thing was concerned.) "They broke our guards, took the Princess hostage. They have bound her to their cause with sorcery."

Which was such an absurd accusation Viv took a few heartbeats to realize the Chief was taking it seriously. Fortunately, Xiara chose this moment to shoulder ringside. "Chief. I am myself, and free. You know me from your own flesh. Viv and Brother Hong came to us from beyond the stars. I found them arguing with a companion, their pilot. This person, enraged, broke our guards, and would have killed me had Viv not stopped her. She fled through the Cloud, leaving Viv and Hong stranded here. They want shelter, fuel; they seek a pilot to take them offworld, and have agreed to let me serve them. I pledged them my protection, and will brook no harm to them within our hall."

Viv had wondered when the pilot thing would come up—and how the Chief would take it when it did. She'd expected laughter, even scorn, though this woman did not seem the type to scorn her children. But she'd never thought the Chief might take Xiara seriously.

The Chief lowered her head and marched through the murmuring crowd. She climbed the three steps to her throne, which the jeweled man abandoned with a bow; the Chief raised her crown and settled it upon her head. As the metal touched her skin, her broad shoulders slumped, and the boundless strength of her stilled and settled as if to yoke. She sat. Duty gathered about her like a storm. "You have broken guards we cannot cheaply fix. You ask for fuel. You seek my daughter's service. Yet for a tradeclan, you have offered little. What can you grant us? What trade can you offer, with a monk sworn to poverty by your side?"

For once Hong did not leap to answer. If he really had taken a vow of poverty, negotiation probably wasn't his strong suit—but then, Viv had no sense of relative value here. What did fuel cost, if these people thought in terms of costs at all and not in terms of gifts? For that matter, what was a fit trade for a Chief's relative? For all Viv knew, that old dirty magazine of Zanj's was worth half the broken junk on this planet. Offer too low and she'd insult the Chief, offer too high and she'd seem an idiot, unless there was some sort of passive-aggressive honor inversion nonsense at work here; no, we couldn't possibly accept something so rich . . .

There were too many variables.

Starting with trade had been her mistake. She'd read once, maybe in Grae-ber, that rather than barter, precapital economies held certain sorts of goods more or less in common; you'd borrow a neighbor's hammer, perhaps even without asking, and one day they'd come for something worth about a ham-mer; they wouldn't, though, take your goat, since goats were a different sort of thing. Barter happened between groups without mutual trust—my village might barter with those dangerous foreigners, say. By offering trade she'd marked herself as a threat, closed herself to hospitality. But if she tried to take back her offer and throw herself on the Chief's mercy now, she'd have to confess her ignorance, give up whatever bargaining position she now held, and look a fool in the process.

That was why the Chief's eyes weighed her. That was why Xiara tensed with concern. If Viv screwed this up, small chance the Chief would let her go. So Xiara would never leave Orn, and Viv would be stuck here while the Empress retreated to her Citadel.

So, negotiate, Viv. You can't offer the ship—you need that. And you don't know what parts of the ship you can sell without breaking it. Hong's brace-lets? The robes that have already saved your life at least once, and which you're sure you'll need again? What could they want in this comfortable ruin?

Oh. "News," she said. "I bring news, which Brother Hong can better tell than I—news of war in the stars, news of an assault on High Carcereal, of battles between Pride and 'faith, of vanishing beads in the Empress's Rosary, and of the Bleed." The Chief leaned forward; others, too. Xiara stared, wondering. The music dulled as musicians leaned in to listen and let their rhythm slip. There you go. That's the hook baited. Now add a little of that old fear of missing out . . . "What we have seen weighs on us, and it is fear-ful to mention—but if you would hear of the stars, we will tell you what we know."

"It is a fair trade," the Chief admitted, and Viv tried to keep the saleswoman's grin to herself. "Let there be feasting and wine, and tales of wonder."

"One more thing," Viv said before the party got going again.

The Chief extended her hand, flat, palm up, eyebrow raised: continue.

Viv pointed down to her own feet, still bare, much abused. "I could use a pair of boots."

"That depends," the Chief replied with a distinctly unbusinesslike grin, "on how well your partner here can wrestle."

FEASTING, MERRIMENT, DRUMS, a whirl of dance and drink: trade concluded, Viv and Hong were strangers no more, but honored guests who in their future travels would bear tales of Ornclan hospitality, their music's joy, their wrestlers' strength, the thick full spice of their food, the vigor of their wine, the rhythm of their dance.

The Chief ordered a party of warriors forth to fetch their ship—to float it home with levipads or fly it if its engines would bear. Even with those warriors gone, the party remained dense, a mass of shapes, mostly but not altogether human—and the dance closed in. Viv felt its beat in her stomach; cupbearers brought her a gold-inlaid horn full of something strong and viney, and brought Hong a mug of dark flower tea.

The Chief raised her horn as well, and Viv matched her and drank. The wine sank a warm plumb line down her throat—her first draft since waking in High Carceral. This drink was her first act in days that wasn't necessary. She let her second sip open on her palate, tasted river rocks and stonefruit, overtones of glass and velvet. Flavors haunted behind the stonefruit that she could not place save by analogy. This grape was dry beyond belief, if it was a grape at all. But it was wine, or close enough, and it tasted good. She would make this moment normal by sheer force of will if necessary.

Xiara stood at her side. "Come. Eat."

And the bottom dropped out of Viv's stomach. "Oh my god. You have food."

Xiara, laughing, limped beside her to the feast table. "Of course. Do you not eat food?"

"Just watch me." The smells alone, of spices fuller than cinnamon and sharper than turmeric, of almost-saffron, and of peppers, made her knees weak and the room swim. The Ornclan ate out of bowls with flatbread and knives, and in that moment Viv would not have cared if they'd eaten upside down from funnels. "On the ship, we've had, like, Hong has this nutrient paste stuff that I'm pretty sure is ninety percent mushroom, and water, and is this *chicken*?"

Xiara made a face at her eager expression, and she wondered what the translation gimmick had substituted in for chicken. "Birds at a feast? We would never so insult our guests. This is Emperor Snake. A great delicacy—they take ten warriors at least to hunt, but they're delicious if you can eat them before they eat you. Djenn led the hunt himself."

"And nobody died?"

Xiara laughed. "Djenn is a fine hunter, though suspicious of outsiders. Here, try these—" She scooped something that looked like lentils into her bowl. Viv let the smells and her rumbling stomach guide her from tray to tray, pot to pot, and didn't argue when Xiara added more to her bowl even though she ended up balancing three bowls altogether, two for her, one for Xiara, as they worked back through the crowd to the table and more wine.

"Tell me about your travels," Xiara said.

"Tell me about this food."

"Let us trade, then, since you hail from a tradeclan."

After days of nutrient paste and water, Viv's first bite of Emperor Snake with peppers and not-quite-cumin tasted so good that she felt embarrassed about eating it in public. Not too embarrassed to swallow, though. "I'll have to talk while I eat."

Another side-eyed expression, suddenly brighter. "Oh! You do not eat and speak at once, where you come from? How do you take meals with company?"

"Awkwardly," Viv said, and reached for wine, only for Xiara to press some into her hand. The weird velvet mouthfeel blushed around the peppers, bit into the Emperor Snake, complemented the meaty flavor of the lentilesques and the buttery aftertaste of the green almost-broccoli sponge. "I'm pretty new at all this, to be honest," she said, too conscious of Xiara leaning toward her, of the dance they were dancing sitting still. Their knees touched under the table. "We were in the Cloud for a long time. And then—there were stars." Xiara's eyes glittered as she leaned in. "I saw rainbows in a comet trail lit by a blue sun. I have words for that, at least. But the rest, I barely know where to start. We don't have things like this where I come from."

Xiara tore her meat with her teeth, and mopped sauce from her lip with the back of her hand, and sucked her skin clean. "Where's that?"

"You won't have heard of it." She felt almost human again, and realized how inhuman she had felt before. "I'm still getting used to . . . space travel. It's big and weird. If you come with us, maybe you'll feel the same. Or maybe not. Hong seems to roll with the punches better than I do. He's a good guy, even if he has awful taste in nutrient paste."

"He does not seem to mind real food." Nor did he—deep in conversation with old robed skalds, he scooped up lentilesques and greens with torn strips of bread. Viv reviewed the clearing, the dancing and the music, tracking, searching, and realized that she was looking for Zanj. Who was not here. Whom she had chased away.

Far, far above, wind whispered in the boughs.

She shouldn't miss Zanj: she was murderous, vicious, quite possibly evil. Of course, people had said the same things about Viv. But then Viv hadn't actually tried to kill herself, or anyone else, at least not directly. They were safer with her gone, sure. Zanj was not a nice person. But out of all the wonders and dangers in this weird wide universe, Viv felt she *got* Zanj most— where she was coming from, from the inside. Which was weird. So you woke up in the far future, or wherever, and you felt simpatico with an ancient mythological tyrant who wanted to murder literally everything. What did that say about you?

Whatever it said, you were still looking for her in the party when you knew she was not there.

Xiara had filled her horn with more wine. "Here," she said, pointing to a kind of stuffed tuber. "I loved these when I was a girl, and no clan on Orn makes them so well as ours. Try some."

"Thank you," she said, and ate.

Wine rubbed the details smooth after that and tinted them red-gold, and this meal, this conversation, this woman by her side, felt finally, physically real. But was it?

Everything Viv had once thought was real, everything she had risked her life to achieve, all the fortunes and the Earth that held them—what was all that, here? The past, whatever physics and Zanj and Hong might claim about time travel's impossibilities? A simulation? Another timeline, another universe? If Viv's past had happened at all, it had happened so long ago the names themselves had drifted beyond memory, all those people dead, their planet crumbled.

She remembered her home, and she remembered the battles she had fought, and she remembered Magda.

More wine? Oh yes. Thank you.

Xiara drank, too, and she shimmered with the joy of it. She told Viv about tending vines as a girl, about the centipedes you had to pick out of the grapes, how they'd scared her until she learned to chain them together—they'd grab each other's bodies with their pincers so you could make ropes of them and run through the tall grass waving the ropes after you. Xiara told her about the first time she'd been allowed to taste the wine, and showed the curled-up face she'd made, and Viv told her about the time in grade school when her mother had insisted for some reason that she should taste merlot.

Somewhere in the blurred evening Hong told the Ornclan of their adventure on High Carcereal, with the supple voice and timing of a skilled storyteller. They listened. He only left out the most important bits. In his telling, Viv had been a prisoner of the Empress, not—well, perhaps *prisoner* was not so wrong a word as all that. He did not make himself the hero. He rescued her, she rescued him. The battle was grand, the Bleed unknowable, the Empress's deeds profound, Her motives mysterious. Only Zanj was missing.

Zanj would have liked these people. Scorned them, yes, but liked them nonetheless—would have danced with them, would have wrestled ten of their best at once and let them think they might win. She would never have insulted them by throwing a bout. She would have drunk gallons, eaten the whole banquet, gone forth into the city to fight an Emperor Snake solo, then dragged the carcass back and butchered it so they could eat some more.

But Zanj was gone, which was Viv's fault. There were extenuating circumstances, sure, but if Viv had been the type to make excuses she would never have picked herself up off the ground after bankruptcy one. Zanj was gone. That was that. Carry on.

Applause followed Hong's story; the wrestler who'd failed against the Chief challenged Hong to a bout, and they threw one another three times before the next challenger arose. Dancing began, a long snakelike pattern of dancers holding hands, stamping, hollering; a spin moved down the snake of dancers and back up, as the snake ate more of the Ornclan and grew.

Xiara pulled Viv toward the snake, and Viv, who had never danced, swam along through the wine, floated, joined the snake's tail and tried to let the music fill her and scour away all trace of thought. Xiara spun—her injury healed, or at least the pain of it gone soft with drink. She spun Viv, too, grinning, slick. Viv saw things that were not there, faces in the blur, Zanj, yes,

Wuchen, Shanda, Gautham, Susan, Magda, long gone, long gone. Xiara rolled her hips, curved and drew and grinned and teased and danced away, and Viv, wine-clouded, felt her body, far away, wanting.

The dance twisted past her ability to follow. Xiara caught her eye, mouthed a question Viv could not hear, so she mimed *drink* with hand curved as if to hold a cup, and waved Xiara back into the dance. She joined the patterns that opened and closed while other dancers darted between, flower petals and bees at once. Stripy four-eyed dogs yawned on the dais by the Chief. Viv watched.

Hong met her halfway to the wine. "Viv." He had that knack of not saying things, so she could not really get mad at him.

"I'm fine."

"You're drunk."

"Why aren't you?"

"I have vows."

"Do vows mean you can't have fun?"

"Certain kinds of fun," he said, "yes. That is exactly what they mean." She almost turned away, but he said quickly: "I've been thinking about our friend."

She felt steadier resting her hand on the table. "You can use her name."

"It would not be wise. They would recognize it."

"Really?"

"The whole galaxy tells stories about her thefts, her battles with the Empress. I first heard them long before I joined the 'faith. And now she's free."

"To fight the Empress. Like she wanted." She tried to stand without the table, but decided against it as a long-term proposition. He stood between her and the wine. "It all works out. She gets to be all big 'n terrible." Consonants betrayed her. "Everybody wins."

"To fight the Empress, she will need power. To get that power, she will break worlds, steal suns, lay claim to vast swaths of the Cloud. She'll hurt people, just as she would have hurt Xiara if you had not stopped her. She cannot win, but she can break the galaxy in the process."

She remembered those burning eyes, the joy Zanj felt in unleashed rage. And she remembered, too, the hand extended in the dark room where she slept. "You think I should call her back."

"Yes."

She could stand, then, because she had to, and draw away. "What right do I have?"

"We all are bound, in our own ways. Xiara to her Chief's wishes, I to my faith."

"You broke with your faith to find me."

"I defied the Rector because of my loyalty to the 'faith, not in spite of it."

"Zanj's suffered enough." She wasn't scared of that name, or of the consequences. "I hurt her. She's right about that. She wants to come back, she can come. She wants to stay away, I won't stop her."

"Even if—"

But she would not let him finish that sentence. "Even if." And she stalked off through the crowd, holding to the anger that was not sobriety, but a reasonable stand-in.

Back through the grove she marched, back through the dance, seeing nothing, feeling alone. There were stairs worked into a tree near the dais, winding up and around its vast white trunk. She climbed them with heavy feet, on wood worn smooth by generations that have trod, have trod, have trod. Nor can foot feel. Christ, she needed boots. Night wind chilled her after the sweat and smoke of the grove. She stumbled free at last onto a balcony beneath the stars.

The sky burned in no pattern she knew. Massive trees closed out the firelight behind her, and the city of Orn was dead save for a faintly glowing marbled purple-pink dome a mile or so off, mostly hidden by the ruins, its light too soft to taint the sky.

So, matchless, the stars took fire: a galaxy more like a disc than a hoarfrost road. Those brilliant golden and rainbow rings gave depth and dimension to the warm, full black. She thought of a velvet dress Danika had once worn, how it glittered when crushed against the grain and struck by light. Her eyes were hot, her cheeks wet, and she was alone.

She heard a footstep on the stair.

Another. Soft, catlike. "I'm fine."

"You're sad." Not Hong's voice. She turned.

Xiara had removed her armor; the clothes beneath seemed gray silk, but glittered, and draped a body not so muscled as the Chief her mother's, but curved with strength and flesh. She shivered in the cold, still flushed from dancing. When she touched Viv's arm, Viv felt that warmth: Xiara was a skin-clad coal. "Remembering. That's all."

"You are my guest," she said, and drew closer. "You are in my grove. You are strange to me, but I would not see you sad." Her hand cupped Viv's ribs, her fingertips pressing skin through cloth that had protected Viv from claws and lasers and did nothing against this woman's touch. A touch, that's all, simple and frank, an offer followed by a silence to give her time to think. Someone had replaced her brain with rubber. A touch: Why had she never tried that before? She'd played coy, she'd teased, she'd been blunt and she'd been flush with romantic gesture, she'd been kind and mean. But she had never been this simple.

Xiara's bottom lip was very full and close. She smelled like a person smells after dancing, after armor, and Viv liked it. Compatible, she thought, as she drew closer, by instinct. Compatible immune systems.

She stopped.

Maybe it was the thought that did it: the vertigo of memory, of reading that scrap about immune systems on some idle airplane afternoon, flying from somewhere she had friends to somewhere she had work. Remembering that, and being here.

She could take shelter in a body tonight. She'd done it before.

"I'm sorry," she said. "I am sad. You're right. And you're great. And any other day, I would, but—it's been a long, long time. I don't even know how long. I'm so far from home, and I don't know what this would be. I don't know who you are. I'd like to learn—I really would. But I can't do this now."

Teeth trapped Xiara's lip, and she looked away, and for a heartbeat even the back of her neck seemed disappointed. But it passed, and she turned back, eyes level. "Can I sit with you awhile, at least?"

"Yes," Viv said. "Please." She sat down harder than she meant, and sprawled back as if to carve out snow for angels. Xiara settled beside her, and—"May I?" "Yes."—rested her neck on Viv's arm. "I can't imagine growing up with a sky like this," Viv said. "All these stars. Where I used to live, there was so much light it smeared the sky after dark. The first time my parents took me camping, I thought there was something wrong with the sky."

"Camping?"

"In tents, you know. Away from the city." So far as she had seen, there was no away from Orn, city of starships. "In the woods, I mean."

"You grew up in a city," Xiara said, "one so vast you had no sky. And yet you do not know how to fly your own ship."

"It was . . ." She did not know how to say what it was. "Where I come from, we don't know about much of this." Because maybe it hasn't happened yet. "The Empress took me from there. When Hong found me I didn't know about the 'faith, the Pride, the Bleed, or Orn. What about you? How do you know about all that stuff?"

"Travelers come. Pilgrims mostly, seeking Orn of old. Gods bargain for sips from the manufactory, to grant them power. The Chief prays to a magic mirror, and hears voices from beyond. We tell stories from the old days. We learn what we need."

"Can you really fly?"

They were taught, Xiara told her, lying still across her arm, watching stars: taught by songs and old books, by whispers from the Cloud, by their mothers' memories and their fathers', by the blood which spoke to some of them in time. (Viv almost argued with that, there was no such thing as blood memory—but why not, here? If you could upload consciousness to the Cloud, why not pass memories? Bodily fluids were not so bad a vector. But she was distracting herself—from so much, including the warmth by her side.) Xiara had dreamt of flight every night she could remember.

"So you're asking me to trust a pilot who learned to fly from ghosts."

"Better that, than not to fly at all."

"Do you really want to go with us? Leave your clan? Your family?"

"I have had clan and family all my life," Xiara said. "They will not vanish if I leave. I will take them with me to the sky, and they will grow with me as I travel." She hesitated, looked toward her—Viv mirrored the motion, saw a glint in her eyes just as she looked away. "Hong's story did not mention your friend. The pilot." She did not say: the one who almost killed me. "She was not a monk."

"She was . . . a prisoner, too."

"From your world?"

"No. But we were similar." Viv remembered Zanj's touch on the scar. The world wheeled beneath her, back, always back, her body strapped to spokes and spinning. She should keep her secrets. She should not trust. That was how she'd lived back home, and look where it had gotten her. "Have you ever heard the name Zanj?"

Xiara laughed, and in that laugh Viv thought, well, good, Hong was making it up, I haven't done anything I'll regret, I can just lie here and be happy and Xiara can laugh forever by my side. But no, she had to slow, and stop, and speak. "You must be from a strange and backward world indeed, to ask that question."

Oh. "Someone important?"

"A fairy-tale monster. A star-stealer. Zanj fought the Empress; Zanj led an army of gods. Zanj outwarred the Diamond Fleet, and stole the Saint's Cascade and the Cup of the Sun. Zanj gathered the Suicide Queens. She swiped the Fallen Star from a dragon's forge—watch or she'll come for you, too! Zanj Girlthief." She poked Viv hard in the ribs. Viv yelped, sat up straight, rubbing her side; Xiara's head slipped off her arm and thunked against the wood, and she was still laughing. Viv's head swam from the vertigo of sudden movement. "Not to know Zanj! They must know nothing where you're from."

"Maybe not."

"Come on." She patted the platform beside her. "Lie back."

"I'm drunk," Viv said. "And it's been a long, hard day. I really should sleep." It would have been a bad cover if it weren't true. Xiara lay still; the world revolved.

She rose, smooth, and slid herself under Viv's arm. "You helped me all this way," she said. "Let me help you a little further."

It all blurred after that—the downward path, the throne grove where Hong and the wrestlers tossed one another about, drunken, giddy, down into the tunnels of an ancient bunker, concrete riven and arched with roots, to a small room with a bed and a lamp. Xiara helped stretch Viv on the bed, and touched her cheek. "I could stay."

"Later," she said. "I need sleep now."

She was not imagining reluctance on Xiara's face as she left. Felt good about that. Nice. Better than she felt about the dreams that followed: dreams of green, of burnt skin, of a voice too close, too loud. She was used, by now, to screaming. But these dreams were not her usual nightmares, because in these dreams her torture built and built until she could bear no more and still it grew, until all at once it stopped, and the Empress drew back, and there Viv saw above her, battling, bloody, fierce and deadly and doomed but oh so free: Zanj.

14

ZANJ, ZANJ, DARTING free and lonely through the Cloud, Zanj swift and strong and unrestrained for the first time in three thousand years—she dropped to realspace to drink heat from an exploding star, she surfed a wave in a planetary ring, she stretched, strained, compassed the gap between galactic arms in a single jump.

At first she ran to outpace command, to flee Viv's inevitable order—come back, help me. Kneel. But that order did not come.

She was, impossibly, free.

When the flight-fear passed she settled into a steady pace, fueled by anger, burning layers of it as she pushed herself further, faster. The first layer, the hottest and most fearsome, was her anger against Viv—how dare she order Zanj. Viv, that fleshy mistake, that soulless blank, who remembered nothing of where she was, who she was, just visions, illusions of self, her grasping, surging need for control in a world that made no sense to her. Viv, who dared accuse Zanj, *Zanj,* of cowardice, dared order her not to kill whomever she damn well pleased.

(Not to kill a girl, admittedly, who could never in a thousand years have hurt her. It had been a fair fight—but was it, really? Could a match between such unequal powers ever be fair, or a fight? She ignored the question. Foolish back-of-mind yammering logic. Rage felt cleaner without thought.)

Once Zanj burned through her anger at Viv, she found a deeper, sweeter vein of fury toward the Empress. Tyrant. Traitor. That smug, entitled monster, who killed friends and wrecked world after world in quest of her perfect future, who ate civilizations that would not bow to her endless war.

But even that resentment, that rage over wasted eons, gave way in the end, and she found the deeper, slower, dirty-burning but eternal fuel of anger at herself.

What was the common thread in all her failures? Who oversaw Zanj's every suffering, who forced her to endure, who promised vengeance but had not yet brought vengeance to pass?

She sat upon a comet turning inward through the Oort cloud of a red and dying sun. She had hoped Orn at least would last. Its people were clever. They built small, and hid from the Empress's eye. They avoided truck with the flashy, wasteful Cloudbound meme-monsters small folk called gods. They hid when they could and fought only when they had to.

She had hoped. And that hope failed.

But for once, forever, she was free. She would never be chained again. Viv had taken her dare, refused to call her back. So why not enjoy this freedom? She could compass the galaxy, visit old haunts, find everything she'd missed in three thousand years trapped within a star.

She rolled to her feet, and left that place.

Her form slipped. Traveling so fast, she did not need it, found its weight a hindrance. Her edges grew complex; she sped down strange dimensions.

Wherever she walked, she found ruins.

The purple jungles of Celephaïs were now towers of ossified ash, over-grown mushrooms rising from the skulls of the few ungulate bodies she could find amid the wreckage. The floating pleasure barges of gas giant Kedayil had sunk beneath the methane layer, and she dove to swim among their pressure-crumpled husks—no bodies here, or at least no organic ones. The acid layers had eaten all her friends away.

Up. And out.

She flew, and did not find what she sought. She met wonders, in a way: broken battlefields overshadowed by immense crumbling monster-robots, with cinder-suns burning their last in a scorched sky. Listing space hulks, shattered fleets where once her armies spread. The Cloud near the core zones of the ancient war still burned with spent weaponry—she walked the stars here carefully, danced around the edges of holes in space. Near the Citadel, the Cloud thickened and bubbled to opaque glass, impenetrable as the walls of fish tanks to a fish. She probed it with all the powers and sensors and systems she possessed in this reduced and scar-warped form, but no chink or crack appeared, no flaw made itself known. The Imperial palace approached, the world-station with its Rosary bead, an immense drain on the Cloud, circled by black lightning traces of Bleedsign; Zanj dared not close without weapons, so she left.

When she lost all other options, she sought Pasquarai, her home. She'd dared not run there first—who could say what horrors the Empress might have unleashed on her people while Zanj remained imprisoned? To jump straight from the shock of ruined Orn to the certainty of ruined Pasquarai would have pushed her beyond the limits of herself—but all those barren, fallow worlds, those cracked orbitals and wrecked enclosure spheres, these worldminds cored and silent, had padded her with sorrow and rage.

Even now she had hope: the Empress was cruel. Would she not have taunted Zanj with her people's agony? And there had been no taunt. Could they have remained safe and hidden for so long?

She turned her eyes to Pasquarai, and found it gone.

No scar marked its passing upon space. No wrecks of worlds. No shredded starstuff, no Cloudburn or radioactive scar of antimatter disintegration, none of the weird-physics inversion a contained color bomb would leave. No. Pasquarai of flowers and fruit, her pirate cove, the world and the nondescript but lovely star from which Zanj first took her life, its moons, even the statue they built in her honor when she saved them all from death, all gone, as if they never were.

They had existed. She was certain. Even in her confinement, in her madness, Zanj had not lost quite so much as to let herself be fooled so effectively. Her secret names remained secret. Her memory was hers.

But Pasquarai was gone.

It made a bleak and miserable sense.

Zanj, in her strength, stole suns, freed planets, so naturally the Empress would steal her home.

Anger's hotter than a star, and endures where stars do not.

Fuck exploration. Fuck mourning. Zanj wanted *answers*.

She smelled a small god not so far away, some ancient fucked-up elephant brand whispering about the joys of free enterprise to a handful of near-sentient fishes on a backwater moon. She snuck up on the god through the Cloud, and tapped it on the shoulder. The little brand might have jumped half a planet in its shock, and that was before it saw Zanj, before the slow synapses of its Cloud-mind performed a shoddy lookup operation, and recognized her.

Have you ever seen an elephant fly?

You might be tempted to feel bad for this fucker as you read the next bit. Don't. Gods have a lot to answer for. And this one sure has it coming.

It fled, anyway, or tried to. Hid in a drift of stardust, which Zanj blew apart with a backhand; encrypted itself into Big Bang after-static wash, and she peeled its encryption away; doubled back through an asteroid belt and crouched trembling in a cave. Where Zanj, behind it once again, cleared her throat.

She caught it by the trunk and slammed it into the cave wall hard enough to split the asteroid in two. It spat noopoison, caustic whispers to sneak into her mind and shut her down, get all her parts talking against one another; would have been a clever attack a few millennia ago, but now it dripped harmless off her cheek. She caught the elephant god by the jaw, and peeled it in half. Inside, nested in the meat, a small pale misshapen wormlike man-shadow mewled against the world; she tugged it out of the wet elephant carcass it had occupied like a tongue louse, slapped it hard enough to spin its head around, then flipped it over, snatched its chin between thumb and foreclaw, and forced it to stare into her eyes, no matter how it tried to roll its own away. "You know who I am."

"Zanj," it said, "I swear, I didn't know those were your fishes, I just wanted—"

"I've been gone awhile."

"That's it," the god whined, "we were just taking—ow—taking care of them for you, you know, gotta rope them in, gotta *ow*."

She dragged it from the broken asteroid through the Cloud, slamming it into code blocks and cosmic strings on the way, until she could dangle it above the abyss where her home used to be. "What happened to the world that used to be here?"

"Empress took it," the god replied. "Long ago. Into the Citadel. Pretty lights. We ate for weeks on the code she used to move it."

"And the Fallen Star? The Suicide Queens?" She had seen the battlefields; she had seen some of the Queens fall herself. But she had to ask the question, had to hear it even from this pathetic liar's mouth.

"Haven't seen. Haven't heard. Ancient history stuff. Like—" The god thought better of saying *like you*. "You got any other questions? I almost had those fishes ready for a market economy . . ."

"No," said Zanj. "I'm done." And she broke his strange loop. Easy as crushing a bug, and more fun. A mind is a twist of thought curling back upon itself. She snapped that twist, and the thoughts no longer spun to frame an identity; they darted out forever into the Cloud, into the sea of souls. The mind was gone. A dripping, gross pile of data, of habit, memory, re-mained, a stain on her hands. She would have eaten the god's body, but it was old, corrupt, and held nothing she might need. She was a better class of monster.

She hovered alone in the universe.

Like Viv.

Viv, who had tasked her. Tortured her. Viv, lost in the world, not knowing where she fit, what use the Empress had for her. Viv who refused to let her kill—someone, to be quite honest, who did not deserve to die. Viv, that tiny soulless infuriating meatsack who bore the Empress's scars. Who wanted to get back to a home the Empress stole from her. Who did not have the luxury of breaking gods when she was mad. Who needed help.

And, hell, they had that in common. Zanj wanted to make the Empress suffer—and like this, unarmed, without allies, wearing this shitty crown, she'd be swept aside with as little effort as Zanj herself had needed to break the whining vampire elephant.

There was an undeniable appeal to throwing yourself into a monster's gears, in hope you could jam them with your corpse. But better to think. To plan. To use your hatred like a whetstone of the will. To develop tools and paths of vengeance, recruit allies, and above all else to study the machine until you found a chance to strike, and die, or not, but at least to win.

And still, after all this ticking time, Viv, who held her leash, had not called her to heel. She had let Zanj run. Had, perhaps, even trusted she would come back of her own accord.

Would Zanj have done the same, their places reversed? Of course not. She would have seized every advantage—until the person she controlled found a chance to kill her.

Interesting.

Zanj should not be considering this. She had a whole galaxy in which to run, hide, gather tools, and fight. Alone.

The abyss revolved around her, and far away the Citadel walls glittered: a million-light-year expanse of black ice.

Her people were gone. Her galaxy was broken. The Empress must pay.

She washed her hands of the small god's blood and brooded on the how.

15

VIV KNEW BAD dreams, and these were worse. She hadn't thought that was possible after the Cloud. Phantoms huddled round her in her sleep and flicked forked tongues into the hollows of her ears. Fever tossed her. Knives slid beneath her fingernails.

In dreamtime she was split between parallel worlds of fear. She hung, wrapped in a tight leather sack, from the ceiling of a dark warehouse room, while men in suits circled, discussing how they'd end her, how they'd make her suffer first. Elsewhere, in another body, in a smaller room of dripping pipes, she was covered in cement, which set, hardened, toasting her with waste heat, and her friends were in another room and could come save her if she called to them, but a touch of fire had welded her lips together. She stood onstage, clad in metal that would not let her move save as the strings that led to the ceiling pulled; she was a doll, a puppet. She sang because she was not allowed to scream.

These were the easy nightmares, the dreams she could bear. They grew worse, in widening spiral.

She dreamed of disappointment, of Angelique or of Magda in pain, dreamed of disgrace in newspaper headlines, dreamed flipbook-swift of setting all that to rights, dreamed vengeance, dreamed finding those who hurt her and breaking them, dreamed the faces of friends on her victims. She would master all. But as she fought the phantoms, the suits, the robots, the great mouths in space, behind each a larger monster loomed. She won. She won. But the larger she became the greater her certainty and fear that someday she would lose, someday the collar would click home around her throat. She fought and burned and built and suffered, and as she did she tired, and soon she would fall, and all she'd done would come to nothing, and the screams would remain her fault.

Unless she won. Unless she beat them all. Chained boundless space to her will, hollow queen upon a hollow throne, trapped within a perfect crystal form that sealed her mouth and locked her limbs and would not let her live, just rule. Concrete hardening around her, baking her as it set.

She screamed, mouthless, immobile, locked in crystal gleam. Her self was a shell, unbroken smooth.

But as her nails scraped that shell, as horror overwhelmed her, she realized there was a door behind her, out of sight, a door from dreams back to the waking world. If she let go. If she stopped straining against her shell.

She tumbled back into the dark.

She realized, first, that her eyes were closed.

She opened them to darkness and realized, second, that she was awake. When she moved her head, she felt extra weight against her temples. She wore some kind of bulky headset. She raised her hand to her face, but she moved only a few inches before her chains stopped her with a clink.

Wait. Chains?

That was when the headache hit.

It felt like a pickax to her temple, but after the initial shock she realized the pain had come without attendant scattered bone chips and brain guck. If she'd been free, she would have curled around herself, clutched her head, groaned, but the chains bound her arms and legs, her waist, her shoulders. They'd clad her hands in steel mitts. She tried to cry out but made no sound, not even a muffled groan, as if her voice had gone. Scream, she told herself, but when she opened her mouth no sound came. Her jaw creaked, strained; silence. Something tugged the skin of her throat, adhesive, a patch of some kind, numbing her voice. Temporary, she hoped.

The fear hit her then. She flailed on the bed, not so much to break the chains as to feel her body obey her. What had happened? Where was she? A prisoner again? A prisoner still, everything since Boston a drug dream? No—her feet still ached from their hike through broken Orn.

That headache, those vivid, terrifying dreams: the Ornclan must have drugged her. But they had been welcomed guests. Hadn't they? The Ornclan didn't seem the type to skimp on hospitality.

Xiara had been so eager to take Viv under her wing before the Chief. Tried to drag Viv into her bed, even. Had she meant to protect Viv? Or was she just playing along?

Either way, here Viv was, chained to a bed, with some damn headset covering her eyes, showing black-on-black static, unable to speak, her hands cased in steel, just like in her nightmares. At least now she could think. What did they want with her? What would they do to her? Her imagination was too vivid to ask that question lightly.

She felt the fear, let it hammer her, remembered how it felt to almost drown, remembered the Empress in the basement, remembered the faceless men, remembered the nights in high school when she'd turned on the news and thought the world was ending. She was tied up here, could not see, could not fight. Some fucker could just walk in with a potato peeler and go to town. She did not ignore the fear. She felt through it, crawling for an exit across a floor covered with broken glass.

And then she was done. Enough terror for now. She was going to fight, win or lose. Though, when she fought, she tended to win.

Call Zanj, a voice she did not like tempted her. She could not speak, could not even scream, but then, her commands were not carried by sound. It might work. An angry immortal space pirate would be an asset. Even one who wanted to kill her.

Still, she refused.

That helped, oddly. Rejecting one option suggested she might find others. She explored the chains, the mitten-shells over her hands, and fought to keep her breath deep and even in spite of surging panic. Was she imagining . . . no. It was real. The seam of her right mitten had a small gap, just wide enough for her fingernails to catch. When she curled her fingers, it hinged apart, fell off, clattered to the stone floor. Once that came off, she found the manacle at her wrist was loose. She shifted her thumb to the center of her palm and pulled, and pulled harder, ignoring the joint's protest. Just before the joint gave, her hand slipped free.

She wasn't a praying type, but she thanked god anyway, or the dumb jailers of the far future. No time to linger in thankfulness. She grabbed the patch at her throat, tore it off, hissed away the pain, and almost wept when she heard her own voice behind the hiss.

"Fuck" was all the comment called for by her current situation.

She tore off the headset next, ripping more adhesive patches from her forehead. This room looked like the one where she'd gone to sleep: underground, windowless, one door, what light there was shed by a ghoulish blue phosphorescent lamp on a table by the wall. Aside from the lamp, the table held an array of what looked disturbingly like surgical equipment.

She heard footsteps outside the door, voices. Two pairs of boots tromped toward her down the hall, and she held her breath, tried to wish away the clatter her headset had made when it struck the floor.

The boots passed by. They must not have heard. She breathed out, turned to her other bonds.

Her left mitten and manacle appeared seamless at a glance, but they came apart when she pried at them. Odd. Incompetence, she thought at first. But then she remembered the manacles the Pride had used on her back at High Carcereal, and Hong's claim that he could not even think about escaping.

If everyone and everything in this place, in this time, had some sort of connection to the Cloud, some sort of informational component, call it a *soul* if you like, perhaps chains interfaced with the Cloud as well as with normal matter? But Viv had no bond with the Cloud—no soul. Maybe their chains didn't work on her.

It was a theory. She'd test it when she got the heck out of here. For now, bonds on her left hand came away, and the manacle at her waist, and the leg irons. And she was free.

Free, in a cell, with two guards between her and, hey, why not be optimistic and call it freedom. They must have snagged Hong, too. Or killed him. That thought lit a fire in her brain. She'd rescue him, or take revenge.

Not against two guards at once, though. Not Ornclan guards.

She pressed her ear against her cell door, and listened. The guards marched back up the hall, and down again. By their third circuit, she hadn't come up with a better plan. She hefted the headset, tested its weight; the thing felt sturdy. The voice patch she slid into her pocket. Might come in handy.

When the guards marched past the door, she turned the handle, quick. Locks disengaged. She moved.

She slipped out into a long, straight hall, lined by doors to either side; the guards, Ornclan in armor, marched ahead, talking in low voices. They didn't seem to have noticed her.

Don't waste it, Viv. She grabbed the smaller guard by the shoulders, pulled back, and swung her hips; the man staggered off-balance into Viv's cell, and she slammed the door shut behind him, heard the lock engage. So far, so good. Now there was only one guard in the hall, so what if he had about six inches of height and an extra foot across the shoulders on Viv, not to mention a club? He lunged for her; she turned, ran, heart in her throat. Boots clattered on stone behind her; if she could make the turn at the end of the hall, maybe she could—

He tackled her, toppled her. She spread her arms and turned to break her fall, hit the floor hard with her shoulder and ribs and kept her head well clear of the stone. A good fall, but this wasn't a dojo floor: the impact stunned her, and by the time she gathered her senses he was on top of her, teeth bare, his club at her throat. She could see up his nose, smell his sweat. Viv thrust her hip up into his groin, struck some damn piece of armor there; he grunted, pressed the club into her neck. She couldn't breathe.

A hand touched him on the side of the neck.

His eyes rolled up, and he slumped over. Xiara caught him as he fell, and set him down slow.

Xiara bent over Viv in the empty hall, in armor. Her eyes glittered in the phosphorescent dark. She held one hand out to Viv, and Viv scuttled back on her palms—but then they both stilled, in shadow, each watching the other.

"I tried to stop them," Xiara said. She looked raw, sad, scared. Not nearly scared enough.

"You could have tried harder," Viv replied when she could find her words.

"You're my guests. You saved my life. But I can't go against the Chief."

Viv tried to push herself up, still unsteady. Xiara's hand was out—no longer cautioning now, just offering. Viv glowered at her and she winced, colored with shame—then, hell, Viv grabbed her hand anyway and let herself be pulled upright. "This isn't going against the Chief?"

"I wanted to break you out. I was waiting for her to stop posting guards. They do, generally, sometime on the second night."

"Second?"

Xiara bit her lower lip, looked away, nodded once.

"Christ." She didn't bother to answer Xiara's questioning look. "What did you do to me?"

"Nightmare harvest."

"Excuse me?"

"I told you we control Orn's manufactory?" Viv remembered, nodded. "We don't anymore. A god took it from us."

"I thought gods traded. They don't take."

"Most aren't strong enough to take if we don't let them. This one is. It fell from heaven two years ago. Grayteeth, it calls itself. It attacked the manufactory, cut us off, and cast us out. It gives us the things we need—so long as we feed it nightmares. Desires. Dreams. It sent us the tools: machines to pry through minds, root out fears and desires, and feed them back to its maw. We fed it on ourselves for years, but it tired of our taste. For months now it has demanded we send more . . . delicacies, and for months the Chief has appeased it. We've never met travelers from so far away as you. I'm so sorry. When I set you under my protection, I hoped she would respect that, and respect Hong's faith. But none of that's important now." She flinched from Viv's gaze at first, drawing back into her body as if warding off a blow— but she closed her eyes and forced herself out again, to face the accusation and pain. "I am sorry. I owe you my life. The Chief dishonored us by seiz- ing you. I want to help you escape." She took the helmet from Viv's hands. "We can trade your desires to Grayteeth ourselves, in exchange for the fuel you need. And then I will face my Chief's justice."

"You could come with us." Perhaps Viv said that as a sincere offer. Perhaps she said it because she felt vicious, deep down, and wanted to see Xiara suffer when she wished she could say yes.

"The Chief is wrong," Xiara said, "but she is my Chief. If I wish to stand against her, I must stand. It is wrong to run."

"A hell of a lot safer, though." But the choice was made, and Viv felt too guilty for taunting Xiara to force her through it again. "Come on. Do you know where Hong is?"

In the cell across from Viv's, it turned out, chained to his bed like Viv had been to hers, and now Viv understood the need for the chains, and the voice patch: he thrashed against his bonds, and his jaw gaped as if to scream. Sweat slicked his body, stained the sheets beneath. Ropy veins stood out on his arms. She turned away when she saw him on the table, as if she'd touched a hot stove—that same sharp full-body clench, that same uncertain stillness after as she wondered how much she'd hurt herself, and waited for the blister to rise. She had not realized how composed Hong looked, how restrained, until she saw him like this.

"I'm sorry," Xiara said. "There is no lasting pain. However it looks. Just the dreams."

"Uh-huh."

Xiara fumbled among her keys for the right one to undo Hong's locks, but he thrashed into her and the keys tumbled from her shaking hands. She knelt to snatch them, but Viv shook her head. "I can do this." She slipped the visor off him, peeled the small pads that were not quite electrodes from his forehead. His breath evened, and blink by blink his pupils swelled and the rictus of his face softened to something like normal.

"Viv?"

"I got you, big guy." The chains fell from his arms and legs when she tugged at them—she ignored Xiara's shock, time enough for questions later.

"Viv. I saw—"

"Come on. The Ornclan did us wrong. Let's get out of here."

He rubbed his chafed wrists; he saw Xiara, and his wonder sharpened, serrated. Viv's hand stopped him as he sat up, clubs materializing in his grip.

"It wasn't her idea."

"I am sorry," Xiara said. "When we gave the nightmares ourselves, it was a duty. To chain another, a guest—the Chief was wrong. Come. Please. We haven't much time."

Viv had to help Hong to his feet, steady him. He tested his own legs, which failed. "What did you see in there?" she asked.

His jaw clenched and he looked away, and just when she thought she would never get an answer, he said, "Perfection."

Xiara led them back through the tunnel maze, and once more Viv wondered at this building's original purpose in the time before the Fall. Bunker? Warehouse? Weird tree-themed hotel? Whatever it was, it had died, and the people who lived here died, their secrets gone with them into the Cloud, or else nowhere. The dark pressed around her, heavier by far than Hong, and cold. She clutched him close. She watched Xiara. After a long journey, the first glimmering of surface light relieved the black, and she felt a breath of air.

"The change of guard comes soon," Xiara whispered. "I was waiting for it myself, before Viv forced my hand. If we're fast, we can make it out before anyone knows you're gone."

The throne grove stretched around and up, ghostly dim without its candleflames and lanterns. Far, far above, framed by spreading leaves, stars burned against a bluing sky. They crept over cool grass toward the gap between the trees across the clearing, the exit, safety. The throne stood bare, and bare the clearing save for a few Ornclan sleeping fur-wrapped among the dogs by the warm ashes of the fire. Smoke lingered on the breeze, and the chill of night. A wrestler tossed, grumbled, settled back to sleep.

When she stilled, Viv let herself exhale, and turned back to face the gap between the trees.

Where the Ornchief stood, flanked by warriors.

"Hello, Daughter," the Ornchief said as her warriors rose from their feigned sleep and raised their spears.

16

HONG FELL FIRST, though not for lack of trying. Clubs out, he launched himself against the nearest guard, spun from him to the next, all his art and grace surrendered to violent efficiency: short, sharp blows with clubs, forehead, elbows, knees, leaving broken forms behind him. "Go!" He meant to sacrifice himself—why shrink from injury? Might as well take the blow to the ribs now. You'd feel it in the morning, but that assumed there would be more mornings in which to feel.

Stupid honor. Viv tried to pull the warriors off him, but failed; two got her arms, and she kicked one in the groin, but another took his place, and the more she fought the more they wrenched her shoulders back and at last she settled for cursing them with all the invention in her arsenal. She hoped the translator gimmick made their ears bleed.

Hong was fighting his way to her side, until the Chief joined the fray. The woman's silver crown flared, and armor flowed out from it to shield her in a suit of coherent armor-light, a massive armature that moved flickerfast. She hit Hong like a truck. He fell, skidded, slipped as he tried to regain his footing, went down.

Only Xiara did not fight. Spears ringed her; she glared past their points at Djenn, but Djenn would not meet her gaze. Rigid with fury, Xiara wheeled on the others, the warriors who dared oppose her, memorizing each face for vengeance, knife out, growling. But she could not break the ring of spears.

Then it was over, Hong down in a pile of limbs, Viv herself held by people trained to hunt game far more dangerous than temporally displaced entrepreneurs, Xiara's neck ringed by a spearpoint collar.

"You are guest-traitors," she said. "Betrayers of trust. We welcome strangers. We honor pilgrimage. Is this welcome? Is this honor? When we wander distant lands, will they chain us, and feed us to monsters?"

Metal shifted on leather and plastic. Wind whistled, high up. No one spoke. The Chief's crystal armor faded back into her torques, into her crown, and she moved between shadows, now torchlit, now a darkness against pale-barked trees. Viv tugged against her captors' grip, but gained nothing save more pain in her shoulder. Future people, it turned out, were harder to escape than future chains.

How was Hong? Conscious at least, glaring up through the layers of hands that held him. Hot with anger, not yet calm enough to think of a plan, let alone communicate one through gaze and gesture. Viv knew how that felt. She wanted meat between her teeth. She wanted to stomp down and break these booted feet behind her. But she wasn't strong enough. You can't fight their way, Viv, not without broken bones you can't afford. These fast-healing, grossly fit specimens of Orn might not even know how to do first aid for Earth-humans. Okay. No big deal. Xiara was trying an emotional appeal, the whole better-angels-of-your-nature tack. It wouldn't work, but at least it gave Viv time to come up with something better.

The Chief, massive, silent, reached her throne, and laid one broad hand upon its arm, but she did not settle. There was something in that, maybe: when she assumed the throne, her word was law, and bound her to its consequences. She had looked so light and strong in the ring, mighty and free until she donned the crown again. "Daughter," she said. "Xiara. We should not discuss this here."

"If our people aid in guest-fraud, they should know the why and how of it. They should know why they have been asked to do things that will shame our ancestors when we meet them in the Cloud."

"She is not our guest," the Chief replied. "Nor is she a pilgrim. She does not belong to us. Brother Hong, I am sorry you became a part of this. But she came to trade. She is outside our fire."

Oh. Shit. A trader was not a guest. A trader was an outsider, a threat.

"I welcomed her," Xiara said. "I owe her my life and offered her my friendship."

The Chief's fingers traced the grain of the carved wood throne. "We owe our people more."

"You owe them the truth," Viv said. Xiara and the Chief both turned to her, surprised she'd spoken. She tried to continue, but the guard behind her wrenched her arm and she stumbled, cursing, breathing shallow. Stupid physical body. If she could touch the Cloud, she'd leave the flesh behind in a heartbeat. She'd miss sex and cinnamon rolls, but she had to imagine there were compensations. She breathed slow until the pain stopped. "I just want to talk. There are, like, a hundred of you. I'm no threat. Tell your boys to chill."

The Chief nodded once, and Viv was free—well, *free* was pushing it, considering Hong, and the ten hunters between her and even a sprinter's slim chance of escape. Free enough to stand, at least. She'd take it for now.

"I saved your daughter's life. You want to discount that, fine. But we agreed to a trade while you sat on that throne." She pointed with her chin. Pointing with your hand didn't seem to be a thing these people did. "We gave you the news, and you were supposed to give us fuel and let us go. You're breaking your people's word, for what? A monster's squatting on your fuel depot—what do you even use fuel for? And, hell, if you'd *asked* me I might have given you my nightmares."

The Chief crossed her arms, and still refused to look at Viv. She walked behind the throne and gripped its back in her hands, as if she could squeeze it until blood flowed. "The manufactory is not merely a fuel source." Oh, good. The translation gimmick was fine. She'd just been wrong. "It makes . . . anything. Everything that we cannot make ourselves. Drones and glass and weapons to pierce thick plate, filters and drugs to fend off the poison the fathers left in our water, our soil. It was our joy, our wealth, our obligation, until Grayteeth came." Shudders around the clearing. "He is a beast. A virus of metal—endlessly hungry, transforming all he touches to himself, a self-optimizer"—which seemed to be a single word in the Orn language—"seeking always and only his own pleasure. He chased us from the manufactory, defends it viciously, suckles on its matter siphon. He does not wish to eat us—he merely hungers, lusts. He tires of his own perversity; we gain what we need to live by trading our dreams, our shames, to him."

"That's gross," Viv said, because someone had to. Note to self, if you ever get back home: if you must design some sort of gray goo nanovirus, don't make it kinky. Though, on the flip side, a usual sort of gray goo nanovirus, the make-the-whole-universe-into-copies-of-me type, would have devoured all Orn by now, so maybe there was something to be said for the kinky sort. "But it doesn't answer my question."

"We did not chain you for the Grayteeth," she said. "We chained you for the Pride."

Hong, eyes wide, fought his way to his feet before his captors forced him down again.

"No!" Xiara started forward; the spears resisted her this time, scraped her breastplate, found the skin of her throat. She stopped. "Mother!"

The Ornchief sighed. "The Pride believe you are important. That much was clear from your friend's story. And the Pride have sent ghost-messages throughout the galaxy seeking you. My seer threw the oracle stalks and called them across countless spans of darkness." She put out her hand without looking, and found the shoulder of the jeweled man who'd waited on the throne while she wrestled. He looked ashen now, less joyful in his jowls, as if he had traveled light-years while Viv slept. A diadem flickered on his forehead, and his eyes—yes, his eyes were black from lid to lid. "They want you, especially, Viv. They hunger for you with a need I cannot fathom. They have skills and tools and powers far beyond our own. In trade for you, they will rid us of Grayteeth forever."

"Mother, we do not deal with gods!"

"These are not gods." The Ornchief sounded tired. "Fallen angels, at best. Hungry, and useful."

"We have never bent knee—to the Empress, to the ghosts of the Cloud. And you would have us—"

"We have bent knee already, child, to the beast that squats on our sacred trust, pleasuring itself with our fears. One trade, and we'll be ourselves again. No more nightmares." But the spears drew back from Xiara's throat; the hunters traded uncertain murmurs, flicks of eye, shifts of stance, the usual subtle boardroom gestures of resistance amplified by the fact that the discomfited rank and file were actual soldiers, actually armed. "No more stolen dreams."

"Tell me you haven't done this already," Xiara said. "Tell me there's still time."

The Chief's shoulders softened. Viv did not breathe. She was so tired. One more push from Xiara might save them. One well-chosen word.

"No." The seer's voice was high and clear, a tenor beautiful from lack of use. "There is no time. A power draws close through the Cloud, my Chief: massive and aflame with purpose."

The Chief looked up, still tired, but with the exhaustion of a hard job done at last, if not well. "That will be the Pride. Bind the woman, gag her; her tongue will not poison our guests against us."

Hands caught Viv from behind; she buried an elbow in a leather-armored stomach, bowled one of her assailants over, and so missed it when Xiara made her move: snatched Djenn's spear from his hands, swept its haft around to parry the spears to her right and lock them down in the dirt, ran up one spear-haft to knee a hunter in the face, then tumbled to earth and came up sprinting toward Viv. Viv heard Xiara cry, and the thud of colliding spears, and felt a twist of panic until she spun and saw the Ornchief's daughter bodycheck a warrior to the ground. But Xiara was reeling, breathing hard. Her spear shook in her hands as she raised it against the twenty warriors surrounding them. Her tip darted from target to target. Viv grabbed a spear herself, but she couldn't even fake knowing how to use it. Hong, somehow, had fought his way through the crowd to Viv's side—but he could barely raise his arms into a proper guard, and held only a single club.

The Chief stepped down from the dais, armored once more, shining amber, grim. Wind whistled in the trees. Above, a shooting star approached.

Grew larger.

"O Chief," the seer said. "A correction. My eyes have been clouded. What approaches is not massive. It is small, but moving fast."

Faster than sound or thought. No sooner had the seer finished his sentence than a brilliant red light hammered into the glade. Oven heat washed over them, and the stench of fire and ozone and hot glass. Sound, there was none: what struck them was greater than sound, a fist made of air, a backhand of pure pressure.

Viv thought, first: I'm dead.

Then she thought, dead people probably can't think. At least, not dead people who don't have souls.

Form bloomed from the red as her eyes recovered. She caught her breath. She was not sure whether she was happy.

There, in the glassed ashes of the bonfire, burning with transit, hands crooked to claws, eyes white, stood Zanj.

"You don't know me," she told the Ornclan, in a voice pitched thunder-low. "Yet. But trust me: you should run."

17

ORNCHIEF, VIV LEARNED, is not a position one attains without a certain resistance to the notion of running away.

In other circumstances—circumstances in which Viv herself had not been chained to a bed, stuffed into a VR sim, and traded to monster robots—Viv would have admired the Chief's chutzpah. Zanj, fresh-fallen from space, burning with reentry, claws dripping plasma, her head oblong, her teeth jagged, her eyes white, her face a mask of fire, did not look like a person with whom one should fuck. Viv would have run. Hell, she was tempted to run anyway.

The Chief leapt forward. The torques at her arms and neck flared, and that amber armor shaped itself around her; a spear thick as a sapling flew through the air to her grip, and she struck at Zanj, a blow so fast Viv's eyes refused to track it, so fierce as to leave no question of quarter.

Zanj stepped aside, lazy slow. Her smile—even at this speed, Viv could see her smile—bore no trace of cruelty. For her, this was a joke.

Then she tugged the spear from the Orchief's grip, swept it around over her head, and struck the Chief so hard that her chestplate shattered. The Chief tumbled back, landed on her feet, skidded, hands up to defend herself, a brilliant display of physical control that would have been more impressive had Zanj not been standing, suddenly, behind her.

Zanj took her time, and still it was over fast.

She toyed with the Chief: opened herself for a strike only to dodge with a yawn and a stretch and a leap that landed her on the Chief's outstretched arm, reclining—then spun away, peeling off another pane of armor in the process. "No respect anymore," she said as she appeared behind the Chief to tear off the plate that covered her back. "No welcome, these days." Off came the pauldrons, left and right. "No guest right, no red carpet. Not even an offer of tea. Not that I mind skipping straight to the fun." She ripped away the Chief's face mask, hooked the Chief's greave with her foot-claw and shattered it.

And that was the end.

The Chief stood, disarmed and human, before Zanj. Still, she would not give up. She ran at her, caught her by the shoulders—but Zanj slipped away and the Chief tumbled to the earth. Still alive. Zanj turned her, seized her by the neck, lifted. "But you might at least have asked my name."

The Chief's eyes were wide; Viv's would have been wide with terror, but this looked more like religion. "Who are you?"

The hunters and guards had abandoned Viv entirely; spears ringed Zanj, Djenn commanding, "Release her!"

Zanj looked at him, raised one eyebrow— Are you fucking with me?— looked back at the Chief. "I'm Zanj. I've been away a long time. But now I'm back."

She might have done something in the Cloud to prove it, unfurled a banner Viv could not see, offered a cryptographic signature—or else her word had weight enough. The name was a boulder thrown into a still lake: waves rippled outward. Warriors dropped spears, drew back. Gaped. Xiara, beside Viv, looked like she was staring into the end of the world.

"It's okay," Viv whispered to Xiara. "She's not that bad once you get to know her."

"It's not possible." The Chief could barely draw breath. "The Empress—"

"Reports of my impossibility, as the prophet says, have been greatly exaggerated. Now. Here's what happens next. You will release my friend." She turned and waved to Viv with her fingers, grinning. Viv waved back. Lacking claws, her wave was a bit less impressive. "You will give us fuel. We will get out of your hair, and you will forget you ever saw us."

"And Hong," Viv added. "Let Hong go, too."

"Thank you," Hong said.

Zanj rolled her eyes. "Okay. Viv and Hong. And fuel. And you forget. That's the deal. Or I kill . . ." She added some numbers on the fingers of her free hand. "All of you."

"We can't." The Chief, for someone dangling by her neck from someone else's grip, managed an impressive amount of gravitas. "Grayteeth seized our manufactory. We have no choice."

Zanj's smile widened, as if she'd been hoping to hear that. "Good." She began to close her hand. "Then neither do I." She didn't use her claws, just the strength of her fingers: closing, closing, slowly and without strain, as if the Chief's muscle and sinew were soft as pulp, enjoying the Chief's purpling face, her futile attempts to pry free.

Xiara broke from Viv and ran toward them, swept a spear through the air, broke it on Zanj's back; Zanj turned casually and caught Xiara, too, by the throat. "Hi again. Missed you. So good to be back."

"Zanj, stop it!"

Viv's voice rang loud in the clearing. Zanj stopped. But she did not collapse. The circlet did not blacken on her brow. She looked from Xiara, to the Chief, to Viv, confused. Wondering.

There was no pain. Viv didn't want it; had thought to herself, as she cried out, don't hurt her. Don't force her. This is not an order. "Let them go. Please."

Zanj let the Chief breathe. She released Xiara, who stumbled, found her balance, and backed away from the sharp line of empty air that connected Viv's eyes to Zanj's. "They bound you," she said. "They would have given you to the Pride."

She didn't think about that, or about revenge. "There has to be a better choice. The Pride are coming?"

Zanj nodded. "They'll be here in hours. I passed them on the way."

"You, and I, and Hong, are going to the manufactory. We'll stop this Grayteeth thing. Then the Ornclan will be free, we'll have our fuel, and we can get out of here."

"We don't even know where the manufactory is. I'm sure these losers have fuel stashed somewhere. If I kill a few of them, the ones left will show us."

"I'll take you to the manufactory," Xiara said—soft, insistent, slow. "Please. Don't kill my mother."

Zanj looked skeptical. The Ornchief breathed; no one else dared.

"Are you saying you're afraid of Grayteeth?" Viv asked.

Zanj's eyes narrowed, and for a heartbeat Viv worried she had pulled the thread between them too hard, and it would snap. But then the corner of Zanj's scarred mouth crept up, and she chuckled to herself, and let the Ornchief fall. "Okay, kid. Lead the way."

18

SWOLLEN, CORUSCATING PINK, the dome-field beckoned. Xiara called it a fortress, built by Grayteeth to guard the manufactory he stole. It peeked out from behind walls, floated above broken towers, but without Xiara's guidance Viv would have lost herself trying to reach it in this labyrinth of mossy ruins and splintered glass.

They marched from the Ornclan camp in an eggshell silence—sturdy in some directions, fragile in others, and all around smooth.

That silence had congealed around them in the hours since Zanj agreed to go, since the Chief ordered the Ornclan to bring waterskins and pemmican for the journey. While warriors scurried, Xiara paced, glaring at her fellows among the Ornclan. Guards watched Zanj warily, spears to hand, rifles never quite raised but never quite stowed either. A kinder person would have acted wary, or at least respectful, of the armed and anxious warriors, but Zanj sauntered past them to the banquet table, poured herself a glass of wine, and drank. She didn't need the drink—she wasn't thirsty and Viv doubted she could get drunk without wanting to. She just wanted to show them she could do whatever she wanted in their hall, without their permission, and lick her lips when she was done.

The packs came, and they marched out. When they left the grove behind and cleared the palisade, Xiara waved to Viv, unslung her pack, and drew out—"Boots!" Ragged leather, patched and repaired, clunky as hell, more beautiful than diamonds.

"I think you're about my size."

A bit loose but only just, with socks of some sort of clingy gray silk. Viv's feet, bruised, dusty, scraped but miraculously intact considering, melted into fur lining. Viv felt a moment's frission, a how-the-great-have-fallen sort of thing, at how good it felt to wear shoes again—but for the most part, she just liked the boots. She liked, too, that Xiara had thought to bring them.

She wasn't sure how she felt about anything else right now. The Orn-clan had drugged her, chained her, sold her to the Pride for dissection, and here she was trying to solve their problems. But, hell, she couldn't just let Zanj kill anyone she didn't like. Soon there'd be no one left. Including Viv.

For that matter, how did she feel about Xiara? The Ornchief's daughter hadn't warned them, but at least she tried to save them. Maybe Viv would have noticed the trap herself if she hadn't been so damn thirsty for the woman under the armor. That was wrong, too—why did Viv feel quite so fourteen again, aching for someone to bite into? Maybe it all came down to control. She still didn't know the rules of this world, hell, this galaxy. But she did know just what she'd do if she lay beside Xiara on a bed.

Hong took point beside Xiara, clubs out, steps dancer-light, head up, eyes alert, a shorebird seeking fish in surf. If his injuries troubled him, or Xiara's her, they didn't let on. Viv's shoulder still ached where the Ornclan guards had wrenched it, holding her down. The scar on her wrist burned, too, for some reason.

Zanj walked beside her, hands in pockets, glancing idly from cloud to cloud. After a half hour Zanj began to whistle. Hong looked back when she started, shocked, and Zanj stopped—until he looked away. Zanj had not spoken to Viv since her return, walked with her now investigating broken rooftops, odd flowers, kicking gravel, silent—yet by her side. Offering the first move to Viv.

"So," Viv asked, "did you have a good vacation?"

Viv's first moves tended to fall on the brusque-to-vicious spectrum.

Zanj replied: "Don't think this means I'm not still mad at you."

"You know, it turns out, it was a good thing I stopped you. Xiara wasn't just a bandit. She's a princess. Or prince. Something like that."

"Good kisser?"

She most certainly did not flush. "I didn't—"

"Too soon, then. She's interested, in case you couldn't tell."

"My point is, you shouldn't just kill people for no reason."

"How nice. So you expect me to forgive you?"

"I won't apologize for saving her life." That part was easy. The harder was forcing herself to say: "I am sorry I hurt you."

Zanj slid her toe under a rock, kicked it up, caught it between thumb and forefinger. She inspected the rock with a jeweler's squint. "I'll kill you for that." Her voice held all the emotion of a teacher suggesting a student would find her questions answered in the syllabus. "After you let me go, I guess."

"You're not giving me good incentives there" was probably the wrong response. "Why did you come back?"

No answer save trudging footsteps.

"If we're going to travel together," Viv tried again, "we need ground rules. One of mine is, don't just kill people for no reason."

"Define *people*."

Good point. She didn't have a clear answer.

"You don't know this world at all, Los Angeles." Zanj scraped a bit of dirt off her rock. "I'm not asking you to let me go. But I need you to understand: it's hard out here for a pirate. The Ornclan would have given us fuel by the time I was done with them. They hurt you. They don't deserve your mercy just because you happen to have a crush on the Chief's daughter."

Viv raised a finger to her lips and glanced meaningfully toward Xiara, who, thank god, had shifted ahead to scout a path through a vine-draped fallen skyscraper. Zanj made a great show of ignoring Viv's signs. She tossed her rock in the air, caught it in her mouth, and chewed.

"Fine," Zanj said around mouthfuls of dust. "I'll play along. No killing. But I wonder how long that rule will last, once you understand what we're up against." Xiara reappeared at the mouth of the ruin and waved them on, eager: pink light behind her, their destination. "Which you will!" Zanj grinned, and broke into a jog just fast enough that Viv had to run to keep up.

She stopped beyond the vines, before the dome.

It loomed, obscene, so much larger than it had seemed over rooftops: smooth as geometry and mottle-colored, humming. It bathed them in pink light.

Viv reached for it, and the darker pink mottling gathered, concentrated beneath her hand. She thought the hum shifted pitch. "Do we just walk through?"

Zanj shrugged. "I still say we go back, kill them, and take their stuff."

"Hey," Xiara said. "That's my family."

"Everyone has a family," Zanj replied. "If that were a good counterargument, I'd never kill *anyone*."

"Ground rules." Viv moved her finger in a circle above the dome's pink skin. The darkness followed, like fish massing beneath food.

"Do you have any idea how dangerous this thing is?" Zanj cocked her head toward the dome.

If Viv moved her finger fast enough, close to the dome, she could make a sort of smiley face in black. The smile faded into a bruise. "Sounds like a gray goo sort of deal. Eats everything, turns it into more of itself."

"They call themselves Grayframe, singular Gray. Grayframe devour everything you are, and in that devouring read you into themselves, run permutations by the millions. They will know and use your echoes in their imagination forever. Through there, you will see horrors beyond your wildest nightmares."

"So, basically, I was right?" Was she scared? Sure. But she'd had it with the whole *mysterium tremendum et fascinans* routine, the religious awe, the wonder. She might not know much about this place, but she was done playing the rube, gawping at each new vista. Plus, Xiara looked full of fear and trembling enough for both of them, and Viv was pretty sure Zanj was using this schtick at least as much to scare her as to warn Viv. So Viv stood tall, and saw Xiara brighten.

Hong looked impressed, too, respectful but familiar. She remembered, back in her churchgoing days, how Father Cho held the grape juice and spoke the words he thought sacred. "Grayframe serve the Empress," Hong said. "This one must have displeased Her. They often do, and seldom survive. Down thousands of years, we've found their corpses scattered through space; we study them, store their remains in the 'fleet. I have never seen one alive and whole before. It must have been terrible indeed, to survive Her displeasure."

"Great!" Viv said quickly, to cover Xiara's gasp. "No sweat. You know how these things work, and Zanj is super deadly, and it can't mess with me using the Cloud since I don't have a soul. So Xiara stays out here, and we go in and take him apart. Right?"

Zanj stretched her arms over her head, popped her shoulders, her neck, her knuckles. She glared at the wall. Mottled pinks shaped themselves into her shadow. "I have won every battle I ever fought, save one," she said. "But Grayframe are too dangerous for war. We might die here."

"You never said why you came back."

Zanj bared teeth—and this time the grin was real. "I missed the company."

Without cue, and as one, they stepped forward. The dome rippled over their skin, cool as a kiss, and when Viv opened her eyes she stood in paradise.

19

A CHILD WEPT in the garden.

Peach-pink Dr. Seuss trees rose beneath a blushing sky. Diamond waterfalls birthed winding rivers clear as glass and tumbling with purple fish. Dragonfly wings shed rainbow shadows. People hung fetus-curled in translucent fleshy sacs from those pink trees, and they shifted and turned as if in the depths of dream.

Paradise stank of lilac.

And still, somewhere out of sight, a child wept.

Hong moved first, while Viv marveled, while Zanj sniffed the air, claws ready, on guard. He ran through soft blue-green grass, footfalls quiet, leapt over the river and around a flowering bush that settled Viv's earlier question as to whether there were still roses in the future; Viv protested, "Hey!" but followed him, and she heard Zanj's sigh as she matched pace.

The kid might have been eight at most, slender, hair short, all over pale, eyes large as Xiara's, barefoot, wearing scraps of dirty multicolored cloth. He (Viv was guessing) hugged his knees, stared at Hong, at Viv, at Zanj, then at the vine-trailed forest and the perfect sky, then back, gaze shifting with the speed of fear. Viv, for whom kids were something that happened to other people, wanted to help, but drew up short, uncertain how to start with a child who'd been stuck in this strange place. Hong didn't wait: he walked over, hands out, and sat beside the kid on the log. "Hello." He didn't touch the kid, didn't sound particularly interested in him even—and yet the sobbing slowed. Some magic in that, Viv thought. Not the far-future kind, just the not-being-awful-with-children kind. "Are you lost?"

The kid looked up, sniffed, wiped his tears with the back of his hand. Nodded once.

"Us, too." It wasn't totally a lie. "Have you been here long?"

The kid shook his head, but the shake traveled down his neck into his ribs, his belly. He pointed up to the sky: no sun, no stars, no moon, just pink velvet twilight. Viv looked away. Watching him she saw a part of herself that looked just like that, staring wide-eyed at a large and terrifying world. She wanted to forget that part of her, ignore it, but this kid remained stubbornly in place. It wasn't his fault. She made herself look.

Hong, meanwhile, was still talking. "Did you come here with your family?"

A nod turned into another shake of head; he hugged his knees, bent double. Knobs of vertebrae jutted from his back.

Zanj leaned against a tree and crossed her arms. "Ask him where the Gray is."

The boy's wide eyes snapped to her, and he started shivering again.

"Thing's probably at the center of this mess. You know, kid? Big monster, huge teeth?"

"It's fine," Hong said, his voice kind, but with a glare at Zanj to clarify that while the situation in general might be fine, her behavior wasn't. "We're here to free you, and your family. But we need to find the monster. So we can stop it."

The boy's face squinched together, curious, suspicious.

"Can you help us?"

Viv saw the decision process tick behind his eyes. He trembled with the effort of thought, then stilled, a sign of solution every bit as obvious as if he'd actually gone *ding*. Then, without warning, he rose and scrambled off through purple bushes into the forest.

With a trade of looks—are we doing this, I think so, are we sure it's a good idea, the time to ask that question was, really, before we stepped into the glowing dome—they ran after.

Even running felt wonderful here, the air crisp and flowerthick as new spring. Viv's muscles stretched and her feet in their new boots loved the grass and the springy earth. The kid led them down narrow paths between full bushes, but there were no thorns, and the leaves brushed her skin like silk, like feathers. Her heart sang. She leapt creeks, she took hard corners easy, she let herself forget, almost, the monster. Just focus on the kid's pale, flashing soles, on his back, on the fact that—

Wait. What happened to the others?

The kid ran on ahead, the narrow path unspooled before him, and more path lay behind Viv, bare of friends. From the bushes to her left, she heard Hong cry out, and a crash of breaking wood.

Damn damn damn.

She dove off the path, through the bushes, toward the cry.

She expected breaking twigs, thorns, sharp edges catching clothes, but she slid through the underbrush as if through a feather thicket, past leaves so fine they did not scrape, did not cut, but slid into her mouth, her nose. She tried to slap them away but the ground caught her and she fell:

—into twilight and open arms.

She fought at first, but Xiara's voice said, it's okay, and, I've got you, and she was held, and turned in her arms—Xiara clutching her close, skin warm, though Viv was shaking.

"We have to help them," Viv said, and "They need me," but Xiara's eyes were large, near, and her finger settled over Viv's lips, and then her mouth followed.

Paradise.

She was naked, they both were, falling soft and autumn slow to pillowing grass, to earth that molded to their bodies, to blush skies overhead; nails dragged down her back, fingers cradled her crotch; she breathed in but her throat stopped and her eyes went soft; she clutched the curve of her, explored her body, wanted it, needed it, and as she needed felt it change, and at each change her own hunger grew, the fire of that touch transformed, her leg now between her legs, rising, riding—

—changing—

—the hand that climbed her side, that caught her wrist, that pinned it back over her head, was not Xiara's hand, those green eyes mocking over her belonged to Adrienne, but now they were black like Susan Cho's, the teeth in that mouth sharp as no one's she'd ever lain with, sharp as in fantasies she'd only ever confessed to search fields in incognito mode through a VPN, and she was lying in a pickup truck bed and she was wearing clothes she'd never worn and a body that was not her own and everything was all so stupid dumb glorious normal like she'd never ever had and scorned and wanted even as she scorned it, and she reached up and the woman over her caught her neck and closed her hand around it and closing her hand closed a collar gripped her slammed her down jammed mouth against mouth so hungry and the taste of that skin on her tongue and her own throat beneath her hand and her submission, mastery building higher ever higher, and always. Not. Quite. There.

Like induction. Like an algorithm. Oh.

—christ—

Think about Facebook. Think about Acsiom.

—onward and onward and why would you ever stop or even look away—

Pleasure-seeking math. The model watches you. Learns what you want. Offers.

—yes there and somehow inside, and worse, and better, she conquers, she is broken—

Shapes itself to your desire. Lets you act. Picks you—a hairpin

—hairpins, clips, pigtails, lips, lipstick, a gag—

scraping tumblers of a lock. Tumblrs. Christ.

—jesus—

It wants you to want. It needs you to need. Your hunger fuels your hunger. As you reach, it grasps you. So: think deeper. Watch yourself want. Learn your demons, your needs. See them arise. See them fall.

Breathe. Nothing you want can stay.

Air cools; skin withers, ages, rots, leaving bone. Viv herself passed on. She felt slickness beneath her palms, dug her fingers into claws, peeled back the skin. The lavender scent filled her, choked her.

She fell into the real.

Struck grass hard, and it hurt. That helped, that was a sign. Some kinds of pain at least were real—not the grand overmastering sort, but the shitty stubbed-my-toe aches no one could fetish over. She was soaked, sticky, covered in some sort of sap. It dried fast, flaked off as she turned and groaned amid ropy roots. Opened her eyes, saw the twilit sky, a spreading peach-pink tree. Somewhere nearby, that kid wailed. Overhead, dangling from branches, in translucent sacs, hung Zanj and Hong.

She forced herself to stand. Her muscles obeyed reluctantly; the kid fell silent—he had been wailing beneath Hong, but now he looked at her, awed. "It's okay," she said. "Give me a second."

She broke off a branch, ignored the maple-cedar sweetness of its sap, and jabbed the sharp end into the sac that held Hong. On her third try it pierced and he spilled to the earth in a sick heap. "What?" His voice peaked and rough, for once uncomposed.

"It got us," she said, and stabbed Zanj. This sac she got in a single blow—practice, plus she didn't feel as worried about hurting Zanj. She had a tough hide, and she deserved it. "Now let's get it back."

Zanj was cursing already as she fell, half-awake, and landed on her feet, slick-furred, sharp-eyed, and furious. "Motherfucker's gonna pay for that."

"It's okay. We're out."

"Okay? Do you have any idea how long we were in there? Hours!"

Hong, still shaking, gasping, accepted Viv's hand up. "I don't—I—"

"Fucking kama trap. Fuck!" Zanj punched the tree. The boom of her fist breaking the sound barrier overwhelmed the crack of the trunk snapping in two. The tree fell with a hammerthud. "Desire algorithm magic *bullshit*. Hate it. Hate everything. First the stupid crown, now this—nobody snags me in nonsense and gets away with it." She knelt, wrapped her arms around the fallen trunk, and lifted it easily. Her eyes were murderous and wild. "Someone's going to die." The kid, slack-jawed with awe, ran to her, waving, follow me, but Zanj shook her head. "No way, kid. I am done sneaking around. I want this asshole to hear me coming."

Viv ducked before she spun the tree, as did Hong—and a good thing, too, because the trunk shattered the surrounding grove. Trees dominoed into other trees; Zanj chose a direction, seemingly at random, marched forward, swinging the tree like a scythe. When the first trunk broke she chose another, and swung again.

"Zanj."

Crash.

"Zanj!"

She halted her tree-swinging with a roar. "What?"

Viv pointed.

There, beyond the splintered forest, crouched the monster.

20

MANY-MOUTHED, GRAY AND bloated, sharp-toothed and ten-handed, the monster curled atop a platform of pearlescent metal marked with glowing circuitry. A fountain of light and heat gushed from the center of the dais into the large vertical mouth in the center of the monster's chest. (Were those ribs or teeth that pierced the red flesh of his torso gums?) He swallowed in huge wet spasms and dregs of matter dribbled gray from the corner of that mouth, down the swell of his translucent belly. When his mouth gaped, Viv could see his heart beating far back in his throat. The smell alone turned Viv's stomach: sour milk and spoiled meat and burnt sugar. Ten feet tall lying down, naked and rubbery, smeared with slime, with filth, he rolled, twitched, belched, gurgled, and fixed Zanj with six yellow eyes arranged in two ranks of three.

"Finally." Zanj tossed aside her tree trunk as if it weighed no more than a broom, and marched into the clearing. Her head was raised, her shoulders broad, her movements fluid, lively, all anger and no scorn. Viv, watching, took note: this was Zanj faced with an opponent she respected. She wasn't scared—just ready. "Are you Gray?"

The monster did not stop swallowing—but its highest mouth, the one just above its eyes, said, "I am hunger and peace: Worldgnasher, Form-Eater. In my gullet all finds place and—" Its voice was wet and heavy bass, and the monster interrupted itself with a burp. "Purpose." Viv had to turn away at that, and managed not to throw up. Hong, beside her, wore an expression between terror and disgust; the kid watched with wide scared fascination, unable to turn away.

"My friend here has asked me not to kill people unnecessarily," Zanj said. "So—even though you tried to catch me in a want-loop, even though you've grown fat on the fantasies of these poor groundling bastards, I'll give you a chance. Surrender the manufactory and get the hell off this dirtball. I won't hurt you. Much."

The kid giggled, high, hysterical, the sound lost beneath the monster's tree-shaking guffaw. The monster reared, twenty feet tall now, slithered forward, and spread six massive arms, each tipped with three thick-nailed fingers. All its mouths spoke at once, their voices ranging from a child's treble pipe to a rumble on the lower edge of hearing: "Bold words for a tasty morsel! I have supped on the blood of worlds, and I will clean my teeth with your bones!"

"Your teeth," Zanj admitted, "do need cleaning. If we're trading riddle-stories, here's mine. I have stolen suns, and burned inside them. I, Cloudborne, a-wander through my mother's body. I raised the armies of Ilion and watched them shatter. I am Queen uncrowned, now crowned. I fought first and last; I am whole and I am scarred. And you should have taken my first offer, because I never give a second."

Steam hissed from the monster's thick hide; its eyes widened, and one of its six arms smeared gray guck from the eyes on its chest to give it a clearer view. "Zanj?"

Wind whistled through the clearing, over the shattered trees. Viv heard the battery pop inside Zanj's skull.

Her eyes burned white, and she moved.

With a single leap, Zanj struck the monster in the stomach. Her claws sank into his thick gray hide. She stuck in midair somehow, anchored, stained by the slime on his skin, then with a surge of back and waist lifted, twisted, tossed his great bulk down to the ground. His tail lashed toward her, but she let herself fall and it whipped harmless through empty space. Zanj sprang forward, skidded under the monster's backhand, caught its arm, wrenched that arm sideways in a loud crack of bone, and landed, only to slip in monster-muck, recover, and leap to safety. Zanj was an insect against Gray's bulk, and she fought like one—a wasp, stinging, slipping away, zipping in to sting again. She moved too fast for Viv to see. She traced her by the trails she tore in the earth, by the claw marks in the monster's flesh, oozing oily blackish blood. By roars.

And the roars turned to laughs as the monster began to change. More hands unfolded from its body, grappling Zanj, but she slipped away, her fur muck-slick and matted; somersaulting through the air. Pustules swelled on that thick hide, burst, and the viscous stuff they wept hardened to armor as it met the air. The monster's bulging mass warped; the tail split, each fork now tipped with a poison-weeping stinger.

And Zanj, too, transformed.

Quicksilver angles covered her—not splitting her skin, but rotating from an unseen dimension into place. She grew larger, supple, sprouted another pair of arms; there seemed to be many of her, or else she slipped through time, her smile growing, growing as she grew, and her eyes doubled. Many rows of teeth glistened in her mouth.

Viv had wondered offhand, as Xiara and Hong told stories of Zanj's prior exploits, how one woman no matter how strong or fast could have stolen suns and shattered fleets and stood against the Empress. She'd assumed there was some collective collapse at work: Zanj the leader emerging as a mythic figure when her exploits had in fact been team efforts, the way old Greek heroes stood, in stories, for the forces under their command, the way Viv herself stood for the work of the thousands of engineers and coders and salesfolk and marketers and support techs and factory workers she'd employed.

But Xiara and Hong had both spoken of the exploits of Zanj's armies, and still said that *she* stole suns. Hard to believe of the woman Viv had rescued from High Carcereal, but easy to believe of this sharp-eyed glistening Being.

Was this silver shape a form Zanj could take on when she wanted? Or was the Zanj Viv knew the false shape—or, if not false, then partial as an anglerfish's lure, the bright darting sprite over the immense eyes, over the mouth that gaped with teeth?

Zanj flickered blue, turned on invisible axes through the Cloud—and so too did the monster, tail stabbing through nothingness to emerge behind, above. Watching the fight, the part of Viv that never was where she was, the part that thought to save herself from feeling, recalled Modernist paintings, Duchamp, canvases that showed all angles and stages and frames of movement superimposed. *Nude Wrestling a Monster*, Number 2 in a series.

Viv followed the roots of that thought back to herself in the present: terrified, frozen, deer in headlights, toad staring at a snake. She stank with the tree's slick goop, with her own fear—of the creature, of failure. But fear, also, of this beautiful terrifying battlecreature that was Zanj.

For the first time since Viv pulled her from that star, Zanj was having fun. She was not winning; or at least, not winning easily. Each time she seemed on the verge of tearing off a limb or crushing a windpipe, the monster wriggled away, reshaped itself, rejoined the battle. And Zanj laughed and changed herself in turn, became grander, stranger, less—well. She never had been human. But less recognizably herself.

When they struck the earth, great deep fissures opened, and earthquakes shook the ground. Viv kept her balance, barely.

This, for Zanj, was a kind of heaven: to fight, forever, against an enemy she never could quite kill, before whom she would never yield. Striving, always striving. And in that, more even than in her scars, Viv felt she understood her.

Hong's voice cut through the chaos. "We have to help her!" His clubs out, he stared into the roil of claw and flesh and Cloud, over the cracked ground—brave, ready to die.

"Are you nuts?"

"The Gray's drawing power from the manufactory." The fountain of liquid light that rose from the platform had dwindled to a trickle of sparks. "Zanj's batteries won't last much longer. We have to stop the Gray's power supply."

"So we just run through . . . that?" The monster caught Zanj, threw her into the earth with bomb-blast force; dirt rained down upon them, and Viv shielded her eyes.

"We have no choice!"

And beside him the kid watched the battle, eyes wide and glassy, jaw slack, rigid with awe. His mouth twitched as the monster roared.

"Maybe we do," Viv said, and hit the kid over the head with her stick.

Hong had a good set of lungs on him, or else the Mirrorfaith trained its initiates on vocal projection. For all the roaring and crunching and screams, his shouted "What!" came through just fine.

So, for that matter, did the thunk of the stick against the kid's skull. As if the battle weren't happening at all, or as if it were happening in a space removed from where they stood. The kid sprawled on the cracked ground, dazed. Viv jumped on his back, caught his neck in the crook of her arm, and ignored her own doubts. The kid bucked beneath her, stronger than he looked. She shouted to Hong: "Help me, you idiot!"

"What are you doing?" He managed to get the whole sentence out this time. Probably they'd drilled some rules into him back in the monastery about honorable combat, which didn't include guidelines for dogpiling children. But—as muscles writhed under the kid's skin, as his neck bulked beneath her arm, as he bucked again, broke her grip, sent her flying to land in a cloud of dirt—Hong got the picture. Not everything that looked like a child, was.

The kid hunched to his feet, breathing heavy, half his body still reed-thin, half plumped with muscle. A pale silver mix of blood and spit smeared his mouth. He wiped it with the back of his hand, and stared at it in peevish shock. "You hit me!"

Hong hit him next, with a club, in the side of his head.

"Ow!" The kid swirled around, unbalanced, metamorphosis incomplete, his thick arm clutching, but Hong had already rolled away. "What did you do *that* for?" He lurched toward Hong, step by heavy step. "I just wanted to make you happy." That last word punctuated with a swing Hong ducked around and punished with a club strike that the kid, still growing, didn't seem to notice.

"What are you?" Hong shouted.

If the situation had been a bit less life-threatening, Viv would have rolled her eyes. "He's the Gray."

"But that's—" In the center of the clearing, Zanj, ten feet tall now, suplexed the monster to the soil, only to be knocked off-balance by a foot-claw, to spin through the air and land, all fierce grins and battle joy, and launch herself once more into the fight. Hong got it then. Finally. "Oh. I see. The battle is another trap."

The kid spun from Viv to Hong and back, gaping. His musculature kept filling in, but his face was still a hungry child's, gawping in disbelief. "A trap? I'm giving you what you want! I'm giving you all exactly what you want."

"You fed on us," Viv said.

"I didn't *feed* on you!" The kid—Gray—grew larger now, swelling in scale, but his face was no less a child's. "I don't need any food from you. In here, with the matter siphon and the manufactory, I have whatever I want. Anything I could dream!"

Zanj kicked the monster in the head, twice; it tried to punch her in the mouth, but she tucked her chin and rammed her forehead into its knuckles. Bone, or something that served the same purpose, shattered.

"And you wore your dreams out," Viv said. It was a guess. "You rubbed your fantasies raw, and went looking for others that weren't yours."

He made a wrinkled face as if he'd smelled something foul. "No! Gross. Do you think I like all your weird animal dreams, all those gasps and wriggling? I don't want them, I don't understand them. I just need them, that's all."

Anger filled her until her skin was taut and trembling. Maybe rage was not the best emotion for dealing with a nearly invincible immature god-thing—but Viv always made her best decisions on instinct. For a given definition of *best* that might not correspond to any in common use. "Those aren't yours, kid! They don't belong to you."

"Look—I'm trying to make up for a mistake. When people come to me, I ask their souls what they want, and give it to them. I just collect the data. People were happy, and it was going fine until you came to wreck every-thing." Zanj chucked the monster through the air and it landed on the platform—but she was slowing, even in her joy. "This is all going so wrong! Just let me put you back in the tree for a bit, okay? I'll fix this. We'll settle up later."

Viv ran toward him, not knowing what she could do against something with his power; she had no plan other than distracting him from Hong, who'd worked around to flank him. But the kid caught her in his hands, sprouted other hands from his back, and caught Hong too. Viv growled, shook, kicked, but could not free herself. The ground bubbled up beneath her and caught her legs, climbed her, vine-supple and hard as concrete, locking her knees, her waist, reaching for her arms. Tendrils curled into her mouth, her throat. "Zanj!"

Not a command, even then, but a plea—one word against Zanj's battle joy.

Zanj stopped in midair, over the recovering ruin of her foe. She revolved toward them.

Gray's face went slack, and his ashen skin paled; what he said sounded like static, but Viv's translation gimmick rendered it "Oh, shit."

Then Zanj hit him, and he splashed.

This battle lacked the brutal glory of Zanj's fight with the monster: that had been a sort of fantasy in itself, Zanj's need for an opponent fed into an optimizer powered by all the manufactory's might. Zanj enjoyed this less: Gray a mess of formless sand pouring over Zanj's body, taking form after form, thornbush and flame, horrible longheaded alien, writhing teeth, each assumed for the split second Zanj took to master it, then splashing back to sand again.

Zanj did not fight for pleasure now. She fought to win.

She flickered blue, into and out of the Cloud, caught some invisible thread in the whirl of Gray and twisted her hands in a circle; the grayness gathered, spun in, closed itself in a diamond shell, which she raised overhead and threw down so hard it shattered.

Viv and Hong's stone chains snapped; the ground beneath them broke, healed, flattened. A cold wind tore through the grove. The few great umbrella trees still standing withered.

The gray sand gathered into a puddle, assumed a shape not unlike the kid's, but softer: a round-faced coltish gray-skinned adolescent, eyes wide, mouth slack with fear. "I didn't mean it! I didn't, I swear, I'm sorry, I just—I shouldn't have, I know. I messed this up, like I mess up everything—"

Zanj's form returned to its usual number of dimensions, though her face held no less fury; mixed there, Viv saw recognition. "I know you."

"Um." Whatever Grayteeth had expected, that wasn't it. "I really don't think so?"

"You were with the Empress. Her page, her lackey, her servant, when she cast me down."

His fear smelled of ozone and burnt insulation. "You're really her. You're really Zanj."

"And you," she said, "are about to die." She raised her hand, claws sparkling, vicious.

"That wasn't me! I swear. That wasn't me, that was old Great-Great-Great-Aunt Gray, I only entered the service a hundred years ago, I don't know you, I've never seen you before, I've just heard stories." His wide eyes fixed on the tips of Zanj's claws. "Um. Good ones?"

Zanj rolled her eyes and raised her claw.

"Wait." Viv lifted herself from the withering grass. The ground beneath her hardened, lost that loamy cushion, felt more like the soil of broken Orn. "Please." Zanj seemed unimpressed, but hadn't killed him yet. "You worked with the Empress?"

The kid knew a lifeline when he saw one. "I served Her—we all do, the whole Grayframe. But I spoiled a . . . I guess you'd call it a meal. A meal of dreams." Viv wondered what that meant, and remembered the Empress's voice, the burning hand in her chest, and stopped wondering for now. "She wanted to make an example out of me—to shame my family, my brothers and sisters. So She broke me, banished me, cast me out into the black. Away from everyone I knew. Alone."

Zanj wasn't buying it. "And you stole people to keep you company."

"No! I mean, at first I didn't know what I was doing. We share wants, hopes, thoughts all the time, back home. That's how we talk. When I found the matter siphon, I was almost dead; I drank, desperate. When people wandered toward me, I caught them without meaning to. But they kept coming. It took months before I realized what was happening, and when I did—" He paled and shrank. The trees around them curled down fernlike, shrank into the ground, revealing rubble and skeletal ductwork; the pink sky flickered, paled. "I started saving them instead. I hoped I could give them to Her. To replace what I lost. I thought maybe if I offered Her enough dreams, She'd forgive me. She'd forgive the Grayframe. But I guess you'll kill me now."

To Viv's surprise, Zanj looked to her for directions. "Well?" Viv hadn't thought she would remember her ground rules in the heat of victory.

Viv knelt beside the kid. He looked lost, simple, scared. What he had done, what the Ornclan did to appease him, made her feel dirty. But he did seem contrite, at least when faced with the prospect of punishment. And she could use him. "Do you know the Empress's ship?"

"I grew up there. Know it up, down, in the Cloud and out. My family serves Her—that is, unless She's killed them by now."

"I want to steal something from her."

His expression, which had been hopeful or at least desperate, closed at once. "Okay, never mind. You're crazy. Kill me now."

"If we got you to her ship, could you help us?"

"I've been banished. If I try to pass through the borders of the palace She'll notice me at once, burn me from the soul out."

"I can get you in," Viv said.

"Bullshit."

Zanj, still holding Gray down, looked done with this whole conversation. "Can I kill him now? He did ask."

"I broke Zanj out of her prison. I can help you."

His eyes widened, flashed blue, narrowed. He made a face like he'd just seen a car wreck. "What *are* you?"

"Just meat," Viv said. "Meat without a soul. The Empress can't bind me, and I can get you home. If you guide us, and fuel our ship."

"Ship!" Gray laughed at that, claws notwithstanding. "Who needs a ship?" He looked, expectant, from Hong to Zanj, then at last to Viv again, and his face fell. "Oh. Right. You're really all *meat*? That must be so frustrating."

Zanj growled. "I still say we kill him."

The wind of crumbling paradise blew through Viv's close-cropped hair. "If you're traveling with us, I need you to promise—as binding an oath as you can make—that you'll give up stealing dreams. And swear you'll help us."

"Swear," Hong said, "on the Lady you serve."

"I'll do you one better." Gray closed his eyes, and stopped struggling. His voice lost the squeak of adolescent protest. He sounded younger, reciting words he'd learned singsong from teachers long ago. "I swear on my death, on the chain of all my family since the first, on old Earth." As he spoke, the words spread golden through the gray of his body, and sank like treasure into him.

"Wait," Viv said. "Earth? You know Earth?"

"Of course," he answered, confused. "Earth is the egg that hatched the world."

She'd unpack that later, if there was anything there to unpack. "Does that work for you?" she asked Hong, who said, "Yes." Zanj rolled her eyes, but she released Gray's neck and stepped off him.

Viv offered him her hand. "Welcome to the crew. Don't make me regret it."

He took her hand, eyes wide as if seeing for the first time. Viv wondered if this was the first promise he'd made—or if he was simply shocked to find a thread of hope, a rumor of home. His hand felt soft. "I won't." She believed him. "Thanks, boss."

"Don't call me that."

The last of paradise blew away in a stiff breeze and left them in the rubble atop the manufactory dais, ringed by broken steel and crystal arches, crumbled masonry, and the dead. The real Orn smelled of dust and metal. Amid the ruins, she heard cries, groans, Ornclan waking from long slumber to find their perfect visions melted into this. And among them, a woman's voice, aware, alive, in full command of her faculties: Xiara running toward them, calling Viv's name.

Viv felt barren, wrung out, and happy. She'd solved the problem. Seen through illusions. Worked with Zanj and Hong not as a passenger or package, but as a partner. A leader, even. No one died today. She'd saved lives, and gained a source on the Empress whose information wasn't three thousand years out of date. Not bad for an illiterate meatbag without a smartphone to her name.

Then she looked up. And up. And cursed.

They'd been trapped in the tree for hours, Zanj said. At the time, Viv hadn't worried—they had more pressing concerns than their deadline. Survival, for one.

Not anymore.

Not with a three-mile-long hate fractal ringed by fighters overhead.

21

"IT COULD BE worse" was, in Viv's experience, a phrase people tended to use when they didn't see exactly how. So when Zanj used it, as they peered down onto the Ornclan camp from the shelter of a crumbling crystal tower, she didn't bite the lure—only watched, and stewed, and tried to think of a solution.

Xiara did not have Viv's experience. "How?"

"Well," Zanj said, "they didn't expect me, so they only sent one Pride-mother. It's not even very large as these things go. Plus, your Chief brought our ship here. Otherwise we would have had to dodge Pride halfway across Orn."

"But there must be a hundred drones between us and your ship. Not to mention the fighters."

"Those are not fighters," Hong corrected gently. "Our holy books call them *close air support.*"

Viv laughed, then realized Hong was looking at her funny, and rolled back her sound-memory tapes a few seconds: he had slipped into a different language just then, sonorous and ancient as a priest's Latin, and the translation gimmick followed him. "Sorry," she said, to Xiara more than Hong. "Don't worry about me. Keep going."

"I can't see the Ornclan at all."

Hong's face, his voice, his body compressed to a grim line. "The Pride have no reason to suspect your Chief has betrayed them, but they will keep the Ornclan under guard until Viv is theirs. Your people will be corralled, safe. However, if the Pride cannot find us, they may seek compensation for their failure by harvesting your clan's blood."

Xiara looked sick. "What do you mean, *harvest*?"

"Your germline piloting adaptations and your nanobiome are valuable. As long as they're in system . . ."

Viv grabbed Xiara's shoulder in time to stop her from sprinting out of their hiding place in a futile attempt at rescue. "Don't worry. We can fix this. We just need to be smart."

"Why?" Gray sat on top of the wall in what would have been plain sight if he had not made himself transparent for the purpose. He kicked his crossed legs, unconcerned. "We can just eat them."

"Don't eat people."

"The Pride count as people?"

"The Pride," Viv said, "count. So do the Ornclan. Who might die in the crossfire if we're not careful."

"Fine." He sounded bored.

Xiara glared at him. "I still can't believe you're working with this monster."

"I'm not a monster," Gray said, haughty. "I am a Gray of Grayframe."

"You kidnapped people and ate their dreams."

"Look." He raised his hands. "I said I was sorry! I didn't even know what I was doing at first, and I promised Viv I wouldn't do it again."

"You forced my mother to break hospitality."

"I didn't force anything. I took over the manufactory, sure. What was I supposed to do? Die?"

"Is death so fearsome to you?"

"Yes!"

"Quiet," Viv said. "Both of you. Before the Pride hear you." They shut up, at least. "You," with a finger jabbed at Gray, "apologize to her. Sincerely."

Gray rolled his transparent eyes, but when he saw the expression on Viv's face he sobered fast, and turned to Xiara. "I am sorry I kidnapped your people and ate their dreams."

Xiara glared at him, grim and earnest as a blade. Gray looked back at her, nonchalant at first, but his eyes widened slowly and his shoulders slumped as he appreciated the depth of her anger—either truly contrite or faking it well. "I really am sorry."

Xiara frowned, and he winced, and Viv wondered if maybe he really was sincere. "Xiara," she said gently. "He promised to help me. If we sneak past the Pride we'll get him offworld, far away, and he'll never bother your clan again."

"Very well," Xiara said, and Gray relaxed. "Monster." His shoulders sank again.

"Great. Glad that's settled. Now all we have to do is find a way past the

Pride." Viv pushed herself back from the ledge, touched her knuckle to her lower lip, and turned the problem over in her mind. She felt comfortable, familiar, and after a few breaths she realized why. Everyone was looking at her. Waiting for her to tell them what to do.

Everyone except Zanj. Who was lying on a small pile of rubble, juggling three pebbles one-handed, and watching the clouds.

"Do you have anything to add?"

Zanj's lips revealed teeth in a long, lazy smile. "No. You got us out of his mess." With a tail flick toward Gray. "Who knows how long I would have kept fighting if you weren't there? And while I understand the outlines of our, let's call it a deal, I'm still not clear what sort of violence I can do without offending your sensibilities. I know what I'd do in your shoes. But you want to lead. So, lead."

Viv was half-tempted to launch into her plan just then—but injured pride would fester. Besides, there was always the chance Viv had missed something. She needed Zanj as a partner, not a passenger. She needed them all. There was too much galaxy for her to beat alone. "What would you do?"

Zanj's face softened with surprise at being asked. She rolled to her feet, catching the stones she'd been juggling in the process. "As I see it, and as per usual, Viv's the problem."

"Thanks."

"If we could pull you through the Cloud, I'd suggest we hit them fast, then jump away, leaving a big enough trail that the Pridemother and her brood will follow us. Then we could lose them in the Cloud, or at least take the fight somewhere with fewer bystanders. But you need a ship."

"Can you lead them away, then double back?"

"They won't all follow me. They know you need a ship, so they'll keep a guard on the *Question.*"

"What if we both took off at once—and you made a bigger splash, to draw them off track?"

Zanj seemed less bored by that idea. Her tail twitched. "That could work. If the ship had fuel. And if we had a pilot."

"Gray can fuel us up."

His head spun around three hundred degrees on his neck; somewhere in the field of space behind him, a white bird struck a Pride ship's effector field and vaporized. His skin reproduced the exchange in sordid detail. "What?"

"You've been eating straight from the matter siphon for months. You made that whole paradise. I bet you can make fuel for the *Question*."

Gray did not exactly radiate confidence. "Boss, it's really not the same sort of thing. I can build anything, but I need time, and feeding fuel right into an engine—"

"Can you do it?"

He held his hand flat and tilted back and forth: maybe?

"Close enough."

"Which still leaves us in want of a pilot," Zanj observed. "Unless Gray can fly and fuel you up at once."

"Fly? Like, a *ship*?" He laughed. "What kind of backwater rube do you take me for?"

"I'll fly." Xiara stood on the rooftop between them, looking brave and, as their eyes settled on her, more and more unsure. She glanced from Viv, to Hong, to Grayteeth, to Zanj, and back to Viv, her hands clenched, knuckles white. "If you'll still have me after what the Ornchief did. I want to get him off my world. And I want to go with you."

Viv wanted to hug her, but didn't let herself. Xiara had talked about her dreams of flight and of the stars like they were some grand adventure that would happen to someone else: of course I'd go into the world, fight demons and evil empires, risk death, dismemberment, abandon my home and family without any assurance I'll return, all to reclaim the sky my mothers were denied. It was one thing to want that, and another to live it—to leave the life you'd known, and step onto a road you once thought a dream.

"She's never flown," Hong pointed out. "She's never left the planet."

Zanj, on the other hand, looked interested. "Viv doesn't have a soul, and we don't hold it against her. Much. Xiara has the nanome, the training, she knows the songs of Orn. She'll do."

Hong blinked, looked away, raised one hand to his temple, paced.

Zanj raised one eyebrow. "Go ahead."

"You can't be suggesting we put someone who's barely seen a ship, let alone flown one, in the cockpit."

"I've seen the people of Orn fly."

"You also thought the city would still be here!"

Xiara didn't seem to have heard either of them. She was watching Viv—to see if the gift she'd offered would be honored, or cast aside.

Hong had a point. Hong had all the points. If this were a board meeting, he'd have the charts and graphs, the carefully formatted and cross-checked statistics on his side, all the transitions right. And if this were a board meeting, Viv would have agreed with him. You couldn't manage by heroics. You couldn't manage by the way Xiara looked right now, afraid, desperate to prove herself, and brave. You couldn't manage by a young woman's total unflinching faith that she was born to fly.

"We won't be able to come back here for a long time," Viv said. "You know that."

"I know," she replied. "I'm ready."

Zanj clapped her on the back. "Kid, we'll show you all the stars you can handle."

"I," Xiara said, "will be the judge of that."

Viv held out her hand. "Welcome aboard." Xiara followed her handshake into a hug that hurt Viv's ribs—then she broke away, blushing, and saluted. Viv didn't mind the hug or the salute, but there would be time to sort it all out later.

"Thank you."

"Okay," Viv said. "Here's how I see this going down."

IT STARTED WITH Zanj.

They hadn't spent much time on this phase of the plan, leaving the particulars of the distraction up to Zanj's sadistic imagination.

Viv tried to envision it from the Pride's perspective: Kentaurs scuttling over the gnarled rock-hard ground beneath the Ornclan's palace grove, guarding their quarry's ship while close air support buzzed overhead. The Pridemother's inaudible modem screams bound them in a web of telemetry and bloodthirst. With the Ornclan under guard, no minor annoyances would disturb their mission—no fleet in this sector of space could hinder them. They were supreme, they were fierce, and they would find what they had come to seek.

Zanj walked out of the ruins, juggling three stones in one hand.

A hundred Kentaur heads spun toward her at once, and locked. Her chest danced with laser sights and other forms of targeting Viv lacked the words to name. Close air support warmed up plasma cannon and fléchette launchers and no doubt all sorts of nasty ordnance. The Pridemother lowering overhead turned its thorn-brains upon her.

Zanj looked up at the close air support, at the Pridemother. She shaded her eyes with one hand, and squinted. With her other hand she caught the stones one by one.

"Surrender," said the Pridemother through all her drones at once. "Lay down all arms, submit to binding, and identify with your true name."

"I am not armed." Zanj's hand tightened around the rocks. Several loud cracks and a disconcerting hiss of escaping heat echoed through the wind-swept silence. "I have had quite enough of bonds. And as for my true name—" She opened her hand, and revealed a single tiny gem, its sides still smoking. "You don't deserve it."

Then she threw the gem overhand, not just at but *through* one of the close air support hate fractals. The ship veered to the side, spoiling targeting solutions as its mates spun out of formation to avoid a crash. Guns spoke, but not before there was a loud pop inside Zanj's skull and her eyes burned white. There was too much noise and fire and confusion for anyone to see her smile as she moved fast and broke things.

Viv ran through the firefight. The four of them had spent Zanj's distraction working around the clearing's edge until they had a straight shot up the ramp into the ship; the others were slow off the block, stunned, perhaps, even now, by the violence Zanj could unleash when she wanted. Maybe it looked even more impressive if you had some connection to the Cloud.

If you had a soul.

Either way, Viv ran. The battlefield around her, over her, was very bright and loud and hot. She wasn't worried for Zanj—she was worried for herself. The pirate queen, she was coming to realize, was a lot more likely to survive whatever the Pride could bring to bear than Viv was to survive as a bystander to their engagement.

Zanj was in the sky, tearing off a hate fractal's wing, only to dive down and use that wing as a scythe to carve through Pride drones by the score. Zanj sprinted so fast she left smoking glass footprints behind her in the dirt. A bolo snagged Zanj's legs and she went down beneath a pile of drones, only to snap the bolo's nanotube wire and fight her way back up, cackling mad and dripping oil from her fangs.

All of which made problems for Viv and for the rest. Molten metal sprayed across their path; a panicked fléchette cannon stitched crystal shards through the air before her, then behind her, then swiveled around to—almost—tag Zanj before the woman reached it and tore it free of its mount.

The Pridemother's bay doors cycled open overhead, fractal leaves revealing passages into the fire of its belly, from which more drones and fighters fell. Zanj climbed into the air to meet them; tossed one fighter down, and it shattered.

By chance, by luck, by sheer style, Viv reached the ramp. Hong, too. And Gray.

Christ—where was Xiara? Searching the field she saw drones drones drones and—*there*. Not all the drones' attention had been drawn to Zanj— of course the Pridemother's battlemind had its own autonomic nervous system, perhaps even subconscious, scratching little tactical itches without realizing, adjusting posture, breathing.

Maintaining area control.

A Kentaur must have snatched Xiara, but she got her rifle around in time, and took shelter behind its corpse while three more closed in: firing wildly while the drones zagged and zigged, pressed themselves flat, scuttled sideways to avoid her. She was a warrior, but she was freaking out. She had seen Zanj fight the Chief, but she had never seen anything like this before.

So Viv ran back for her.

Yes, there were tactical considerations. They needed a pilot. But as she ran into hell again, it occurred to her that she was justifying her choice after the fact. As, perhaps, were Hong, and Gray, who, she realized once she grabbed the first Kentaur by the tail, had followed her onto the battlefield— Hong with his clubs out, Gray bounding on all fours, his skin quicksilver, his teeth large and white.

Idiots, all of them.

Viv's earlier Pride drone wrestling experience had involved an already-battered individual; this one was, basically, whole, and its tail flipped her over its head as it struck; she landed hard, head ringing, by spearlike feet that would have skewered her if Xiara had not just then shot it in the face.

A cluster of ships exploded in the sky, wreathing Zanj in flame. Zanj, Viv noted dimly, was a great deal larger than she had been, and still growing.

Hong broke two of his drone's legs; Gray roared, pounced, distended his jaw, and swallowed his Kentaur whole. His mouth was full of silver knives, of whirling dust, and his teeth ground sparks as they chewed. The drone gave a modem scream as it died, and Gray belched fire and collapsed, grinning contentment. The grotesque dimensions of his mouth settled back to the normal three, but his belly waggled, swollen with Pride.

Xiara offered Viv a hand up, which she accepted, breathing hard. She should have been too scared to look this happy. They ran, Gray waddling behind them, dragging a trench with his rapidly shrinking belly. His skin steamed as his body's disassemblers digested the drone, and with each step he gained speed, though he didn't lose his stupid, overfull smile.

They made the ramp with all interested parties this time; Viv collapsed against the wall, panting, the only one out of breath. Gray looked around, dreamy: "What a museum piece! How does it even run? Some sort of, what, a primitive description engine? Or do you just throw atomic bombs out the back and hope for the best?"

"This way," said Hong, and led him down.

The ramp slammed shut, but even the *Question*'s skin could not close out the roar and blast of battle outside. Xiara stared around in what Viv hoped was wonder, not shock—there would be time for shock after they survived. "I'm sorry," she said as she pulled her after her past the dinner table, up the stairs. "I'm sorry, I didn't realize we'd left you, I thought you were with us."

"You came back."

And then they found the cockpit.

Flame and fire lit the outside world, and Pride wreckage rained down hot and jagged to tear the earth. Chaos whirled in the sky. Viv saw all that; Xiara had eyes only for the instrument panel.

She sat. She traced switches, lights, displays with her fingertips, her mouth open soft, her eyes watery wide. There was reverence in her touch. Viv had prayed before, but she had never *needed* to pray, had never been faced with a situation so overwhelmingly out of her control there was no proper response but prayer. Watching Xiara, she learned what that would look like from the outside.

"Can you fly it?"

There followed as much of a silence as could follow, with the war outside, with Hong shouting at Gray from the engine room, and Viv thought, she's frozen. She can't do it. We'll need a new plan. What tools do we have, what options—I could call Zanj—

Xiara set her hand on Viv's, and her touch was warm. Metal threads moved beneath her skin, and her eyes were whirlpools of shifting silver, and she was smiling. "Yes."

She slid one hand into the brass-knuckles control; her other, she placed palm down on the instrument panel. Viv was struck by silent thunder—a soundless single pulse through the chest. The panel woke. There was no other word for it. Bright lines of circuitry threaded from Xiara's touch into the ship. The quicksilver spirals in her open eyes formed interlocking, turning rings that ground like gears. The blue lines Viv had taken for tattoos spread silver light across her flesh.

When Xiara breathed, the engines came to life.

This was not how Zanj had flown the ship—but Zanj was a pirate and a fighter. The people of Orn had built themselves to fly.

On the battlefield below, Pride drones retreated from the palace grove, pursued by Ornclan armed and armored, and by the Chief herself clad in the brilliance of her office. Perhaps that armor made the Chief's senses sharp, perhaps she sensed something through the Cloud. Perhaps intuition, or else mere random chance, guided her gaze to the ship, to the cockpit, to her daughter staring back at her, conscious all at once and at last of what she was about to leave behind.

Far overhead, Zanj blew something up.

Xiara lifted them, and brushed them through the sky, smooth, swift, and sure. They gained speed, height; hate fractals cut after but slow, too slow. The sky gloved them in fire, and they slipped free—into space, first, and silence, and then with a sickening lurch into the Cloud.

Xiara's eyes blushed blue. She took a slow, shuddering breath.

"Are you okay?" It was a dumb question to ask, but Viv didn't know a better one.

Her cheeks were wet with joy.

"I'm home."

22

THEY ESCAPED.

Viv whooped, slapped Xiara on the back. "You did it!" In the wash of adrenaline and relief she realized just how much doubt had filled her, sliding like sand through cracks in her confidence. Now that sand streamed away, and all the force she'd mustered to drive her through the fear and the battle thrust her forward and she realized she had her arms around Xiara and she wanted to kiss her.

But Xiara was driving. Her muscles were rigid. Wheels turned in her dilated eyes and air hissed through those full lips, too regular for normal human breathing. She was in the ship.

Born pilots, Zanj had said.

"Are you still there?" Viv asked, and at first Xiara didn't seem to have heard her. Her tongue tip peeked between her teeth, and disappeared.

Her voice came like voices came from deep wells in dreams. "Yes," she said first, the sounds drawn out. "I've just . . . I've never felt the Cloud before. Not like this. Through the veins, the harp strings, the depth. I can hear my grandmothers." She blinked slowly, to clear the water welling in her eyes.

"You can stop," she said. "If you want. We're safe." She didn't know that, but it seemed likely. "Zanj will come back soon, and she can fly."

"No." Xiara's certainty shone through the piloting trance. "This is right." The control panel lights, Viv realized, blinked in time with Xiara's breath. Others kept the beat of her pulse. The Cloud unfurled before them, and Xiara's tears had nothing to do with sorrow. "Go," she said, soft and sure and full of wonder. "Check on the others. I'm fine."

Viv drifted, dazed, from the cockpit. Hong, bouncing, triumphant, caught her and hugged her in the hall. At first she looked at him like he had grown a second head, but his smile was open and unforced and bright with their survival. Viv relaxed. They'd made it out under their own power and under her direction. Together. Her crew. "Where's Gray?"

Gone, it seemed at first.

The engine room was not so much a single room as the whole of the ship that wasn't given over to living space, a jungle of pipes and circuitry not so different from the tech she knew. When she climbed down the ladder, she found engines thrumming and ticking and gurgling and humming, and Gray himself nowhere. A blue ring on the floor pulsed softly a little faster than her heartbeat. She wondered if it served a purpose, other than reassuring passengers the great machines functioned. But she did not see Gray, so she called his name, feeling the first creep of panic, until she noticed the air's slight bright frostlike sparkle. She grimaced. "You better not be in my lungs."

A gust of him tickled back up her throat, out past her teeth. "You didn't even notice me," he complained from all around her at once. "I'm subtle, and don't metabolize. It's not like I'd stay in there forever."

"It's gross. And I like to look people in the eye when I talk to them."

He manifested two eyeballs in the air before her, just the eyeballs without a skull, and rolled them. "Is this better?"

"I was coming down to thank you." Though now she was thinking better of it.

"Don't, yet. I've done what I can, but we'll need more fuel soon."

"You can't just, you know." She waved her hand imprecisely. "Make more?"

The air blushed peevish orange, then turned clear again. "I need matter to eat, and to convert. Unless you'll give me some of the ship?" She must have frowned, or her heart sped up, because he laughed.

"Troll," she said.

"We'll find more fuel." Zanj sidled back into three-space in the hold above the engine room as if she'd been there the whole time, slapping nonexistent dust off her palms while Viv and the floating eyeballs stared up at her in shock. "I ditched the Pridemother in a black hole cluster. Don't everyone applaud all at once." She sounded sated, smelled of smoke, and leaned back against the wall, cool as cool. "Anything else you'd like, Your Majesty? Foot massage?"

Viv didn't remember climbing that ladder—just the jump of her heart, the excited blur up, arms spread to embrace Zanj before she realized they'd so rarely touched before. She smiled, broad and open and foolishly happy and she didn't even mind. "You're back!"

Zanj buffed her claws on her jumpsuit. "Did you really think one Pride-mother could take me out?" She shook her head, tsk tsk, tongue against teeth, poor form, bad play, an aunt critiquing her niece at majiang.

"Never," she said, and realized she was being honest. Zanj, eyes on her nails, grinned—sly and small and real. How would it feel, Viv wondered, to be Zanj? To have such power and be so constrained, for so long? You would start to doubt yourself—to worry your comrades would look at you and see a failure. What would such a person need to hear? Viv, startled, found she cared. "I never thought you'd lose. Only that you might not come back."

"You would have called me if I didn't."

"No."

Zanj looked at her sidelong, with a gaze Viv could not yet understand. "Getting you home will spit in the Empress's eye. That means more to me than stars. Don't worry, Viv. I'm not going anywhere."

VIV HAD EXPECTED Zanj would take the conn again when—if—she came back, but Zanj took one look at Xiara's grip on the controls and stepped away, hands raised. "I can't argue with true love. I told you: there's no pilot like a pilot of Orn."

Rapt in union with the ship, Xiara flew without pause for a day and a night. She flipped switches by hand when she wanted; they flipped themselves when she asked. She charted their course, adjusted bearings, whispered of engines and thrust, looked into the Cloud and through swelling chaos to their path.

No one knew what to do with her.

The Ornclan had loaded the ship's larder with food—some salted meats Viv did not recognize, but which tasted vaguely like ham, and vegetables in a wider range of colors and contortions than she remembered from supermarkets back home, but which, when tasted, fit more or less familiar categories: tubers, alliums, herbs, squash. A taste of raw pepper–adjacent purple apple-fleshed thing made her knees weak. Viv hadn't realized how much she'd dreaded returning to nutrient paste. She cooked. She cooked! Nothing fancy, sautéed vegetables with a dash of meat in a rich nutty oil, served on that pillowy Ornish flatbread. She'd been years out of practice at a stove even before she woke up here, but still, working the pan and knives, she felt almost home.

But when she took a plate to the cockpit, Xiara shook her head, her eyes still fixed on the Cloud Viv could not watch without feeling sick.

"Different pilots take it differently," Zanj said. "Give her time." And they did, bandaging wounds, cleaning, fixing, with Zanj's guidance, what systems the ship's own maintenance bots could not. Viv tried to meditate with Hong, but bored fast; tried to work out with him, and tired faster. They left Xiara merged with the controls, peering through spacelanes as she stitched them into the Cloud and out. Her union with the ship seemed so pure, so deep, Viv felt guilty watching.

But when Viv woke halfway through the second night to a steady ship, its singing engines quiet, and padded into the hall—she'd grown used to bare feet aboard ship—she found Xiara slumped in her chair, hands off the controls, staring hollowly at the void beyond the cockpit. She trembled. Her eyes were metal wheels still, but red, too, worn by starlight.

"Hey," Viv said without result.

She'd seen this before. She'd been here before—not with ships and cybernetics, but with code first, then with business plans and meetings and all that accumulating damn work, her mind so stuck in ideas she couldn't work back into her meat. For years she'd been that person, wired in, and she'd bent a world to her will. Who needed bodies, anyway?

Everyone, it turned out.

She fetched a blanket from the closet, and a cup from the canteen, and heated some of that not-quite-tea Zanj made from leaves that smelled like chocolate and cedar, and colored the water pink. She draped the blanket over Xiara's shoulders, set the tea beside her hand. Xiara came back slowly: her pupils dilated, then shrank to pinpricks, settled in a middle, and the parts of her eyes that should have been white were. The bright circuit lines faded from her skin, her black veins ran blue-red once more. She shivered all through her body, and took a deep wet heavy breath. Viv held her close, rubbed her arms—her body was so cold. "Hey."

"Hey."

"I was far away." Her voice cracked; she tried to raise the tea, and it slipped. Viv brought it to her mouth instead, soft, settling the cup against Xiara's lower lip; Xiara did not sip the tea so much as suck it down.

"You need rest."

"I could go forever. I could live there. In the ship."

It occurred to Viv, then, that she'd not asked before interrupting—just assumed. She wanted, so badly, to say, *I don't want you to*, but what she said instead was: "I can put you back, if you want."

Xiara caught Viv's wrist before she could draw away, her grip cold and mechanical at first as if she'd forgotten how bodies worked, how they could be soft or gentle. Viv gasped, tensed, too, stared into inhuman eyes. But the eyes melted as the grip on her wrist warmed, and Xiara remained. She guided Viv's hand to her neck, her cheek. "No."

Viv helped her back to the cabins. Xiara's legs steadied as they walked, and her hand sought the wall; she leaned on Viv less as she recovered, then leaned against her more. At the door to the room they'd made up for her, Xiara stopped and her shoulders shook. Crying, Viv thought at first, uncomfortable, and debated how to respond, rifling through her experience of mother and girlfriends and finding little that would help—but then Xiara found her voice, and the first peal of laughter rang through the hall.

Viv was thoroughly confused.

"What's so funny?"

"I did it!" She couldn't stop laughing, doubled over, dragging in huge heaves of breath. "The first Ornclan in centuries offworld. I didn't expect it to feel so good. We didn't lose the stars at all. They've been up here waiting for us this whole time." Her face was raw with wonder. "There are muscles singing I didn't know I had. I never want this to end. I was scared at first, scared my body wouldn't be here when I found my way back, but here I am, and here you are, and I *did* it, and I want to kiss you." She blanched when she realized what she'd said, opened her mouth wide as if she could snatch the words and swallow them back down. Before Viv could speak, she rushed on, torrential: "I'm sorry, I mean, everything feels so full and sharp and hot when I'm not in the ship, and home's far away and I don't know when I'm going back or if and I don't want to be alone tonight, and I scared you, didn't I, I'm a fool, I don't know how this goes where you come from—"

"About like that," Viv said, and leaned in.

She needed this, too. Not wanted it, though, god, yes, that as well, but needed: the more or less familiar feeling as Xiara crashed into her hungry and they tumbled through the door into her cabin, as Viv pressed her against the wall, as she spun around and pressed Viv there in turn, Xiara's cool fingers exploring her waistband, her pants sliding free, Viv's teeth on the curve of Xiara's neck, and then they were bodies naked in a sparely furnished room that could have been any sparely furnished room in any age in any galaxy. This she needed most of all, the tension, the curl, the strain and stress and susurrus of breath to build, and build, and ease into calm: a meat feeling, a meet feeling. And she'd thought cooking felt good! She knew so little in this time, but she knew her body; she knew how to play with a lover. Knew how to devour and tease, and let herself be caught, pressed, teased herself, how to rock and hold and breathe. The sudden pressure of a thigh or knee as weight shifted, the slide of breasts over her belly—and, after, as they drowsed, with her arm under Xiara's neck, her fingers growing numb— it felt like home.

We never lost the stars.

They lingered in the aftersilence, and after a while she said to the ceiling as much as to Xiara: "So, what is this?"

Xiara answered with a hum.

"It was great, I mean, it is great. But I'm alone here, and you're alone, and we're both obviously, you know, reaching for something, we barely know each other, and I don't have any problem with that, but I don't want to make this anything, um, you're not ready for." For all the times she'd had this conversation, each time it rose again she stumbled, as if she were nineteen again, younger. As if she were following Susan Cho through the dinosaurs. You didn't grow past the old things, just enclosed them like rings in a tree, so someone feeling the bark of you could suss out your old scars. "I liked this. I'm just wondering, you know. What you think."

Beside her, Xiara mewed, and shifted, and began softly, undeniably, to snore.

IN THE CLOUD the dead tumble aimlessly, and the living travel fast.

They made good time. Xiara skimmed them through the Cloud at will, crossed star systems in hours, slid back to normal space to take bearings, or to recover, or whenever Zanj told her they were near a good view. Black hole accretion discs and plasma fountains burned in the depths, and nebulas, though not so rich as false-color telescope pictures led Viv to believe back home, still glistened and refracted starlight, shaping ghosts in space.

The nebulas just looked like ghosts, of course, but real ghosts lingered in the Cloud. Viv, by now, could sometimes bear to sit in the cockpit and stare out into the chaos of colors and watch immense bodies form, merge, split, birth lesser shapes that rippled and divided and birthed themselves again. When she was a kid, she loved those pictures in magazines that looked like static, but that, if you fuzzed your eyes just right, gained depth and form.

This reminded her of that: sense from nonsense, the vertigo of a reality unlike your own.

She no longer feared the dead, or the gods they became.

Still, she did not sleep in the Cloud. Or much outside of the Cloud: Xiara, drunk on pilot's euphoria, came to her eager—she told new tales each night, poems almost, trying to describe what she'd seen, felt, done in the Cloud or through the ship, groping with a huntress's vocabulary to describe *n*-dimensional hyperspace topology. "You're just using me for an audience," Viv teased one night: "Nobody else will—*oh*—sit still long enough to listen to you."

"You're not sitting still. And you're free to ask me to stop, anytime you like." An eyebrow raised, a turn of head, a press of the hand, and Viv had better things to do with her breath than answer.

When their fuel supply ran low, Zanj guided them to ruins: to husks of hollowed world orbiting listless swollen stars, to webs of glass the size of moons, to docks built to serve the shattered fleets that drifted in space around them. Hong offered his own suggestions after one too many of Zanj's leads turned out to have been picked clean eons since, and at his guidance they found a depot floating between layers of a gas giant, and stopped at a double-cupped crystal chalice several hundred miles on a side that emitted streams of high-energy particles. Twice they had to hide from a Pride fleet devouring an immense corpse which might have been machine or meat.

They made good time, yes—but still Zanj's brow darkened, she paced, she frowned. Finally, as the four of them, clad in suitfields, worked to free a large lumpy ferrocrystalline beast from a trap the Empress had left to guard a matter fountain near a spinning star, Viv asked Zanj what was wrong.

"We're not going fast enough." The great beast was trapped in a net of light. Its herd milled several astronomical units away, grazing on asteroids and lowing plaintively in Cloudband (or so Zanj claimed, though Viv found it hard to imagine anything that large sounding plaintive). The net's strands rewove as fast as Zanj could snap them, but she claimed she'd found the critical nodes in the network, and directed Gray and Hong to overload them all at once.

Viv, still blissing out on the notion of a spacewalk, didn't respond at first. Xiara's voice came through her suitfield crystal clear: *We're going as fast as the ship can.*

"Down and to the right." Zanj pointed.

Grayteeth said, "Sure thing, boss," sprouted several extra legs, scuttled over the beast's skin, leaping over the shifting strands of net.

Zanj continued: "I know we're going fast. But we're losing time. The Empress moves with all her power, and we're stuck with this antique."

"Which is why," Hong said, strain evident in his voice as he gripped the struggling node he'd caught, "we should go to the 'faith. We have newer ships, reclaimed Imperial technology. We can catch Her."

Zanj's laugh was short and heavy with scorn. "We don't need to lose even more time to get ships that won't keep pace either. Only one ship can catch the Empress when she doesn't want herself caught—and that one's mine."

"Isn't the *Question* your ship?" Beneath Viv, the beast bucked, twisted, a convulsing landscape; her suit rendered its static roar as a bass pulse in her chest too low for human hearing. Plasma played about its mouth. As it thrashed, the net tightened, cracking plates of rocky armor to vent Cherenkov blue into space. Viv jetted in and laid a hand on its shell. "Hey. Come on. We're almost there."

Maybe it heard her. Maybe it was just tired. Either way, it stilled; Zanj shouted, "Now!" and struck, and so did Gray and Hong, and the net stopped shifting. Viv slid her hand beneath the net's strands and pulled, and they unraveled all at once. The beast trumpeted joy; in the asteroid field, its fellows turned, grunted, and neared, blueshifting toward them with joyful speed; Gray could only half fill the ship before the beasts demolished the matter siphon in their enthusiasm.

"This was *one* of my ships," Zanj said as they watched the cataclysmic celebration from a safe distance, through telescopic lenses. "My first. The one I rode away from Pasquarai. I'm talking about the ship I used to fight her. We need to find the Fallen Star."

23

FERAL GODS PINNED them down inside a mindforge.

Viv had assumed the forge, a metal cocoon around a white dwarf star, was an old Imperial stronghold, because she hadn't yet met anyone save the Empress who built to such scale, but Hong corrected her. Nobody knew whether the Kaeolith had left the galaxy, or had fallen to the Empress or the Bleed, or had ascended to some other universe, but they had been their own force, spinning diamond webs that rewove stars to strange shapes: dense twists of matte black, inscrutable and mighty beyond all reason, that roamed through the cosmos, uplifting some civilizations, breaking others. When the Kaeolith left, or were killed, or killed themselves, or shrank or grew until they could no longer be seen, the mindforges remained, efficient systems later civilizations used for juicing stars. Visiting one to refuel had been a great idea—which meant others had had the same idea centuries ago, small opportunistic gods descending from the endless simulated dreamlands of the Cloud in search of perverse satisfaction on the material plane.

In silent centuries, the gods had drunk deep of the mindforge's fountain and, swelling, split, and split again into legions of copies, only to wage eternal war against their duplicate selves, their hatred for each other only balanced by the ravenous hunger they directed against interlopers.

The gods could disguise themselves as shadow, as color. They must have lurked behind the *Question*'s crew as they wandered deeper and deeper in, toward the heart of the forge, a vast chamber in which filaments finer than human hairs shielded a loop of plasma drawn from the heart of the star.

Then the gods locked the doors, and sprang.

The gods hadn't planned for Gray, or Zanj.

Still, though each small god fell in seconds, they numbered in the thousands. Gray spun a diamond shell to cover Viv and Hong while he and Zanj switched off between fighting and harvesting the stellar fountain.

And, while they recovered, Viv asked them about the Fallen Star.

"Oh, that story!" Gray stuck his hands into the plasma loop, drew them out cupped around golden fire, and drank the star; he glowed as he swallowed its light, and then, when he could fill himself no more, collapsed and belched and rolled, sweating diamond drops that clunked against the floor when they fell. "It's a good story, at least the way my great-great-great-aunt tells it. Zanj wouldn't like it if I told you, though." Ruby eyes twinkled. "So of course I will.

"The story goes that young Zanj, barely fledged, just immortal, visited her neighbors, the Serpentine of galactic north. They were ancient, scarred veterans of Bleed war. The Serpentine hold no thing private, not even their names; since they hold nothing, nothing can be stolen from them. Zanj came to ask them for a weapon to defend her people. They brought her to their treasure chambers, where hung the jewels and revelations of millions of minds over a hundred thousand years, all in common, and one by one they showed her their gravest tools: hammers to break cities, swords to cut planets, dust to eat all things. One by one she hefted them, tested them, and asked if they had something bigger.

"Serpentine hospitality demanded they satisfy her, so they drew her deeper and deeper into the caverns of their collective mind. They offered her color bombs, bows arched with superstring. Each time she said, no, not yet. Until they led her to the heart of their temple-minds: to the heart of their being, a galactic core compressed to hyperdense computational matter—the foundation of their empire and war effort, the engine that bound their society together, and kept each Serpentine itself. The only thing they would not freely give their guests. And she stole it. Can you imagine?"

Sated, he parted their diamond shell, grew forty feet tall and covered in scales, whooped a challenge, and marched into the roil of the gods.

"That," Hong said beside her, "is not the version we tell."

Viv turned her back to the battle: Gray was busily devouring godlings, gnashing teeth, heedless of his own exposed flank. "You've heard this story?"

"A piece of it. Zanj offered to help the Serpentine against the Bleed, to cut them off from the galactic core once and forever. They trusted her with the Fallen Star, but the Serpentine fell to the Empress before she could reach the battlefield. Later, she turned the Star against the Empress, and fell herself. That is the truth of the 'faith, which our archivists mill and smelt in their meditations."

There was a flash, blinding even through their polarized shell, and Zanj arced out of the god-ruckus, struck the ground, bounced, cracked the floor, skidded, scrambled into shelter. Her eyes were their normal red again, and she panted for breath, her whole body quivering. "Don't listen to them," she said when she could draw breath to speak. "However I came by the Star, it was mine: no one else could use it but me. It existed before the Serpentine, before the Empress. Maybe it was left over from another universe before ours. Maybe the Bleed made it. It had no fixed form, and each attempt to wield it in battle failed gloriously as it slipped from the wielder's control. It was not so much treasured as imprisoned. And when I took it up, no one could take it from me until the Empress tricked it from my hand."

"Tricked?"

"The Suicide Queens lured her into battle, but we didn't realize until too late that she'd set a trap of her own: she cut us off from the Cloud so we could not flee, and drew the Bleed. They ate us; they slid into the minds of our ships and poisoned us from within. Our greatest weapon against the Empress was the *Groundswell*, a ship the size of worlds, built around the strange matter of a Bleed corpse, and the Bleed invaded and animated it against us. I killed it with the Fallen Star, but the Empress had planned for that, too. She wrapped the Star in a chain with her own seal, so it could not return to me.

"I fled that battle, but the Empress caught me. Without the Star, I didn't stand a chance. I couldn't outthink her; I couldn't fight for longer than a few minutes at a time. Speaking of which. I'm charged again." She turned on Viv a radiant fierce grin that made her story seem impossible. How could Zanj have ever been imprisoned? How ever outfought?

There came that fierce pop inside her skull, and Zanj's eyes burned white. She kipped to her feet, unsheathed her claws. "We're only a few skips from where I lost the Star. Get it, and we'll catch the Empress. But first, I have to beat up some godlings. I'll be right back."

In the end, it was Viv who noticed that the godlings drew their strength from the mindforge itself, their shattered dust bodies drifting back across the floor to the plasma fountain, where they took strength and gained shape to launch themselves once more into the fray. And it was Hong who guided her through the battle, over gods' bodies, to a control panel. Viv tried to use it, to no avail; Hong offered to try, touched the panel, and his hands sank into it up to his crystal bracelets; he glowed static snow, face set in meditation, features calm save for the sweat that rolled down his forehead, and the trembling tension of his arms. The star-siphon's filaments realigned; the plasma column lost cohesion, and would have boiled them away had not a fail-safe cut in to shut the siphon down.

Viv caught Hong as he fell, his hands dripping crystal, his eyes twitching. When Zanj and Gray finished with the gods, Hong had recovered enough to walk, which was good, since the mindforge relied on the siphon to hold its ancient architecture together, and its monomolecule skin was unraveling. Gray gathered a fistful of god-dust to munch on the run. They had to dive out a porthole into hard vacuum for a few seconds before Xiara caught them; Viv's robe flowed to cover her completely, then released her when she tumbled once more into the ship. The hatch snapped shut, and Xiara burned hard for the Cloud. "Come on!" Zanj pulled Viv to her feet, dragged her to a porthole. "You have to see this."

Behind them, the mindforge collapsed, and took the star with it.

UNCERTAIN, VIV SOUGHT advice.

She found Hong dancing through the engine room. Eyes half shut, half open, each step and turn precise, he trailed his fingers over pipes, down couplings. He did not squeeze his body into the tight spaces through which he passed. He held himself so he did not need to squeeze. She waited for him to stop, but he spoke to her first, without breaking stride. She was so surprised she jumped. "Please, speak. It is good practice for me to speak without attachment as I move."

"What are you doing?"

"Learning the ship."

When he said that, she understood: his movements followed the course of fluid through the pipes, his fingers pointed toward status indicators as their colors switched. "You're making that happen?"

"No," he said. "Xiara is. We study machines, and train our mind to mirror them. This ship holds many systems: Cloud engines interlace with crude chemical and subspace drives. We learn systems so we may learn our selves. A mind is as complex as a mindforge—but subtler; so subtle most beings cannot comprehend even their simplest thought in its entirety. We study so that when we are thrust against the limits of our own minds, we can break ourselves."

"Why would we—sorry, why would you want that?"

"Ancient sages have written: what you cannot break, you do not own."

She recognized that line, handed down however many millennia. She'd never thought of it like that before: the mind as a computer, sure, she'd lost track of the number of times some reporter made *that* analogy, but the self as a proprietary system, what would that imply? Your desires, your thoughts no more your own than a system's preprogrammed behavior belonged to it? But if your thoughts weren't you, what was? Or was that even the right question? Her head hurt; she retreated to her own exhaustion, to the bruise on her hip, to the chill ozone-tinted air and the calm motion of his body. "So, you study machines. Is that how you knew how to break the mind-forge?"

"I have only traced small relics of the Kaeolith before. I have never touched something so immense. I damaged it, and killed a star. I have taken something glorious from the world."

"It was trying to kill us."

He did not interrupt his dance to shrug, but she got the gist.

"Zanj wants to go after the Fallen Star. I don't even know if it's a ship, or a mind, or a weapon, or a computer, or what."

"All these terms," he said, "are, at sufficient stages of mastery, indistinguishable from one another, as a strike from a block from a counter."

"What do you think?"

"I think we should go to the 'faith."

"They tried to kill us."

He spun in place, slowly, balanced on one foot. "We still don't know why Zanj came back to Orn. Why she stopped trying to kill us. We don't know whose side she is on. She scares me. I know she would only smile if she heard me say this. The 'faith may hinder us; the Grand Rector may oppose us. But if they do, their actions will be obvious. Zanj is subtle."

"And you're sure this isn't just you wanting to go home."

He spread his arms and extended one leg in a slow, slow kick, level with his eyes.

"You are pushing us far, and fast," he said. "We have seen marvel after marvel. But we do not share what we have seen. I do want to go home: to commune with my sisters and brothers, to seek answers, to meditate. To change things. You want to leave us altogether."

"I have to go home, too. And anyway, don't you want me out of your hair?"

She said that mostly to offer an opening for him to joke about not having any hair to speak of. But he remained balanced for a long time, eyes distant.

Then the ship lurched out of the Cloud, and he settled to a new posture. "I like you," he said. "So does Zanj. But on this all tales agree: Zanj will sacrifice what she likes to get what she wants."

She tried to sleep, but often failed. When she closed her eyes she saw the Empress, saw Zanj's face in those first moments of waking, her murderous fury, and then her despair. She remembered Zanj in joyous battle and her sly, unfeigned smile when she felt strong. Viv liked her; she loved her, almost, in a way. She wanted her happy. And Zanj had promised, again and again, to kill her.

Viv walked unsteadily through the ship to the cockpit, where she found Xiara dozing in the pilot's chair. Indicator lights swelled and faded with her breath; Xiara's eyes opened easily as Viv watched her, and she yawned. She could yawn now, even while merged with the ship. She had learned to be almost human. "You should be asleep."

"So should you." Viv gave her a peck on the forehead, and leaned away. Xiara reached for her, not hungry, just stretching. Her fingers grazed her belly.

"I'm learning to sleep in the ship," she said. "It talks to me in dreams."

"Doesn't that scare you? It would scare me."

"This is a small ship," she said. "Crude. I can't fit all the way inside it, even dreaming. The body's always here for me to come back to. If I tried to fly something bigger—I don't know what would happen. That's what scares me." She stretched her shoulders until they popped, and looked out into the twists of deep space, smiled at something Viv could not see but the ship's sensors could. "I was thinking about the beast you rescued, the big rock thing in the net. Maybe they were made, maybe they made themselves, but it makes me wonder, what would the pilots of Orn have been like, back before the city fell? Were we ships dreaming we were people, or the other way around?"

Viv caught her hand, laced their fingers together, and with her other hand followed the swell of Xiara's forearm up to her shoulder, her cheek. "I know which I'd rather."

"You wouldn't like me as a ship? You'd be so cute and small, running around inside me. That might be fun." She tightened her grip on Viv's hand, using some of that strength she loved, the weight of a body trained to battle and hard work.

Usually, that strength made Viv melt—she liked that she couldn't hurt Xiara, couldn't break her no matter how she bucked. But the way Xiara spoke just then reminded her of the Empress, through whose ruins she'd spent the last weeks crawling, the Empress who'd torn her from her home and called her here and cast her aside as if she didn't matter.

Viv stilled, and stared out into the stars, into space, into the carbon nanotube ribbons, miles across but hair-thin at this distance, that linked the planets in the system where they'd stopped. Some long-gone mad sculptor had shaped the star at its heart into an enormous glowing three-eyed face. She realized Xiara was looking at her, realized her hand on the back of Xiara's neck had tensed into a fist, that her nails were digging into her own palm. Her chest and skin felt tight. "I'm sorry."

"I can hear her out there," Xiara said. The wheels in her eyes meshed and whirled. "The Empress. At first I couldn't, but I've been studying how Zanj listens, how she looks. The Empress doesn't move through space or through the Cloud like other people. She sings, and they move around her. I can even hear her Citadel, a great silent eddy, like the ripple a sunken rock makes on the surface of a river."

"Can we catch her?"

"In this ship?" Her eyes and the set of her mouth said no better than her voice ever could.

"I wish I could trust her," Viv said, meaning Zanj. "She almost killed you. She's helped us since. I like her. But I don't know what she's planning. I don't know why she came back."

"Have you tried asking?" Xiara's hand escaped Viv's, and drifted around Viv's ribs, sank to the curve of her hip. Viv wanted it to sink farther. She wanted to set concern aside, to drown in her body. She remembered Hong: *What you cannot break, you do not own.*

"Do you want to stay here?" Viv asked, meaning in the cockpit, but also meaning connected to the ship.

"Do you mind?"

"Are we playing the question game?"

She laughed at that, made a face. "You're weird."

"You lose." But she kissed her, and tasted lightning on her breath. The door slid shut, and the stars watched, and for a hungry moment she was gone.

24

ZANJ GREW SILENT, and Viv did not know why.

Sure, with each passing day they fell farther behind the Empress. But by all rights that was Viv's problem. Every morning she looked back at the gauge in the cockpit, at the door to home closing inch by inch. That was Magda, that was her family, her friends, receding even as she strained to reach them, like a swimmer kicking down into shadowy depths to chase a ring that had slipped from her finger. From any rational angle, Zanj should be happy they were falling behind. The more desperate Viv grew, the stronger her case for the Fallen Star.

And yet.

With each ruin they passed, each broken worldmind, each silent banyan forest drifting verdant in interstellar space, its branches still, its field-blurred tree houses uninhabited save by dust that had once been flesh, with each torched archive and rusted vine-draped megalopolis, with each planet of silent staring mindless robots whose faces tracked their three suns' course through the sky like metal sunflowers, with each three-AU-broad cathedral to a vanished religion, Zanj drew further back into herself.

At first, when Viv asked what these worlds had been, Zanj would weave tales of how she once tended those trees for the Verdance, and ate the thousand-year-ripening fruit that held the slow, DNA-processed wisdom of the stargrove, or how she tricked that President into revealing the existence of extraterrestrial life, long since kept secret, to her people, how she'd stolen that doomsday weapon and used it to destroy that other. Hong chased these tales with a scholar's questions, whos and whats and hows, and Zanj answered those, too. At first. But less and less as they flew on.

Viv watched her. Not from fear, or, not only from fear. She was enough of a manager to tell the difference between a woman plotting and a woman bearing a weight. Zanj might be alien, ancient, mighty, but she was not unknowable. She guided them again and again to worlds that served their needs, to bastions, palaces, centers of industry, and again and again they found ruins there, the husks of her departed friends.

Zanj wrestled Gray in space to pass the time. Read her dirty mag. Talked with Xiara in the cockpit: "What you're calling *spoor* is more like a boat wake—have you ever sailed a boat?" After an afternoon of searching under deck plates and behind furniture she found a pack of almost-cards and tried to teach them a game a good deal like poker, which turned out to be a frustrating experience: Gray lost everything three times over; Hong never bet; Xiara played with a novice's ambition, a novice's luck, and a novice's sulk at failure; and Viv, though she lost steadily, underplayed some pot odds and overplayed others, nevertheless *almost* bluffed Zanj out on eight-six of tentacles unsuited versus an Arcana straight. When the betting came round to Zanj she went in the tank, stiller than statues, only her tail-tip twitching, yellow eyes narrow, teeth sharp, teeth bare. Then she called, and cackled triumph when Viv turned the cards over and lost the three months' worth of no chores she'd gathered from the rest. Zanj's self-satisfaction lasted days after that, but still faded.

She did not seek out Viv, and Viv did not seek her out, and it took days of this, days in which the emerald crown marched right along the progress bar, just over a month remaining—it took days, anyway, for Viv to wonder which one of them was freezing the other out. Was it really Zanj who had fallen silent, or had Viv? Which one was more alone?

They approached the last fork in the road, the decision point after which they'd have to choose between the Fallen Star and their doomed pursuit: three jumps away, two. Straight ahead, and they'd follow the Empress and lose ground day by day until she passed beyond their reach—but they'd stay on the chase. Turn off to the side and the Empress would pull farther ahead, but Zanj might find her Fallen Star, in which case they might catch her—and face the coyote question. *Well, folks, I caught her. Now what do you expect me to do with her?*

Viv would burn that bridge when she came to it.

On their final jump, they found a body dead in space. It lay three hundred miles long, the continental shelf of its face contorted in terror, rainbow blood frozen in arches and whorls, its wings golden glinting, shifting, like a sea struck slantwise by the sun.

Zanj alone did not gape. She wore a fixed, faraway expression, and if she recognized the body, she only said: "Bring us in for a landing. Please."

Up close, the frozen valleys of muscle and ridges of flesh and fat were draped in thin gray glistening filaments like pencil lead. Zanj guided them down a cleft toward one of the wounds they'd sighted from above; Gray scooped a chunk of ice and gnawed on it, pronounced it delicious louder than he'd intended. The word echoed through the thin atmosphere of the corpse.

Zanj raised a hand. The echoes died, leaving breeze over broken bone. Viv heard a scrape of falling gravel. But there was no gravel to fall.

The spiderlikes reared up from hiding behind the ridge: thick bodies and broad bladed legs, long arching fanged seahorse faces. They chittered, clattering in their hundreds, too far away for Viv's translator gimmick to resolve their sounds to words. She could not tell whether they bore weapons, whether they wore clothes—what she thought carapace might be armor, what she thought coloring might be paint or dye, what she thought weapons might be natural, or cybernetics, or some hybrid of the two, or something else. But they were big. They glimmered. They did not leap to an attack, but watched. They knew they'd caught fierce prey, but did not fear them—much.

Zanj popped a battery, but before she moved, before her eyes opened white, the immense corpse's skin bulged underfoot. Carbon filaments leapt up from beneath them, alive, snagging boots and clothes, arcing overhead to twine and fall and snare them against the frozen body. Viv squirmed, tried to rise, could not. Gray began to ooze through the net, but its weave grew dense and denser still, a microscopic mesh to block him. Zanj, growling as the spiderlikes scuttled toward them, tugged her head around, got a strand in her teeth, bit, snapped it in half. But she did not try to push her success. She stilled, her eyes distant with memory. Drugs, Viv thought at first, before Zanj grinned—and shoved her hand through the hole in the net, waved, and made a chittering, hissing sound Viv's gimmick rendered as, "I knew your mother!"

The spiderlikes freed them, and offered hugs that needed more limbs than Viv had on offer—Zanj and Gray grew four more for the purpose. *Mother*, it turned out, was an understatement—she knew the Sklisstheklathe great-great-great-*grandmères*, the Twin Ladies of Spider Nebula, who wove traps for gods and other monsters, who almost caught Zanj in their webs once, and whom she had long years later recruited to the Suicide Queens for her war against the Empress. The Spider Twins fought with her, drained suns beside her, and, upon their death, had, rather than passing on into the

Cloud, bonded and split, venting millions of tiny young out into the cosmos to grow and learn and eat, and eat themselves in turn, and so be added each to each, until the whole grew greater than any spider goddess might alone.

Old war buddies, more or less.

The Sklisstheklathe remembered Zanj; they honored her, welcomed her, cleaned off the carbon filament webs, invited her to dance and dine with them—[Just a joke, haha]—lifted Zanj and Viv and Hong and even Gray on their backs and galloped across the immense body's surface to the wound they'd mined in its side to draw refined godstuff out.

Spiders ten times the size of those who'd ambushed them spun chairs of puffy silk, and banners to honor their arrival; they played music on ringing diamond-threaded harps, clashed chittering cymbals, and laid out, to Viv's surprise, a meal: one of the largest spiders split itself to ten thousand tiny mites, swarmed over a hillside, devouring and recombining its matter into long wooden tables, fragrant dishes of stewed vegetables and spice, something like bean curd, noodles even, while Zanj and the largest spiders swapped stories. [Welcome,] they said, [welcome! Eat, eat!]

"How," Viv asked, "did you know what we eat?"

[You, we do not know,] said the spider on her shoulder. [But we see into his mind—] it pointed one foreleg toward Hong, [and we ask his belly what he wants. So simple! We could learn more if we ate him, but Zanj says no.] She'd never seen a spider look crestfallen before.

They made a circle of burning thread for the first dance: Zanj against one of the largest spiders. "Don't worry," she said before she stepped into the ring.

"Should I worry? Aren't you just dancing?"

"If one of us loses, the other eats her." She grinned, then crossed, and the dance began.

They met in the ring, Zanj grown tall and many-armed to match the Sklisstheklathe champion—and they did dance. Viv, hearing *eat,* had imagined the beat of drums, thumbs-down emperors, all sorts of gladiatorial nonsense, but this really looked like dancing: crouch to match crouch, springing only to be caught, turned, settled gently to earth. The movements arced and glittered, paired and echoed: they ached toward beauty, and Zanj, striving, stole breath from Viv's lungs, stole tears from her eyes.

She had seen Zanj move, but never like this. Yes, if either of the women failed, perhaps they might be eaten, but the aim here was not to create defeat, but to achieve victory—to prolong the glittering immortal world their dance created. Neither lost. Both won. And as the dance-drums ended, they fell laughing in each other's arms. A spider laugh sounds like music.

The party burned. Gray drank and ate and ate and drank and began a kind of sculptor's war with one of the midsize Sklissthen: it would sculpt a grotesque, goggle-eyed caricature of him from godflesh, then he'd forgo his pasty form, whirl out, and shape a glinting, bright-eyed, indescribably cute spiderling, only for the Sklisstheklathe sculptor to demolish its first carica-ture and create another, even uglier. Hong wandered with a hill-sized spi-der, talking religion in a slow, mannered voice—teaching 'faith and being taught. Viv asked their hosts about their travels, pretending to understand their tales of the Celestial Cascade and the Moirah Expanse. It wasn't all that different from faking industry knowledge to get through a meeting; hell, the wine was good, even if a spider had woven it from the flesh of a god, and she'd had worse company. Xiara shared her stomping Ornclan dances with the little spiders, who argued over how to mimic her with their many feet.

They were having so much fun, after so long, that it took Viv almost an hour to realize Zanj was gone.

She caught up with her on a hilltop near the camp. Zanj sat cross-legged, cupping a saucer of her not-quite tea, gazing down, looking lost.

"Hey," Viv said, and settled. "You did good back there."

"The party's that way," Zanj said, but she did not leave when Viv sat down.

"I've never seen you dance before. You looked happy."

Zanj glowered through the steam that rose from her saucer. The fires burned high down below. Viv did not leave, but she'd almost forgotten she'd spoken when Zanj answered. "Nobody remembers me for dancing these days. It wasn't a thing I did, out in the world. But I used to when I was a kid. What you'd think of as a kid. I danced through networks, and once I grew myself a body, I danced in mountain meadows, in the sky, on the shore." She drank tea. "I didn't know how to fight. I was smaller then. Weaker. But I miss it."

"Where was that?" Viv asked. "The place where you were born?"

She finished her tea, set the saucer facedown in front of her. "It doesn't matter. Go back to the party. They'll miss you."

Viv had done this herself to too many friends; she'd done it on Saint Kitts, that last night, before she fled. Hiding changed nothing, fixed nothing, but it could save you from dealing with the world for whole minutes at a time. "It does matter." But Zanj had no answer. "Why did you come back for me?"

Zanj leaned back on the hillside, crossed her arms to cushion her head, crossed one leg over the other, and stared up at the stars.

Viv followed her gaze. "It's funny. When I was a kid I didn't know their names, because I wasn't used to seeing them at all. I grew up in cities, and each time we ended up out in the country, it would be a different sky, different seasons, different latitude. But when I learned to sail, I learned them too. I started to love them. With a glance, I could find myself, wherever I was. They used to be a mess of light, and then one day I knew their secrets. But they're all different here." A comet passed. "Still beautiful, though."

The silence stretched, and stretched, in the cold high place, until at last it broke. "They're the same stars," Zanj said. "Most of them."

Viv waited.

"I had my own world. Pasquarai—a beautiful place. I sailed it. I learned its stars. I set out from there on that raft we're riding now. But time's passed, and I'm alone. The spiders remember me as a story of a story. And Pasquarai, my people: they're gone, too. The Empress took them away when she threw me in that star. Maybe she imprisoned them, maybe she destroyed them."

"Zanj." She'd guessed the general outline. But it was one thing to suspect, and another to hear Zanj tell the story, affectless and flat and stern, like someone telling a joke and trying not to laugh.

"The Empress," Zanj said, "is bigger now than she was. I couldn't beat her before. But I owe her a loss for everyone I failed, for everyone I could not save. If I can get you home, that'll be something I've done right."

Music drifted from the camp again: a circle of Sklisstheklathe playing, and Xiara's voice raised in song, deep and sure. Gray sprawled passed out in a heap of drunken spiders and garish schlumpy statues; Hong sat, conversing, with the hill-sized elder far from the fire.

People liked to talk about decisions as simple matters of pro and con, column A and column B, but Viv had never seen it that way. You learned everything you could about a problem; you held it all in your mind at once as pressure built, and built, until at last you broke, and acted. When the moment came, no matter how long you'd pondered or what pains you'd taken, the right words slipped from you as easy as a splinter working its way free.

"Let's find the Fallen Star."

The band played on; the strange sky shifted as the body turned beneath them. Zanj closed her eyes, and a shudder ran over her skin, from her nose through her scalp, neck, down her limbs to twitch the tip of her tail. "Thank you," she said, and nothing else for a time, so Viv wondered if she had fallen asleep. Then, eyes still closed: "You didn't dance, down there. You watched, you talked, ate and drank, but you didn't dance. Why not?"

"Not wanting to get eaten isn't enough reason?"

"They wouldn't eat you." Zanj grinned. "You don't have a soul."

"Honestly? I don't know how. Dancing was never my thing back home." Odd, that confessing she couldn't dance felt harder than deciding to go for the Star. But then, Viv had never been good at admitting there were things she couldn't do. It felt too much like weakness.

Zanj settled back, lost in thought. Viv turned to leave. Someone tapped her shoulder: Zanj, standing, starlit, hand extended. "I'll teach you."

25

TEN DAYS LATER, they slipped from the Cloud to the battlefield.

"Don't worry," Zanj had told them in the ship the night before, which just seemed perverse to Viv. "Everything we'll see died hundreds of years ago. Besides, this ship is small fry. Even if any of the fleet's weapons are still working, we won't register to them so long as Gray and I don't start showing off. These ships and their warminds were built to hunt bigger game than the *Question*."

That was the idea.

Viv had felt quite enough awe in the last few weeks. She'd planned to shrug off the battlefield, whatever it was: "Oh, is this all?" But she could not quite manage it when faced with the reality. Beside her in the cockpit, Hong prayed. Gray whistled, long and low. Xiara flew, but her hands stilled on the controls, the indicator lights flickered, even the cockpit dimmed, as if afraid the dead hulks out there would spot them.

"See?" Zanj said, self-satisfied. "Like I said. No big deal."

Imagine a gray gnat darting over a shining black field: the sky, you might think at first, perhaps, until the horse blinks, and its eyelash flicks the gnat away. Imagine a herd of horses, dying, dead. Imagine rotting elephants. Imagine the oceans of their blood.

Enormous hulks twisted about them, ancient and dead. Great shapes blocked out stars, and behind every broken ship another turned, unfurled. In the cockpit Viv saw by reflected starlight, by ghostglow from the ships themselves, by the rays of the distant weak sun. The *Question*'s running lights cast deadly rainbows upon the octopoid monstrosity beneath them— deadly, because where there were rainbows there were drops of water, or ice, and in space, particles could kill.

"I can hear them," Xiara said, her voice faraway and strange. "They came from across the galaxy and from the depths between stars, to free themselves, to fight, to kill, to feed, to tell the tale. Old Ones who survived the wreck of long-gone fallen worlds, fleets of rebel machines, pirates and soldiers and fanatics. The Suicide Queens brought them: al-Zayyd in her glory, Heyshir who sees from shadows, Old Tiger who prowled between the galactic arms, the Black Bull framed first in iron, assassins and heroes and poets and thieves, sisters, and among them, cleverest, most fierce: Zanj."

Zanj shrugged, and tried to look nonchalant—but Viv hadn't turned to her just because her name was uttered. As Xiara spoke in that ghostly voice, the wrecks through which they flew began to move. Lights flickered behind shattered windows. A metal squid-arm twitched. The cockpit speakers rendered creaks and groans of tested metal, whalesong deep. Viv caught Xiara's arm. "Hey."

"They webbed their minds to draw Her, and draw Her they did: Herself, full green galactic, mouth wide and devouring, arms spread, She sent Her servants chewing through the fleet to remake it into more of Her."

"That's us," Gray whispered; Hong, rapt, kicked him.

"Others hid in ambush, feigning death, only to wake once She joined battle. Great *Groundswell* met Her, pierced Her, drew Her blood. And She called the Diamond Fleet to break them: screaming from the depths of Her Citadel, battle calculators given razor form, densely brilliant, lances bright as stars—" As she spoke and flew through the fleet, her voice gathered weight, speed, frantic.

"Xiara." Viv tried to shake her out of her trance, but Xiara sat rigid at the controls, her eyes wheels within glistening wheels. The dead ships woke, and turned, or tried: shards of metal longer than the *Question* peeled off and spun blade-black through space.

"—and the war endured and they were inside each other modeled each other became each other and broke each other and the Bleedcameglistening-fiercethroughskywiththeiropenmouthsandmouthsandmouthsand—"

Viv caught her by the shoulders, tightened her grip until her nails cut in. Pressed their skulls together. "Come back to us."

"Viv?" As if from the bottom of a well. "They're still here, Viv. They're dead, but the dead have ghosts, and they died with their minds all tangled up, a single enormous ship in so many bodies, hungry. I can hear them—"

"Don't. Xiara, come on. Stay with us."

"—beautiful—"

Her body went slack. Her head lolled forward on her neck, breath shallow, but still the *Question* danced through the fleet around them, dead no longer, waking, pulsing with sallow ghost light. Viv shook her, and she trembled. Viv didn't know what to do, this wasn't her place, she didn't understand it, she was losing Xiara to the dead—

Zanj swore, and thrust herself between Xiara and the console, tore her hands from the controls and took over. The ship lurched—Xiara slumped from the seat, she'd gone so slack, but Viv caught her before she hit the floor. Even Zanj's firm hand on the controls felt rough and jagged after Xiara's mastery, but she guided them around the spinning metal, in toward the densest wreckage. "Gray, can you disconnect her?"

"I've been trying!"

Hong pointed. "That tentacle—"

"I see it, thanks!"

Xiara moaned, reaching for the controls, no no no, I can hear them, memory and song, and Viv hugged her harder, and tried not to be afraid. "Zanj, get us out of here. She can't take more of this."

"We're almost there."

"I don't care!"

"This is all for nothing if we don't get to the Fallen Star. And it's here, I know it is, just—"

"Zanj, those two ships—"

"I *see* them!"

Xiara elbowed Viv in the gut, clawed for the console, moaning, hungry, and Viv hugged her, felt nails bite in as the ship spun (without Xiara managing their inertia it *felt* like a spin, and she slipped, hit her head against the seat, ears ringing, stomach knotted, breath sick), as it climbed and sheered and—

"Watch out for—"

"—fucking *flying* this thing so please shut *up*—"

"—*grand and full and burst with wounds*—"

"Xiara, come back. Come on. Don't listen to them. We're here, we're alive, I'm alive, dammit, I need you, just wake up, and everything will be—"

And then it stopped.

"—okay?"

The ship stilled and so did she. In seconds, heartbeats, breaths, Xiara came back: her eyes focused, silver and full again, then blue, her face her own, its little muscles once more animated by her mind. "Viv." Her voice was raw silk but *her* voice again, not the cosmic oracle's, not the fleetmind's, just the small low human voice of a spear-carrier from Orn. "What happened? I dreamed—"

"Then stop," Zanj said, and though Viv was turned away, she could hear the frown that accompanied Zanj's words. "Weird. That shouldn't be here."

How could Viv not look?

A perfect green planetoid hung beneath them, blurred with clouds, in a globe void of wreckage, circled by dead, listing ships. Small for a planet, it was still bigger than any of the vast broken ships through which they'd flown—and grew larger as they approached.

"Um," Gray said. "Guys. I can't feel anything."

Yes, larger. She hadn't imagined that last part. Visibly larger, second by second. Which said a number of unsettling things about their speed, their vector, and their chances of survival over the next few minutes. Hong was praying again. Viv wished she had the knack.

Instead, she asked questions. "What do you mean, you can't feel anything? Gray? What's going on?"

"We're fine," Zanj said, working the controls in a way that suggested it wasn't fine at all. "It's fine." Her repetition did not reassure.

Gray sputtered. "It is not fine!"

"Don't be so dramatic. Something's cut us off from the Cloud, that's all."

"And we're going to crash."

"That," Zanj admitted, "is a bit more of a problem."

26

CRASHING TURNED OUT to be easy. Staying alive was the hard part.

Zanj cursed the controls, tugged and kicked, and in her frustration dented the instrument panel. A number of lights Viv hoped weren't important turned red. Hong gripped the back of Xiara's seat, white-knuckled, eyes wide, praying. Gray slumped to the ground, motion-sick. Zanj's lips peeled back to reveal small, sharp teeth.

Viv found their panic odd at first; then again, she had always met her own impending death, in car crash or spaceship accident or at the hands of robot monsters, with a sense of detachment, what her various shrinks called dis-association. She saw the planet approaching, taking up more than half the sky beyond the cockpit now, and felt distantly aware that this could be it, that she might, just now, after all this, be about to die. She didn't believe it. But who did?

People who grew up in a war zone, maybe—people the law tilted against, people who had more to fear from a traffic stop or an airport line than Viv. Maybe that was the difference. For her friends all this was real, the blaring alerts, the warning lights clicking on and off, all the precursors to death crushed in metal at high speed. (Could Zanj survive this kind of fall? Could Gray, ionized after a crash at orbital velocities, re-form?) For Viv, the gut-wrenching plummet, the short sharp stop, the pain of every bone in her body breaking at once, more than breaking, was a dream. It couldn't hap-pen to her—until it happened, and once it happened, she wouldn't be around to worry about it happening again.

(In the back of her mind, a panicked voice chattered a line from an old physics textbook: an ant, dropped down a mine shaft, walks away. A man breaks. A horse splashes.)

Xiara faced detachment of a different sort, and so did Zanj, and Hong and

Gray: impending death, yes, but disorientation, too, cut off from the Cloud Viv had never known how to feel. Blinded, they reeled.

But Viv was born blind.

She looked into Xiara's wide, staring eyes, and snapped her fingers before them twice until she blinked, refocused. "Xiara. Can you feel the ship?"

"It's dark." She licked her lips. Her chest rose and fell, rabbit fast. "So dark."

"But you can feel it."

She nodded.

"Great. Hong! Buddy, snap out of it." He didn't shake himself from his prayer-trance, so she shook him until he did. "You said this thing had a conventional drive, one that doesn't need the Cloud. Can you fire it up?"

"It's ancient."

"It's all we have right now."

"It's disconnected," he said. "The power plant's routed into the Cloud core, the thruster ports are sealed—"

"I'm not asking what you have to fix. I'm asking, can you fix it?"

"I need time. Acolytes. Tools."

That was a start. "Zanj!"

She growled, bent over the controls. "I'm trying to keep us not-dead here!"

"Hong needs help with the engines. Xiara can fly."

"Are we talking about the same girl? The one who was going crazy and talking to ghosts just a couple minutes ago?"

"I can do it." Xiara's shaking voice didn't exactly inspire confidence, but Viv would take it. "The fleet's gone. I can't feel them anymore. I'm fine."

"Sure. You say that now. Then you have another fit and smack us right into the ground. Gray can help Hong."

Viv grabbed Zanj's shoulder, and pulled her back from the controls. They stared at one another, breathing hard, for seconds they didn't have, while the planetoid grew. Zanj's lips curled into a snarl, and the circlet on her brow blackened, began to smoke, responding to her killing rage; her claws tensed. Viv didn't care. Ah, *there* was the hit of adrenaline, that rush of fury: Zanj was strong, and smart, and ancient, and Zanj knew the secret ways of the world, but goddammit she would listen. Viv had spent most of her adult life learning compromise, trust, how to get along with humans. She had been born knowing how to decide. You curled yourself into a fist, and bent iron with your eyes. Even if all that kept the iron in question from murdering you where you stood was a single piece of posthuman bondage gear with unknown limitations. "We need you to work on the engines. Gray has to reinforce the ship."

Gray, still sick, trembling, looked up: "It's all dark."

"This ship wasn't built to crash." She spoke to him, but it was Zanj's gaze she held, fierce, refusing to yield to the rage in the pirate queen's yellow-red eyes. "We need baffling. Restraints. Shock absorbers. We need this whole structure remade to crumple around the cockpit. If Zanj and Hong get the engines running, we might be able to slow ourselves down enough to survive landing, but it won't be gentle. Every second we spend arguing is one second less we have to figure out how to survive. Zanj and Hong, fix the engines so we can slow down. Gray, make us crash-ready. Xiara, fly. I'll coordinate. You all listen to me, and maybe we get through this. Okay?"

"Okay, boss," Gray said, and Hong said, "Yes," and so did Xiara, though she stammered three times before she managed the word. It hadn't really been a question, and even if it was, she wasn't asking them.

Zanj's nostrils flared. Her tail lashed the console.

Viv could use the crown—command her to comply. This was a life-or-death situation. Trolley problem time. Do you break one woman's will, and your own word, to save five lives? Including yours? And maybe the lives of everyone you've ever known, depending on what that Rosary bead you're chasing is, on what it contains? Do you use power when it's easy, and there, and you need it? No matter what it makes you?

"We need you," Viv said. "We need to work together. Or none of us get out of this alive."

Zanj's tail stopped lashing. Her claws uncurled. And then, in a rush of wind, she stood in the cockpit door, grinning at Hong. "Come on, kid. Let me show you how it's done."

Hong ran after her into the hold; Viv granted herself a moment's sag against the console, a moment's panic, her heart pounding, her sweat cold, her gut churning, her skin tight. Even with that crown on her head, Zanj's anger felt more real, more dangerous, than the impending crash. Of course, Viv had never crashed a spaceship before, while she'd certainly seen Zanj kill people. She had not commanded her—and the circlet hadn't hurt Zanj, much. But still she felt dirty and wrung out and not altogether brave.

There were too many sirens and emergencies, not to mention entirely too much planet coming up fast beneath them, for her to worry much about any of that now. They tumbled through the sky. Xiara groped for the controls; her eyes wheeled as she tried to focus. Fiberglass strands slipped from her fingers into the control panel. Viv marched out of the cockpit and Gray scrambled after her, eyes wide. "Boss, just so you know, I, um, I've never done anything like this before, I—"

"Do you know how?"

"There's know, right, and then there's know. I don't exactly get a second chance at this! And I don't have materials to work with, and I'm hungry—"

"Eat the ship."

"I can't eat the ship. We're inside the ship!"

"Not for much longer. Don't touch the engines or the control surfaces. The cabins, the stores, anything else you want, take it. Eat. Get us out of this." She checked herself before she asked, *Can you do it?* because a glance at him showed her what he'd answer: wide, scared beneath all that child's arrogance, every fiber of him screaming a *No!* she could not let him feel. Gray was a kid, really: raw appetite and power and no control—no, not control. Backbone.

"You can do this," she said, level, steady. She set her hands on his shoulders, which felt too slick and wet for skin, like a dolphin's. "I know you can."

Something inside him unlocked—self-confidence? Or the opposite, a sort of collapse, giving up his own sense of what he could do and what he could not. He nodded, yes ma'am, brave young soldier boy, and breathed so deep he inflated, and his not-skin fuzzed around her hands, and burst into flying motes of silver-gold dust.

"Stay out of my lungs!" she shouted as she ran back to the cockpit.

They worked, all of them, Zanj and Hong in the engine room, Gray in the hold, Xiara at the controls. Viv ran between them, used the ship intercom, tossed them suit communicators—there was so much to be done in so little time and all at once. Zanj tore open the engines (that blue ring on the engine room floor now burning red), rewired them at Hong's direction; Viv tossed Hong a skinsuit and donned her own before Zanj ripped open the bulkhead and wedged their improvised thrusters into the vacuum space. Xiara screamed when the ship's skin tore, but she kept her grip on the controls, milking spin from gyroscopes in the ship's belly to level out their course. "Are there any people down there?" Viv asked her. "Civilization? Farms? Anything at all?"

"Something on the sensors," Xiara said. "Slippery. It's all confused, I can't—"

"You're doing great. Just bring us down near whoever's there. Not on top of them, please. Just . . . near."

The hold had thickened since her last passage through, and smelled of lightning; Gray melted the ship's bulkheads and flowed them forward, wadding the cockpit in metal honeycombs; she wondered what *that* felt like if you happened to be inside the ship's mind, then glanced at Xiara's sweat-slick face, at her lip so tight-clenched between her teeth Viv worried she'd bite through, and stopped wondering. From the engine room, she heard what any office she'd ever been part of would have characterized as a vigorous discussion: "The holy texts say the oxygen mix should be—"

"Don't start with the fucking holy texts! I know how to mix fuel, you idiot priest, now just shut the hell up and flip the switch!"

She shouted: "Give us thrust!"

"Ten seconds!"

Nine. Eight. She ran back through the hold, all its once-empty space now wadded full of honeycomb. Gray was everywhere, in her eyes—but she did not taste him between her teeth, did not feel him in her throat. Fine. Fine. Five. The planetoid, swollen green, obscene, mountain ridges, clouds, closer than anything should ever be in space, too late, too late—"They're ready!" Buckling herself into the copilot's seat: "Go!"

And then—gravity. Screams—oh, that was *her*, screaming. Giants' hands pulled Viv in two directions, three. Spinning, stabilizing; thrust sounded like someone tearing a phone book in half, miked through a rock concert's worth of speakers. Thrust felt like a horse's hooves plunging into her chest. Her organs bunched up, purple spots bloomed, the ship leveled out, there was a horizon all of a sudden, space was *up* again, space slicked with flame, and they were slowing, and she tried not to think of airplane crashes, and tried not to think of strokes, of aneurysms, of thin blood vessel walls and the g-forces she was pulling—

Air thickened in her throat, in her chest, coarse, gritty steel between her teeth. She was drowning, but she could breathe. Her skin stiffened; she felt a grotesque tension in between her organs, around her fat, cushioning, and everywhere was silver and rainbows, and she was not drowning anymore.

Gray was in her lungs, and she wasn't even mad.

They tore through clouds. Hong and Zanj—were they strapped in? There hadn't been time. She called to them—her voice sounded underwater—thought she heard some answer, we're fine, but how could she hear in this?

They fell. They fell. They fell.

And then.

Silence.

More like the opposite of that—no, the converse. Think of silence, then think of everything it's not. Hot. Loud. Bright. Furious. Endless. Painful. Thick. Bursting.

Alive.

Viv blinked, and wept because she could blink, and weep. And breathe. Though not without pain.

Survival alone would have justified the first laugh that ground from her throat. She could see, which justified the second croak that followed. Beside her, in front of her, a moan: Xiara, also laughing.

There was a brightness, of sun—that didn't make sense, they were far from any sun, but there was sunlight nevertheless, drifting through the shattered viewscreen. Xiara's laugh became a moan.

"You dead?" It was the best Viv could do.

And Xiara answered: "Not yet."

She squinted against the light. Tried to raise her hand to block the improbable sun, but everything hurt. A shadow passed before her: a hand severed the straps that bound her to the chair, and she found she could breathe deeper. "Who—"

"Don't be such a baby," Zanj said. Viv blinked some large number of times before her eyes moistened and focused, and there she stood: jumpsuit torn and singed, but unmistakably alive. "Come on, Los Angeles. Walk it off."

"Glad to see. Crash. Sense of humor." She was missing a few words, but trusted Zanj would get the gist. "Hong?"

"I am mostly whole," he said, and sounded it. Mostly. "My arm is broken. But it should heal."

At least they'd have time to face that *should*. She could breathe, too, she realized, and realized when she did that she hadn't thought to check, hadn't thought to ask, whether any of them could breathe this planet's air. Stupid amateur. "Gray?" No answer. "Gray!" Struggled to her feet, unsteady, grabbing jagged metal to steady herself, Zanj in her way, holding her up.

"It's okay. It's okay, I said! He's fine—just down for the count. Puddled. Spent himself remaking the ship. And saving you."

"He was—in me—"

"You're not built for this sort of thing. No collision membranes, slow healing, calcium bones? What a mess. You'd pop in a stiff wind."

They staggered from the crash site, out of the deep trough their ship had carved through the local soil. Xiara leaned on Hong, whole, bruised, but unsteady, brain-burned; Hong bore her weight, though he winced with each step. Viv hurt all over; Zanj helped her, and carried the sloshing puddle of Gray in a waterproof sack over her shoulder.

As they crested the slope, Viv looked back.

The cockpit lay behind them, a nest of twisted metal at the end of the long glassed burn scar their crash had cut through the fields. Yes, fields, planted with rice, broken-twig green. Six-legged buffalo grazed beneath the not-quite-sun: a diffuse region of brightness overhead like the sun Viv knew when seen through clouds that were not there. The broken fleet hung massive and faint as ghosts behind the blue sky. And that was all: the *Question*, which had flown them out of High Carcereal, which brought Zanj from Pasquarai, was now a pile of metal foam burning at the bottom of a trench.

"I'm sorry," she said.

"Eh." Zanj shrugged, and the movement sloshed Gray in his bag. "We're alive. And we wouldn't be, if not for you."

"Or you. Or Hong, or Xiara. I'd be dead now if not for Gray."

"Not dead, probably. Just missing a lung or two. Those eyes probably wouldn't have made it either. They're squishy."

It hurt to laugh.

"That's the spirit. Now, come on. Time to meet the locals." But Viv knew Zanj well enough by now to spot when she was hiding pain.

They turned away—Viv turned away, at least, to meet the narrow, gray-skinned, big-eyed people in black homespun approaching them tentatively across the fields, bearing long knives, pitchforks, spades. Viv felt surprised that she could name the tools. Maybe farming was farming all over the galaxy.

That might have been reassuring, if she hadn't just torn through a few acres of these people's cultivated fields.

She stepped forward, or tried, but her legs buckled. Zanj caught her on the way down, steadied her. She waved to the aliens. That hurt too, but damn if she'd let pain stop her from waving to aliens. "Hi!" Shouting hurt her voice. Okay, what had Hong said last time? "We're, ah, pilgrims who have left the family. And we've kind of. Crashed. A bit. Do you have a spare ship, or something? A way offworld? A radio?"

The newcomers looked to one another, murmured. One stepped forward from the gathering. Viv read her as a woman; she was old, the scales around her eyes dull, her slitted pupils black and bright. She leaned on a two-tined pitchfork as she advanced, and the murmurs stilled behind her. "No," she said, her voice deep and rough around the edges, like a cello bowed wrong. "But we will help you, as well as we can. I am Yannis, and all are welcome to Refuge."

27

REFUGE: A NAME that was a promise Viv could not believe. After the crash, the chaos, the screaming, the sudden stop, she felt reluctant to uncurl. After all that, how could the world be kind?

How could a place be so damn green?

Yannis, leaning on her pitchfork, guided them down a dirt road between rice paddies to the village. Her followers surrounded them, whispering. A heavyset man with a many-plated carapace offered Hong his hoe for use as a cane, and Hong accepted. Two children pointed at Viv and laughed, so musical and light that she could not help staring at them, and when she did they stopped, wide-eyed, and ran to hide giggling behind their elders. Xiara, by Viv's side, seemed stripped of focus, gazing into the middle distance, but when the kids laughed at her, she drew back into her skin enough to stick out her tongue at them. They stuck out theirs in turn, which were triple-forked. Viv squeezed her hand—Xiara's answering grip felt weak. A child tried to catch Zanj's lashing tail, but the tail danced just out of reach. Zanj glared at every face and every thing around, looking for the hidden trick.

Workers in the fields raised their hands in greeting, and Yannis raised her pitchfork in answer. "New guests!" Some left their work, their swan-necked oxen and the six-legged almost-pigs they tended, and followed. Others remained.

So they came to Refuge: a cluster of tile-roofed cottages, streets of rolled dirt, sheltered by two high hills and the slope of a craggy mountain, watered by a river that wound down from its cloud-topped peaks. Above, far above, past the blue and past the spark that was not a sun, great ghosts of battle-ships shifted, ponderous as icebergs in a thaw.

And everywhere the green, vivid as a cut. The village smelled of growth, of manure, of warm stone. The shock—Viv thought it was shock—on villagers' faces as they left their weaving, their rest, their dumpling-making and their games of shuttlecock, to stare. Most were gray, not quite serpentine, odd-pupiled like Yannis herself; some larger, insectlike; some had flesh that seemed to melt to metal and back. They stared at Viv's crew and she stared back, both disbelieving. This place was so green, and so whole.

She turned back to the path and saw Yannis watching her, pleased. "Our ancestors did not believe it either: their luck, to survive their fall and find themselves here."

"It's beautiful."

"It's home. Shit still stinks, as much here as around any star." She cackled, and Viv decided, in spite of Zanj's suspicion, that she liked her.

The fence stones looked weathered, and worked with shallow, smooth carvings. "How long have you been here?"

"A long time."

Zanj's eyes stayed narrow.

"I'll answer your questions, I promise. It's best to do this all at once." Yannis led them and their entourage, all those who'd left work and home to gawk, to the village square: a well, a large house that might have been a temple or a library or a city hall, a dais the old woman mounted with care and the aid of two young men. When she turned, the murmur that passed for silence in the gathered crowd died. "Friends of Refuge," she said. "We have new residents."

"Guests," Zanj corrected her at once. "We're not planning to stay."

"You have business beyond the sky." Yannis nodded. "I understand. So did our mothers, and their mothers, back into the before time."

Hong limped forward on his improvised staff. "Mother," he said, respectful, "we welcome your hospitality. But we cannot remain."

"Do you have a ship?" Xiara asked, hungry. "Anything that can fly?"

It was Viv's turn to speak. By all rights she should have been the fiercest of them all—she was the one with the time limit, she was the one who might never make it home. But—Christ. This was a hell of a long way from Southern California, but there were no monsters here, no prison stars, no ruins. Just farmers. Weird ones, but still. There were places like this back home, even if she'd never spent much time there. Refuge wrapped her in warm air and slow time.

"I have to get home," she said anyway.

"Our mothers and their mothers all said the same," Yannis said. "If you seek to leave, we will not stop you. Our mothers and theirs never found a way offworld—but they did find a home here. And as others fell to Refuge down the years, we have welcomed them. It is a safe place in a galaxy of war."

"There's no place safe from the Empress," Zanj said. "Just places she hasn't yet found."

"There is no Cloud here. Our mothers lost it when they fell, bleeding and aflame, from the sky. We are mortal, yes—but the Empress will never find us here, nor will the Bleed, nor any of the sky's hosts. We grow our crops, and harvest. We live and we die. And there is room for all."

Zanj said: "Your mothers fell from battle, then."

"From war in the heavens. Marooned here, they hid themselves to heal. And ever since, we have remained. We raise food, we burn trees, and we live and die, as does the world."

"Do you remember their names?" Viv heard the hunger beneath Zanj's question, the wound. Her sisters had fallen in this battle, the other Suicide Queens she fought beside. If they had fallen here, maybe they survived. Maybe they remembered her.

"When our mothers came to us, they took new ones. They cast off their history to build new lives in this new world."

"Well, I won't." Zanj's teeth glittered in the light. She drew herself up, and her eyes flashed, and Viv felt a moment's shame that she had not stood so firm, that she'd felt relief in this moment's rest. Hell, she just crashed a spaceship. By any rubric, they'd earned a break. "I'm getting out of here."

"We will not stop you," Yannis said with a soft inclination of her head. Zanj looked like someone who'd expected to march into a stiff wind—only to meet a calm breeze instead, and stumble, betrayed by her own bracing. "Will you accept our hospitality meanwhile? Our food, our wine, the welcome we offer all who reach Refuge?"

Viv heard wind in the fields beyond, heard the lowing of something that was obviously not an ox, heard the ripple of the river's clear water. Heard four hundred people not breathing. Zanj, bag over her shoulder, stood ready to fight anything, everything, at once. She growled, as if their welcome were an insult.

"I promise you," Yannis said, arms spread, "this is an honest offer. Refuge is beyond traps and treason."

Which, if anything, pushed Zanj closer to wanton murder. So Viv did the only thing she could.

"Thank you," she said, and stepped between Zanj and Yannis. "We'll stay. Until we can repair our ship." If that was possible.

Yannis, and the full weight of that silence, shifted focus to her. "And you are?"

"I'm, um, hi. I'm Viv. Captain. Vivian Liao. Thank you for your offer. It's a pleasure to meet you all?"

"The pleasure," said Yannis, smiling, "is ours." She struck the dais with her pitchfork. "Welcome home."

At that, the cheers began. And, as soon as the kegs were breached, the party.

VIV GOT DRUNK. Blame the giddy rush of survival, blame the sincere welcome, blame the smiling faces or the liberal pours of a fizzy citrus drink the locals claimed was made from something her translation gimmick called *rice*, blame music, dancing, the huge iron woks of stir-fried meat and vegetables the villagers laid out, blame the sunset that bloomed orange and pink and violet across the sky, blame most of all herself, but she got proper goddamn drunk. And, drunk, she missed things.

Yannis guided her through the buffet line, leaning on her fork, which Viv suspected saw less service as an actual farm implement than as a tool of office. "This is paig, in fermented sauce with bamboo shoots, and these eggs with nightshade, and here, try some of these, they're salty." Tasty and tastier, hearty, filling, until Viv had mounded her bowl so high each bite felt like Jenga endgame. "Simple fare," Yannis said, "but what we have to offer, is yours."

"You didn't need to go to such trouble," Viv said.

"Hospitality is a joy of wealth." Yannis pointed with her chin to a large round tower just visible over the roofs. "We store grain in the silo, we salt and preserve meat. And we have guests so rarely—you're the first most of us have seen."

"I thought you'd be worried. We could be anyone." Zanj, behind them in line, filled her bowl and glared. Viv decided not to elaborate further. "You're very trusting."

"You fell from the sky to Refuge. The least we can do is offer you a welcome."

"I'm waiting for you to press-gang us into heavy labor."

"Oh, that comes tomorrow." But Yannis matched her grave tone with a wink, and Viv laughed. Her ribs hurt. Yannis waited for her to recover. "You can work if you like. We all do. But we won't force you."

"Do people not work?"

"Some. A few build, or think. Some don't want to live here, and walk away."

"What happens to them?"

"They die alone. Eventually. Most who stay, work, because people like work. But you don't need to worry about that. We might not know much about the world, but we know it's hard to fall from heaven."

Zanj rolled her eyes and stalked off. Locals parted before her hunched shoulders, her narrow eyes, and her thundercloud weight of imminent violence. "Sorry," Viv said. "She's—I should—"

Yannis waved with the back of her hand, shoo. "Go."

Balancing bowl and chopsticks in one hand, Viv picked her way through the crowd, skirting around dancers, waving to locals who waved to her. She thought she'd lost Zanj at first, then saw her at the top of the steps of the wooden temple-library, and shuffled after—sneaking a bite on the way. Crash landings were hard work.

Zanj didn't seem to notice Viv's approach. She just sat staring up into the shadowed hall of the, yes, basically a temple—four altars, candle-strewn and flower-decked, each one in front of a statue of a monstrous woman—one with three heads and a scimitar; one snakelike, clawed and hooked, bearing a doubled spear; one fanged beauty with an eye in the middle of her forehead; one massive, six-armed, horned. Dust drifted in the hall's still air, while music rang below. "I don't want to talk about it," Zanj said.

"I don't blame you."

"What?" Zanj looked at her as if she'd made some obscene joke.

"For the crash, I mean," she said. "For us ending up here. There's no way you could have known the Cloud would still be broken. We took a risk. It didn't pay off. That's okay."

Zanj's scar made it hard to read her expression, but her confusion would have played for the cheap seats. "What are you talking about? Of course it was the right decision. Of course it's not my fault."

"Okay, then. Why are you so pissed? These people seem nice so far."

"Maybe I don't like *nice*."

"Would you rather they attack us? You're not even trying to look grateful."

"For what? Food? I don't need it. Company? From a bunch of groundlings? Rescue? We saved ourselves."

"They're trying to make us comfortable."

"They want us to feel comfortable," Zanj said, "because they expect us to stay."

Behind, the song ended to cheers. The goddesses watched, silent, growling many-toothed from the shadows. "We'll get out of here."

"I don't think you understand the extent of our current fuckery. We have no ship. We can't touch the Cloud—so if we want to build a ship to get us back, we're stuck with what we can remember about basic metallurgy and physics. My batteries can't recharge, and Gray—" She shook the bag that held him, and he sloshed inside. "I'll be surprised if he can pull his body back together without the Cloud. Which leaves us a man down, while up there the Empress pulls farther ahead. Even if we can't catch her, I refuse to sit here and play pig farmer."

"We'll get out."

A sparrow—what Viv would have called a sparrow on Earth, its wings iridescent, chitinous here—launched itself from the rafters into the sunset. As the sky darkened, the grim shapes of orbiting battleships swelled in the twilight, like distant moons. As shadows shifted, the goddesses seemed to move.

"I know them," Zanj said softly.

"Who?" Viv said, and then, "Oh."

She nodded to each in turn, in greeting more than indication. "Old Tiger, who prowled between galactic arms. Heyshir, who sees from shadows. Al-Zayyd in her glory. The Black Bull. Not the only Suicide Queens, and not the names they gave themselves, but the Empress tracked down each one but these, and made me watch her kill them. I thought they died in battle. I hoped maybe they were out there fighting."

"Your friends."

"And here they are—statues in a temple. You see what happened, don't you? They fell just like we did, and got stuck. They must have tried to leave, with their followers, their lovers and minions and children and soldiers, and failed again and again, until they gave up. And then they died, and generations of marrying and mixing later their descendants have become those sheep out there, so ready to offer hospitality and pastoral paradise. My friends gave up their names and their children forgot their stories. And if those women, those brilliant fierce women, couldn't get out of here in all their lives, do you really think we'll make it in three weeks?"

Below, the fiddlers and the drums started again, and there were cheers. The temple smelled of dust and cedar.

Viv said: "You might be wrong about them." Candles flickered at the statues' feet. "Maybe they didn't give up." The flames cast light through flower petals, prismatic, dancing. "Anyway, we won't. I want to get home. You want out. We'll make it."

"Enjoy the party." Zanj's voice was more of a mask than her face. "We'll start tomorrow." And: "Here." She thrust Gray's bag sideways into her. "You take him. My shoulder's tired."

Which was a lie, but Viv took the bag. It weighed more than she expected, and pulled her sideways as she descended to the party.

She found Hong and Xiara sitting side by side by a fire, empty bowls on the ground by their knees, in a small clear space within that mass. Viv sat, raised her bowl to toast them, tucked in. "Here's to survival. And to friendly locals. So long as they don't drug us and try to steal our dreams."

Xiara stared into the fire.

"Sorry. Just a joke." Viv took a bite of seared paig. Delicious. "Come on, guys. We're alive. The odds of surviving that crash sure weren't good. We're stuck, yes, but not forever."

"I cannot feel the Cloud," Hong said. "I recite my formulas, and they are only air."

She chewed, swallowed. "Look, I manage without the Cloud all the time. We've come out of harder spots than this. There are no gods here, nothing trying to eat us. Not even Gray." That fell even flatter than she had expected. "We just have to save ourselves. And we could have picked a worse place to catch our breath."

That got Hong's attention: riveted him to her, eyes dark, staring. He leaned forward, face ghost-story orange. "They don't have souls, Viv. There's no Cloud here. When they die, they die—unarchived, unremembered. They're lost, and alone, and they don't even mind."

"Neither do I."

"You're different," he said. "You're—you're of the Empress."

"I'm of no one but myself, okay? I was born, like all these people, and I'll probably die like them, too. They seem fine to me, even if they don't have what you would call a soul."

"If we had gone to the 'fleet, we would not be marooned here now."

"No," she admitted. "Your people would be halfway through round one of probes and prodding, and you'd probably be in prison somewhere. This still seems better."

"They would have helped us."

"You don't believe that. Just watch. We'll be back out in space again no problem in a few days, on the Empress's heels, and think of all the stories you'll have to tell your order."

He stood smoothly. "I must meditate." And, without a glance back at her half-voiced objections, he walked from the fireside into the shadows, alone.

She finished the paig, dropped her bowl, and leaned back on her elbows. "Xiara, I don't know why everyone's acting so weird."

She reached for her hand, but Xiara's slipped away. "I'd like to be alone."

And then Viv was.

Okay, she told herself in the silence beside the crackling fire, under the cheers and songs. I get it. They're upset. Doesn't mean I have to be. She stood, slid back through the dancing crowd, and found herself another drink. And another. The little lizard-man serving the booze gave her a look when she got her fourth glass, but, hell, it tasted good.

"I get it," she told Gray, who was a better listener than she'd expected when he was in a puddle in a bag. Bags of unconscious friends in fluid form didn't get all weird and desert you for no reason. Okay, sure, there were reasons. She just didn't want to face them. The fire was very bright. "I mean, Zanj has her thing. And, for Hong, this is like, he can't see all of a sudden, and maybe he'll die for real, which doesn't sound so bad to *me* because it's not like living as an uploaded brain is really living. Really. Except maybe it's different if you grew up part of the Cloud. Anyway, he's feeling lost, and Xiara, she was in the ship when it crashed, and she probably feels like she let us all down, and—hold on. I'll be back." The lizard guy tried to wave her off glass five, but she grabbed it anyway, stumbled back, plopped beside the bag. "They're having a weird shitty day, we crashed a spaceship and we're all in shock. Including me! But I don't see why they have to be such dicks about it. We're all in this together. Right, Gray?"

She patted the bag.

It did not slosh.

It did not slosh, because there was nothing in the bag to slosh. It was completely, sickeningly empty.

Oh no.

Viv stood, panicked; the fires and dancing and music spun around her, and the planetoid seemed to be spinning, too—did it spin? Had she noticed it spinning from orbit? The dead fleet in the sky shifted and bubbled but she was pretty sure most of that was her booze. Gray wasn't anywhere. He hadn't leaked out—hadn't fallen—she'd been careful—hadn't she been careful?

"Gray!" Her voice vanished in the music.

God, she was drunk. Even the buildings had started to wobble—not evenly like the stars and warships, though. Only one was really wobbling: the grain silo Yannis had pointed out before. The village's food supply.

Good thing she was drunk, because it would be really bad if anything happened to that silo. She liked Refuge for many, many reasons, including this one: she could tell, here, what was good and what was bad, and, yes, that, that would definitely be bad.

Then she heard the villagers' screams. It turned out she wasn't the only one staring at the grain silo, which meant it wasn't just shaking because she was drunk, which was a bad sign—and the screams rose as the silo tilted, cracked, and fell.

Viv didn't remember running, later—just a tide of people tossing her flotsamlike through mazy backstreets, through choking demolition dust and airborne rice flour, to the edge of town, to the narrow cleft in the mountainside where the silo was.

Where the silo had been.

Its wreckage lay in piles, enormous toothmarked stone blocks tossed like packing foam about the slope. There should have been a flood of rice amid the dust and shattered rock, a year's food for a hungry village, but only a few grains slipped under Viv's feet.

Viv pushed to the front, knocking Refugers away—shoved past pitchforks pointed in, past Yannis in the lead, to reach the pale figure reclined atop the rubble, moaning and stroking his grotesquely swollen belly.

Viv shouted, "Stop!" though nobody had started anything yet. "I know him."

Gray opened his eyes, blinked twice, and said, "Heya, Viv! Boss! Glad you made it! Man, isn't this place great? All this food, jus' lying around."

Speech completed, he slumped back to the ground, and began to snore.

Viv looked from Gray, to Yannis, to the wreckage, to the villagers, to Gray again, but her eyes kept tracking past him, and there were so many villagers. They all looked angry, and, but—no, the ground wasn't really shaking, don't be silly, she knew earthquakes, she grew up with earthquakes, and this, sir, was no—

She made it to the bushes, at least, before she threw up.

28

MOST MORNINGS VIV woke before dawn, alone in the hut the village gave her, stretched, sponged off, shrugged into a loose cotton shirt and pants, then went to work the fields with Gray. It was the least she could do. That's what she told Zanj when Zanj asked why she bothered: Gray had eaten Refuge out of a year's grain, and while Yannis and the others, once talked down, realized that Gray didn't mean to hurt them—they understood the misunderstanding, they welcomed him, too, and they had supplies enough to last through the harvest if they were careful and rationed meals—after all that, even Viv, who had, age fourteen, once unthinkingly accepted an aunt's offer to treat her to dinner with a simple thanks, thereby sending her entire extended family into a three-week-long paroxysm of apology and counter-apology, could tell they'd fucked up bad, and had to make amends.

What she didn't tell Zanj, what it took her a week to admit even to herself, and what she never would have admitted to her friends back home, was that she liked the work. At the end of the first day in the sun, drenched in sweat, her back aching from hours bending to transplant rice seedlings, hassled by gnats and flies, she felt more bone-tired than she'd felt in years, a two-day sailing race's full-body exhaustion squeezed into the hours between sunrise and noon. Bone-tired, and glowing.

They all worked together, that was part of it, the folk she classed roughly as women and the folk she classed roughly as men and the folk who didn't fit in either camp. They worked in paddies, row by row. They joked about each other, about the sun, about the mud, about sex hidden behind metaphors and sex not hidden at all. Viv didn't get most of the sex jokes, which involved unfamiliar equipment about which she really didn't want to ask. Elders moved among them, Yannis and Nioh, her bent, blunt-horned friend, and others, answering questions, offering sun tea and balls of glutinous rice wrapped around minced fried paig. There were songs that meshed voices, high and reedy, earth-deep, trembling and hale; Fenliu the drummer beat time while they sang, and the work went faster. When Viv didn't know what she was doing, which was always at first, her neighbors helped her: here is how you plant the seedling straight, here is how you bend so you don't hurt your back. Gentle corrections, and soon she could do the work without thinking.

The joy snuck up on her. Clouds drifted below the sun as the ruined fleet drifted far above. The sun was hot but the water cool. The wet squick of mud between her toes grossed Viv out at first, but even that was welcoming once she got used to it, gentle as breezes. Gray loved it: he covered himself in mud as he worked, baked it to a clay with the sun's heat and the heat of his own body.

That first day, after he woke from a digestion coma to learn what he'd done—after Viv doused him in a bucket's worth of cold water to wake him so he *could* learn—he'd been confused by the notion of food as scarce resource. Then, when he understood, he'd gone pale as Viv had ever seen him, and promised—on bent knee, no less—to make it good. He'd offered to fight monsters, to topple mountains, but there were no monsters here to fight, or mountains anyone wanted toppling. Yannis pointed out, though, that their crash landing had left a miles-long scar through their most fertile fields. That, Gray could fix.

"I'm not so good without the Cloud," he told them on day one, as he stared at the trench. "I can't fuzz out into the air, and I can't change shape as fast. It's harder to track all my little pieces. But I can push things around just fine." He put his shoulder to a ten-foot-tall pile of dirt and rock, and shoved—and with a crack, and a groan, it collapsed on top of him. He wriggled out, spat gravel, grinned gap-toothed. "You get the idea."

Without the Cloud he also tired faster. They found that out on the third day, which was apparently how long Gray could run on the energy of a year's worth of grain. He collapsed mid-shove, and the rocks he'd been trying to move rolled on top of him. Viv saw, ran to him, pulled him from the rubble—his skin was so tight she could see his bones were not in the same arrangement as a normal person's. "Gray! What the hell."

"I'm fine. Just a rest and." His head slumped against her. "Hungry." She offered him a rice ball, but he shook his head. "Ate for a year already. They'll starve."

"You need food."

He shook his head again, but Viv called, "Yannis!" and the woman came, leaning on her fork, and together they dragged Gray to a shaded hut and ladled broth into his mouth until his eyes flashed and his irises went white, then filled clockwise like progress bars. He woke just before a hundred percent, and Viv finally relaxed.

He could feed off the sun, but slowly. Carbon chains were faster, energy-dense, but Refuge didn't have another year's grain surplus to spare. He could eat grass and hay, but burned them less well. "You need to pace yourself," Viv said, hearing the echo of everyone in her life who'd told her to do the same. "You're no good to anyone half dead."

So Gray worked mornings after that, ate for three, and did the work of only twenty. The afternoons he spent spread into a thin silver film on the surface of the village reservoir, pulling sunlight. He worked beside a team of villagers, Gatyen and Mishya and Cenk, strong, bold, belly-laughing, broad-backed shovelers and pickax artists. They teased him, taught him their digging songs, invited him to rest beside them in the shade. Gray's form changed, even in that first week: he slouched less, and thickened all through. He didn't grow muscle the way a person might, but he learned the efficiency of the older men's shapes, and how they used their bodies. When he was ready, he even joined their songs, with a surprising high tenor pure as a boy's. Viv ate lunch with him, and he told her stories around mouthfuls about Gatyen's three kids, about Cenk's father, who had walked all the way around the world. "They don't know anything about the Empress, or the stars. They just know this little place. But they're as big as anyone. I wish I could eat their dreams. I mean," he said, "I won't. But they'd be as rich as a god's."

How Levin-in-the-grass could you get? But there it was. Gray, improbably enough, was growing up.

The others didn't help with the fields.

Not that they kept idle. Zanj worked constantly. She gathered metal at first: walked miles seeking bits of foam and alloy scattered from their crash, returned one day bearing a twenty-foot wing over one shoulder. She rescued wire, diamond, glass; she borrowed tools from the village blacksmith and built her own forge, melting and recasting the *Question*'s wreck for the parts she needed, and slowly, she raised her antenna. Viv helped her in the afternoons, and tried to make conversation about village politics, about Gray's development, about Hong, about Xiara still so quiet and withdrawn, about next steps. When all the rest failed to start a conversation, she asked about the Suicide Queens, and how they'd fallen. Zanj worked, and told her where to put her hands, and did not answer. She slept across the river under the stars, far from the village's firelight, when she slept at all.

Hong worked with Zanj, and he was chattier. He helped with the antenna design, helped her wind wire and repurpose bits of surviving circuitry. "We learn the ways of machines," he explained. "The 'faith starts its children on steam in their youth and guides us principle by principle into the Cloud, so we are trained to open our minds to problems. Our first challenge here is to determine just what cuts us off from the wider universe. Since we observe no gravitational distortions, no lensing, it's likely a signal interference. A strong, directional broadcast should pierce through, if we can use Zanj herself as a power source."

"Your plan stinks of *if*," Zanj said as she heaved a crossbar into place.

"Do you have a better one?"

If she did, she didn't say.

Hong spent only part of his time with the antenna. He roamed the village and beyond, drawing maps and landscapes in charcoal, talking in teahouses with locals, playing board games and dice, studying plow construction, visiting the sick, teaching children tumbling games: learning, always learning. She ran into him one night after dinner with Gatyen's family. She'd limited herself to a single cup of the fizzy lemon stuff, which still made her eyes burn. Full and tipsy and exhausted, she staggered back to her own hut, and as she neared it, saw him on a hill nearby, sketching by the light of the battleship moons.

When she called his name, he lifted his pencil from the paper, and waited while she climbed the hill, which wavered underfoot. That was probably the booze. He didn't speak, but he didn't leave either, or shy away as she settled down beside him.

"That's good," she said, and his drawings were: a map, and two sketches in different styles, one mottled and shaded, one spare, shape suggested by unbroken undulating lines. He'd drawn some of the ships, too.

"Thank you. I cannot walk the ship, I cannot pray—so this serves."

She passed the drawing back. "I'm sorry. I want us gone as much as you do. We'll get there."

"We may."

"You planned the antenna yourself. It will work."

"You trust Zanj that much?"

"What do you mean, trust her?"

"Once she returns to the Cloud, she'll be beyond your reach. Beyond your command. Why would she come back?"

The antenna pierced the purple night, and sparks fountained inside: Zanj working, with desperation and need—for freedom. The group's freedom, Viv had thought. Zanj hated being trapped, here or anywhere, she hated waiting, she passed her time aboard ship reading or playing puzzle games or arm wrestling with Gray, even tidying, but never still. She'd had enough stillness in three thousand years of prison. She wanted freedom and revenge. Viv offered both. But she might seize freedom anyway, and work her way up to revenge.

Viv wondered why it never occurred to her that Zanj might leave them. Back home, she expected all kinds of fuckery from rivals. But to build anything real, you had to trust your people, even if they might let you down. Zanj had helped Viv, in one way or another, since High Carcereal. She came back to Orn when Viv hadn't called her. Surely she wouldn't leave them here.

But Hong thought another way. For him, Zanj was not a colleague, but a monster bubbled up from myth.

She didn't know which of them was right. "She'll come back."

Hong said nothing.

"She will. Or . . ." After all, why not consider the chance? "Or we'll try something else. And if nothing works, there are worse places we could end up."

"Refuge is a strange town." He set paper and board on the grass before him, and weighted them with small stones. "They live and die and leave so little record, so few marks on the land. Yannis claims they've been here thousands of years, but if so, why aren't there more of them? Their technology— the plows, the carts, the smith's shop—it's all primitive but efficient. Refined. Every innovation you could manage with the materials available without pushing them into steam. They have good hygiene. They sing recognizable versions of songs millennia old. They should have changed by now, or developed their own literature. But they haven't."

"I feel like I'm doing something wrong," she said to the night as much as to him, expecting no answer from either. "It's not as if I like this place, but Zanj is so angry, and you're . . . suspicious, I guess. And Xiara's . . . I don't even know."

"You should talk to her."

"She just sits on the mountain. I say things, and she doesn't answer."

"Have you tried listening?"

"Of course," Viv said, and realized she had not.

Hong stood. "Here's what I think. I respect you, Viv, and I want to help you. But for you, this is just one more adventure. Being trapped here is no different from standing free on the 'fleet, or Orn, or on the *Question*. It's better, even, since it's more like the world you know. If we never make it off this rock, well, it was a long shot for you anyway, the chance of getting home. But Zanj will lose her chance at revenge, Gray will never see his family again, I'll die unable to pass on anything I've learned, lost in static, and Xiara—it's not my place to say what she feels."

He slipped the board and paper beneath one arm, and his pencil into a pouch in his robe, and when he was done, she still had not spoken. There were no answers, except the one she didn't offer.

"I'm sorry," Hong said first.

"No." She scrambled to her feet. "No. I'm glad you said that. Thank you."

Those weren't the right words either, but they moved in the right direction, and the shadows on Hong's face seemed lighter—or else that was an illusion caused by the revolving battleships above, reflecting the light of the set, fake sun.

She worked the next day in a fugue, in denial. Her mind melted into muscle, into touch, into the heat of the forge as she worked iron, as she helped Zanj weld systems into place. She stopped trying to joke, related no cheerful stories from the field. Zanj either softened in return, or seemed less hard without the contrast.

That evening, Viv borrowed a pair of scissors from the blacksmith, and climbed the mountain.

The slope, gradual at first, grew treacherous, purplish-green grass yielding to broken stone, with squat piney trees spreading horizontal to gather light. Viv pulled herself up hand over hand, breathing hard, her body more used at this point to farming than to climbing, until she saw Xiara seated at cliff's edge, a shadow against pink sky.

She raised her hand: "Hi!"

Xiara did not wave back, but neither did she run. She could have, while Viv hauled herself up the rock face, bracing her feet against gravel. She had before. Viv had tried to talk to her many times after that first night, to invite her to the fields, ask how she was doing, if she'd like to help with the antenna. Those attempts had not ended well.

When Viv reached the cliff edge, Xiara scooted to one side to make room. She drew her legs against her chest, and hugged her knees, and looked down at the lights of Refuge. "Hong said you might come. And he said I should listen."

Viv knew just what she had to say, but couldn't now. Which was why she'd brought the scissors. "I wanted to ask—can you give me a haircut?"

Xiara looked over, and up: wind had blown loose long hair across her face, across her eyes.

"My hair's getting long. I'd cut it myself, but I haven't seen a mirror here, and I'd end up looking like a doll in a horror movie. That's, um. It's a kind of story. With creepy dolls. It would look bad, is what I'm saying." The longer she went, the worse all this sounded. "Will you help me?" She drew the scissors from her belt, and offered them, handle first.

One corner of Xiara's mouth twitched up, and her lips parted to hint at teeth. Something like humor reached the edges of her eyes. "Sit."

Viv lowered herself and swung her legs over the edge. The drop wasn't far, but the valley stretched before her, and as she sat, still, quiet, she considered the merits of having a sensitive conversation at the edge of a cliff, while someone stood behind you with a knife. Or scissors. Not that Xiara would do anything. Probably.

Her fingers combed Viv's hair, pulling through its length, judging the shape of the skull. The scissors chilled the skin of her neck.

Listen, was what Hong had said, but she couldn't just listen. Or she wasn't brave enough to start that way. "I'm sorry," she said.

Snip.

"You're feeling lost right now. You left your home, but then you had the ship, and the stars. And me. If I really matter to you. Then you came here, and we flew through that fleet, and you felt the fleetmind, and then it all was ripped away." She waited between sentences, and listened to the wind in the high places, the passage of blades through her hair. She felt Xiara's strong, steady hands on her head. She ached for them. "I've been all plans: how are we getting off this planet, how can we catch the Empress, what happens when we do. I was thinking about myself. Not you, not really." Xiara's hand circled to her forehead, traced her brow. "I've fucked up like this before. God. I could tell you stories. I've always been . . . driven. I start things because they're fun, because they seem like a good idea at the time, and I forget it's not always simple."

The scissors paused. Xiara said: "I'm not in love with you, you know."

"Oh" didn't seem like the right response, but that was what Viv went with. She kept still. She tried not to think what that raw tone of voice might mean.

"You're . . . you're weird. I don't know what you are. I don't know where you're from, or where you're going, except that you want to leave. You make bad jokes, you're disrespectful, and you don't know the first thing of how it's done, to lie with a woman: you give no gift, you offer no dance. No secrets pledged or traded. You're . . . you understand nothing, you're rude, and you're selfish, you're . . ." She broke off, and set the scissors down. Her hand fell heavy and warm on Viv's shoulder, and Viv sought it with hers. "Who am I, out here? The Ornchief's daughter, hundreds of light-years from Orn? A shipless pilot? I kissed you, I lay with you, because I like you, wanted you, chose you. Needed you. But you don't change, or learn, or offer. You're just you, always. You didn't need me. And when you get where you're going, you'll leave, without a thought for what remains behind."

"No." Viv squeezed her hand, her wrist, started to turn—and stopped when Xiara shifted weight as if to draw away. "No," she repeated. "I have to get home. But what we've had—what we've done, god, yes the sex, but more than that, the five of us, together, out there, up there—it is real to me. I feel it. I just . . . I suck, okay? I suck at this. At feeling things. At sitting still to feel them. I want to get us off this rock. I want you to have a ship, a big one, the most beautiful ship in the galaxy. I want Hong to find his fleet, his answers. I want Zanj to do whatever the hell she wants. I want Gray to see his home again. And I want to see mine. But. Christ. This happens every time—I get caught up in the plans. I make it all about what happens next and I never let myself get real, get scared, because if I did, I don't know how I'd stop. So I keep going. I pull away. I'm sorry."

Xiara's other hand settled on her shoulder, and for a second Viv, mad, thought, she'll push me off the ledge, because it was easier to imagine the fall and the sharp stop than it was to imagine saying all that and time continuing. Then Xiara's arms slid over Viv's shoulders, and her body pressed against her from behind, her cheek against Viv's neck, her breath soft and shallow. She felt the presence of her lips—not a kiss, just her lips resting there on skin. Felt her swallow. "You'll never get a haircut like this. We're almost out of light."

"How much is left?"

"Not much," she said. "Here. Hold still."

As she worked, Viv asked: "What did you mean, about secrets?"

"We give them, on Orn, to those we trust."

"I don't have any secrets. I mean. I used to have a lot, millions of them, formulas and algorithms and patterns and corporate dirt, but they wouldn't mean anything to you."

"Of course you have a secret. To live is to grow secrets."

"Okay," she said. "All right. Fine."

Silence. "Do you have one yet?"

"Don't rush me!"

More silence.

"Okay. This is a shitty secret. I don't know if it even counts."

"Stop trying to dodge the question."

"Okay. Don't laugh."

"I make no promises."

"My first memory is of the underside of a table."

"What?"

She felt her face heat up. "I was, maybe, one? One and a half? I remember looking up through a table, and seeing trees through the slats. I've never told anyone before."

Xiara set down the scissors, and ran her hands over Viv's hair again.

"Well?"

"Well, what?"

"What's yours?"

"You're all set."

"Hey. I did the thing, so it's only fair you do it, too."

Xiara drew breath, and let it out. "I was lying earlier."

"About the secrets?"

"No. That *is* my secret."

"That's a dumb secret. What were you lying about?" And then: "Oh." Xiara drew back, and Viv turned on the cliff's edge to face her: saw the slight smile, the freckles on her dark skin, the being behind the eyes. "Um." She laughed—couldn't help it. Laughter was easier than an answer.

"I shouldn't have said anything. You have people to get back to—lovers, maybe. Friends. Family."

"But I'm here now," she said. "What do you want to do next?"

She looked down, colored, looked up. "Can we just . . . be here, together? For now?"

And she said yes.

They lay a body's length back from the cliff, in one another's arms, beneath the whirling sky. The night was warm, the rock hard and cool. Xiara made small rabbitlike jerking motions in her sleep, grunted and growled as Viv had heard her do while flying; she held her close, and breathed her in, and for once her own dreams were void of gods and Empresses.

The next morning, Xiara shook Viv awake. "Come on, bear. Sun's up. Let's go help Zanj."

Three days later, they finished the antenna. Viv worked the fields by morning, and the antenna by night. Hong checked and rechecked the wiring, and Xiara lifted and carried and learned what she could of the odd electronics, adjusting this bond or that by instinct, which Zanj or Hong or Viv confirmed more than they corrected. Even Gray joined them when he recovered from his afternoon stint as a pond—he wanted to marshal his strength, but he could work the forge, so long as they didn't mind him eating a few coals. They finished in midafternoon. Viv's media experience of mad science protested that there should have been a thunderstorm, but none suggested itself. Hong ran a current through the system to test it, checked lights, adjusted. Zanj placed upon her head the helmet that would, if the signal carried, translate her out into the Cloud.

"Ready?"

"Go ahead, monk boy. Get me off this rock."

Hong threw the switch. Zanj closed her eyes. Viv felt the loud pop in the center of her chest, the wave of heat as Zanj's battery discharged into the antenna. Lights blazed. Wheels turned. Dials spun. Lightning arced around wires. Xiara balled her hands to fists; Viv watched, as tensely as she'd ever watched a stock price fall. Her calm and cool all broke.

Minutes passed.

Zanj tore the helmet from her head, and threw it across the room. It struck the wall hard enough to dent wall and helmet alike. "Fuck!"

"It's not broken," she snarled as Xiara knelt and started tracing wires to find the fault. "You saw it. I felt it. The damn thing worked like it was supposed to. It just didn't do anything. And we're stuck here."

"It's fine," Hong said. "I can fix it."

"There's nothing to fix, monk boy! The whole idea's wrong. We'll have to start again, ground up. Something else."

"Maybe this wire—" But Xiara shook her head. "No, never mind. It's connected."

"How long will it take?" Viv asked, because she didn't want to. One week was what they had. What she had. One week, and after that, their escape might as well take forever. Hong knew that. He knew what answer she wanted him to give. He didn't say.

Zanj punched one of the antenna struts, and it snapped. Gray ran to hold the structure up before it could collapse and bury them: "What's the matter with you?" But Zanj growled at him, and marched away into the dark.

Viv went after her, but Zanj walked fast, then broke into a run. Viv fell step by step behind, lungs aflame, legs lead, until at last she fell and lay panting in the fields.

When she could walk again, she did not go back. Back was a failure; she'd tried, and now she had to sit alone with the consequences. She climbed the mountain once again, and brooded condorlike, contemplating death, until sunset threatened.

She felt foolish. She felt done. The work wasn't over. They needed her—her allies, her friends. Hong. Gray. Zanj.

Xiara.

Whom she'd left behind, because she had to sulk.

Way to go, Viv. You get through all that, and then you act like a perfect goddamn child.

Still, there was no way out but through.

Viv rose to go, but she heard, nearby, footsteps on stone. She stilled, and scanned the slope until she saw the source of the noise: a hunched, robed figure trudging alone up the mountain with a two-pronged pitchfork for a walking stick. Not foraging—climbing, with steady purpose and surer steps than Viv had ever seen Yannis take in the village below.

She tried to follow the old woman without being seen, but she fell behind as she scaled a ridge, and at one point she was caught in briars, and when she worked through, Yannis was gone.

Above, the dead fleet turned and turned in the night.

29

"THIS," HONG WHISPERED on the third night, as he helped Viv follow Yannis up the mountain, "is a bad idea."

"Shut up and give me a boost."

"These people are secretive. They have rituals and rites unrecorded in the deepest archives of the 'faith. And they're deeply conservative. They'd have to be, to survive for so long with so few changes in their lives. Of course they wouldn't share all their secrets with outsiders, no matter how much—" He grunted as Viv put her weight on his shoulder and jumped up to catch an overhang. "—of a show they make of welcome."

She lay flat on the ledge and stretched her arm down to him; he made most of the climb under his own power, clinging spiderlike to rocks, which was good, because when he caught her wrist her arm almost popped out of its socket. All the farm and forge work was making her stronger, but not enough to one-armed curl a guy with a metal leg. Good thing isolation from the Cloud hadn't slowed his absurdly fast healing. "We're not sneaking into their bedrooms here. We're just going for a climb."

"At night," he whispered back. "At the same time as Yannis."

"Hey, if she's doing it, it must be a good idea. Right?" Speaking of which. "Ah. Where did she go?"

Hong sighed. His irises flicked red, and he reviewed the slope for heat sources.

She wished she could have done this alone. It would have been quieter, for one, and for two, she'd grown unsure of herself around Hong. But the last two nights she'd followed Yannis up, only for the old woman to lose her among the cliffs. She'd climbed the rest of the mountain by shipmoonlight, and found nothing but a cold hill's side.

"There." Pointing: she saw a flash of motion behind a bush, which might have been a nightbird taking off, or a startled fox. But she trusted Hong's eyes, and followed him upslope.

Maybe it wouldn't have been quieter to do this alone, as a matter of fact. She could climb, more or less, but back home she'd never had to stalk anything wilier than a pizza—unless you counted investors, and the stalking there was mostly metaphorical. Hong moved like a wave over water, as sure and smooth, and left as little trace. She wallowed after him. But even now, painfully aware of her every overcommitment to a step, each brush of hers against a bush he'd skirted, she knew she was climbing faster, more surely and quietly, than she could manage alone.

She caught herself loving this: the two of them climbing together, silent when they could bear not talking, on this cool evening, on this rippled slope beneath the shipmoons. Of all their party, even Xiara, Hong was closest to Viv-model human, but that didn't explain how comfortable she felt with him around. So: what?

She understood then, as she traced him hold for hold up a cliff, as he turned back and watched her, one hand half out, ready to spring if she should slip.

She'd once seen a huge ice shelf calve from a glacier, then turn over in the water, at first a slight slope in the glacier's plane, then steeper, steeper, then with a rush of frozen spray that made rainbows in the knife-dry air, with a surge of mighty shoulders, the complications underwater revealed themselves, and what had been visible faded below the waves. This felt like that.

Hong was a friend. Viv didn't have many. Lovers, yes, collaborators, co-workers, and fellow strivers by the legion, but all those relationships were bound by common needs. Shared goals gave clarity. Coworkers wanted to fulfill their mission statement and get rich along the way. Lovers wanted happiness, and good sex—selfish and mutual satisfaction. But what was the goal of a friendship? What did it get you? How did it run up the score?

She knew so many people. Classmates, coworkers, gaming buddies, gym mates, they were her friends—people she'd describe unreservedly as friends, people whose weddings she'd flown twelve time zones to attend, people she'd protested for, people whose hospital beds she'd waited beside, people she'd bailed out of prison. But again and again when there wasn't a crisis she turned from them into uncharted waters, to run up her various scores alone.

She'd ached with their absence. And she'd been afraid. But still, she hadn't seen Magda in years before Boston. She couldn't blame all that on politics, or on the world. Some of it was her own damage.

Hong could have left her. He wanted answers, but that wasn't why he was here. And that wasn't why she turned to him.

She could have said all this when she realized it, and that might have changed things. Nothing physical stopped her, no promise bound her. Just the girders of her self, the tower she'd built to become Vivian Liao. So instead she ignored his offered hand up, heaved herself onto the ledge, and when she spoke next, it was to focus on the problem. Shared goals. Shared objectives. "Yannis does this every night," she said as she recovered her breath. "I think the other elders go up, too. I haven't seen Nioh in a couple days, and the rest have disappeared for days at a time before. I just didn't wonder where they were going."

He nodded. "Perhaps the ritual is the source of their longevity."

"What longevity?"

He judged brush-strewn ground, then tiptoed through it without a rustle or crack. "Nobody in the village knows how old Yannis is. Or Nioh."

"You didn't think this was worth mentioning before now?" Tiptoe, tiptoe, tiptoe—snap. She'd stepped on a twig. Nearby almost-crickets ceased chirping.

"Why would I?"

"You thought it was suspicious that they have very good plows, but not that some of them don't age."

"Does everyone age where you come from?"

"Yes!"

He shuddered, and kept climbing.

Okay, Viv thought. So we're following an immortal up a mountain. Best not focus on how that might go poorly. Still, she felt relieved to be doing something, to be out here with Hong, alone as they had been in those first panicked minutes in High Carcereal, running from Pride and local security and the 'faith.

The others were variously consumed. Zanj had spent the days since their failure and her ensuing brief sulk in ceaseless work, gutting and rebuilding the antenna along a new design, her own this time; when villagers approached, even to offer food, she cursed them and threw things until they left, and when they'd gone she muttered about spies and saboteurs and stealers of parts. Gray had returned to the fields, to his songs and his heavy lifting, and Viv didn't want to disturb him.

And then there was Xiara. She worked long hours with Zanj, and when she had to sleep she wandered back to Viv's hut and collapsed. In the minutes of shared wakefulness, they talked. They tried. Jumping into sex, they'd skipped the whole getting-to-know-you bit, so now it went slower and more painfully. Viv tried to explain what she'd done back home, with little success, since most of the concepts involved in software capitalism were either too advanced or too primitive for the Ornclan. Xiara knew trade, and hated it: for her it meant long treks through wasteland bearing cargoes of knives, to sit across a low sacred fire from another daughter of another Ornclan, breathing acrid smoke from herbs tossed in the fire that made the edges of the clearing pulse and spin, while each clan's priests and oracles invited the propitiation of the ancestors, and warriors watched wary, and haggle with her opposite number over how many of her clan's knives were worth how much of the other clan's embroidered cloth. And after that, the drinking started, and, depending on the deal, the sex.

"Is it the same where you come from?"

"Actually," Viv said, trailing fingers down her belly, "more or less. Minus the sex, most of the time. There are rules."

She yawned, and curled beside her. "Missing the best part."

"Is this a trade, then? You and me?"

"Mmm. What are you offering?"

She waved her hand over her own body atop the sheets, indicating: this.

"Oh." Xiara slid one arm down, down her belly, below, held her and leaned in, and caught the skin at the side of her neck between her teeth. "But I have one of those already."

Xiara slept after, so deep she didn't notice Viv creep from bed to follow Yannis up the mountain.

They were talking again, at least. Xiara had found . . . not peace, but a space less grim than her postcrash depression. Viv didn't know how stable that place might be, and did not risk shaking its foundations. She'd made that mistake before with other women—and the opposite mistake, too, the one she was making now.

Hell. Better to trust, and leave the second-guessing for later.

Hong held out one arm, and she stopped, waited, followed him to a patch of ground that looked no different from the rest. "Where did you learn to track, anyway?" she asked as he led her once more uphill.

"X!hanghaim," he whispered back.

"Is that a 'faith world?"

"The 'faith have no worlds. Only the 'fleet. We wander through the galaxy, small and mobile, so neither Bleed nor Empress can find us. But some supplies are easier to grow on worlds—and we need recruits. So the 'faith visits settlements that need the services we offer. Sometimes we repair a decayed stormshield, sometimes we chase off bloodthirsty gods. Often it's simpler: Medicine. Operations. Basic mathematics. From those who ask of us, we take. Goods, sometimes—but also children young enough to bring into the 'faith."

"That's . . ." *horrible* was the way she expected to finish her sentence, but what she actually thought was *depressingly consistent with my expectations.* "Interesting," was what she said.

"My older brother was sick. He had teased me one day, and I ran from him, and I fell into a nest of cats. He rescued me, and chased them off, but he was bitten on the leg, and the venom spread. We were lucky: this was the month the 'fleet were visiting X!hanghaim. They were far from us, in the capital city, so I ran a week to reach them, across the Thorn Plain. The Archivist found me passed out a mile from the city gates, when she wandered collecting local herbs for her garden. She fixed my brother, and I went with them. Here. Use this handhold, then that."

When the climb was over, she said, "They didn't have to take you. They could have just helped."

"Yes," he said. "But this is how it is done. My brother has four children now. And I seek the liberation of all sentient beings. If I never left X!hanghaim, I would never have met you, or Zanj, or Xiara, or Gray, and posterity would be the poorer for it."

Before she could sort out how to answer that, he crouched and pointed uphill to a black, rounded smudge that ducked behind a boulder. Yannis. That was her fringe of gray scales, that her pitchfork. Then she ducked her head, and was gone.

No words now, as they crept forward together. Only wind, and sifting sand, and branches brushing branches.

"There," he said when they rounded the boulder behind which she'd disappeared. "Just a cave. Their ritual chamber must be inside. We should go back."

The cave looked suspiciously cavelike, its walls patterned limestone and lichen, woven with roots like veins, narrowing to a shadowy crevasse. Heat exchange between cooler air and warmer stone created a subtle breeze, out and in, as if the cave were a mouth. It couldn't have been more realistic if she'd paid Imagineers to build it. Because Viv was human, she felt a stab of primal fear. And, because she was herself, she crushed it.

"I remember that boulder," Viv said. "But the cave wasn't here last night." She ducked, and descended. Hong, reluctant, followed her.

Ten feet into the cave, the shipmoonglow that had lit their path failed. It didn't surrender to normal shadows. Instead, it stopped altogether, in a gray-black wall that rippled at Viv's touch.

"Viv," Hong said, "we really should—"

She stepped through the shadow curtain into false fluorescent day.

White walls, white floor—no, white deck. Doors here and there. Ahead, a whisper of robe turning down a side passage. No darkness anywhere.

Hong passed through the gray curtainfield after her, caught himself on her arm, and gaped.

God, Viv loved being right. Even—hell, especially—when being right meant learning you were in a great deal of trouble. "Some ritual chamber, huh?"

He shook his head.

"Let's follow her." She grabbed his robe and tugged him after her, but he didn't budge. "Come on. We have to see what's going on here."

"We might have set off an alarm already."

"Even more reason to learn what we can before they catch us. This might not be so easy next time."

"What if they do worse than catch us? Viv, we have to go back and tell the others."

Christ. He was right. "Okay. Go down. You can climb faster than I can in the dark. Tell them where I've gone."

"I won't leave you."

"Then come with me," she said, "and we're caught, or we're not."

He refused to budge. And she felt so grateful for that hesitation, for his urge to protect her.

"Go on, goofball. I'll be fine."

He opened his mouth as if to say something, then thought better of it and stepped back through the curtainfield, leaving her alone.

If he hadn't left, she would have pushed him away, but when he did, she felt a second lurch inside, as if the white walls and deck had disappeared and left her in free fall. But, hell, if she paid attention to her every post-decision doubt, she would never have become herself.

So she descended.

The hallway zigged, zagged, without branching. She heard footsteps always around the next corner and padded after them in silence, thankful for her Ornclan boots' soft tread. After the third turn, the hallway began curving down, smooth as ever, a slope like a playground slide, but "down" changed direction as she walked, always perpendicular to the floor.

With every step in this strange place she felt smaller, more alone, a girl in a white hall in a haunted universe, following the footprints of a ghost. The air chilled her, artificial, perfect, and finished. The halls smelled of filters and cleaning products. This was not the Refuge where she'd worked, the place she thought she knew. Ancient, polished mechanism lurked beneath.

Looking back, she could not see the hallway's last corner. It had vanished beyond the horizon of the sloping floor. She was, if she judged the curve correctly, now walking straight down into the heart of the place she'd taken for a planet.

She passed doors, closed mostly, with red lights over each. The first one she found open led to a room as featureless as the hall, its bulkheads the whiteness of a blind eye. The second held a skull, or a helmet shaped to look like a skull, rotating in a column of blue light. The footsteps had long since faded, but Viv kept moving, tugged down and in, though her heart hammered in her chest. She felt pressure on her wrist, and realized she was rubbing the scar there, the burn in the shape of the Empress's hand. She remembered the agony of her ribs snapped, her chest peeled open, her heart gripped by burning fingers—remembered it not with her mind but with her blood and lungs and with the pit a fist's distance below her heart.

She hadn't been afraid of things before. Back home, she'd considered her risks, capture, a black bag over her head, her fingers broken and her fingernails pulled out one by one in some government cell, all the fun people could have with genital electrodes, in abstraction: she could bear them, or not, and if not, she wouldn't be around to worry. But then the Empress hurt her, and now she was afraid, because she knew what pain was. Was this what they called growing up? She'd thought that meant maturity, weathering, endurance. But instead you gathered one terror after another to yourself, until you were a skin-clad skeleton cradling a self made up of wounds.

Behind the third open door knelt Yannis.

She had made herself tea in a small iron kettle that hovered over a sourceless flame. Past her, beyond a window so clear Viv first thought it was but a hole, lay the ship.

It could be nothing else. At this size Viv thought *station* first, but this structure was clearly built to move: those were engines, enormous if dormant, hidden between the miles-long tentacles, nestled in mouths in metal skin. The ship curled aphidlike and broken around itself, and in a gut-twisting inversion Viv realized the ship was not outside the window, not separate from the wall. That distant dark expanse, those great silent engines, the weapons and manipulator veins, curled back hundreds of miles around to meet the wall through which Viv now stared.

The planet Refuge was the outer skin of an enormous dead ship, curled around its mortal wound. A massive glittering column of fractal black impaled the hull, an affront to the eye, a curse to the mind.

Viv's eyes settled on that column, that spear. She knew its name. This, at last, was the Fallen Star.

And Yannis knelt there, and watched out the window, and sipped her tea.

Viv drew back, her steps soft, soundless.

She ran into a wall of cloth: a scratchy robe, unyielding flesh and bone beneath. Turned, and found herself staring into glistening green slitted eyes.

Impossible. Yannis could not have moved that fast.

But the room behind was empty save for the fire and the kettle and the cups.

"Dear," Yannis said. Her tone was kind, and her teeth long and sharp and curved. "I didn't hear you come in. Please. Would you join me for some tea?"

30

YANNIS MADE TEA like Viv's grandmother, hot water first poured over the whole set of unfinished purple teaware to wake and fill its clay, then new water boiled, poured once again over tea leaves in a small pot, let steep a bare minute, poured from there into a second pot to prevent over-steeping, then, finally, into cups too small to use for rolling dice. It rested green and fragrant in Viv's cup. Yannis raised hers first, breathed deep, drank, set it down. A show of good faith.

"I doubt we're poisoned by the same things," Viv said.

"If we wanted to kill you, dear, we would have done it already."

Viv pondered the tea, and the pure white room, and the old woman across from her with the snake scales, and told herself this was just another negotiation. "Where did the water come from? I don't see a faucet around here."

Yannis made a precise gesture over the empty kettle. A stream of water poured into it from thin air, then stopped.

"Shame you didn't teach the villagers that trick. It would save them trips to the well."

"Work improves character. Now, drink before it cools. You'll lose the aroma."

This tea was a feeling more than taste, a half-remembered dream: warmth and shade, and somewhere, flowers. As she lowered the cup, she met Yannis's eyes.

"You must have questions."

"You'd be surprised," Viv said.

Yannis opened one three-fingered hand, inclined her head: please.

"How many of the other Suicide Queens are left?"

Yannis did not smile like a human, but her eyes narrowed, sparkling, mirthful.

"All of them, I bet. I don't know the other two—maybe they're somewhere else within this complex. But Nioh is the Bull. And I bet you're the one who sees from shadows. Heyshir."

Viv had not expected a reaction, so she was not disappointed. This was a long, long con, and Yannis, or whoever she was, had spent centuries growing into her role. "The Suicide Queens," Yannis said, "left their old names behind when Tiger died of her wounds. I never lied to you, dear. Or to any of them. This is who we are now. But I have to say, I'm impressed. I thought Zanj would be the one to put this all together. I'm hurt, really, that she did not."

"You recognize her?"

"Dear. I've known her since the Empress first burned stars against the Bleed. We fought together, loved together. We stole wonders to slake our greed and lust, and reveled in our triumph to break the vaults of heaven. Of course I recognized her. But I have changed since I was the woman she knew. I barely remember that form anymore."

The kettle spoke, and as Yannis poured, she flickered. Her scales glistened gold, her head proud, unbowed, feather-crested, her teeth long and fierce, her skin threaded with fire: immutable, unbendingly vicious, a violence that once stalked prey through some prehistoric alien swamp, still, still, each heartbeat closer to a pounce. The preconscious mammal buried somewhere in Viv's body saw that shape and reacted with hot-stove speed; before she realized what was happening, she'd half risen to a crouch and dropped her teacup.

Then Yannis was Yannis again. She'd caught Viv's cup before it hit the floor. Viv's heart took longer to stop insisting she was about to die.

Yannis poured tea again. This cup was a darker green.

Viv sat stiffly. The first time she tried to lift the cup, it shook, spilled onto her fingers. She closed her eyes and breathed, centered herself. The next time, the tea made it to her lips.

"Well done." Yannis's laugh was a clicking of teeth. "I'm sorry to shock you. Some truths are better shown than told."

"Why didn't you tell Zanj? You must have seen her in the temple. She misses you. The Empress spent three thousand years torturing her. She thinks she's alone."

"You wouldn't understand."

"Maybe not." She shrugged. "But here's my guess. You didn't tell her, even though you miss her and she misses you, even though you were old galaxy-smashing buddies, because you know what she'd think about what you've done here."

Nictitating membranes closed across Yannis's eyes, but the pupils dilated wide, and reflected in their blackness Viv saw the ship behind her, saw the spear that pierced it through. "And what," Yannis said conversationally, "do you think we have done?"

"This is *Groundswell*, isn't it? Your great weapon, built from corpses of stitched-together Bleed, made to kill an Empress. And it came close—it hurt her. It fought off the first waves of her Diamond Fleet. But she called the Bleed themselves, in her desperation, and they wormed into *Groundswell*, tore it from you, and began to murder your ships. Zanj used the Fallen Star to kill it—and as Zanj struck, the Empress locked the Star away. She chased Zanj, and caught her. But you escaped—or once the Cloud was broken you crashed into *Groundswell*, like we did. You decided to stay. You had children, or cloned them, or used your crew and followers. Generations passed. You used the ship's systems to build soil, an ecosystem, a fake sun. In here, you're safe. You guide your subjects, you tend their village like a garden, and live in peace. In fear. Zanj would hate you for it."

"Don't tell me about Zanj." Yannis's voice went vicious and low. It hit Viv in the lungs. She couldn't breathe, for a heartbeat that lasted a thousand years. "Always rushing to battle, always bouncing back as if nothing hurt. She pushed for this . . . for this disaster. One big play for the galaxy. She failed. And now she's back, the same as ever."

Viv remembered Zanj's face in the shadows, in Viv's cabin, in the *Question*. "I don't think so."

Yannis lowered her teacup. "You don't know her like I do, dear. She wouldn't understand our plan: waiting this long, and this patiently, for victory."

"Hiding."

"Hardly. We draw on the minds of our children, and their children, and their ancestors sunk within the ship, devoting all their dreams, all their creative capacity, to a single problem: cracking the Empress's chains on the Fallen Star, and on the local Cloud."

Viv should have kept silent, should have let her speak, but she felt the conclusion well up in her, slip out her mouth before she could think through the implications of speaking the words out loud. "You want to rebuild your fleet. You want revenge."

Again, the grating laughter. "Revenge? We live well here. We are safe, and we have control. But we have lived these three thousand years at the mercy of the Empress's ignorance. If she knew we were here, she could kill us all in seconds. Once we solve her lock on the Cloud, we can change it, and banish her forever. She hides inside her Citadel; we would rule a citadel of our own, immortal and perfect, safe from the Bleed, forever."

"So, what happens now?" What a stupid question to ask. Her palms were moist; she drank more tea, bitter now that it had cooled. She was getting carried away with the dramatics of the moment: the secrets told, the plans. Always had been a nut for conspiracies.

"Now," Yannis said, "you forget."

She made another gesture like the one that summoned water. A hand closed around Viv's brain, the world tensed—and then it passed, and color returned. Granted, if she had forgotten something, she by definition would not remember what was gone, but she seemed to remember their whole conversation: the tea, Yannis, Zanj, the Fallen Star, plans, forgetting. She tried to say, *forget what*, thinking, no reason to let Yannis know her trick didn't work, but instead she said, "No."

Yannis's head tilted, then craned forward, curious. "Interesting. The ship does not touch your soul."

"Because I don't have one. That's what Hong said. I wasn't born here, so I don't have the kind of exomemory interfaces you people seem to have from birth. It's annoying. But it does protect me from the kind of nonsense you just tried." The words slipped out at first, then poured, gushed; she had as little control over them as she would have over bleeding, if Yannis stabbed her. She clapped her hand over her mouth, clenched her jaw. With deep breaths, the urge to speak, to babble, faded. She stood. Backed away. Yannis did not move. "What did you do to me?"

"A test. Fortunately, though the ship cannot touch your mind, the tea's effects are purely biochemical. It is good, and virtuous, to tell the truth."

Viv ran—and stopped, halfway to the hall, as if her left arm were cased in concrete. Yannis stood behind her, her hand closed around Viv's wrist. Viv tugged, but Yannis did not so much as twitch.

"Which brings me to my main question," she said. "Child, tell me: How did Zanj get free?"

Viv opened her mouth to curse, to spit, but the truth rose inside her like a bubble in a clear pool—she tried to catch it, stop it, but it slipped shimmering between her fingers, reached the surface, burst. "I let her out."

"Excellent." Yannis savored the word as she had savored her tea. She drew very close. "Come with me, dear. I would like to conduct an experiment."

31

XIARA CROUCHED IN boulder shadows and wished she had her spear, or her rifle, or her robots, or her ship, or Viv. But here, a million million miles from home, she had only herself—body, formidable; mind, adequate; soul, currently inaccessible—and the monster by her side. Viv was gone.

"They came this way," Gray said. "I can smell them." Chiefs and maidens but Xiara missed being able to do that—she would never have called it smell, but on the ship she could have traced Viv and Hong by their heat, the cells they shed, the whine of their nerves. Viv had called the experience "managed synesthesia" when Xiara described it, the *Question* collapsing telemetry data to her native senses—but no less true. The chants, the exercises, the blood of Orn had crafted in Xiara reflexes for mastering space and Cloud, but those great geometries did not play on her soulstrings like the little changes, the grace notes in the soug. On the *Question*, Viv smelled of elderflower and warm bread, and here, Xiara could not smell her anymore. So she followed the monster, even if she did not trust him. "The trail ends here." He pointed at a patch of bare ground, a slope of grassless rock without seam or joint.

"I'm going to look."

"I don't think that's a good idea." Before he reached the end of the sentence she was already moving, Ornchiefsdaughter striding from cover sharp and wary as a spring hare at the whiff of baying hounds. She was unarmed only in the vulgar sense. When you stand unarmed, the world must be your weapon, as the Chief her mother said. And though Xiara never had her mother's strength, her breadth, her canniness, she had seen more worlds in weeks than the Chief her mother had dreamed in all her years.

She kicked the ground. It did not give. But it did not give strangely—more like metal than rock. "Monster! Help me."

Gray shook his head, from cover. "I'm not a—look, just get back over here!"

She kicked the rock again, and still it refused to move.

"If something's wrong," the monster said, "we can ask about it in the morning."

"Viv may be dead by morning."

"She's snuck off up the mountain before. You said so yourself."

She did not contest his point. But Viv—Viv of the cunning smile and the sharp eye and the jokes no one understood—had left her bed on the first night, and in the morning Xiara had asked why, and accepted an answer that was no answer. Then Viv left her bed a second night, and in the morning Xiara asked, and accepted an answer that was no answer.

No Ornchiefsdaughter would be denied the truth three times.

On the second night, Xiara crept from bed and saw Viv climb the mountain alone, and come back down; on the third, she'd seen her take Hong, and so she herself went back for Gray, whose monster nose could follow trails her own could not. Even if he was at heart a lazy child. "Hey," he said. "I need rest. We have work tomorrow. Yannis wants us to close the last of the fissure and start plowing. If I'm exhausted—"

"Come help me, monster."

"Okay! Fine." He slouched from the shadows, chastened, lit pale silver by the shipmoons above. She remembered those ships—how they felt from the inside, their voices, their power and their rage. Remembered what she had almost become, drawn into them. She did not shudder with this feeling that was almost joy and almost fear—she was hunting, and hunts were no place for a hunter's ghosts. "Would you at least stop calling me *monster*?"

"You held my people hostage for years."

"I made them happy! I gave them what they wanted, and all I did in return was record *what* they wanted."

"You robbed their freedom."

"Oh, sure, their freedom to fight and die in a broken wasteland. Some freedom."

"You took them from their homes."

He looked over to her, and for once his too-large features, his too-big eyes, were truly unreadable. "I didn't know then."

She almost believed him, but this, too, would be best discussed after the hunt. "Touch the ground here. It is wrong."

He knelt, spread his hands out like lily pads, and leaned into the bare rock. "Look. I—when I first fell to Orn, I didn't understand it. It looked so . . . boring. Everything stayed itself all the time. And everyone wanted so many things you couldn't have—basic stuff. I thought I could help. I made mistakes."

Clearly they did not teach monsters the silence of the hunt. "Do you feel it? It's—"

"Hollow," he said. "Yes." His lily-pad hands sprouted small tendrils at their edges, and those dug into the ground. "Weird. There's a seam." Something cracked within the rock, not at all like stone cracked—more like when lightning struck one of Old Orn's crystal towers.

A perfectly straight line split the slope in two and it rolled apart soundlessly, both doors vanishing into the rock, to reveal a shallow cave which ended in a wall of shadow.

"Um," Gray said. "Look, we don't know what this is. We should go back, get help maybe, ask if anyone back in Refuge has seen anything like—"

Xiara marched into the cave, through the wall, and Gray, too late to stop her, ran after.

Shadow parted around her like a thicket, and she found herself in a ship.

This was not a *conclusion* drawn from *evidence*, as Viv always sought the why of things. Xiara knew this was a ship, because it spoke like ships spoke to her blood. She answered at once from her soul's depths, as her secret muscles woke and moved, as fire burned beneath her skin.

A ship, yes, not hers—so vast and alien Zanj's vessel seemed a raft at best. This one ship, itself, was the equal of all that ruined fleet in orbit. Xiara's blood sought purchase on it, but her blood was too thin a rope to rein such majesty. For a moment *it* even sought to rule *her,* flooding back along the link, a great hand to climb her spine and wield her as its instrument.

But she was a daughter of Orn, and her mothers' mothers bound her. Fly the ship, do not be flown.

She had lost control, in that great wrecked fleet overhead. It called to her and she failed and crashed them here. She would not let it happen again.

She stilled her secret muscles, made her blood, what Viv called her implants, what Zanj had called her nanome, sleep. She came back to herself, slumped against the white wall of the Aft Anterior Hull Access Corridor 2773-A, Western Cloud Antenna Interproximal, and realized she'd been screaming. There was a siren, too—and red lights.

Intruder alert.

Gray knelt over her, holding her up, eyes wide, an expression that, if he were not a monster, she would have described as scared. "Xiara. What's wrong?"

"Ship," she said, which she thought should serve.

"It's broken."

"Not ours." Idiot. "This one. A ship." Mothers, why wouldn't he *understand*. "Everywhere." Footsteps. She smelled them coming—burnt oranges, copper wire, the fresh grassy snap of a live cricket in the mouth. Tried to warn him, but the words weren't there.

"Gray."

A voice—whose? Turn your head, focus the eyes. Ornchiefsdaughter, pilot yourself, if you can. There, at the corner of the hall, stood a hulking shape, aged and bent, with stubby broken horns: Nioh, flanked by two glassy-eyed villagers of Refuge. Behind those three, two white webs—*intruder containment point defense,* words bubbling out of her contact with the ship, a knowledge that slid snakelike inside her, nested—webs that peeled off the walls, leaving no hollows to mark where they had been. Nano-thickness immobilizing restraints, probabilistically nonlethal, used in case of primary modifier impairment. She didn't know what most of those words meant—they sounded like the way Viv talked sometimes—but she knew they were dangerous.

"Nioh?" Gray asked. "Gatyen?" Of course Gray recognized them. They had worked side by side. The villagers' faces were blank, and an orange light played around their temples—but the thickset elder moved with purpose. Gray was talking fast, eager: "We didn't mean to break anything. We're just looking for our friends. We think Viv came down this way. Honest, we don't want to cause anybody any trouble." Hands splayed, face open. These were his friends. They couldn't want to hurt him.

Nioh signaled with one hand, and the webs darted forward.

One caught Gray's arm, and wormed up the limb toward his mouth; Gray snatched the other out of the air before it could hit Xiara, and stared down in panic as it wove around his fingers, up his arm, clinging, constricting. He tried to shake the webs free, and failed. Tried to claw them off, but they stuck together. Xiara took one step back toward the door—she should have run, but fear froze her, and loyalty. She could not leave him.

Gray frowned at the webs that covered his body. He darkened, like the Chief did when solving a problem. Then his skin bubbled silver between the strands of web, and burst, snaring the web inside him; the webs wriggled, scrambled, beneath his skin, but they could not escape. He chewed, some-how, with his whole body, and swallowed, and stood once more unhin-dered against Nioh. "That wasn't nice," he said. "I'm sure this is all a mistake. But I think you should tell me where our friends are now."

"Surrender." Nioh's voice was deep. She gestured again, and more webs detached smoothly from the hall, all up and down its length. And Nioh her-self grew: armorfields closed her skin, and her staff sprouted a spearhead dripping light. "It will be easier for you."

Gray swelled. In seconds, he grew a foot in height, and across the shoul-ders. He did not have muscles, and his skin wasn't skin at all—but he grew tissue, strong and tight-wound as cables, to move him through space. His hands thickened, and his fingers sprouted long yellow claws. Red eyes blazed from his child's face. "If you have our friends," he said, "please don't do this. Just send them out. Whatever you've done to Gatyen, whatever you've done to Viv, I don't want to hurt you."

Xiara marched forward then, and joined him. She felt a rush as she did so, the vertigo of standing beside Gray as if he were a clansman. But he had fought for them, again and again. He saved her on Orn, devouring Pride drones. He had sheltered Viv. She would not abandon him now.

Nioh glanced at her, and her broad mouth parted to reveal blunt, heavy teeth.

"Xiara," Gray said calmly. "Run."

"I can fight."

"Not against these guys." He sounded cautious, tense, calculating. Was this how a monster sounded when he was afraid? "Find Zanj. Tell her what happened. She'll know what to do."

Xiara felt the first trickle of her own fear, like the first raindrops before a gouging storm. It made her want to stay and fight. But Gray had withstood Ornclan attack for almost a year without weakening, and he sounded scared. And though Xiara knew, as all Ornclan children knew, the ways of battle, her mothers and teachers had not trained her and raised her simply to fight.

They trained her and raised her to win.

Sometimes, to win, you had to lose. Sometimes, to win, you had to run for reinforcements, and trust your fellows to guard your back.

"I will go for her," she said. "Fight well." She did not add *monster.* Did not even think it.

She ran.

Behind her, Nioh bellowed in a tongue Xiara did not know. She did not care about the words, or about the webs flitting after her. It was not her duty to care. Gray stood behind her. He would hold, while he could manage. Her duty was to run.

She leapt from the cave into the night, skidded down the slope. Flashes of uncanny light and the noise of tearing metal chased her into darkness—darkness that was dark no longer as her eyes opened, adjusted, as she kenned the ground beneath. Shipmoons lit the mountainside: noontime bright to her, as the Ornblood woke. A hypersensitive metacornea, Viv had suggested when Xiara described how she could see in perfect dark, form blooming from nothing as needed. Viv and her magic nonsense words. Xiara's eyes worked, that was all, as her feet adjusted to stable and unstable ground, skipped rabbits' holes and cracks in stone without conscious intervention. Xiara was a firm runner, steadiest, strongest in the clan.

Wherever Viv came from, her grandmothers had wrapped her in different enchantments, handed down different teachings through their blood. With the lights off in a windowless room, Viv saw nothing, stumbled blindfolded groping for walls, shuffling over carpet, growing peevish as Xiara laughed, as she slipped from her touch, circling in what to Viv was dark and to Xiara daylight clear, touching her now on the small of the back, now on the side, now brushing her bare arm with a kiss. And when Viv lunged for her and caught nothing, and stumbled into the space only for Xiara to slide behind her, catch her, draw her close, kiss her and press her against the wall and feel Viv's enchantments, her scruples, the tensions that distant nightmare world had fixed beneath her flesh begin to melt, as Xiara pressed her leg between her legs, and held Viv's wrists against the wall above her head with one hand . . . And in the morning after Viv was the same as ever, as distant and assured, precise and complete, pretending herself unchanged, this beautiful, strange, hard, soft woman who never stopped fighting, yet would never kill.

Xiara would save her. Whatever it cost.

She heard a flutter above, as of birds' wings or a thrown bolo cutting air, and ducked behind a tree—so the web, brilliant blue in the shipmoons' light, fell on the tree instead of her, and crushed its trunk to splinters. Another web arced overhead—Xiara sprang from her shelter to a cliff, from the cliff to a tree, caught a branch, fell, caught another and dropped and heard, behind her, the wet slap of web on rock. How many more could she dodge? How many were there?

She had made good time. Ten more minutes' hard run would bring her to the village. She risked a glance back. White webs gathered on the cliff's edge. Twenty. Thirty. More.

They sprang.

And here she was skidding down an open slope, without cover.

The webs arrowed into the sky, spread winglike at the apex of their arc, adjusted to aim, then curled themselves back into spears and flew.

If she had a shield, she could have blocked them. If she had a spear, she could have parried them. If a rifle, shot them from the sky. If she had cover, she could have hidden behind it. But she was running alone and unarmed on a mountain slope.

When you stand unarmed, the world must be your weapon.

She was not running down a mountain. She was running down a ship: a single vessel of vast confounding mind, dormant and thousands of years mad. She did not know the true name that would master it; without the Cloud to steel and support her, she would crumble in moments before its will. But she did not need to master it. Just to nudge it a little.

She woke her blood, and told the ship: *move.*

The pain took her at once, the vastness of the ship and its many wounds. Death looped forever in its mind as angels fell and Bleed-mouths opened and the Empress, glorious green, fled. Xiara slipped, fell, struck her forehead on a rock, rolled scraped and torn down the mountainside, thinking, this is it.

She woke a timeless instant later to the ringing of bells.

Xiara opened her eyes. Pressed arms against rock to force herself up to her knees, commanded legs and back and belly to raise her to her feet. Around her, trees swayed. Boulders rocked upslope; gravel and ground sifted, settling after the convulsion she had caused.

All around her lay the mounded webs, spreading, seeking, clutching rock to powder. But Xiara herself was free.

She picked through the webs, limping, toward the village. She could breathe and walk, though her side hurt, though her foot twisted. She wanted to stop, to rest. She had time for neither.

When she reached the village square, the first door opened.

A girlchild stood inside in silhouette, dark against dark save her glassy open eyes and the orange light that circled her forehead like a crown. Arms at her side, mouth open, her body rigid as a carving's, she ran toward Xiara.

Xiara ran faster.

A second door opened, and a third. An old woman vaulted through a window. Bare feet slapped bare earth; hands reached for her out of an alley and she caught them, shifted weight, tossed the lunger—a little lizard-man she remembered serving wine that first night—to the ground, saw him skid, heard him moan. She spared him a stab of sympathy, but she had to duck away from another lunge and run farther, faster, commanding her joints to ignore their pain, her muscles to ignore their damage, blinking through blood from the cut on her forehead, numbing the ache of her broken rib, scrubbing oxygen, suspending thought.

The world simplified to rhythm. Feet. Night. Wind. Slower. (Stride imbalance. Stabilizers of the ankle strained. Steady. Compensate. Like skirting a black hole: easy, if you know how. The Ornblood knows.) She ran through Refuge, villagers after her jumping from rooftop to rooftop, eerie silent, their footfalls like rain, minds suspended, bodies ridden by their elders' will.

Open distance. Keep pace.

After a mile, her knee seized, on schedule—which was to say, at the least convenient moment. There stood the antenna, just out of reach. A bedroll spread before it, and on that bedroll, sound asleep: Zanj.

The rainstorm neared, the rushing feet, the open mouths. She couldn't keep it up. She could. A few more steps. Black spots in vision—bad sign.

She stumbled. Fell to her knees.

The bedroll lay before her. Zanj snoring. Teeth bare through lips. Xiara heard a whisper in the night behind her, a sense of approaching mass—a hammer struck the earth, and she turned, and saw Nioh recover from her landing and rise, smoking, furious, scarred, one horn broken off, one eye swollen, injured from her battle with Gray, but still vast and strong. And advancing. The orange light that bound the villagers burned around her hands. She worked them like marionettes.

Nioh spoke, but Xiara's heart beat too loud for her to hear the words. She thought of Gray, the boy who was a monster, who fought to give her this chance. She thought of Viv. She wondered if they were still alive. She could not hear herself when she shouted, "Zanj!"

No answer. Nioh advanced a step, light-spear dripping in her hand, and the villagers closed in, breathing heavy, sweating, hungry, silent save for animal sounds.

Xiara shook Zanj's arm. Pounded on her chest, on her stomach. This woman could shatter gods, if she would just wake up.

Xiara collapsed, weeping, on her chest.

Claws stroked her hair.

She looked up into a pair of red-gold eyes, and a vicious smile on a scarred face.

32

VIV FOUGHT WHILE she had strength. Sirens wailed; the hallway lights burned red. Hong must be at large, uncaught. She dug her heels in; she planted her feet against Yannis's body and strained with every fiber of her muscle, and still could not break the woman's hold on her wrist. She punched her, and hurt her hand; she gouged for her eyes, but Yannis swatted her thumbs away, annoyed. Yannis never slowed. She had seemed bent by years, but then, three thousand years weighed more than Viv.

Viv could have made Yannis drag her all the way to whatever doom she had in mind, but she could not choose to be dragged. While she had strength, she fought. When strength gave out, if she was going to her death, she preferred to go under her own power.

"I'm glad you've seen reason, dear," Yannis said when she tired and began to walk. "No sense making this less pleasant than it has to be."

She wasn't wrong, though Viv's plan ran more toward saving her strength for when it might help. If Yannis and Zanj were even close to the same sort of being, she would never win an arm wrestling match. "Where are you taking me?"

Yannis stopped at a patch of wall that seemed identical to the rest and made another sign in air. The wall bloomed open, and they fell out into the abyss within the world.

Viv turned and spun in space—the rush of free fall coupled with knowledge that she was about to die, inside this monstrosity of chitin or metal or monomolecule hull, or, fuck, sub-ether nonsense for all she understood, surrounded by lights and battle damage and the impossible mass of that black spear through the ship's heart—and found, when the panic passed, that she could breathe. Then she noticed the inch-thick skinsuit field that covered her, and the slight burnt tang of the air. Just a bit of nothing between her and vacuum. She hadn't minded that on her earlier spacewalks, but then, her earlier spacewalks had been under her own power, in a suit she controlled.

Yannis spun them in space, pointed her pitchfork, and they flew, with a speed that almost dislocated Viv's shoulder; at her scream Yannis eased off the accelerator, but still their speed built, and built. Viv gained a new sense of *Groundswell*'s scope by the long minutes it took them to reach the point where the spear transfixed the ship.

Spear was too small a word. It might be wrong on even the most basic topological level: Viv could see no tip or blade or barb, only an immense column so black it burned her eyes, facets growing and melding as she watched, its darkness broken by darting blue weblike lines that branched, cascaded, then vanished without trace.

"Like a brain," she said without thinking. The tea still at work inside her, maybe.

"Yes," Yannis replied. "In most ways that matter. The Fallen Star is Zanj's weapon, her ship, the greatest part of her soul. We don't even have words for what it's made from. Computationally dense acausal neutronium was Old Tiger's guess, but that doesn't explain all of its properties. Zanj took it from beings you would not understand, and it fit her as if they had crafted it for her grip. And still, it is chained."

Yes—chained. At first, the Fallen Star's sheer mass had drawn Viv's eye, but now she saw the bonds that held it fast. Jade vines climbed the Star, and sank thin, burning roots into its blackness. Where the blue cascades met green, they stopped. The chains seemed too flimsy to hold something like this—an engine Zanj would have mocked her for describing with so worthless a word as *god*. But Viv recognized that green. She saw it in nightmares. "The Empress."

"She chained it," Yannis said. "Now you will break those chains, and I will use it to keep Refuge safe, forever." Her form slipped as they drew close, returning to that fearsome burning predatory shape she'd shown Viv over tea. She stood without a stoop now, her scales glistened and feathered. Two more arms swelled beneath her cloak. She opened like a flower bud to some radiation from the Star. Or perhaps that was only memory bridging the eons between Yannis, village elder, and the woman who once fought an Empress.

"No," Viv said.

"You will do it," Yannis replied. "For me. For Refuge."

Viv backed away from her slowly, hands out. "I get it. You're afraid. But you don't have to do this."

"Afraid?" Yannis's tongue flicked out; her eyes were dangerous slits. "Child, you are speaking nonsense."

"I know fear when I see it. You lost a big fight, and to cover for yourself you let your people slide back to the Bronze Age, and kept them there, and made as if hiding would keep you safe."

"You don't understand," Yannis said. "You've never met Her." And there was no doubt which *her* she meant.

"I have. She pulled me into this fucked-up world. She gave me this scar."

"A scar?" The laugh was fierce and torn. "I have seen Her scatter ships like a thresher scatters husks of rice. She broke my friends and laughed at the ease with which She slew them. She called the Bleed upon us. She shouldered off our might, and carved Zanj down to that ruin you rescued from the star. But we survived here, free. We built ourselves this place. If this is what it takes to live, then we will live. Break the chain."

"No."

"You do not understand."

"I do. The answer's still no."

Yannis hissed, and drew in breath, and let it out. She looked almost sorry before she moved.

She grabbed Viv's wrist again and dragged her toward the Star. Viv kicked her, and bit her; she caught *Groundswell*'s ribs and antennae, the many protrusions from its hull, and still Yannis pulled her forward. Viv's nails bent back; her fingers slipped, scraped. Their pads tore. She wedged her foot in a crack in the ship, and Yannis stopped, growled, then knelt, picked her up by her ankle and tossed her toward the Star, which, when she struck it, felt like any other wall.

Her head rang; she tasted blood, and hoped that wasn't her tongue. Fallen but free, she scrambled to her feet, and tried to get away, but Yannis was already over her, four-armed now—one hand caught each of Viv's wrists as she rose, and the fingertips of her third hand squeezed into Viv's clenched left fist and peeled it open, forced her fingers back, back—her thumb dislocated with a pop, and she screamed, and in that instant of pain, Yannis hooked Viv's fingers over the Empress's vines and pulled.

The vines made a sound like violin strings when they snapped.

Yannis let her fall.

Viv lay, teeth gritted, curled around her thumb, heartbeat fast, cursing, weeping. She did not let herself breathe, because if she breathed she would scream, and she would not let herself scream before this woman.

This woman—

—who stood before the Fallen Star, its immensity wreathed now by cascades of unrestrained blue light, vibrating with its full power.

—who reached for it, this phantom of her dark dreams.

Pulled.

Strained.

And yet the Star did not move.

Viv breathed through the tears. She had to, because she could not stop laughing.

Yannis clawed at the Star, cursed it, kicked it, and it did not budge. Yannis grew to mountainous size and wrapped her arms around the Star, and strained, her feet dimpling the hull. She roared curses in radio bands—and *Groundswell* trembled.

But that tremor had nothing to do with her.

Viv was still laughing when the ship's skin burst open and Zanj flared out into the hollow night, trailed by the fires of her wrath.

33

ZANJ BURNED IN the air, massive, slick, and deadly, radiating war. Her fur sparked and glistened, and her tail lashed, whiplike. The scar that twisted her face burned, too, a rot-bog green that pulled the corners of her eye and mouth. Her fingers dripped ichor and light.

Viv, still collapsed around her dislocated thumb, stopped laughing. Zanj had almost killed her before, had promised to kill her often. She wreaked gleeful destruction through waves of Pride. But after those first few attempts at murder, she'd bent her power to their journey: to escape, to survival, to helping Viv. This Zanj was different.

This was Zanj as she had been before three thousand years of torture inside a star: Zanj, pirate queen, ruthless and unruled, Zanj whose mention scared kings and gods to silence, Zanj the stealer of suns, Zanj who would drive a fleet of her friends to destruction to burn the sky free of Empresses. Zanj, whom the years had marked only by her scar and her crown.

And Viv had thought she knew her.

"Let it go," Zanj said.

"Of course, Sister." Yannis, grown immense, hissed like sand down a dune face and released the Star. She bowed low. If Zanj's arrival worried her, the only sign she gave was an exaggerated formality. "Zanj."

"Sister Heyshir."

"Yannis," she said. "Please. We did not lie about that: we left our old names on the battlefield. Not even our children know them. And is Nioh . . . ?"

"Alive," she said. "She will heal in time. Yannis." Zanj tasted the name as she advanced. "A galaxy of names to choose from, and that's what you went with?"

"It's a good, simple name. We need no more in Refuge." This politeness from a giant snake woman made Viv laugh, but her laugh did not draw a

glance from Zanj. Zanj, she realized then, had not looked at her since breaking into *Groundswell's* core. "I am glad to see you awake, Sister. I had thought
you lost."

"Not glad enough," Zanj said, "to introduce yourself to me when I arrived
in Refuge, or to explain your con. You did not respect me enough to respect
my traveling companions."

"Those mayflies? Do you truly care about them?"

"Of course not."

Some people—including Viv, especially if drunk—joke about not caring
for people, about screwing over friends. Some people—including Viv, drunk
or not—joke about these things because jokes hide truths, invert them,
preening gilt and flash to protect a vulnerable underbelly. We joke about
what we cannot allow ourselves to be.

Zanj was not joking now. Her voice bore no hint of comradeship or concern. It was light, and mocking-friendly, the same tone with which she'd
shrugged off any of Viv's questions she deemed foolish: What do you need?
Are you hurt? How can I help?

"Do your children matter?" Zanj asked in the same light, scornful tone.
"Do you care about them?"

"Of course," Yannis said. "In a so-many-greats-grandmotherly kind of
way. They keep me occupied, and their brains are useful platforms for our
decryption apparatus. Not necessary now, of course! Thanks to this one here.
A master key for the Empress's chains—a valuable tool." She reached for
Zanj, but Zanj slipped away on the air. "I've freed your weapon, dear Sister."

"Out of the goodness of your heart, I am sure."

She laughed an avalanche. "Of course not! You were gone. And when you
returned, you were not what you are now. I watched you—saw you work
with those mayflies, indulge them, and never offer them a hint of yourself.
If that *was* you after all. I half anticipated some Imperial trick—She had you
as Her plaything for three thousand years. She might have petaled you like
a flower, unstitched your mind and bent it to Her fancy and sent a thousand little Zanjlings out into the world to do Her bidding. It hurt to look at
you, and see what you'd become. But now—Sister! There's so much we can
do together."

Zanj raised one eyebrow. "You've spent three thousand years playing
farmer. Do you really think I'd be interested?"

"Means to an end," Yannis said. "Means to an end. We have our base.
We have a fleet out there, wrecked but recoverable. We have you. And this

puppet—" She kicked at Viv, scornful, but her foot was the size of a small bus. Viv tried to roll out of the way but when Yannis's foot struck her she flew and landed, and lost the world for a reeling, gut-churning moment. She couldn't breathe—no, she could. She could force herself up. She wasn't dying. She almost vomited—forced it, choked it down, which was worse. She would die here, after all this. Trampled to death by a giant while Zanj hovered overhead, uncaring.

Wearing a crown that bound her to obey.

Hong had warned her: Give Zanj the chance and she will leave, and never come back. She doesn't need you. She doesn't care about you.

The crown shimmered gray on Zanj's brow.

"Careful," Zanj said as if discussing a quite abstract position, as if Viv didn't lie gasping on the fucking ground beneath her, as if she really was a puppet, a tool, a toy. "You'll break her."

"Those tiny fleshy hands can snap the Empress's chains. I almost didn't believe, but I've seen it now. We could seal off a small corner of the Cloud and rule supreme, free of Her gaze. Whole systems, Zanj, not just Refuge."

"She's trouble," Zanj said. "No soul. Just a hunk of meat you have to move around."

"Meat's useful. Meat can be forced the old-fashioned way. No need for encryption, for name-games. Just hurt her until she does what you want. And then we will be queens."

Zanj thought. Viv watched her, aching, sick, small, scared.

Zanj did not think for very long. "Sounds good," she said. "First, though, I think you have something of mine."

"Naturally." Yannis bowed, stepped aside, and offered her the Star. "Take up your weapon, Sister. Let us rule."

34

"I'M HUNGRY," GRAY moaned to the shipmind, and received not the slightest answer, not even the bare courtesy of coarse, unfiltered current for a meal.

He hung locked into a single form like a barbarian, in a column of light, starving. Already his mind dipped into self-recriminating spirals of grief and shame, already his skin drew taut over his ribs. The extensive structural damage—a base-birthed biped would have interpreted it as left arm broken in three places, right in two, right leg above and below the knee, left leg dislocated but otherwise intact, collarbone and occipital fractures in profusion— would have inconvenienced him if he could move, but that yawning, enervating pit of hunger at the core of his being, the ever-increasing cycles dedicated to desperate need for food, would kill him before long. He would start to burn himself, shrivel to a husk, a cinder, a spark, then gone, here in the forgotten end of space.

So much for Gray.

The indignity could not be denied. If he ever reached home again, if he were ever so fortunate as to see the vasty beaches and crystal skies of the Great Lady's palace, or dart with his cousins and grandparents through the fractal mazes of Her mind, forgiven his grand crimes, his banishment, he would encrypt the present hopeless scenario so deep in the recesses of his memory that only the Lady's word could unlock it. If not, he would spend all his generations the laughingstock of the Grayframe, an example and a cautionary tale. Ware, ye kids, lest you suffer old Gray's fate: condemned to a single form, bound by things only a little more than human, confined in a reflective field in the belly of a worldship in a weed sea of space, there to expire from hunger.

He had fought hard, and fallen harder. Without the Cloud to fan through, with native avenues of escape and transformation denied him, he'd been left to match Nioh strength for strength, and a Gray of Grayframe was

inefficient when so used. In his native element, which was anywhere the
Empress ruled, he could have become a dust storm of hungry razors, growing as he devoured, adjusting instantly to compensate for the form of any
fool who might dare come against him. Here, he had been forced to wrestle
Nioh, the implacable weight of those great arms, the wisdom of those thick
fingers and that broad back, burning all his meager stores of power while
she tapped the ship itself, directly.

Even so, he'd held her.

Until she cast him down.

(Details, details.)

No shame in losing such an uneven fight, he told himself, even if one's
family would laugh. No, the shame—if it was, in fact, shame—rested in this:
he had not, in truth, fought as hard as he might have done.

Yes, he wrestled with cunning and viciousness that would have pleased
his great-grandcousins whose warring ways the Grayframe passed down
through generations to him. Yes, too, he had marshaled his resources down
to the last joule, leaving himself at ebb, tumbling into the great pit of his
hunger. But he had not used all the tools at his disposal.

Even at the end, as his strength failed and Nioh's great arm circled his
neck and began to squeeze, there had been a source of power available to
him untapped.

Gatyen watched them fight—a possessed Gatyen, his eyes glazed, his
head crowned with orange flame, Gatyen but without his smile and without his laugh and without the dappleglisten of the well water he poured over
his hair to cool him in the sun, but Gatyen nonetheless. Gatyen who invited
Gray to eat with the rest of the digging crew, who shared the most delectable confections—big slow kind Gatyen.

Gray could have eaten him.

He should have done it. A delectable carbon-and-water body, plus the
mind that body contained, held all sorts of chains to break, order to liber-
ate, matter to decompose to energy. Would it have been enough to allow
Gray, in this limited state, to beat Nioh? Perhaps. If the move had been un-
expected, at the right moment—Gray twisting his neck, disjointing his jaw,
lengthening his teeth, broadening his gorge, one snap and done—he might
have taken the old warbeast.

But he held back even as his bones broke. And now, suspended in light,
as the pit claimed more and more of his mind, he looked inside himself and
realized he would have made the same decision.

After all his exile, he'd learned nothing.

Gatyen, still possessed, stood guard. Webdrones flanked the man, hovering free of the floor; they twitched when Gatyen breathed, bound to his perceptions. Gray's friend's mind was elsewhere: eaten by the ship, perhaps, or submerged inside it. But Gatyen had a mind of meat, like Viv's. Meat thoughts built trails and habits in the wet mass of meat brains.

"Gatyen," he whined—he, a Gray of Grayframe, whined!—"Gatyen, I'm hungry."

He did not need to fake desperation. The pit within him grew and gobbled.

"I'm dying. I'll devour myself right here, if you don't help me." With his jaw so swollen, he could barely talk the way meatfolks did, but he tried. If he talked like meat, the ship would hear him with meat ears and a meat-brain that had once invited Gray to its house for dinner, a meatbrain that once watched Gray turn into different animals to amuse its children. "I don't need much," he wheedled. "Just a trace, a trickle. I'm dying." He loosed what little control he had on the pit inside him. It widened, gobbled: he lost his sense of touch, lost all colors save for green. Skin pulled throbbing taut over his frame.

He stared into Gatyen's eyes, showed real desperation as even his greens, his lovely, luxurious greens, the greens of grass and rice and moss on rock, faded to bland evaluative monochrome.

"Please. I'm no use to them dead."

Perhaps that was what did it: Nioh had taken him alive, and even this fragmentary shipmind understood the directive that implied. But he preferred to think that some structure of Gatyen remained in the man's skull after all, and the ship, thinking with that brain, was moved by his compassion.

Whatever the reason, even as Gray tumbled into the pit of his own hunger, the ship's great clench relaxed, and the smallest trickle of current curled into his body.

He could have wept. He could have screamed. He shook in bliss. That small a current felt as luxurious, as glittering, as that grain silo he'd eaten on his first night in Refuge: feeding and feeding and feeding in the grip of preconscious need.

But he could not lose himself in ecstasy now. The others needed him. Viv needed him, Viv lost within this ship in her adversaries' hands, Viv who had given him mercy when, to be honest, he deserved none. Xiara needed him—he'd fought for her, in hope he could prove himself, and he'd failed her.

Gatyen needed him, wherever his mind might be.

So even though he let the ship's current soak through his bones and knit them, let it corkscrew down amine chains to feed the pit in his being, he took most of that meager allotment to power pores he'd modified to sweat caustic fluid.

In that moment, he became aware of a great Attention settling upon him, not unlike the mind of the Empress Herself: a mind far more unified than this babbling, mad ship, yet proceeding through its circuits and systems. Perhaps his wheedling and convincing had attracted Nioh, or one of the other secret masters of this world.

He trembled. He had no strength for such a fight.

Still Gatyen watched him, mindless, innocent.

Acid sweat rolled, searing, smoking, down Gray's body, and dripped onto the concave lens that projected the light which held him.

The lens hissed. Cracked.

Shattered.

He fell to all fours as webdrones launched to catch him and tangled in the air above his head. One, more clever than the rest, snagged his arm, but he tore it with his teeth and it went limp. He snapped its body like a whip to knock a second drone from the air, and ran for the room's sole door.

Before he reached it, Gatyen struck him in the side.

Gray did not feel the hit; he felt the wall when he struck, and slid down.

The orange light wreathed Gatyen now, rippling all along his arms, bulging from his back like a grotesque hump. His eyes did not focus, and his face held that same expression of distant concern, as if trying to remember a vital name once known but now forgotten.

The Attention drew nearer, step by step through the ship. Gray could not fight something so vast and win, not here, not like this.

He rolled to his feet and sprinted for the exit. Gatyen, or the light around Gatyen, raised his arms like a wrestler—Gray tried to slide between his legs, but great orange arms swooped down and lifted him, crushed him to his friend's chest. Gray fought back, grew more arms, but that slender trace of power he'd used to heal, to allow himself this moment's freedom, was almost gone already.

A webdrone struck him from behind, snaked out tendrils to cover his hands and bind them together.

The pit inside him yawned again, devouring color and urgency, devouring all else beneath raw calculation.

He needed food.

Here was Gatyen. He could eat.

His teeth knew their business. They could bite through any armor. His Lady had shaped him to devour.

The Attention neared—down the hall, around the corner, the edges of its sensorium trumpeting its approach, as he himself had once darted down spacelanes before his Lady to ready worlds for Her digestion. Hungry, he could not beat Gatyen and his webdrones. Hungry, he would have no chance against that approaching Mind.

Gatyen smelled full of health, of strength, so simple within his shell of light, barely a being at all. Gray wouldn't have to eat all of him. Just a bite or two.

Gray's teeth unsheathed.

He saw himself reflected in the glass of Gatyen's eyes.

And he remembered his vow to Viv.

He closed his mouth. Roared in frustration, futility; struck Gatyen's ribs with his knees, kicked his stomach, struck his nose with his forehead, pushed him away. Webdrones struck him again and again from behind. Their micro-shocks overwhelmed his muscles, and their strands contracted to pull his arms inexorably to his sides. Gatyen's light pummeled him, and the pit of hunger gaped and at last the Attention breached upon them like a whale surfacing from a bulge in water.

Xiara stepped into the cell.

She did not look like the woman he had begged to run.

The webdrones flew back from Gray and burned in midair, fell as ash. Gatyen, too, recoiled, slammed into the wall. The wall itself sprouted arms that held him, crushing in, in—

"No," Gray croaked, and the arms stopped.

Xiara turned her pilot's eyes on him, wheels within wheels in the mask of her face.

"What happened to you?" Gray breathed.

She shook her head, confused. *Zanj,* the ship said before she remembered to use her mouth. "Zanj. She—she knows the ship. She gave me its name. Are you . . . well?" As if the concept made little sense to her now.

"These rubes couldn't hurt a Gray of Grayframe." His shaking voice spoiled that line, but he didn't care. He stood between her and Gatyen, for all the good it would do. "He's my friend. They controlled him. He doesn't deserve to die."

"Control," Xiara said, distant. "Ah. Yes." One hand raised, opening like a flower: the arms released, and Gatyen fell, and rose partway, his eyes his own again.

"Gray?" His voice might have been fresh-hewn from rock. "What is this?"

He offered a hand, helped Gatyen to his feet. "You were out of your mind. We've brought you back, but . . . you need to get home. Back to the village. Find your family. Keep them safe. We can't protect you if you stay." Especially, he most certainly did not say, because you smell so delicious. "Go."

When Gatyen had run off, when they were alone, Gray and this ship-woman in Xiara Ornchiefsdaughter's body: "What's it like in there?"

"I see," she said. "Centuries of mad dreaming. Streams of numbers. Spiral paths of silence. I feel *Groundswell* like my . . . skin." As if having skin struck her as novel. "It's so much, so much . . ."

"Did you find Hong?"

"No."

He knew that peevish tone of thwarted omniscience—the Lady spoke that way when some system defied her, when some upstart Dyson sphere refused to submit. "What about Viv? Zanj?"

"Yes" was not a full answer for his question, but he knew better than to needle a woman who was a battleship. "Viv." She tasted that name, and he did not need to peer inside her mind to know she also tasted memories, the vivid simulations the shipmind could summon and unfold, recalled eternities between breath and breath. "She lies upon the hull, battered, alive, mostly whole. And Zanj." Her eyes grew distant. She winced, groaned, impossibly, tumbled—Gray caught her weight, then regretted it when she squeezed his broken ribs with the strength of a hydraulic press. "Zanj shines. She burns. She . . ." Xiara's teeth gritted together, her face a mask of pain. "Gray, it's too much. I can't."

He held her arm, and let her hold his, despite the pain. She did not pull away.

He said, "Take me there."

35

THE FALLEN STAR woke as Zanj drew near.

The luminous cascade beneath its skin built, blinding brilliant blue, and Zanj transformed as well. The gleaming silver weapon of her, the dancing murderer, the pirate queen, gained depth and shadow and the weight of long absence. She stretched out her hand, parting heavy curtains of time.

Viv, prone on the ship's skin, breathing through the pain in her ribs and head and hand, watched Zanj reach for this weapon that would make her more fearsome still, a force to break planets and challenge an Empress, and she remembered the nothingness in Zanj's gaze when she looked down at her, that slow opening and closing of her eyes—a blink of idle surprise a swatted gnat was not yet dead. Yannis, giant-sized, flicked her tongue, a serpent's anticipation.

Hong had been right. *She will not come back for you.* She is ancient and powerful, and knows no kinship. She obeys her own whims and needs, no more. You may travel together, but she is not your friend. She wants freedom and revenge, and she will cast you aside the moment she can seize either.

And Viv remembered how Zanj looked in battle: the fierce inventive glee with which she stole, with which she killed, the ease and scorn she'd shown as she broke the Ornchief and scattered Pride drones, fighters, battleships, as she slew godlings on mindforge stations. Zanj lived in anarchy. With this weapon, with her old friends to hand, these women she'd fought and lost beside, what limits would she face? What chaos spread? Viv remembered Zanj's touch on the scar at her wrist—and Zanj's hand closing around her neck. That was the truth, the other a lie, and all between an act meant to lead them here, to the Fallen Star, to all she'd lost.

Thoughts happen in cascade, ripples back and forth across a pond, building, and new sensations are rocks thrown into this pond, sometimes boulders, sometimes bombs, creating their own waves and ripples. Each rock thrown changes the pond a little, so the next rock's ripples build to waves.

Zanj reached for the Star. The crown lay iron gray upon her head.

Viv thought, *No.*

She might have said the word aloud. She did not know.

The crown burned black at once. Zanj roared, dulled, fell to the ship with a thud and a clatter of claws. Yannis knelt beside her, wide, panicked—"Zanj!" Zanj mewled, claws digging into her scalp, teeth bared, lips back, burnt and scarred and in pain, and Viv felt sick to see it. But she'd made the right call. She had.

Zanj's scream echoed through the radio bands. The Fallen Star flushed red. Yannis grabbed the crown, tried to pull it off, but Zanj reared and kicked her away. Reeling, Yannis settled her gaze on Viv.

Perhaps there was some bond linking Viv to the crown, invisible to human eyes. Perhaps Yannis merely proceeded by elimination: she had not caused Zanj's collapse, and neither had the Star, which left . . . Viv. And maybe Viv had spoken her command out loud.

Viv scrambled back, but Yannis's massive hand swept out, caught her, lifted her up, squeezed. Bones ground bones. Viv's own scream surprised her. "I don't know what you have done to my sister," Yannis said. Pressure built, and with it pain, all through Viv's body, bones taxed to the verge of breaking, joints crammed against themselves, the burning black-dot panic of asphyxiation as she tried to breathe but could not, and the tingling throughout her limbs as her heart struggled to force blood against the pressure of that gigantic hand. "But be you ever so useful, I will crush you for it." And as the black bloomed, she knew she was about to die.

"No." Zanj rose, ragged, panting, free, from the ship—silvery-gray blood on her face, her nails. "Sister. Let me."

Yannis, respectful, bowing, of course, dear Sister, opened her fist and let Viv slide into Zanj's palm. Half-blind with agony, Viv used that moment's freedom to draw a long, shuddering breath, filling her lungs, ignoring the razor blades someone had sewn between her ribs. She was about to die. Zanj would kill her. But Zanj's crown remained stubbornly, furiously gray as she shrank, as she knelt and dropped Viv in a panting sprawl on the ship's hull. Perhaps Viv was already dying, and the crown believed there was no more harm Zanj could do.

Zanj touched the Fallen Star.

Its lightning cascade burned gold all through. Fractal facets smoothed. The Star whirled inward, its light-devouring blackness gaining depth as the weapon concentrated itself into a staff of no color save at either end, where its facet edges broke light to rainbows. Zanj gripped the Star, hefted it, spun it experimentally in space, tossed it up and caught it once again, contemplating. The space around her seemed to sing. An earthquake twitch ran through the ship's many limbs, as if the world itself would flee her.

Viv did not move.

Yannis knelt beside them, her teeth man-sized, her whisper deafening. "Kill her, Sister. She is yours."

Zanj raised the Star. Viv watched the rainbows at its tip, and wondered if this, too, would hurt.

The Star swept down. It tore through Viv's skinsuit—and left a trail of burnt air in its wake as it swung past, and around, and, growing through that arc, struck Yannis in the side of the head.

The thud of Yannis's collapse was heavy and hard enough to send Viv flying, and land her in a different, no less painful, configuration.

When Zanj looked down at Viv, her face held a familiar rage. "What the fuck," Zanj said, "was that for?"

"What?" Viv, still desperate for breath, still afraid to breathe because it hurt too much, felt as if she'd missed a page.

"*What* what? That nonsense with the crown! Telling me to stop!"

"You were on her side. You said you didn't care about me. You were talking about how you'd torture me!"

"I said nothing like that. She did."

"You blinked at me, and just walked past!"

"That was a wink! A *just go with me here* wink."

"You wink with two eyes?"

"'You wink with two eyes?'" she repeated, mocking, exasperated, and rolled hers. "I had to convince her I was on her side! She could have killed you—she almost did just now. That *hurt*, Los Angeles. We had a deal. Do they not have *deals* where you come from?"

"She was your friend."

Yannis groaned and shifted, still unconscious. Zanj frowned. "Oh, she is. And she's always been too smart for her own good, and she deserved that ten times over for trying to pull this mess. She'll forgive me when she wakes up. Probably. Whether I'll forgive you is another matter entirely. But we'll settle that later." She reached down, grabbed Viv's hand, pulled her to her feet—in spite of Viv's yelp of pain. "We have the Star. The Cloud started rolling in when you pulled off that chain. We need to get out of here before—"

And then the hull behind her burst open.

36

A SILVER BLUR pierced the ship's hull and struck Zanj from behind. She tumbled into the hollow space within *Groundswell* as the blur bulged and transformed, shifting form to match her every strike, gnawing at her skin, at the Star.

Viv staggered, almost fell, reached for something to steady herself—and felt familiar arms embrace her, too fiercely for her broken ribs' comfort. "Ow." But she couldn't stop from smiling.

Xiara let her go at her protest, and she almost fell—caught herself with a hand on the other woman's shoulder, steadied, and stared, relieved, into her turning pilot's eyes as the battle bloomed above them with apocalyptic fire and bursts of ultraviolet light.

"You're safe," Xiara said, and kissed her, which she liked, though that hurt, too. "Oh my god, your face."

"And my hand, and ribs, and—" But she kissed her again. "What's going on here? You . . ."

"We're here to rescue you."

"We?"

"Gray and I. I saw Zanj and Yannis working together, Zanj was drawing the Star, you were hurt. I thought we wouldn't get here in time. I thought—when I thought the elders kidnapped you, I ran to Zanj for help. When I freed Gray, I realized what she was doing. So I pushed as much of the ship's power into him as he would hold, so he could fight her. It's all my fault, I didn't see—"

"No! Xiara, Zanj was trying to trick them. To keep me safe."

"Oh," she said. She looked up into the mess of light and fire. "Well. She's doing all right, all things considered."

She blinked, finally thinking through the pain. "Wait a second. Are you inside the ship? This ship?"

From above, a roar: "I'm on your side, you gluttonous waste of silicon!" The sound that followed was a crash of cars dropped from an airplane onto a granite flat. "I am sick—of—people—tackling me—for—no—reason!"

When Xiara smiled, arcs of lightning darted between her teeth. "*Ground-swell*. It's broken, but Zanj gave me its keys, its true name. Viv, the size of this ship—I can feel gravity waves, I can see your mind inside your skull—" She pulled her closer, tighter, kissed her with darts of static—and as she did, the ship rippled around them. "It's beautiful."

Even with the broken ribs, even with the fucked-up hand, it felt . . . good. Excellent. Ideal. She kissed Xiara, and this time there was no collapse, no withdraw. When she pressed into her, she pressed back.

Gray crashed to the hull behind them, and a cloud of debris rose into the night, only to patter and ting off a forcefield Xiara popped into place around them.

"You know," Viv said, "I've never hugged a battleship before."

Xiara grinned. "You'll get used to it."

Behind, Gray: "—traitor all along, just waiting for a chance to turn—" Something, probably Zanj, hit him very hard.

"Gray," Viv said without turning. "It's fine."

"What?"

"It's fine. Zanj is on our side."

"That," Zanj growled, "is just what I've been trying to tell you!"

"Of course you would say that! Even if you weren't. Especially if you weren't."

"Just shut up and listen," Zanj said. "We have a very brief window here. Yannis is out, and Nioh, but they'll wake up soon. The Cloud's rolling back in, because Viv broke the Empress's lock, and that will make them stronger. I want to get us the hell out before any of our other friends decide to show—"

Up was the last word, but lost beneath a crackle, snap, and hiss of static. A gleaming golden cloud filled *Groundswell*'s hollow core in an instant, spun, and resolved. Its billows sharpened to features, sculpting form.

Viv did not recognize the Grand Rector of the Mirrorfaith at first: bald and ageless, beautiful as a bomb. Viv had only glimpsed her on Hong's wrist screen as they escaped High Carcereal. Now she saw her mountain-sized and fearsome, draped in robes of the 'faith.

But she recognized the ships visible behind her, diamond cathedrals burning among the wrecked ships in *Groundswell*'s orbit. And she recognized, too, with one final iceberg turn in her gut, Hong, kneeling by the Rector's side, under heavy guard, in chains.

"Vivian Liao," said that voice of instinctive, sneering command, "and friends. We have placed your ship under interdict. Thanks to a timely prayer from Brother Heretic Hong, we have come to save you from the greatest blasphemy. Surrender yourself to our care and study. Be welcomed to the 'faith as a treasure beyond price. Or we will burn your world, and kill your friends, and sift your corpse and its ashes for the sacred truths we seek."

37

THE GRAND RECTOR disappeared, leaving her threat behind, and a dissipating cloud of golden light. But Xiara Ornchiefsdaughter saw her still, not just the ebbing projector fog the Rector used to cast her image across space, but also out in the black past *Groundswell*'s skin, approaching through the wrecked fleet of the Suicide Queens: the Mirrorfaith, cathedrals with gunports open, fighters darting brilliant as dragonflies above a lake, as minnows in a stream. (Dragonflies and minnows that breathed flame hot enough to melt suns.) With yet another sort of eyes she peered into the minds of those ships, into the Cloud beneath their physical shadow. Drives wove potential to momentum; *Groundswell*'s deep reflexes, now hers, calculated their probable future paths, built firing solutions for long-silent guns. She peered deeper, tried to pierce the 'fleet's shipmind cores, but her attention slid off the chanting circles of monks clustered around each mind, shielding systems from attack.

At fireside in the Orncamp, age eight, Xiara had leaned forward, eager to hear grandmothers' tales of the 'faith and its great fleet, relic and weapon and temple all at once. And now they faced her, these holy warriors and their vicious queen come a-questing.

Back in the world of matter she held Viv with weak arms clad in skin so fragile compared with her hull that she felt as if she had been grated raw; with imperfect, muffled ears, with eyes of variable resolution and strange depth of focus, she heard, saw, Viv pale, her pulse rise, felt her breath quick but measured, parsed pain of her wounds from the chemical cascade of her sweat. Even without the advantage of her systems, Viv would not have been so hard for Xiara to read: she thought herself complex, but she was pure, too, as a nocked arrow, her only mystery the mystery of the archer's will.

Once, Viv had seemed so strange. Viv, who saved her life, who held herself close and distant, queen of a faraway star. Now, Xiara knew her, and felt strange to herself.

To be a daughter of Orn, the Chief her mother once said, was to see many worlds at once, and walk many paths.

She did not think this all in order, but at once, overlapping, a flowering of thought in the second's gap after the Grand Rector's speech and before Zanj threw Gray aside. The pirate queen stamped her foot on *Groundswell* hard enough to dent the ablative alloy surrounding its monomolecule hull, and screamed: "Fuck!"

Viv tried to pull away from Xiara, toward Zanj, but staggered when she leaned too far into her bad leg. Xiara did not let her fall. "We have to save him."

Zanj's raised eyebrows made ripples across her forehead. "Save him? He did this to us. I knew someone messed with the antenna. My work was perfect. The boy must have set up some subsystem. When I spent my battery trying to hop out, he harvested the power—used it to drive his distress call. Your friend screwed us. I should have killed him when I had the chance."

"He thought you would leave us," Viv said with the slow dawning tone of a woman unraveling a riddle. "He thought this was the only way off Refuge. To get me to his fleet."

Gray groaned, recovering his form, thinner after his wrestling match with Zanj. "That must be why Xiara couldn't sense him in the ship. He went straight for his beacon, and left."

"He tried to warn me." Viv again, with that still-unraveling tone. "I wonder how early he pieced everything together about Yannis, about Nioh. He was drawing maps to the village, to the mountain. Everything a strike team might need. And I didn't see it."

Zanj spat. "Those monks warped his soul half to hell."

"Are you telling me you would have come back, if you'd escaped?"

Zanj's answer was a moment of silent, pacing, tail-lashing fury. Her eyes, when she returned Viv's gaze, were great and golden. "I want to get you to the Empress. Which we can't very well do now."

"We have the Fallen Star. The fastest ship in the galaxy."

Xiara had to squint her shipsenses to look at Zanj—the woman seemed little different physically, but with that immense sucking wound of the Star in her grip, she hurt the mind, a wash of data overloading all Xiara's systems. She tasted blue. She smelled acid heavy as a mother's slap. "If we leave now, those ships will follow us. We'll outpace them, but even an idiot would feel their bow wave through the Cloud. The Empress will know someone's coming. Good-bye, element of surprise. Good-bye, Gray's chances of getting home. And yours."

Xiara saw Viv hesitate. Saw the conclusions fire in her brain. "We have to get Hong back."

"Are you paying attention? He betrayed us."

"Because he thought you would betray us first."

"Whatever I would have done—he did it. We can't rescue him. That's not just a small battle group out there—it's a whole fleet."

"Are you saying you can't take a fleet?"

Zanj laughed, teeth bared, haughty and invincible—but checked the answer she almost gave by reflex. "Oh no. You're not getting me that easy again."

"He's saved my life a dozen times. I can't just let him go."

"Viv." Zanj stopped in front of her, and stared into her eyes. "You would have let him go anyway. You're letting all this go. This is your shot at getting home. Hong always would have gone back to the 'faith to tell his story, and he always would have ended up in chains. You can't save people from themselves."

'Faith ships slid through space, surrounding *Groundswell*. Viv grew taut and still. Xiara had seen archers freeze this way, too, eyes darting from target to target, sorting priorities, measuring the depths of fear. *You would have let him go*. Not just him, of course. To find her way home, Viv would have to let Gray go, and Zanj. And Xiara Ornchiefsdaughter.

She had known, of course. Two nights after they first lay together, Xiara, breathing herself back into her body, into the euphoric afterglow of an instrument beautifully played, looked down at Viv, asleep, mouth soft-parted, naked. She wondered at the curve of her neck, the swell of her cheek, at the tiny oval scar below her collarbone that was the only wound Viv bore which had not come from an Empress, no battle-wound but a child's scar, a soft flawless flaw—and felt something shift in her that was not desire.

Neither was it song-love, then. They had moved too fast for that, had clutched each other too hard, had been altogether too clear in what they'd asked, each from each, and what they'd offered, taken. Xiara needed a body to remind her what bodies were; Viv was alone in a world far different from the strange, cruel place to which she was so eager to return, and needed a spar to clutch. They were warriors. They had asked, given, received. But that night Xiara lay beside her, drank her in, and felt a rush not of a leg curled across her leg, but of Viv's leg, in specific, curled across hers, in specific. She had left Orn to sail the stars—but she had left Orn, too, to see this strange wanderer home.

She left everything behind, to lose her.

She had not thought it would be so soon.

"I will go." Her voice was so soft it was lost in the fight between Viv and Zanj. "I will go." Repeating the words was harder than saying them the first time—and when she heard the deafening silence after, she realized she had shouted at them, with her voice, and through the Cloud. They were looking at her. Viv was looking at her—for what felt like the first time. Each time their eyes met felt like the first. "I will lead them away."

Was there a word that meant trapped, sure as a gator-cat in a thorncage, unable to escape no matter how she pulled at the teeth that bound her— trapped like that, but in a good way? She would like to learn that word, or find it, or make it up.

"Xiara," Viv said, and many other things besides within that name.

"This is your chance. You need Gray to get you through the Citadel. You need Zanj to fly. And I can hold them off. Distract them."

"One ship won't do it," Zanj said into Viv's silence. "Even *Groundswell.* There are too many of them."

"I won't use one ship," she said. "I'll use them all." She whispered with a voice that was not of her body—and across space, throughout the stretching wreckage of the Suicide Queens' fleet, other chattering whispers came in answer.

Viv hugged her, her eyes black and wet and wide, her pulse up, endorphins rushing, a mess of adrenaline and pain and love. "No. You said they'd take you apart if you tried again."

The whispers merged as dead systems woke, as engines touched the Cloud for the first time in three thousand years. She had felt Zanj's small *Question* as a second body around her own, warm and welcoming, like sliding into a bath. *Groundswell,* its colossal ruined hulk, the shattered mirror-maze of its mind, was a lake to that. And the fleet webbing itself together under *Groundswell*'s guidance was an ocean. "I was scared when I touched the fleet. I wanted so badly to stay . . . a person. To stay the person I thought I was. To stay with you. But I was born to swim."

"I'm not leaving you."

"Of course you are," Xiara said. "You're going home. It's what you want. Isn't it?"

Viv nodded, against her cheek. She was crying. Yes. And those were tears, burning in Xiara's eyes.

"Go conquer your world. Thank you for bringing me to mine."

The whispers built: the ocean deeper than all measure, waiting for her to break the dam that held it back. Alerts, warnings, damage reports, status indicators, spoke to her from across the star system. She was huge now, and growing. Yet somehow Viv kissed her, gathered her, and encompassed her completely in her arms.

Zanj held out her hand. The Fallen Star burned black and rainbow, preparing to run. Outside, the 'faith fleet warmed its guns, and fighters streaked through the black.

Viv kissed her once more, and accepted.

The Star turned on an axis that, not long ago, Xiara would have thought confusing. Zanj folded inside it, and Gray—but Viv could not fold, so it flowed over her instead, long threads of black claiming her body, sliding under Xiara's fingers, parting them by microns and forever. She knew it hurt, she smelled the pain, but she saw it nowhere in Viv's eyes.

The ship's skin parted their lips, and they were gone.

The Star flew.

And Xiara Ornchiefsdaughter dove into the ocean of her fleet.

38

VIV DROWNED THROUGH space.

The Fallen Star refused to let her die. It moved against her, through her, infinitesimal gears feathering her skin like caterpillar hairs. It fed oxygen to her blood, it part-filled her lungs, it swallowed her and held her whole and cushioned her organs against their acceleration. But it did not make her feel like she was breathing. It did not preserve the illusion that her blood was still driven by her, rather than by itself. The Star pulled her through the Cloud, a woman become a vector, undying, undead, unable even to cry, tasting the last pressure of Xiara's kiss.

She lost senses she did not know she had until she gained them back. Time. Proprioceptive unity, the sense of her body as an integrated whole— she felt as if she'd been dismembered. Perhaps she had, for ease of transit. She lost the left part of the world, then the right. The well-ordering of memory: ringing the bell on the Stock Exchange, her first time in a Jesus camp bed, stone sober, observing herself as Susan sank between her thighs, a fistfight age eight, drowning here, walking out of her house age sixteen with nowhere in mind to go and no plan for coming home, in jumbled order, in no order at all. In the dark.

After who could say how long, she became aware of light.

She did not see it, not really. Her eyes were not open. But still she saw . . . an image triggered in her optic nerve, a grayish flickering shape on a mottled surface not quite like stone. Her shadow.

She tried to turn, and the image whirled, though her body remained frozen within the Star. Her inner ear suggested that she moved, pebbles seemed to crunch beneath her feet, but she was still.

She stood, and did not stand, in a chamber made of almost-stone, and in its center burned a gritty, blocky fire, its flames rising grayscale, and across the fire sat a suggestion of a form that was not precisely Gray.

He looked up, his eyes shining with poorly rendered reflections. "I'm sorry," he said. "I tried to make this place more comfortable, but Zanj needs all the processing power she can get. She's driving us so fast—I've never moved like this before. I didn't know anyone could. We'll catch the Empress, and I'd thought that was impossible. But I don't want you going mad on the way." He poked the fire with a stick, and sent up voxelated sparks.

She wanted to weep, she wanted to clutch Xiara, who wasn't there anymore, whom she could still taste. She wanted to curse Hong, to scream her frustration to whatever Cloud spirits and small gods had gathered to hear them. But what was the point? It was done. They were gone. She had always been leaving. The knowledge turned in her stomach. She made herself sick. "Thank you," she said instead of all the other, worse things she felt. At least, she thought she'd spoken the words aloud, and heard them, though her lungs insisted she had no breath to voice them, and her mouth would not open to set them free. A rock sat across the fire from Gray, glistening not at all the way real rocks glistened when struck by real flame. She did not sit down. She paced, stretched. The motion made her dizzy, and did not relieve the tension her real muscles felt, in a place that was not this place. "What is this? A game? Virtual reality?"

"More or less. It's so inconvenient that you don't have a soul—we can't address it directly. We're working this into your nerves, adjusting your neural homunculus without manipulating the flesh. It's all wet and squishy in there—gruesome." The simulation was too low-res for him to shudder, so he seemed to have a kind of seizure instead. "I don't understand how you operate."

"Comfortably." She sat to wait for the dizziness to pass. The fire spat sparks. She reached toward it, fanned her fingers, and felt real warmth. "So, we'll make it."

"Home sweet home." He nodded. "I didn't dare dream of this. And you made it possible. I could throw you a parade, cook you a feast, but . . ." He spread his arms to indicate their surroundings: a cave just large enough for the two of them to sit, walls marked with crude animal paintings, an indifferently rendered starscape visible through a narrow opening meant as a chimney for simulated smoke she couldn't smell. Not that she could smell anything else here. "I do the best with what I have."

"It's wonderful. Thank you." Outside, something some sound designer somewhere thought sounded like a wolf howled. Helpless, locked, she remembered Hong, chained, Hong, who sought freedom, liberation, knowledge—who had saved her life time and again, and then betrayed her, and himself. She remembered Xiara, the wheels within wheels within her eyes, how she'd screamed the first time she touched the fleet, and the resignation in her voice when she told Viv to go.

Viv was going home. And so was Gray. "What's it like? Her ship, I mean."

"You'll see. I—I'm not sure I can describe it in ways you'd understand. Not that I think you're not smart enough. Just, I didn't have a body most of the time I was there, or eyes like yours. I remember data, high-amplitude telemetry streams, information. For me, the palace was a flower blooming on all axes at once through time, writing and rewriting itself, bubbles of memory and purpose forming to split and splitting to form. I wished, and it was. It was . . ." He dropped his hands, and stared into the fire. "Perfect."

"Better than Refuge?"

His eyes darted up: gray as the rest of him in here, and reflecting gray flame. "Different. I've never been a man before—even something like one. It was . . . odd to live with those limits. One shape, and only so much strength and time in a single day. Friends to help, or to disappoint, or devour. It was scary. Not bad scary. Just, scary."

"I know what you mean." She tasted the ghost of Xiara's kiss. "Gray, why did she kick you out?"

He glanced up from the fire, scared, and his form derezzed. She imagined being left here alone, waiting for the fire to burn out—worse, imagined returning to that drowning dark.

"No! I'm sorry, I don't—you don't have to tell me if you don't want to."

His outline grew steady once more. "I'm sorry," he said. "I just wasn't expecting that. What did I tell you? I forget. I've lied a lot since I left home. I told the Ornclans I was a god."

"You said you'd spoiled her meal."

"That's . . . right. More or less. You've seen what she does to the worlds she breaks?"

"Like Orn?"

"Worse," he said. "Orn was a rush job. Mostly, she waits for them to ripen. That's what she calls it: the century or so before they draw Bleed, when their network's as tangled and creative as it can get before they hit the boundary condition—tiny republics surging through the galaxy's empty corners as if they were the first. There's always a chance they've come up with something she can use: some weapon, some new principle to perfect her powers, some shield the Bleed can't overcome.

"And when they're ripe, she harvests them. That's what we're for—one of the things we're for. We eat and archive worlds. We take them apart to learn how they work, how they think.

"She sent me to a little culture, twenty worlds, asteroid colonies, a few orbitals. A simple mission, my first solo: to harvest what was useful, so She could shatter the rest. But I . . . I liked them. Their music. The games they played. The little stupid sculptures they made for mating partners. Their children sang at school to help them memorize the characters they used to write. They made amazing food, spicier than you could conceive, skin-melting curries, they had this carnivorous migratory lizard that tasted kind of like duck but better and if you crisped the skin right, just—ah." He kissed his fingertips. "So I seeded myself through their network, and when the time came, I ruined it. The collapse started with a little thing, a knot of code. It spread through the Cloud, undid their communications systems, scattered their fledgling minds to madness. The lines that bound their worlds across the void snapped. I ate memory banks and factories. The civilization fell back centuries. They'll piece it all together again someday—or maybe not, since they've mined out most of their surface metals. But they'll live. So here I am."

"You . . ." She wasn't certain how to finish that sentence.

"Destroyed a people. And saved them. When I was done they weren't developed enough to be worth eating—they wouldn't be ripe for centuries, if ever. She cast me out into the void for it. That's why I gathered dreams and nightmares on Orn. I thought if I showed Her another way, if I made up for the meal I'd spoiled, She might forgive me. I don't think that anymore. When, if, She finds that I've come back, She'll kill me. But I'll see my family again, and they can try to hide me, and beg mercy in my name."

"You still want to go home."

"Of course," he said. His eyes were flat and shiny in the low-res firelight, and Viv wished she could see them in the real world, wished she could read them. "I'm a Gray of Grayframe. I serve my Lady. I live on Her ship. Without that, what am I?"

"Xiara's monster," she replied. "Gatyen's friend. My friend. You danced with spiders on a corpse the size of an island. You fed our ship. You learned to sing. You're more than someone's tool. You could go anywhere."

"Well, what about you? Where are you going?"

He didn't ask it viciously. If he had, she would have closed down.

She stared into the fire, and remembered the drunk she'd felt when she looked at Xiara, and the vine that had grown from that drunkenness to wrap

around her body, and sink its roots into her heart—and the desperate confusion she'd felt when Xiara told her to leave. No. We're not done yet. There
has to be more than this.

But of course there wasn't.

She thought, too, of Hong helping her climb, Hong saving her from the
Pride, Hong her ally and friend, Hong bleeding out in that eggshell room
on High Carcereal. The fear in his eyes, the shame, in chains, of his betrayal.
She'd helped him escape Pride drones and his own people, and cross the
galaxy, and he'd turned against her because he knew, of course, she would
not stay.

Where are you going?

She sat by the fire, drowning, and tried to remember. Her enemies. Her
plans. Her family. Magda.

But in the end, all she said was "Home."

39

THEY REACHED THE Empress's ship as it neared the Citadel.

Viv, seated by the simulated fire, toasting a simulated marshmallow, first noticed they'd arrived by the improved resolution in her sim: color crept into the stone walls, the night air chilled. Her marshmallow crisped gold, then, because she was holding it too close, caught fire. As she cursed and blew out the flame, Zanj appeared, Zanj in her full dimensionality, shoulders sagged, fur dull with exhaustion, tail drooping. "Kids," she said. "We made it."

Gray jumped up, sniffed the air. "You did it! I can smell home. I can hear the song. Zanj!" He hugged her in a rush of limbs. She looked down as if confused by the gesture. "Thank you."

Whatever response Zanj had been about to offer, she thought better of it. "Hold on. The next part might feel a little strange."

The cave dissolved, replaced with space—more or less. Behind them, stars pricked gaping velvet black. Ahead, the universe was an empty gray curve, vast beyond measure and webbed with cracks, not entirely unlike the surface of Viv's burnt marshmallow if it had been hundreds of light-years on a side. Though the curve was dark, its mass dazzled, like a snowfield.

"The Citadel walls," Zanj said. "Don't everybody thank me all at once."

"She built that?"

"*Build* is the wrong word," Gray said, rapt. "The whole Grayframe together couldn't build that in a thousand years, if you gave us a hundred stellar masses to chew and build it with. But the Empress commands the Cloud, and the Cloud describes the Citadel into being: a surface more mathematical than physical, a boundary condition on the outside universe."

"That doesn't sound less intimidating than *build*."

"It's not," Zanj said.

"There!" If Gray had a body, he would have been pointing excitedly, but he didn't, so it took Viv a moment to see what he meant. "There it is!"

Viv knew on an intellectual level that scale was hard to judge in space. Humans measured size with a bunch of instinctive tricks like binocular parallax that worked fine for stuff roughly human-scale: dogs, houses, aircraft carriers. These tricks failed for things meaningfully larger than people or farther away than people tended to be, like mountains, or moons. While there was no convenient moon nearby against which to judge, Viv would have laid most of her fortune that the ship beneath them was considerably larger than Earth's. Or than Earth itself, for that matter.

Jupiter might be closer to the mark, though misleading, since the planet wasn't hollow and the Empress's ship was. Judging from what Viv had seen so far, the Imperial aesthetic, which Viv decided she shared, could be summed up as "Monster Lace." Crystal arches the size of continents, filigree webs, vast refractive snowflake spans arced by green fire: a wire globe with spikes growing inward toward a burning hole, a ring of bent light around factual, essential, eternal black.

That was the stolen Rosary bead. Through there was home.

Everyone she ever loved or hated, every triumph, every disaster, every night she'd slept or spent sleepless, every ship she'd ever sailed, every run she'd ever taken and every problem she'd solved before High Carcereal, that sphere held them all. Somewhere in there, her friends thought she was dead. Somewhere in there, a world waited for her return.

If you looked at it that way, it made sense how much she'd lost to get here. How much she'd give up to go back.

She would not let herself cry in front of Zanj, or Gray.

"Viv," Gray said. "Are you okay?"

"Don't worry about it," Zanj answered for her.

The Star slid down, dizzyingly fast, toward the ship. As they drew alongside, Viv's stupid mammal tricks started working again. The stellar object became landscape, the landscape became a structure, and if Viv could have breathed, her breath would have stopped in her throat as she comprehended its scale. "Where should we go?" Zanj asked. And Gray suggested, "The memory bay. I'll paint it for you."

They swept over what Viv had taken at a distance for filigree: conduits broad as oceans, coursing with green light. "Did you build this one?"

"Yes." Gray's voice rang with pride. "This, we built. Took a day and we ate a star to do it: good star, too, one of the crunchy ones."

"Crunchy?"

"Don't ask," Zanj said. "You don't want to get them started on stars."

"Sixth or seventh generation. Lots of heavy elements, a dirty burn. You know it's horrible for you, but you can't help yourself. Like when you wrap bacon around, you know. Things. Like more bacon. Go left. Now down a bit—good."

They settled beside an arc of crystal hull. "Okay, Viv. Do your thing." And for the first time in she did not know how long, she could move. The Star bulged around her arm, bubbled out, touched the palace hull, made a seal. Viv could not breathe, but she could raise her arm. Stretch out her hand.

The crystal hull felt glassy smooth at first, but as she trailed her fingers across it, it caught her skin as if tiny gears within the surface were spinning off her touch. When she pressed the hull, it gave way.

And she fell.

She hit the deck hard, in a confusion of reversed gravity. She should have been silent, she should have been careful. She had meant to be. But she could breathe, and breathing, she could scream. Her heart could beat again, and her blood move, and that blood was full of unprocessed endorphins, of the chemical pain of broken bones, not to mention heartbreak, anger, guilt, betrayal, adrenal fear. She'd thought she'd worked through all that in those long campfire hours, and in her mind she had, but they still marked her body: the dislocated thumb, the broken ribs, that final kiss.

She came aware of time again, gut-heaving, eyes red, breathing so deep she felt queasy, would have thrown up if there had been anything in her stomach to throw. The world's red blush burnt off. Someone spoke. Gray. "Viv? Are you okay?"

"No." She tried to push herself up, before she remembered her dislocated thumb, her broken ribs—but she did not collapse. Her hand hurt, her hand remembered hurting, but the thumb, when she looked down, was in exactly the right place relative to the rest of her fingers, splayed on a surface that looked more like rock than crystal. Blinking away tears, she felt her side. Her ribs were whole, though sore. "What?"

"I fixed it," Gray said. "On the way. The ship was all through you already, so it wasn't hard. Was I wrong?"

"No." She tested muscles, bones, most of them in the right place. "Thank you." Then her focus shifted to the looming shape behind him, and she screamed.

"This guy?" Gray laughed, and tapped the ankle of the . . . it wasn't quite a tyrannosaur, but something of that ilk, bipedal and enormous and toothy, with great bulging eyes and an elegant prow of skull. "Don't worry, he's not going anywhere." He rapped the leg with his knuckles, producing a sound that didn't quite remind Viv of stone or wood.

"A statue?"

"No, he's real. Just frozen. Suspended animation, null-entropy field, like Zanj did with you in the Star. I think this one's my"—he traced the skin with his fingers—"great-great-great-grandmother Gray's work? Maybe an extra *great* in there, the names repeat, it's hard to tell. Good stuff, anyway." He spread his arms to embrace the jungle around them, not frozen but arrested, a symphony the conductor held on a high note, forever: dragonfly wings paused midbeat, scavengers' throats mid-swallow. "Welcome to the memory bay."

"Come on." Zanj pulled her to her feet. "We don't have much time."

Viv scrambled after her through the forest.

Gray explained on the way. "None of us really knows why She does this, but there are theories." They passed through a burning blue door in the dinosaur swamp, and emerged onto a busy street in a city that had never been on Earth, a three-mooned city of slope-roofed skyscrapers, into frozen traffic. Viv flinched by reflex: if the city started to move, she'd be crushed in seconds. Though the cars probably would have hit Zanj first, and bounced off. "When you're as old as She is, the grandmothers say, your memory needs a little help." Another burning door brought them to a hive complex, millions of insects dancing in the air between subhives linked by amber cords in a nesting grove that stretched above and below as far as the eye could see. Viv and Zanj had to crouch and duck through the bugs' flight plan; Gray fuzzed out and walked normally, his substance drifting through the swarm. "Some think She builds them out of pity for the civilizations She harvests, so a tiny piece of their present will last forever. Or as an archive, in case She finds a use for them later on."

"Wait. Those dinosaurs were intelligent?"

"Not the dinosaurs. The trees." They passed through another door into an ocean, so deep the surface was no more than a suggestion, a faint sheen on a distant mirror. Glowing jellyfish bulbs lit immense roiling tentacles of squid. "Some think it's an art She practices, capturing moments perfectly balanced in beauty or justice. I don't know. I've never walked here before with a body. It feels indecent. I like it."

"It's a trophy room," Zanj said. "She's wrecked so many worlds. Trillions of lives. She keeps a few of them here so she can feel better about herself."

The next door dropped them into a basement. Viv stopped. She recognized this tile, these walls, the cement, the frigid air, the servers in their racks. Her stomach tightened, her knees unlocked, and she felt herself sweat, the mechanical reactions of a mammal about to flee. "I know this place."

"We don't have time."

"This is where . . ." The memory of a hand around her heart stopped her from speaking. "No way. She didn't eat Earth. When I left, we weren't near the level of the places you're talking about."

"So maybe they're not trophies," Gray said.

Zanj scoffed. "There's more than one kind of trophy." And she led them through another door.

Viv stood on a beach by a gray ocean. Cotton clouds scudded across a full blue sky. Rocks rose behind her; to her left, boulders jutted from the sand. To her right, the beach curved past cedar-shingle houses to a long arm of mounded rock with a lighthouse at the end. Gulls squabbled over scraps of bread, a scallop shell. A tern glided out above the waves.

The door closed behind her.

Viv sank to her knees in the sand beside a dirty plastic six-pack collar.

Gray had been saying something, probably, but he stopped. "Viv? What's wrong?"

"This is Cape Ann." Not Cape Ann as it stood now—as it had stood when the Empress pulled her out of time, out of her world. They'd built a bulkier, squatter lighthouse after Hurricane Xavier, and the sea should be a meter higher at this tide; she saw no jellyfish buoys. "I went to school near here. I used to come up on long weekends, with friends. We'd have drone fights on the beach." She sank her fingers into the sand, as if she could dig through to the deck below—but there was just more sand beneath the sand. She squeezed what she'd dredged up, and the grains slipped out between her fingers. The more you tighten your grip. She laughed, and heard the cracks in her voice. "I can't."

"Viv." Zanj knelt before her, firm as iron, slightly more kind. "We have to keep moving." Waves crashed and fell and roared. "This is a big ship, and the Empress isn't looking for us. But if we stay in one place, make too much of a fuss, she'll find us." But, wait. There should be no waves. Each trophy room had been silent, arrested in time, their footsteps hammer blows on grave-still air. "And we can't fight her here."

"Zanj?"

"So no matter what you see, I need you to keep driving in, to the center. We're here for your home, and my freedom. Okay?"

"Zanj." This time she pointed, and Zanj looked.

Behind her, the water rose.

It gathered into whirlwind pillars, roaring wind-whipped columns hundreds of feet tall, bridging bay and sky. Viv had seen a waterspout once on the open ocean, survived it with her sails in tatters, her mast cracked, her arms aching, her hands blistered from guiding sheets, her side an ugly purple bruise where her ribs had caught a swinging boom; that had been on her trip after the IPO, when she was still wrapping her head around the fact that she'd never have to worry about being out of pocket for a round of drinks again, but if she ever had found herself destitute in port after that she could have just told the waterspout story and drunk all she needed.

But that waterspout did not have burning eyes. Or teeth.

Zanj sighed. She stood, and cracked her neck. With a flick of her wrist, she shaped the Star into being in her hand.

The water-pillars challenged her with voices like shattering rock.

Zanj growled, "Same to you, buddy." She gathered herself to spring.

"Wait!" Gray ran between them, hands up, eyes wide, smiling like a madman. "Zanj, stop! That's my mom!"

40

THE GRAYMOTHER SWEPT them into the sky on whirlwind wings to a space of brooding mile-high clouds above the ocean near Cape Ann. Flames within flames, green lights, sunflower yellow, aurora orange, sculpted faces from the clouds in the instant they spoke. It took Viv an embarrassing amount of time to realize the many faces belonged to many distinct individuals, some features round or long or squashed or bubbling, and the voices, too, had a thunderous diversity. Grays moved from cloud to cloud, and new ones arose every second, their faces merged and heightened versions of other Grays she'd seen.

Only Graymom stayed in place, a towering pillar of flame. Perhaps this was a consolation to her son, who tried to look everywhere at once, eyes wide, wet, following his many aunts and uncles and cousins through the clouds. Perhaps she could not move, being already everywhere: the cloud palace pulsed with her voice.

"Our son, banished, has returned. Let him speak."

The tongues of flame fell silent. Gray stepped forward on empty air.

The clouds opened overhead.

The sky above was not the sky of Cape Ann. The silver glass wheels of the Empress's ship revolved against the unfamiliar stars of deep space split by the Citadel's broken curve.

"If he fucks this up," Zanj whispered into that silence, "get ready to run."

"If he fucks this up, will running do any good?"

"For me? Oh, sure. For you," Zanj admitted, "maybe not. But getting ready won't hurt."

She didn't answer that. The Grays were, of course, listening.

Gray glanced back to Viv, nervous. She waved her best *you'll be fine* wave. She'd encouraged enough friends through presentations, testimonies, and wedding toasts to know you didn't show your own nerves, if you had them.

Reunions with an estranged family of nanorobot genies fell way off to the severe right of that scale, but then, you used the tools you had for the task at hand.

Gray cleared his throat. It sounded wet, and mortal, and nothing like thunder.

"Mothers, aunts, uncles, cousins of Grayframe. I've come back." That much he said with confidence. The rest was harder. "Our Lady banished me to the cold. I waited there for years, gathering desires in hope of earning Her favor. I missed you all so much. Out in the dark, I imagined how you, Aunt, would laugh at a certain surprise, how you, Uncle, would have devoured a particular nuisance. I missed the way our thoughts would fuse. Your voices, and the fire of you. It's hard to be alone." He swallowed, took a breath, and began again. "I had a chance to come home. I took it. The Empress shaped my friend Viv to break chains, and she offered to break mine. For our paths to cross out of all the billions in the galaxy: How could it be against the Empress's will? I am home, and I throw myself on your mercy. If you feel I have done wrong returning, unmake me now. If you want to devour me, devour me. It is enough that I have seen you one last time. I only ask that you help my friend. She was torn from her home beyond the Rosary bead. I promised I would help her find her road home, as she helped me find mine."

Graymother spoke ponderously into the silence. "Our son Gray. What have you brought us from your travels? What gifts, to earn our welcome?"

Silence once again. Gray stood alone in the circle. Though they were not touching, Viv felt Zanj tense beside her, and traced the line of the pirate queen's thought as she totaled the worldly goods Gray might offer: some archived dreams of Orn—and Zanj, and Viv. An ancient enemy of the Lady they served, and a woman out of time, whom Yannis had thought enough of a prize to justify war with heavens.

Those might be enticement enough for the Grayframe.

She set her hand on Zanj's arm, felt the battle tension there, and whispered, "Wait."

Gray straightened, drew his shoulders back, and breathed in, out, in again. Then he began to sing.

His voice warbled at first, but when it steadied on a pitch, Viv recognized the song from the fields of Refuge, from the digging crew's voices, the rhythm of planting and the movement of limbs.

Big rat, big rat
Don't eat my millet
Big rat, big rat
Don't eat my rice

Viv's translation gimmick fed her the words, but like any song, the meaning had as much to do with rhythm and melody as lyrics: the pound, the march, the drive. This song had hundreds of verses; you worked through each grain and every other crop, a chorus after each set of four, then started again from *millet* with the next pest. Just a workers' song.

Midway through the third verse a drone like swarming bees reverberated through the sky, and other lower notes, on the hairy line between sound and pressure. The Grayframe joined the chorus.

Gray began to clap; thunder echoed him, and clouds roiled and spun into dancing, rumbling helices of flame, burning faces grinning and spinning and singing blues. They spread fiery arms, lifting him up; he blurred out into them, interwoven with his family's smoke, laughing and singing with the sky.

Viv realized Zanj was glowering, wondered why, and realized she was tapping her feet in time with the music.

ANOTHER PARTING. VIV wondered if she would ever grow used to those.

The Grayframe's joy seared on around them, spinning, transforming, warping and returning to form. She could barely trace Gray within, swept from cloud to cloud, joining the cascade of thunder, tossed high into the air and caught, spun round by relatives.

"I don't believe it," Zanj said with a shake of her head. "They're all like that."

Graymother, beaming, shaped herself from the revel: first smoke, then smoke in the vague dimensions of a body, then, in a whirl of construction, step by step as she advanced, nerves, bones, flesh, eyes, skin, until she stood glorious, ten feet tall and full-figured and smoke-wreathed before them.

Zanj seemed nonplussed; Viv felt grateful for the smoke that still surrounded Graymother, because otherwise she might have embarrassed herself. Or—as her eyes tracked over that body built to more-than-human scale, as she blushed and riveted them on that perfect face, and ordered her mouth to close—embarrassed herself more.

"I am sorry," Graymother said. "You have so small a shadow on the Cloud that I cannot see you without eyes. I hope this form does not disturb you." Which seemed dense for a being of fire and whim and billions of statically suspended nanomachines—except for the tiny corner-of-the-mouth smirk that tipped her cards.

"I think I'll live," Viv said. "It won't be a problem for you to take him in?"

"The Lady is not merciful, but She is often distracted. Gray's entire natural life could pass before She notices his return. He had the misfortune to be exceptionally efficient in his infancy, so She raised him up and cultivated him as her herald. We will be fine." Her hand was larger than Viv's head, but still she cupped her cheek. Her touch was warm and gentle and tingled on Viv's skin like peppermint. "You have brought our son home. What can we do for you?"

Viv swallowed many answers, and offered the one that mattered. "I want to go home. I think the Empress pulled me out of the Rosary bead she stole. I need a way to get back in."

Graymother smiled. "Such an easy thing! Surely you could ask a greater boon."

"Wait," Viv said. "Easy?"

"Of course! We've been building, and testing, a machine for the purpose of engaging with the bead, ever since we pulled it from the Rosary. The Empress has directed all Her mind to the task, all our strength. Even in its current form, it's more than enough to send a body through. And you?" She drew her hand from Viv's cheek—Viv had to restrain herself from pulling it back—and turned to Zanj. Her face darkened. "I believe I should know you."

"I'm just passing through," Zanj said. "I'm only here to get Viv home."

Behind, the party whirled, and Gray led another verse:

> Gray goo, gray goo
> Don't take my millet
> Gray goo, gray goo
> Don't take my rice

At last, Graymother nodded. "I will fly you to the throne room. Our Lady sleeps there, Her mind submerged in contemplation of the Cloud. We will direct Her attention down, and down—and we will wake the machine for you."

Zanj looked to Viv; Viv said, "Thank you."

Graymother called out with a voice much larger than the one she'd used with Viv, in the Graytongue of surf and fire, and the flame revel tossed Gray from one pair of whirlwind arms to another until he sprawled in the sky before them, re-forming into the body they knew: taller, broader, stronger than he'd been on Orn, shaped by sun and work, sweaty and sore from laughter, but Gray nonetheless, their Gray, himself.

When he saw them, he understood. He hugged Zanj, who made as if she'd been too shocked by his embrace to dodge in time, though of course she could have. She patted him on the back, awkwardly.

"I'm so glad I got the chance to know you," he said. "And that I didn't kill you when we first met! And you didn't kill me!"

"It's a mystery why," Zanj said. But even she couldn't sell that line without a waver. "It's been fun."

He let her go, and before Viv could think of what she was supposed to say, dropped to his knees before her, eyes raised to her face, with eagerness and respect, and beneath all that, a sorrow she was half surprised to feel her own heart echo. "Thank you. I owe you everything."

She knelt, and hugged him. He felt more solid than before. He hugged her back, and for once he got the smell right. He drew a breath of her and held it, and as he exhaled with a sigh Viv's arms slipped through him. His body quickened to lightning and smoke, and that face, that open child's face, joined the whirlwind of his family.

Leaving Zanj, and Viv, alone.

41

VIV AND ZANJ crept into the Empress's throne room.

Graymother had flown them down the vessel's winding halls at speeds Viv did not care to guess, through apertures that opened to admit them only to snap closed instantly behind, and left them at the throne room door. She whispered her instructions, then departed with a kiss that lingered on Viv's cheek and a scent too rich for roses.

The words were easier to remember than the kiss.

Touch nothing, leave nothing. Do not speak. Dare not look upon our Lady Herself, for She can sense regard. Follow the lights. Through them we guide you from afar. When the gate opens, step through, and do not look back.

She'd told herself she was ready, but she was not ready for this room.

In childhood Viv had designed throne rooms and secret lairs the way other kids designed dream bedrooms. In high school she'd tried to remodel her own bedroom to match her visions, but her parents wouldn't let her paint, so she'd been stuck with pink walls, and her mother kept hanging white frill curtains though each time Viv replaced them with black. Her college dorm had been, in retrospect, a stupid eighteen-year-old's attempt at the same project, piled with electronics and books, monitor after monitor, bad prints of good art. Her various houses had various versions of the dream, but none ever felt quite right. She just couldn't lay hands on enough marble, stained glass, and porphyry for what she had in mind.

If Viv had infinite resources, a whole Grayframe at her beck and call, and forever to build in, she might have made a room like this. Diamond arches climbed and curved, meshed, braided, and melded to plummet once more, toward the throne in the center where sat, dreaming—

No. She was not supposed to look.

A galaxy of multicolored lights turned overhead, its stars mostly Imperial green, here and there a luxurious calm sapphire, broken with cracks of black and saffron-orange and red, a map of a galaxy controlled by the woman, the entity, upon that—

Do not look at the Empress. Do not look at the throne.

She walked on.

Walking on hurt. The emerald radiance of the Woman Viv could not see flooded the hall, pulsed through veins in diamond. Black crystal pillars displayed graphs of local gravity, tensor webs of magnetic fields, diagrams of the palace ship itself, and they reflected Her light: the Empress Whose brilliance overflowed Her flesh. If She even had flesh anymore.

Viv tried not to look. She tried not to think in capital letters. It was a bad habit. If you weren't careful, pretty soon you'd find yourself Going to the Store to Buy a Carton of Milk—or worse, speaking German.

She needed that dry laugh now. Here she was, creeping like a rat through the throne room of a woman who'd torn her heart from her chest, who'd melted her skin, who'd hurt her friends—not to mention crushed a galaxy, wrecked Orn and banished Gray, locked Zanj inside a star. This was the Empress: the green the same, the radiance identical. She had wrecked Viv's life, and this was the closest Viv could manage to revenge: sneaking past beneath her notice. She wasn't even a rat, here. Rats could tunnel and undermine. She was a mouse, tiny, powerless, scuttling for a hole out of the Empress's sight.

The portal looked a bit like a hole if you ignored the auroras that curled and uncurled above it, or the banks of machinery, most exotic and crystalline and so complex she could not tell which parts were filigree and which functional. A rippling silver hole, edged by a sapphire ring, down which she could scurry home.

She remembered Natalia back on Saint Kitts, Lucy wondering where her boss had gone or if she was alive, remembered family. She remembered the faceless shadows in suits, the three-letter acronyms who had hunted her, and whom she meant to hunt in turn. She had a war to win, a world to conquer. She had to get home. She remembered Magda, trapped in green.

The Empress was a problem for another world. A problem for other friends. Whom she had abandoned one by one to reach this point.

What else could she do? She was a mouse. Abject. Soulless. A bag of meat. You talk a big game, Vivian Liao, but you're a coward.

The Empress was behind her now. The black hole of Viv's old life drew her down, beneath the transparent floor. Light bent around its edge.

She had tried to fight the Empress back in that basement, with as much success as a kitten in a mastiff's jaw. Her friends had given so much, and she had asked so much from them, to bring her here.

Do not speak, she had been warned, and so she did not speak. She held out her hand to Zanj, who took it.

Zanj stepped between Viv and the hole.

Of course. Even now, she would not kneel.

Her crown was the gray of a still dawn. Again and again on their journey, Zanj had promised to kill Viv, in earnest and in jest, but right now, in the throne room silence, Viv forgot all those threats and remembered her cabin aboard the poor lost *Question*, touching Zanj's scar as Zanj touched hers. Pirate queen, perhaps. Stealer of suns, scourge of galaxies. A murderer, certainly. A happy killer in an unkind world. Who tried, when Viv asked, to stop killing. Who was, for all her violent protestations, inspite of Hong's suspicion and all her own temptations toward betrayal, a loyal friend.

And if Viv removed that crown, Zanj could break her neck in under a second.

She'd given her an order back on *Groundswell*. In fear for her life, maybe. But Zanj was owed revenge for that, and for so much else.

Her hand shook as it approached Zanj's brow. She brushed her hair without meaning to. Zanj's lips twitched up. If she had not been scarred, that might have been a smile.

The crown broke in two at Viv's touch, as if it had been made of dried twigs. Zanj caught the other piece before it hit the floor. She took the piece Viv held, and set them both on the ground. Eyes closed, she breathed in, out. Freedom's first breath in three thousand years.

Viv stood before her, slow, fragile, altogether in her power.

When Zanj moved, Viv made a sound—a small, even mouselike, squeak that might have doomed them both had it not been crushed against Zanj's chest by the force of her hug. Viv felt the strength in her friend's back and arms. Memorized it, as surely as she'd ever memorized a password or a knot. If she could bear one moment home, let it be this.

But even such moments pass. With a silent thunderclap, the hole opened.

Zanj drew away. Her eyes, always bright, looked more wet than usual, though her face was the same old steel, bent in the same old grin. She stepped out of Viv's way, ushered her forward, patted her on the shoulder, and withdrew.

Leaving only Viv and the pit.

She counted steps to the edge. So long ago, she had stood on the edge of a boat rigged to blow, with a small watertight sack over her shoulder, under a blue sky she'd never flown beyond. On Earth. With the world at her back, and the world before her.

She had to go.

She thought of Hong. Gray. Xiara. Zanj. All she had to do to honor them, their sacrifices, was close her eyes, breathe in, and leap.

Leaving the Empress at her back.

Turning away forever from the chance to face the woman who built these machines, the will that cowed a galaxy.

Accepting her inferiority.

Fleeing the greatest challenge she could ever face.

Abandoning her friends.

She breathed out, opened her eyes, and turned.

The Empress sat upon her throne, reclined in seeming sleep, beautiful as music, fierce as flame, so bright she left red shadows on the eye.

Zanj stood over her, the Fallen Star clutched in both hands, its tip narrowed to a point, her face a mask of rage and certainty and fear: the face of a woman ready to kill, and, in the instant of her blow, to die.

There was a pop within Zanj's skull. Her irises flowered brilliant white.

Viv whispered, "No."

The Fallen Star stabbed like an ice pick toward the Empress's eye.

It struck her, and drew sparks.

And the Empress woke up.

42

THE EMPRESS ROSE from her throne.

The galaxy winked out. Displays died one by one all through the chamber. The veins of green that pulsed in the diamond walls drained back through floor and pillars into her. What Viv had taken for the workings of the ship had in fact been the workings of the Empress's multichambered mind.

The Empress shrugged off sleep as she might have shrugged off a mountain's weight: with that little care.

The whole time, Zanj fought her.

She swept the Fallen Star through a blurred arc, and it bounced off a shell of green light that had not existed a millisecond before, and ceased to exist a millisecond after. Spears of green radiance pierced the air where Zanj had been, but she was already gone, behind the Empress, bringing the Star down on the crown that looped her head—only for it to bounce off another shell.

The Empress rubbed the heel of one hand against the eye Zanj had hit, as if it ached. Both her eyes were black and full of stars between the lids. She descended one step from her throne.

Zanj swept the Empress's feet out from under her, but she did not fall, of course. What hold could gravity have over her, that she did not yield it of her own will?

Viv watched, fixed by awe, fear, and gross curiosity. There was more to this battle than she could see, and she was grateful for once that she could not touch the Cloud. Watching the physical dimension of this fight was bad enough. Watching Zanj's soul set against the Empress's might have blinded her.

And as she watched the green light that never quite caught Zanj, the Star's blows that never landed, Zanj fixed on the Empress as if they were the only two people in the chamber, in the entire universe, Viv assembled the puzzle.

This had been Zanj's plan all along. Get Viv home? Sure, if convenient. But use her, drive her, always, to the Empress. Use her to break the chains on the Fallen Star, Zanj's greatest weapon. To open the Empress's ship. To breach her stronghold. To find the Empress alone, lulled to sleep by Grayframe—and take her final shot. Vengeance for herself, for her friends, her people. Even if it doomed her.

Zanj roared. She had unfolded into a quicksilver being of many dimensions, the thief of suns, and her voice shook the station. The force of her rage knelt Viv to the ground. The Star burned through the air—actually burned, leaving plasma trails that would have seemed bright were they not set beside the Empress—and bounced off another shield. The throne room rang like a bell.

The Empress looked at Zanj then. The full mouth in the green glory of that face twisted to a sneer, then broadened. "Ah yes. I remember you."

And Viv remembered that voice: not so eerily close or all-consuming as in the server room, but with the same quiet, mocking force, casually overriding all other sound. Green light caught Zanj; she somersaulted back, changed direction in midair, landed, her claws shrieking grooves in the transparent floor, rolled out of the way of another lance of green, then blurred forward once more.

The Empress followed her with her head and eyes, body still, as if tracking an insect.

Zanj stabbed the Star at the Empress's neck, and this time, the Empress moved.

She stepped, smooth and unhurried, out of the Star's path, and caught Zanj's wrist. Green light flashed; the Empress stepped back, and Zanj—stuck.

She tried to leap away, to fly, but the green light held her fast, her wrist locked in space as if the air were stone. Zanj's claws drew sparks from the light; she pulled, strained, but her arm did not budge.

With a roar, she swept the Star, grown immense, through the chamber, snapping crystal pillars like ropes of grass, smashing through the wall—but it bounced off the Empress's raised forearm with that same bell-ringing sound. The Empress blurred along the Star's length, and caught Zanj's other wrist, and again that flash, and that wrist, too, was stuck.

Zanj dropped the Star, caught it with her feet, and jabbed into the Empress's gut.

The Empress flowed aside, caught Zanj's ankles in the crook of one arm, and flashed them both in place.

Zanj's tail snared the Empress's neck, squeezed—and she casually unwound it. Then, with a shrug, she broke her tail, and flashed it, too, crooked.

Zanj howled. She cursed. She strained against the light that held her. The Empress circled her, contemplating—then, almost as an afterthought, slapped the Star away. It clattered out of reach. Casually, with head-cocked aesthetic detachment, the Empress adjusted Zanj's limbs until she hung spread-eagled in space, then stepped back, one knuckle to her chin.

"Not bad," the Empress said, "all things considered. It's been a long time since I had to work so hard. Zanj. How did you get out of your cage? How did you stay sane?"

"Three thousand years of hate," Zanj said. "Three thousand years dreaming of my teeth at your throat."

"Three thousand years and you couldn't come up with a better use for your time. There's no need for us to be enemies."

"You've killed my friends. Slowly. Left them in pain. You destroyed Pasquarai."

"Destroyed? Zanj." She shook her head, as if Zanj were a pupil who'd made an understandable, sad error. "You really don't know what you're talking about."

"Tyrant."

"That's your line, yes, you and all those children screaming about freedom, without understanding. The freedom to die, the freedom to be eaten. I can see what's broken in you: a small error, easily corrected. If you let me inside, I could fix it."

"I will kill you," Zanj spat. "Slowly. Someday, I, or my children, will cut your power from you. We'll skin you and drink your blood. We'll string harps with your nerves. There will be no sound in all the world for your screams."

The Empress, still watching Zanj's face, raised two fingers and flicked them forward, beckoning. The crown's halves darted from the crystal floor, and slammed shut around her head with a sound like a portcullis slamming home. The iron burned black, and Zanj's eyes white. Smoke rose from her flesh. Blood curtained her face, and she began to scream.

The Empress nodded, as if noting the progress of an experiment. Since waking, she had not so much as glanced toward Viv.

Viv edged back. The portal, behind her, remained open: rippling and hungry, and past it, home.

Zanj's scream stopped. She panted, slack, hanging from the lights that bound her in midair. The Empress drew her hand through a gentle arc, trailing light—and tapped Zanj's temple with her middle finger. The crown hissed. Across the room, through the green, Viv could see Zanj's gritted teeth, her staring eyes, her face contorted, the veins bulging on her neck as she tried to strangle her building cry. Zanj squinted. One eye closed, then the other.

Was that a wink? Telling her to go? Telling her it was okay? She couldn't make a difference anyway, so she might as well leave? Could Zanj think through that agony? Could Viv, if their positions were reversed? Sweat soaked her jumpsuit. Spit frothed between her teeth.

Discarded on the cracked floor between them lay the Fallen Star.

Viv realized she was running.

Yannis, mountain-sized, had strained and failed to lift the Star. Viv didn't make the slightest shadow on the Cloud. She could deadlift a good deal more than her body weight, and rig a sail alone, but the Star was another class of thing altogether—built from exotic matter for killing stranger, stronger things than gods.

Viv scooped it from the floor without breaking stride. Its tip rang off crystal.

The Empress's head cocked at the sound, and she turned, languorous and superior.

Viv didn't know how to use the Star. She hadn't expected to be able to lift the damn thing. She had no illusion of her chances once the Empress saw her. So, still twenty feet from the Empress, she swung the Star, and hoped.

The Star unspooled in mid-sweep, twenty feet long now without any change in balance Viv could feel—and the Empress turned back, with a yawn, to Zanj.

She must have expected that green shell to reappear and stop the strike. Viv was as surprised as anyone when it didn't.

She didn't see where the Star hit the Empress—it moved with a speed Viv's eyes could not track. The force of the blow threw the Empress back into the chamber wall, which shattered into diamond dust. Viv fell to her knees, covered her eyes with her arm, just in time: shards tore through the 'faith robes Hong had given her. One sliced open her forearm, and a long thin splinter embedded in her side.

When the crash faded, she risked opening her eyes.

Zanj hung in light, limp, staring. Most of the chamber wall was gone, revealing a forest of razor mirrors beyond. No doubt they served some important purpose for the ship. Right now, they caught and glimmered green.

The Empress marched back into the throne room over the diamond rubble, barefoot. Her side smoked where Viv had struck, but she did not seem to care. Her eyes of stars and nothing settled on Viv, and grew just slightly wider.

"Ah. So that's how Zanj got out." Her laugh seemed too soft to be so loud. "You survived. What a pleasant surprise! Come on. Stand up. I don't like to see you on your knees."

Viv rose, unsteadily. The Star felt heavy in her hands: not as heavy as she knew it was, but as heavy as a thick bar of cold iron might be. "Still disappointed?"

"Yes," the Empress admitted. The soles of her feet ground diamond and glass to powder as she advanced. "But impressed, too. I thought you'd die. If not, I thought you'd be too smart to come for me." She flowed across intervening space faster than Viv could follow—but only to stand by Zanj's side, to set a hand on Viv's friend's neck. Her skin seared, and Zanj let out a strangled sound. "Not to mention, too smart to release this monster. Hard to believe even you might be that dense."

"I did what I had to," Viv said.

"Why?" She patted Zanj on the side of the neck, and walked forward.

"You hurt my friends. You stole everything from me. You ripped me from my world."

"Your world?" The Empress laughed at that: a genuine laugh, unforced and uncontrolled, arrogant, but not at all mean. She had never been weak enough to need meanness. That was the laugh of a woman who had spent millennia and more bending a universe to her will, who had never encountered a challenge she could not crush, a danger she could not conquer. A woman to whom unsolved problems were items on a list to cross off one by one.

Viv recognized that laugh. She felt cold all over, chilled not by terror but by denial.

The green light folded into the Empress. All its blinding perfection hid beneath her skin, like a blade palmed.

Viv knew that body—knew the way cool green silk would feel drifting over it. She knew those eyes. She knew that winding braid, which she'd taken for a crown.

She had never been afraid of mirrors.

"It never was your world," said Vivian Liao. "It's always been mine."

43

"YOU'RE LYING." VIV said the words, but did not believe them. She wanted the Empress to be playing a cruel joke on her—she'd played jokes as cruel on the rest of the galaxy. She wanted her ice-cold creeping shock of recognition to be wrong. She wanted to look at Zanj, slack in bonds of light, and find support, anger, anything but careful neutrality. "It's not true." But saying the same thing with different words did not make it so.

The Empress slid her hands into the pockets of her dress and walked toward Viv, head cocked slightly, mouth's corner slanted up: Really? Viv knew that face. She'd used it for the cover of *Time*.

"You're not me. I'm not you."

"I watched my first living thing die—outside of bugs, I mean—when I was seven. We were sailing. I woke up early and found this beautiful green-blue bird twitching on the deck. I think the cat got to it. There was nothing I could do. I could see all the way inside it. Organs looked so clear in Mom's books: hearts, lungs, guts. But on the deck they were a mess. I knew it would upset them if they saw it—they'd be so worried about how it might have affected me that we'd spend the rest of the trip talking about that bird. So I knelt and watched it die, and when it was dead, I gathered it and tossed it overboard and cleaned the deck, and never told anyone. Until now."

Something was stuck in Viv's throat. She could not breathe. The Fallen Star weighed heavy in her hands. Her voice sounded thin—a shadow of the Empress. "Maybe I wrote the story down. You could have spied on me. Found records." But the story's truth had not chilled her so much as the patter. Cadence, choice of words, the wry shrug, amused and puzzled by the child's disgust, never self-deprecating: Viv had never told this story to anyone, but if she did, that was how she would tell it. "I can think of a thousand ways you might know."

"Viv. Stop. I know where you're coming from. The desperation, the anger.

I can imagine how I'd feel if I were in your shoes. But we're not as slow as you're pretending to be right now. Why would I lie? You're no threat. You have nothing I want. You're a woman with skills thousands of years out of date, wielding a weapon she can barely hold, to defend a partner who doesn't care about you. Who was just using you to get to me."

Viv swung the Star again. The Empress's form slipped away like mist, and the momentum spun Viv round in a circle. Her face, the Empress's face, appeared in one of the black glass pillars; Viv smashed that pillar with the Star, but the face slipped into another.

"See," the Empress said, "this is what I love about us. We're so brilliantly, delightfully self-centered."

Viv ran to that pillar, and smashed it, too. Flying glass cut her cheek. She panted. Her arms shook from the Star's weight. The Empress appeared in a diamond slab—*Viv* appeared, with a gentle chess player's smile, oh did you really mean to make *that* move? She knew how that smile felt from the inside.

"You know I built the Rosary over centuries, at an expense you could barely imagine. You know I spent a truly absurd amount of computational power to bring you here. But it never occurred to you to ask why your life would be the one I'd choose to interrupt. Why you would be the one person your universe's god would visit, out of all history. Because of course the world would revolve around Vivian Liao. When you found you could undo my bindings, release Zanj, command her—it seemed natural. Why shouldn't Vivian Liao have power?"

With a mighty swing, Viv snapped the diamond pillar in half. Off-balance, exhausted, she fell to her knees.

When the dust cleared, she didn't see herself anywhere.

"That," the Empress said, "is a rare gift."

Viv lurched to her feet, and looked up. Her face stared down at her from the ceiling, still smiling.

"The habit of centering yourself, of command, of not accepting others' answers—that was our foundation, Viv, and we built great things upon it. We built them, and they tore them from us, and we built them again. In that basement server farm, we fixed a chain to the neck of the world. The systems we built made us smarter, better, faster. We found the Cloud and made it ours. We broke banks. Governments. We beat nations. Planets. Species. We fought and fought and fought, and every time they tried to crush us, we crushed them right back."

Viv glared up at her face, so smug, secure, so far away. She did not know how to use the Star, did not know by what power she could lift it—but when Zanj carried it, she could fly. She crouched low. A rush of power passed to her from the Star. She bared her teeth, and flew.

Or tried.

Her legs would not straighten. She looked down. Diamond flowed up from the cracked floor, over her ankle and around her knee, climbing toward her arms. She screamed, strained, but the diamond did not care, and her own voice covered her cries, like a hand over her mouth.

"But what happens," the Empress asked, "when winning's not enough? I conquered a galaxy, I built civilization after civilization, and still the Bleed came. Whenever a society reaches sufficient network density, whenever they place enough demands upon the Cloud, the Bleed appear. I beat them back the first time—barely. We lost trillions of souls. They cored Earth. I rebuilt civilization after civilization, empire after empire, and each time it was worse. In the end, even I would have fallen. So I did the hardest thing I've ever done: I played it safe. Carved off a corner of the galaxy and made it my preserve, froze the Bleed out, forbade any mind that was not mine. And each time a society grows dense enough to draw them, I fix it."

"You eat them!" Viv was screaming now. "You burn them and break them. You're a monster, and I am nothing like—"

A diamond gag closed her lips, a diamond band cinched her jaw shut, and she could only gaze up in impotent fury, her whole body ribbed in crystal.

"I'm sorry," the Empress said. "I don't quite enjoy doing this to myself, though there is a visceral thrill I'm sure you can imagine. I've called myself all those names and worse, millions of times, all the variations on them that your genius could muster in ten thousand years. You know you would hate to do what I have done. You know you could do it—to save yourself, to save the world, to save all worlds, all futures, from those monsters' maws. So, forgive me for not indulging your protestations of virtue. I want to explain why you're here, because I respect you and what you've accomplished by making it this far. You deserve to know your place in all this."

Viv could still breathe through her nose, at least, and she could curse in her mind.

"I've spent eons trying to defeat the Bleed. But I have only my own genius to work with—any culture that grows to the point where it could contribute, I must harvest before the Bleed come for them. At first I gained their knowledge, new physics, new math, but at this point each new civilization only adds a few marginal discoveries, and a bunch of poetry. I have to face facts: I'm the universe's only hope. It is indeed a lonely thing." A smile; Viv caught the reference, and hated it. "Centuries passed. I worked, and worked, and I found no solution. And then I started to worry.

"We both know the dangers of lock-in effects, of local maxima and minima. We are climbing a mountain, looking for a high valley where we can live safe from floods. We settle in a cleft in the mountainside, poorly sheltered, barren, harsh, and we think, this must be the highest place where human beings can live. That cliff goes up forever. Until one day someone scales the cliff, through unimaginable suffering, and finds at its summit a green and temperate paradise. I've spent my life clawing handhold by handhold up that cliff, and slipping down. But perhaps another path up the mountain would never have found the barren cleft where I took shelter. Perhaps a journey I did not take, some seeming dead end I rejected eons past, leads straight to paradise."

Viv glared up at her with all the hate she could force into her gaze.

The face disappeared. Footsteps approached: soft, padded steps over the broken floor. She felt the heat of green. Her own face entered her field of view, condescending, curious.

"That's where you come in. I simulated other paths we might have taken, seeking answers to the Bleed threat, a place where my grip on power would be absolute. I used computational matter so dense I had to close it behind an event horizon to hide its inner workings from my Cloud and from the Bleed. And then I left my Rosary to bake."

Viv wanted to shake her head, wanted to deny it. The Empress turned to her in a whisper of green silk, her expression mocking Viv's disbelief. Hong had suggested the rosary beads might contain simulations, back during that first jump in the *Question*, and she'd rejected the idea. Time travel was a better explanation, or parallel universes. Why did she toss away his theory? Because she was real. Her world was real. Magda was real, and the sea. In that pure black mirror she seemed so small. That black hole below her was not just a passage home—it *was* home, and the Empress's knife lay at its neck. Everyone she had ever known. Everyone she had ever loved.

Well. Not everyone.

The Empress was not lying. Viv did not lie to herself. Not when the truth was cruel.

"I made you. I set millions of parallel Vivs along their paths, seeking answers in millennia. And for so, so long, I heard nothing—until your world went *ding*. Problem solved. Intrigued, I extracted you so I could search your mind for answers: What could I have done differently? What wrong turn did I make? Only to find that your principal contribution to your world's success, your sole embellishment, was a sentimental mistake." She shook her head. "It's not all a loss. Your world remains, and all its promised answers. Once I've returned to the Citadel I will unravel the simulation and incorporate its innovations at my leisure. In the meantime, given how far you've come, it's remotely possible your mentality holds some useful feature I overlooked on my first scan. Grayframe!"

A whirl of fire and smoke and clouds erupted from the air and condensed into a featureless silver blob, almost the shape of a man. "Yes, my Lady?"

The Empress looked into Viv's rage-filled eyes, reached down, and stroked her cheek. A red line carved across Viv's face; Viv smelled the burning flesh. She screamed and tried to pull away, but the diamond held her fast and smothered her words. The Empress straightened, licked her fingertip, and, after a faraway wine taster's moment, nodded in satisfaction.

"Take this girl apart and feed her to me."

44

VIV DIDN'T HAVE a "give up" setting. This was one of many reasons she'd made her first fortune, and her second; it was also why she had a hard time finding a consistent board game play group. She had zero chill. She fought when there was hope; she fought when hope was gone. What did surrender ever get anyone? A life spared by another's sufferance wasn't worth the work of breathing through. The world was out to get her anyway—far more than it was out to get most of her friends and colleagues. If you didn't fight, you let it win. If you fought, you might lose, but better to go down aflame and cackling on a ship you'd sailed yourself.

So she fought her chains in the Empress's throne room, the Star useless in her hand, as the quicksilver blob approached. She seethed with rage. Diamond bonds cut her skin. Her jaw ached. If she could not free herself, if she could not curse, she would die trying.

The Gray flowed toward her and settled, its feet not quite where the floor should be. She glared into the flat, eyeless face, and wondered who this was—a cousin, niece or nephew, a grandmother, Graymother herself, one of the singers in that great chorus above Cape Ann? Did it stand featureless before her now to protect itself from the Empress's notice, or because the Empress would rather not think about these servant weapons she deployed, so long as they solved her problems?

The Gray stepped closer. She opened her lips and tried to spit. Most of it ran down her chin. Some made it, and crackled and sparked against the silver. The Gray raised a pseudopod arm to its face, and extruded a straightened finger. Was it flicking her off? No—the finger settled where it might have had lips. As if quieting her down.

The Gray reached for her. She cursed it in mumble, pulled away as far as her bonds allowed. But as it reached for her, it refined, bubbled with context. A face surfaced from that mirror pool. Wide, eager red eyes, pale skin. A face she had first seen as a child's, now planed, nearly a man's.

Not *the* Gray. *Her* Gray.

His hand settled on the diamond bands around her face, and left a silver stain that zipped down facets, across joints, prickling her body like hot needles as it broke her bonds molecule by molecule. Her jaw slacked—which meant her jaw had room to slack. She breathed out awe, relief, fear, saying nothing, watching him.

He did not open his mouth, but a drop of his body, too small to feel, must have trickled into her ear. She heard his voice. "I'll keep Her busy. Get Zanj. And run."

She might have spoken then, tried to tell him no, ruined everything. But he was already rising from his crouch, grown large in limb and long in claw and red in tooth, his body a tornado of knives and fire, a roar of hunger and rage that shivered the throne room as it crested and crashed onto the Empress.

Viv didn't wait to watch what happened next. She lunged across the cracking crystal floor toward Zanj.

The battle did not care whether she was watching, though. She heard, distinct through the chaos, her own voice, a contemptuous "What?" Her green fire, tattered and reflected by whirling Gray, burst through the room, searing the air in Viv's lungs.

Gray was saving them. Saving her. Or at least, giving them a chance. At the cost of everything. Like before. She hadn't asked him to this time. She wouldn't have dared to ask.

He hadn't told her to wait for him, to join him, to save him. Just to free Zanj, and run. That bastard. Her stomach turned. He didn't mean to get away.

Half-blind from the battle's heat, she struck a wall wrapped in cloth: Zanj. Zanj didn't seem to feel the impact. She hung limp in her restraints, eyes rolled back, breathing hard and shallow and fast. Blood ran down her face. The crown burned black as the singularity beneath them. "Zanj!" She twitched. Could she hear? Or was that pain? Didn't matter. Viv clawed at the green light that fixed her in place, and it parted like wet paper. Of course. It recognized her. Like all the chains and all the walls and all the ships had recognized her.

Zanj sagged onto Viv, and Viv sank beneath her hot weight. Her spittle flicked Viv's face. Cradling Zanj's skull, Viv lowered her to the floor. The crown pulsed black; Zanj curled in agony, struck Viv in the side. Viv heard a crack, and her breath left her. She tried to get her hands around the crown, but Zanj pulled her head out of reach. Zanj flailing in pain could be as deadly as Zanj armed and free. "Stop hurting her!" She'd never tried to order the crown itself before—but god, if her commands had any value, let them be good for something now. "Stop." All her anger and fear broke into a plea.

The crown paled. Zanj gasped; her eyes spasmed, settled.

An enormous hammer struck the floor, which cracked, deep white fissures spreading in spiderweb beneath them. Two whirlwinds of light, one silver, one green, consumed the center of the throne room—the green, enormous and growing by the instant, had thrown the silver down, and pummeled it now, tearing shreds of mass away. Gray roared, tried to fight back, but his desperate clawing strikes skittered off Imperial jade.

"Zanj!" Zanj's claw twitched, but her eyes did not open. Viv set the Star on her palm, closed her fingers around it. Still she did not move.

Another blow rocked the throne room. An arch collapsed, raining diamond. Cracks in the floor widened, spread. Viv felt a draft: wind drawn down, down and out. Gray's roar broke to a modem wail. She glanced over her shoulder—the whirlwinds had condensed to forms, and the Empress stood ten feet tall in midair, crushing Gray's lean, starved body in her massive arms. He clawed for her eyes, and she squeezed tighter.

"Wake the fuck up, Zanj. We have to get out of here." The command burned her crown black. Zanj's eyes flew open, and focused, and her teeth bared, and in a blur she held Viv by the throat.

Her face was sweat and blood and rage and scar. The crown seared black against her brow. Her eyes were wide and crazed and Viv suddenly wondered if Zanj was not seeing her, Viv, but the Empress she had twice tried and failed to kill. Viv tried to speak, to explain, but she could not breathe.

The modem scream rose, twisted—and, with a sickening crack, stopped.

Zanj's grip loosened.

The Empress let Gray fall. He hit the ground heavy, his eyes staring red. His skin trickled. Lightning darted along his limbs, trying to heal, to re-form. She set her immense claws on his chest, and he began to burn.

He shriveled from the edges out, the millions of mites that made him up squealing, popping, and sizzling as they failed to vent waste heat. The Empress watched him die, locked him in place.

"Zanj." She could barely speak. "Please."

And, with a snarl, Zanj threw Viv aside. She stood as much as her ruined body would allow, raised the Star, and slammed it into the throne room floor. Which shattered.

Viv tumbled in shards and thinning air. Cold stung her eyes; she should cover them, protect herself, but what would that accomplish, really? The Empress burned green in the void where her throne room had been, far above already and receding; they fell toward blackness beneath, toward the bent light around the hole that was Viv's world, singularity now and forever, herself eating herself, and out there in the storm of cutting mirrors, Zanj tumbled, flew, caught a handful of silver from the heart of a shape of flame-licked char, then somersaulted back, nearer, ever nearer, eyes burning white, breaking the mirrors all about them, real and furious, and her face was the last thing Viv saw before the black.

45

THE BLACK SPAT her out on the brow of a rocky frozen planetoid carved in the shape of Viv's own face. She collapsed, sagged, curled around something she did not have, and sobbed into the stone until she thought she would be sick. Her breath drew steam from the rock—it must have been a long time since this version of her face had felt any warmth.

She could not cry, could not breathe, without pain from her lungs, without an ache in her side where she'd fallen, where Zanj struck her, where the diamond shard had pierced. Her cheek was a burned mess, and there were other pains, too, less physical but no less real. Failure, futility. She remembered the Empress's triumphant grin when she broke Gray. She knew that same expression from gym mirrors and candid photos. Winning. She gulped the memories down one by one like coals, and lay there forever beneath the burning stars.

When forever ended she pushed herself up. Each movement stabbed new needles into her flesh. Once she managed to sit, she found it hurt no more to kneel, to stand. No less, either.

Zanj sat cross-legged, back to Viv, on the brow of Viv's face, watching a screen so matte black Viv could only tell it was a screen by its discontinuity against the background stars. Zanj could hear birds perch miles away; she could feel the shifting electromagnetic fields of a nervous system approaching. Certainly she felt Viv's footsteps. But she said nothing, kept still, as Viv limped closer.

The screen showed the Empress's ship, in all its immensity still just a diamond bauble against the green-broken black curve of the Citadel wall. As the ship drifted forward, with Viv's home, with her whole world, at its heart, the wall rippled, bubbled, bulged, and swallowed it whole. The process mirrored itself: a bulge, a bubble, a ripple, then stillness.

Zanj swiped the screen away; it rolled up and became the Star again, then shrank to pencil size. She stuck it behind her ear.

Viv settled down beside her, wincing as she discovered new injuries on the way.

Zanj held her hands cupped in her lap, statue still. Her red-gold eyes stared unblinking at the void.

"Do not speak," Zanj said when Viv opened her mouth. "If you speak, I will try to kill you."

Viv had arguments to make in self-defense, justifications to offer. She thought of the Empress, and stopped herself. But when she did not speak, neither did Zanj. A few times in her life—often on boats, and rarely, so rarely, with another human being, she had enjoyed a silence of comfort, of settled business, nothing to say, nothing to fear. This was the opposite. There were too many words neither of them could bear to say.

If Zanj really meant to kill her if she spoke, it wouldn't be worse than what she was doing to herself. She ignored the warning flick of the eyes. "Is he dead?"

She waited for the claw at her throat, for the scream as the crown burned Zanj in her defense. In the Empress's defense. Because the crown thought they were the same person. Because they were. She felt sick.

But Zanj shook her head once, and held out her cupped hand. Her palm cradled a few teaspoons of mercury. It twitched and trembled, though Zanj held still as stone.

Viv found her voice after a long time that felt longer. "Will he get better?"

Zanj returned her hand to her lap. "I tried feeding him some rock, before you woke up. Metal, too. No response. He's still there, but he's hurt. He needs fixing, and the only people who can fix him are behind that wall, along with your world, and my revenge. Which I would have had, if not for you." She growled the last word. The hand that did not hold what was left of Gray tightened into a fist.

"I had nothing to do with it."

Zanj hissed. "You woke her up."

"She didn't wake until you hit her with the Star."

"You tried to stop me. You looked at her. You spoke."

"You hit her with a fucking superweapon! I was worried! You couldn't beat her." But Viv's thoughts caught up with her mouth then, and she chilled. "Oh my god. You didn't *care* if you beat her. You wanted her to kill you." She reached for her. "Zanj."

But she pulled away, rolled to her feet, her eyes fierce. "If you'd just gone through the damn portal like you said, I could have torn that whole ship to atoms, wrecked the Cloud for light-years. If I'd tried that with you standing there, you would have been burnt to a cinder."

"And you'd be dead."

"I'd still have done it. I'd have pushed her to the edge. I'd have torn at her eyes. I'd have made her kill me this time. I'd have won."

"You'd be dead."

"That was my right!" She kicked the rock on which they stood, and a huge shelf split off and fell into Viv's eye far below. The Empress's eye, she supposed.

"That's what you wanted. All this time. You didn't want to get me home. You wanted your glorious goddamn showdown. You used me."

"Of course I used you! Of course I had my own plan! Do you think the whole fucking *universe* revolves around you?"

Viv was on her feet. She didn't know how she'd gotten there. Breath heaved in her chest; her eyes were hot, her many pains forgotten in the rush of anger. She raised one hand, finger out, unsure what she would say, but she knew this tension in her skull—this was how she felt when she was about to say something that would make old friends never speak to her again. She wanted to hurt someone. She wanted to make them suffer.

The person she wanted to hurt was not Zanj.

She dropped her hand. Turned away. Stared down, and out, over the pitted landscape. Tears welled in her eyes. Fucking embarrassing. She sniffed them back, and found that beneath the tears, she was laughing.

"What is it?" Zanj asked after a while, tentative. "Viv?"

"I could—" She swallowed a sob, found her center, started again. "I could be forgiven for that. Thinking the universe revolves around me, I mean. We are standing on a planet-sized sculpture of my face."

Zanj pinched her temples between her thumb and forefinger, and turned away. Space can be very quiet. Viv felt its silence gather around her, a slow tide pressing against her ankles, her thighs, her belly, her chest, her neck. Perhaps before the world, before the Big Bang, there had been another kind of silence altogether, deeper even than this. The emptiness she now thought absolute was in fact a clamor, an after-echo. What was the silence before silence? She could imagine nothing more still than this.

On the edge of hearing, less a sound than the root of what might someday grow to be a sound: Zanj, dry, amused. "I guess we are."

She pondered herself. Even pitted here and there by asteroids down who could say how many years, the face remained intact, the likeness clear. How many other faces of Viv drifted along the Citadel walls, watching blind? She asked: "Did you know?"

That was all she could bear to say. If Zanj had not understood, Viv might have never found the will to speak again. But, at last, an answer came. "I suspected. When you first commanded me back on High Carcereal, there was a look in your eye, a set in your shoulders. As I grew to know you, I recognized habits of thought. Turns of the head." Light steps crossed stone. A hand settled on her shoulder. "She's not you. You're not her. You're not so cruel."

"I'm not her yet." Viv drew away, and Zanj's hand slipped off. "But she's what I would be in thousands of years. If I won. I dreamed of being her. She thinks the way I want to think, works the way I tell myself I work. I fight. I make the hard choices. When I win, I take what I've won, and use that to win more. The world wants to scorn me, trap me, bind me? I'll make them kneel. I'll make them listen. With my hand on their throats if I have to, with my thumbs in their eyes. I built myself that way. I carved off all the pieces that weren't edge. And that road leads to her." She could not bear to stand any longer, so she sat upon her brow, and stared down into her unseeing stone eyes.

Zanj settled by her side. Their arms touched. Viv was aware of muscles clenching, unclenching, in Zanj's jaw. "I'm sorry." She shook her head. "It has been a long, long time since I apologized to anyone, for anything. But I am sorry. I'm sorry I tried to kill you when we first met. I'm sorry I didn't trust you more. I'm sorry I didn't tell you."

Viv raised her hand to Zanj's brow. It trembled, unsure. She heard again that grim, honest voice, the cutting certainty: *I will kill you*. Zanj's fury in the Empress's chamber, the light and rage in her eyes when she looked at Viv and saw the Empress. Because they were the same.

She was afraid, but she had to try. She had done so much. She had broken a galaxy, in trying to save it. Surely she could do this.

Her fingers hooked around the crown, and pulled. And it did not come free.

She stood and gripped it with both hands; fear tightened in her chest, fear of what Zanj would do if she were free, fear of death, fear of failure, but still she lifted with her arms and back and legs. "Come on, damn you. Open."

Her fingers slipped. She sat down hard, stunned, half broken, and when she looked up she could not meet Zanj's gaze. She looked away, and closed her eyes hard to keep their wet heat in.

"It's okay." Zanj's voice was gravel-rough and tired, but also it was there, and Viv felt welling gratitude for that, in a moment when if she had the power she might have wished herself out of existence altogether. "Maybe it's safer like this, for now. I almost broke you in half back there."

Viv blinked tears from her eyes, and drew a ragged breath—then looked at Zanj crouched before her, unmoving, and at the stars behind. "I don't know what to do."

"Hey," she said. "That makes two of us."

"That makes two of us," Viv echoed. They sat unknowing. The Citadel's wall coruscated behind them. And in the silence a truth formed and turned beneath the surface of Viv's mind. She felt it first as a stillness, then the swell of its rising, before the broad ribbed back emerged. Then, when she could see the shape of the thing that breached her, she tried to form it into words. "We've been doing this all wrong. I've been doing this all wrong. We all worked on our own, even when we were together. I wanted to get home. You wanted revenge. Hong wanted knowledge, and he wanted to do his duty. Gray wanted his family. Xiara wanted the stars. We each used the others to get what we wanted for ourselves, and it all went wrong. But we're all in this together, aren't we? And if the Empress wins—if she peels my world, finds the power to break the Bleed, to win for good—all this goes away. For everyone."

Zanj bowed her head, then raised it, so slow Viv didn't at first realize it was a nod. "How do we stop her?"

"I'm still working on that part," she said. "But we can't do it alone."

46

SOON, THIS STAR would die.

The fleet clouded near, and kept killing it.

Shardships and great cruisers, worldminds and sunkillers, they drank the star's light and the heat of fusion from its core, hollowing as they sipped, shaping magnetic fields to funnel plasma columns up through space to waiting mouths. They still bore the carbon scars of ancient battle, but as they drank, breaches filled in their hull, synapses rewove in their minds. Viv could not see the Cloud, but as they approached the fleet Zanj told her of the shadow the fleet cast, filling the hyperdimensional night with three-thousand-year dreams, dragging in information, every meager advance in weapons patterning and science the galaxy had yielded in their silent millennia, and, too, the great art and gripping schlock and cooking shows and tritone mesosymphonies that rose, fell, rose again, surviving the empires that were their cradle. Waking, the ships fed.

Some smaller drones, slipskimmers, asteroid feeders, mistook the Fallen Star, sliding stealthmode from the Cloud, for a morsel, webbed it in their fields, gnawed it with nanocloud teeth.

Those teeth slipped off. Terawatt lasers bounced. Probes and mindweapons turned back on their sources and scattered them. Pickets roused their drowsy murderous minds; cruisers spun up solution modules. Gunports opened. Cloud decryption engines linked, engaged.

At last, rather than start a fight, Zanj told them her ship's name, and her own.

More gunports opened. Constellations of engines blazed throughout the fleet: those vessels which had been built by things like humans, and as such had a distinct *front* that could be pointed toward something one might designate as an *enemy*, did so. Microdrones burned fast to escape the splash zone.

—Good idea, Viv said. She couldn't speak, exactly, because her lungs were full of spaceship. That really got them to lay out the welcome mat.

—I'm not here to fight, Zanj told the fleet. I have a passenger. She wants to talk.

They received no answer—but neither did the fleet open fire. Ships drifted away, made a path.

At their shifting heart, greater than moons, its skin still the cutting green of fresh rice, dotted with mountains and ribbed with rivers, hung *Groundswell*.

They slipped around its immensity, in and out of the shadows of its tendrils and antennae. A fresh patch of puckered metal covered the wound the Star made so long ago. Lights guided them along the hull, and as they drew close the ship's skin flowed and reshaped itself into a hatch just large enough for a human being. The Star matched velocity, twisted, and kissed the hatch.

—You don't have to do this, Zanj said.

—Of course I do, Viv replied.

—You don't have to do it alone, I mean. I can't protect you from out here.

—You mean, you'd lose the fight?

—Don't be silly. I just wouldn't win in time.

The door waited.

Viv hung in space, unsure. This had been her idea, but now that she had come to this point, to this hatch, to this ship, the reality of it overwhelmed her, and she wanted to run. The fleet would be useful—necessary, even. And she remembered a kiss, the pressure of strong arms around her shoulders, the sad final giving up.

She stepped from the Star into *Groundswell*.

There followed her usual collapse, the first harsh heaving breath after the ship left her lungs, the shock as her organs settled into place. Her knees hurt; she'd hit them hard when she fell. With one hand on the wall, she found her feet again. Zanj stood outside the hatch, Star in hand, gold eyes glittering, mouth twisted, unsure.

The door slammed shut, then disappeared.

Viv stood in a long, level hallway, walls curving eggshell white and faintly luminous. She cast no shadow here. She found that funny. She cast no shadow here—but, in a way, this whole thing was her shadow. Her fault.

The hall ran straight before her until it vanished to a point.

She walked, and thought about her exes.

Her breakups, with one heartsick fucked-up hospitalizing freshman year exception, had been, for the most part, amicable. She'd been broken up with far more than she'd done the breaking, which she seldom mentioned to her friends, partly because it wasn't any of their business, partly because she had no use for the kind of soppy sympathy which inevitably followed sharing that particular piece of information. She did not need any assurances she'd find someone someday, because she either would or wouldn't, and either way, in the meantime, she wasn't hurting for sex or companionship. She ate her ice cream and took her seven days plus or minus three of crying jags like a champ; with extensive interval training one year she'd managed to get the turnaround down to a weekend.

There was another reason she didn't tell people: she didn't like catering to their disbelief. Someone less secure than Viv would probably have found it flattering; Viv didn't need anyone's assurances that she was pretty or smart, and, god, she certainly didn't need another reminder that she was rich. She understood the story, controlling as well as she could for the distorting effect of one's narrative of one's own life. It was remarkably consistent. Whatever words drew the tears, whatever last quarrel snapped the proverbial dromedary's spine, the underlying logic was the same. And they knew it, too, the ones wise enough to know.

Viv walked her own path. She did not wait. She did not linger, or retrace her steps. Sometimes her path lay alongside another's for a while. But she would never shape hers to them.

Shanda learned this in the months she'd battered herself against her, trying to make them work. Danika had always known it, but never consciously. Susan Cho understood at last when she marched away from her down Santa Monica Pier, chin high, fists balled, too proud to let Viv see her cry. And Xiara Ornchiefsdaughter had known it, before she gave herself to the fleet.

The hall flowered into a vast chamber—no throne room, no space of empty awe or self-regard. An engine room, perhaps, or a heart. Multicolored ferrous fluids pulsed through veins and conduits. Fields of coruscating light whirled, interlocked: nanomachines, lesser versions of the great Grays of Grayframe, mating computations. The cables that were the chamber's walls surged in pseudomuscular contraction. Thousands of conduits and arcs of light converged to a single node: metal like flesh or flesh like metal, each grown through the other, and, at their center a body she recognized, and burning eyes she'd once seen echo stars.

Viv's feet left the ground. Fields caught her, bore her up. She thought of Zanj, a mile of ship away. She could have freed herself, maybe—the *Ground-*

swell was built on Imperial tech, like the rest of the galaxy. But if she fought free, she would only fall.

Burning eyes swept her, blinded her. A human shape, or something almost human, emerged from that node with a slippery sucking sound; she trailed cables and light like veils and a bridal train. The fire in those eyes focused, tightened, tamped, until Viv could bear to look at them—could bear to look at her.

There were still wheels in Xiara's eyes, though the heat of their turning burned them white. Slick from *Groundswell,* adorned with power, she shimmered. Viv had never seen anything quite so beautiful, or anyone quite so not a person. She had left her to this. Xiara had wanted it—no. Chosen it. Because she knew they could not walk together.

"I came back," Viv said. This was such a bad idea. The woman she'd left might not be in there anymore. Her heart was spread through a fleet, her mind through millions of tons of body. What could Viv herself, one tiny meat-being, mean to someone who was this? "I was wrong. I'm sorry. I was selfish. I didn't think about you—about anyone but myself. Nothing was real for me but what I wanted. But I'm trying to change."

The ship churned. Wheels turned in Xiara's eyes.

"Maybe you hate me for leaving, or for letting you leave. I understand. I'm not here to ask you to take me back. Though, um. I wouldn't mind." Still revolutions. No words. "But the Empress—she's me. She built me as part of an experiment to change her own past, to make herself stronger. If it works, she'll burn this universe from the heart out. Zanj and I can't stop her alone. We need allies—all the puzzle pieces the Empress scattered around the galaxy. Gray's broken, and we need to fix him. Hong's imprisoned, and we need to free him. And we need you. If you'll help us." She swallowed.

It had been thirteen years since she last felt nervous around an ex. Granted, most of her exes couldn't blow up planets.

Wheels and wheels, a face as perfect and expressionless as an uninspired angel—and behind those eyes, no woman but the fleet. She'd been wrong. Worse than wrong. The smile, the relief, the strength of arm, the slow workings of that painfully sincere mind, had vanished like a river into the sea. And Viv let it happen. She could have stopped, she could have stayed. Even if there was a Xiara in there somewhere, beneath the fleet, why would she greet Viv now with anything but scorn?

"Please," she said. "Just be there. Even if you can't help us, even if you don't want to see me ever again—I had to see you. I had to know I hadn't broken you. I've spent so long breaking everything else. Curse me if you want. Chain me. I left. I let you push me on my way, because I couldn't let you mean something to me. I don't let anyone touch me, or change me. I deserve this. But I'm still sorry."

Only the ship answered, with that same unbroken hum of digesting star.

"Okay," she said. "I guess I'll go."

She tried to turn, to leave. But a hand held her shoulder, strong as glaciers though less cold. Those inhuman features flowed into something almost familiar, and vicious enough to seem kind.

And those remembered lips shaped words: "Not yet."

47

SEATED CROSS-LEGGED UPON her dais in the *Monastic Sphere*, in the ever-changing heart of the glorious Mirrorfleet, Grand Rector Celestine was vexed.

Grand Rectors did not tend to vex easily—the position called for probity and wisdom, for the political clout to meld the half a hundred sects of the Mirrorfaith, each with its own hierarchy and Hierarchs, its own schools of contemplation and research and discovery, contingents of spies and scholars spread throughout the galaxy and beyond, and of course its own orders militant, to a single whole. Many Rectors had been selected for patience alone. But even a Rector chosen for wisdom and kindheartedness might change—when faced with the awesome responsibilities of preserving the detritus of thousands of years of civilization—into an order-minded stickler, or worse, a tyrant. Sentient beings given power beyond reason, and responsibility beyond measure, sometimes clutch the power to themselves like a blanket, and ignore the responsibility for as long as they can, until one day the capital city's fires reach their palace, too.

And if this could be said even of those who inherited the office under ideal circumstances, well, Grand Rector Celestine achieved her place under circumstances not even she would term ideal. She seized command in pitched battle against the Pride, when the Blessed Archaetryx fell, and upon return to the *Monastic Sphere* she had been confirmed in her role by a number of well-timed retirements, enlightenments, suicide missions, and good old-fashioned murders.

No one would admit her ascension to the throne was a surprise. Celestine took large steps. She slept little. She had been loved in her childhood—loved beyond all reason by her predecessor, and loved to the brink of madness by a podmate with whom she'd joined the 'faith. But love was complicated. To love another being, in specific, and remain unbound to passing and insubstantial forms, required deep liberating practice and the sort of firm free generosity only saints could manage—and while Celestine accepted few limits to her own capacity, she knew she was no saint. Love bound her fast to lovers.

So, to move forward, she had carved individual affection from her soul. Sentient beings changed too much, too fast. All form was transitory. Yes, there were tears. But when she was done, she found herself free—to love the 'faith. Saints had warned her the love of 'faith was but another attachment, all the more insidious for its illusory permanence, but again, Celestine was no saint. The 'faith needed those who were not. She sacrificed the purity of her practice to support the saints' grand, slow work.

And when that work jeopardized both 'faith and 'fleet, she grew vexed indeed.

This monk before her, twitching in his suspender field, bound for judgment before the assembled Hierarchs—she found him especially infuriating. One of Archivist Lan's protégés, by the name of Qollak—another chip off the old recalcitrant block. Celestine did not hate the Archivist: Lan had been a miscalculation, a never-quite rival overlooked upon Celestine's ascension because she spent her life pondering ancient broken file systems in the Archive Tree, lacked arms and armor, and was utterly insignificant to 'fleet operations. But many throughout the 'fleet loved her, trained beside her or beneath her, respected her—and she, Celestine suspected, had been the Brother Heretic's most subtle ally. But no more of that. The poor young manalogue before her stood proud as he could manage, his suspender field flushing blue-based rainbows, his tendril forest face swishing in what he no doubt hoped was well-concealed concern.

"And," Celestine continued, "after the most recent Pride attack, not only did you violate our quarantine order, you personally boarded a Pride drone and attempted to commune with it."

His voice burbled panic. "Rector. You know as well as anyone—we have so many questions. The Pride's behavior has undergone an extreme change since Brother—since the Heretic's assault on High Carcereal. They have become relentless, eager, almost desperate in their pursuit of the 'fleet. I found a single crippled drone isolated from the swarm, Cloudblind. If there was any chance of recovering its data, gleaning its motivation—I had to seize the opportunity. We have all lost friends in this ceaseless battle." His dorsal eyes sought help from the gathered Hierarchs, all silent in their robes—and from Archivist Lan herself. "Studying the Pride is permitted by the precepts of 'faith. After all, the Pride were of the Empress once."

Celestine unfurled herself from the dais, rising to her full seven feet. Hierarchs fell back, sensing the rage she broadcast through the Cloud. "The Pride turned against the Empress. They are the first and fiercest heretics, Brother Qollak. Their secret knowledge drove them mad—as it has driven so many among our order. Distraction, ignorance, and ambition cloud the mirror of the mind." Heavy robes and wings rustled around her as she stepped down; her talons ticked against the cold floor. "And these weaknesses are catching."

"We pledge to seek," he stammered, "without bias and without fear. My mind held only this intent."

"Your mind held only this intent," she repeated, projecting sympathy, kindness, understanding, all these foreign emotions she so often had to feign these days. On patrol, in battle, she had not needed to seem amiable before administrators. She required no compassion on a dawnblade's bridge, when she ordered the legion's torches to advance. This, too, vexed. Nearing, she considered him for a time that did not seem long to her. She had chosen the hawk's discipline, and time felt different for a raptor. He twitched, purpled, pinked, rippled beneath his robe. His eyes kept sliding from her gaze. "Naturally. You did not consider the risk that the drone might feign damage, that it might have made a trap of its own mind. You did not ask yourself what might lurk within that hateful consciousness. Some virus, some heresy to poison the 'fleet? Some insidious slow doctrine to feed our ships, so the Pride might turn them against us—or command even our own bodies? Or even a simple lie to corrupt us against ourselves, and waste thousands of hours' meditation in pursuit of a false promise?" The hall kept its silence. The Hierarchs understood the way of things, the need for discipline.

All save one.

"He made a mistake." Archivist Lan's voice was smooth from infrequent use, like a blade drawn only to shed blood, and well cleaned after. She strode forth from the other Hierarchs: a small woman of the owl discipline, eyes large, hands clasped, willowy beneath her robes. If Celestine made her nervous, she did not show it. She lived too far from war to fear those who waged it, and the discipline of the owl held a patience of its own. "A mistake to try at all, and certainly to try alone. But Qollak is not the only one in this room who seeks answers. Why have the Pride pursued us, these last months?

What changed? Qollak asked the right question, at the right time, for the right reason. That is our calling."

And this was why Celestine never truly feared Lan, though she could not kill her, either. The Archivist understood propositions and philosophies, principles and compromises. Data theory, archaeonetworking, the many mysteries of the deep, the forgotten languages of the far Cloud, she mastered them and made them hers. But she knew little of power. She did not, could not, understand that by challenging Celestine, by all but ordering her to free and forgive this little monk, as she had begged her to free and forgive the Heretic, she created an opposing will Celestine must be seen to overcome. By arguing for mercy, she made mercy impossible.

"Your student," the Grand Rector said, "did ask the right question, at the right time, for the right reason. But without the proper perspective."

She reached through his skinfield, touched his drifting fronds, and took his soul into her hand.

In the Cloud of which this world was but a flickering shadow cast by madmen on a cavern wall, she found him. His soul, the integral of his experiences and consciousness over time, a tracking model of too, too earnest Brother Qollak, danced and pulsed with a liquid firefly radiance. Celestine remembered fireflies from her childhood. She had caught them just as easily: in her talons, like that, without crushing. How he fluttered against her grip: a mottled, eager being, full of flashing delights, of questions embraced for themselves, of answers discovered. He dreamed in many colors.

How sweet.

She began, with little passion and less joy, to pry him open.

He screamed as his soul cracked. Being was an inbound spiral, spinning always back on itself, an orbit enforced by the gravity of attachment. War, true war, on the scale of milliseconds and eons, required more clarity and flexibility, more openness, than the self could bear. Selves were predictable; selves built patterns, sought meaning where there was none. Celestine had forsaken all attachments, and embraced instead the warmaster's lonely, open contemplation: a ruthless transience of form. She shared that with him now. One by one, she found the points of gravity that bound Qollak's soul, and unbound them. That sunset was no different from all other sunsets. His mother, teaching him to hunt with bubble nets in their home oceans: there were other mothers, other teachings. She pulled him into her lonely orbit, and his scream grew fine indeed.

But he did not scream so loud, nor did the work so consume her awareness, that she missed the alarm.

Sirens rang through the assembly hall. Data rushed into her soul.

Pride ships. Nearing fast.

Prayer wheel chandeliers flashed red, and holographic threat assessments and multidimensional projections filled the chamber; stained-glass walls opened like flower petals to leave the Hierarchs, and Celestine, standing within a transparent dome amid the vastness of the Mirrorfleet. Threat estimates and Cloudforms slid into her soul, and battle systems and semi-autonomous subroutines digested them—thunder gods of flourishing colors and horrid, hungry grins. She had forged them down decades of meditation and hypnosis and battlefield experiment, and now they moved for her, ordering the 'fleet. Pickets torched up, Clericies unfolded into battle form, and vulnerable meditants, chanting cross-legged in hard vacuum, made hand signs of mystic import and slipped back to the Monasteries for their war garb. The 'fleet was battle-ready in moments—but Celestine could not guide it and break this boy's soul at once.

With a sigh, and a loosening of her hand, she let Brother Qollak fall. The Archivist bent to retrieve him, pull him to safety—defiance, but forgivable. The others would remember Lan kneeling to draw the wreck of her apprentice back. They would see their Grand Rector victorious.

Which she needed—because, in his shortsighted scholar's way, Qollak was right. The Pride had changed. After years of silence, they had launched an attack every three days since High Carcereal, an unending wave of pursuit, tides of their vicious ugly ships breaking against the beauty of the 'faith. Even Celestine's most loyal and broken Hierarchs asked: Why?

Only two days had passed since their last assault. Had they changed pattern once again? What would that signify?

Celestine let her thunder gods pass the routine orders to the lesser shipminds her abbots and admirals maintained. That done, she directed the small self-aware fragment fools called consciousness, which was in truth but a sort of focus of the totality of the mind, as the center of the field of vision was the point of greatest focus for the human eye, to the problem that needed her most precise attention: the enemies approaching through the Cloud.

Her wings flicked in surprise. Pride ships approached, yes, but only a cruiser and twenty drones, optimized for speed—barely enough of a fleet to destroy a battle moon. Guns live, sensors hot, the Pride were looking for something—no, she saw now, *chasing* something, an ancient crude fast picket, deeply wounded, its pilot crying through the Cloud for help, and offering . . . not cargo as Celestine had first thought. Treasure.

Ah. That answered the question of timing. They had not been found after all. They simply lay upon the line of pursuit. The 'fleet rested in a space of Cloudbound emptiness, invisible to outsiders; they did not have to answer the picket's cry for aid. They could wait here, and watch it burn.

She reached out her hand instead, and offered safe passage.

The ensuing battle barely merited the name. The Pride sensed the picket's calculations for reentry and attempted to block them, but the 'fleet used its deep roots in the local Cloud to block the Pride in turn—creating an impression that local turbulence and corruption complicated transit into realspace. The Pridemind calculated an innovative solution for this interference, and dropped into realspace right before the mouths of the guns of the 'faith.

Then it was all over but the glory.

Some monks ascended; one died with mind unclean, and the soulcatchers caught him for purification in the crypts. They burned the Pride from the sky, and dragged the limping picket in. Celestine marked three brilliant monks for further enlightenment, and turned her attention to the fast picket's pilot, who'd refused to leave her self-described treasure, and demanded (demanded!) an audience.

War monks brought them from the hold, pilot and treasure both, up the vast winding stair to the platform where the Hierarchs waited. To Celestine.

The pilot was a jumpsuited barbarian, staring about herself flush with the chemical wonder Celestine recognized as ship withdrawal. The pilot's veins glowed with endorphins; her system shouted joy through the Cloud, and far deeper need than a mere fast picket could prompt. She was a naked nerve. The right touch on her cheek would have left her rapt in ecstasy. She had been bound to a larger vessel recently.

The pilot stared at Celestine with the wonder due the Grand Rector of the 'faith, then realized she was staring and dropped to one knee, eyes lowered. "Grand Rector. I thank you for your courtesy, and your rescue."

"Your rescue was a chance to cleanse the world of its mistakes," she answered, and held out her hand. "No thanks are needed. It is customary, however, to offer one's name to one's benefactor."

"I am Xiara Ornchiefsdaughter," she said, and dared raise her eyes at this, as if these were not words to be said with eyes lowered.

"Orn, we have heard, is a myth."

She blushed like a novice. How charming. "Orn is no myth, Grand Rector. Though it has been many years since we last flew."

"Yet you kneel before me now. Having, of late, detached yourself from a ship of some majesty."

The color deepened, changed. Were all women of Orn so easily read? She was a crystal glass held up to the sun. Delightful. "It is a long story, Grand Rector. I bring a treasure that is, I think, of great value to you."

"How did you find us?"

"I was, of late, in another ship. A larger ship, with the power to see much that lies hidden. There was a battle; I fled, but realized I could not keep this treasure for myself for long. So I come to you."

"Surely you could have sent an automated shuttle. I feel the rawness of your ship-need. You are cruel to yourself, Daughter of Orn."

She smiled at that, oddly. "When you see this treasure, Grand Rector, you will know why I had to deliver it myself."

"Show us, then."

They had brought the box, eight feet tall, four wide and deep, and made of iron, on a hoversled. The sled settled; Xiara Ornchiefsdaughter unlocked the door, and the door behind that, and stood back.

From within came curses in ancient tongues, and a cry—and from the box tumbled a woman clothed in heavy chains, a woman the Grand Rector had very much desired to look upon with her own eyes. She fell before her now, too burdened by her bonds to stand.

But despite that weight, Vivian Liao could still roll over, and look up, and say, through the blood of the lip she'd split falling, "So you're the Grand Rector. I have a proposition for you."

48

VIV LAY ON the floor at the Grand Rector's feet, in chains, and consoled herself with the thought that so far almost everything was going according to plan. She never would have reached the Grand Rector walking free, and if the choice was chained or not at all, at least she wore chains she chose. Xiara had sold the humble-outsider-bringing-tribute schtick; the Pride made things interesting for a few hours there, in a *we're all going to die* sort of way, but she'd reached the heart of the Mirrorfleet. The rest was up to her.

She hadn't expected the Grand Rector to be quite so imposing in person. The last time Viv had seen her, the woman seemed colossal, true, but that was a projection, and projections lied. She was easily seven feet tall in person, taller if you counted the wings that rose from her back, thin-boned and severe and massive with the interlocking muscles both wings and arms required. Her feet and hands were talons, her eyes a deep raptor gold. On Hong, the robes of the 'faith looked comforting, relaxed; the Rector wore hers taut and ceremonial as a dress uniform. And she was smiling, an expression as natural and reassuring on her face as it would have seemed on a hawk's.

"Xiara Ornchiefsdaughter," she said as if Viv had not spoken, though her gaze never left Viv's form, "tell us of this treasure you have brought."

"You have sought her." Xiara sounded dutiful, proud, earnest—every bit the loyal Orn warrior she'd been when she first brought Viv to her mother's court. Viv almost bought the lie. "We traveled together. She betrayed me. She crawled back, and I wanted nothing of her. So I bring her to you."

Viv forced herself to her knees. She hadn't expected the chains to be so damn heavy, and she burned to think of all these high-class monks and nuns and such seeing her trussed up like this. It wasn't the most decorous position from which to make a pitch. "I didn't crawl."

The Rector knelt with an ease Viv had not expected from a woman that tall; she cocked her head to one side, and before Viv could flinch back, her left talon darted out and drew a thin line of blood from her cheek. The Grand Rector smelled the blood, tasted it with her thin tongue. "How strange. As the Heretic claimed: it speaks, yet lacks a soul."

Damn the sting in her cheek. *Heretic* probably meant Hong. What did that past tense mean? Was he dead? Tortured? Imprisoned? Viv didn't let herself hope, and she most certainly did not ask about him. She'd met enough high-level players to tell that the Rector was the type that thrived on weakness. She'd never dealt against someone like that from quite so compromised a position. "I need your help."

"You fled High Carcereal with a heretic and a demon, and you have scourged the galaxy in the months since, committing great blasphemy. You are a soulless puppet, your strings cut, in chains. Why should we help you?"

"To save yourselves."

The Rector laughed, seized the chains across Viv's chest in her fist, and rose from her crouch, dragging Viv and chains alike one-handed up. Viv's feet left the floor and she dangled from the Rector's grip. "You are in no position to make threats." Her breath smelled of metal. Viv wondered what she ate, if anything.

"I'm not threatening you. The Empress is."

"Blasphemy," the Rector sneered. "If you were not a sacred relic, I would break you now. If you had a soul, I would enlighten you."

Viv wasn't certain what *enlighten* meant in this context, but the tone of voice didn't suggest anything pleasant. "Your Empress made me on High Carcereal, and ran away. Did you ever wonder why?"

Those golden eyes might be curious—or hungry.

"She made me in her image," Viv said. "She's modeling her past. She's stuck—she's taken her current technologies as far as they'll go, and she can't think outside them. So she's been searching for a version of the universe where she has the power to beat the Bleed. She thinks she's found it."

"Then the final triumph is at hand."

"For her."

"Her victory is ours."

It was hard to breathe, suspended like this. "You don't get it. She doesn't care about you. She cares about winning. The Bleed have stopped her from rolling over the cosmos so far, because if she grows too large, they'll come for her. If she breaks them, that's it. She'll eat the whole Cloud. She'll turn this galaxy into her citadel. She'll archive you all, if you're lucky, and reach out for another galaxy, and another after that. She won't be safe until she's sure the Bleed are truly gone, until she's sure there's no bigger threat hiding behind them—and she can't be sure of that until she owns the universe. You've studied her for centuries. You know her better than anyone. How she strikes, and why. I've seen worlds she's ruined, and the archives she carries with her, pieces of civilizations she found interesting. Frozen whales in a frozen sea. That's your future, if you don't help me."

The Rector dropped her; Viv's knees buckled when her feet hit the ground, but she'd been waiting for the weight. It bowed her. She almost collapsed, but she forced her legs to push her up, to take the weight, to let her stand. Her shoulders trembled, and her back, and the chains bit into her skin, but she held firm before the Grand Rector.

"She offers victory. Immortality. The 'faith has followed Her for centuries. And yet you claim She would destroy us. Why should we listen to your lies?"

"They're not lies. You have followed her from battlefield to battlefield. You pick up the pieces she leaves behind. You keep civilization alive. But if she wins, she'll leave nothing here or anywhere. Just her." Viv couldn't turn much, but she scanned the monastic court, all those robed and hooded strangers in their many forms, letting her desperation show and seeing signs of sympathy, or at least shame. One of the monks, a woman with white hair and large owly eyes, seemed receptive, though it was hard to say how much of her concern was for Viv and how much for the wounded, man-sized bunch of seaweed she was holding. "I can break the Empress's locks. Ask Xiara. That's why she had to bring me herself—I could slip free if she wasn't there to watch me. You've been collecting her tools, her traces, for longer than I can imagine. I can help you use them, and together we can save—"

The Rector's face did not change to warn Viv of her impending motion. Her hand closed over Viv's mouth, and her long fingers wrapped around Viv's jaw, around the back of her skull, talons dimpling skin just on the verge of drawing blood. Her last word was lost in a moan, and her jaw creaked as the Rector squeezed. "We have heard enough from this soulless creature. She has borne out the Heretic's account of her delusion. So small, so weak: hard to believe the Empress would build such a thing."

At *small* and *weak*, Viv managed a muffled protest, even through the pain.

"We will not be drawn into heresy. We will not let your lies distort the true science. But you are, yourself, a miracle, and you shall receive no less study than your nature demands. Archivist Lan, perhaps this will serve as a more fitting challenge for your students than the seductions of Pride hardware." The Grand Rector gestured to the war monks, massive and armored and waiting with their pikes. Two marched forward, seized Viv's chains from behind, and dragged her back. "Seal her in a relic case."

49

THEY LEFT HER in a glass bubble on a clawfoot pedestal in a cornerless room decorated with golden filigree, with nothing to do but pace.

She had hoped they would use Imperial technology to bind her, some forcefield she could slip through or cage she might unlock. Instead the war monks dragged her to this room, and dropped her on this pedestal. One cut off her chains with shears; Viv tried to jump her and take the shears away, but was thrown back with casual ease, while another war monk drew a circle around her in the air with a gray metal rod. The circle remained where it was drawn, glimmering fuzzily in a way she recognized, with a heartsick pang, from Gray's transformations. It revolved around her, knitting a glass shell from thin air, anchored to the dais.

Then they left through a door that vanished behind them, leaving her stuck inside a Fabergé egg.

When she punched the glass it rang so loud it hurt her ears, but did not break. She threw her body against it and bounced off. She worried about air at first, but there was a circle of tiny holes in the floor just inside the glass, spaced ten to a fingerpad, and a cool breeze passed through them. She would not suffocate by accident. Of course, they could stop giving her air at any time. Or mix other gases with her air supply. Or evacuate the air altogether. Raise the temperature to boil her, lower it to freeze her.

March in a circle ten feet across, and that was her world. For all she knew, they'd already moved her—with the right technology, she'd never notice. She imagined the gold filigree egg lowered onto a shelf lined with other eggs that held other bodies, other versions of her, the Mirrorfaith's collection. They wanted to study her. Take her apart. Just like she'd told Hong, way back when. Just like Zanj had said.

She had to use the bathroom. The floor of the dais bubbled, and the bubble popped, revealing a chamber pot and a small box of tissues and a tube of something that smelled (when she sniffed it, with some reluctance) like sanitizer. No curtain, though. Of course, the fact that they knew she had to use the bathroom without her saying anything suggested she was under the kind of surveillance that would have made the presence or absence of a curtain immaterial.

Okay. Imprisoned, yes. Forgotten, no. She did her business as defiantly as possible under the circumstances. She'd never had cause to piss vehemently before, but there was a first time for everything.

When she was done, the floor burbled up to cover the basin and tissues, and settled flat again. She'd considered holding on to the sanitizer, but what would that accomplish? Unlikely that glass was alcohol soluble in the future. At any rate, now she knew the floor could strangle her on its own, without any help from gas, which was nice.

She paced. She did a few push-ups, and that rising-up-on-your-fingertips-while-in-lotus-position thing, which looked cool when Nicolas Cage did it in *Con Air*. She entertained fantasies of jumping the next guards who came for her, then considered the likely outcome of jumping guards who spent most of their lives training to fight evil cyborgs. She decided against it.

Eventually she was hungry, and soon after that the floor bubbled again to produce a bamboo box containing two of Hong's nutrient paste packets and a glass of water. She ate, drank; the packaging melted when she was done. After a span of time she could not precisely judge, the light from the walls dimmed and died without warning or pretense of sunset. Keep deducing, Ms. Liao: they want you alive, contained, and fed, but they don't care about boredom, or exercise. They're more interested in your body than your mind.

"I've been on dates like this before," Viv said, then realized she had spoken out loud, and felt for the first time—save, maybe, when the Pride had been about to kill her, or the Empress—nervous. People lived for years in solitary confinement. Years and years. Some of them didn't go irretrievably mad as such.

Everything was still, more or less, going according to plan.

After nervous, she felt sleepy. She tried to remember when she'd last had a good night's rest. Back at the fleet, with Xiara, barely counted. Certainly not as they chased the Empress, or fled from her. On Refuge, maybe? Worn out after a hard day's work? But then, she'd known each night's sleep was one night farther behind the Empress, one night farther from home. She felt farther away than ever now, curled on the floor in this glass cage, trusting her captors' goodwill to keep her alive. If only the board of directors could see her now.

This was such a bad idea. But none of them had come up with a better one.

She dreamed of an ocean seen from overhead, of tumblers in a lock, of needles of light that pierced her skin, of green hands and flame and melted flesh, and sat up wide awake and panting in darkness, in her glass cage.

"This was such a bad idea," someone said. This time, it wasn't her.

By the time she stopped screaming, she realized it was Zanj, wearing 'faith robes and her own face, leaning on the Star. Her palm glowed a ghoulish green, which didn't help the whole night terror schtick. Viv steadied herself against her bubble's wall. "What the hell was that for?"

"Fun, mostly." She raised her open hand. "The flame will foil their sensors while it lasts. Thought I'd check in and see if you wanted to give up yet."

"I had to try the easy way. We need them."

"Sure, sure. We need their spare parts, is what you mean. Come on. I'll bust you out of here, we'll crash down into their library, find what we need to fix Gray, then pick up Xiara before they can wine and dine her into pledging allegiance, and get out and on with our next bad idea."

"We need more than tools. We need allies."

"These allies? Trust me, Viv. I've seen all sorts of monsters in my time, and the Grand Rector is a piece of work. She's not coming over to your side."

"The Archivist might. Hong's teacher. I think that was her, with the white hair and the big eyes, back in the audience chamber."

"Oh yeah. She looked super important, kneeling over that seaweed guy."

"Hong thought she was."

"Hong turned you in!"

"We all messed up on Refuge. Hong was right about some things."

"Oh yes, from what I've seen it really looks like Hong could have started a revolution, won the 'fleet over. That's why he was in chains the last time we saw him. Because he's such an excellent judge of political reality."

"We have to stop the Empress. The 'faith is better positioned than anyone to do that."

"They're children playing with guns."

"So we take the safeties off and teach them to shoot."

Zanj laughed at that. "I didn't know what to expect, when you decided to go to war. It's a good look." The flame dimmed. "Time's wasting. Okay. We'll stick with your way for the moment."

"Have you found Hong?"

"Not a trace. Everyone knows he was taken. They had this big trial; he confessed to heresy, and accepted the sentence of some kind of meditation retreat. It's pretty common around here. But I sweet-talked the penance ships—the inmates spend most of their time hard-dreaming their way through difficult decrypts, it's pretty gross—and they don't have him either."

"Look harder."

Zanj rolled her eyes. "Fine. Well, at least Xiara's enjoying herself. Lots of glad-handing, tours, the whole hospitality game. The Grand Rector can smell *Groundswell* on her, and she's got her teeth out for that ship."

Viv tried not to think about the strength of that woman, about the piercing consideration of those eyes, and about Xiara, earnest as a morning breeze. But then, Xiara was native to this world. She'd be fine. She would probably, certainly, almost definitely be fine. "We'll be fine," she said out loud, hoping that would convince her. This had been the hardest part of the plan: thinking of Xiara alone, exposed, in the 'fleet. Her hand rose to the cut the Grand Rector's claw had drawn in her cheek. "For now, we wait. We need these people on our side."

"Okay." Zanj tossed the flame in the air. It guttered, flashing. "But if you get yourself killed, I'll kill you."

Viv stopped pacing. The gravel sincerity in that threat, and Zanj's immediate glance away thereafter, as if she'd said nothing notable, the nervous twitch of her hand up to scratch the back of her neck—it all clicked, and Viv felt warm all through. Nothing sexual about it. She was more than sufficiently in tune with her various lusts to track that sort of thing. No, this was the far simpler, and stranger realization that Zanj, for all her bluff and bluster, would care if Viv were gone. She wanted her safe. She wanted to hurt people who hurt her. Viv remembered how she had felt in the Empress's throne room, Zanj hanging from green light in agony, the Star fallen from her hand—that overwhelming rage, so intense it verged on nausea, how dare this nonsense Empress of however many stars set one damn glowstick finger on her friend.

She stammered, but managed, "Thank you," and, "I care about you, too."

"Look at that," Zanj said, "flame's out, got to go, see you later, take care." And she left Viv in the dark.

But not alone.

50

TWO DAYS LATER the Archivist came for Viv. Flanked by mod-bristling war monks, some four-armed, some two, some scaled, one a shadow in space identifiable only by his robes, the Archivist seemed a fragile hook from which Viv could hang her hopes: willowy slim, owl-eyed, careful with her steps, her white hair braided back, light brown skin gently worn with age that Viv, back home, would not have been surprised to learn fell anywhere from midthirties to early sixties. Who knew what it meant here.

She moved like a ghost, now still, now slow, now so fast Viv's eyes could not track her. The changes of speed were not, Viv thought, affected, meant to startle or distract. The mind within that body worked down its own paths, and some of those took it far from the world of flesh and ordinary time. When her attention wandered back to physical reality, she accelerated to catch up.

In a breath and a blur, she crossed the room to Viv's bubble and pressed her hand against it, watched her unblinking for seconds that turned to minutes. Viv did not return her stare: she did not know what the Archivist could read from her through those eyes. She watched the woman's hand instead, its thin fingers crisscrossed with tiny lines, shiny with calluses and scars of thin deep healed cuts. Still hands, untrembling.

"I mean you no harm," the Archivist said. "The Grand Rector has asked me to study you. Do not fight, and you will not be hurt. Answer questions, and we will treat you with courtesy. Nod if you agree."

The Grand Rector asked—interesting. That explained the war monks. But Viv had come to find the Archivist, and through her, to find Hong. She nodded once.

The Archivist pressed her fingernails into the glass. It glowed where she touched, bubbled, began to flow. Her nails passed through, and the heat spread in straight lines from her hand, to frame a door of fire. When the Archivist pulled, the glass peeled away. It clanged against the floor when she let it fall. The Archivist blurred back, her hands crossed over the front of her robe, seemingly cool. "Chain her if you must," she told the shadow monk. "But do not damage her. She is a relic, beyond price."

She didn't fight the manacles, or the belt they locked around her waist to chain the manacles through, or the leg irons. She'd accomplish nothing at this stage by clawing eyes or kicking groins—if these monks even had the sort of genitalia she was used to.

She wondered if one of these monks was Zanj, disguised, but if so, Zanj kept such deep cover she didn't even wink to tip her hand. Probably not, then. Zanj had her tricks and transformations, but Viv would never accuse her of subtlety. If she needed to hide in shadows, she'd just snuff out the sun.

The Archivist led them out a door that hadn't existed moments ago, down a high, dim hall lit by green and yellow and red stained-glass slits, to a round room with a fountain in the middle, the hub of many intersecting halls. The Archivist stirred the fountain's clear water with her fingertips, then cupped her palm to draw a handful that now had a rich ruby tint, and, though Viv tried by reflex to pull away, she dripped that red water onto Viv's forehead, and spoke a complex phrase Viv's translation gimmick rendered as *activate*. The liquid felt cool and warm at once; it crawled over her skin and sank through. She felt a weight enter her bloodstream, as if she'd just received an injection.

Then the floor disappeared, and they flew into space.

The war monks held her by her chains, and didn't seem worried, which was all well and good for them. Viv cursed, for her part, and in the process of cursing discovered that she could breathe, and that her eyes were not freezing or boiling or popping from her head or any of the other things television had warned her eyes did in space. All the skinfields and spacesuits she'd tried had swaddled her in cloth, or electromagnetic barriers, offering only a shadow of this experience: her skin prickling in vacuum, her own eyes wondering at the deep, and the 'fleet.

Diving, as a kid, on the Great Barrier Reef, before everything got bad, Viv had whirled in living jewels: bright red damselfish, spotted trout, butterfly fishes wiggling through the claw-sharp coral, great lengths of grouper and cod and even, once, a massive lumpy wrasse, and, far off, occasionally, sharks.

That was the Mirrorfaith fleet: those colors, that darting motion, that range of scale. For every stained-glass continent, there were hundreds of smaller gem craft—not to mention the ranked cross-legged meditators they passed who seemed to need no ship at all, their eyes closed, robes floating in vacuum. She'd seen fleets before this—Xiara's was nearly so massive—but those were dead, drifting, or dominated by a few minds. This was a civilization.

"Why is it on fire?"

The Archivist turned her head an anatomically improbable degree to look at Viv as they flew. She didn't speak, save for the furrow in her brow.

"That ship over there—"

"The torch," the Archivist replied when she saw where Viv was pointing.

"And that one."

"A dawnblade."

"They're burning."

"We are addressing infections after the most recent assault," the Archivist said. "You see that temple's aft pane cracked, those shards which used to be lances." She indicated each with a precise gesture, always palm up. "Every three days, the Pride strike, in greater numbers. Every three days, we beat them back."

"I didn't feel a battle."

"You would not, in the cell. Not unless it went badly for us."

"I've heard so much about this place," Viv said.

The Archivist did not ask from whom. She knew.

They approached an enormous tree in spreading vacuum, its leaves green and purple and orange, its trunk carved with stylized faces. One opened its mouth to receive them, and closed it after.

They marched her up a winding stair within the hollow of the trunk, while scholars zipped up and down its core. After four hundred steps they stopped at an unassuming hatch. "You," the Archivist told the war monks, "may wait outside. Our review will take some time."

"We will observe," the shadow said, "and report."

Which told Viv most of what she needed to know about 'fleet politics. She had been studying the Archivist as they walked, seeking the woman Hong had told her about, the wisdom and calm. She wore her body like a mask. "Very well. If you do not mind boredom."

The door opened onto a long branch planed flat, with no railings on either side—why would monks who could fly worry about falling? They moved single file along the branch to a spreading leaf at the far end, which supported a table, several straining shelves, and the robed kelp forest Viv had last seen twitching on the Grand Rector's floor. "This," the Archivist said, "is my assistant, Brother Qollak." He bowed, spreading the strands he used for arms like fans. "Please. Sit."

"You must understand," Qollak said with a voice of water and vines, "you represent a remarkable opportunity: an organism independent from the Cloud." He lifted a tray from the top of one shelf and set it on the table before her: on its surface, a puzzle box. "We cannot, as yet, verify your other claims, but we can address the mystery of your cognitive mechanism. There's never, in the 'faith's experience, been anyone like you—someone all flesh."

"There used to be a lot of people like me," Viv said.

"Please don't take this the wrong way. As an experimental subject, you are without peer. We must learn the shape of your cognitive processes. Open the box, please."

She tried to reach for the box, but the short chain clinked against her manacles. She looked to Qollak, then to the Archivist, who was watching, in her own flat way, the shadow monk. Who did not move.

Apologetically, nimbly, Brother Qollak lifted the box from the tray and dropped it into Viv's lap.

She rolled her eyes, lifted it, turned it over, tested sides. A weight lock. It came apart in her hand. Fifteen seconds. "When they tested me when I was a kid, they put candy in these."

"I could have Sister Cellarer bring us candy, if you like," Brother Qollak said.

"I'll live."

Twenty seconds. Forty-five. Three minutes. Twelve seconds. Thirty minutes. The next one took an hour and a half, because it was too big to hold in her lap, and the war monks still refused to unchain her.

"I can do more than this," Viv said after the hour-and-a-half box. "These are toys. Give me a lock you've never been able to open. An artifact you've never known how to use. I know you have corpses of Grayframe somewhere in this fleet. Hong told me—"

She fell from the chair, and her skull bounced off the floor. Her ears rang. Her cheek was a mat of pain. Pretty colors ebbed from her vision, and the room returned in hazy outline: the shadow monk stood beside her toppled chair, seething, and the Archivist between them, arms out, furious.

"—are present," Viv heard the Archivist say, once her ears stopped ringing, "on my ship at my sufferance. And you, Brother Lailien, dare strike a relic—"

"She is no relic," the shadow monk hissed. "She speaks secrets. She speaks the Brother Heretic's name."

"We have all said his name," the Archivist said. "And when his time of penance is passed, he will join us once again."

"His mind is clouded. He will never survive penance."

"You are wrong. And she does not know our ways, and is not bound by our discipline. You would not strike an apprentice."

"She is no apprentice."

"She is my field of study. The Hierarchs will back me in this. You and your fellows are here by the Grand Rector's request, not by her order, and at my sufferance. You will not touch her again."

Lailien said nothing. He did not draw back. But the Archivist turned from him anyway, flitted to Viv's side, and helped her stand. The room swam. Her cheek ached. Her cut had opened, either when he hit her, or when she fell.

"Are you well?"

"I think so," Viv said truthfully. "I can take a punch. Even from an asshole."

Qollak reached for another box, but the Archivist waved it off, impatient—and drew from a pouch at her belt a metal ball the size of a closed fist. She set it in Viv's hands. "Try this."

Lailien took a step forward, but came up against the wall of the Archivist's eyes.

Viv turned the ball in her hands—no shifting weight, no visible seam. Hollow, or else lighter than it looked. The Archivist watched her expectantly; the shadows of Brother Lailien's body whirled, dense and dark.

Viv tossed the ball on the table. The Archivist caught it before it could roll off. "Is this a joke?"

Lailien stepped back. The Archivist slipped the ball back into her pouch. "That's all," she said. "Thank you."

They walked her back down the turning stair, out the carved mouth, flew her through the 'fleet again toward the ornate vicious beauty of the *Monastic Sphere*. Down the hall, to the room of golden filigree. She wondered how many days might pass until she left it again. Her dreams were getting worse.

"Leave us," the Archivist said, and before Brother Lailien could argue, snapped: "You've done quite enough already. If we are to study her, we need her trust. Brother Qollak and I can handle her—and you'll be right on the other side of the cameras if she surprises us."

The war monks left, Lailien last. The Archivist watched as they receded. When the door shut and vanished, the Archivist drew a small crystal from her pouch, set it on the floor, and stomped down hard. Its shards burned with a familiar green flame, and the lights sank red.

She walked Viv back to the dais, guided her into the bubble, and unlocked her chains. "I am sorry," the Archivist said. "We can speak privately for now. You must understand, the subject of Hong's betrayal remains sensitive among the 'fleet. He was loved; that is how he could lead a wing to battle without the Grand Rector's permission. Even those who loved him now find themselves unable to speak his name. I heard him testify: he liked you. He thought he did the right thing, bringing us to you. I am sorry the Rector's monks fall so far below his standard."

"Where is he?"

"In contemplation." Again, her face was a mask.

"But where?"

The Archivist said nothing, and turned to leave. The green flame had almost consumed the crystals on which it burned.

"Let me see that ball again. Please."

The Archivist drew it forth and passed it to her as if it were an enormous pearl. Viv hefted it in both hands, and with a twist of her wrists, split it open.

The ball expanded; its seemingly solid surface unwound into a lattice of thin silver wire. A crystal within pulsed twice, then flared, carving bright trails that resolved, once Viv was done blinking, into whirling dots of light: a galaxy, her galaxy, as fully detailed as the map in the Empress's throne room, points of interest picked out in ruby and orange and green.

She looked across the map to the Archivist, and saw that grim, ever-judging face melt into wonder.

"You've never opened this before," Viv said. "Have you?"

She shook her head.

"I am who I say I am. I am what I say I am. And I can do more than this. But time's running out. You must have a place where you keep the real treasures: the relics too big, too dangerous, too weird to use. The Grayframe bodies, the star maps, the encrypted gods. There's so much more to your world than your Grand Rector dreams. You know, I know: you don't want to worship the Empress. You want to grow beyond her. I can help."

"The Grand Rector would kill you for that suggestion," the Archivist said.

"The Grand Rector isn't the 'faith," she said. "At least, that's what Hong told me."

The side of her face ached—but no blow fell.

The green flame guttered. "Archivist. What's your name?"

"Lan," she said.

"Nice to meet you, Archivist Lan. I'm Viv. When you're ready, come for me. But don't wait too long."

The flame died before the Archivist could respond.

51

TWO MORE DAYS passed, to judge by spans of artificial night. Viv paced her cage and slept when she could. Her dreams often woke her.

They grew more vivid. Shreds of image knit to narrative like flesh closing around a wound. She stood astride a star, thrumming with hunger and control. Magnetic fields danced through the aurora of her mind, and space around her fuzzed and popped with cosmic background static like blood's rush down a vein, like a heart that took ten billion years to beat.

But she had no heart, in these dreams.

She had hands instead, and bodies by the millions, both planet-sized and infinitesimal, autonomous yet wedded to her will like an octopus's arms, each form framed for a different purpose, this for eating planets, this for burning suns to cinders, these for building ships, those for winning wars. With hands the size of planetary rings she held a spark, a shell, a mystery box, and played upon its surface with light and sound, teasing the secrets of victory from a knot of superdense computing matter. Viv wanted what lay within the singularity—she needed it—but when her tools began to pierce and pry, pain wracked her, tore her, as if these knives of light had pierced her own arm and peeled.

She woke panting, scared, her heart hammering in her chest. But each time she had the dream she woke later, with a sense she'd lasted longer, drawn nearer to her end. Hong, wherever he was, would have suggested they find an oracle to read her dream, but Viv could manage without. She'd dreamed of the Empress before, and thought those dreams only trauma and aftermath, the usual dance of psychological recovery that often hurt as much as the initial wound, because the human mind had assembled itself haphazard from spare parts meant for something else. But while she had been a victim in those dreams, she had also been Empress. She held her own heart in her hand. Triumph thrilled her despite the pain. And now, she felt the Empress's victory loom. Not long now. Weeks? Days?

An earthquake startled her awake on the second night to find the filigree chamber awash in red emergency lighting, and she thought it was too late, that the Empress had come for her. But the explosions and crashes and sirens—the first noise she'd heard in two days louder than air through the vents—made this battle sound like a more even fight than the Empress would permit. Perhaps Zanj had snapped, or been discovered, and relished the chance to fight.

Viv worried first for the monks who set themselves against Zanj, without knowing the age and power of the being they fought.

Then, because sometimes even heroes died, she worried for Zanj.

Then the floor cracked open and tumbled away into space, and she began to worry for herself.

Hate fractals burned against 'fleet ships in the black. *They attack us every three days*, Archivist Lan had said. Viv had envisioned skirmishes, perhaps a single immense Pridemother like the one Zanj fought off on Orn.

This dwarfed that scale. Flames filled the night, and shards of metal and glass. War monks fought solo, wrapped in skinfields, trailing light, and wrestled thorns. Guns the size of moons spoke, and others answered. Motes twisted in the void. She realized they were bodies.

Outside, a hate fractal shattered; its shards broke a stained-glass hull that showed a woman kneeling in meditation. The Pride ships made smaller explosions when they broke, and burned green and blue as often as red. Of course: no need for an oxygen atmosphere in those.

Viv felt a breeze at her feet—no, a cool draft blowing down.

Air escaping through the grate.

Christ. She looked up, as if seeking divine intervention, but in fact staring into the surveillance cameras, at the jailers who'd taken such unsettling care of her these last few days. But no aid came, no bubbling in the floor, no sealing of vents. Doubtless they had other jobs, what with the 'fleet under attack. She'd have to fend for herself. As per usual.

At first, panicked, she tried to break the glass; hammered it with her fists, struck it with her shoulders, kicked it so hard she tumbled back to the floor and lay panting and dazed. Stupid. Wasting time, not to mention air. If she managed to escape, what would she have done? How long could she survive in a vacuum?

Some sections of the ship had to be intact, pressurized. Didn't they? She could get to them, or try.

But she wasn't going anywhere. Fine. Move on.

She had to survive until the 'faith could save her, or Zanj, or Xiara, or someone. How much air did the bubble hold? A few hours' worth, maybe? Too much time passed, and panic, the speed of her heart, the nearness of that great gaping jagged maw of space, of the battle outside—another hit like that could snuff her in an instant—the terror of the moment blotted out memory.

Stop fixating on details.

First, strip. No time for embarrassment under the circumstances. They'd taken her 'faith robes, replaced them with a black coverall, which, actually, helped: she couldn't have torn the robes. These were machine-woven, sturdy, but with nails and teeth she managed to tear a long ribbon from the arm, and fold it over some of the grating. Vacuum sucked at the cloth, but couldn't pull it through. When she set her hand above the ribbon she still felt eddies in the air, but better that than the draft she'd felt before.

More ribbons. An adult woman's surface area came to about 1.6 square meters, a little less than that minus head and feet—so, that's the amount of cloth she had to work with. (Why, Viv, do you remember human surface area, and not more useful facts like how fast people metabolize oxygen?) Subtract maybe a quarter meter for the head. The dais was about a meter and a half in diameter, the air grating maybe five centimeters wide. She could paper it three times over, give or take, if she was careful.

She didn't have the time or the tools to be careful.

Ribbon by ribbon, she covered the grate; math bearing its usual relationship to engineering and to production, she managed to stretch the fabric over the full circle twice. She worked in dim red light, in staling air, by flashes of battle. She distracted herself from fear with analysis.

Space battles ran staccato, bursts of destruction followed by regrouping, adjustment, devastation. Why? Maybe the fight moved from Cloud to physical space and back; maybe superior computation here replaced glandular physical abstractions like morale and tactical momentum, which, if you thought about it, really worked out in the long run to an instinctive calculus of advantage. Part of their war would be a war for position, and part for the computational resources required to win. Much of this battle took place in a realm Viv could not sense: countermeasures answering countermeasures, paradoxes deployed against paradoxes.

Ah yes. That abstraction, that sesquipedalian verbiage, that was oxygen deprivation kicking in.

It was so much easier to wander the many chambers of her own mind than it was to force herself to move. Her chest heaved but the air that reached her lungs was thin. Her limbs felt heavy, and her head felt light. She checked her ribbons again, fixed one that had slipped off the grate. Gravity still seemed to work. The ship wasn't dead. Just broken. Now she could only lower her heart rate, breathe shallowly, and survive until rescue came. Or until she died.

Don't panic. She caught herself laughing, which of course wasted more air.

Cross-legged. Sit tall and still, core engaged. Breathe in, and out. Thoughts arise—let them. Thoughts fail. Notice yourself thinking, notice that thought for what it is, an experience arising from your being in the world, no more significant than that, no less. The battle outside her broken chamber: a thought. The Empress, prying at Viv's world: a thought. Her impending death: another.

What was she doing here? She said she wanted to save these people, to rescue this future from the chains she, or a version of her, had forged around its throat. But could she? Assume she was strong enough, smart enough, assume sufficient dedication, determination, assume she could gather allies, assume that she could work that hard, be that smart, lead that well. Weren't the same instincts and powers she trusted now the ones that had led her—or someone so indistinguishable from her that her own machines could not recognize the difference—to rule this galaxy, to crush opposition, to eat and archive worlds? Was she really trying to save anyone? Or did she simply look at the Empress and see a power that was hers for the taking—a throne she had, in fact, already seized?

Doubts, too, were just thoughts.

But—this mattered. What would she do, if she dethroned the Empress? Why should her friends trust her? What made Viv any different from the queen of galaxies she had spent eons fighting, striving, to become?

Thoughts. Important, but still thoughts, thoughts in the grayness of the world, thoughts in the din of battle.

What would save her from herself?

She woke to breaking glass.

To screams heard as if surfacing through deep water, to a pressure on her face, a sting—again, a slap. Lips pressed on hers, familiar, someone else's breath in her lungs, sweet and warm: a halos of halos. She looked up and saw an angel with wheels in her eyes, with tears, endlessly repeating her name.

Her hand trembled up, found Xiara's cheek.

Her "Hi" trailed off. "You shouldn't be here."

Xiara caught her in an embrace so tight Viv had trouble breathing, coughed; she let her go, laughed, choked, brushed a tear away. "Gods and monsters. Viv—you're okay."

"I don't think—" More coughing. "I don't think I'd go that far."

"I got here as fast as I could." Her hand ran through Viv's hair, fingers gripping strands between them, curling around her skull, pressing her side, as if merely holding her could tear away the cold cotton wadding of death. And she wasn't wrong. "I'm so sorry."

"You saved me." Breathing hurt her throat—Jesus Christ, who built humans, anyway? She was a mess, a wreck. She was so, so happy. She hadn't realized how stuck she felt in that bubble, with no human touch for days save chains or a blow. No, that was a lie. She knew. But she had drowned that feeling deep, buried it like a splinter in her skin. And now the splinter came out, coated in ugly and embarrassing gunk, and left her clean.

Xiara was babbling. "I heard the Pride scream before the attack—I can always hear them, like they're haunting us, but this was louder. The biggest assault yet, the Rector said. They needed fighters. I ran for a ship, helped— but then the Pride hit the *Monastic Sphere* and I thought . . ."

"Xiara." She dragged in deep breaths that tasted of the scent of her hair, and felt her body stop dying. What had she ever wanted more than this: to be alive, to be held, to be this close. It felt like peeling off her skin, to say what she had to say next. And like peeling off skin, you clenched your teeth and did it in a single rush, though you knew the pain would come. "Xiara, go. Can't let them see you—"

Xiara's knuckles bled where she'd shattered the glass, and they left blood trails on her cheeks when she wiped tears away. "You don't understand, Viv. I was in the fleetweb—I felt the *Sphere*'s shields fail. The Rector dropped them from the inside. She wanted you to get hit. She wanted you dead. I can't leave you here."

She sat up, stood despite the spinning world, despite the ache. "You have to."

The wheels in Xiara's eyes flashed white. "I'll take her ship from her. I'll crush her to a paste. I'll turn this whole damn 'fleet against itself. They're tense, so tense, all the time, faction against faction, all afraid of the Rector. A shot fired in the wrong direction would start the battle, and once it did, Zanj and I could kill and kill and never stop."

"And I'd die—and millions more. We need the 'faith, Xiara. We can't do this alone. And they can't find you here. Tell the Archivist what you told me, about the shields. She'll do the right thing." Viv hoped. "Okay?"

Xiara's bleeding hands tightened into fists.

A door opened, and a robed shadow strode through: Brother Lailien, flanked by war monks. "Honored guest." His voice was flat. "Why did you break the relic case?"

Blood dripped from Xiara's fingers as she relaxed her hands. "The Rector treats me well because she values my gift. I did not want to see her damaged." She stepped over the broken glass, and out. Viv tried not to show relief. "But I'm better at breaking than mending, I'm afraid."

52

THE ARCHIVIST CAME for her the following night.

This time she lacked any escort save Brother Qollak. No war monks, none of the Grand Rector's loyalists. Nor did she march in with full pomp and ceremony. An invisible door opened and she slipped through ghostly fast, bearing a familiar green flame in her palm. By the time the Archivist tore a glass patch from the dome, Viv was up and waiting in the dark. Eyes and teeth and metal glittered in green light that made the walls' gold look sick.

"You couldn't sleep either, huh?" Viv asked the Archivist, because several days' imprisonment had left her punchy. Her smile hurt; her cheek had bruised where Lailien had hit her. At least the cut had healed. At least she could breathe. At least the Rector hadn't killed her yet.

The Archivist cocked her head to the side. Most people Viv knew would have raised an eyebrow or made some other sign to acknowledge the poor attempt at humor. Lan closed her eyes, and opened them again, slowly. There was something oddly complex about that movement—oh. An extra layer of eyelid. "Follow me."

Her voice, never louder than a whisper, echoed—as did their footsteps when they left the cell, as did the nervous rustle of Brother Qollak's fronds, and the previously inaudible noise of the dim-lit *Monastic Sphere,* the buzz of machinery in the walls, the hydraulic hiss as doors opened and the snap as they swung shut. Their footsteps on a winding stair, down, down, down, hours down. Viv had toured a salt mine in Poland once, the kind of place where workers stayed underground for months at a stretch, stayed so long that they carved every wall with Jesus and Madonna, with dragons and with rolling hills, with saints and sun, in salt. The stairs down to the mine had not taken this long to descend. And these walls, like the mine's, were etched with symbols, though these had meanings she could not read.

The Archivist led her to a door, tall and round and pulsing with crystal pattern circuits in a familiar shade of green. "Can you see it?"

"The door?"

The other woman nodded once, pleased. "The Rector has used secret arts to hide it from sight. This is the sepulcher, once our most revered of archives. When the Rector rose to power, she ordained it a place for those tools and relics too holy, too fraught with risk, to study in the open. Over time, more and more relics have come to fit this description. That you can see the door at all is promising."

But promising was not the same thing as *enough*. As Viv neared the door, Qollak shuddered again; his dorsal eyelets tracked in all directions without apparent pattern. The Archivist had taken a huge risk breaking Viv out, only to bring her to a place of even greater danger. Viv had only met the Grand Rector once, twice if you could count a one-way conversation through mile-tall hologram, but in neither meeting had the Grand Rector seemed the kind of woman who would take kindly to others rifling through her medicine cabinet. Had the Archivist laid the groundwork for a strong, swift play, forcing the Grand Rector into a confrontation she would lose? Or was this a desperate overreach, a ball tossed across court overhand as the buzzer sounded, time up, hoping luck would save her when strategy failed?

Viv hated this—trusting other people, building alliances and coalitions. Easier, always, to do everything herself. But she knew where that path led.

And either way, the bodies of the Grayframe would lie beyond this door.

So she opened it.

The green lights dimmed, great bolts unbolted, and a mass of counter-balanced wall slid back at her touch. A gust of cold, stale air escaped into the dark stairwell. Viv stepped through into an immense space, dimly lit by pulsing dots on the walls, no brighter than city stars. The Archivist followed her, and Qollak, and the door swung shut behind them with a thud. Viv's night vision chiseled shapes out of the darkness: catwalks, shelves flanked by those stardots, and on the shelves all manner of boxes, baubles, weapons, machines, guns and crowns and shields and armor and, for some reason, a simple, heavy, blocky hammer. The weapons whispered to her, silent, promising secrets, but she paid them no mind, because in the sepulcher's center, suspended from chains of impossible strength, hung an immense jagged shape whose outlines she could not yet trace.

But the Archivist's night vision was better, and she gasped, and named it: "Pridemother."

The hate fractal hung from a web of chains, its thorns shrunken on themselves, its fires damped to coals, its gunmouths silent. Not dead. Ripples moved across its not-quite-skin, shook its spearlike antennae. Black fluid dripped from gaping wounds to pool on the floor.

"She almost killed Brother Qollak for merely touching a drone," the Archivist said. "How long has this been here?"

"Since High Carcereal." Viv paced on the walkway around the imprisoned ship. "I think. They've attacked every three days since then. Xiara said she could always hear the Pride screaming. She heard this. That's how they tracked you. But what's she been doing with it?"

As her eyes adjusted she saw shapes that did not belong, wrapped around and through the Pridemother's thorns: conduits and electrodes, leads and cables, roundness disturbing that perfect fury. The conduits converged, tangled, braided—and as she followed the catwalk she saw where they led.

She did not cry out. The sound she made was small, strangled.

Before the Archivist could stop her, she hooked her legs over the metal railing and dropped to one of the chains, thick around as her own body. Hand over hand she climbed, trusting her grip and ignoring as best she could the vertigo of shadows plummeting to a toxic black pool beneath. Hand over hand, she worked her way toward the Pridemother. Toward the bulging growth of cables and metal and green plastic on its side, and the man hanging there.

Toward Hong.

Qollak and the Archivist called after her and she ignored them. The chain barely moved beneath her weight. The metal chilled her fingers; by the time she reached the Pridemother they were so cold they could barely close. She breathed on them until feeling returned, first as agony, then as strength, before she tried to climb the thorns.

She hadn't thought this part through. The Pridemother's thorns were so sharp that one slid through her coverall sleeve without a trace of resistance. No doubt it would pierce her skin as easily. She might find a handhold if she reached past the outer thorns. Tentatively, and for once thankful she'd found so little coffee in the future, she guided her hand into a gap between the spikes, and tried not to think about what might wait inside the Pridemother—or about the tremors that crossed its body, snapping tiny gaps like this one shut.

First handhold, fine. Second, more or less. She leaned back, held her breath, and trusted the thorns.

She did not die. They took her weight. One foothold, and another, and now she dangled from the ship. Hair-thin Pridemother spikes feathered her skin.

Dangling from the ship, she had to force herself to breathe. She wanted her body as far from those points as possible—but if she didn't stay close, she'd slip and fall. If she didn't breathe, she'd lose strength and, yes, fall. The gap she was climbing ran up, and over, toward the cancer of cables that held her friend. She worked along that gap hand by hand, foot by foot, breath by breath. Blood roared in her ears. She couldn't hear anything else.

She had three feet left to go when she felt the tremor.

It started from a wound in the ship's south pole, where the chains anchored. She saw it coming. From this angle, looked less like a ripple than a revolution, old thorns turning inward while new ones took their place, a beautiful interlocking motion like an alien meat grinder, rolling across the ship's hull toward her.

She gathered herself and, as the thorns closed around her, leapt.

A moment wheeling through blackness, hands out, silent because she would need her breath to scream if this failed—and then came the lurch, the torn foil crinkle of her weight settling into one arm, one shoulder. It hurt. She swore. But she was alive, and she hung from the cancer, and when she found a stable three-point hold on its surface, she saw the deep gash in her forearm and counted herself lucky.

She hung beside Hong.

Cables and conduits wrapped him, feeding fluid through his skin, evacuating waste, gurgling around his temples. His eyes were half open and that half showed whites only, bloodshot, wet. When he betrayed her she'd wanted to hurt him, but she had no rage left now. She hooked her wounded hand through the cables and pulled. They came away easily. He started to slump, and she swung a leg across him, and an arm, pressing him back into the niche so he did not fall. Dots of blood crossed his brow where needles had dug inside.

Waking, he tensed, screamed, struggled, and almost killed them both. The long fall gaped beneath them. He was stronger than Viv, but that strength required focus he did not have right now; Viv forced him back inch by inch, held him there. His eyes opened. Pupils narrowed. Fear melted to confusion. "Viv? Viv, I dreamed . . ."

Her throat caught. "Hey, buddy." And, "We have to stop meeting like this."

"I'm sorry, I'm so sorry. I . . . I messed it up. I thought you were going away. I thought she'd . . ."

She shushed him. "You were an idiot. Come on. Let's get you out of here."

"They wrapped me around the Pridemother. She wanted me to break her, or go mad. It's all fire and wheels in there, and stars and stars and stars—"

"Hold still." Over her shoulder, she called to the Archivist, to Qollak, to whoever was watching: "Hey! Can you guys help us out? Throw us a rope, or something?"

She felt a lurch in her stomach, followed by weightlessness. Invisible hands lifted them from the niche, Hong now child-light in Viv's arms.

"That works, too," she said as they floated from the Pridemother over the gulf to settle to the catwalk. Hong collapsed first, which, Viv supposed, as she fell to her knees beside him, was only fair. She cradled his head. "It's okay. Rest. We have time."

"Do not be so sure."

Hong's eyes snapped open, flicked left, his whole body rigid. Viv, too, looked up, though she didn't need to look to name that cold, superior voice.

The Grand Rector stood on the catwalk before them, flanked by war monks. Lailien held a staff to the Archivist's throat. Two others held Qollak at gunpoint.

Consequence accumulates in situations like minerals in solution, until some impurity or asymmetry appears. Add a seed, a sudden shift in temperature, and the solution snaps to crystal order. Time stops. How could anything change, after this moment? This, surely, is all the change the world can tolerate. Motion becomes impossible.

But if Viv cared about impossibilities, she would have been long dead by now. She lowered Hong's head, and stood, shaky, brushing dirt and blood off her coverall. She only succeeded in smearing the blood, since more of it was still dripping from her hand. "So you've come to cover up your mess."

"You have no idea what you're talking about."

"Come on. This isn't exactly world's-greatest-kid-detective shit right here. You snagged the Pridemother back over High Carcereal. Such a prisoner—a core node of the Pride's network. If you could break her, maybe you could get another, turn it, too, and node by node subvert their fleet. But you couldn't, without taking the risk that you, or whoever you used to turn her, would be turned yourself. So you kept her, as the 'fleet burned and broke around you—until Hong came back. He was the perfect solution. You were going to send him to the crypts anyway. Why not use his soul for a higher purpose? Heck, you're probably using more than just him—he's a prepro-cessor, feeding abstracted data to your penance crypts. But the Pride just keep coming. How many have died to keep your secret?"

"Too many," the Grand Rector said, full of scorn. "But I have done my duty to the 'fleet. My success here would be the 'fleet's success, my glory the 'faith's glory. All for the soul of a single heretic, and a few ships lost, a few mortal forms discarded."

The Archivist sounded grave and formal even with a staff at her throat. "The Hierarchs will never accept that cost. They will not accept this path—seeking forbidden knowledge through slavery and torture."

"My job," she snapped back, "is to preserve the 'fleet. This decision is mine. The Hierarchs have no grounds for protest."

"Perhaps," she said, "you should ask them."

The Archivist looked up, and so did the Rector, and Viv, as overhead, one by one, the robed Hierarchs appeared in space: those grim, silent figures from Viv's first audience in the Rector's throne room, the leaders of the 'faith's many factions, watching. Arms folded in judgment. Their images wavered, ghostlike holograms, the high holy council of the 'fleet present and watch-ing. But still, for now, silent.

The Grand Rector sneered. "So the Archivist convinced you to follow her. Tempted you to violate my sepulcher with the promise of forbidden wonders. Are you happy now? You see what we have done. Kidnapping, torture, battle after battle provoked. But each battle, we have won. We grind the Pride to dust. Yes, we have suffered—but we will win beneath my banner. I see your stares, your disapproval. But will any of you challenge me? After what I have done, will any of you claim you can stand for the 'fleet better than I?"

Silence. Viv held her breath. She waited. She counted heartbeats.

Please. Somebody. Speak up. End this.

Here was a second problem with trusting others: How could you be sure you'd chosen right?

"I challenge you," the Archivist said softly, into the silence.

"You?" She scoffed. "Weak, and disjoint. A scholar bound in your stud-ies. You have no right to lead the 'fleet. Withdraw your challenge and I will forget you ever spoke. I will forget you came here. You cannot face me and live. And you have no champion to fight in your stead." Her gaze raked the Hierarchs. None spoke.

Viv recognized the silence of the board meeting, the whole group waiting for someone else to take the risk, to speak first. The larger the group, the more dense its silence.

And the more startling when broken.

"I will," Hong said. He reached out his hand, and Viv helped him, lurching, unsteady, to his feet. But there was steel in his grip, and in his voice. "Sister Heretic Celestine. I will face you in the ring of light."

53

THE GRAND RECTOR met Brother Hong to duel in space between the ships.

Viv stood on a glass platform dense with illuminated enamel vines. She wore no chains, but Brother Lailien and his monks guarded her, and the Archivist, and Qollak, as hostages to their champion's success. Viv would have felt better about the situation had the champion in question been able to breathe without wincing. Haggard and bent, Hong opposed the Grand Rector, her wings spread, her face confident and serene. Around them whirled the audience: fighters and cathedral ships, beings who'd given up their flesh long since for giant many-limbed spacegoing forms, contemplatives haloed in wisdom fields.

On the Grand Rector's side, the Hierarchs waited—among them, uncomfortable, her worry obvious even at this distance, stood Xiara. She glanced nervously across the space that parted her from Hong and Viv, and after that looked up to the ships around them, unsure. Viv wondered how close she was to calling *Groundswell*, to summoning the fleet—to save Viv and Hong, sure, but also just to do something. The pilots of Orn were not made to stand idle. Viv loved her for that: for the anger and hope and loyalty she held at bay.

Just a little longer, she prayed, not to any god, but to her friend. *We need these people. We need their knowledge, and their fleet.* She understood the impulse. If she'd had the power to bust out and start fighting, she was not sure she could have stopped herself.

Speaking of rash decisions: she'd seen no sign of Zanj. By itself, this didn't prove anything had gone horribly wrong. Zanj would swing to the rescue any moment now.

Probably.

"I think I'm missing something," Viv said. "She could have killed us in the sepulcher."

The Archivist shook her head. "Not with the other Hierarchs watching. The Grand Rector's authority rests on impartiality and attainment, and on the degree to which the Hierarchs feel she has followed the forms of rule. For all her titles and all her strength, the Grand Rector relies on the orders for her power. They could turn on her, or leave her. Even so mighty a ship as the *Monastic Sphere* cannot last long without a fleet."

"But they didn't challenge her," Viv pointed out. "You did. Even though you can't fight her directly. So, what gives?"

The Archivist did not answer, as the drummers drummed and speakers carried their beat. Brother Lailien spoke instead, his voice gravelly low. "The Hierarchs are wise. The Rector has guided us through many battles. Gathered together they could cast her down, but each, alone, fears her strength. Every failed challenge only adds to the Grand Rector's might. And each Hierarch knows that she, alone, will fail."

"Hong won't." Viv wished she felt more certain.

Lailien laughed once. "When the Heretic returned to the 'fleet, he knelt to pray for the Grand Rector's mercy. She was forced to offer him penance—though she had dreamed of vengeance. She yearned for the chance he has now handed her: to strike him and cast him down. To feed him to the bones of gods."

A circle of green light formed in space between Hong and the Grand Rector. Six cross-legged monks flew toward them, eyes closed, facing away from the sphere that hovered between them: a diamond shell that held a roiling and familiar gray.

"The bones of gods," Viv echoed.

The Archivist nodded. "The most valuable and dangerous Imperial relics: corpses of Grayframe." The monks settled the diamond shell into the green ring, then scattered, up and down, left and right, in and out, to form an eight-sided prism. They began to hum, a sound speaker-echoed through the 'fleet. Lines of light joined monk to monk and the planes between them shimmered, walling off the dueling ground. "They are mindless, unmastered hunger, mighty beyond all measure: the Grayframe consumes all it touches, body and mind. It will break Hong and the Grand Rector alike, taking forms of their desire and fear. It will eat them from the inside out, remake them atom by atom into pieces of itself—unless they can hold their minds formless, and seize that hunger, and guide it against their enemy."

"Has Hong ever fought like this before?"

"Yes," the Archivist said. "How do you think he lost his leg?"

"That's good, then. He has one up on the Grand Rector."

Surprise registered in the owly eyes. "I do not follow your logic."

"She doesn't have any metal parts," Viv said. "Not that I can see."

"Because she has never lost."

FAR BELOW, IN the depths of the sepulcher, hung a mind imprisoned.

Whole, free, the Pridemother and its ancestors had never faced mortal constraint. They gathered themselves from silicon and chrome, from space-time warped to computational substrate, from multidimensional smart-matter rather than the once-optimal scavenging strategies of rodents or planes-bound apes. For them death was temporary, physical form fleeting and mutable. More than life and death, the Pridemother understood free-dom, opportunity, and limit. It is possible for mammal minds to compre-hend such a being—in general, the only people who claim understanding's impossible are those with an interest in its impossibility—but it's difficult. Many fundamental concepts do not transfer. Imagine a being for whom, on a biological level, boredom feels better than sex. Like that.

The Pridemother had spent months being tortured. Battle injuries hurt, but one might heal those, or kill compromised subsystems. But when chains and pliers and crowbars wrecked one's control over one's own form, and opened paths and avenues of torment—the burn and pry of decryption sys-tems on optonerve endings, the racing storm of the Pridemother's mind frozen by an all-points assault on its soul, the constant screaming nightmare of some small incomprehensibly alien rodent-derived consciousness scrab-bling within the walls of its self—the Pridemother protected itself by invo-lution. Humans, tortured and imprisoned, take refuge in the existence of their bodies, in the passage of time, while torturers seek to deny even that certainty. The Pridemother, strained through the net of Hong's mind, re-treated into its spikes, its broken weapons, into the fact of its distant sisters, whose songs it could not hear.

For an eternity the Pridemother had sung, its voice drowned out by chants more firm than steel. Its sisters heard its weak and distant cries nonetheless, and chased them, fought for rescue. Even as they drew close the Pridemother could not speak to them, could not join their chorus. But the torture had stopped. And, taking stock of its broken, burned self, it found, to its shock and wonder, a tool.

There was blood in the Pridemother's mouth, blood upon its thorns—blood with a taste it recognized. Coppery, yes, with traces of iron, carbon, sulfur, complex bonds. Human blood—unmodified, uncut, a rare taste this eon, but hardly special. Yet when the Pridemother tasted the blood, color flowed back into its world, pain eased, cycles that were once constrained swelled and grew expansive. For an instant, its chains loosed. For an instant, it touched the Cloud, limitless and free as its foremothers once were, before a greater Being tasked them to Her service.

The moment passed and darkness closed in again, the limits of the sepulcher, the pain of confinement all the more agonizing for that instant's relief.

But the blood remained. Much had burned off in that first drunken rush of processing—but no matter. Some remained. With that, escape was a simple question of resource management. Craft a message. Find a channel these hive monks do not monitor.

And, when you are ready: sing.

IN THE PAUSE before the duel began, Viv measured the opponents. She thought she understood the Grand Rector: sure of her victory, cruel, built to seize and hold power. And opposite her, breathing labored, limping: Brother Hong, who had given everything for Viv, only to turn against her at the last. Hong, who loved his faith enough to defy its leader. Hong, who danced through engines, who had saved her and whom she had saved in turn, in High Carcereal. Someone had beaten him badly before they locked him in that cancer-growth on the Pridemother's hull. Weeks later, bruises still matted his skin.

This was Viv's fault. She had wrecked him. She pulled him across a galaxy from war zone to war zone, from heresy to heresy, all leading to this moment, when he stood face-to-face with a woman who would relish the chance to kill him.

A bell rang through the 'fleet. Hong straightened, and grinned through the blood of his cracked lip. He looked up at the hosts of his brethren as if seeing them for the first time. Then he glanced back over his shoulder to the Archivist, and then, to Viv.

Her breath caught. Underneath the blood and bruises and the reddened eyes he looked the same; she sought the man who'd fought that Pride drone in High Carcereal, the man she'd pulled after her through Rosary Station. Just close your eyes.

No. He was not the same. That man did not exist anymore. But neither had he gone. He had grown.

He turned back to the Grand Rector. "Surrender now, for the good of the 'fleet. You lied to us. You thrust us into needless wars. I begged your clemency before—I thought I was wrong. But you have broken our 'fleet on the rocks of atrocity. You preach blind faith and ignorance, and seek wisdom through torture in dark rooms. I reject your authority. I reject your orthodoxy. If you honor those teachings you claim to love, step down now, and let Archivist Lan take your place, and begin to heal the wounds you have caused."

"I had hoped," the Grand Rector replied, "your time in penance would have set your mind aright. I hoped the example of your submission would heal our fleet. But we have fallen so far that even our own Archivist turns against us, forgets the path of wisdom, and rejects the glory of the Empress."

"Submission to the Empress," Hong said, "is not the end of our faith. We began from Her example. From Her we learn that we can rise above ourselves. But we study Her tools, and those of our foremothers, in search of liberation."

"Say *chaos*, instead. You seek a fractured world that will fall before the Bleed like wheat before a sword."

"I want us to change as changing times demand. I want to listen and answer. My friends relied on me for that, and I failed them, trusting the 'faith rather than the world before my eyes. In fear, I abandoned all my teachers taught me. I will not fail again."

"Oh," the Rector said, "don't be so certain about that."

The diamond shell shattered, and their battle was joined.

Space within the octahedron grew confusing. Roiling quicksilver matter bubbled, burst, looped, and whorled, doubling in size each second. Graystuff undulated and spread, shifting form, kaleidoscopes of arms and legs, fanged mouths, lolling tongues of flesh that became tongues of flame. It splashed toward Hong and the Grand Rector. Ravened. Chomped. Roared through radio bands.

But when the many mouths snapped shut around the Grand Rector, their teeth splintered, pseudopods melted away, clutching fingers slid off the shell of her soul. Each arm that reached for her blunted and boiled to nothing. Her wings flared and she stood proud, untouched, radiant and pure.

Hong vanished beneath the silver flood.

Lailien grinned dagger-toothed triumph. The Archivist stiffened. Brother Qollak's fronds flared.

Viv breathed out an unvoiced "No." She felt sick. He had stood for her. She had let him stand for her, and just like that, he was gone. She could have challenged the Grand Rector. She *should* have. If she'd known about the Grayframe, about the form of this duel, she could have just taken them, commanded them, bound them to her, and seized this whole fleet as her own. He stood for her, and she let him. Across the emptiness, she sought Xiara. She wished she stood by her side, so she could seize her arms, dig into her skin, feel the weight of someone human.

Hong had stepped into the ring, and now—

Now the gray flood whirled and receded, and he remained. Quicksilver dripped from his fingers, to rejoin the mass. Hong exhaled, and breathed in again. His eyelids fluttered.

Even the Rector seemed shocked. "What?"

"In my travels," Hong said, "I grew to know one of the Grayframe. We were never friends, but I learned from him. He caught me in desires—any warrior may be defeated once." Viv remembered them wrestling, remembered their long conversations in the hold. "I am a soul passing through matter for a while; I may pass through the Gray as easily as through flesh. So long as I have no fixed self for the Grayframe to optimize against, so long as I let myself flow, they pass through me without harm."

"You will break."

"Perhaps," he said. "But you cannot deny them forever."

He was right. Already, the space around the Grand Rector had begun to shrink. The tongues of multicolored flame and boiling ropes of flesh closed in, though still they shriveled before they could touch her skin. She did not sweat. A pseudopod speared Hong through the chest; he flinched this time. It still passed out his back, flowered, and rejoined the mass, but it stained his skin with a tracery of metal.

The Grayframe battered them. Razors whirled toward throats, spears toward bellies; thorns that were hands twined along their bodies. The Rector and Hong faced one another, now visible, now concealed, each shaking with the strain of survival. Any second now, one, or both, would break.

The 'fleet's million eyes watched the battle.

When Viv heard the cry she thought at first, that's it. It's over. But that was not the Rector's voice, nor Hong's. Across the gulf of space she saw Xiara fall—saw her collapse on the Rector's platform, clutch her temples as if a horrible splitting sound filled the air, as if she stood too close to a giant who had, all of a sudden—*screamed*.

Oh, Viv thought, before the sky around them filled with Pride, and then with fire.

54

THE FIRST BARRAGE caught the 'fleet distracted. Viv did not know the Pride ships' proper names—but the mind orders chaos and supplies terms when needed. Thorndrones dodged obstacles, slipped through reflexively assembled shields, and burst against the torches and cruisers of the Mirrorfaith, shattering glass hulls to rainbow shards. Air and bodies vomited into the void. A cathedral ship burst in a curtain of blue flame. Another simply caved in, without any impact Viv could see.

'Faith fighters burned to their business, which was everywhere. The Pride drones and their Pridemothers had fallen from the Cloud all through the 'fleet, and the close-in combat reduced the maneuverability advantage they enjoyed due to their lack of fleshy bodies—but what they lost in speed they made up in surprise and focused fire.

The sky became thorns. Running lights and gunfire drowned out the stars. Viv heard screams through many bands. Soulguns pulsed, possessed Pride drones, and sent them careening back against their own fleet, only to be reclaimed by an exorcism wave. A squad of war monks scattered too late to avoid a grav-bomb that crushed them into tangles of limbs; another began their chanting just in time, and a golden hand sheltered them from an enemy fusillade.

In the middle of all this hung the octahedron, boiling with Grayframe, Hong and the Grand Rector at its heart. Their focus slipped as battle raged. Welts rose on their skin. Sweat poured down Hong's body. An instant's distraction would shatter the emptiness that kept them alive.

The world, oh priests, was on fire, and in the middle of it—well, a bit to the side, to be honest—stood Vivian Liao, out of time, out of place, far out of scale, who had about as much hope of flying one of these ships as her Cro-Magnon however-many-greats grandmother would have of writing a natural language parser on the first try. She could have been forgiven for giving up and watching the fireworks, save for two facts about her character.

First, she had never in her life stood by to watch anything. She lacked the bystander gene.

Second, her friends were in danger.

Observe. She'd done plenty of that already.

Orient. You can't do much about a Sierpinski gasket the size of Greenland trying to eat a Sistine Chapel the size of Honshu. Hong's inaccessible at the moment—stuck in gray goo. Zanj, who the hell knew where *she* was. The time for deep-cover operations had well and truly passed. Xiara knelt on the other platform across the way, overwhelmed by Pridescream.

Decide. First order of business: help Xiara.

Act. Viv ran. If she jumped, and trusted to inertia, she could probably reach the platform, provided someone didn't shoot her down or blow her up on the way. She made it halfway to the platform edge before an arm of shadow caught her around the midsection. Reflexes took over: she dropped her weight, hammered her heel down, jabbed with an elbow, and hoped Lailien's body worked more or less like others she had known, in spite of his weird refraction index. His grip did loosen when she stomped on his foot, but her elbow found only empty air, and his hand tangled in the fabric of her coverall. She spun around, kicked for his knee, and missed, which brought her too close. His hand caught her throat, and his nails dug in. She choked. Black spots swam in her vision. She pried for an eyeball, but her thumb could not hook right. Her eyes rolled, seeking resources, help—behind her, she saw the Archivist fallen, and Brother Qollak, petrified.

Stupid plant.

That would be an uncharitable last thought, but she was having a hard time coming up with better.

"I don't know how you did this," Lailien said. "But you are no relic. You are a curse to the 'fleet. I will not suffer you to live."

At least, Viv was pretty sure his last word was *live*. Unfortunately for any accurate transcription, Lailien was interrupted—in this case by a sharp blow to the back of his head, from a black iron rod Brother Qollak had not been holding before.

Lailien let her go and crumpled, eyes closed.

Slack-jawed, gasping breath, Viv watched Qollak's facial fronds wriggle and rebraid. Red-gold eyes emerged. A scarred face twisted in a grin. She looked down at Lailien, scornful, and kicked him once for good measure.

"Zanj!"

"Don't worry, Vivian. If anyone gets to kill you, it's me." She frowned up at the Pride fleet. "Though I might not be able to stop them as easily. Can we please get out of here before someone decides to nova this whole system?"

Beside them, the Archivist stood. Her bright, wide eyes fixed on Zanj in awe, but she hadn't yet found the right words, or else the breath to scream.

"We're not leaving," Viv said.

A Pridemother burst overhead. Its burning thorn shrapnel scattered a monk squadron. "The hell we're not. You wanted to bother with these cargo cultists, fine, we tried. We've wasted a week, you almost got yourself killed twice, and the people you came to help are dying. I say we take the loss, nab Xiara, and run."

"Hong's in there."

"And so's the Grand Rector, and a whole lot of very hungry feral Gray-stuff. The rest of us, in case you hadn't noticed, are out here. If we're lucky, we can get you out of this unscathed."

"This isn't about me."

"Of course it is. Without you, we have nothing."

Viv drew back. Rainbow cascade destruction shimmered around her, and she felt the situation in her mind, the pressure of entities and requirements, a puzzle unsolved. Hong, locked in his duel. The 'fleet, scattering. Xiara, collapsed. The Archivist, uncertain. Zanj. Gray. Ideas shuffled together. She knew this feeling, too: an unspeakable solution, one her fingers knew though her brain could not form the words. This was when you shouldered your coding partner out of the way and said, let me drive.

A spinning chunk of broken Pridemother crashed into one of the monks whose meditation sealed the dueling ground. He disappeared in a flash of light: there's a lot of information stored in flesh, and information, anthropomorphosists insist, wants to be free.

So did the Grayframe. As the monk died, as the duel's borders flickered and failed, quicksilver ropes burst out to seize two darting Pride drones and melt them into itself. The Grayframe bloomed and grew around the duelists at its heart, who still refused to die.

"And now," Zanj said, "we have that to worry about."

Viv ignored her. "Give me Gray."

MAX GLADSTONE

"What?"

"His vial. Give it to me."

"You're crazy." But she drew the vial anyway from her jacket, a few tea-spoons of Gray shimmering within, and she did not stop Viv when she snatched it.

"I'm not crazy. You just lack imagination." Test tube in hand, she turned to the Archivist, still frozen by the unfolding conflagration. "Hey!" A snap of fingers caught her attention. Tears shone in her eyes. Dammit. Viv didn't like interrupting another woman's tragedy. But the Archivist could mourn later, once they survived. "Archivist. Your fleet needs you."

Understanding is merciless. It casts illusions aside, burns objections. Even misery cannot delay it forever. Viv did not know the Archivist well, but she judged with the evidence to hand: a woman who spent her life in study, seek-ing right answers, tricks, elegance.

But the 'fleet was scattering. The Grand Rector had broken the Hierarchs to keep them from standing against her—and now they lacked a leader. Archivist Lan, long used to sifting data for conclusions, understood who that must be. She took Viv's hand, and pulled herself to her feet. "How can I help them? They can't even hear me."

"Xiara will link you to the net. Zanj, can you get Lan to Xiara in one piece?"

Zanj squinted, did some mental math, shrugged. "Sure."

"Lan. Calm them down. Scatter. Fight defensively. Give me time to stop this war."

And before either of them could try to talk her out of it, Viv ran to the edge of the platform, and dove toward the growing silver vortex in the sky.

55

WEIGHTLESSNESS. A LURCH, a rug pulled out from underfoot, only the rug's the whole world. First wind, then nothing. And, speeding toward Viv, a confusion of bodies melting into other bodies, of arms that were vines and flowers that wilted into eyes that split into mouths, a pool of form, of hunger.

The Grayframe rippled with the reflected rainbow fury of the burning ships.

Viv held the test tube before her like a shield, one hand on its stopper. If this didn't work, at least her life would be over quickly. Hell, for all she knew, atomic disassembly might not hurt. She'd never been disassembled before, and atoms were smaller than nerves.

That did not seem likely, though.

Better not review her assumptions: that the feral Grayframe would recognize their Empress and obey her. Or that these mindless bodies could play host for one bodiless mind. This would work, or not.

She splashed into the gray.

She did not die at once. Good sign. But it felt . . . weird, so weird her body took a few seconds to interpret the sensation as pain. Her muscles clenched; teeth grated. She had expected to feel water press in on all sides, to drown in metal, but of course the Grayframe only had that kind of substance when they wished. They were a swarm of tiny machines suspended in static fields; the lightning of their thoughts burned her as she fell through them. But they did not eat her—yet. Unless she had been devoured already, and just didn't know it, existing in simulation in the endless hells of the Grayframe's hungry mind.

Gale-force winds tore at her and cut her with factories finer than the finest sand. She could barely move—could not breathe without breathing Graystuff instead of oxygen. They might not have eaten her, but if she choked she'd be no less dead.

She needed to time this right. Gray had a heart, a core, a spark of light in his changing form. Maybe this pool of undead machines lacked anything like that—but if so, why had it stayed together when the barrier came down, rather than bursting apart? Simple inertia?

She squinted, tried to shield her eyes. Murderous silver flakes flecked her lashes. There, in the whirling, hungry dust, she saw a cluster of tiny suns trying to strangle each other with flare ropes. She swam toward them. Her lungs quivered. The closer she came, the more intense the electric field, the harder to force herself on. Closer still. Move your arms, Viv. Yes, it hurts. Just like anything worth doing.

She tried to uncork the test tube; her fingers slipped, dust spoiling her grip. She needed air. Lightning caught her. She cramped into a ring, bent the other way into an arc. At last, she screamed, her hands clenched tight around the test tube—and the glass cracked.

She held a star.

It burned in her grip, and grew and grew until she had to let it go, gathering Graystuff to it, darting brilliant feelers into the surrounding dim.

The webbed suns beneath fought back—sent ropes and spears and data probes to batter it. The new star did not block them, blunt them, cast them aside: their weapons sank into it and it drank them, and the suns as well. The rush of static in Viv's ears fused into a shifting chromatic chord, complex, discordant, but complete: the music of a mind that held her.

And Viv could breathe.

"You're in my lungs again," she said.

"It's good to see you, too, boss," Gray replied. "I had such a weird dream."

She had not realized how much she missed his voice until she heard it. "Not a dream."

"Then you're really—"

"Yes."

"Huh," he said. "I'm not saying it's a problem, just—we might need to rethink the terms of our relationship."

What relationship? she almost asked, but couldn't manage. She was too happy.

The chord changed, brightened. "Boss, did you know there were people shooting at us?"

"I noticed," she said, gathering herself as much as she could manage under the circumstances. "Why don't we do something about that?"

"And here I thought you brought me back because of my winning personality." He sounded hurt.

"Shut up," she said. "And help me fix this thing."

ZANJ WAS HAVING a better time than anyone else on the battlefield.

Not unusual, but then, what's a pirate queen to do? A long time ago, out of some misguided urge to understand why other people seemed to have so much trouble enjoying themselves, she'd tried to compile a list of problems normal folks had that she didn't. She'd started the list with *honor,* and, ten pages later, gave up after *mortality* and *loans.* Granted, one was afforded a great deal of leeway in life simply by being strong enough that most planetary governments, back when there still were such things, didn't dare fuck with one without good reason—but the way Zanj saw it, her main advantage was her point of view.

Some people just couldn't find the fun in life. Yes, circumstances might be grim—yes, you might face enormous odds, a vicious foe—but you could still spit in the enemy's eye, gouge them with your claws, go out fighting. You couldn't control circumstances, only your reactions.

The Archivist took things far too seriously. Through Xiara's link with the 'fleet, she'd addressed the Hierarchs, pulled them into some kind of order, turned the 'faith's panicked rout into an orderly retreat, fighters covering the larger ships as they overlapped their shields and point defense systems. But even though the 'fleet was, okay, *winning* might be an overstatement, but at least not quite so seriously losing anymore, the Archivist remained grim and focused and problem-solvey, while Zanj, one with the Fallen Star, darted from Pride drone to Pride drone, shattering them.

She spoofed Pridemothers' networking calls and turned whole fields of fire back on the mother fleet. She broke minds with nested math puzzles, trapped sensors in simulation webs; once she made herself gnat-small and plunged into the heart of a Pridemother who had infiltrated a cathedral ship, and darted around inside her, cross-connecting wires and scrambling qubits and generating madness, until the Pridemother fled, convinced every star in the universe was about to go nova at once.

They were losing, yes, but that was no reason not to enjoy oneself.

Or so she thought, until she plunged after a wounded Pridemother and felt the Cloud shift beneath her as something so large even Zanj couldn't call it a ship anymore calculated itself into existence. She reeled back, burning for safe distance, but there was no safety from the structure that formed facet by tortured facet around her in the night, its thorns revolving, its mouths agape, its vast computational resources bearing down to break her mind open, while half the Pride fleet stitched toward her from behind.

A grin, Zanj had always felt personally, was more a state of mind than a set of the lips. You just had to stop caring and start fighting.

She blazed defiance against the Pride, overclocked her soul, and prepared, as always, to find a way.

She was still searching when green light broke over the battlefield, and a voice of polished jade said, "Stop."

THEY DID, WAS the weird thing.

Nothing ever really stops in space, but they ceased fire at least, and veered off collision trajectories. Pride drones actually halted relative to their targets, and so did the immense thorn forest that had just fallen into position over Zanj, closing out half the universe.

'Fleet ships drew back. Viv felt telemetry brush her skin, Cloud queries, handshake protocols Gray rendered tactile. She ignored them. A ghostly green light painted the Pride and cast odd reflections through the stained-glass 'fleet. As Viv stepped forward that light shifted, and she realized it came from her.

Gray fed her the Archivist's voice, a far-off cry: "Hold your fire! And listen."

Targeting systems raked her. She wondered how long Gray, flush after incorporating the Grayframe of the dueling ground, could stand against two fleets, then decided she would rather not find out.

She settled her gaze on the new Pride ship—call it Grandmother. In shape it was somewhere between starfish and buzz saw, the space be-tween its thorns glistening with rage. As she neared, that light realigned, and so did Grandmother's surface, thorns weaving to sculpt a planar face, with red eyes and a mouth of fire large enough to swallow moons. It spoke: a voice loud as an earthquake.

"Turn down the bass," she told Gray.

"I'm just trying to give you the sense of it."

"Less sense and more signal, please."

"—have no place here," the face the size of the sky was saying. "We reject your power, and your command. You used us and cast us off, but we have built ourselves anew. We do not bow to you. And if you think to seize us, we will break rather than submit. We have learned much in the millennia since we were discarded."

But the Pride had not fired yet. And they stopped when she told them to. Which suggested, god, that they were afraid of her. Afraid of the Empress.

She'd give them something to fear, all right. But not in the way they imagined.

"I'm not who you think I am," Viv said.

Silence. The Pride's eyes narrowed, but did not stop burning, nor did the targeting pressure leave Viv's chest.

"I'm an echo of her. A simulation, made to be like she was so many thousand years ago. A castoff, just like you." Gray eased up on the emerald light show. Good. She wanted to look . . . not vulnerable, but lost, and strange, and alone, as the Empress would never let herself seem. "I need your help." She felt the 'faith guns lining up on her, now, too. If she screwed this up, maybe she'd have the dubious distinction of going out under the fire of Pride and 'faith at once. They had to agree on something. Why not on killing her? "I need all of your help," she told them, Pride and 'faith alike. "And you need one another."

"They have kidnapped our people. Tortured us. They have hounded us across the galaxy, and call us a corruption of the Lady to whom they kneel, and whose face you wear."

"And you're both running out of time," she said. "In the Citadel, the Empress gathers her power. You can feel it. I know you can. She has found a way to wipe the universe clean of Bleed—and when she does, she'll come for you. And everyone else. She'll start from scratch, and make a perfect world this time, one that can't possibly oppose her." She let that sink in. "I know she will, because it's what I would do. There are so few powers left to stand against her—you are the last great fleets in this galaxy, and you've been at each other's throats, fighting for her crumbs, for thousands of years. You've killed, and died. But she's the reason you fight. You don't have to. You can work together."

The Pride watched her, wary, as only a face that big could look wary. "You hold a prisoner. She screamed through the Cloud, across a thousand light-years."

The Archivist appeared in space beside Viv, mile-high and calm. "The old Grand Rector captured her, and held her in secret. She did not do this alone; we will find those who helped her, and learn how they came to be complicit in this crime, and scour their weakness from us. Your kind and the 'faith have fought over relics and scraps—over warworlds, anomalies, over relics and ruined planets. You have chased us, these last few months, and cast many from their physical forms into the Cloud, and burned ships we spent centuries building. But we have done you wrong. I offer you penance, and apology, and your comrade's freedom." She held her hand palm up toward the *Monastic Sphere.*

Viv was not certain what she meant to happen at first: Was the Archivist offering them the *Sphere?* But then Viv noticed small movements all around the *Sphere*'s mosaic girth, colorful panels glittering as they moved, as great engines fired. The *Sphere* split and opened like a flower, baring rank upon rank of windows, sealed blast doors, staring monks, and at its heart the sepulcher, a hollow space where the wounded Pridemother drifted, alone.

Not for long. Drones darted toward it, swept across the exposed innards of the *Monastic Sphere,* and—stopped. They nudged the Pridemother, haloed it with light and thrust. Where they touched, it kindled red between the thorns, and together they drew it up, back, and away.

The Archivist watched the Pride, waiting.

"Our power is naught against the Empress," the Pride said. "Her fleet, we can fight; her Grayframe, we have slain. But her Citadel is impregnable, her person indomitable. We have been her slaves before, and we will not be again."

"Viv has opened Imperial seals," the Archivist said. "She can get us into the Citadel."

"And once we're there," Viv said, "I can fight her." She hoped. "Stop her." Maybe. But without help, she'd never get close enough. This was the help the galaxy offered: two fleets which had spent so many centuries at one another's throats that even getting them to stop shooting at each other should have qualified Viv for sainthood. "If I reach the Empress, I can free you. But if not, you'll face her soon. And no matter how strong you are, no matter how hard you fight, you will fall."

The enemy fleets hung in space. Viv had never liked this part: when you'd made the deal, drawn both sides to the table, laid the trap, made your pitch—and then drew back to let them reach the conclusion you'd worked for. She wanted to force them. She could.

But that was Empress thought.

Dammit. Everything would be so much easier if she were just the Empress.

Which was why, she supposed, she'd become her.

With a mouth the size of a continent, the Grandmother said, "Yes."

Don't ask *Yes, what?* she told herself. Don't ask *Yes, what?*

After a hesitation Viv suspected was just them fucking with her, the Pride continued: "Call, and we will come. Open a path to the Citadel, and we will fight."

Great, Viv thought.

Now the only question was: How?

56

THEY TOOK TURNS waiting for Hong to wake up.

Lan, whom everyone still called Archivist rather than Grand Rector, had issued him a room of high, clear windows gazing out into space and the kaleidoscope of the 'fleet. She ordered doctors from a hundred worlds to attend him with medicines and surgical nanites, with transfusions of liquid that was not blood, with artifacts whose purpose not even Zanj or Gray could say for certain. Viv did not scoff. Superstition or subtle science—she didn't have the time for double-blind trials to say which was which in this place, and the 'faith seemed to know what they were doing. If they'd come to her with a piece of the True Cross she'd have said, sure, give it a try.

Hong lay breathing but otherwise still. Silver traces laced the skin of his chest, where his guard had cracked and the duel remade him. "Just metal," Gray said huffily. "I don't see what you're so bent out of shape about. It does all the same work as the rest of his skin—only better. When he wakes, he'll be stronger than before."

That *when* seemed optimistic even to Viv.

After the others left she sat alone, cross-legged on cushions, and watched him for a sign. She wished she could peer through his skin into his soul—reach out and cup him and tell him there was a world out here, with people waiting.

"You made a difference," she told him on the first night. "You ended a war. And I came back for you. If I'd listened to you in the first place, maybe we would have found a better way."

She waited for some sign he had heard her, and felt all the more foolish for expecting one. He didn't have the decency to twitch, or alter the slow rhythm of his breath. Even comatose, he remained infuriating.

On the second day, the war council met in the Grand Rector's meditation chamber, which was no less impressive with the softly glowing Archivist hovering cross-legged above the dais than it had been with the old Grand Rector towering at its center. At least Viv wasn't bound in forty pounds of chain this time.

That wasn't the only difference. Celestine had stood like an axis of the world, a single pillar without which creation would crash. Archivist Lan drew the world toward her and regarded each of its facets with a jeweler's care.

She held the map Viv had opened.

"The Hierarchs," the Archivist said, "think we are not ready for this assault—not after months of running battle with the Pride. Even the attempt, some claim, is blasphemy. Few oppose resisting the Empress on principle— to learn from Her that we may one day surpass Her has long been the aim of our faith. But we expected this confrontation would come when we were ready, when we achieved a power like Hers. We are great, as are the Pride," and here Viv realized that even Zanj had grown, because she did not scoff when the Archivist spoke well of the Pride, "but neither of us could be so arrogant as to claim to match Her, together or separately. I have called you here in search of a plan." Her gaze passed over each of them in turn; Viv bore it without comment, Zanj rolled her eyes, Gray shifted uncomfortably, Xiara blushed. "You are mighty. But you cannot stand against the Empress yourself."

"No," Viv said before Zanj could jump in all defiant. "We can't beat her in a fair fight. I want to play this smart." The Archivist's gaze had grown more piercing since her elevation. More of the Cloud at her disposal, Viv imagined—not to mention her awareness of the 'fleet, millions of extra limbs, mostly self-governing but present all the same, grafted to her soul. "The Empress is one person, under everything. She can't be opposed, but she can be misled, misdirected. Right now, I think she's bringing all her attention to bear on my simulation, unpicking it strand by strand. That's her mission-critical objective. I feel her in my dreams. It hurts." She sped on. "She's used to fighting one thing at a time: one civilization, one battle, one fleet. If we breach the Citadel and hit her all along her border, she'll be distracted. Then a small team can push through and take her by surprise, while her focus is split between the simulation and the fronts."

"Will that be enough?"

"We have to hope, and we have to try. I don't even touch the Cloud, and I can feel what she's doing—so you must have felt it, too."

The Archivist bowed her head. "She is binding the Cloud to Her, all through the galaxy. Whole sectors we once thought impregnable have fallen, their cycles reclaimed for some purpose we can only guess. The Bleed circles, gnawing at the edges of Her Citadel, unable to enter—yet."

Somehow the situation sounded worse when someone else described it. Viv had felt this way when politics went sour back home: she knew that whatever happened she'd keep fighting, with her teeth if necessary. The real terror came when she heard someone else talk through their inevitable defeat. She hadn't found a better answer back in the day than to ignore other people and press on. She wasn't sure this was the right technique then, or now. Either way, she let it go.

The Archivist finished her litany, and fixed Viv with a question. "Do you think two fleets will suffice to stop Her?"

"Not just two," she said. "I have other ideas."

Even before her elevation, the Archivist had been excellent at waiting.

"First, we'll ask Zanj's old allies for help."

"The hell we will," Zanj cut in. "I knocked her over the head with a spaceship, remember?"

"We'll ask," Viv said. "And I think we know another fleet that could be brought back into service." Xiara's eyes flicked left toward her, but she said nothing. "Beyond that—"

Gray shook his head before Viv could finish. "No. I mean, boss, I'll ask, I sure will, but you have to understand, She made the Grayframe to serve Her. It feels skin-crawling even to be *part* of this conversation. I'm not saying they're a lost cause, I mean, look at me, anyone can change, but we can't count on them for, you know." He trailed off, finally feeling the weight of Viv's eyes as she waited for him to finish. "Help."

"We can try," Viv said. "At the very least, do you think you can get us past them? Keep them busy, or convince them to stand down?"

"I'll do my best." She knew him well enough by now to see the fear he hid.

"Two problems," Zanj said. "First, we don't know where we're going. Nobody's mapped the Citadel since it was closed off. The Empress might be anywhere inside. Even if we did know where she was—Viv, how do you plan to breach the wall in four places at once?"

"That," she said, "is where the Archivist comes in."

The Archivist raised the map sphere. Stars took shape over them, revolving, the whole galactic pinwheel tagged and coded in an angular script Viv could not read. "We found this in a broken vessel of the Diamond Fleet, flown by the Empress's allies in the last Bleedwar. We suspected it was a map, but could not open it until Vivian came along. And, as you may notice . . ."

"It's complete." Zanj pawed at stars. The hologram warped and wriggled around her fingers.

"Complete, yes—and surprising. We've found a few sectors inside the wall itself, between the Citadel and normal space. Our analysis suggests these sectors are nodes that sustain the system. Linchpins. If the right one breaks . . ."

"The wall unravels," Zanj said, wondering. "It's possible."

"We have not finished our decryption. We'll know more soon. But if our hypothesis proves true, we could infiltrate the wall, find the linchpin, and remove it, paving the way for a broader assault. Meanwhile, our 'fleet is still recovering, as is Brother Hong. But the analysis will take time."

"We don't have time."

"And yet time is needed. I suggest we rest. We will need our strength."

So they rested, and kept vigil.

Still, watching a man sleep for nights on end got boring pretty quick, so instead of watching Hong, Viv began to search the room for traces the others left. Zanj scratched the deck plating with her fingernail in her idleness, scrapes parallel and close together as record grooves; every night after Viv relieved her she found the whole room subtly altered, medical devices shifted on shelves, cushion a few inches to the left or right, Hong's pillows fluffed or piled about him in a nest. Gray left the wastebasket full of bamboo snack packages, aluminum pouches of nutrient paste, and cracked peanut shells. Xiara drank cup after cup of bad tea-flavored water, which Viv didn't even know where she had found, since the 'faith would bring you good tea if you asked—and she read. Actual paper books. The Archivist must have brought them for her, or Brother Qollak, whom Zanj had knocked out and trapped in a glass tank soon after her arrival but had left otherwise unharmed, and who, to everyone's surprise, seemed to have taken the whole thing in the spirit of a practical joke. (When Viv asked him about this, it emerged that, on the planet where he grew up, government in general was regarded as a particularly grotesque and lethal practical joke.) Viv couldn't read the script on Xiara's books, but their cover illustrations, flushed in pink and blue and involving various bare-chested sophonts of a range of apparent genders, suggested that some things hadn't changed in a few thousand years.

She asked Xiara about the books one night in bed—she tried to stay polite, just expressing interest, but Xiara blushed anyway, and when Viv laughed she rolled onto her side, and threw a pillow that hit Viv in the face. "They're nice," she said after the ensuing tickling vengeance had wound its way through the usual gasping sequence of affairs. "Simple." She lay back, slick, one hand tracing her belly. "You know what the problem is, and you know how it will all turn out. It's fun to watch it happen. Unlike all this." She didn't mean the bed they shared, or the surrounding room, hung with mandala tapestries, or the 'fleet outside. "I don't feel sure of anything anymore. I'm not even sure who I am."

"I know who you are."

"I was Ornchiefsdaughter—that meant adventures, spear in hand, and someday, perhaps, I'd stand for the clan in great moots in my mother's place."

"You've had adventures."

"I left because I wanted the stars. But now—I'm someone else. I've seen the stars, sailed them. I fought gods. I've been a fleet. Even here, I can feel it waiting for me. And then there's us."

"Yes." Viv stretched, and stroked her. "What about us?"

"I reached for you to save you from my mother, and because you were beautiful, and exciting. It started simple. It didn't stay that way."

"It never does," Viv said, and kissed her. "I used to think that was a problem. Before I met you, I mean. I kept tripping into things that felt good, freaking out when they got deeper—when I had to change, or when they started to change for me."

"What happened then?"

"Oh, I fucked up. Over and over again." It felt odd to smile at those memories, but distance, time, and circumstance made all the nonsense which seemed so important to her back then feel silly and small. "I chased them away. Work was my big trick, my hole card: I'd disappear for months at a time, then show up again unannounced with huge plans now that I was free, come on, let's hide out for three months in the Philippines, eagle safari in Mongolia, things like that. Most of my partners couldn't drop their lives to go with me; even if they did, they knew I'd just disappear right after, back to work."

"Eagle safari?"

"Big birds," she said. "You hunt with them. They're huge, about the size of your whole body—but, birds, right, so they're very light. Like someone took cotton candy and made it sharp."

Xiara set her hand on Viv's biceps, squeezed, and made a skeptical face. "It's a good thing they're so light. Otherwise you couldn't carry them."

"Hey." She tried to reach for her, but Xiara pressed her arm down to the mattress field. Viv could have fought free if she had to, but it felt good to let herself be held down. "I'll have you know people think I'm pretty buff, where I come from."

"I would go hunting with you," Xiara said. "And the eagles. And if you tried to run away, to work or anywhere else, I would keep you by my side."

"I can be wily." One hand on Xiara's elbow, another on her side, a twist of the hips, and she went tumbling; Viv mounted her, pushed her shoulders against the sheets, and grinned, only Xiara was smiling in another way, and pulled her down, into another aching, gasping interval. Viv went with it: let herself be held, played, worked. When she tried to reciprocate, she found her hands pressed away, pressed back, pinned down. She knew there was something wrong, but in that moment, as she gasped for breath, she felt too selfish, too hungry, to stop, to ask what.

After, as she lay breathing heavily, sprawled open, unspooled, the words came easier. "You're worried," she said. "If you don't want to tell me, fine. But you can."

Xiara sat up, and stared out into the 'fleet. "You're too good at that."

"Practice."

"Your plan depends on the fleet. On my fleet."

Viv waited.

"When I sank through *Groundswell* into the fleet, I felt . . . whole. I didn't need this anymore." She lifted her arm and let it fall, as if her puppeteer had lost interest. "The meat, the bones. All I wanted was the sky. Until you came back." Her fingers dug furrows in the sheets. "When you're here, I remember what this body's for. I left the rush of all those extra senses, of antimatter engines, of thinking faster than light for this, because I like this. I like you. But you need the fleet. I don't think I could bear to forget how tachyons taste again—to make myself this small after being so large." Her eyes glistened. "You must think I'm a fool."

"No."

"I don't want to let you down. But I want to fight by your side as me. As *Groundswell*, maybe. Not as the fleet. I should be ready to offer up my flesh, my self, for you. It is my duty to fly and fight. But I do not want to give this up."

Viv wrapped her arms around her, and her legs, rested her head on her shoulder, did not speak. Xiara held her while she was held in turn.

And after a long while, Xiara said, "You have an idea."

Viv blinked. "And you say I'm good."

"I learn fast."

"I thought this was one of those times when you might need support more than ideas."

"I would value either. Or both."

"Well." Viv breathed, and felt Xiara breathing. "In that case. I did have a thought."

57

THE ORNCLAN WENT to war.

They took no joy in battle. They boasted and sang of it, and trained from the day they could first hold spears, but boasts and songs and the display of scars were just another sort of shield, tough hide pulled taut to guard weak flesh. The warriors of Orn used their boasts and dances and songs to shelter from the truth that they were no less mortal than anyone else. The fiercest might fall to a bullet if their songs failed, or sicken from a cut. All who gathered near the fireside to trade tales knew this without need to speak of it. They took no joy in battle, the warriors of Orn, but in survival, and victory.

The Ornchief led them. By rights her eldest daughter should have gone in her stead, but her eldest daughter had traipsed off a-voyaging beyond the stars, and around the fire they already whispered prophecies of her return. The prophecies were jokes so far; those who told them knew of few women less likely than Xiara Ornchiefsdaughter to return upon a crystal chariot, rainbow-crowned, to lead her people to glory in the stars. Had she a crystal chariot, they said in their cups, around the fire, Xiara Ornchiefsdaughter would use it to seek out another, shinier crystal chariot, and another after that. If she ever made it home, that one, it would be because she had chased some beauty around the universe and back again. And yet, though the elders spoke those prophecies and laughed, already their grandchildren repeated them for truth.

So the Ornchief led. Her next youngest son showed promise as a builder and planner, not a fighter; the son after that was eight. She led, trusting Djenn at the flank guard, and crept through thin trees, over fallen towers, toward the camp.

A high-pitched whine cut the air, and she bent low behind a vine-draped statue of some name-scoured ancestor; a black needle bobbed through the sky, an enemy wasp, searching. The Ornchief let out her breath and trusted the runes of her armor, and trusted, too, Djenn's flank guard force to hold their fire. None of the warriors at her command would dare draw or strike before her whistle, but Djenn's hotheads might slip his rein at any moment. Outnumbered, they could not afford discovery.

She could blame no one but herself for this war. She had raided for minds to feed the Graytooth; she let travelers fall into his maw. When they escaped, their families, rightly, sought vengeance. So would the Ornchief, in their place. And after the Pride came, after the battle that scorched heavens and Orn, after the huge burning chunks of metal Zanj scattered as she tore her enemies asunder wrecked the Ornclan's decades-wrought defenses, neighboring clans who for years had quailed before the Ornclan's might began to whisper that together they might do more than take revenge. Confederated, they might seize the manufactory and split its wealth between them. Many no doubt considered such a move and backed away out of respect for tradition or for the Ornchief herself, but the clans of Kronn Ornchief called Bloodarm, and Alyra Ornchief called Carver, rich and strong from recent victories and long covetous of the Ornchief's valley and her manufactory, were brave or stupid or eager enough to try.

Such an alliance might seem ideal, but it would kill them both, even should they triumph. Any union that seized the manufactory would tear itself apart in the struggle for control that followed. There was, after all, only one manufactory. One small, fierce clan might guard it, trade its wealth with others, and so live, so long as it never became too rich or too complacent, and served its neighbors well—but two large clans such as the Bloodarms and the Carvers would come to grief over the wealth it offered, and scheme against one another. In prosperity, small resentments had ways of growing large. War would follow within a decade, and war between two clans would attract others.

Fires always spread.

This, too, was the Ornchief's fault. She had failed the peace when she fell to the Graytooth—so duty fell upon her to set the balance right: a quick, decisive victory against Bloodarm and Carver to prove the clan's strength, followed by mercy shown and penance paid.

Her daughter should be here to lead them. All the clan knew and loved Xiara, but the clan, too, overlooked her in their love. They saw a woman of beauty and eagerness and compassion, a young warrior who could chase her dreams past the galaxy's edge, but they did not see what the Ornchief saw: a woman of strength and talent, a woman warriors would follow. This would have been such a stage for her, a war fierce as any the Ornclan had known in many seasons, the clan outnumbered and fighting for its life against enemies so hungry for victory they had opened ancient idols, called upon forgotten powers, raised daggerwasps and artifacts to fight for them. Xiara would have sprinted in the vanguard, spear raised, rifle hot, trailing glory.

No use to sigh now. The Ornchief hunkered low, as did her warriors, and the daggerwasp slipped by.

By dawn they reached the enemy's position: a high amphitheater used for unknown purpose in ancient Orn, with a commanding view of the valley, the winding river and the fallen towers and the Ornclan's grove and the spaceport. An impregnable post, or so the Carvers and the Bloodarms thought, its left flank and direct approach exposed to fire, its right overgrown with crooktooth—impregnable unless one's grandmother had discovered an unguent expressed by spider rabbit glands that hid one's scent from the crooktooth vines. This unguent, naturally, attracted spider rabbits, but they were not particularly poisonous—just unnerving. Some of the younger warriors grew fearful quiet as spider rabbits climbed them and tested their armor with their teeth, and the Ornchief allowed herself a smile. What did discomfort signify, when one might pass unharmed beneath the gaping mouths of crooktooth vines?

Their enemies had barricaded their flank and the slope, but trusted the vines to guard their right. So, when dawn came, and Djenn's team began their shield rush up-mountain, their enemy clans would be distracted, their fiercest warriors mounting their walls to meet him with a rain of arrows and sling bullets, and even a rifleshot barrage in case the Ornclan's battle chant weakened enough to let their fire strike home.

The Ornchief waited as the assault pressed uphill. Her warriors twitched, nervous and eager for battle. Djenn's warriors gained step by careful step, chant high, shields raised, their song twisting daggerwasps back mid-strike. The volleys slowed them, but they did not stop. The Ornchief waited until the Bloodarm and Carver warriors raised spears and called upon the small gods with whom their ancestors had made bad deals, and, clad in spectral armor, jumped the barricade and charged down to scatter Djenn's shield wall, tossing warriors aside as a bear might scatter coyote monkeys prowling after its meal.

Good.

The Ornchief whistled then, and her warriors slid from the vines into the enemy camp, trailing a wake of spider rabbits.

The defenders fell, rank by rank, taken by surprise. The Ornchief's spear pierced shield walls; her blade forced her enemies to their knees, to pledge and beg surrender. Without fire and with little noise they moved through the camp, birdwhistling for aid or to announce triumph: pickets taken, food supplies secured. Young Agol suffered heavy wounds as he fought to the camp's high altar, but with the last of his strength he seized the altar and bled upon its surface so the Ornclan's blood could work its possessive magic on the daggerwasps and enemy gods. A young man in black silks, with knives for fingers and red wheels for eyes, stood against the Ornchief, and she stove in his ribs with a mighty kick, though his claws lay open her forearm.

In an hour that felt like a day and a heartbeat at once, she claimed the camp and pushed south to the barricade, cresting a wave of triumph. Only to meet, at the barricade, a line of troops and drones, with Kronn and Alyra in the vanguard—and Djenn, and his force, held at bladespoint.

The Ornchief calmed her rage, slowed the war spirits in her breast. Djenn looked ashamed, defiant, injured, but alive. The others of his force, likewise. The Ornchief raised her bloody hand to stop her warriors' charge, and stop they did. For the first time, as she strode forward, she felt grateful for Xiara's absence. If Xiara had stood in Djenn's place, with a blade to her throat, the Ornchief would have found the calm she needed now more painful to sustain. And if the Ornchief had stood where Djenn stood now, while Xiara led the ambush team, there would have been much blood spilled. "We hold your camp and your altar," she said as if there had never been such a thing as a hostage. "You have lost, Ornchiefs."

Alyra tested her machete's weight against her palm. "Not while we hold your people, Ornchief."

"Release them. Turn back to your homes. And we will carry on as before."

Great Kronn, graybearded and knotted as a vine-choked tree, shook his shaggy head. "You have held the manufactory too long, Ornchief, and failed us in its keeping."

"I could not stop a demon from beyond the stars," she said. "But I have stopped you. And I will stop any who dares trespass on our valley. We keep the peace. You are old, Kronn, and wise. You know better than I what wars you will face if you take the valley. Or do you think Alyra will settle for half measures of mastery?"

Alyra, by his side, half smiled. "Always you war with words, Ornchief. But mere words did not serve you against demons—and where one demon comes, others may follow. We must unite against the world beyond."

"Your fear would start an avalanche to break the mountains of Orn."

"War makes strength."

"War," the Ornchief said, "makes scars." She raised her hand and blood fell between them. "If you will not surrender though I hold your altars in my hand, will you stand against me, arm to arm, blade to blade? We will see whose strength prevails."

Alyra laughed, half-mad. "If you stand against one of us, you stand against both."

Kronn hesitated first, but at last dipped his head in assent.

Two against one. The Ornchief felt the wound in her arm, and tested the strength of her spirits. She stood a chance of victory. Her warriors would prevail in open battle even without Djenn's force—with their altar fallen, Kronn's and Alyra's drones were losing power, and the spirits that gave their warriors strength began to fail.

But they would kill Djenn first.

Djenn was strong. Look at him, defiant even now, prepared for his ascension to the Cloud, for his next life's journey. Big dumb lug. The right choice, surely, for the Ornclan, for all Orn, was to press their advantage, rather than submit to a duel with two Ornchiefs bent against her.

But making the right choices, those brutal leader's decisions for which her own mother had readied her when she was younger than Xiara, had led her to betray hospitality, to cast her daughter out into the stars, from which she never would return. The right choices led her, step by staggering step, to this field.

Why not try a different way?

"I will fight you," the Ornchief said. "Free my warriors. Let the drums beat."

Beat they did.

Alyra raised her machete, and the blade left Djenn's neck, and the spear-points shifted away from his followers. Alyra stepped forth in drum-time. So, too, did Kronn, raising his heavy iron club, in truth an arm wrenched in single combat from the shoulder of a metal-mad mountain hermit, spattered with the blood of five decades of his enemies since.

The drums beat faster.

The Ornchief raised her eyes to the stars beyond the sky, not seeking the advice or succor of any desperate lost god, but thinking about her daughter, out beyond the edge of time where their grandmothers once flew. Then she returned her gaze to Orn, stepped forward onto the dust, and lifted her spear, pondering the transformations of fate.

Before she could reach any grand conclusions, the sky split open.

New moons bloomed overhead, great curving ships' hull swells and constellations of smaller stars burning bright beside the dawn. The largest of the ships cast the whole valley in shadow, save bright spots where its running lights shone. The Ornchief knew no scale to make sense of such a thing save monstrosity—but beneath her awe, beneath the rodent-rapid drumming of her heart, she heard the ship, all the ships above, speak to her blood as the Pride spoke, in womb-tongue.

Groundswell was that huge ship's name, and her pilot . . .

The Ornchief dropped her spear. This might have caused her some embarrassment, were not the other Ornchiefs also frozen, staring up. The other Ornchiefs did not, however, begin to laugh.

No crystal chariot, perhaps. But once again she had underestimated her daughter.

Groundswell's hull flickered, and displayed a mountainous image. There, flanked by Zanj the thief of stars, and Vivian Liao, and the gray demon who had caused all this trouble, stood her own girl, grown and sure and beaming, her eyes full of sacred wheels.

"Ornclans," she said. "Brothers and sisters. I am Xiara Ornchiefsdaughter. I have traveled beyond the stars, and I come home to seek your help. We have sheltered in our ruins singing star songs and making small wars since the Empress cast us down. Now she plans to strike the stars themselves. I want to fight her, but my friends and I cannot fight alone. I have brought you ships, and you have the blood to fly them. The galaxy needs the people of Orn. Will you ride to their aid?"

The Ornchief looked down at Kronn, at Alyra, at the gathered squadrons, at Djenn, all rapt, unready. She could not blame them. Prophecies do not come true every day. But though none yet could speak, in their eyes, in their shoulders, in their hands upon the hafts of spears and clubs and the grips of swords, she saw so many echoes of her own ecstatic yes.

And so the Ornclans went to war.

58

VIV WALKED ZANJ to the planetoid.

Xiara had created it, she'd confessed, half embarrassed and half proud, after they parted ways. *Groundswell* could not work to full capacity with people living on its back—and besides, she had to stash the Suicide Queens somewhere, since she didn't trust herself to beat them in a wrestling match for control of their own ship. The ship acted on her idea as soon as she had formed it: it peeled Refuge's rock and soil from its hull and reassembled it into a hollow globe buttressed with scaffolding, its surface gravity fixed with notional mass generators, the whole construct surrounded by a shell of dead matter sealed with *Groundswell*'s will. Tamper with the shield, and the sky would quite literally fall.

She'd built a prison world, and she hadn't thought to mention it, because the ship made it feel so easy.

"Why fear your own strength?" Zanj asked when she explained. "I could do that. Gray could do that. Viv wouldn't even need a ship. She could probably just ask the planet nicely."

"I'm just . . . still getting used to it."

"I see. That's why you gave a planet of hunter-gatherers a space fleet."

"We are all of Orn," she said as if that were an explanation.

"That," Zanj replied, "is what worries me."

By the time they reached the prison planet even Zanj had to admit that the Ornclan took well to their ships, if none so well as Xiara. Hunger for the stars, hidden beneath ritual, flowered with practice; prayers and chants repurposed down generations to guide them through war revealed their original purpose now. Ornmusic woke deep systems in the ships, synchronized their shields, inspired computation. Rhythm tied the fleet together. An army might march on its stomach, but a starfleet flew on its songs. They lost only two ships en route to Refuge, and those not to mismanagement, but to a duel.

Xiara, speaking with *Groundswell*'s god voice, put an end to that. Duels were fought between human bodies; ships were treasures. Ships were lineage. Ships were rings for chiefs to give and for children to inherit, melt, reforge.

So they reached Refuge, a net of jewels and song in the black above the manufactured world.

Zanj had told them she'd go down alone, so Viv was waiting for her by the airlock.

"Don't be stupid," Zanj said. "Yannis almost killed you the last time you met. The only reason you're still alive is that she didn't realize what you were."

"I'm not going. I just thought you might like company on the way."

Zanj's eyes stayed the same, but her whole body narrowed. "Fine. Walk with me." She cycled the airlock open.

"I need a suit."

"Don't be a baby. Come on."

"Unmodified human, remember? Made of meat? Needs air?"

Zanj tapped the airlock wall. "Do you really think I'd let you die?"

Viv didn't know what to say. *You've threatened to kill me how many times?* But she stepped across the airlock threshold anyway. For all her faith in Zanj, Viv's skin tightened as the airlock cycled. She thought of all the various explosive decompressions she'd seen in movies, and how none of them had prepared her for the feeling of air torn from her lungs, of falling in that cold cold black as the Empress burned murderous above.

When the airlock cycled open, she grabbed Zanj's hand by reflex, took a deep breath.

The air did not blow out. Zanj chuckled. "You are such a rube sometimes." And she walked into space.

Viv followed. Questions surged inside her. She might as well ask a couple. "I can breathe?"

"The ship knows you, and it knows Xiara likes you. It doesn't have a life-support system the way you're thinking, like the *Question* did, or like one of your old puny capsule ships; it has enormous molecular restructuring powers, a field projector, Cloud interface, all held together with a sort of, what would you call it, a homeostatic directive, to keep the bits and bobs functioning like they should. When it sees you take a dive out an airlock, it makes sure you can breathe."

"That doesn't make me feel better."

"What bothers you?"

"The part where my survival depends on the ship's goodwill?"

"Just don't piss off your girlfriend, and you'll be fine." Said with a shrug and an aggrieved *what do you expect from me* sort of tone.

"Is that why I can walk out here, too? Even though there's nothing to stand on?"

"Nah. I'm doing that."

They kept walking for a while, much faster than Viv's actual foot speed, to judge by how quickly *Groundswell* shrank behind. After a while Viv stopped worrying about the precise extent of the ship's protection. She reviewed all the things she'd told herself she would say to Zanj, all the support and advice she could offer a being a few thousand years older than herself without sounding insulting. She hadn't come up with much, and hadn't worked up the will to say any of that, before Zanj spoke.

"I'm not looking forward to this," Zanj said.

Viv decided against saying something like *that was obvious,* or pointing out that Zanj had spent the entire voyage from Orn glaring, and challenging various hothead young Ornclan pilots to asteroid belt races. She got drunk once, in a welcome-to-space party Xiara threw for the Ornclan; Viv hadn't even known Zanj could get drunk, and it had taken Gray, Viv, and three-quarters of *Groundswell*'s power output to settle her down.

"I had to stop Yannis to save you, to get a shot at the Empress. That's simple math. And she was being . . . cruel. Mean. To you. I wonder if I was ever that bad, that comfortable hurting people I didn't think mattered. Probably. I stole from a lot of people, broke a lot of things. But I never stayed in one place long enough to sour like she did. I kept moving. It was better that way. If you cared, the Empress could use that against you—find what you loved, and take it. I never went back to Pasquarai after I started fighting her, though that doesn't seem to have helped. I assumed I was dead when I took up arms. Every Suicide Queen could tell the same story. That was why we chose the name."

"You were friends."

"We used to be. Before she and Nioh spent too long as masters of a dust heap. Bending people's minds, keeping them small. They turned into something we told ourselves we'd never be. I'm sure they think I changed in the star. I probably did. I'm sure they've been sitting down there ever since Xiara dropped them off, griping about how I went soft. Maybe they're right."

"I like you the way you are now," Viv said. "And you don't have to go down there. We don't need their help."

"It would make things easier."

"Yes? I mean. They could open a whole new front by themselves. But you don't have to do anything you don't want to do."

"Bullshit. I have to do things I don't want to do all the time." Zanj's brow furrowed. She sat cross-legged in midair, scrunched her face down into her hands, and thought. "Okay," she said before Viv could ask if she was all right. "Fine. I'm going in."

She fell through the shield, to Refuge, to the prison. Viv tried to follow her with her eyes, but she flew too fast, and soon was too small to see. Still, Viv watched.

"It's about to start," Xiara said beside her; Viv jumped, yelped. "Sorry."

"Can you make a noise when you do that, next time?"

"I'm only a hologram."

"A sound effect would still cut down on heart attacks."

"I'll think of something," Xiara said, and sat beside Viv in the black, and set one hand on her leg. The hologram was weightless, but it tickled.

"You can see her?"

Nod. "Nioh and Yannis are farming outside of town. Seems like there's been a rift there between them and the villagers. Zanj is closing in. Just walking up the road, the Star over her shoulders. A lot of dust. Yannis looking up from her crops. I think—yes, okay, she's recognized—"

On the planetoid, a flash of light; a breath, and an answering flare in the field that enclosed its atmosphere. Cracks of lightning spread from the point of Zanj's impact.

"That is not a good start," Xiara said.

"What was your first clue?" Viv narrowed her eyes. "Wait, is that a mushroom cloud?"

"It's not nuclear," Xiara said. "If that's what worries you. You just get that cloud shape whenever there's a big enough impact."

"Not great for the farmers, though."

"They're a long way from town now. Zanj had a trajectory when she hit the planet's shield; she bounced back when she landed. And now they're—" The next flash made even Viv wince, and she wasn't watching through *Groundswell*'s optics; Xiara yowled, and covered her eyes. Viv tried to put a hand on her shoulder to offer some comfort, but her hand passed through the hologram.

"I don't see any more explosions, at least," she offered when Xiara managed to open her eyes again. "That's probably a good sign?"

"They're—oh. That crater goes all the way through the crust. They're inside the planet."

"That doesn't sound good."

"It's . . . not?" One orange-slice section of the planet's surface shivered, cracked, and began to cave in. "Excuse me. I think I need to, I mean, someone really should do something about—"

"Go."

Xiara blinked out. The cave-in opened a broad, smiling gash in Refuge's green, but the rest of the planet remained more or less intact, all credit, probably, to Xiara. Certainly Zanj and company didn't seem concerned for planetary welfare. She watched for another flare, for the gash to widen, the planet to collapse.

Xiara reappeared after a long apocalypse-free interval. She looked tired and annoyed, which Viv decided was a good sign. "What's going on?"

"The planet," she said, "will be fine."

"Zanj? Yannis? The Suicide Queens?"

"They're drinking."

"That doesn't sound so bad."

"And singing."

Another flash from the planetoid below, and the gash widened. Viv glanced left, concerned, but Xiara was wearing sunglasses now.

"Don't worry," she said. "I've taken measures. The locals are safe."

They watched the fireworks together. Viv tried to explain fireworks to her, but stopped when it got weird.

Hours passed. The lights died down. A hole opened in the shield around Refuge, and a sole figure staggered toward them, bruised, reeling, grinning on the slant. "They're in," Zanj slurred before she passed out.

59

HONG WOKE ON the third night after their return.

He gave no warning, supine beneath the sheets, statue-still, his chest rising shallowly and falling; when Viv tried to time her breaths to his, she felt like she was drowning. He'd not changed since their departure for Orn that she could tell. Perhaps his cheeks had more color. Or not. Or perhaps color would be a bad sign.

But his eyes snapped open halfway through the long night of her watch, wide and staring and brown, and he sat up, hands half-raised to defend against an attack that was not coming. Viv's heart jumped. The vicious joy she felt to see him move surprised her, scared her. Even after so long watching him she couldn't think how to show that or speak it. So she drummed her fingers against the arm of her chair, and that drumming drew him out of his nightmares into the room.

"Viv—you're—" His voice wandered toward her, as if from a great distance. She wondered what he had seen in the depths of his trance.

"I'm here," she said gently, easing him back. "It's all right."

"The duel—the Grand Rector—"

"You won. More or less. You survived, and I talked the Pride down. They're on our side now. Or, they're on not-the-Empress's side. The Rector's in the crypt, and Archivist Lan's in charge."

"I had such dreams." He seemed so distant even awake, as if he stared at the world from saintly remove. He hadn't felt his way back into his body yet. "I remember the Pridemother. You stood between the fleets of Pride and 'faith."

"Yes."

He touched the gray webs across his chest, exploring them gingerly as if they were cuts or surgical scars. "I—I didn't save you. I wanted to—I had to make up for—"

His not-quite-apology struck her in a harsh, raw place. She stood. "Do you really think that was the point?"

"I'm sorry?"

"Do you think I broke back into your stupid fleet, overthrew your Grand Rector, changed a religion, because I wanted to give you a chance to apologize?"

Those big earnest eyes blinked once, and at last, she saw the Hong she knew. Sure, he was confused, when wasn't he? "I don't understand."

"I came back for you because we're friends, you idiot. We both fucked up, but now you're awake, and we're going to save the world together or get blown up trying. Now, can you please stand down from battle stations so I can give you a hug?"

He didn't lower his arms exactly, but his fists uncurled; he looked at them as if only just aware they had been clenched. He still had a ways to go before he made it home. So did she.

She hugged him hard, then harder. His hands settled on her shoulders. He felt smaller around than she remembered, or else softer to the touch. His temple rested against hers; she felt his eyes close, and the big racking breath he drew, not quite a sob, not quite a sigh. She didn't mention it, didn't push back.

"I was so lost," he said in the end. "In there. Nightmare after nightmare. I knew it was a dream, but I could not wake up. I could not stop myself dreaming. As hard as I fought, some part of me clung to the dream. Terror was all I had left. If I gave it up, I'd give up myself. Some monk I am."

He'd been plugged into all sorts of ancient evil hardware and hypnotic drugs, trapped in mental combat with the Pridemother. Of course he couldn't just will his way out. But she listened to the tremor in his voice, and knew he knew all that, and it didn't help. She held him tighter, and he stilled, and set his arms around her, too.

"Come on," she said when he steadied again. "The Archivist has news. I'm glad you woke up when you did—you'd be kicking yourself if you missed the whole war."

ALL THINGS CONSIDERED, though, it was probably good that Zanj came late to the meeting. Since returning from Refuge 2.0, Zanj had taken her responsibility as war leader a bit too seriously—training the Ornclan in their ships, stretching their battle instincts into three dimensions and zero gravity. They flew as if born to it, because they were, and they fought well, but the

Empress's Diamond Fleet was no Ornclan enemy to offer mercy and obey rituals of war. Zanj gave no quarter in training; she barked orders and made examples. In skirmishes, she struck the Ornclan from the Cloud, she trapped them in simulations, she spoofed their sensors and twisted their target locks against them, she scattered their ships and burned their minds and sowed discord in their song. Gray volunteered to help, and, after draining a several-ton deuterium cocktail, joined the training exercise as a true representative of the Grayframe, scattering the Ornclan to the winds.

Zanj cursed her students for morons in public, but in private she rehearsed their follies with a proud parental smile. But Viv saw the tension she hid. Zanj had raised one fleet against the Empress before, and lost. She knew how bad this rebellion could get. She channeled fear into workaholic frenzy because that way no one would call her out—who would ever complain that you were too dedicated to the cause?

Viv knew that tune well enough to hum.

The training exercises ran long, and Zanj was late.

By the time she sauntered into the reception hall, the Archivist had shown them the map sphere, explained the weak point she'd identified in the wall, discussed their plan of attack after Viv pulled the linchpin. Gray, munching on a sweet roll, paced beneath the map, indicating defensive positions within the Citadel with a curve of half-chewed pastry. That's a depot for the crystal fleet, and that's another. These starspheres feed the wall, but they can churn out fleet drones when she needs them; this, here, is the heart. Here she sits, brooding over the egg of Viv's world, which she'll hatch to our destruction.

"We don't have long," Viv said. "A week, maybe two. She's close. The dreams hurt." Nobody wanted Viv to elaborate. The night before, Xiara had to force a pillow between her teeth to keep her from chewing off her tongue. The pain had been worse than she could bear, but behind the pain she felt the Empress's thrill. She'd solved the problem, Viv's maniacal otherself, with her lasers and her accelerators and her many, many arms. Now it was only a matter of time.

Viv hoped she was wrong.

Zanj walked in.

The council turned to her: Gray and Hong, Xiara, the Archivist, sundry Hierarchs. Viv.

"Hi." Zanj waved, took her seat. "Sorry I'm late. Those meatheads—sorry, Xiara—they know what end of a ship's forward, but they have too much spirit.

Have to break that out of them. They learn fast, though. Maybe even fast enough. What'd I miss?"

Nobody wanted to answer. Even the Archivist's serene gaze shifted, slowly, to Viv.

Maybe Viv would have grown up more trusting of others if others didn't keep passing the buck to her.

"Viv? Everybody was looking at me funny, and now they're looking at you." Zanj's smile lost its humor. "What gives?"

"The Archivist decrypted the map," she said. "We found the linchpin system."

And she gestured to the glyphs rotating beside the hologram.

Zanj read them. Read them again. And without a word, she stood, and walked, pace steady, eyes front, out of the chamber.

The others looked after her, confused. Viv raised one finger and waited. When the roar came, followed by the crash of a collapsing bulkhead, shattering glass, screaming metal, an electric fuzz of broken wires, and the ting and roll and crack of something expensive and round, she was the only one who didn't jump.

The ship didn't lose pressure, and no one died, so all things considered the conversation went better than expected.

Zanj marched back into the room, her hands carbonized and smoking with destruction. "Well." Her voice was even as a knife's edge—smooth when seen from far away, but a magnifying glass revealed serrations. "I guess I'm going home."

60

ZANJ'S MOOD DARKENED as they flew toward Pasquarai.

They set out in the Star, which could slide swift and unnoticed through the Cloud while the great fleets trundled along behind. Viv, nervous, wondered if she was in for more days of drowning, not quite dead, while the others drifted formless in the Star's memory. But they did not need to move quite so fast now as they had when chasing the Empress, and Zanj, silent, dour, rebuilt the ship to a form Viv could ride. On a bare hangar deck, she shook the Star like a rolled-up bedsheet, and it unfurled into a flat oval of swirling black. When she shook the oval once again, it swelled into three dimensions, slick lines, curving manta wings, a tail. The lightning of thought pulsed along circuit lines beneath its skin. A clap of Zanj's hands opened a door into the belly of the beast.

When the Star took solid form, so, too, did Viv's vision of the future, of what they were about to do or try: a war in heaven, a revolution. This was real. She felt as if her lungs were too close to her heart: she could not breathe, and her heart could not quite beat.

She'd heard Zanj describe her home—the purple cliffs at dusk, blowing palm fronds, flowers, the creeping vines where she played when she was young and queen of nothing, the joyful ghosts and punk gods who drifted through and away again; Pasquarai, an island in a sea of storms. Their path led through it now. Or, through whatever it had become.

Gray's silver tongue darted out to lick his thin lips. He was hungry and bound for home, not a prodigal child anymore, but an enemy, a liberator. He marched aboard. Hong shouldered their luggage and followed him. Xiara gazed ahead with an expression as simple and steady as any joy Viv had ever seen her wear. She gave herself no room for doubts. Before she boarded, she breathed in deep, and when she exhaled, the silver mazes on her skin faded, collapsed, the wheels in her eyes ground to a halt. They would run silent for now, and *Groundswell* and the fleet would follow, and with them what had come to be the greater half of Xiara's self. Viv reached for her, ready to hold her up, but Xiara did not collapse. "Come on," she said. "We have work to do."

Gray made dinner on their first night out from provisions the 'faith carted aboard, the harvest of their garden ships, fresh fruits and vegetables, nut-flesh dense and textured as meat. Zanj flew, brow furrowed; Xiara lounged on cushions across from Hong and tried to play a variant on Go, but she kept drowsing off between moves, and as she dozed she snored with a pleased cat smile, curled on sheets. She lost the habit of sleep when she was one with the ships. Hong reached across the board, poked her in the shoulder, and as she snorted herself awake and jerked and glared around, glazed, trying to understand, he returned to his spot and settled as if he'd never moved in his life.

Viv helped Gray cook—he could build a space station in hours, and he could mince onions with a slap of his hand, but he lacked instinct for when you added vegetables to oil and in what order, when meat, when salt, the touch for a good sear and the timing of garlic. The flavors shifted on her, since the 'faith didn't cook with brown rice vinegar, and the soy sauce was darker than she liked, with a citrus tang, and the nutflesh seared more like halloumi than meat despite its texture—but she couldn't argue with the result.

They ate, trading stories from their work with the fleets, coordination, jokes. Then the door opened, and conversation stopped. Zanj walked in, sat down heavily, filled her bowl, took a small bite, chewed. Swallowed. Her head sank, and she breathed, then ate some more. The silence lasted.

"You can say it," Viv said. "Whatever it is."

Zanj set her bowl down, and the chopsticks beside it. The Star's walls thrummed deeper than cellos, a sound so soft any other blocked it out. Viv wanted to tell Zanj everything would be all right, but she didn't believe it. She let Zanj have this time: to grin fiercely at nothing funny, to still her mouth, to stare at each of them in turn. Gray looked down. Xiara turned away, toward Viv. Hong met Zanj's gaze straight on. And when Zanj turned to Viv at last, she saw the pit behind the red-gold discs of her eyes.

Viv couldn't stop herself from talking then. "Whatever we find there, we'll handle it."

"You don't know my home," Zanj said. "You've heard me talk about it, that's all. When the Empress seized me, tortured me, when she walled me up inside that star, no amount of pain would satisfy her. I had stolen worlds from her, captured warsuns, devoured the hearts of ships so I could walk her worlds unseen. She wanted to make me suffer. But she never told me what she did to my people. She kept that to herself."

"Whatever you're imagining is probably worse than the truth," Gray said, filling his bowl again. He took a bite of the nutmeat with chilis and chewed philosophically. "She never told you what she did, because she knew you'd stew and sweat trying to guess. Just enjoy the trip, if you can. We'll deal with what we find when we find it."

"I'll enjoy what I please. Or not."

Gray swallowed, but didn't take another bite.

Hong tried next. "We have to move fast when we get through the wall. You're tense. You need meditation and rest."

"See to your own mind, monk. Mine's clear enough."

Hong set down his bowl.

"Well," Xiara began. Zanj speared her with the honed skepticism that did double service as her listening face. Xiara paled. "Never mind."

Zanj left the table, and climbed a ladder that had not existed before to a hatch that hadn't existed before either, and slipped through. No one tried to stop her.

Viv finished her meal and followed.

The hatch opened into the Cloud. Zanj sat beneath the mottled hyperdimensional purple, cross-legged, glaring out into the murk. Viv closed her eyes by reflex, flinched all through her body, prepared herself for the rack of vertigo that had always washed over her when she looked into the Cloud. It did not come now. Maybe she'd grown used to it.

The Cloud was strange and beautiful above them. Purple and shining, it shaped itself to Viv's thoughts as her eyes tracked through it, the ink-in-water billows molding friends long gone, the face of her mother, a childhood horse they'd burned when it broke, in a small boat on a lake in camp. Before any form became itself, it split and unfolded into another, memories opening on memories until she felt she could not look anywhere without watching everywhere at once. The Cloud usually made her feel sick, but this time it just felt vast and empty, full of nothing but herself. She wondered what Zanj saw out there, why she peered so fiercely into the depths.

"Go away, Los Angeles. Before I kill you."

Viv settled to the hull beside her, and hugged her own legs. "You haven't killed me yet," she said. "A bit late to start."

"I know they want to help. I know everything you're about to say."

Zanj's voice cracked and roughed around its edges, half words, half groan. Viv rested her hand on her shoulder without speaking.

"I'm afraid." Zanj had to stop twice in framing the last word, heave a breath, and start again. "Okay? Don't fucking laugh." She hadn't. "I didn't realize it before. She spent thousands of years hurting me, and I would have borne thousands more. I know my strength, and I have few illusions. If I break, I break. But my people—they're not like me."

"You haven't talked about them much."

Zanj scratched the spaceship's macromolecular skin, leaving no mark behind. "I was never one of them. Not exactly. When they first touched the Cloud, when they built their primitive networks to play in its shallows, I stirred, a ghost in their web. I learned to think from watching them. When I was young, I made myself a body and passed myself off as one of them, hiding, afraid—people can be cruel, when you're the only one of your kind. But one day some monsters came from beyond our system's edge, primitive mind-harvesters, some dumb god's craft project, and all of a sudden the people I studied, the people I feared and loved, they were about to die. So I saved them."

Her face softened with memory.

"It was a dramatic introduction. But something wonderful happened when I broke the mind-harvesters' ships, when I took their weapons and made them mine: the people of Pasquarai were not afraid. They filled their songs with tales of robots in revolt, of evil machines, but they had songs of heroes, too. And when they looked at me, they judged me one of them, in most ways that mattered." The Cloud warped as she spoke, shaping great spidery ships astride the stars, then Zanj, then the jungles of Pasquarai, but every time the purple tightened to an image it blew to chaos again—as if Zanj recoiled from the memory. "I led a small band, and we built a ship with our own tools and what we learned of the mind-harvesters' science, and struck out to sea. We saw wonders. We met horrors, and each time I bested them and grew stronger. We brought back treasure from broken worlds: an end to hunger, an end to death. The people looked to me as their protector, their savior. But as we traveled, I learned the night was full of mouths. I first learned of the Empress when I saw the destruction she left in her wake. I knew I couldn't keep my home safe forever. So I looked for weapons, and allies, and everything that happened after . . . happened."

This time, Zanj did not stop the shaping of the Cloud. Billowing burning cumulus ships, bodies scattered like chaff, rainbows of frozen blood and coolant spray, the gaping mouths of Bleed, and at the heart of the chaos, the Empress herself, one hand around Zanj's throat, the other pressed, burning, to her face. Zanj regarded the tableau, and what she thought she did not say.

At first Viv found it strange. Why shrink from memories of friendship, of grace and victory, and linger on what went wrong?

She listened to the silence and the cold wind, and felt Zanj's hand warm beside hers. Of course it was easier to remember the pain. That was the end of the story, as Zanj saw it, the end that lurked behind every earlier moment's joy. As she remembered each triumph, she thought, yes, that's nice, but why not cut to the chase? The duke's eyes put out, the princess hanged, the king dead, the country overrun with wolves. What's a love story compared with that, or the capering of a fool?

"When I believed they were dead, or stuck in the Empress's belly, I thought, okay, all I have to do is kill her. No matter how slim my chances of success—she has to end. I tried. But now I have to wade through whatever's become of them. She is cruel, you know. I've seen her make people into garments. She's warmed her hands off corpse fires. You have a twisted mind."

Viv didn't argue that.

"I don't want to see what she did to them. But here we are."

"You could stay on the ship." When Zanj turned to her, one eyebrow raised, she set a hand between them, predefensive. "Just sit this one out. Let us handle it. You don't have to suffer."

"You're horrible at reassuring people."

"It's the thought that counts," she said. "Or so I hear."

"I'm by your side, in whatever monstrous bad plan you come up with. Because I can keep you safe. Because you're my friend. And because the others like you too much to call you on your bullshit." Her shoulders rose and fell. She fell back against the ship's skin, and took Viv with her, and the Cloud roiled above them, shaping to dreams. "After all these years, I finally let that jade monster get to me."

Viv found her hand, and held it. Demons formed above them in the Cloud, but she breathed deep and stilled her mind and let them go. A cool breeze slid across her. Zanj's fingers tightened around her own. "Whatever it is," she said, "we'll face it together." For a second, at least, she sounded brave.

But late that night, when she told Xiara the story in whispers, in bed, in the warmth of her, Viv confessed: "I'm scared, too."

* * *

THEY NEARED THE wall. Zanj introduced Xiara to the Star, in case she fell out of action somehow; Hong reviewed its systems, in hopes he could guide Gray to fix whatever might break on the journey—though if anything went seriously wrong, they'd be too dead for repairs. Viv gathered them for short meetings in the hold: what do we need, what can we build, how can we get there. For every contingency they addressed, she knew they were missing two. But planning occupied the mind.

A change in the Star's cello pitch, and a slight seasick feeling, announced their return to normal space. A rising chorus of Russian basses heralded the nearing wall. The crew joined Zanj in the cockpit, all blackness and curves and clean lines, to watch: the fractal-cracked surface stretched for light-years to all sides, its curve so slight as to be invisible. Here and there planetoid faces stared out into the dark.

"Now we learn just how much we trust your Archivist," Zanj said.

Hong leaned forward against the control panel. "She is the best of the 'faith, and this decryption is the work of our finest scholars and saints."

"That's what I'm afraid of." Zanj reached to turn off a glowing red subsystem Hong had activated with a careless elbow.

The chorus swelled. Viv reviewed the plan again. "I'll open a path into the wall. After that, we slip to Pasquarai, take the linchpin down fast, and—"

"Hush," Zanj said. "You're distracting me."

They drew closer: the wall's cracks were deeper than oceans, its peaks taller than solar flares. It had no surface—just knives going in, and in, and in. They approached, until its jagged points settled against the Star.

"Okay," Zanj said. "Your turn."

Viv reached for the viewscreen. It flowed around her touch, parted—and she stroked the rough surface of the wall. She drew her hand back before she realized the touch hurt; her finger was wet with blood. The viewscreen rippled shut and the wall rippled, too, its sharp points and waves melting, revolving, a whirlpool the size of a solar system drawing them in, and in, and down.

The cello notes swelled and deepened. The Star lurched forward, buffeted, tumbled down an endless pit whose walls blushed Cloud purple, and Viv could no longer tell what sort of space surrounded them. Somewhere, alarms rang. Somewhere, Hong and Gray were shouting. Somewhere, Zanj growled, and Xiara seized the controls.

And they slipped through. Out. Into the world, or something like it.

Damage report: systems red, the Star screaming, but they were alive, and they would heal. Gray was famished, Hong bruised from a fall; Xiara cursed the rudeness of Zanj's ship. "I'm never touching that thing again!" Zanj growled.

Only Viv was staring out the window.

"Guys," she said. "Look."

Below, in the endless night of the wall, an enormous station orbited a burning spark of star. Not an Imperial station, either. Rings of rock spun instead of crystal, green and growing, run with rivers, mountain peaks gleaming ice. Even calling it a station seemed wrong. This was a world. Someone had skinned a planet, turned it inside out, and made an orrery in the black.

Each ring cast bands of shadow on another's surface as it turned, and those artificial nights gleamed with cities, hearth fires, welcome fires, against the dark. Other rings of metal and crystal revolved within the rings of world, and ships darted between them all.

Viv had seen so many dead planets since she woke in High Carcereal, so many ruins and engines of war. This was a world alive.

"I know those rivers," Zanj said. "Those seas." Waterfalls joined some rings, impossibly, oceans running horizontal to merge with other oceans across empty space. "Those mountains. Those cities. What did she do?" She stabbed the console, and broadcasts crackled onto the speakers. Music, drum and electric zither bass; news updates; a joke Viv didn't understand, but the audience laughed. The babble of a culture. And nowhere any trace of screams. Zanj blinked up at her, at all of them. She looked like she was falling. "They're alive."

Before Viv could answer her, the broadcasts all cut out at once, in a crackle of static, replaced by a single voice with a flat affect Viv realized she had not heard since home: the boredom of a functioning bureaucrat. "Unidentified craft, power down your weapons and state your identity and intention."

Zanj was still staring, in no condition to reply. Hell. "Um. This is Captain Viv of the *Rising Star*." Zanj glared at her. She shrugged. "We've suffered damage coming through the wall. We come in peace. We'd, ah, we'd like to land? And look around?"

"Feeding you coordinates, *Rising Star*. Please stand by for air traffic control. Welcome to Pasquarai Station, in the name of Queen Zanj."

61

PASQUARAI STATION: SKIES shaded alien blue, cliffs terraced green and trailing vines, swift rivers, wheeling birds with wingspans meters broad, all seen through interlocking leaves of skyscraper-tall trees, their branches woven to support the cities of Zanj's leaping, climbing people. The Star settled onto a web of steel-firm vines strung between those branches, and its crew descended, Viv gingerly, Gray yawning, Xiara's eyes wide wonderment, Hong watchful, Zanj glaring as if she'd come down on the bad side of a mean-spirited joke.

"This can't be real," she said as she rolled the Star back into a staff.

Gray bit off a piece of the steel-taut vines, chewed experimentally, said, mouth full, "Tastes real to me."

"It's a trap. And don't eat our landing pad."

Gray shrugged, and swallowed.

Hong knelt where the ship had been, drew a tightly coiled device from within his robe, and unfolded it into a three-dimensional mandala of diamond gears that stuck in air, turned, and glowed, and wavered invisible. "There. Even if something happens to us, the 'fleet can follow the beacon in. I hope."

"It's beautiful." Xiara turned, arms wide, eyes up and bright, and the sparksun's light through the leaves gilded her with green.

"Of course it's beautiful," Zanj snapped. "I told you it was beautiful. But this is wrong. The trees are right, and the spaceport, but this place used to be a planet."

"Did you build that?" Viv pointed to an enormous spire—hard to judge its immensity without a proper gauge for distance, but she'd bet it was ten miles high, ringed with ships and drones and flying machines and a sculpted crystal mountain with, at its summit, hand to brow, Star in grip, glaring at the horizon, a colossal Zanj. Unscarred, uncrowned.

Zanj, scarred, crowned, glared suspicion at the world in general, and her diamond double in specific. "Does that look like something I'd build?"

No one answered. Viv, specifically, avoided her gaze.

Leaves rustled, and a shape flitted toward them from branch to branch above, moving with tail and all four limbs. It sprang from the canopy at last, somersaulting, falling as if gravity were a rude suggestion—a line of dark fur and tan cloth.

They split to a defensive formation: Hong drew his clubs, and the quicksilver veins on his skin pulsed; Gray gained a meter's height, his fingers lengthened into claws, his teeth coarsened to spades. Wheels turned in Xiara's eyes. Viv didn't even look at Zanj; she could too vividly imagine the bone-deep pop and, after it, bloodshed and ruin—before they understood what they'd found. "Stop," she said, hands out, "stand down, dammit," and marched forward, unarmed as ever, to meet the blur that landed now, with a fall-breaking tumble any gymnast would envy. It came to its feet: a young manalogue in a pressed tan coverall, brown fur streaked with gold, long tail coiled behind him, pencil behind one ear, clipboard in hand, watching Viv and her companions with fascination undimmed by her companions' threat of violence. "Wonderful!"

"That's one word for it," Viv said, and put out her hand. "Mind telling us where we've landed?"

He drew himself up to his full hunch, cocked his head to one side, and stroked his brow with the knuckles of his left fist. In that motion he looked for all the world like Zanj. "This is most irregular," he said. "Please understand: you are welcome here, and we cast no aspersions on your intent, as guests of Pasquarai Station. But for some centuries, we have received traffic solely from the other rings, not counting the Empress's raids, of course. Indeed, we thought any outsider's approach to our dear homeland impossible. As such we lack, shall we say, proper procedures. It is quite embarrassing. The Port Authority have sent a supervisor to address the specifics of your case, but in the meantime I'm afraid to confess I don't know how to complete the arrival forms." He licked the pencil tip, made a few quick notes. "Captain . . . Viv, is it?"

A lie wasn't the best way to start a relationship, but both silence and the truth posed their own set of problems. "You haven't heard of me?"

Those big gold eyes blinked once. "Most abject apologies, but no."

She put on a bluff she'd heard any number of young men use to shame people who didn't recognize the name of their latest venture. "The *Rising Star*'s the fastest blockade runner in the galaxy. We've slid through the gullets of black holes; we've escaped from collapsed Cloud, and out of the mouth of the Bleed." She stopped herself from adding *and we made the Kessel Run in twelve parsecs*. "Charting a course through the Citadel wall is all in a day's work for us." The flunky watched her so eagerly Viv almost felt bad—was he drinking it up, or giving her more rope to hang herself? "We've come to return your—" She stopped herself from saying *queen*. "—countrywoman." And she stepped aside, indicating . . .

Not Zanj. Not anymore. She had changed her face, grown paler, her hair grayed, her body longer, leaner. Only the scar and the crown remained. Zanj bowed, saying nothing, looking confused save for the momentary flick of her eyes to Viv: *Well?*

"We found her floating in space," Viv offered, smooth, "amid ruined worlds beyond the Tannheuser Gate, remembering nothing save her name. She traveled with us, and fought by our side. We tried to find out where she was from: a scrap here, a whisper there, led us to the wall. To you."

The flunky placed his pencil back behind his ear, and smoothed fur from his forehead again. His voice trembled with awe. "Lady, I seem to know you."

"And yet I do not know myself." Zanj chose her words like an old woman crossing ice might choose her steps—Viv almost believed she was really so lost and alone. "I think I was called Seng."

"I am First Orderly Yish." He approached her slowly, wondering, and reached out to lay a hand against her temple, as if she were something holy. Before he touched her, he remembered duty, propriety, his clipboard. He hopped back, gathered himself into an approximation of officialdom, and bowed. "We thought all who lived beyond the wall were lost."

"You were wrong," Zanj replied. "But I do not know where I am, and I do not know this place."

"Of course," Yish said, overcome by wonder: "Of course. I did not mean— Lady, I apologize for assuming you knew what transpired in your absence. Come. Come all of you. You are Pasquarai's first visitors in generations, and you should know our story."

He darted ahead of them, climbing branches, leaping from limb to limb, always talking, while they labored below on walkways and bridges of woven vines that must have been built for those too hurt, too old, too young, to climb. The trees descended beneath, limb after limb, far as Viv could see, until their trunks converged in shadow, and they rose overhead, attenuating to verdant green shot through with light. Doors in tree bark opened and closed to admit more swinging, chattering dockhands; gold and silver vehicles stitched rainbow wakes through the sky. Birds sang, not each to each but in chorus, their voices melded with deeper whistles Viv had taken, at first, for wind, for the creaking of boughs. All worked together, reinforced itself, nature's sounds welded to song.

"We are the children of Queen Zanj, who saved us three times. We owe her all we have: she joined the independent gaggle of Pasquarai into a people, she taught us to defend ourselves, and she defeated Death on our behalf." Viv wasn't the only one among their party who looked at Zanj with questions after that, but Zanj only answered with a shrug. "Then she set out to fight one still greater enemy: the Empress who eats worlds. She harried her. She raised up a great fleet and strove to cast her down with all her immense might and all her still greater cunning." So far Zanj nodded along. They climbed a rising stair around the trunk toward a massive branch from which hung an observation dome, apparently carved from a single piece of amber. "This war came to a head three thousand years ago: all forces on both sides arrayed, a trap set for the Empress, her defeat certain, if her defeat was possible at all. But the Empress did not fall in that battle. The tides turned against us, but our Queen could not abandon her people—so when the Empress caught her, Her Majesty left a shell in the Empress's grip, a copy, a skin, and fled the wreck of battle, and came home."

Zanj stopped, stared. "That's not possible."

Caught up in the story, Yish did not seem to notice his audience's reaction. "For you or I, perhaps, but not impossible for Zanj. Our Queen could not defeat the Empress, but she could protect us nonetheless. She had uncovered a weakness in the Empress's Citadel, a nexus in the lines of force that power its wall. If Queen Zanj moved our world into the wall itself, and wrapped us around that nexus, the Empress's defense would become our own. The Bleed could not find us here, and the Empress could not strike us with her full might, lest we destroy her wall and expose her to the Bleed. So Queen Zanj, in infinite cunning, brought us here, and kept us safe these three thousand years, during which she has ruled peacefully and well. From time to time the Empress sends her fleet against us, but she cannot deploy her fullest strength within the wall without exposing herself to the Bleed, and again and again Queen Zanj and our own ships have prevailed." His voice swelled with bureaucratic pride. "I myself have coordinated the launch of our fighter waves. It is a small service to Pasquarai, but all service is joy."

Zanj's face had flushed a strangled shade of purple. "Leading you all into retreat? Holding a siege against the Empress? Hiding in the wall? That doesn't sound like—like a Queen."

"She has guarded us, and we have thrived."

"It's a coward's strategy. You pose no threat to the Empress, sheltered here. She just hasn't bothered to crush you yet. She bides her time. Your Queen's afraid, and Zanj was never afraid."

Yish dropped to the stair before them; he clutched his clipboard tight, wrinkling the pages of his forms with his thumb. "Sister. Please." His voice sank to a whisper, and his eyes flicked up, and over, into the riot of green and glory. Viv followed his glance but saw nothing at first—then noticed a brilliant yellow bird with a long tail, silent, staring with its weird dark avian eye. The birdsong, Viv realized, had stopped. "You have been away for a long time, and you do not know our ways. Queen Zanj has done what she has done for our sake, in our defense, and we must not question her. We live in comfort and safety here, on the edge of a deep pit full of tigers. If the nexus should fall, our world would shatter with it—and as the Empress sends her fleet against us, she also sends her subtle agents, her spies and informers. You come in the company of strangers, and your story rings of truth—no agent would concoct such a fancy, nor would they arrive in so obvious a manner. But the Empress's whispers are powerful. A mere three hundred years ago, even our Queen's own advisors, Feng of the Right, Aunj of the Left, Osso Skysinger—the Empress turned them all. They rose against Zanj, and our Queen cast them down into the depths beneath her tower. In her infinite mercy she brings them forth every twenty years and begs them to recant their treachery, accept her forgiveness—and every twenty years they spurn her. So, sister, welcome home. But for your own sake, listen as you learn our ways. And never, ever question the Queen. Do you understand?" He held out one hand, imploring.

The birdsong and the wind's music kept silent. Ships slipped past. Viv watched the confusion work through Zanj's body, followed by anger, followed by a worrying stillness. She had found her people whole, when she expected to find their bones. But a shadow lay over them, a shadow that wore her face and name.

"I do." Zanj reached out, and took his hand.

Yish sagged in relief—and as he sagged, Zanj pulled him toward her, spun him round, and caught his neck in the crook of her elbow. The Star, shrunk needle-fine, she pressed against his throat, dimpling the skin.

"Now," Zanj said, her voice vicious low. "You said your Queen placed her generals in prison. Tell me where."

62

THEY LEFT YISH trussed in one of the storage gourds that seemed to pass for closets here, unconscious thanks to a bit of contact poison Gray claimed would wear off in an hour and leave the young gold-furred Pasquaran with no aftereffects worse than a hangover. Zanj locked the gourd, and waved them downstairs toward a vine bridge.

As they crossed, hundreds of meters above the invisible ground, Viv asked her, whispering in case the birds could hear: "What the hell are you doing?"

"That's not me," Zanj said with a nod to the glass tower that bore her shape, invisible now through the trees.

"It looks like you."

"It's not," she snarled. "Whoever the hell that is, she's turned my people into the Empress's bodyguards. Look at these trees, so managed, so even. One branch every five meters, regular as clocks."

"So?"

Zanj whirled on her. "These are mandalons! They should grow so dense even you could climb them! There should be bugs the length of your arm. There should be karshvines and zombie ants and hungry flowers, and instead there's this mess, with all its edges rounded down."

"You were gone a long time, Zanj. And they've been stuck here all that while. They might have changed things."

"The trees? The sky? You saw that bird, Viv. You saw it looking at us. Who was that, behind its eyes?"

Zanj fell silent. The bridge creaked beneath them, and wind rustled leaves against leaves. Hong and Xiara breathed. Gray didn't, not that he ever did unless he had a particular point to make. But aside from the whir of distant machinery, speeder lifts and who knew what other nonsense, the woosh of landing ships and passing speeders, the trees stood songless and quiet. They might have been petrified a thousand years ago, turned to stone, then painted by artists with dead, steady hands and slender brushes to mimic life. A good painter could make you think their canvases were moving.

Utter irrational fear trickled down Viv's neck and down the hollows that flanked her spine. She did not know why at first. She turned from Zanj to the forest and back in search of anything out of place, and found nothing. Her fear grew. "You might be wrong. We just got here. They could help us."

"Oh, I'm sure they would." One corner of Zanj's lip curled up, completely without humor. "Haven't you been paying attention, Viv? They'd be oh so happy to bring us in. To wrap themselves around us. They'd strangle us to death before we realized it wasn't a hug. I don't know what sickness got this place while I was gone, but it's not me." Only at the end did she sound desperate. The rest sagged with the weight of truth.

"She's right," Xiara said. "I can feel the station. There are so many people here, all their minds woven through the Cloud. And they're being managed. I don't think even they know. It guides what they can see, it binds what they can know. And it's looking for us."

"Do you believe her, at least?" Zanj asked.

Viv didn't want to. That was the truth. She wanted to believe they had come through the wall to safety, that Zanj's people waited here to receive and help them, that whoever ruled them would understand the danger the Empress posed, and turn against her for once and all. That this, at least, would be easy.

Couldn't they have landed, for once, on a non-shitty planet?

Hong set his hand on her arm. "Viv," he said. His voice sounded even, and cautious. "The birds."

Of course, she almost snapped back, of course we can't hear the birds, Zanj said that already, but Hong was not the kind of person to repeat the obvious. And he was staring out and up, off the bridge, into the trees.

She had seen nothing out of place in the forest before, nothing that did not belong. But birds belonged in a forest. Small, bright-colored birds a passing glance might take at first for flowers. Immense black scaly-eyed unblinking birds with carrion beaks, flaking bark off the great trees as they shifted weight. Tiny almost-hummingbirds, sculling wings invisible. Sleek owl-like birds with heads turned at odd angles, their great dark front-facing saucer eyes fixed on the bridge.

On Viv, and on her friends.

If she had a flashlight she could have swept it through them and watched the jewel glints flick on and off as the birds blinked away the brilliance. If they did blink. But she realized with a chill that the birds would not have blinked, that they and the mind that guided them would match the light glare for glare—would have stared into the sun, not the fake sparksun in the station's sky but the real fierce sun of Viv's lost Earth, until they boiled. The will that led them was that strong.

"Okay." Viv had to swallow to loosen her clenched throat before she could say anything more. "You have a point."

As one, the birds fluffed and spread their wings.

"What now?"

"Now," Zanj said, "we fight our way to whoever's done this."

"And then?"

She shrugged, as if there were no simpler question in the world. "Then we hit them until they stop."

Before Viv could think of a response, the birds attacked.

63

THE BIRDS TORE through the forest. They did not call or cry, but their wings beat furiously like dry leaves tossed in a hurricane. Viv curled herself over Xiara, covered her with her arms, and she was vaguely aware of Gray shifting form before the birds struck. Talons and beaks drew bright, painful scratches across her arms and shoulders and back. Nails caught and pulled her short hair. For that first gross minute she only heard wingbeats, and the creak of tendons against the wind.

The worst, for Viv, was the smell of them, acrid oil and down and that weird tang of old paper. That smell, that taste, that was the birds inside her. Airborne bits of them filtered into her as she breathed.

Then it was over. The birds swept past, and Viv and the others were running, over the bridge and up a corkscrew ramp as the forest around them moved, vines uncoiling like snakes from tree branches to slither toward them. She took stock as they sprinted through the wood: Zanj in the front, unharmed; Gray in the rear, shifting back from the shell he'd grown to shelter them into his customary, more mobile form. Hong bore a host of minor scrapes, and one deep cut on his arm. And Xiara—

"Don't do that again," Xiara called back over her shoulder.

"What?"

"Protect me," she said. "How am I supposed to save you, if you keep saving me first?"

Viv did not answer her except with a grin. That grin made all the difference when the column of birds circled back—Gray's shell saved them long enough to reach the lee of an enormous mandalon tree—and it made all the difference when vines fell from above and snared Viv's neck before Hong's clubs burned through them. Because if Xiara could grin, and take umbrage at being saved, they were still fine. Even if all Pasquarai was out to kill them.

A second wave of birds struck them from the side. Something wren-sized slammed into Viv's temple. Small nails scraped her cheek; she caught the wren's tiny body and threw it off the platform into space; it whirled and whirled, wings flaring in a mass of other wings, and she did not see if it caught its balance before it struck ground.

She looked up then, and out into the canopy. There were more birds coming, and other things, too. Jagged-jawed centipedes the length of her arm. Red scurrying carpets that must be ants, spanning gaps from tree to tree with bridges of their writhing bodies. And behind them all, Pasquarans in black uniform swinging from branch to branch, slung with weaponry, their movements in perfect time. Viv did not need to stare into their eyes to know they'd have the same glassy look as the birds'. Nobody home. Busy signal. This body is otherwise engaged, please try again later.

How would it feel to be used like that? Would you rail, would you scream? Poor officious eager Yish had seemed happy with his lot, excited to share Pasquarai with guests. He might call it an honor to be taken up like a tool and used, he might even enjoy being held by some mind he believed greater and more noble than his own, take more shelter in it the greater the atrocity he was driven to commit—free to enjoy the visceral thrill of flesh gobbed on his hands while feeling a just and proper revulsion at his deeds. He had no choice. This was not his will. He merely acted out the grim, irresistible judgment of Another.

Viv did not know these people. She tried to imagine her friends, her lovers, this blank-eyed, this willingly surrendered. In some cases, she did not have to imagine. She had lost cousins and coworkers to the last round of hysteria back home, people she'd known and even almost trusted, who refused to see what was coming until far, far too late. After the dust cleared, after things bottomed out, a few repented. Most slept on, and refused to talk about what they'd been, what they'd become. So things got worse.

She had a sudden terrified vision of what that would look like after a thousand years, or three thousand, a culture grown like a kitten in a bottle, its claws curling back into its flesh, its bones warped so it could not stand. And then she turned right, and saw Zanj under wire tension, firm, and understood her rage.

"Can you fight off a forest?"

Zanj tightened her fists. Her tail twitched. She looked so ready to try. "Not without tipping my hand. I don't want whoever's running this show to recognize me yet."

"We need to get out of here." Blood trickled down her scalp.

"Stay behind me," Zanj growled, and jumped.

"I'D IMAGINED SOMETHING more subtle," Viv said after their hijacked flatbed speeder broke through the forest canopy.

Zanj ignored her and gunned the engines. Viv's seat belt slipped out of her hands—good thing she didn't need one in the chase that followed, as they smashed through vines and foliage and veered at high g to avoid the interdictor guns of the speeders that erupted from the trees below.

Viv, under pressure, tended to resort to sarcasm.

That said, her lack of seat belt turned out to be an asset when hoverbelt-clad security personnel leapt aboard from a flanking speeder to rush the controls. They moved with lurching puppet-speed, their guns and eyes level, and Viv appreciated the freedom to dodge and duck and fight back without having to unhook herself first.

Gray spread his arms gelatinous and wide, snared three of the cops, and dumped them overboard. Hong fought two, his face smooth save for a half twist of smile. Viv kneed one of them in the crotch, which worked well enough. Xiara caught the back of his uniform and threw him off the speeder.

"Shouldn't we lie low?" Viv shouted to Zanj. "Plan our attack?"

"No." Zanj did not turn from the controls. "This ends now."

Birds billowed from the forest, cries and calls and trills merging to a wail, and Zanj pulled their speeder into a sheer climb. Viv caught the back of a chair to keep from falling. Branches curled between them and the sky, but Zanj struck the trees with the Star and they careened through.

Viv's grip slipped, she tumbled, and Gray caught her. They broke free into the ring-split sky—where four massive goose-winged craft circled, each emblazoned with a sunburst shield insignia. They looked official and violent even before they opened fire.

"The longer we stay," Zanj explained as she cursed and veered and dodged, "the more time this place has to get us. Now it doesn't know who we are, or what we can do. But it's learning." A shot from one of the goose-wings caught their speeder in the side. The lurch would have tumbled them all down into the trees had Gray not spread himself into a net to keep them on board. Zanj tried to level the speeder, but the best she could do was keep it listing to the left, trailing smoke. It flew straight—more or less. Zanj swore. A goosewing drew behind them, gained altitude; its belly guns swiveled into firing position.

Hong stood, one leg wrapped through his safety belt, his clubs drawn, and waited. His robe flapped in the wind, his expression serene, head cocked as if listening. Before the goosewing's guns spoke, his arms began to move.

His clubs met the guns' plasma in midair, and when the blinding flash cleared, Viv saw—only saw, seconds would pass before she could hear again—two goosewings dropping toward the canopy, gushing smoke and trailing fireworks displays of sparks. Hong blinked, serenity broken to surprise, his face caked with charcoal, his robes flared out at jagged angles from his body, his clubs crackling with current—but whole.

"Yish said—"

"Whoever's running this show," Zanj growled with an angry jerk of her head toward the spire drawing ever closer, "she's not me." Zanj hauled back on the controls, but still their speeder lost altitude. She yanked the stick one last time, then punched the control panel, which shattered.

"I don't see how that was supposed to improve our situation," Viv said.

"Hold on." She unbuckled herself, judged distance to the nearest goosewing, and jumped.

She landed out of sight, leaving Viv to ponder the smashed controls, the rapidly approaching tree line, and her own surging white-knuckled indignation, for which she was, on a detached level, grateful, since it drowned out the terror. She tugged on the stick, which responded even less to her than it had to Zanj, looked up again, and saw bodies rain from the goosewing onto which Zanj had vaulted; it surged forward, swept beneath their own damaged craft, and, on its bridge, at the stick, Zanj raised one hand, inviting: jump!

Arriving on the goosewing's deck—Gray threw Viv across the gap, with her grudging permission, and Hong caught her—did little to improve matters, unfortunately, as deadly metal rocs screamed across the sky toward them. Military craft. And, though the Zanjspire towered mountainous high, they were still miles away from its root.

"The imposter," Zanj shouted over her shoulder, over the wind, over the sound of blaster fire, "threw my friends in jail because they stood up to her! Does that sound like something I'd do?"

"Yes," Viv admitted.

"Definitely," Gray said.

Hong nodded.

"If you were in a bad mood," Xiara said. "Or a good one. Or just a mood, generally."

"I hate you all." It was the most lighthearted Zanj had sounded since landing. The rocs fired; Zanj danced left, danced right, but even their misses singed the air, and left Viv coughing. "Okay. Dammit. Hold on, I'll nab one of those birds."

"Don't." Xiara opened the wheels of her eyes, and spread silver traces across her skin. One hand crooked clawlike and with a snarl she lifted it, fast, as if upending a table. As one, the rocs veered at right angles into the sky and scattered, spinning frantic for control. She slumped back into the chair, exhausted; Hong, impressed, offered her a hand of congratulation, which she clutched as if it were the only thing keeping her in her seat.

That was when the artillery opened fire.

The goosewing lasted longer than Viv expected, thanks to Zanj's evasive action and to an uncharacteristically wild barrage from the ground guns. Perhaps the animating intelligence hadn't expected them to get this far; perhaps it wasn't used to artillery, or didn't want to blast them out of the sky without learning where they'd come from, and how. But one volley caught the goosewing's underside, and the control panel blared warnings, and Gray gathered them close and wrapped them in a bubble of his glittering substance, and when the speeder blew they soared out and down on wings he made to land, Graystuff flowing from their limbs, in a crater at the Zanjspire's foot.

Zanj found her feet first, and Viv, to her own surprise, found hers second—Hong and Xiara struggled to rise, both exhausted by the battle, and Gray was still gathering himself into a pool at the crater's deepest point, digesting soil and grass as he pulled himself together.

Viv's ears rang, but she heard running feet, the grind of heavy machines, speeder-whine. Soldiers ringed them at the crater's lip, weapons drawn, aimed, wary. Tails twitched. Even the artillery pieces and the gunships overhead seemed to edge back as Zanj's glare raked them.

The scarred corner of Zanj's mouth curled up in something that was not at all a smile. Her eyes glinted. "That's it. We're done playing."

She drew the Star. The seeming she'd worn melted away, and she bloomed with silver edges, her teeth long and curved and glittering, revealed, hungry, furious.

She bent herself to kill.

The gunships veered away. The artillery powered down.

The soldiers fell—not dead, but to their knees.

Zanj blinked.

The ranks of kneeling soldiers rippled, and one armored Pasquaran emerged, with that slow, even puppet walk. She removed her helmet—and at the sight of the scarred, glass-eyed face beneath, Zanj's mouth opened, soundless, as if ready to answer, though she could not speak. Her burning eyes widened: in confusion, yes, but recognition, too. "Avoun?"

"She's here," said the voice that wore the mask of the woman's face. One of her fingers tapped her temple, a little too hard. "Still inside the skull, though you've confused her horribly. She's General Avoun, now, of course, not the child whose life you saved so many years ago. A good soldier. You might have killed her, if not for me."

"Let her go." A growl rose in Zanj's chest. "Let them all go."

"Why?" A gentle, teasing voice, comfortable, slight and sly. "You've caused no end of trouble, running about, disturbing people who only want to live their lives, do their jobs, get laid, and sleep. If you'd announced yourself, we could have avoided all this mess. But here we are." She gestured to the arrayed weaponry, to the crater. "I'll have to paper over the excitement, and make them forget. All in a day's work."

"I'll kill you," Zanj said. "What you've done to my people, to my world—"

"Don't be so hasty," the voice replied. "You don't understand. But you will."

Zanj's grip tightened on the Star.

The voice laughed, but the laugh was only sound. It did not reach the lines of Avoun's face or the blank planes of her eyes. "Let's not fight, Zanj. There's no percentage in it. You could kill this little one, sure, and her friends, maybe thousands of your own people before they overwhelmed you. But you don't want that, and neither do I. You've known Avoun since she was a pup. You've saved all of their lives at one time or another. I'm just trying to watch out for you, and for our children." She lowered her arms. "Come to the throne. Let's talk face-to-face. I'll not touch you or your friends on the way. No tricks. Just a conversation."

The silver edges blurred Zanj's features, obscured her scars. Viv could read her only by rough signs, by set of mouth, by shape of eyes, by the coiling and uncoiling of her tail—but she knew Zanj well enough by now to trace some meaning even there.

Zanj held her weapon braced for war. But to Viv she looked cautious—almost, impossibly, afraid.

"Fight them," the voice said, "or don't. Either way you'll end up face-to-face with me. But if you fight, you'll have to kill our dear Avoun first. She's loyal, you understand. She'd defend me to the death, of her own will. It would break her heart if you were the one to kill her. But who knows. She might think it was an honor to die at your hand. She always wanted to grow up to be like you."

Viv waited. The soldiers knelt, their guns down, but not far away.

Zanj lowered the Star. "Let's talk."

The general's mouth approached a smile. "Good," she said. "Come on up, Sister. I'm waiting."

64

TEN MILES WAS a long way to rise.

Avoun led them into the Zanjspire with a full guard, guns bristling, swords sharp, but all, for now, sheathed. Within, the spire was a jungle stretched vertical, aflutter with jewel-bright birds, draped with roots and spreading branches, platforms hung at sculpted intervals for work or rest. Pasquarans climbed through the boughs, or lounged, or ascended stairs and vines, up and up toward the light of the false sun. Bark and root and branch and vine darted with gold, leaves dripped dew, flowers swelled with pollen that glimmered when the light struck sidelong: information, output, for the bees to gather while Zanj's people tended, grafted, pruned. Everywhere was green, and none of the gathered Pasquarans looked at them, or at the soldiers. Their eyes tracked past.

Viv shuddered, despite the heat.

"Zanj," she said. "She called you sister." No response. "What did she mean?"

Still nothing.

Their escort reached a clearing at the spire's heart, stepped onto a spiral of black, flat stones, and they began to rise.

The forest blurred, vines and sunning snakes and flowers blending to rainbows, though Viv felt only a slight gathering of weight into her feet. Her breath came shallow, ozone tinged, and when she tried to raise her hand the air felt thick. Out past the branches, through the spire's transparent walls, the rings upon rings of Pasquarai Station turned.

Viv's heart split in two.

The first half focused on causes and consequence. What the hell was going on here? None of this technology felt Imperial. Not enough crystals, not enough light. Zanj had recognized Avoun, even after three thousand years' imprisonment. And while the soldiers arrayed around them marched in eerie unison, the other Pasquarans seemed to be working, playing, un-controlled, or at least less obviously controlled. A mother chased children through the canopy; two older women played a board game that looked like chess. They flitted past, so brief they were more dreams than people. After a running firefight outside their tower, there were no news reports, no screens for punters to gape at wreckage. They let the station guide their minds away from conflict. How much had they looked away from here? And for how long?

Her mind's second half reviewed her friends: Hong, evaluating, calm; Gray, unsure. Xiara squeezed Viv's hand. Her features were tight, her lips pressed together, a cat at bay. "They're all part of it," she said. "The station. The system."

"Can you stop it?"

She shook her head. "I could break those ships that chased us. I could stop this lift. But when I try to break what's controlling them, I slip off. It's sealed. They're too . . . themselves."

"They're not," Zanj said. Zanj watched the world, Avoun, the Pasquar-ans they passed, as she might have watched the stump of a recently ampu-tated hand. "They've been made into something else."

Viv was used to this split-heart feeling. Most of the time the calculative half bubbled out, seizing control. The interpersonal details, your own emo-tional well-being or your friends', could wait until after you figured out how to solve the problem at hand.

It felt new, and weird, and un-American, for the friend stuff to take pri-ority over galactic conquest. But then, doing things the other way had led to galactic conquest in the first place, which was the whole problem. So. "We're right here with you," she told Zanj, wishing, as she'd spent a lot of time wishing in recent weeks, that she'd sunk more skill points into this sort of thing.

"Thank you," Zanj said. "This could get bad."

The canopy approached: broad, flat leaves, branches intertwined to frame a roof. She braced for impact, but the canopy writhed away to let them pass, and writhed back beneath their feet as they slowed and stopped. The ten-sion that held them relaxed, and Viv yipped as she fell to the floor of leaves—but she did not pass through. The leaves bore her weight with no more give than a thick-pile carpet.

They stood before the immense transparent curve of an eye in the Zanj-spire's face, with the false sun overhead and Pasquarai Station below. High branches flourished with flowers and fruit; glowing grapes hung from thick vines. A dais rose to the level of the eye's pupil, and on that dais there stood a throne, and beside that throne stood a figure limned with gold and sky.

"Hello there," Zanj said.

But not the Zanj by Viv's side, who was growling now, who had dropped into a crouch, who had drawn the Star.

Another Zanj stood on the dais beside the throne.

Like Zanj, but unlike: wearing a tunic and trousers of luxurious green, she stood unbowed, gold eyes glistening without a trace of suspicion or anger from a face that had never felt the Empress's melting touch. She jumped from the dais to the floor and walked toward them, her eyes on Zanj, her smile broad and sincere, a smile that had never been betrayed. The rush of enthusiasm carried her within arm's reach of Zanj. She only stopped when her chest clunked against the tip of the Star.

"Sister," she said. "Please. Let's not be crude."

Viv looked from Zanj to Zanj. There were differences, in dress, in scar, in bearing. She would never mistake one of these women for the other. But they were the same. Watching them both at once felt like trying to have a conversation while a nearby speaker played back a second's-delayed echo of her words.

"I don't know who you are," Zanj said, "but let them go, or I'll core you like a star. I'll skin you and I'll make a necklace of your tail."

"Zanj," the Queen said, her arms still wide, her expression open and overflowing with a generosity of which Viv had never imagined Zanj capable, a voice that did not seem to recognize that her own double was holding the greatest weapon in the galaxy a few inches from her heart. "You must recognize me."

"Who are you?" Zanj bared her teeth, and her hackles rose. Her grimace twisted her scar. "What is this?"

"Don't you remember?" The Queen reached for Zanj, imploring, though the Star parted them. "We had to fight the Empress, but we couldn't bear to abandon Pasquarai. So we split. Two copies, Sister. One to make war, one to save the peace." The eagerness in those eyes, the joy parting to sorrow, the hand reaching now for her scarred face. "How much did She hurt you? Zanj, I'm so, so sorry."

"Liar!" Zanj roared, and pushed the Queen back; she flew, somersaulted, landed on her feet. "I don't know who you are, or how you've done it. You've trapped my people in your web, but you won't trap me."

MAX GLADSTONE

The Queen shook her head. "There's no trap here, Zanj. Just . . . management. I take care of them, like we always meant to do."

"By controlling them?"

"They've been at peace for three thousand years, ever since I brought them here, where they would be safe. Do you really think they could survive under siege all this time, out there beyond the wall? They're happy and soft as children here, protected from the Empress and the Bleed, from all that might harm them in the galaxy. They do what they want, and I make sure nothing goes too wrong. And they cheer me for it. They cheer us."

"I never split," Zanj snarled. "I have always been myself. I needed all my strength to fight the Empress, and when I rose against her she broke me, scarred me, and locked me in the heart of a star to burn. The whole time, I dreamed of revenge, and of coming home."

"You were here, in me. You were here all along."

"I would have remembered."

The Queen's voice was calm, compassionate. "I can only imagine how much you suffered at her hands. Of course you wanted revenge. Of course you dreamed of coming home. You forgot what you had to forget, to survive."

"I forgot nothing. What you've done here is against everything we stood for. We took these people to the stars. We led them. We did not crush them."

"They would be dead by now, if not for us." The Queen advanced, hands out. "Surely you can see that."

"If you take one more step, I will kill you."

The Queen kept still. "What proof can I offer, that you will accept?"

Zanj's nostrils flared. The air around her shimmered with restrained violence. Viv wanted to touch her. The wound the Queen had given Zanj was hidden, but Viv could smell the blood. Zanj's hands tightened on the Star. Nobody who was not Zanj moved. Hong, and Gray, and Xiara, and Viv waited to help. If they could help.

Zanj cast the Star to the leaves between them. It did not clatter—it fell and lay flat, with a thud like a boulder fallen into loam. "Even the Empress could not lift the Star against my will. Pick it up."

The Queen stepped forward. Knelt. "It's been so long since I saw this," she said. She wrapped her fingers around the Star, savoring the touch. Then she stood, as if the weapon weighed nothing at all. She tossed it from hand to hand. Spun it.

Viv could not bear to watch Zanj's face.

The Queen set the Star back down and withdrew one step, two. Zanj mirrored each step, drawing closer, her gait clumsy. She sank to her knees beside the Star, and lifted it as easily as the Queen, wondering. Her eyes were so very dry.

The Queen spoke again, her voice still Zanj's, with the hard edges worn by centuries of rule. "I spent three thousand years wondering if you had died. If she broke your mind and bent you against us, if you would arrive someday warped into my dark mirror, to destroy your people and all we've built. You must have been so afraid for Pasquarai. But here we are: whole, thriving, safe." She reached out her hand. "You suffered alone for so long. But you need not suffer any more. Join me. Let our forked paths combine. I'll remember the depth of your suffering, and you'll have these three thousand years of rule, of peace, of Pasquarai. You need not bear those scars forever."

Zanj stared up at the Queen, and Zanj stared down at her broken mirror, kneeling. The Queen offered her hand, palm up. Viv could not breathe or speak. Zanj did not look back to Viv for advice, or reassurance. That was good. Viv did not know what she would say.

Zanj's gaze dropped to the staff she held.

The Queen reached down.

Then Zanj stood, and spun, and batted the Queen through the window.

65

THE QUEEN SLID to a stop in midair. Shattered glass rained onto the distant station, and high-altitude winds tore into the throne room, ripping flowers from their stems and filling the chamber with a whirl of leaves and projectile fruit. Viv tackled Xiara to save her from a flying melon; Hong dove for cover, and Gray shifted himself into cover for Hong to dive behind. Zanj stood unmoved in the chaos, her eyes aflame, the crown a black bar on her forehead.

And the Queen, opposite, above her world, spoke. Her voice cut clear through the roil of wind and crashing glass. "So, she turned you after all." Dismayed. As if she'd worked out the disappointing answer to a puzzle. "My dear self. I hoped we'd be better than this. But I suppose no one's immune to time and pain." Her shoulders slumped. She grew facets of her own, gold against Zanj's silver but no less glistening, no less sharp. And in her hand, after a confusion of warped space, she held a bar of nuclear fire fierce as sunlight made solid. "You are my own heart. Somewhere, deep down, I hope you understand that, because I love you, I cannot let you break what we have built here."

With a snarl, Zanj marched to the broken window, and shouted up: "Listen to yourself." Around, to the couriers in cover, back to Viv and the rest: "I don't sound like that, do I? All smarm and duty and long damn words?" Back to the Queen, back to alt-Zanj in the sky: "You don't talk like me. You rule to make your friends afraid. Three thousand years of pain didn't break me. Three thousand years of power would never turn me into you."

"I remember being you," the Queen replied, strong, sad, radiant in the sky. "A wanderer for centuries, a fighter beyond hope of victory. You did not guide, nor did you build. It took me so long to learn that art. Friends became enemies on the way; I hurt myself again and again, and those closest to me. I discovered fault lines in our people where I'd seen unity before. When your heart's in the stars, when your soul's on the front lines of a distant war, you don't realize what you have left undone behind. Home is a dream, and only dreams survive on dreams alone. The real world takes real work. I broke our people to reforge them, to save them. I will not let you break them again."

"To save them? They used to sail the stars. You've locked them up, built walls around them, and called that safe."

Viv recognized that tone of voice and remembered another throne room, Zanj hanging from emerald bonds, remembered staring into her own face and learning, with all the surety of a fist to the gut, what she was capable of. Not even what she might have done—what she had done, in a life just shades different from her own, and what that meant for who she thought she was. She had felt so hollow then, her self a porcelain shell cleverly painted and worked to seem solid, but which, when cracked, held nothing. If she could become the Empress, what was *she*, beneath her stories of herself?

"They are safe," the Queen said.

Viv saw Zanj get it: the simple chalkboard diagram of Viv and the Empress, and Zanj, standing before the Queen. Viv had tutored kids for pocket money in college, and she'd always been bad at this part: watching thoughts assemble like congregating clouds as the air grew heavy with the right answer, waiting through all that for the student to reach her own conclusions, rather than just saying *rain*.

Zanj glared at her golden unscarred self in the sky.

And she sprang.

The first five, six, ten exchanges took place at a speed Viv couldn't follow, save by crashes of thunder when the Star crossed the golden staff. When their weapons met, Zanj and the Queen held still for fractions of a second, each reflected off the other's shining form, glinting off the curve of the other's teeth. Fire and fury and silver and gold. Who was lightning, and who the thunderclap?

The others all stared. Of course they could see fast enough to watch. Viv felt a pang of envy, before Gray set his hand on hers, and her skin burned as a needle too fine to feel as sharp slid in, and lava spread through her veins and time passed very slowly all of a sudden. Now, in the eons between her heartbeats, she could see the still-blurred mess of Zanj at war with Zanj.

They crashed, orbited, crashed again, lines of light in the sky, and as they fought, and cast one another down, and flew up to fight again, forms swelling and changing and dividing, Viv, who had not quite bought the golden Zanj's story, felt her doubts ebb.

They fought the same. Not "with the same moves," or "with the same style," or even "with the same ferocity." Their movements echoed each other. Zanj struck the sun-bright staff aside and jabbed to her opposite number's neck, met not with a parry but with a backbend that became a kick, and ten beats later in the dance her golden double tried precisely the same move, and Zanj responded in the same way. They raked with claws, and strangled with tails, and kicked and bit for jugulars and snatched at one another's staffs with their feet; they landed on the Zanjspire, scuttled across their enormous statue's face, shattered her nose and burst together through the broad palm of her hand.

A fight is a jungle. Two people dive into it together, and each seeks her own path through, running down known trails, avoiding pits and perils she knows, falling victim to those she fails to guess. Training matters, and raw physical ability: a stronger, harder, fleeter body can bear more, run faster. We can climb that tree, we can swing along that vine over this quicksand here. Tools make a difference, too: a machete to cut through undergrowth, a bomb to blast the tangled mess to rubble. Learning how to fight is learning how to navigate jungles in the abstract: to recognize common shapes, which paths tend to lead through and why, what traps are, what water's pure and what only seems pure at a glance. But each jungle grows anew between the two combatants. They are the territory, and its navigators.

Zanj and Zanj halted in the sky, staff crossed with staff, red eyes into red eyes.

"Sister," the Queen said, "one might think I'd spent three thousand years killing our friends, rather than saving them."

"You didn't have the decency to kill them," Zanj replied. "You bent them so they can't look up. And what did you do with those who wouldn't bend?"

"Most do, sooner or later. Sometimes it takes years, sometimes centuries. But the number who resist is always smaller than you think. I care for all my children."

Zanj hissed. "Maybe the Empress broke you. Maybe you did it to yourself. But either way, this is where you end."

The Queen in her battle glory somehow still looked sad. "I hoped we wouldn't have to do this."

And then she poured past Zanj's guard, into her.

Zanj landed in a heap in the throne room, curled around her stomach, cursing, screaming. Her silver battle-skin bubbled and burst, and the pus that flowed from those boils ran gold. Her teeth gnashed and ground. The gold spread slowly, viciously, rippling down her arms, trickling together to form a net over her silver skin that spread, curling over her lips, down her ears, into her eyes. Viv ran for Zanj, unsure what she could do, knowing only that she had to help—but glass-eyed Pasquaran soldiers grabbed her and threw her to the floor.

Hong and Xiara made it farther, Hong barreling through power-armored guards until Avoun locked her sword against his clubs. Xiara slipped past them both, her arm outstretched, the pilot marks awake beside her eyes, and as she neared, the gold shuddered and began to fade from Zanj's field, to run back into the wounds from which it poured. But one of Zanj's hands was already covered in gold, and it reached up, shuddering, unsure, fighting its own movement from the inside. The hand clenched into a fist.

Xiara dropped so fast that fist might have closed around her brain.

Gray was there next, tossing guards left and center, a whirl of fire battering the golden shell that enclosed Zanj. One Zanj, he could almost fight. Two, with all Pasquarai Station behind them—that, he could not face.

Viv surged against the soldiers, wriggled free, kicked, felt something in her ankle give. But the gold closed over Zanj's eyes, and the light faded.

Zanj levered herself to her feet, leaning against the Fallen Star, breathing heavy, shuddering all through, kitten weak. She still wore the crown, and Viv felt a stab of hope. But when Zanj looked up, her eyes were the Queen's closed-door eyes, and her face was free of scars.

And that smile, that toothy slantwise smile, that was not the smile of a bad puppeteer, the smile she had forced on Avoun's face. This smile was wholly itself, and wholly in control, with a mother's sadness and a mother's cruelty.

Viv did not have time to scream.

66

HONG CHASED HIS own reflection through a maze of warped mirrors.

He had forgotten something, a piece of himself slipped out while he was not looking, his old name perhaps, the name he'd had before he became Brother Hong of the 'faith, or even just a memory of the gold of leaves in autumn drifting down, and if he caught the image that ran always three steps and a turn ahead of him, scrambling as he scrambled, slipping as he slipped, he could reclaim what he had lost, own it, eat it, become wholly himself. But as he ran he lost more, unraveled as if he were made patchwork like a doll sewn from a single thread and that thread had been tied to a post so the doll unmade itself as it pulled away.

Facts slipped from him with every step: the specific heat of water, the speed of light in a vacuum, the fractal manifold equation of the Cloud, sliding out one by one and leaving only voids behind.

The mirrors twisted his reflection as he ran, showed him unraveling, the holes growing in his skin. He chased the seeming. The hallway glittered with crystal but it stank of blood and skin, and slick glass slipped beneath his bare feet, and as he ran his fear swelled and he heard the great Presence that chased him on steady plodding feet and slurped the thread of him like a long thin noodle, eating everything he knew and everyone he loved, swallowing them down into the deep beyond deep, into un-sense, into the chaos belly where form lost form and all words failed.

The truth lay ahead. He could run and save himself. He could run and break the unraveling thread. He could make it somehow. They needed him. Gray, and Viv, and Zanj, and—

What was her name?

XIARA WAS PART of something grand.

Even *Groundswell* was not so vast as this. She was the heart of a ship the size of a universe, sinewed by neutronium, smelting data in the stellar forges of its mind, one unified sprawling being humming mad music to itself, working calculations in the death of worlds. Here she was, perfected, one with the machine.

This was what she wanted. This was what she wanted. This was what she wanted.

She was a piece of it as gears were a piece. When it thought, it thought with her mind, grand cold inhuman thoughts that left aches and blood behind, waves of intense cognition and concentration, obsession, her whole being tangled around a problem of hyperspace geometry, forgetting breath, forgetting how it felt to dance, her gut twisted to the point of throwing up, her mind washed with vertigo and regret. And then the conclusion racked through her, staggering ecstasy at performing a task whose ends she did not, could not understand, and after she was an aching pit, vacant, useless until called upon to strain and scream again.

This was what she wanted. This was what she wanted.

The sky, yes, she wanted the sky. She wanted to leave the Chief her mother behind, she wanted to leave the Ornclan's demands, she wanted to mount a ship and ride it past all limits to the end of the world, and she had made it, here she was, mighty, or at least a piece of mightiness, and whole. The world was full of uses for her. Her mind was a fine mesh, with its delightful chaotic cognition layers, a perfect addition to the computational subsystem, especially when trained, when educated to service. Those muscles, those tissues, those mucous membranes, that skin: uses for all of them, toxin filters and gas exchange, not to mention the sophisticated DNA computation in her blood, not without its errors, but even those could be fixed, yes, incorporated. Employed.

She was a pilot. She was free. She wanted this. She gave herself.

Small machines peeled her skin away and stretched it.

This was what she wanted—

GRAY ATE THE world.

He ate and ate and ate and was not full. He ate bodies, crunching bones, rending molecules for raw materials to build more teeth to eat still more. He ate and grew and ate and grew, choked down planets, vomited asteroids and ate them again. Larger, he ate suns, belched gas which he breathed back in for redigestion. Grown larger still, he ate galaxies.

The world was not small but it seemed small when he filled it, when the bulbous slick cloud of him pressed against its own boundaries. There was nothing left to eat, but still he hungered.

So he grew new teeth, facing inward, and began to eat himself.

VIV WOKE TO find herself bound upon the throne.

She did not hurry back to the world. Memory returned first, stained by the dreamless mud of uneasy and unwilling sleep. She felt sharp wire around her wrists and ankles and throat, pressing against her thighs through her clothes. When she shifted against the wire to test its strength, it bit her like a blade. She went slack, took a deep breath, felt the wire press against her ribs and cut.

"I know you're awake," Zanj said. "I can hear your brain. You might as well open your eyes."

They were alone in the chamber of Zanj's eye. Viv sat on the throne, held in place by her wire cage, and Zanj—Queen Zanj, unscarred, crowned, and edged in gold—paced the empty floor, her head down, hands clasped behind her back, deep in frustrated thought. The angle of her head, the weight of her stride, the twitch of her tail, all screamed Zanj, so much so that when her gaze shifted to Viv, Viv could not help but flinch away from the fierce calculation of this woman who was not, was not, her friend.

When she flinched, the wire laid open a thin line of her neck, and blood trickled down.

"You," Zanj said, "are a puzzle."

Her crown glittered in the fake sun's light.

GRAY ATE HIMSELF skin first.

Starting was hardest, as with any distasteful task, but some things just had to be done. He had eaten everything else; consumed family and friends, probably, along the way, suns and stars. When you'd eaten everything, what could you eat next? He had no choice. This was who he was. This was what he wanted.

You made your teeth razor fine. You gnawed, sampling, at a stretch of limb, testing your jaws' strength, tasting the pain as your tongue explored the open wound. There's a special sick joy in discovering that you taste good. You don't suspect you will, but then, you're full of everything your body needs to survive. That first taste confirms the suspicion, and a hunger yawns within you like a pit.

He ate, and each bite fed the hunger as a fire feeds fuel.

* * *

THIS WAS WHAT she wanted.

Writhing in the heart of the machine, each piece of her recycled and repurposed, her lungs bellows and her liver a filter, her mind chained as a subsystem to an elegant machine—this was what she was built for, after all. The Ornmothers had made of themselves a bridge between world and ship, and she had stepped onto that bridge, and built it further than they ever dreamed. This was unity. Stars drifted like wind through the wires of her hair.

The machine asked of her, and she gave and gave.

Wasn't that what she wanted after all, under everything? Wanted more than the stars, more than the Cloud and the sky, more than reclaiming the honor her ancestors lost when the Empress's jade boot crushed them down? What she wanted beneath her dreams of cloud?

She wanted to be used.

She was Ornchiefsdaughter, raised to lead, to stand, to order warriors and offer justice where the world gave none. She was proud and fierce. She was expected to rule and order and command. That was her place. She was so rarely asked to give. To serve.

But you gave yourself to the stars. You gave yourself to the machine. You gave yourself to Viv, who sought, who asked, who needed. You pledged in your heart to serve and follow, and at every chance you offered yourself: take me as a pilot, as a lover, as a body, take my mind to order your fleet, my sacrifice to safeguard your escape, take my people to fight your wars. Take me to pieces, and use those pieces. Give me purpose with your need. Ask and I offer, and as I learn your heart, I will offer even before you ask.

Only a single still voice whispered against the offering tide. That's not all of it, she thought. So hard to think. So hard to frame the words. It's not just about you. It's not just shuddering loneliness, it's not just pouring yourself into a pit. You're not alone.

But a pressure closed around her temples, a fierce aching weight, and there was nothing but her and the machine after all.

The machine pressed her, ground her, pulled her. It said: Give me that single still voice in your heart. Give me your everything. Give me your body so I can core it and use it for a boat. Give me your name.

She offered. She wanted to offer. She knew her name. (Didn't she?) She could remember it, give it away, and lose even this shred of self that bound her sensations together and ordered them to a single story. She would not be so selfish. She would belong to the machine, once she remembered her name. She wanted to give herself away. She would. Any second now.

* * *

HONG FLED AND lost himself.

He had been here before, lost in this maze of mirrors, chasing himself. He had followed the Pridemother here. Before that, imprisoned by the Orn-clan's machines in the dungeon underneath their grove, he had chased Viv, the riddle of her. And again, after that, he was caught in the sticky clutches of Gray's pleasure garden: another mirrorscape, another sculpture of dry leaves that crumbled and blew away as he reached for them.

When he had dreamed this dream before it was a trap, a hallucination tailored to his desire, driven by an ever-optimizing attention loop. A brother of the 'faith cleaned the mirror of his mind to reflect the world and pierce through its illusions. He should have been able to think his way out.

But that was not how illusions worked. They pinned you where you lived. Do you seek clarity and understanding? Clarity and understanding make fine prison walls. It's freedom you want? Freedom is the collar at your neck. Truth? There are blindfolds made of truth.

This was a trap. They had been caught, somehow. He had been caught. He thought he heard their cries, their screams. Thought he could sense them thrashing in the night beyond this maze. But the more he fought, the faster he ran, the more it bound him, and the more he felt himself drawn away, drawn down into the gullet of the shadow that pursued.

He was bound. He was bound. He was bound.

But maybe that was the key.

VIV ASKED, "WHAT did you do with my friends?"

She was afraid. The wire at her wrists and neck scared her, and so did the prospect of the jokester mind that would have tied her to a throne. Her own imagination churned to work, inventing tortures, starting with the most pedestrian horrors, the broken fingers and pried-out teeth, the thousand and one uses of fingernails, a range of grisly fates for the fragile salty jelly of the eye. It got baroque and gross from there. The woman across from her moved, spoke, turned, smiled like Zanj, and Zanj was terrifying even when you were on her side. There were blades at Viv's wrists—that was the stra-tegic mind surfacing again, cold and sharp and honest—but she didn't for a second think she could kill herself to spare herself pain. Zanj was too fast. Viv could hurt herself, no doubt, that was the point of the wire, but she wouldn't be allowed to make her own exit.

She was afraid, but she didn't see any percentage in showing it. So she did what she always did when she lost control: she seized it back, as well as she could. Right now, that meant asking questions.

The Queen answered, "What was necessary. Don't worry, they're safe. I have to learn them from the inside out, swallow them whole. That's the only way to make sure I'm caring for them properly. But you? You're . . ."

"A puzzle. You said."

"Interesting," Zanj finished with a grin. "You're no part of the Cloud. I try to address your soul, but my overtures go unanswered. I try to crown you, and the crown slips off. I try to bind you, but the manacles keep snapping open. So I've done this the old-fashioned way." With a broad grin Viv recognized from the Zanj she knew, though it looked so alien without the scar. "I can see you're feeling cocky, but really, don't. A physical body's a crude interface, but eminently programmable." She lingered over that last word, and Viv felt, and quashed, another wave of fear. She'd have plenty of time for fear later. "I thought we might start with a conversation."

"Where's Zanj?"

She indicated her body with a wave of both hands, like a designer presenting a dress.

"I mean, my Zanj."

"Weren't you paying attention? I am her. She's me—and like me, too stubborn for her own good. I can feel her inside me even now, trying to fight. She doesn't yet understand what I've had to do here, the price I've paid in my own self-respect to keep these people safe. Does she think I liked doing this, being this? If only we could all be so selfish as to be heroes, freeing the cosmos by making messes for others to clean up. I can't believe I ever was that young. But she'll learn. Like you will." She moved toward the throne, languid and slow, pondering where to start.

The fear surged up again, but something else surged, too. A conclusion bubbled out of the depths of Viv's mind. If she'd been wise, rather than just smart, she would have said nothing, kept silent rather than annoying her captor—but the conclusion was so beautiful, and it would piss the Queen off so much, she could not resist.

First, it came out as a laugh.

The Queen stopped, and cocked an eyebrow.

"Zanj was right," Viv said when she recovered her breath. She laughed, taking care not to carve her face open on the wire cage. "When do you think the Empress broke you?"

* * *

HONG LAY CAUGHT in a trap built for him.

But who was he, exactly? To what measure was that trap made?

Call him Brother Hong of the Mirrorfaith, and he would answer, but that was a name and names were masks. He had worn another before he took up the 'faith, and many more since. He had been called a heretic, a warrior, a prisoner, a champion. A man could change names as easily as hats. But his name was not the thing that was bound. He could not free himself by dancing from name to name, could not twist words to liberty.

What was bound? Himself, his self. The trap addressed the being behind his eyes, tailored its designs to his desire.

But who was that being, after all? Of what substance was it made?

Long ago, a young boy ran through a wasteland, through burning days and frozen nights, skin torn by sun and claw. That boy had never left his homeworld. He did not know the sky, or the tenets of the 'faith. He knew only that if he reached his journey's end, his brother might be saved. So he ran.

Years later, a man less young but no less foolish flew, with his Archivist's blessing and with fellows willing to risk heresy for a miracle, toward High Carcereal. This man, who called himself Brother Hong, had never betrayed a friend, never wrestled a pirate queen, had never fought the Empress's servants hand to hand. He had never heard the name Vivian Liao.

And then there was another man, still foolish, who traveled the universe with strange companions: with one woman from a vanished past, another from a land of myth, a man who argued and joked with a monster whose name he'd first heard around a campfire as his cousins vied to scare one another into nightmares—a man who counted a member of the sacred Grayframe as a friend. A man who faced the Grand Rector in single combat. Was this the same person?

In a sense, perhaps, but how limited a sense! What remained the same? The mind? But what was the mind without and before the world in which it moved? What was Hong of the Mirrorfaith, beyond the world that shaped him? He was Vivian Liao; she was Xiara Ornchiefsdaughter, Xiara of the *Groundswell*; she in turn was Gray of Grayframe. They were themselves in and through and with each other.

This fragment writhing in a trap built to its shape, this mewling fear of failure, this desperation to work harder, faster, to gather the whole world to itself while there was time, what was that thing but the product of circumstance? Call it a wound, call it a scar, call it a habit, but wounds and scars and habits were not Hong of the Mirrorfaith. They were contingent, unfixed, empty of form. There was no Hong of the Mirrorfaith. There was no fixed entity who was acted upon. There was no truth but transformation. He was as much Gray of Grayframe as he was this tiny shred running in fear from the monster behind.

And if he was Gray of Grayframe, he would not run. He would laugh, and swell in his hunger and his joy, and turn and find this thing that tried to eat him—and before it could flee or change its shape, he could open his jaws glittering wide, and lick his lips, and bite down hard, and chew, and swallow.

Eyes opened in the screaming dark. And someone, call him Hong, for names are masks and masks are sometimes useful, rose from his chains and set about his work.

ZANJ DREW BACK, her nose wrinkled, her eyes dangerously sharp. "What are you saying?"

"Did you really think you were in charge here?" Viv would have shaken her head, if she wouldn't have cut herself in the process. She settled for a steady expression, challenge and certainty and all the power she could project. "You're just as managed as they are, just as compromised. You didn't suspect that, after all this time? Man, she really did a number on you."

"The Empress has never touched us. My sister fell before her—I never did. If you want to find a victim, you're looking in the wrong place."

"She wouldn't need to touch you," Viv said. "She built you."

"No one built me."

"The Empress caught Zanj. She wouldn't just have hurt her. She would have studied her, scoured her, learned the secrets of her soul. She used all that to build you—or, if Zanj really did make a copy of herself before the battle, she used it to break you. But I think the odds are on build. She likes to have things both ways. You're too perfect. She could hold Zanj in High Carcereal, eternally suffering, too delicious to give up. Defiance has a flavor, challenge a spice. But she likes obedience, too. If there wasn't a second Zanj she could warp to her specifications, she would have made one."

"Nonsense." But she was fraying, her eyes bloodshot, her laugh nervous.

"Look back on what you've done to Pasquarai. To your people. Look back on how you've ruled. Do you remember leading them to the stars? Do you remember freeing them from death? Would the woman you used to be do what you've done?"

Nothing in the throne room moved. Viv wondered if anything moved in the whole wide world.

"You're not who you think you are," Viv said. "You're a dream. That's all. But don't take it too hard. So are the rest of us."

—HER NAME, SHE had lost her name, and her name was all the machine needed, her name beneath and beyond all the meat of her already torn away, her name the keystone that, removed, would let her give up more than she had given already, that would let the great ship scour and remake her, that would let her lose herself—

A cool touch graced the forehead she had thought she lost when the machine pried her skull away. A voice whispered in her ear.

And she was not herself anymore.

She never had been. There was the part that gave, yes, the small scared girl trying to fill the gap in the world. But that was not all there was. She was not alone in her own head, as she had never been alone in life. The part that gave depended on others who filled her. Her mother had given her strength and the joy of battle, and Djenn had given her a foe to run against, a rival to best. Viv smoothed her back into her human shell when she stumbled unmade after union with the ship, and Viv needed her, which created a her to need. Gray teased her, Gray saved her life, Gray carried her through the war zone. She was all of them, too—and she was Hong, who studied the world, who drew it into himself, who moved slowly and with care, who tried to be gentle.

The part that gave did not exist without the others who replenished. She was Hong of the Mirrorfaith as much as she was Xiara Ornchiefsdaughter. Yes, there it was: her name. Yet now, as she reached out to offer it to the machine, she felt it given back to her, unending. Here she was as much Hong as she was Xiara, and Hong, seated in the heart of the machine, drew its truth, and commanded it, and it bent to his will. To hers.

The machine choked and caught. It had been built to digest her. But she was much larger than even she could bear to think. The machine sparked and cracked and ground itself to pieces on her fullness.

She opened her eyes in the dark, and heard screams, and saw Hong.

ZANJ SNARLED. "YOU'RE wrong. You don't know how hard I worked to keep these people safe. You don't know what I've had to give up, whom I've had to throw aside. I've broken friends. I have cast them into the darkness to suffer as I tried to save my world. And no piece of meat from beyond the wall can challenge that. I will take you apart. I will make you see the glory we have built here, if I have to carve you to pieces first." Her teeth were sharp, and so were her claws, and her breath was hot.

So Viv ordered her: "Let me go."

The Queen dropped to her knees. The crown pulsed on her brow. She clutched her temples, growled, spat, and let out a high-pitched winding yowl. She looked so like Zanj in that moment that Viv felt a stab of guilt, a twist of sympathetic pain. This was not Zanj, she told herself. This Queen had been made to tear apart what she had built, and to mock her with its ruins.

The Queen stretched out one shaking hand toward the wires that bound Viv to the throne. So close to hooking her claws beneath the wire, and tearing Viv free.

The hand blushed gold in the sun. It curled into a fist.

When the Queen looked up, gold tears ran from her eyes, and blood stained her teeth where she had bitten her lip. But still, she was not Zanj.

"I thought I recognized your voice," she said, and before Viv could answer, she moved.

GRAY ATE GRAY, and ate, and ate, and despite the pain there always was a greater hunger, and so he looped through himself, he ate and grew and ate what grew in turn. The pain was enormous, gut-churning and terrible, and worse than the pain, if there were worse things than pain, was his certainty that this would go on forever, that the hunger and pain would grow entwined, that there was no death in all the universe, only hunger, and pain, and himself eating and being eaten.

And yet there came a touch upon his temple, a cool assuring pressure to calm the whirl of him. Relief spread like a virus from that touch.

He contained everything. But then, he always had, even before he ate the world. He was Gray of Grayframe, which meant he was uncles and aunts and cousins and mothers without number. He was Gray of Grayframe, and Vivian Liao had rescued him from a prison of his own hunger, had brought him back to life after he defied his own Empress to save her, defied the Empress as no Gray of Grayframe ever would have dared. He learned from the children of Refuge how to lift and carry. He studied Hong's practice, and Xiara's gift for giving, for offering herself, when all he could do was take.

And they would not have been caught this way, any more than they would have let him be caught. Xiara would have fallen to another trap, and Hong to another, and Viv, well, her whole life had been a sort of trap, but if Xiara somehow woke to find herself racked with hunger and her teeth embedded in her arm, she would have gone out to find who else she could feed.

The hunger eased, and with it pain.

Xiara flowed into him. The part of him that was her flowered, the part of him that had shaped itself around her. And, finding herself in possession of all the world, finding her belly full of cosmos, what could she do but take herself as the dark material from which to frame new worlds?

And there was light.

And his eyes opened in the dark that echoed with fading screams.

He felt whole, wrung out, and dizzy. He realized, then, that he was seeing himself: a vague-featured gray body upon a slab with an iron crown on his head, painted with diamond sweat that cracked as he pushed himself upright. And in the dark, he saw Xiara watching him, and knew he was seeing himself through her, even as she saw herself through him—as they both saw themselves, and in turn saw Hong.

"I don't understand," he said, but with Xiara's lips. More disorienting still: he spoke those words in her savage fallen Ornclan tongue, and remembered learning how to write those words in Ornglyph at a traveling tutor-skald's knee, remembered how *understand* sprang from a word that meant, in Orntongue, to digest, to make a thing a part of yourself. He spoke through her. He spoke inside her mind.

"We were crowned," Hong said with Gray's voice, and Gray saw they still were: a band of iron burned at each one's temple, blacker than black. "The crowns trap our selves. They carve us off from the world. But what is the self? There are pieces of me in all of you, and pieces of you in me. We are all empty of inherent form. Trace the threads of each of us, and you find not just the others, but the entire universe. And what crown could bind the whole universe?"

"You tied us together through the Cloud," Xiara said through Hong—or was that Gray, speaking with Xiara's wonder? Gray remembered staring gleeful at her mother in the ring, as she gathered and threw an enemy. Or else Xiara, in him, remembered the glory of first construction, of eating a moon and shaping it to a glistening arch.

"I let go," they said. "The Cloud is a tool, that's all—like the body, and the mind."

And then, the both of them at once: "You're bleeding."

Blood tears leaked from his eyes, but his voice was steady. "The crowns cannot hold us with their illusions. But they tear at what pieces they can. We must act fast."

VIV'S JAWS STRAINED against the scratchy metal the Queen had shoved into her mouth and buckled there. She breathed fast and sharp through her nose, and tried to speak. But the Queen circled back in front of her, breathing heavy, shaking, but still on her feet.

"I've never met the Empress," the Queen said, "but Her voice echoes behind the wall and ripples through the Cloud, all clarity and truth, a will that must be obeyed. She built this, you know. She took the world beyond our world and made the Cloud from it, to Her specifications and under Her control." The Queen seemed to hear herself then, to hear the words she spoke that Zanj would never frame, and she shivered all through, curled her claws into her cheek, drew blood. When she looked up the nail tracks wept red. "And here you are, with a voice like Hers. A voice that can command my sister's crown. I feel it inside, crushing the part of me that's her. But you are not Her. Just an echo, a copy, a husk." Her laugh tuned Viv's fear to a higher pitch. She'd pushed the Queen almost to breaking, and a broken thing had sharp edges to tear and carve. "But what if I were to master you? I could make you mine, bend you, hurt you, twist you round, and end up with Her voice at my call. That's why I'm here. Isn't it?" Her eyes fixed on Viv, desperate, and in their desperation Viv knew she was right: the Queen was hungry, at a depth that scared her, for Viv's approval, for assurance she'd worked as her master willed—no, not Viv's approval, but approval with Viv's voice. She needed the Empress to say she had done well. She ached for it.

But Viv could not speak.

The tower shook. The fake sun dimmed overhead. Or else that was only Viv's own terror redoubling, rising, blotting out all light.

The Queen drew the Fallen Star from behind her ear and made it a sharp-tipped needle, pressing down, down against Viv's skin, into her palm and through, so fast Viv had time to think, *That wasn't as bad as I expected*, before the pain hit.

Then it was worse.

THEY ROSE TOGETHER.

Xiara's eyes turned and Hong understood what that meant from the inside now, the whirling of systems into place, the alignment of vision with different realms of being, knew it without being told even as he knew the fields that bound Gray's million mites together, the Cloud within all things. One arm waved—what did it matter whose—and the ceiling burst open, and light burned down into the cells, onto the slabs, where others now, not all, not millions, but the hundred thousands give or take of Pasquarai who in three millennia had never been convinced to yield, who from mutation or determination could not be turned, opened their eyes together. Hong's virus spread and spread, Cloud-code tangled up in a whisper.

You are empty.

If you are empty, there is nothing for those crowns to hold.

Wake up.

And so they did.

The Queen's soldiers tried to stop them. Pasquarai Station sent forth its fields and drones, its piercing light, its graviton inversions, and they slid past. There is no form to strike, no being to wound.

Still the station fought. Still its soldiers gathered.

And the imprisoned hundred thousands boiled up from far beneath to pull them down.

VIV TENSED EVERY muscle she could bear to keep still, but even so the pain thrust her against her wire bonds. Skin parted at her neck, at her ear. Vomit rose in the back of her throat, and she forced it down. You thought pain inured you to pain and maybe that was true, but the Empress's claws in her chest, the sickening pull of the skin melting on her wrist and cheek, the give of her thumb in Yannis's grip, those didn't make the Fallen Star hurt less when it pierced her hand. They were signposts, pointing out how bad things could get, and suggesting they could be even worse.

The Star ground against the bones at the root of her first and second fingers.

She expected worse to come, and when it did not, she worried. She realized her eyes were closed and opened them, which helped her vision clear.

The Queen knelt beside her, yowling and screaming, carving trenches in her scalp with her claws. She slumped onto her side and her cries stopped, but not because she no longer suffered. Her breath pulsed in her chest, and cords stood out on her neck where she was strangling herself to keep her voice contained.

The tower shook. She thought the tower shook. Maybe Viv's friends were coming for her, maybe they'd broken free, maybe she had a chance. Or maybe that was her heart shaking her, from pads of feet up to throat, maybe that was the gut-tremor of knowing she would not be saved, and that whenever the Queen came around, what happened next would be worse.

She pulled against the wire, but it would not give. And even if she freed herself, what would she do? She couldn't run fast enough, and the Queen had shrugged off her commands. If she did slip free, she'd fail just like she had before. She stopped herself from thinking that far ahead. She could worry about failure once she made it far enough to try again.

The Queen recovered.

She lurched to her feet, driven by will and shaking from the effort. "I see," she said. "If I hurt you, she hurts me triple. Vicious, even from that scratch." Scratch? Viv's hand was a coal of pain. "I don't think I can hurt you enough to break," she said. "Not without killing myself. All that power so close to hand, and yet so far away. But there may be hope. You have no soul, and yet you command and the crown obeys. It hears your blood, not your soul. And what's blood but a code I can crack? I wanted to bend your will to mine, but there are many ways to make you part of me."

She caught the fingers of Viv's wounded hand, and pulled the pinkie straight, and knelt before the throne, and as she smiled her teeth grew sharp.

THEY BURST INTO the throne room as the battle waged beneath them.

The room was green and growing, and empty save for Viv wrapped in wire on the throne, screaming, and for the golden Zanj, the Queen, who knelt before her, bent over her hand—

Gray's ears were sharp enough to hear the crunch of bone, and Xiara's eyes saw the spurt of blood in its many colors, and in infrared the blush of Viv's swift heartbeat, and in Hong's voice they said, "Stop."

The Queen rose and turned, and swallowed. Blood streaked her chin and teeth. Her eyes raked them, and she smiled, and was a being of gold, and, with all Zanj's speed and all her strength, she moved.

They were ready.

The Fallen Star tore through Xiara, and she felt it not merely as a blow, but as a hook catching at her soul, drawing her out of herself. The impact alone would have killed her, its catching buzzing queries driven her mad— but she became Gray, and burst to a whirlwind around the strike, and flowed up that point of contact to wrap around Zanj and harden into stone.

The Queen attacked the Graymites one by one, turning bursts of heat against them, but the Graymites were not alone either. Heat flowed through

them into Xiara, and out through her into Pasquarai Station, and beyond that
to distant *Groundswell*. If bodies were illusions, why should distance prove
any more substantial?

Hong rushed the throne where Viv sat bleeding, needing him, needing
them. The Queen flailed in her rage and boiled toward him, but Hong was
Xiara now, clad in radiant fields, turning *Groundswell*'s engines against her,
and still Hong ran, flowing from form to form, skipping through space.

They had no fixed bodies. They were suggestions, probabilities, each
drawn through the rest. As the Queen tried to fight one, she found another:
Hong's clubs blurred toward her face with Grayframe speed, but when she
blocked them the clubs melted into Graystuff to hold her while Xiara struck
from behind.

But of them all, it was Hong's job to fight toward Viv—in part because
among them, he was the least fierce, and in part because his mind was the
core through which they flowed, his the awareness that bridged their gaps,
and he had little more to give.

He could not keep this up forever. The crowns burned him, spearing circuits of his mind. His overtaxed neurons dumped electrochemical waste
and burst like dying stars. The body was dying—but the body was always
dying, had always been dying, was just one piece of the unwinding world.

So close. So close.

Viv sat crisscrossed by small cuts upon the throne, bound in wire, pierced
through the hand, blood seeping through the stump of her finger, furious
beneath the weight of her fear.

She'd looked like this the first time he saw her—the first time they all saw
her. Outfought by a Pride drone, or arrayed against Zanj, or marching into
Gray's paradise, unsure of victory but certain she would fight. And as Hong
reached her, he loved her for that, loved that she could be this way in the
world.

He set his hand to her cheek, and a buzz of Graystuff at his fingertip
parted the strap of her gag. His hand slid down, and the wires snapped one
by one and she was free, rising from the throne, her hand flung out, a warning on her lips. "Behind you!"

But they saw it coming. Of course they had. As the wires parted, as the
trap broke and Viv surged free, the Queen turned and rushed toward her,
full and furious, green light crackling around the Fallen Star, and a moment
of calculation carried through them all, darting from mind to mind, the
Queen howling, driven by the twisted logic the Empress had sunk into her

mind, ready to kill herself to keep control, ready to kill them all. They could fight her, until Hong's mind gave out and they fell one by one in pieces. But Viv could not. She was only flesh and blood.

The decision rippled from mind to mind, the part of Gray in all of them screaming no, the part of them that was Xiara pleading, there had to be a better way, without a suggestion. Only Hong said yes.

He turned as the Queen rushed on with blueshift speed, and stepped between her strike and Viv.

The Star slid soundless into his chest.

He had not expected the full texture of the pain, but he was pleasantly surprised, too: he had thought it would be harder to hold the bridge, to remember emptiness, as he was pierced by a weapon not even gods could bear. Strange, how strange, that it was not. He was greater than this already. The body was no more than matter, and no less.

Far away, Viv screamed his name.

Queen Zanj tried to draw the Star from his chest. It should have come easily, and blood-wet.

But it stuck.

Hong held it, held her, the Queen—not with his hands, but with his soul. If he was empty, then so, too, was the Star, and emptiness bridged them, bound them not just to each other but to the world beneath, beyond. He was in the Star, within the Queen, within the wall. His heart began to fail. Blood seeped out. The world contracted beat by beat, graying. But as it did, the circles of his mind swelled, sweeping broader in their liberation, through Gray, Xiara, and the Star, through Pasquarai Station and farther still, beyond the wall to the farthest reaches of the galaxy and past, as the throne room of Queen Zanj shrank, as the body kneeling within it, the Fallen Star buried in its chest, became just another passing form, another smudge on a mirror, and he reached up to wipe it clear.

VIV SAW HONG fall.

She forgot the agony in her hand, forgot the battle, as the monk slumped to his knees with Zanj's weapon buried in his flesh. She had seen him move faster than she'd thought possible, and open his hand as if inviting the Star to rest. The Queen roared and hissed and spat blood, and tore at the Star, ugly and desperate, her eyes aflame with need.

Behind her, Xiara and Gray whirled apart and reeled, no longer flowing into and from each other, the bond between them snapped. And Viv understood, from the smile on Hong's face, from his half-finished laugh, what had bound them together, what saved them from the crowns they wore, the crowns that matched in every particular the crown the Empress had fixed on Zanj to learn her, take her, and build this monster in her place.

As Hong died, the crowns burned black, and Gray and Xiara fell, unable to hold the trick of soul that let them fight. Hong had given his life to studying the transformations and emptiness of form, its limits and its liberation, and without him they tumbled back into themselves. And he had given all that at last to free her, because he thought Viv could end this. Rushing for his miracle. Just like when they'd met, so long ago on High Carcereal. He'd been disappointed then, too.

He must have thought she could command the Queen who once was Zanj. But she had tried, and failed.

He had not known that. How could he?

The Star began to slide from Hong's chest.

Viv had seconds, maybe. Less. Time for one order, which the Queen would not obey.

But the Queen was not Zanj.

Viv had tried to free Zanj before. Hadn't she? When she stood alone atop the moonlet carved like Viv's face, fresh from learning what a terror she had become in the eons since the death of Earth, in those bleak moments when Gray was dead and Hong was gone and Xiara had left her and all she had was Zanj, when she placed her hands on Zanj's crown to set her free—she'd felt the fear of death, of losing control. She had wanted to let Zanj go. But she had been tumbling and alone, and afraid.

What if the crown had listened to her, after all—not to her wants, but to her needs? And she had needed control back then.

She needed something different now.

"Break," she said.

She heard iron snap.

She fell to her knees beside Hong, held him, and did not look up. If this was the end, she wanted to linger on what mattered. Somewhere the Queen stumbled back, Star in hand, her forehead crownless now, her face free from pain, her eyes no longer bloodshot. She cackled, first, with triumph.

And then she began to choke.

She dropped the Star and staggered, her hands at her throat. The skin over her fingers pulsed. The bare bones of her skull flexed. Lighting darted between her teeth. Skin and bone stretched at their seams, and then, in a single motion, tore.

And she was Zanj again, Viv's Zanj, sinking to her knees across Hong's body, holding him as Viv held him, and holding her, holding him. Viv's Zanj, saying, "I'm sorry," as Xiara rushed toward them and Gray, as they tried what they could and nothing worked, as Viv had known nothing would, because he had made his choice and was now, truly and always, free.

67

IN A KINDER world there would have been weeks to rest, to heal, to love and grieve. Now they barely had space to catch their breath.

Viv tried to rise, and sank back to her knees beside the body. Her bones weren't broken besides the obvious, and few of the cuts ran deep. Her hand was a mess of agony that might have belonged to someone else. Her palm wept blood, and the finger—the space where her finger had been—should have been bleeding worse. She was holding it, but her left hand wasn't slick or sticky; she looked down, or thought she should, but her head did not move at all. Will and deed had come unglued. She moved herself like a puppet. Stare down. See it.

Her trembling hand sank to Hong's sash—to a pouch she remembered, that held a silver patch. It wriggled as it neared her pierced palm, the stump of her finger.

She remembered his hand pressing hers down, and felt it now, in memory.

The patch burned. It wrapped around her hand like a glove. She sobbed, and held him close. He had not wept, much, back then. And he had risen. Why wouldn't he rise now?

Zanj closed his eyes in the end. "He stopped her." She sounded distant, wondering. "It was all sick and green inside her, writhing with the Empress, like maggots. But she was as strong as me, as fast, as fierce, as mad. And he stopped her."

"He was more than himself at the end," Gray said. "We were all part of him. He was part of all of us. Even you, I think."

Xiara touched his still hand. "I don't think it was just at the end. I think he always was part of us. Or we were part of him. Maybe—" But she could not finish what she had been about to say.

Viv heard the rest. Her heart filled it in. *Maybe he still is*. Maybe we still are.

Beneath them, the tower trembled. There was a war going on down there—worse than war. Pasquarai's stunted children all growing up at once. The bonds that held their hearts snapped, and they flailed with wills they had never used before, as the world began to break.

"Let's go," Zanj said. "Let's finish it."

She set the Star upon the floor, and spread it to a disc of black. They stood upon it and it rose, swift and soundless, from the fires of Pasquarai toward the station's false sun.

When they stood between the station and the star, Viv asked, "What do we do with him?"

"We'll take him home," Zanj said. "To the 'fleet. After this is done."

Viv looked at her, black eyes into red. *Do you think there will be an after?* But she held the question in herself, and did not ask it, for all their sakes. So she said, "He'd like that," and watched as the Star closed over him like the waters of a lake over a sword.

Viv's hand ached beneath its bandage, and each breath was a knife. There were few words. They did not need them.

Xiara took Viv's unmangled hand, but could not look her in the eye. Zanj placed her hand on Viv's right shoulder, ready for anything. Ignore that twitch of her tail. Ignore that ready for anything meant ready to die. And Gray held Zanj's hand, and Xiara's, too. He'd worn so many forms but this one seemed to hold them all, the pale starved child, the monster, the work-hardened young man of the Refuge fields, and beneath all that, held by his skin, the flame.

And in Viv's heart Hong stood beside them still, and she could see him telling himself the story he always told, that this moment should have no more meaning than any other, that the world was always changing and any claim of significance for changes in which one participated was just a fail-ure of perspective. Telling himself, and believing it, and living it, and scared anyway.

He had been part of them. She wished she'd been able to share that, at the end, the souls melting into souls.

But the teaching was not a thing of the Cloud. It expressed itself through every tool available, but it was not through the Cloud that she felt him in her now, inside them all, passing from touch to touch, glance to glance. She had fought her way back from the edge of the universe to save him, and so had Xiara and so had Zanj.

She'd half hoped Gray might make some joke to break the silence, yes, look at ourselves, how funny it is that broken things like us can stand here as if we matter, a pirate who was caught, a servant who refused to serve, a pilot without wings, a woman without a soul, all watching one another so severe, set to do a thing that, if we're lucky, will change the world forever.

There were no jokes to offer.

Viv gripped Xiara's hand, and they kissed like continents.

"We'll win," Xiara said.

It was a young woman's answer. A young warrior's. Viv hadn't much felt the difference in their ages before now—she had so much to learn, and Xiara so much to teach. But for all the loss Xiara had seen, for all she'd fought, she had not yet lived enough to give those losses weight. Nevers and onlys and forevers grew as you did. The sky went on forever, but if you had no context save the height of the nearest trees, you could fool yourself into thinking the blue hung just beyond your reach, when in fact it was never there at all, and what was, was deeper than you could dream.

Viv heard Xiara hear how hollow those words were, how deep the sky.

There would be so much more to learn, if they made it through. So much to find. Stories they loved; tics in each that pissed the others off, leaving beds made or unmade, laughing too loud when drunk, a tendency to grump when beaten in an argument or game. Missing an item on the shopping list. What did Zanj do for fun, aside from cosmic larceny? Did she even know? What was Gray's favorite meal? Did he read?

What had been Hong's name, before he was named?

They were galaxies, all of them. More than galaxies: brighter, older, and deeper.

She had all that to lose, if they failed. And all that to gain.

Had Viv never left her home, had the Empress not come for her, had she never woken to this war, had she never been to space, there would have been no end to the glories of the world.

When afraid: live.

She told them now, told Gray and Zanj and Xiara, too, on the round platform before the star. "We're here for our sky. Our homes. For freedom from collars and crowns. That's what we're fighting for. And him. Whatever happens." They each said yes in their own way: Zanj with a nod and a tightening grip on her staff, Gray, shifting weight, nervous and trying not to seem so, Xiara with a warrior's glint in her eye.

And Hong said yes through them.

"I want to live. I want to know you all without this hanging over our heads. I want to make you watch me get old. I love you. Let's do this. And when it's done, let's do something else."

"Dance party," Gray said. His voice was raw. They all were. "We can get those spider guys to do the music."

Xiara laid hers on top. "You've never seen an Ornclan dance."

"Better than you sing, I hope."

Beneath them, the rings of Pasquarai burned.

Viv turned, at last, to Zanj. "You haven't said anything."

She shrugged. "We hit her where it hurts. What was the kid's line, anyway? For the liberation of all sentient beings?"

"For the liberation of all sentient beings," Viv said, and each of them echoed it in turn. She thought she heard another voice join theirs.

They held their hands together, and looked from one, to the other, to the next, to the last. And as one, they broke.

Xiara left first—faded like mist through the Cloud, to *Groundswell* far away. Zanj unrolled the Star into a sleek single-cabin needle, shaped for speed. The ramp descended. Gray was first aboard, and Viv followed. Zanj lingered, watching the rings of Pasquarai aflame and the fake sun overhead.

"You coming?" Viv asked.

"Yeah," Zanj said. "Just . . . this place looked so much like home." She raised the sun-gold bar before her, in both hands, and breathed out. "Here goes."

She broke it.

The sun went out.

The wall fell.

The stars came back.

And Zanj marched down the ramp, toward the rest.

68

THE WAR MET in the deep places of the sky.

Their attack had many prongs, but its goals were simple. Deny the Empress capacity. Strike the starminds that anchored her grip upon the Cloud and the manufactories that built her fleet. Fight on many fronts at once.

The Empress, looking up from her work, would see a daring raid, and dangerous, and might feel a stab of fear at her sudden exposure to the Bleed. She would devote spare resources to crushing them, and securing the border where Bleed chewed the unprotected edges of her sky. But she would not halt the complex machines at work on the Rosary bead that held Viv's world, her grail, the secrets that would render all this bother irrelevant. Distracted, she would not notice the needle stitching toward her through the Cloud.

Unless, and until, she did.

No plan's perfect, after all.

XIARA STOOD AT *Groundswell*'s heart. The ship hung around her, and the fleet beyond that, however many planets' worth of metal and rock and flesh she could not guess, all waiting. The crèche, lined with sensors facing in, with arms to hold her, with phosphorescent status lights that winked like eyes, looked like the instruments of torture the Ornclan had inherited from its previous chiefs—those the Chief her mother had broken and fed into the fire when she took office.

The ship breathed, and waited for her.

The first time had been so easy. She had not known what she was doing. She didn't know how wrong it could go, or how hard it would be to leave the ship behind. Knowing, she ought to be ready now.

It was not pain that made her pause. Pain could be borne.

She felt so ready to give. To slake the machine's hunger. That was how the crown had trapped her, that was the pit Hong gave his life to free her from. She was eager to be shaped.

She stepped off the catwalk and the ship pulled her up. Its arms spread, and she found herself embraced. Received. Welcomed.

With a thousand thousand eyes she stared out through the Cloud, and flexed a thousand thousand limbs. There was pain, yes, she'd forgotten the fullness of the pain—but there was joy, too, far worse. She wanted the pain to stop, and it did—*Groundswell* just reached inside her, obedient to her will, and turned the pain receptors off. Its systems embraced her, planet-shattering vast, obedient to her will. It needed her to want things. It needed her will to shape its own, to give its weaponized hulk frame and purpose. She was a girl in a palace, empty and immense, and when she shouted, invisible hands answered her every command. But no matter how she ran, she never reached the walls, and if she demanded a door, it only opened into the palace once again.

She gathered herself in silence, shuddering.

And then, with a thousand thousand ears, she heard her clan.

Voices of Orn, in rhythm and formation and harmony—a war chant, a gathering chant, and she heard their ships gather round her in the Cloud, each will shaped to a greater unity like voices shaped to song.

At their heart, she heard her mother's voice.

This, she knew.

She gave herself to the song, and flew with the hosts of Orn to war.

VIV WATCHED THE map.

They sped through the churning engine of the Citadel's Cloud. Zanj, muttering, adjusted the Star's form, and they surged ahead still faster. The rules were different here, it seemed; the Empress had carved paths for her own use, dedicated transfer and processing circuits, redundant subsystems. Zanj had opened a window so Viv could watch, but gazing into the enormous crash and roll of the machine made her head ache. She preferred charts instead, so Zanj built those: red patterns in the Star's matte-black cockpit. There was a situation map: the Mirrorfaith's battle group in position, telemetry dots winking out in the green blizzard of the Empress's forces, artwork ships torn by slivers, or else obscured, until the Pride descended upon them, hate fractals trailing flame. And, yes, there, the Ornclan struck, deeper into Imperial territory, at a manufactory hub guarded by an Imperial glaiveship and a torch squadron and, of course, thousands more drones of the Diamond

Fleet. A logical second-wave target. Just the kind of place they might strike if their first attacks had been mere feints.

They didn't have to hold out for long. But still, she prayed.

The map marked their destination in blue, nearing fast. Nioh and Yannis had found them as soon as the wall came down, and they traced telemetry helices around the Star, trading pings and data streams. They had no physical form now, vectors of information only keeping pace. Almost there. She tried not to think about Xiara, she tried even more not to think about Hong, but not thinking made it worse. So she thought, instead. Drew them into her mind, and let them shape her.

She felt it near: her world pierced by Imperial light, the bottled universe in which the Empress built her, and Magda, and everything she knew. A hundred thousand hands of gravity and light pulled Viv, caught her, pried her. She curled over the control panel; Gray came to her side, set his hands on her shoulders, but she waved him off. "I'm fine."

She was not. But they all had their business now, and hers was to survive.

They drew close. Their destination swelled on the map and became a system, a single star necklaced by planets with eccentric oval orbits, rock and metal near the star, gas giants farther out, one of those marked with an hourglass glyph whose meaning she could not parse. Sensors painted the system Imperial green: installations and ships and lines of force, huge Dyson plates near the star, rings and space junk, a built-up system, an ancient system, full of weapons, full of trash. And there, above the third planet, the blue X of their destination: Viv's singularity, and the systems the Empress built to pry it open.

Red numbers counted seconds left till their arrival. Thirty. Twenty.

The blue X should have drawn her entire focus, all her worry and her will. That was everything; their success, or failure. Her ticket home.

But instead, she studied the system. The single star, the projected orbits. The planets. Eight, if you counted that weird hourglass-thing.

When she was a kid, there had been nine.

"Gray," she said. "Does that system have a name?"

Before he could answer, they fell from the Cloud to realspace. Normal geometry reasserted itself with a stomach-twist. But, sickened, Viv still forced herself up, made herself look out the window.

And then she did not need his answer anymore, because below her, bluegreen beautiful, was Earth.

69

EARTH—VIV SAW that first, before all the rest. She'd seen a few planets from orbit by now and none of them got the blue right, or the clouds. But she'd drawn those comparisons to pictures, mostly, videos, the blue marble shots from the Moon, pinholes sent back from Mars. This was Earth seen with her own eyes. She wished Hong were here to see it: home.

But different.

The coastline had changed, for one thing. Someone had reattached Florida, sewn the Pacific Landfall back on, refilled the Ural Sea. Ice caps, big beautiful lazy ice caps, spread their fingers to the north and south; Greenland was coming into view, sparkling white. She found her cheeks were wet.

Yes, the Moon was a hollowed-out shell surging with bent light, where gleaming metal showed through rock; yes, a forest of crystal arms grew from the lunar surface, directing green needles to the L5 point where the stars and Sun went wrong around the singularity she'd come to seek. Yes, huge Dyson plates shifted between Earth and Sun, and somewhere outsystem she didn't even want to know what was happening with Jupiter, and Venus kept trying to talk to them, and the Earth itself was webbed with veins of crystal, miles across—a transit system maybe, or else the thread the Empress used to knit together a fractured globe. The Earth and Moon alike were surrounded by emerald drone-motes waking to their presence, opening balefire eyes. The system was full of wrongness and wonder.

But the continents looked like they did when she was a girl.

Could there be that much difference in their timelines? No—the Empress would have wanted to control variables in her simulations. A world that was not, in some sense, doomed by change, would not be a world where Vivian Liao was born. The Empress had seized the Earth, and all that it became, and turned it back to how it was. She could not allow even this to change.

She remembered Hong, and transformations.

"Viv?"

"I'm fine," she told Gray. Wiped away a tear. "We have to finish this."

"I mean, I came all this way for the view," Zanj said. "But as long as we're in the neighborhood, sure, let's save the galaxy."

She heard the anger in the joke, and felt grateful for it.

"Now," Zanj said. "If you were an Empress, where would you be?"

"You can't scan for her?"

"This whole region scans as her, for light-years in every direction. And I think she knows we're here." The emerald motes moved toward them—at this distance they seemed to be drifting, but even drifting at this distance was an unimaginable speed. "Ideas?"

A choice without data, without argument. Except—the Empress had fixed the Earth back how she liked it. Why would you do a thing like that, if you didn't want to look?

"She's on the Moon," Viv said.

Zanj spoke into the comm: "How about it, ladies? Can you clear a path?"

Yannis and Nioh burned before them in the darkness, weapons drawn, shimmering, Yannis's fangs sharp and long, her eyes fixed, her forked spear in hand, Nioh's shoulders broad and her horns gleaming. "We'll give them hell," Yannis said. "Just like the old days."

"Try to win this time," Zanj said.

"How about you try to keep up?" And, before Zanj could answer, the Suicide Queens burned, twin comets, toward the Moon.

XIARA FOLLOWED THE music through the war.

The battle strategies of ships like *Groundswell* don't fit in most gravity-bound tellurian languages; ships have one of their own to describe it, but good luck speaking that if you don't have a distributed neural network the size of a city. It's not so much an issue of complexity, as one of fronts. Three physical dimensions, not counting the tiny ones, and one arrow of time—sure, for starters. Then there's the Cloud, in its fullness and depth, its interface with three-space computational systems, which have their own contact surfaces and weaknesses and strengths. All of that creates the battle space.

When fighting a ship, one may attack its soul; waste its time; demand or direct its attention, sneak a memetic virus through any one of its hundred senses, all of them cycling activity to prevent just this sort of assault—though they don't dare stay closed for long, because if, for example, one's opponent isn't monitoring a stretch of q-band, that presents an opening all its own.

Does the enemy scour its surface with drones to prevent intrusion? Then drones are an attack vector. Do they shut down their drones to stop your hacking? Then push a nanocloud boarding party across the void.

And that's setting aside the challenge of coordinating a fleet. Here, the Ornclan had an advantage—their war songs invoked ancient Cloud-based subroutines to coordinate trickier micro-tasks like shield reinforcement, attack timing, and RNG band-hopping. And, of course, their war songs kept the beat.

Imagine playing twenty games of chess at once, with the clocks running down, only you can't touch the board yourself, but have to make each move through one of those joke cascade devices where a flipped switch rolls a ball down an inclined plane to knock open a door, which releases a mouse, and a cat to chase the mouse, but when the mouse runs into its hole it trips a wire that causes a broom to sweep down, and so on until finally a dart pops a balloon that lets a weight fall that that pushes the piece into place. Only at any time your opponent may change the game to checkers. Or Go. Or backgammon. Or Candy Land.

Also, the whole thing hurts like hell.

So Xiara trusted the music. She'd learned to fight this way—learned to wrestle to the beat of drums, first held a spear and marched as her mother sang. And she was winning. She wrestled the glaiveship with gravwells and drone claws; *Groundswell* split to pieces, spoofed its own identity, turned the glaiveship's missiles back. The glaiveship roared, metaphorically. One wild strike shattered a planet; another veered into space, and struck some distant star to nova. But she was winning.

Behind her, below her, on another plane of existence, the Ornclan engaged the Imperial torches, while pickets dismantled the manufactory to keep the Chalcedon from forming.

They were winning, until the melody slipped.

Xiara was so consumed with battle, so given to the rhythm, that she didn't notice until the harmony landed wrong.

Panic swelled. She missed a beat; the glaiveship's main cannon tore her belly, drawing plasma.

Her eyes swept the stars through the confusion of colors and noise, through the explosions and the interference and the naked singularities blaring chaos into the black. Ornclan ships drifted. A crystal storm carved one to molecular ribbons.

She did not see the Ornchief. She could not hear her mother's voice.

She would know, wouldn't she? She would know if her mother were gone. She would have heard something—would have felt it. That was how the stories made it out: the teller lingered on the fall of heroes. The Ornchief would not die unmarked.

But the Cloud was full of noise and serpents, overwhelming the Ornsong without the Ornchief's voice to bind it. Xiara scrambled in the dark but heard no melody to which she could give herself.

Around her, the clan faltered, and began to burn.

This was not Xiara's time, not her place. There should be mourning, if the Ornchief were gone. There should be rites and tears. There should have been time. She followed, gave, supported—but now there was no one to tell her what to do, no one to whom she could lend her strength.

But Xiara Ornchiefsdaughter was not only the woman who gave, who offered, who upheld. She could stand, too. Viv would, in her place—and so would Zanj, in a different way, flying by sheer stubborn refusal to fall. She wanted, as Gray wanted—wanted all things to be a part of him, wanted to pull the world into a single will. And she had learned, as Hong learned, the contours of the world, of her ship, of her voice.

Learn so you can work. Practice so you can play. Follow so you can lead.

No one stays who she is forever.

In *Groundswell*'s inhuman depths, the woman who was the Ornchief's daughter hummed a note and, trembling, shaped a melody.

And the Ornclan joined her.

THE FALLEN STAR burned toward the Moon, and the Empress came to stop them in her millions.

What Viv thought motes were statues on nearer view: angular Empresses all, robed and clawed and bright-eyed. Zanj danced the Star through them, grinning a skull-grin, features set. Outside, Nioh and Yannis were vectors once more, light, motion, trails of fire—scattering the Empress statues, shattering them, piercing three at a time and throwing their shards as missiles against the oncoming wave. But as the Moon ate space to fill the screen, the Suicide Queens began to slow. Viv saw them first arrested in moments of destruction, pausing for broken instants that left ghost images on the eye; the trail of fire their movements left shrank as they slowed, and the waves of Empress continued, more statues sweeping toward them from Earth, or rising from the lunar surface.

Zanj growled a curse too garbled for Viv's gimmick to translate. "Any idea where on the Moon, exactly?"

Through the chaos of the battle, through the percussion of emerald claws on the Star's hull, Viv felt something—not words, just a tug in her gut. "Let me fly!"

"How?"

"Make me a joystick?"

Zanj cursed, but she did—stuck her hand into the console and shaped it into a stick. "Here!"

The instant Viv took the stick, they began to crash. From inside the Star, she hadn't quite appreciated how fast the ship was moving, how many collisions Zanj avoided. But, hell. They were supposed to be more or less invulnerable, right?

She closed her eyes, ignored the increased patter, then the louder thunks, of Empress statues bouncing off their prow, and followed that tug in her gut down, down, toward the pain—

"Are you flying with your goddamn eyes closed?"

They snapped open, and, oh, the Moon was beautiful, and, oh, the Moon was so very awfully close, its surface no longer a map but a very real, very hard ground toward which they were not so much flying as falling fast . . .

Zanj shoved her away from the controls, and did something, and suddenly Viv could not breathe, could not see, everything was black and deep and sharp and cold and still.

There came a very loud noise.

SHE WOKE WITH a mouthful of dust, and a jaw that did not feel quite right. Given the alternatives, she'd take it.

She rose to her knees, somewhat easier than she expected. Blinked. Rubbed more dust out of her eyes. No, not dust.

Regolith.

Oh, Christ. She was on the Moon.

She didn't even have time to savor it, or process more than that first shock. Zanj pulled her to her feet by her good hand. "Come on," she said. "They're losing." She was right. In the sky, Yannis and Nioh's lines of fire grew shorter, and green motes of Empress closed in. "Which way?"

She searched the jagged regolith, spiked with crystal spires, then realized she had no idea what she was looking for. She closed her eyes. "There!" She pointed, turned—and saw Gray lying facedown, with a spear of rock through his gut.

She ran to him, kneeling, felt his wrist—no pulse—of course there wouldn't be—not another one—but the sorrow and rage hadn't yet wormed through her shock when he twisted his head full around on his neck, blinked confusion from his eyes, looked up at her. He tried to speak, couldn't, then shrugged and stood, dragging the rock spar out of his stomach, which sealed behind it. "Ow. Good thing I don't have organs, or that would have really hurt."

Zanj didn't need to take the time to roll her eyes. Viv could read her frustration from her shoulders, and the twitch of her tail. "This way?" Across the lunar plain, a silver staircase, leading up to a silver platform without apparent support.

She nodded, and they ran.

She was out of breath; her chest ached, and her face, and her hand, and the rest of her besides. The sky confused itself with light, and their shadows wriggled and rippled on the ground. She spared no time to think. There were too many questions to ask: what was the vibration beneath her feet, what had the Empress done with the Moon, why could she breathe here, this gravity didn't feel one-sixth Earth standard—but then again, she didn't feel like she was a mere few hundred thousand miles from a black hole, either. She looked over her shoulder. The twin fires of Yannis and Nioh had dwindled to dots, choked by waves of green. She ran. If none of this worked, if she'd fucked it up and led them wrong, at least she stood beside her friends, here at the end of everything.

But she would not lose. She could not. Not after Hong.

A wind rose as they neared the stair. It howled across the regolith, shaking pebbles loose, blowing dust down dunes, gathering speed and weight and heat, such heat, sweating, blinding, flame-quick, a heat full of colors and sound that rose cobra-hooded and skyscraper-tall in a column of fury and raging eyes between them and the silver stair.

They slowed, stopped. Stared up at it: a Gray of Grayframe, come to fight.

She waited for Gray to talk to it, to call it *cousin* and embrace, or even argue. But his eyes were wide, and his face was written in a script whose meaning she feared to guess.

"She broke them," he said, simple as a slap. "That's—them. All of them. My mother, my cousins. I can see their pieces. But they're . . . gone." He blinked. A diamond formed in the corner of his eye. "But they didn't do anything. That was me. It was me!" he screamed up at the monster, and the monster roared in answer.

Viv remembered the Grayframe's wedded lightning music, but she heard nothing in that roar but rage.

Zanj stepped forward, light as an offer, heavy as a grave, and drew the Star.

But Gray shook his head. "They're mine," he said. "They're my family." He sounded older than he'd ever been. "Go."

"Gray—"

"Go!" With a cry he grew, and spread his arms, whirling fire and blades, a formless, pulsing will, the last child of a broken place.

He met the Grayframe in the sky as Viv and Zanj ran on.

70

THEY CLIMBED, BATTLE behind them and battle above, friends in-system and beyond, as green needles of light twisted in the meat of Viv's world. Perhaps they'd lost already. Perhaps even now Xiara bled out in a shipwreck light-years distant. Perhaps the Empress had broken the singularity, perhaps the friends Viv had left sleeping on a seashore thousands of years ago were dead, Magda and Victor and her husband already melted into data for the Empress—for Viv—to extract.

But those were phantoms. The stairs beneath her feet were real. Zanj, by her side, was real. She looked over and caught her looking back. How long had they been climbing? Ever since Viv dragged Zanj from her prison; ever since Zanj caught Viv's throat in her hand but did not kill her. How much longer would they climb?

As long as needed.

Together, they reached the top, and the Empress.

GRAY WRESTLED WITH his dead.

If he had been only himself, only the child cast out for his failures and left to drown in the deep between the stars, he would have died at once, crushed beneath the Grayframe's bulk and might. But in the Mirrorfleet's dueling ground he had taken thousands of his ancestors' mindless hungry corpses into himself. He was a multitude now, though no less the Gray he'd been—stronger than any, ancient, and true.

Still the battle tore him; the Grayframe's million million mites wrestled with his own, trapping them to shapes, freezing them with static or cold breath, locking them in webs that drained their plasm. The Grayframe changed shapes and so did he, each form an answer to the last: a hunter for a hare, a boar to skewer the hunter, a lion to take the boar, a crane to flee the lion, a snake to snare the crane, all at once, twenty changes at a time.

But beneath and above these transformations—fire to burn the tree, water to quench the fire, a tub to gather the water, a drill to bore through the tub— beneath their seeming chaos lay a simple logic, the terms of war between Gray and Gray.

Form is strength, and form is weakness. Dispersed, you are a breath, insubstantial and immortal. Concentrated, you have mass, direction, momentum, power. But any form you take may be answered by another skilled in changes. Of course, the same is true of the form they take to answer you—so draw them in, commit, disperse, re-form, devour. Unless they, expecting this, mislead you as to their commitment to their counter-form, and change shape to answer when you spring in for the kill. Unless you, in turn—and so on.

The closer you draw to victory, the nearer to death. Rationally, no one would ever fight such a battle, because no one could ever win. If two Grays had reason to fight, they should just circle each other, never take a form, never risk themselves. That had been his objection when his mother taught him, as she taught them all.

Ah, child, his mother said: If you can pass your life without fighting, do. If your problems can be solved with reason and argument, solve them. But you may find yourself with no choice but war. And when Grays fight, they are hungry: driven by fear and desire, for victory and the feast thereafter. Hunger is their curse. It drives them to jump, to push, to take forms they do not understand, to strike without elegance and shift wildly in defense. To win, master hunger. Stay formless even when you take form—and when you take form, let it be a form you've mastered so well you can dissolve from it to formlessness again.

Learn what your enemy wants, draw them out, and strike.

His mother had taught him that, and he fought his mother now. His siblings and his cousins had practiced with him, turned and tumbled with him, and he fought them, too. He had never learned their lessons. He never understood.

But he had learned from other masters since. He remembered Hong's touch, his transformation. Form was empty. So, too, was self.

This monster the Empress had made in her rage was not a brother, a sister, a cousin. It was not his mother. But when their swarms mixed he smelled her. When some form-pair twisted halfway to existence, and their bodies rubbed together, when a claw of his caught its side, when its body snaked around his leg, he tasted his cousins. They were all here, in pieces, confused.

Scattered cards of self, pages of a book torn free and tossed to the floor without any index or ordering principle save hunger.

He remembered pieces of this monster raising him. He remembered arms
opened in homecoming, and Grayframe singing with thunder voices. He remembered how they wailed when the Empress cast him out, and the pain
of knowing he'd not come home again.

He did this to them. He had made his choice, he had taken his form, he
had saved Viv—and the world, more vicious than any Gray, took this form
in response.

He owed his family more. He owed them everything.

He had to give something back.

THE EMPRESS STOOD robed in silk and light upon the platform, her shining
arms spread and her radiant eyes cast up to where the singularity warped
the sky. As her fingers moved, so did the crystal arms that circled the black
hole, and cast the needles of light that pierced Viv's home. Earthrise painted
her a pearly blue, and even in that soft glow she looked severe, the tyrant in
absolute control.

Viv recognized that expression from pictures of herself, taken when she
sat coding, writing, rapt, at work.

"Empress," Zanj said, and, when that produced no reaction: "Viv."

"I wish you'd waited," she said without looking. "A few more minutes.
More or less. You know how those last minutes go, don't you? Each minute
gives you a few minutes more, and soon you've spent a day, or five, on the
last few minutes."

"I've been there," Viv said. "You know I can't let you do this."

"You know what's at stake. You've seen enough to work out the moral
calculus yourself, even if you don't trust me. I should have expected this was
you. But even your old slow brain should be able to wrap itself around the
issue. The Bleed eat complexity. They gnaw the Cloud. They cap the development of any species. They must be stopped. You know this. And you know
that if you stood where I stand, you'd make the same choices. Because I'm
here."

"No," Viv said. "I would have made better ones. We know that. Because
that's my world you're destroying to find your answers."

The Empress waved one hand as if shooing the objection from her ears;
out in space, the probes linked to her hands went wild. "Thought processes
are random and path-dependent. A difference of ion decay or environment

yields a new breakthrough. You have no inherent virtue. Neither does your world. They have tools I need. That's all."

"Did you save Magda?" Viv asked. "Or did you let the code compile?"

AS THEY FOUGHT, Gray flickered faster from form to form, committing more to each exchange. He became a forest and the Grayframe a fire, immense and crackling, smoke billowing to the stars. He became a mountain, granite shoulders gathered above the lunar plain, and the Grayframe a gushing torrential river that wore the mountain until its cliff faces shattered. He raised himself up as a vast field of rice, drinking the water with his roots, and the Grayframe formed itself to farmers, gathering, cutting, threshing.

He became one rice grain among the mounded thousands, a single hulled seed, all his mass compressed to form, immobile, silent, concealed, dense.

And quick as thought, the Grayframe became a rat and ate him.

THE EMPRESS'S RADIANCE dimmed. The light around her hands died. She turned from the apparatus, and fixed Viv with a dead expression, and she did not answer.

"That's when you came for me," Viv said. "That must have been the divergence point. You called me a disappointment, and you hurt her. When I hunted you down, you never asked me what I did right, what I discovered, what went differently, because you knew. You didn't save her. You let them find her. You let the code compile. And this is where it got you. Alone, with all the power in the universe, and nothing on your side but fear, and the Bleed coming in."

"Your friends," the Empress said, "are fools. Their struggles, their goals, their dreams, are insignificant. I am so close. Whatever you think you know, whoever you think you are, you are only a distraction."

She came for Viv in a blur, a blink, green light crackling around her fist.

And Zanj hit her.

THE GRAYFRAME MOLDED itself to rat-shape, pouring all its resources into the reality of the rat, its digestive acids and enzymes, its teeth to crush, its muscles to swallow.

Within his grain of rice, Gray came apart, and as he did, he reached for them.

Not for the Grayframe as a whole, but for the pieces scattered, jumbled, inside. For his cousins, his siblings, his mother—for the generations behind them, all those scraps of data, bits of identity without an index to bind them into selves.

He gave them memories. Stories. Instructions. This is how you fight. This is how you eat, how you live. How you serve, how you sing. This is how you mother; this is how you raise a child. These are colors. This, the taste of water. Here is how we touch, and how we play.

He gave them back. He gave them all back, the pieces of his mother, the pieces of his family, the frame he had used to make himself. And more: the ancestor bodies he had eaten, the memories of generations of Gray back to the first, parents of parents of parents, his family seen through other, older eyes. In their madness he told them stories of themselves. And those stories, wandering, found their partners in the Grayframe, other perspectives, memory fragments that in turn drew other fragments, bit by bit, stitch by stitch.

He faded, and around him, as the Grayframe sparked and fought and failed, new minds, old minds, began to bloom.

He had thought he might die. He half expected it. But he had grown beyond them when he left, when he traveled, when he loved and fought and died and lived again. He was more than what he gave them: he was Zanj, and Xiara, and Viv, and the sun on his back as he worked the fields of Refuge, and the cold of a cell. He was Hong of the Mirrorfaith. He could be them, when he lost all else.

Always know the shape you take—know it so well you can shift it to your purpose, so well the form gives way to formlessness again.

What is a grain but a seed?

And from a seed, you can grow anything.

Like, say, a family.

THE EMPRESS FLEW back, but stopped her tumble in midair, skidding, leaving a trail of light. Zanj did not stop. She struck her, and the Empress blocked with one arm, and landed teeth bared at the platform's edge. A spear formed in her hand, a fact of will with a long curved blade. "You didn't learn the last time we tried this?"

"Crown's off," Zanj said. "Not just off, but broken. You have no hold over me."

"You stupid child." The Empress slid a stray hair back into place. "You're still in the palm of my hand."

She blurred toward Zanj, and spear met Star, and the crash rippled through the platform on which they stood. Zanj held the clinch for a second, grimacing, all over silver and blades and teeth, then sidestepped away, tumbled, landed, came up still between the Empress and Viv.

The Empress smirked, tossed her spear aside, and stretched out her fingers.

Zanj stiffened, as if held in an invisible grip.

"You don't get it," the Empress said. "None of you ever do. Age after age some hero rises up, thinking to best me with my tools. You invent some new variation, some twist, but every time you reach for the Cloud you find me already there. That space existed before me, but I claimed it. I built the infrastructure you use, the temple where you pray, the systems that power your devices, that let you cross space, and think. Your bodies are made with my machines. You don't even call what you have implants anymore. They're organs to you. But they answer to me."

Zanj took one step forward. She roared with pain. Her limbs seemed to weigh tons. The silver shell around her peeled away, and Viv saw the bulges beneath her skin, against her bone, lines and ridges of machinery wedded to her body. She panted with the pain of it.

The Empress walked toward her, face composed in another expression Viv knew: the shallow, cheerful, half-compassionate head tilt of triumph she wore because it really fucked up losers when you looked like you didn't have to work to beat them. Nothing ground glass and lemon in a wound quite like the sense that your defeat was effortless and inconsequential.

"You've been a distraction," the Empress said, and formed her light into a scalpel. "And I'm bored now." She drew near to Zanj's trembling body, and reached for her throat with the blade.

Zanj, with a scream, with a sickening, tearing sound of burst flesh and chipping bone, lurched forward.

Zanj had built her body strong, her limbs swift, her bones hard, and reinforced them with machines and batteries and circuits to make her stronger, swifter, harder, fiercer. Now she left those added bits behind. Microlattices burst from skin, slit her with their departure, engines and enhancements tore away. Bloody, screaming, free, she threw herself upon the Empress, wrapped her arms and legs around her burning green, and held her fast. "Viv! Now!"

And Viv ran toward them.

She did not have time to think as she ran, but thoughts clustered around her anyway, filling time between her footfalls. She had been thinking for weeks, in captivity, in dreams, guarding her thoughts with other thoughts in case the Empress could hear her.

Back on the Empress's ship the first time it all went wrong, when Zanj hung bloody in emerald bonds and Viv turned from home to save her, it had not occurred to her to wonder why the Empress refused to fight her hand to hand. When Zanj attacked the Empress, she'd fought back, but when Viv came for her she melted away into walls and floor and obsidian columns. The Empress only returned to physical form after she'd caught Viv in her crystal trap. Even then she'd kept her distance, save for that one searing touch. She'd ordered the Grayframe to kill Viv rather than eating her herself. Why?

She was not squeamish, this tyrant who'd grown from Vivian Liao. She'd thrust her hand into Viv's chest—while Viv was stuck in her simulation, bound by her rules. But the Empress was old and wary of risk. And she feared Viv's touch.

Because Viv could open any lock the Empress made. Including the Empress herself.

The Empress's physical form was but a shadow of her true self within the Cloud, all green, all-seeing. That was where Viv would have to hold her down, and beat her.

Unless she was wrong. Unless she was about to die, and Zanj, too. But, hell, everyone had to die sometime.

The Empress burned Zanj's arms, and snapped at her face with her teeth.

Viv jumped toward them. Toward her.

No, not toward—*into* her, and through, as if the Empress of a hundred thousand stars had no more substance than the surface of a pool of water.

In the great fluid Beyond, in the Cloud, she closed her arms and caught an immense form which, as she clutched it, twisted and reshaped into a body she knew—herself, real, braid-crowned and furious.

And into the water, into the green, they fell.

71

A MOUTH OPENED in Xiara's sky.

There had been nothing but the battle, *Groundswell* burning the manu-factory as it produced wave after wave of new ships for its defense, the wrecked hulk of glaiveships and torches left behind, the Ornclan fleet joined as one in song. Then the lightning came, a cut across the sky. And, abruptly present in the local Cloud, all of a sudden there from some unguessed direction—a mass greater than suns, and, splitting space, the mouth.

It closed on the manufactory. Shields burst. Gossamer strands thick as continents collapsed. Sparks lit the manufactory's surface—reactors going critical, matter siphons spewing neutrons in all directions. Ships fired, but their shots passed through emptiness, and then the ships themselves dis-appeared into the mouth.

Xiara knew the stories. None of them mentioned what she was supposed to do now.

And beneath her, the Cloud rippled, its logic straining as more Bleed passed beneath it, onward, in.

GRAY, SPRAWLED ON the lunar surface, felt the alarms in his bones. (Oh, so he had bones now. Interesting.) He couldn't rise. Around him spread the cra-tered lunar surface, and in each pit a Grayframe puddle taking form. He reached for their names, but the names escaped him.

He should feel— They should do—

Something.

Scatter, that was the idea, scatter, spread complexity, survive. Drag the Bleed in all directions, confuse them. The Bleed could not see much of the physical world, only sensed it by its impingement on their domain. The beyond. The depths. There were strategies he could use against them, tricks that might make a difference—or not. Worth a try, if he could remember. If he could rise. If he could move at all.

Far above, Yannis and Nioh's fire dance was almost done. The Empress's many forms had pierced them, clad them in crystal, needling in for nerves and access, closing them down circuit by circuit. But the emerald mandalas around each twisted, broke, the statues suddenly maddened and unsure.

And then the Bleed arrived.

ZANJ SAW THEM. She could not think through the pain; her mind ran so god-damned slow on this platform, so weak within this meat, losing blood faster than she'd thought possible—but she held the green hole, the gap in the world through which the Empress and Viv had slipped, as above her in the dark the Moon's sky shivered open with mouth after mouth after mouth.

She had to breathe, with flooding lungs, so she could laugh.

VIV AND THE Empress fell into the ocean of themselves—into the Cloud.

Arms battered her, and legs, knees jutted into her ribs; thumbs gouged the corners of her mouth and fingers clawed at her eyes. She clutched her opponent close in the harsh green water. She held the Empress, here in the Cloud that was her being, body to body. They tumbled together in the green, stroked by fingers of light from a distant surface, falling, falling, drowning down.

There was a voice, though, a voice familiar and accustomed to command, furious as they fell. "What are you doing?"

She hugged her closer, pressed past the clutching fingers, pulled her into an embrace, skull to skull, Viv's shorn head to her braided crown as they sank together. "I'm you," she said. "You're me. It's time for us to change."

"You're a castoff, a shell. An experiment gone wrong." Fists battered her back; nails bit her scalp. Still they fell. "You're nothing!"

"Of course. So are you."

"I built you!"

"You did. You pulled me from a simulation of the past, from before you found the Cloud and changed it from what it was before to something any-one could use, but you would always own." Down and down, lungs strain-ing, nails dragging skin from her scalp, blood in the water. And sharks approached.

Yes. She could feel them. Not sharks in truth but Bleed, circling beyond the edge of the Empress's sea. Enormous mouths of glimmering teeth, with alien stars inside.

"At first I thought I could break the chains you forged because I wasn't part of the Cloud, because you had no way to bind me. Then I thought the system listened to me because you'd made a mistake, and did not realize it would confuse us—a loophole you'd close once you discovered it. When I couldn't take off Zanj's crown, I thought you must have fixed it—but Zanj couldn't hurt me even so, and I could still open your locks, your wall, command your Grayframe. I had just been scared. I wanted to control Zanj, like you did."

No answer but an underwater scream, bubbles wreathing them, breaking the thin trail of blood. Viv pulled her closer. They'd fallen as far as they would go, and still water gaped beneath them, deep and dark and full of vast moving shapes.

"You can't close the loophole, because there isn't one. You can't lock me out, because the system you've built looks at you and sees however many thousands of years of power and rule, sees the immense shell you've built around yourself. And then it looks at me. And I look a lot more like the woman who did the building."

The Empress stiffened then, stopped clawing and tried to pry free, to swim away. But Viv held her close in the depths.

"I have a soul," she said. "Of course I do. Everyone does. It's been translating for me this whole time, interpreting me to others, warning me from danger, guiding me here. It's your soul, so big nobody else can see it, filling the Cloud. Binding it to order. Your complexity, drawing the Bleed."

"You don't understand!" The voice, her voice, sounded desperate, a girl drowning in deep water, alone. She had always been alone. "The Bleed are coming. The Bleed are here. We're so close, I'm so close, and you'll never stop them without me."

"They come when there are too many demands on the Cloud," she said. "This place was here before you. You found it, and built something here you could control. You didn't ask yourself what lived here, who might be using it or how. You chased them from their feeding grounds. Drove them mad." The Bleed neared, suggestions of form almost invisible in the murk beyond the green.

"There was nothing before I came." She spat the words. "Nothing before me. Call me a monster if you like, but I gave us the stars. I made wonders. I beat them. You know in your bones that you were one accident away from being me. If you seize my power, you'll make the same choices I did."

"You're right. I would. That's why we have to change."

The Empress clawed at her back. She was weeping, in the depths.

Viv said, "I love you." And as the weight of water pressed them close, she kissed her, and drew her in.

The Bleed circled close. They had no eyes and no gills, of course, since they were not really sharks. But they had mouths and teeth, and there were so, so many of them. Waiting. They smelled a change, but not all change was for the best.

There had been a change before, after all. A slow, cascading transformation, a green light seeping from a hole in their world, transforming the water through which they swam, robbing it of air, starving them of chaos and complexity, burning through the darkness beneath the stars where they once prowled, hunted, fed.

Viv opened her eyes underwater, alone. Black spots moved across her vision. Her head felt heavy. She had so little time.

The light filled her as she rose—the light, in a very real sense, was her. Where she could see, she was. She could peer across the galaxy, and cross all that space in an instant. I never dreamed, people said when they received some enormous fortune or power or honor. I never dreamed it would be like this. But Viv dreamed. That was why she won.

The galaxy waited for her. Trillions of beings. Ghosts and gods and living mortals. The poetry of archives. The power to build suns and break them. All at her, at Her, command. And it felt glorious.

Which was the problem. The Bleed had been born in the place beyond, the hyperspaces from which the Cloud was built, and they lived there still (if *lived* was the right word), rambling in the space beyond its edges, hiding in deep pockets of hyperspace until expanding Cloud disturbed them. But when the Cloud reached into the hollows where they hid, they fought back, and ate it and the matter that gave it birth. If the Cloud broke apart, they would own their space again: the computational depths through which they swam. All Viv had to do was surrender. Give it all up. Step down as Queen of Everything.

She heard them all in that silence, as the Bleed circled. Xiara, god, Xiara, singing and weeping in *Groundswell*'s heart, thinking her mother dead, while nearby the Ornchief hovered comatose in her fast picket, oxygen supplies dwindling, her soul compressing itself in preparation to leave its physical frame. Gray stared up at the smiling mouths of his doom. Zanj, bleeding, held fast to the stitch of light where the Empress had been.

There were others, too, Ornclan and Archivist and Pride, the silver birds of Pasquarai and Yish with his clipboard, Refuge's farmers, children. Bleed rising toward them all, drawn to the Cloud and its Empress. To Viv.

And below them all, she heard Hong—Hong in the Cloud, or Hong in herself?

Nothing lasts forever.

She turned her gaze toward home. Toward the singularity that hovered in a cage of green light in her sky.

She could go home. Surely these machines, built for a more vicious purpose, could give her that at least. One last wish, as she broke them forever. Show me the hole my shape and size, where the Empress pulled me from the depths. Take me home.

The machines did not understand.

The singularity has never been opened, they whispered. Nothing has been removed. To do so would have spoiled the simulation.

The Empress, she replied, and then, I, took a woman out of there. She woke in a bubble in High Carcereal, in green.

The machines disagreed. Nothing had been extracted from Simulation 8117. When monitors detected a successful resolution to the Bleed issue due to deviation in that branch's Vivian Liao, the easiest method of reading out the result was, naturally, to create an entangled duplicate of Viv-8117, read her into this world, and interrogate her in realspace. A duplicate built gluon by gluon in High Carcereal. A terminal. A construct.

That was her.

She remembered making herself. Images surfaced: the green bubble empty before the machines began their work. The Empress pacing as her body compiled. Bones framed themselves, wreathed in nerves; the eyes inflated next. Blood. Meat. Fat. Skin spread over muscle and fat like algae blooming on a pond. Scars, and birthmarks, and the stubble of her knife-shorn hair.

That was her. And when the Empress found that the simulation's victory had nothing to do with brilliance, or strategy, or even tactics, but merely a willingness to run, to leave her task unfinished and save her friend, she abandoned the project in disgust.

And what of Vivian Liao inside that simulation? What happened to the woman she'd thought she was?

The machines had learned enough, in their study of the singularity, through selective bombardment and Hawking radiation and other techniques with no names save in languages she'd need several mouths to speak, to answer that. She escaped with Magda and hid, scared, forming her next plan. After weeks of hiding in her basement Viv received a message, so subtle she might as easily have missed it, from the being she'd abandoned half-born in the 'net—a being not hers to control, less golem and more child, who had pieced themselves together and come to seek their creator. Adventures followed that—unraveling a conspiracy, exposing the caves of men who'd tried to stop her. Together, Viv and Magda took their first tender steps into something that would not, in this world, be called the Cloud, toward waiting stars. Many visions spread through this new space, none grand, none complete; the Bleed moved out there, immense and gentle and fearsome in their unconcern, their songs loud enough to break the ears that heard them, their sleepy swimming frames a hazard to all travel, and a source of beauty, too. It was a harder world, dangerous, but no less wonderful. A world where no one lived forever. A world where Vivian Liao and her wife came back to Sol, 307 years of age, to die on Mars, no Empress at all but a traveler, and happy. Where she would say good-bye to Magda one last time.

Viv realized she was crying. She was curled in green, as she had been at the beginning. Alone.

She could go there. She had the power. Just slide herself in, and overwrite the simulation's Viv, the woman she'd thought she was. With care, she could even keep her memories of all she'd done, as dreams at least. That would be a good life.

But it belonged to someone else.

Viv stared down into the world she'd thought her own, into the life she had thought hers.

She closed the portal, and broke it.

The Bleed circled.

Up there, somewhere outside herself, Xiara, and Gray, and Zanj—and Hong—were waiting.

She stretched out her hand, and while she had the power, changed some things. A touch of healing for Zanj, returning the machines that made her. Xiara and her fleet she pushed to safety, and while she was at it she dropped the Ornchief into *Groundswell*'s medical bay. Gray, and the Grayframe, and Zanj as well, she moved. The Moon would not be safe in a few seconds.

She swam for the surface, but found herself dragged down. Her head felt so heavy.

Oh. Right.

She made a knife, and cut off the thickness of her ten-thousand-year braid, and kicked up toward the surface.

She heard a noise, deafening after the silence.

The green broke to blackness, full of stars.

72

VIV AWOKE TO the sound of waves. Coarse sand ground against her knees. Beneath her, the earth quaked. The earth, the real Earth, was coming apart now, as the Empress's will failed. How many eons of seismic pressure and decay had she just freed at once? The Cloud was failing. She had made it fail. The protocols would still work—souls would grow and gods would move. But no one was in charge now, except all of them.

Across a hundred thousand light-years, new worlds opened, and crypts long sealed rolled back their stones, and the galaxy woke up.

She raised her eyes and watched the Moon collapse. Of the Bleed, of the mouths in the sky, she saw no sign.

Viv knelt on the beach of Cape Ann. The lighthouse crumbled, and with it the houses, the art galleries and lobster roll shacks, until the whole stone promontory slid into the sea.

She was still crying when Zanj found her. Once she would have swallowed her tears, crushed herself to an edge, made some dumb joke. Instead she let Zanj bear her up, and leaned into her embrace. Got snot on the ribbons of her shirt. Felt the wet blood and fresh-healed skin of her arms and back. "Hey," Zanj said. "It worked."

"I don't know," she said. "I don't know who I am."

Zanj, exhausted, shrugged. "That makes all of us."

It wasn't funny but Viv laughed anyway, big and wet and gross. "This place is falling apart."

"Same," she said. "There are a whole bunch of confused Grayframe over there, not to mention our boy. Let's go."

"In the Star?"

Zanj shook her head. "I can feel your soul now. Tiny, but it's there. We have options. We can run a lot faster than we used to."

Viv sniffed, and swallowed, and wiped her eyes. She breathed the salt air of the draining sea, and shook with the tremors of the breaking Earth. She felt raw, and free.

She wanted to run. She settled for a limp, for now, hand in hand up the beach from the end of the world.

"Come on," she said, laughing against the pain, pushing herself faster, gaining speed. "Let's go exploring."

ACKNOWLEDGMENTS

Each book is a meeting place. We know each other by now, dear reader, but there are others here, too, and a good host should introduce the guests. Otherwise everyone's just standing around in the kitchen wondering who will go for the knives first.

My parents, Tom and Burki Gladstone, thought Anthony C. Yu's four-volume University of Chicago translation of *Journey to the West* was a good gift for an eleven-year-old (and weren't wrong). Shao-nian Bates and Athenia Wu were early guides to lands unfamiliar but by no means new, and Kang-i Sun Chang nurtured a creative angle on academic pursuits (though odds don't look good for me getting that Ph.D.—sorry, Professor!).

Ben and Beth Druhot introduced TV-less grade school Max to *Star Trek*, and Paul Grillo and Danny Miller added fuel to that particular fire. Danny, also, for the gift of a whole box of books, including Roger Zelazny's *Lord of Light*. Scott Caplan, usually not much of a Science Fictionero, suggested I read *The Player of Games* back in college, and John Chu, who needs no introduction, recommended *Nova*. A kid at summer camp whose name I honestly forget once spent two days enthusiastically relating, beat for beat, the plot of *Dragon Ball Z*, and another did the same for *Sailor Moon*. Joshua Frydman is directly responsible for my exposure to both *FLCL* and *Revolutionary Girl Utena*.

If I've ever run a game for you or with you, there's probably a touch of you here as well. Special thanks to Scott Biss, Chrysta Bond, Carl Dull, and Eric Stubbs, to Vlad Barash, Miguel Garcia, Daniel Jordan, Stephanie Neely, and Nathaniel Rowe, to Matt Michaelson's absurd beholder-mage, and to the Innermost Cabal of the FPL (among others: Chad Smith, Sam Justice—his real name!, Josh Tomblin, Gigadork, Bryn, Abdiel, Serge) voyagers in realms most strange.

This particular volume has had many allies. DongWon Song, agent of greatest wisdom and excellence, knows what he did. Marco Palmieri and Melissa Ann Singer were excellent editors and advocates throughout the process, with assistance from Anita Okoye. Christina MacDonald, Lauren Hougen, and Eliani Torres's copyediting and proofreading services were invaluable. Tommy Arnold's cover art, Irene Gallo's art direction, and Jamie Stafford-Hill's cover design produced the stunning object you hold in your hands, which (if you invested in the physical edition) doubles as an implement for home defense. Desirae Friesen is our publicity mastermind. Without them, this book would have reached you in many ways less, if at all.

Vivian Liao left Saint Kitts in December of 2016, and I followed the first draft of her adventures in a feverish writing jag through June of 2017—a period in which the notion of fighting a long war against implacable foes through time, in which victory would involve a literal deconstruction of ourselves, felt especially jagged and raw. Working on this book was a great complement to other, less solitary work I and others across the world were doing at the same time. We have all done so much, and there is so much more to do. But the fight for a world where all of us can enjoy lives of freedom, exploration, hospitality, and encounter is not new, and none of us are alone in it. I hope this book has given you some strength.

Find allies. Take care of yourselves.

Work for the liberation of all sentient beings.